WHEN SNOW FALLS

WORLD BUILDING AND CONTENT WARNINGS

BECAUSE OUR MENTAL HEALTH IS IMPORTANT AND EPICS ARE COMPLEX!

When Snow Falls is a much darker tale than both *Following the Snow* and *Snow on the Summit*. For a list of Content Warnings, please turn to the back page of the book.

World-building information and pronunciations can be found on For tneaux.com

TO YOU.

YOU ARE WORTHY.
YOU ARE POWERFUL.
YOU ARE A FUCKING GODDESS WALKING THE EARTH.
TAKE UP SPACE.
SING THE SONG.
DANCE THE DANCE.
AND IF YOU DON'T FEEL LIKE SMILING... DON'T

MONWYN
BASILIA
PENU
Eira's Rift
COLPASS
CORDILLARIA
STORMRI
MOONLEDGE
SINNONBREAK
RUINS
OF HAIN
LENNAN
L
BALDORVA

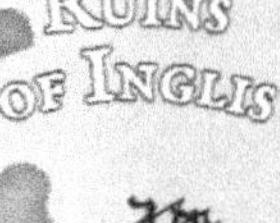

SILVERSTEP
SNÆRSHADE
NORTIA
VERUS
THE RIFT
RUINS OF INGLIS
MYNDER
GAEA
RUINS OF TALEER
SOLNNA
ÆRTA
N
W
E
S

CONTENTS

TEMPLE OF VERUS HIERARCHY

THE MANTLE
Religious Head of Ærta

DEVOTEES
Mantle's council and kingdom advocates

OBLIGATES
Chosen children committed to Ærta's betterment

PRIESTESSES / PRIESTS
Religious practitioners

ACOLYTES
Priestess or priests in training

ÆRTA'S PANTHEON
MAJOR GODS

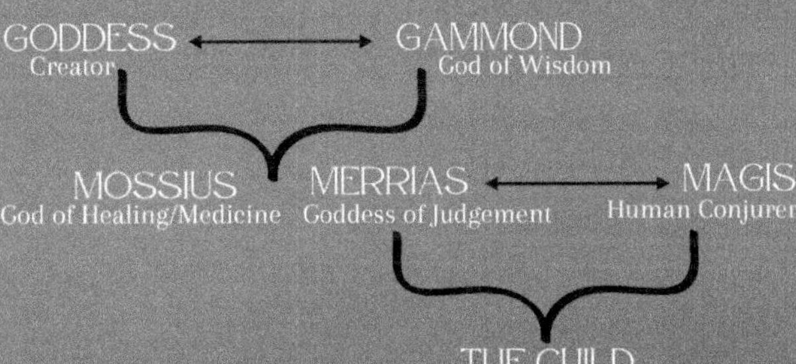

MINOR GODS

DERROS: God of the Seas

LYKKSUN: Goddess of Sun

JOSA: God of Music

MARESSA: Goddess of the Forests

VIKTOS: God of Thunder

THORAMIKA: Goddess of Metallurgy

CHAPTER ONE

THE WOODS

CATO

"No, brother mine, what I am saying is that of the prospective matches you have sent to me, the closest I came to selecting a potential spouse was a lesser noble who contorted herself into the most awkward of positions. Lykksun's divine kneecaps—the woman would just drop to her back during a leisurely stroll through the garden and toss a leg over her shoulder. Can you imagine staring at a face whose chin perched upon their own rump? Disconcerting business, that."

"I do not see the problem, Aberus." I glanced up at my older brother and shrugged, reining in the laughter that threatened to spill over.

Disgruntled brown-black eyes, a replica of our mama's, stared back at me in disbelief.

I tsked at my mount and rode closer to his side. He straightened in his saddle, back stiff.

"The *problem*, littlest brother, is that a queen must possess a noble bearing. She should be strong yet solemn and present herself as pious, inspiring her people with her regality." Aberus circled his gloved hand in the air, mimicking the flourish of a courtier in curtsy. "Going twat up in the middle of afternoon tea is not a commendable trait in a stateswoman."

"Is it not?" I asked, noting the position of the moonlight that filtered between the treetops. *I would gladly sever another toe to see my woman twat up instead of the massive loaf who rides beside me.* "You prefer something more docile then?"

My mountain-sized brother mulled over the question, taking too long to answer, as he always did. A full minute later, his weighty head of curls bobbed up and down.

"Docile, loving. Devoted like our Auntie Lilium is to Uncle Septimus."

I huffed aloud, floored that he would believe such blatant falsehood. They were both miserable in their marriage. One just hid it while the other fucked who he pleased in Monwyn's underground Den. *Depraved bunch of reprobates. How one could stray from their chosen is beyond me.*

Gods, Ambrose probably had Eira there now. Since their Joining, he compromised her time like she was his personal attendant. No Monwyn husband spent as much time with their wife. *My wife.*

Eira.

I smiled to myself, thinking of the day she brandished that knife in Scion Greggen's smug face. My chest swelled. Never had a Monwyn contingent been inspired to such heights—even the octogenarians were moved to wield their canes at her command.

"Ah, you will, without doubt, enjoy brother Ambrose's new wife then—a proverbial paragon of morality. Virtuous in every way. Soft."

I chuckled to myself.

Aberus would catch Eira in one of her righteous fits sooner rather than later, and I prayed to the Goddess I would be there to witness it. She would rant and rail, and those cheeks of hers would flush pink as she stamped her indignant feet. Gods, those tits would heave and bounce and—

Fuck. Get a grip, Cat.

"How wonderful. I cannot wait to make her acquaintance. When Mama visited and told me he meant to marry, I was in shock—absolute shock, I tell you. And when it was revealed that she was neither whore nor showgirl, Catommandus, you could have felled me with the flick of a finger."

Mmmm. Eira played a whore once. She could play one again... my personal attendant. She would backhand me across the jaw for using the term whore, but—

"The fuck you say, Aberus? Back up. When Mama *visited*? This whole time, you and she were meeting, and you kept it from me? I was the Protector, you giant dick, sworn to keep you safe from any who'd dare seek you. For fuck's sake, our sweet biscuit of a mother is a godsdamned mastermind to have pieced together your whereabouts... and her heir is just as deceitful it would seem."

Aberus swiveled around to face me. His cheeky grin took up more than half of his cow-sized head.

"Brother Cato." He paused for effect, placing his hand over his heart. "She located me within three days of you setting me up in that old hunting lodge."

I shook my head, grumbling. "I should have become a Scholar like I wanted."

It was just another shitty reminder that my operations were not as infallible as I assumed.

Over his shoulder, Aberus scanned the forest, and I used the time to adjust the bulge in my pants. Thoughts of Eira consistently left me with a stiff cock and currently smashed into the pommel of my leather saddle—it was less than pleasant. There were two more days of distracting myself before we reached the next safe house; gouging someone's eyes out, or remembering the rancid stench of Scion Ozius's head presented at court, were my go-tos for erection deflation. Daydreams of the woman who was *my* wife, in all but the legal sense, were agonizing.

Since leaving, I spent my days in the saddle, concocting ideas that would allow me to spirit her away from the palace for a duration of more than six hours. And though many of my plans ended in fucking, they began with adventure. I wanted to watch her eyes light up when I took her to visit the fire mountain or hold her hand as we swam in the cave pools of Basilia. Even when I rested, back against a tree, the snores of my ogre-sized relation in my ear, I could imagine my head resting in her lap as she read to me of the new mineral deposits found in southern Monwyn.

"Listen." Aberus pulled back on his reins and raised a hand.

In a split second, my dagger was in my palm. I focused, listening for any sounds indicating the presence of man or otherworldly beast. The wraiths had been rampant on the road east but had luckily kept to the skies, chasing after bats and terrorizing the owls. There were no shrill wails here, no growls or screeches. I inhaled deeply. The air was sweet with the scent of evergreen. No odors signifying a troll or ogre in the vicinity.

I scanned the tree line, which revealed nothing more than swaying branches and the glowing eyes of a fox at hunt.

"It is nothing, truly, Cat. Just the paranoia of a man who looks for his corruption-addled father to appear from the mists and conjure me into an early grave." He sat back in his saddle, and we resumed our trek. "Do you recall the day he nearly drowned me for pinching that pie from the palace kitchen?"

"I do." I nodded. "But to be fair, you were reaching into the oven with your bare hands like a fucking toddler might," I murmured.

A fist smashed into my shoulder, nearly unseating me.

"Do not take his side, petite princeling. It was at your urging that I take the pie in the first place. Chubby cub of a boy."

"Aberus, do you require a reminder of how easy it would be for me to remove your gigantic ass from that horse?"

"Still sensitive about your height?" He pursed his lips and bent them into an over-exaggerated frown. "Catommandus, a girl will grow to love you one day, even if you yourself did not grow above five foot and nine."

Jokes on you, motherfucker. I yanked my heather blue cap more snuggly over my cold ears and readjusted the hidden leather spaulder that had, moments before, covered my shoulder. A hit from Aberus was as stunning as being whacked by a troll. *A girl does love me, brother, and she is everything that is magnificent in this world.*

I rubbed my chest absentmindedly; a hollow feeling had settled there the moment I stepped foot outside of the palace. Demoted from the Protectorate... the realization that I *could* have then Joined with Eira, if my own schemes had not prevented it. I was entirely adrift without the woman who stole my heart—not *stole*—woke it from its self-imposed slumber.

This must be pining... Fucking revolting.

"Cat, describe to me again the look on Uncle Septimus's face when Father handed you the title he craved for so long. Euphoric, you said, lips parted, eyes hazed... Goddess, do you suppose that is also his sex face?"

I doubled over, fake gagging.

"I do not want to imagine that. I wish to keep the food firmly in my stomach."

"Th-the mushroom water you forced upon me? I think it would serve its purpose better on the ground. Why you brought nothing palatable is beyond—"

I pulled my sword and slid off my mount before he finished his sentence.

"Aberus, go!"

Something was out there. The way the branch snapped. It was not in accordance with the innate sounds of nature. Animals did not halt their steps when stepping on a twig—they carried along on their path or ran if startled.

This was man, or it was magic.

"Cato, remount, we will run."

"No, Aberus, I will hold them off. Go now. Do not turn back!"

Shadows emerged. A crescent of adversaries moving forward. The outline of their armored bodies shone like silver slivers, illuminated by the faint light of the moon.

In a bent-legged stance, a prickling surge of adrenaline spiked in my body, preparing it for battle. The swell used to make me anxious, make my palms sweat. Now it brought me a sense of elation, second only to coming between Eira's velvet thighs.

"Cato, there are too many. I will not abandon you."

He was no coward, Goddess bless him, but the chivalric-minded Aberus never knew when to flee. Never.

My excitement turned to true fear. Keeping Aberus, next in line to the throne of Monwyn, alive, had been my singular focus for the better part of a decade, and now he was making that chore difficult.

I took two measured steps forward and raised my blade. I would *not* allow Merrias to greet him this night.

"Aberus, tell Ambrose to take care of Ei—"

"That will not be necessary, Your Highness." I recognized Lemder's voice immediately but did not lower my steel. I trusted no one this night, not even my guard, the father of Eira's beloved lady's maid.

"Why have you tracked us? Speak now or forfeit your life," I gritted out between clenched teeth.

Lemder continued walking toward us, raising his hands in front of his barrel-shaped chest, showing he bore no weapons. He remained silent.

"You have chosen death, I see."

I stretched my neck from side to side. It would take a stronger blow than normal to remove his head from his thick bull's neck. Luckily, I reveled in a challenge.

Lunging forward, I arced my weapon, aiming to bring it down on the back of his neck, right above the knob that I knew would protrude at the base of his nape.

Lemder fell to his knees, hanging his head.

I pulled my steel, seconds from severing the tether that kept him tied to this realm.

His stance was one of supplication.

Confusion cluttered my mind. Lemder was a proud man.

"What has happened? Speak."

He shook his head, shuddering as his chest collapsed with a deep exhale.

"Speak now. That is an order!" I commanded.

His head snapped up, and his mouth dropped open, unshed tears caught in the moon's diffused glow.

"King Burchard is dead. Long live His Majesty Aberus, King of Monwyn."

CHAPTER TWO

EVEN IN DEATH

EIRA

"He died as he lived—casting the otherworldly scourge back into the nether depths. The corruption was upon us, citizens of Ærta, but Burchard protected the innocents of Monwyn in his final act upon the soil," the priest intoned, a hand placed over his heart.

He died because of me.

"I am no innocent, and a priest who speaks falsely should be—"

Ambrose pressed my face into his chest, cutting off my words.

"Let the rift that now bisects our grounds be ever a reminder that She Who Knows All favored her mountain children. Saved by her grace, while the deplorables remain in the netherfrost! She has defeated evil once again, and our most blessed monarch took up a sword by her side: the Goddess's general. He, no doubt, stood upon the Arbiter blade and has found his reward in the cradle up above."

And here I stand, a killer who walks among the living.

Imella

Lilium.

Little satyr.

Burchard... My Nan—Gray eyes, torn throat, lips sewn. Remembering the catalyst for my rage caused my nauseating guilt to wane, at least for the moment.

"Stop it now," Ambrose hissed into my ear. "Cool yourself immediately. I'll not be scorched twice in one day."

I breathed deeply, recalling the frigid temperatures of Nortia—imagined lying in a drift of freshly fallen snow. I tried to control the heat, truly I did, but like it did every time I conjured up my beloved companion's image, my body's temperature rose, the pain of the memory sublimated to heat.

Firewalker. Nether Daughter.

"We now inter His Majesty Burchard in the state yard mausoleum, to rest amongst the storied Monwyns of history past. I would venture to say that his contribution to his kingdom and to all of Ærta stands heads above those of any other."

I twisted around and gazed upon the shrouded body of my father-in-law, my co-conspirator—my papa when my own father was in hiding with my mother.

The wind whipped around the white—the color of mourning in these parts—linen covering and sent its bottom edge, and the servants bearing his body, into a tizzy. The pallbearers, also garbed in brilliant white tunics touting finely embroidered chains of white flowers, did their best to keep the covering secure so as not to reveal his burned and broken body.

I maimed him... I took his life.

I'd already decided. When my strength returned, I would exact revenge for my pain and for the suffering of my men, Cato and Ambrose, who had both parents ripped from their lives in a single, terrible night. The Primus-King would have his daughter, and with her would come the end of his charmed existence. Not swiftly, mind you. No, he would remain alive for as long as my blood could sustain him. His punishment would endure—

"Ouch, goddessdammit!" I yelped as Ambrose pinched the sensitive skin of my ribs.

"I am sweating through my best silks, wife, and pearlescent ivory shows every imperfection already. Calm yourself and resume your normal temperature post-haste."

"Unhand me and you will cease your sweat!" I scolded, keeping my voice low.

"So that you can set the temple to flame? I think the fuck not. Besides, you can barely stand on your own, and, like your hair, you are an absolute mess. Should I let you fall into a heap on the ground? Is writhing in a lump of misery a funerary custom of the North?"

If I didn't love this fucker.

One... two... three... breathe, Eira.

The priest—the very same man who presided over our Joining—held a torch to the massive stone bowl perched upon a granite altar. Small bits of parchment containing the prayers and well-wishes of thousands of citizens burned. I focused on the bits of paper and watched their edges catch, glowing red and orange in the gloom of an overcast morning.

How I longed to see the lush Gaean forests engulfed in similar flames. To walk behind the inferno as it raged and spread on its way to consume the kingdom of filth.

"Oh, dear," the priest muttered while looking left and then right.

His torch sputtered out, extinguished by the winds that howled through the yard between the temple and the tall, black-marble obelisk that would serve as Papa Burchard's place of rest.

But not Imella's. Not his wife, Goddess be with her.

Hating the misogynistic kingdom just a little more, I entered my alternate realm, the one that mirrored this one but only allowed *my* presence.

Since I had become the shade and battered the world around me that bloody night, entering was as simple as imagining myself there—I followed the shadows behind my eyes and emerged in a strange solitude. Here, my body no longer felt weak, though this state would not heal me as the shade form had. No matter how hard I tried, I'd been unable to take *that* form since the Nether Lord made his presence known.

It was interesting being able to watch the world revolve around you, and manipulate it with none the wiser. Did any others share this gift?

I watched Ambrose as he held me, a pillar supporting my broken husk. He was resplendent in his pearlescent vest and matching long coat. So entirely beautiful with his hair pulled back, braided, and held in place by the silver coronet of a prince sitting atop his noble brow. The studs of sapphire and rosettes of ruby somehow made his eyes greener.

Barring the burn mark on his cheek, my husband's sacrifice was hidden—his chest bore a swath of angry blistered skin where he had held my fevered body as the nether god appeared, and the discoloration of frostbite mottled his calves.

Ambrose was the sole reason that I had not set out on my premeditated path of destruction already... and, I suppose, the three broken fingers on my right hand and four on my left. Clean breaks all, but I felt as useless as a newly born Nortian babe, swaddled in layer upon layer of puffy furs. My furs, however, were inches of thick bandaging.

I moved toward the priest and wrapped my hand around the smoldering torch handle. The flames reignited, surging high enough that the priest recoiled in alarm.

Father Burchard deemed himself most comfortable manipulating water, but fire was *my* element.

Firewalker. Nether Daughter. I repeated the Nether Lord's words, a constant litany in my mind.

The mountain of parchments sparked and roared as they exploded into a ball of orange and yellow tongues, lapping three feet into the air.

The wide-eyed priest shrank back and then fell to his knees, tossing the entire torch into the offering bowl.

He raised his hands to the sky.

No, it's not your Goddess, man of the cloth. She *is benevolent, peaceful, and loving. I am not that.* The long line of my ancestors may have followed the light—I was on a different path.

Firewalker. Nether Daughter.

I moved around the priest on silent feet and rested my hand on Papa Burchard's chest.

Why would they cover him and keep all from bearing witness to the violence he endured?

I lifted the shroud and gave it a fluttering shake. The gathered assembly would think it the wind.

Gasps and cries came from the assembled crowd.

"Goddess, we see you!" the priest cried out. "We are your children to command."

Oh, Papa.

Turns out I could cry in this realm.

His perpetually dry skin was sallow and his cheeks sunken. I smoothed my hand over his face. The recent growth of a few-day-old beard peppered his jaws, but his eyebrows and head were still totally bald. I brushed the shorn side of my head where the magical explosion had taken half of my hair.

Thank you for treating me as your own.

The loss of our Infinite Bond was profound—in the same way that sudden illness or injury can highlight the miracle of having one's health. In this case, though, the change was tangible, like a portion of my æther was missing. Though we shared it for only a short amount of time, it was only after it ceased that I understood how utterly safe it made me feel. The knowledge that someone was there, even if they weren't, physically speaking.

Servants scurried to replace his shroud.

"Let us pray as we seal our beloved monarch, our blessed provider, into his eternal home on Ærta. May his soul rise to the cradle, to be nurtured by our Divine Creator."

I backed away as the servants lifted the platform on which Papa Burchard rested and made my way to Ambrose. Could he feel me? I swept my thumb across the hands that held my body, still tucked into his chest. His lashes lowered. With both Cato and Aberus gone, he bore the weight of the world. He was second in line to the throne, but the only representative of the royal line currently at court. It fell to him to reassure the citizens of Monwyn and plaster over the mess I had made. As far as I was aware, he had yet to shed his own tears.

I stretched up, placed a kiss on his chin, and smiled to myself when his brow lightly furrowed.

I reentered my physical body.

The pain drowned out my tender feelings, leaving in their place the ache of every bruise from my wrist to my elbow, the constant throb that accompanied my broken bones—it had rendered me useless for three days.

I was supposed to be a "fully fueled" vessel of æther, Goddess touched, but my body remained so very human, and now, the only man who had had the knowledge to answer my questions was being sealed away for eternity.

I shivered in Ambrose's arms as a stone mason shuttered the open hole that now contained Papa Burchard's remains. *Gross.*

"I don't like your burial customs at all," I murmured. "This is nasty."

"Too reverent? Too solemn for my fire-breathing harpy?"

"Too... yuck." I hugged Ambrose closer, disturbed by what I was witnessing. "His body is going to... to—"

"—rot," he said matter-of-factly.

"Yes, and in such a small enclosure. All dark and dank. It makes me sick really, just the thought of it."

"What backward custom do they practice in Nortia?"

I bristled, pushing against his arms, but he held firm.

"Well, nothing rots there. It's too cold. We burn our dead or bury them at sea. Either way, you are returned to the earth." I glanced down at the ground, feeling wearier than I thought possible. "Not shoved on a shelf to get all gelatinous and stinky."

Ambrose lightly gripped my chin and tilted my face up to his.

"Is this about Nan, wifling?"

My throat constricted. Despair crept in, hugging its sickly arms around me, squeezing the air from my lungs.

I nodded.

"I don't want her shelved and bricked in, or... or put in the ground, Ambrose. I can't... just can't stand the thought of it."

His soft lips grazed my forehead.

"I understand, but Eira, it is simply not possib—"

"His Highness Ambrose, first in the line of succession to the Monwyn throne, will lift his voice in prayer," the royal herald cried.

"Come." My husband gathered me into his arms and carried me to a seat atop the tall dais erected in the yard. Banners of white floated above us, snapping in the wind, reminiscent of the clouds gathering in the sky.

From this vantage, above the crowd, the faces of what seemed like every Monwyn citizen from here to Colpass stared back at me. Dozens in the assembly—men and women alike—wept openly into their handkerchiefs, and all but a handful wore the blue baldrics that, Ambrose had explained, got sent to households every time a child reached the age of four. Citizens and royals alike would wear them at coronations, funerals, and when marching to war. The wealthy paired theirs with tunics and fur coats, a million shades of cream and ivory... the poor, over whatever was warm.

Ambrose stood before the gathering, tall, proud, every inch the crown prince.

"The day has come when my father's silence stands more powerfully than the voice he raised in ruling Monwyn. He kept his faith, even in the face of great turmoil, and therefore a Wreath of Valor will lie upon his grave," Ambrose's steady voice rang out, echoing off the temple walls, carrying beyond the throng.

The crowd pressed in, craning their necks when two children—twin boys—appeared, bringing forward a wreath of pine and dried lavender. Guards stood watch, holding their spears horizontally across their chests, forming a walkway running from the back of the temple to the gravesite.

"Long live King Aberus!" Ambrose shouted, as the children lifted their little arms and hung the circle of greenery over its new home. The wreath formed a ring of purple and green, framing the boldly chiseled name: BURCHARD.

Though the stories would speak of his valor in defeating the Nether Lord, the wreath would remind me of his embrace as he pulled me back to humanity and away from æther-fueled nihilism.

"LONG LIVE KING ABERUS! LONG LIVE KING ABERUS! LONG LIVE THE KING!" the crowd roared in response.

"Long live Prince Ambrose!" a man shouted from the far right.

My heart fluttered.

"LONG LIVE PRINCE AMBROSE!" the masses chanted back—full-throated acceptance for the adopted son. He had won them over, not by royal decree, but by steering the ship of state with a steady hand. My husband's chest swelled as the chorus continued to carry around us—he deserved the praise.

The priest bowed, walked down the short flight of steps, and then it was over.

The crowd departed, and Ambrose appeared by my side, sweeping me up into his powerful arms once more.

"I can walk," I said, more impertinently than intended.

"And I need something to occupy my hands, wife," he snapped back.

I nodded and kept quiet, contenting myself by running my less broken hand down his thick braid. The intimate gesture soothed me as he leaned into my touch.

We walked across a mausoleum-scattered yard and rounded several smaller stone obelisks until we reached a rectangle of ground separated by a wrought-iron gate.

Three red-robed priestesses came into view, their robes billowing around their ankles. They stood in prayer—hands to forehead—surrounding the covered body of Monwyn's forgotten queen.

Imella. Stronger than any man, braver than an army standing on the cusp of war.

Her man Hughes and a handful of older nobles formed a horseshoe around the spot where her body lay on a short table next to an open grave. I tensed—the small muscles in my ribcage contracted painfully.

"Is... is that where she will..." I pointed to the cavern of mud and dirt.

"It is, Eira. Be still. Your heart is fluttering as fast as a bird's wing."

"Please, Ambrose, please don't sit me near it," I whispered, hearing the panic in my own voice. The muddy hole reminded me of the basalt quarry... and of the deep chasm that splintered the back grounds of Cordillaria. Maihon, the groundskeeper and his daughter Mae had lost their cabin to my fury, swallowed whole into the ground.

Firewalker. Nether Daughter.

We passed through the gate.

"Set her chair on the far end, Jance." The guard, Levaunt's nephew—Goddess rest Levaunt—snapped to Ambrose's command. After his harrowing rescue of a collapsed Ambrose and my broken, unconscious body, Protector Septimus had appointed the young man to our personal detail. I stared at Jance and prayed his path would be easier than his uncle's. Burchard had been a handful to keep in check... and Levaunt, faithful servant to the end, was one of the sixteen who fell that night, his body impaled upon my black shards as he sought to protect his sovereign.

Jance favored his elder—deep-colored skin that reminded me of the jet gemstones that stood proudly in the centerpiece of the Nortian crown. Kind brown eyes that reflected gold in the light. Lush, full lips and the lithe musculature of a boy on the cusp of adulthood. He probably left the mines only a year or two ago. Levaunt would be proud of his nephew.

I turned my attention back to the much smaller funeral, avoiding looking directly at the hole in the ground.

The aged priestess, with wispy gray hair and thin skin, bowed her head.

"She bore the future of Monwyn. Five children in all, brought into the Goddess's earthly paradise. From the body of the late monarch Burchard, she mothered two boys: Aberus and Catommandus, and three dutiful girls: Odella, Borka, and Pansy."

And?

"There is no greater gift to a husband than for his wife to bear…"

Fucking, and?

I could no longer hear her, her voice blotted out by my growing rage.

I mustered all the strength in my legs and rose to a shaky squat, willing my thighs to hold me upright, if only for a minute.

"And?" I shouted, my voice startling those at prayer.

The gray-haired priestess, who wore a large blue medallion in the middle of her chest, looked at me askance. How could she not understand why I was shaking with fury?

Ambrose rushed to my side and placed himself in front of me.

"And nothing. Hush," he warned, placing a heavy hand on my shoulder, and forcing me back to my seat.

"This is outrageous. You are her child, just like the others."

"*Not* a child of her body," Ambrose said. "Sit."

I tucked my bandaged hands under my armpits and stewed while he turned back to the proceeding. The main priestess raised her hands to the sky while her assistants worked to tuck a white shroud tighter around Imella's body.

"And I can think of ten things she accomplished that were more profound than pushing out your big-headed brothers."

Ambrose's hand shot back, sealing itself over my mouth.

"Let Merrias judge her accordingly as she stands upon the blade. Let her rejoin her late husband Burchard and may they both find peace in the Goddess's bosom. May she rest." The women laid their hands upon Imella's body and, in unison, breathed deeply, expanding their chests to full capacity.

"May she rest," they prayed in harmony.

The crowd broke up and moved off as three men with shovels advanced from where they stood, only a few yards away.

Ambrose cut their path short and held his hand out, palm open.

"Begone with the lot of you. Jance, see the consort back to the carriage."

"Ambrose what are—"

"Silence, Eira. For once, just..." His voice faded as he turned away from me.

Jance packed me up and into his arms, expending much more energy than Ambrose or Cato ever had to. He wobbled under my weight as he bore me toward the waiting carriage.

Peering over his armored shoulder, I located Ambrose, fearful of the moment I let him out of my sight. No one was safe. *Nowhere* was safe.

I watched as he placed his crown upon his discarded jacket, and then pulled his lifeless mother into his arms and held her like you would a sleeping child.

He rocked her gently, his cheek against her shrouded forehead.

My broken heart shattered as he released her and lowered her into the ground. My sorrow amplified as he pulled a blade from his boot, and took a lock of her hair that peeked from under her covering.

A gentle rain began to fall as he stood.

The sky wept as he began filling the grave, each shovelful laid carefully and with reverence, like a prayer given motion.

"Here we are, consort, and just in time."

"Thank you, Jance," I whispered, longing to be back at Ambrose's side. Praying that Cato would soon return.

"You are welcome, consort. Now, don't open that door yourself. Hang on a moment. I have everything under control and will see you up in no time. Just a second. Just need to grab this right here."

I smiled inwardly as Jance propped his knee under my rear. Unlike his stoic uncle, he kept a continual stream of words flowing from his mouth. Even as he wedged me into the side of the carriage for additional support, he continued yammering on about the confusing weather patterns we'd had as of late. Eventually, he wrestled the door open.

"Right on up now. Hang on. Let me get these skirts. I forgot about your mangled fingers. They told me you walloped a centaur, and he stomped all over your hands. That was brave, but ladies should not take on beasts. Embroidery, yes, maybe even light gardening, but beasts, no."

"Ahem."

Jance stiffened and whipped his head around. Dropping my legs, his hand went to his blade.

"At ease," I cautioned, patting his shoulder. "This is Hughes, Imella's guardian. He's received approval from the Protect—Prince Catommandus to be near my person."

Jance shuffled from side to side, still holding me protectively.

"Mmm, maybe, but not from Prince Ambrose. I'm afraid, sir, I will need you to back away before I am forced to run you through. I am an excellent swordsman, so I have been told by countless brothers-at-arms. Cam says I'm the best in the garrison with my spear, but the sword suits me just fine as well."

Hughes took three precise steps backward and then stood his ground. He held the sides of his cloak wide and then spread his fingers, showing us he bore no steel.

"Nope, I am very sorry. I'm sure you are a decent fellow, but that still will not do. Not at all. Just a moment." Jance huffed and puffed and hoisted me up near his shoulders. With a grunt, he placed me gently on the carriage bench seat. He nodded curtly, and then spun. "Right then, draw your blade, sir." He unsheathed his sword and pointed it directly at Hughes's chest. His fighting posture was a replica of Cato's in every way: left foot forward, knees slightly bent.

"As I have indicated," Hughes spoke in a volume so low I had to open the carriage window to continue understanding him, "I have no weapons upon my person."

"Stand down, Jance," I called out. "Truly, he is a man of sound character!"

I could practically hear the wheels turning in the guard's mind. He twisted his toe on the stone path, deepening his stance. Not once did his weapon tilt or dip.

"Cannot do it, consort, no rising in the ranks for the fellas who cannot follow orders. I follow orders and I have been ordered to 'bludgeon any man who nears my wife until their brains run from their ears as liquid.'"

"Hughes," I called out, "take another step back and quickly tell me what you need."

The slight man did as I asked and stepped backward without taking his eyes off the weapon at his chest.

"Troth Eira, after our last meeting, Imella extended my contract and named you her beneficiary. The terms of *her* contract have been fulfilled, and I now enter your service."

You couldn't have pried the brows off my hairline with an icepick.

She left me my own man. Ambrose will flip!

"Well, Hughes, my first order is as follows: make yourself scarce and then beg an audience with His Highness Ambrose. He is not a man to have another near his property. That's me. I'm his property. And if you haven't noticed, Jance takes his orders to keep others at bay *very* seriously."

"As you wish." Hughes inclined his head and then backed up slowly. Only when he neared the iron gate of the burial ground did he turn on his heel and walk away.

Rain began to fall in earnest—the gloomy sky darkening.

"Sheath your sword, soldier, and stand under the temple's overhang so you don't turn to rust."

A steady pitter-patter of droplets sounded on the carriage's roof, picking up in intensity.

"Yes indeed, consort. If you need anything, just ask. I will be less than three feet from your person and have no issue..."

I poked my head out the door, not caring as the rain splattered across my cheeks and ran through my hair.

Covered in mud and soaked by sweat and storm, Ambrose kneeled at his mother's grave, palms covering his eyes.

CHAPTER THREE

A GENTLE KIND OF LOVE

EIRA

"**W**ill you take me to see them?"

Ambrose held me on his lap while he lathered the soap in his hands. The warm scent of cinnamon and orange awakened my senses as he scrubbed his fingers through my hair, navigating around the arms that I held above the water's surface.

"Eira, we have gone twice already. Once before the sun rose and the moment we returned from the burials."

"I know. It's just... shit, I *don't* know." I tilted my head back, and he thoroughly rinsed my long tresses, making sure none of the cleanser made its way into my eyes.

"That is the most sensible thing you've said in days."

He sighed, and I turned my gaze to his, pleading. He responded by placing his hands under my elbows and holding them up for me as he pulled me against his chest. The relief to my straining muscles was immediate, but not so the tumultuous thoughts circling my mind.

He held me in silence until the water began to cool.

"Wife, had I not seen the ice-babies with my own eyes... No, I am still not convinced this isn't some nightmare." Ambrose reached for a cloth and passed it under my arms and over my breasts. "And remember, Bem watches them. If anything changes, he will alert us immediately. Feet."

He floated me off his lap and onto the sunken bath bench. I dutifully poked my toes above the water, and he pushed a soapy finger between each of the digits. When clean enough to pass his inspection, he pressed his thumbs into the soles of my feet and rubbed.

I closed my eyes.

"Eira?"

"Yes?"

"Cato will soon return."

"When?" I jerked up, splashing water over the tub's rim. My pulse quickened. "How much does he know? Is he aware of—"

"Septimus sent the missives. I only know that he and Aberus will arrive and was not permitted to know more... to ensure the safety of Monwyn's young king. There is, if you recall, a long history of brothers slaughtering brothers here, so information—reliable information—will be a commodity more precious than malachite."

Sharp-footed pixies walked the length of my spine, causing bumps to spread across my skin.

"You don't suspect that Aberus or Cato would be capable of fratricide?"

Ambrose pinched the bridge of his nose, suds clung to his beard.

"My mind has been working non-stop considering the what-if's. If the two *natural* brothers were to fall, could Septimus make a claim to the throne? Will he pit them against one another? When Aberus is installed as king, will Cato step up as Protector again... per tradition? Is my life in danger... a non-blood brother easily cast aside?"

My Goddess. The relief that accompanied the news of Cato's return flared brightly, only to dim an instant later.

"Is Aberus the type of man who would commit such an atrocity?" All I knew about the eldest brother was that he was a big man like Ambrose, and that he'd been secreted away from Cordillaria while Cato deemed their father a threat to his life.

"I have met Aberus only a handful of times since Mama and I moved to Colpass. I do not know his mind or his heart, but on those rare encounters, he was an absolute marvel of a man. Confident, well-spoken. Men would cower in his presence when we took to the halls. Do you have to poop?"

"Oh, for fuck's sake." I dropped my head back and wondered again how life had come to this. I should be at the gates of Gaea, laying siege to their filthy fucking kingdom, not being nursed by my contract-husband. "You are not, and I will repeat it again, are *not* wiping my ass."

Ambrose inhaled, expanding his chest to full capacity. He propped his fists on his hips.

"Eira, your bowels are on a tight schedule. How will you see to your hygiene all bound up and dysfunctional as you are?"

"Like I have for the last three days, Ambrose." I stood, arms above my head, and walked the length of the tub, not willing to have this conversation.

"Which is how? I imagine you tossing the linens over the back of the chair and dragging your butt across it like a dog would his itchy ass on the grass."

"Not discussing this," I said in a sing-song voice. And I certainly wasn't admitting that his musing was almost exactly what I'd been doing. The headrest of the chaise was too tall, but the curved bath faucet was the perfect height.

"What about Allaine? Why would you not command her to wipe—"

"She is mourning a brother. One that *I* killed," I shouted, immediately regretful. The æther gathered in my stomach and squeezed, forcing bile into my throat. Her kin had been one of them that night, cutting up the little satyress and desecrating her body. I'd not mourn *him*... but I grieved for his sister.

"She is not aware, Eira. There is not a soul alive who would accuse you of murder."

I whipped my head back around.

"Because you ordered the witnesses slain, Ambrose!"

He shrugged and pursued me, but I evaded him and paced across the tub again, arms held high.

"*Septimus* saw them killed, Eira. I just agreed with him. It was much safer to sell the gods-were-angry-and-shoved-the-Nether-Lord-back-to-his-frosty-domicile story. Could you imagine what would happen if I told the world that you got angry, conjured yourself into a little black puffball and shared in amorous congress with the Lord of Demons to produce some creepy snow-spawn?"

Fucking Ambrose. I stepped up onto the bench and tried to knee-climb from the tub. I had to get out or risk a fight that I didn't want to have.

"Ambrose, see how long you remain upright if you accuse me of having sex with the nether god one more time." I placed a careful foot onto the bathing chambers marble floor, making sure I had solid traction before—

Two hands settled on my rear, lifting and guiding me until both my feet were firmly planted. How a man could be so mind-blowingly infuriating and so damnably thoughtful at once was—

My cheeks parted.

"Ambrose! What the nether?" I yelled, tucking my buns tightly.

I huffed loudly and marched to the column around which Allaine had cleverly tied a towel. I shimmied and shook against the pillar, drying myself the best I could while shooting eye daggers at my husband.

"I am merely investigating your ability to see to your own cleanliness," Ambrose said. He wound a perfect towel turban about his head, padded from the tub to the closet, and returned with a hideous yellow nightgown. This fashion failure had layers of finely tatted blue lace covering the bust and each wrist, and bows of the same hue sewn around the hem. I'd look like a broody godsdamned hen. "You are my wife. I will see to your comfort. I am the one who will ensure you are..." his voice drifted away.

I stomped over to where he stood and held my arms up like a toddler—my cloth-covered fingers looking like fat sausages—but Ambrose was no longer a participant in our conversation. He just stood there, silent, looking across the room. A shadow flitted across his face, and, for the briefest instant, I glimpsed the extent of *his* exhaustion.

My shameful indignation dissolved.

"Ambrose? Sweet love? Other than the Monwyn sport of thrones, your inept magical wife, or your own horrific losses, how are you?"

I attempted to get close to him, but he pursed his lips and went about dressing me like an infant, reaching into a rolled-up sleeve and pulling out my arm.

"I'm fine."

He turned and walked out of the bathing chamber.

I shuffled after him, patting down the lace that gathered under my chin, trailing his reticent Highness through the common room, and into his quarters.

"Ambrose." He threw the bedcovers back and ignored me. "Ambrose, you bull-headed brute, listen to me." I stomped my foot on the floor once and then again.

He sat down on the bed, scooted to the middle, and then angrily stabbed a finger toward the mattress.

Of course.

It was time for cuddles.

I wriggled in sideways, my clumsy movements pulling the bottom sheet free from its corner tuck and exposing the mattress. I ignored it and elbow-crawled to his side. It's not like I could fix the damn thing with my pillow hands. I laid my head on Ambrose's fuzzy chest and felt him deflate a second later.

He needed touch, required it to feel whole and settled.

"Tell me..." I nudged him with my nose and then blew at the hair on his sternum, the way I knew he liked. "Talk to me, my handsome prince."

He let a long-held breath go.

"Nothing is imminently pressing; I assure you that I am—"

"Creator's tits." I bit his nipple smartly, and his sharp shriek pierced my ear. "Will you just spit it out? I know you, Ambrose. And I want to be there for you as well."

"Fine!" He rubbed his peaked flesh and shot me an incredulous look. "I am feeling insecure about Cato's return. Are you happy now? Would you like me to divulge *all* of my self-doubts, Eira?"

I hugged his middle and held him tightly in my bandaged arm.

"I'm worried too."

His lips settled on my hairline.

"Because you are unsure of his feelings after our triumvirate of tupping? That's what they call it when a ram and ewe fuck, by the way... tupping. You are afraid it is *my* muscled arms he will run to, instead of your fleshy bits?"

Ohmygods.

"No, I... I don't think that will be the case." I shook my head as my cheeks flushed, remembering that night. That profoundly amazing eve. "No, for me it's solidly because I... killed his parents, and Ambrose, Cato loves you. He's told me so himself."

"Yes, but *how* does he love me? Things are different now, and we've not been able to speak since we shared our tumble in triplicate." Ambrose sighed. "There is a second rule when involved in a tangling triad. Do you remember the first one?"

"Yes. Leave no one out."

He painted the tail of his hair back and forth along my collarbone.

"Correct. And the second is to talk through the experience during *and* afterward. During, people get so wrapped up in their feelings and performance that they forget to communicate... After, they tend to turn all prudish and keep their thoughts under lock and key. You know I live to tailor an experience; I require after-action debriefing, status reports... an alphabetized list of positions and angles that did and did not work for each partner."

I stretched my neck to plant kisses along his beard.

"You are ever thoughtful. And you weren't able to speak to Cato after?"

"No. I was not. Eira, it was too important that he reach Aberus when Septimus was named Protector. Nothing else could take precedence." Ambrose trailed his fingers along my bent elbow and fidgeted with the bandages that reached below my wrists. "We spoke briefly while he gathered his belongings, and then he left. He was gone within the hour, and you were ill and *my* priority."

I brushed my lips over his perfect pectoral, relishing the texture of his soft skin.

"You are the best caretaker, Ambrose." I inhaled his spicy scent, finding comfort in his closeness. "I suppose we will worry together, then. I have a host of sins to atone for when it comes to him. My actions in the Den, my actions with Septimus... the chaos that followed."

The silence stretched between us.

"Tell me that thing again," Ambrose whispered into my hair.

"What thi—"

"You know... that thing you say to me now."

I smiled, even if he couldn't see it. This had become an additional part of our nightly cuddling ritual.

"Oh, that I am thankful that the Goddess placed an above-average contract husband in my path?"

"And," Ambrose pressed.

"And that he is a big-headed Monwyn asshole?"

"Go on..."

"And that I love him?"

He wiggled beneath me, snuggling into the pillows.

"Yes, that's the one. Good night."

"Good night, husband." I chuckled to myself as his whiskers rasped against my cheek for our goodnight kiss.

And I did love him.

Not in the same way that I loved Cato. Not with a driving, raw intensity... but with a warm, all-encompassing glow that somehow snuck its way into the center of my heart.

Ambrose shut his eyes, and within minutes, his soft snores filled the room. How men could fall asleep so fast still confounded me—almost as much as the innate need in them to appear strong for the sake of others. For a man who never shied away from speaking his mind, he'd done little in the way of grieving his losses. And I *knew* he was feeling them intensely.

I shifted and tried to pull away, seeking to relieve the pressure on my bruised hip—another gift of my rage-filled murder spree—but even in his sleep, Ambrose held me tight.

Oh, well.

I looked into the dim room and focused on the dull, radiating pain in my leg.

My fatigue was overwhelming. It had been for days. But I knew no rest would come.

I settled back into the pillows and stared off into the distance.

Just as my lids lowered, I caught a movement in the room's dark corner.

The small black shade floated from the far side of the chamber as it had every night since the Nether Lord's appearance. It stopped directly above my face.

If this night was like the others, it would hover there until dawn, a physical representation of my sins.

CHAPTER FOUR

HUMPS AND BUMPS

EIRA

For three nights, now four, the shade and I faced off, hostility pulsing thickly between us, the glug of a severed vein. The semi-sheer cloud of darkness lingered above my nose, never touching me, which somehow made its threat more ominous.

I'd seen one like it float out of a soldier's body when I detached him from his mortal home, but unlike this one, that man's spirit had shot up toward the sky and dissipated—perhaps on his way to meet Merrias and her Arbiter blade—may he be cast into the freezing nether. He could writhe in the biting frost for the rest of eternity, and I'd never regret slaying him. I shivered in revulsion, seeing all over again the satyress's lavender eyes and small horns, her head split by the swing of an uncaring sword.

This spirit or soul was lingering on the earth—I assume to ensure my demise. A vindictive guard, or maybe it was Levaunt, Goddess bless him, angry that his life ended with my loss of control... or that the same unbridled power killed Burchard, the man he swore to protect.

I was so godsdamned tired.

When the sun came up, or when a lamp flickered to life, the spirit blinked out of sight, but I had a feeling it didn't stray far from my person. Perhaps it lingered in this realm to oversee my penance, plotting revenge during the day, while I smiled and played the part of royal consort. At night... torture. A torture so delicate that no one could see the damage inflicted. The shade stole my concentration, my wit, my patience—it was a wonder I could function in civilized society at all.

Well, angered spirit, the jokes on you. I don't need any help making my nights a living nether.

My fault. All my fault.

Imella.

Lilium.

Nan.

A queen. A mother. A servant.

That's what the Primus-King's note had said—the poisonous snake.

He took their lives because *his* queen, my mother, his child bride, ran from him and brought me safely into the world.

Nan had just been in his way.

Memories were *my* implements of torture.

The æther stirred in my chest, sending waves of heat down my arms and torso. I'd always run hot, but never like the intense burning of when the Nether Lord cracked open the ground. His frost hadn't touched me. If anything, it calmed the fire, making it bearable.

Show me the daughters of Gaea. That's what I'd asked him. Show me my half-sisters. And then what? Kill them? Take tea with them?

Fuck. I just needed to rest, then I could think with a modicum of clarity.

I turned in Ambrose's embrace and wormed my way toward the edge of the bed, hands as always, in the godsdamned air.

The soul-shade flew in front of my eyes, startling me.

"What do you want from me? My death? You won't have it! Begone with you." I struck out with my blanket-covered foot but missed when Ambrose yanked the covers back, snorting unhappily.

I lashed out again and, to my surprise, my bandaged fingers passed straight through the little cloud, its nebulous form never changing.

"You want me to stay awake until I die of fatigue? Trip down the steps because I can no longer function? Go meet your fate, coward, puff-demon!"

I wrestled my way from the bed and surged to my feet. My hands burned, stinging like a hundred match heads against my flesh.

The æther bolted through my limbs.

I'd burn the shit shade to powder, dissipate it altogether.

Rearing back, I balled my hand and struck.

I dropped to my knees, the pain of closing my fist, moving those broken bones, enough to fell me.

The soul bobbed up and down, laughing in the face of my failure, and shot toward the door.

"That's right. Leave this place, face your judgment, and accept the consequences of your miserably lived life."

The spirit stopped dead in its puffy tracks. It swelled, increasing in size, tendrils of dark matter dancing in a halo of doom.

"Fuck, fuck, fuck!"

It hurled itself my way, a menacing streak bent on destruction.

I dove to the side, landing hard on my shoulder.

"Where are you?" I thrashed around on the floor, desperately trying to spot my adversary, damning myself for not fully dousing my lamp.

There. A flicker!

The shade flew to the other side of the bed and then whipped around, poised for attack.

Goddess alive.

Like it was a breathing entity, the cloud shrank and then grew, doubling and then tripling in size.

"Leave me be!"

"Eira?" Ambrose bolted upright, blindly reaching out for a weapon.

"No!" The soul-cloud shot out as if fired from a crossbow, on a collision course with my husband's head. "Sleep!" I screamed.

Ambrose fell backward, hitting the bed like a pile of stones.

"You will *not* take another from me." Not Ambrose, not the lowliest maid in the palace.

I charged, willing my thighs to maintain their strength.

The spirit turned tail, streaking into the next room. It knew well what it had wrought—Cowardly in life, cowardly in near-death.

I gave chase, tearing through the common room, kicking away the chair in my path.

The cloud blinked through the exterior door. Did it think that would protect it? That a fucking wall would thwart my retaliation?

I hammered my hand down on the handle and threw the door wide.

Jance's eyes went snow-owl round when I slapped a wrapped palm against his cheek.

"Sleep!"

He dropped in a loud clamor as his armored body met the floor. I lunged for his spear, attempting to pry it from the fingers that still clung tight, hindered again by my useless hands. I chewed at my bandages, tearing one until I could firmly grip the wooden spear shaft.

From the periphery of my vision, I glimpsed the nether puff rounding the corner of the hall. I cocked my elbow and launched the weapon, invoking the ferocity of Merrias herself, biting back a scream. A fresh agony lanced through my fingers, throbbing in time with my heartbeat.

A miss.

I ran, tripping once on my stupid nightgown's long hem, and grabbed the ill-launched spear that rolled along the marble floor. The soul shade flitted down the stairs, and I trailed it, keeping the course, descending two steps at a time.

Momentarily, I lost sight of my nemesis, but reacquired its path as I hurriedly doused the lamps intermittently placed along the corridor.

"Are you afraid now, fleeing as you are?" My feet slapped loudly against the cold marble of the grand salon's floor. The heat radiating from my body warmed the tiles as I passed. Sweat ran down my cheeks and dripped onto the frilly-breasted nightgown, causing the lace to droop sadly.

The shade jumped and jolted, fearful of my prowess, flying through the back door of the palace.

"Not today, demon plague. This. Ends."

Using both hands, I twisted the door's steel lock and kicked the wooden panel wide. Torrential rains greeted me, cold and blinding. No matter, though. I was impervious to the chill.

"Halt! Consort, do not take another—"

Fuck no. I stopped for no one.

I dug my foot into the floor, pivoted with all the strength in my hips, and swung the spear into a wide arc, careening toward the as yet unidentified target. The blunt side of the heavy spearhead caught the man right below his chest plate, connecting with a sickening thud against his lower stomach.

He doubled over, clutching his middle.

Before he could recover, I thrust my hand into the space between his gorget and helm, seeking the delicate skin of his neck. He could nap with the others.

"Fuck!" The tip of my finger splintered. Reset just days ago, the sharp stab of bone against the inside of my flesh, made my stomach lurch.

Through tears I opened the eyes that had on reflex closed tight.

The guard raised his hips, arching into the air... and then slammed them into the floor.

"What in the actual..."

He repeated the action. Lift. Slam. Lift... slam.

"Oh gods alive, Eira, you stupid, low-level-bullshit conjurer."

Like the inchworm I'd only read about, the guard hoisted his rear in the air and brought it down against the marble so violently it propelled him forward. The metal splints of his cuisses scraped across the floor, the sound echoing in the empty room.

"Un-fuck! Unfuck this instant," I cried, mangled hands covering my mortified face. "Goddess, please, it was not the command I intended."

My prayers were in vain.

"Gods"—*hump*—"preserve"—*hump*—"me!" the soldier begged in a voice somewhere between a sob and shriek.

Up and down, he hammered his pelvis into the marble.

I pillowed his cheek with one hand and placed the other on his rear, hoping to prevent him from injuring himself. His head mashed my fingers on his next downward fuck.

"Shit! Shit, I'm so sorry. I didn't mean to—"

A forceful gurgle followed by an intense and putrid stench stole my breath from my lungs.

"No." I snatched my traitorous hands back while looking on in horror. "Divine Mother, make him stop. I don't know how to make it stop."

The guard hunched himself across the floor, dragging his feet through the liquid shit pouring from the waist of his arming pants.

I doubled over, gagging and heaving while trying to keep up with his impressive pace.

Don't speak, Eira! Fix this. Think in reverse, like Papa Burchard taught you. What's the opposite of sex-defecation?

Streaks of greenish-brown ooze painted the gleaming marble as he hump-crawled his way toward the exit.

"He-lp, m-e!" the man begged. "Witch!"

"I'm trying!" I sobbed. "Gods, hold still, please. I need to think!"

Hand over hand, he tugged his pounding hips over the threshold.

He couldn't escape. I couldn't risk him alerting anyone else. I lurched forward, grabbed his foot, and yanked.

Like a penguin belly skimming on an ice-covered pond, he glided back along the shit slick.

"Ouch!" His steel sabaton bit into the flesh of my shin. I misstepped and my heel skated. "No, no, no."

I went down hard, landing on my hip, body smearing along the floor as it rode along the refuse track. Even then, I refused to relinquish his foot and held tight while I was hump-dragged through the sticky slop. I crawled over the guard's legs and clutched his thigh. My arms jerked in the rhythm of his thrusts.

"Strength of Nortia." Tears raced down my cheeks. "St-strength of, of Nortia." Mucus dripped from my nose. Shit cascaded over my hands.

My head jerked atop my neck, and then... projectile vomit waterfalled onto the floor, mingling with the already present filth.

"Save me... someone!" the guard screamed hoarsely. "Help!" With his every desperate plea, his bowels erupted, liquified sludge now coating him from rear to foot. And still he humped—nearly ripping my arms from their sockets.

My stomach churned; saliva flowed from my lips. I retched again, and my tears continued. The entire situation was wholly out of control, and Papa Burchard cautioned me *never* to conjure when I was unstable.

I breathed in deeply, sputtering hard, choking at the excrement and mess.

"Please, Papa." Burchard's face appeared on the back of my lids. Smiling, pearl-colored eyes, those wrinkles, and a shiny bald head. I closed my eyes. I looked for the shadows, letting his cracked-tooth smile be my guide.

"Soothe," I breathed, both for the guard's benefit and mine. It was the word that seemed right. "Let us both be soothed."

The humps slowed.

"Gentle now, let's get back to normal, you and me."

The shit stream running down his leg lessened its pour.

I dropped my head back, resting it on the floor for just a few blessed seconds, sobbing freely as I did so.

"You'll need to drink lots of water," I hiccoughed. "And contact the healer when you can rise. Can you keep this a secret? I need you to say yes, or... or..."

I inched my way up to the man's face, where he blinked his eyes at me ever so slowly, an expression of absolute peace on his red-flushed face.

"Yes," he whispered, "or you would have to kill me, vile sorceress." His pale-green eyes were unfocused and euphoric. "I understand."

"Good," I told him. "Good, soldier."

I smoothed my shit-soaked bandaged fingers across his sweat-coated forehead. His eyes closed, and his breathing became even and slow as I watched him drift off. I held my unbandaged fingers under his nose, worried for a moment that I'd "soothed" him into his last breath. But the airflow was steady.

I struggled to my feet and peered into the rain-soaked night—

"My gods..."

CHAPTER FIVE

PINE FRESH

EIRA

I faced the magnitude of my failings.

Holy Mother above.

I'd not seen the back fields of Cordillaria since the night I became the shadow.

Had Ambrose purposefully filled my time to keep me from seeing it? *"Eira, I require your assistance in selecting my formal wear stockings. Wife, help me choose which shade of white will send the message 'mourner and man of the crown.' No, no, to the front gardens. They are picturesque as winter settles in around them."*

A jagged and deep chasm stretched from the private fields where Papa Burchard's favorite vegetables would grow—*What would they grow there now?*—all the way back to where Maihon and little Mae's cabin once stood. Praise the Goddess that they managed to get out when he saw the flames.

The smell of my soiled dress was nothing compared to the overwhelming stench that clung to the air even days later. The aroma of smoke, char, and death made my eyes water profusely, a relentless sting. Even in the heavy rain, the acrid combination was so pervasive that, as I breathed in, it sapped the moisture from my mouth and lungs.

I forced my feet down the stairs, taking one step at a time, telling myself to turn back, but knowing the Goddess led me here to face my truth.

The earth bore dark stains of scorch and soot where the black fire had melted the snow and burned away the grass and bramble beneath it. Even the dirt itself was a discolored gray. I looked beyond the first few feet of wreckage to where hundreds of slits in the rock and soil flanked the yawning tear in the earth; palm-width holes marked where the shards of my black fire had punctured the ground. Sixteen had perished, impaled on those shards—my powers did not discern between guilt and innocence.

Steam rose from my rain-soaked gown. The heat bloomed in my chest and radiated its way down my limbs as my overflowing emotions transmuted to warmth.

I stumbled forward, my bare feet sizzling on a thin layer of ice-topped mud.

And there, just in the distance—

I choked back a sob.

A perfect circle clear of any debris at the mouth of the rift. The spot in which Papa Burchard had brought me back from the brink... That part I remembered well. I had given up and, in doing so, gave myself permission to destroy.

I walked into the circle and ran my toes along the flat surface.

"Because it is what papas do, Marmot," I whispered to the night. "Sometimes, the one we need to be saved from is ourselves."

Sweat gathered at my temples, and the æther settled like a bronze ingot in my stomach.

Up ahead, illuminated by the light of the moon, my tiny shed came into view. Cato's gift. Large pieces of its glass roof lay heaped in a pile. Beyond that—

"Who goes there!"

Snap!

Energy exploded through me, cycling around my body.

A guard patrolling the grounds peered around the shed's far corner, squinting his eyes, searching for what he *thought* he'd seen—which should have been me.

I floated, hovering above the footprints where my feet had rested just seconds before.

The guard marched forward, lamp in hand, casting macabre shadows on the rain-soaked soil.

"I said who goes there!" He came forward with his other hand secured around the hilt of his sword.

His toes nearly touched my sunken footprints.

Shit, shit, shit!

He peered right through me, squinting and chewing on the side of his mouth. He stood so close that his foggy breaths danced with the boundaries of my shadows.

"Fucking squirrels," the soldier muttered before resuming his unhurried pace and rounding another corner.

Close. Too close.

I didn't understand this part of myself, but knew it was imperative that I learn more. Heightened emotions and now, apparently, being startled, then pop... I'm a cloud. Was the heat an indicator? I tried to remember what happened the first time I took this form, but all I retained from that episode was rage. There was no thinking, no methodology in how I moved or where I soared. The predator within me released itself, and the basest of my instincts took over. I hunted. I took.

But now, I just hung.

I couldn't feel myself in this form. Couldn't talk. It was like being in my mind, but with no physical body to command.

The guard appeared again, and I fled backward. Reflex.

Don't think Eira, just move. Let go.

Go.

Go, please?

A sparkle in the distance caught my attention. No, not a sparkle... a glisten. The cracked but not entirely shattered window of the healer's shed glinted like an Ærtan-bound star in the dark of night.

I moved forward, curiosity a motivator.

Slowly gliding over the patches of grass and rain-melted snow, I rose gently until I was eye level with the eave of the roof, noting the beauty of the fractured-glass spiderweb that ran its length. From up here, I could watch the circling guard and—

If I could breathe, I'd have gasped—I had all but forgotten.

The demon-shade.

It hovered and bounced and shot back and forth between the trees a short distance away. Its erratic movements were eerie and irregular. It was a monster from my nightmares. Creator above, was it perhaps another conjurer? Not a spirit at all, but another with the ability?

As if it had heard me, the black wisp thrashed around, swirling. A cyclone of threat. It swelled, sending its shadow tendrils surging in all directions. Onyx tentacles reached out like those of the giant squid said to lay waste to the fishing ships as they sailed across the Penumbrean sea.

Holy fuck.

It shot forward, a massive projectile barreling toward me.

Before I could think, I reacted, slamming myself into the glass roof, doing my damnedest to filter through a tight crack. I couldn't fight a shade... I just learned to move.

The demon-shade narrowed itself into a deadly point, netherbent on spearing me just as *I* had attempted to impale *it.*

No, no, I—

Snap!

I flailed, no longer weightless.

Just as I remembered I had lungs, a concussive smack stole my breath. My head struck the thick glass pane with a crackling pop—a noise that all Nortians feared. My head lulled to the side as, like a boot pressed to thin ice, white veins stretched across the roof, racing away from the point of impact.

"Mother Merriasssssss!"

I plunged through a jungle of leaves, tangled briefly in a web of ropes that slid painfully against my skin, and then hit the ground, landing hard on my back.

"Oof." The air rushed from my lungs, and I feared blindness until I recognized that the flat leaves of a viny growth obscured my vision.

The door slammed open, knocking loudly against the shed's wall.

An armor-clad guard peered into the room. Another man rounded his shoulder and held up a lamp, casting a soft glow throughout the room. Both examined the broken glass and then the floor.

I didn't dare breathe.

"Finally, it gave. Protector Septimus said it might. Nothing in here will mind, though. I'll inform the sergeant at first light."

The man that stood behind him nodded, and the door shut, once again casting me into darkness.

"Mossius above," I groaned while wiggling my toes to see if they remained attached. I ripped at the vines and flung them to the side before attempting to sit up, hanging my spinning head between my hands. My healed hands.

Like the last time I took the shadow form and returned, I was whole again. Also like the last time, my clothing had burned away. My skin felt tight and clean, comparable to the afterglow that accompanied a vigorous scrub.

I plucked a shard of glass from my forearm and sensed more than saw a rivulet of blood trickle down to my elbow.

"Dammit." I twisted to my side and a rush of vertigo hit me so hard the room spun in circles. Whether it was a symptom of uncontrolled æther or a minor head injury, the remedy was the same; I tucked my head between my elbows and applied pressure to my temples until the spinning ended. "Alright body, stand up. Let's solve our own problems."

I groaned like my Gram used to do when getting out of her rocker. Carefully, I toed the larger shards of glass out of the way before fully planting my feet. Once standing straight, I brushed my hands down my rear and then my thighs, assessing for damage. Miraculously, there were no additional wounds.

Scattered foliage crushed and crunched under my soles as I crept to the door. I peeked out of the tiniest slit I could manage and noted three guards chatting around a barrel. One struck his knife against a chunk of flint, and sparks jumped atop a pile of kindling mounded over the barrel's rim. Their faces glowed as they stood in a circle, holding their hands out over the growing fire. Lucky for them, the rain had stopped.

Welp.

There was no way I'd be able to walk out unnoticed with so many on patrol, especially now that the grounds would be lit by the ever-growing flames.

Oh, well. Ambrose would find me... or maybe Septimus would. *Gag.* I hadn't laid eyes on Monwyn's new Protector since he'd cut Lilium from the balcony where her body had swung.

I closed the door carefully and then folded in on myself and let my head rest against the threshold.

Steady, Eira. Let the memory in and let it pass.

I groped the wall until my fingernails clanged against a glass chimney and then slid them down to the chain that held the attached striker. I quickly lit the lamp and turned its dial to ensure only the softest glow cast onto the rows of tinctures and supplies housed here.

I held my arm up to the light. The glass had pierced my flesh deeply and the cut still leaked a thick stream of ruby red. It needed addressing. A quick search revealed a stack of clean linens, and another scan, clot powder. Though I was no fan of the previous healer—may Merrias judge him fairly—his organizational skills surpassed that of any I ever dreamed of having.

Clot powder was the best. In Nortia, we keep buckets of the stuff on hand for fishing hook and spear injuries, of which there were hundreds per day. My mother also used it in her poultices if she needed them to cling to the skin—she even used it to thicken stew. I sprinkled the white substance onto a fresh bandage and wrapped the linen around my arm, using my teeth to secure the length.

I breathed aloud into the room of plants and paced back and forth. My wounds had healed, but my weariness over the demon-shade, remained. I supposed I could try my best to salvage something and fashion it into a weap—

My heart.

It ceased to beat.

"Nan... oh, my Nan."

Just there, beyond the mess my crash had created, was a makeshift morgue.

Her precious body and the bodies of two other unburied men lay upon a grouping of tall tables in the back of the room. The low light of the lamp barely caressed them, but highlighted just enough of their bodies to tell the story of who they once were.

Ignoring the danger of the debris-covered floor, I ran over the shards and fronds in the middle of the long shed. Glass fragments slit my skin and punctured my soles, but the pain of those lacerations didn't compare to my internal anguish. I covered my mouth, pressing my fists to my lips, afraid my cries would alert those who would take her from me once again.

My legs trembled as I took in her prone form.

"Here you are," I whispered. "They told me you were at the temple, my Nan."

Even in death, she was the most beautiful sight.

"They've left your hair a mess." I circled the table and ran my fingers through her dark locks—tracing the few silver strands at her temples and forehead, which stood out starkly in the long mass. "I'll fix it. You'd never be caught in public without it smoothed to perfection. And they've left your nails filthy."

I tucked her hand into mine and brought her palm closer to my face.

"You should have been washed already. You should have been anointed. These Monwyns know nothing of sanctity."

Laying her arms gently back to her side, I went searching, pushing fat, green leaves out of my way, and stumbling over a stack of clay pots.

"There." Stacks of buckets, reaching as high as my head, flanked a spigot on the far-right wall. I filled one with freezing water and then made my way to a collection of vessels, where petals and bits of foliage were soaking. I didn't know which herbs a Nortian priestess would use when anointing the deceased, so I pulled a random bottle and uncapped it, holding it under my nose. The soft-yellow concoction smelled heavily of rose—decidedly *not* a Nan smell. Too floral. I uncorked a green-tinted jug and sniffed. My eyes crossed. Nope. Its scent was astringent and left my throat burning—vinegar and something stale. I moved to a third vessel, a wooden keg, coopered tightly with copper rings. Raising up on my toes, I leaned over and took a whiff.

An embrace that no longer existed in this realm enveloped me. I could feel her strength and remembered the potency of her unyielding love.

Pine—a basic, common, and utterly northern scent.

I closed my eyes and let the sharp yet sweet aroma settle around me.

It was home. It was our kingdom—the mighty palace and the small game huts that housed rabbits and chickens. We used the tree's sticky resin in its purest form to coat and waterproof most of our belongings. There wasn't a homestead that didn't smell of it in some capacity—strong enough to burn your nostrils if freshly applied, fading to a refreshing evergreen after a few weeks.

The keg was too heavy to lift, so I rocked it until the silky amber liquid sloshed on the ground and coated my toes, capturing a healthy glug in the bucket of water at my feet.

Nearly out of breath, but ever determined, I searched the cabinets and shelves for a taper so I could see Nan better. I located a few slim candles, lit them from the lamp, and then used their own melted wax to secure them to the wooden table behind Nan. Surely the legless soldier who lay upon it wouldn't mind sharing his space. My eyes drifted to the clean cuts that severed his legs from his hips.

I swallowed down the lump in my throat.

I did this to him. My fury, my shadows. The intense heat of my black fire must have cauterized his flesh as the shards impaled him. Where his legs should have connected, large, multi-colored scabs sealed empty hip sockets.

"May you travel safely through the stars as you seek Merrias's judgment." Raising my hand to the man's face, I drew my oil-covered thumb across his forehead in the shape of a crescent. I smoothed his open eyelid down to match his closed one, the pine-scented oil helping to adhere it to his cheek.

Nan. How was it possible that I could ever feel whole again, knowing that her body no longer housed her soul? I looked closely at her nakedness and dipped my hands into the scented liquid.

Perfect oval face. Skin that was near poreless, even well past forty. My fingertips brushed over her full cheeks, holding them for a moment, and then feathered down her chin.

"It's the blubber that fills in the cracks, my girl," I said in my best approximation of her voice.

I closed my eyes and forced my shaking hands lower.

The slice at her throat was clean of the blood that had once coated it, leaving only a thin line—it could have been mistaken for a wrinkle. She couldn't feel. I knew this, but when the pads of my fingers came to rest on the evidence of her end, it was like I couldn't be *too* careful, too gentle. With delicate movements, I outlined the length of the slightly swollen mark.

"Nanetta, widow of Kennt, lover of Kan Keagan, friend of Vonnie... co-companion of Eira. I anoint you, cleanse you." My hands, working of their own will, slid down her chest, over her large breasts and the curve of her belly. She was heavily bruised right below her rib cage and again, in a cluster of gray splotches covering her hip. "You enter the cradle pure and worthy of the Goddess's love."

Her oiled skin glistened like the Nortian sun at noon, reflecting off the inky blue waves of the sea. I dipped into the pine-scented liquid once more, ran my hands down her arms, and then went to work, using my own nails to remove the grime from beneath hers. She'd not tolerate such uncleanliness. The dried blood reconstituted as I swept it away, turning her fingertips and mine pink.

"Is this his blood, Nan? The Primus-King's? Did you gouge his flesh and rip his skin?" I rinsed her until the discoloration was gone. "If you didn't manage to leave scars upon him, don't worry. I will for the both of us."

I washed her legs and feet, rubbing deeply at her heels just like she used to love.

"Nan, do you remember the day I learned the traditional dances of the four kingdoms? You were my partner, and Kan Keagan clapped out the beat and called the steps. I trod gracelessly all over these toes. 'Eira, you clumsy codfish, pick your feet up, my girl; mind your shuffling.'" I spread the oil over her broken toenails. Blood had dried around the damaged cuticles of her left foot. "And then you huffed at me until Kan bent low into a perfect courtier's bow and asked you to dance. You circled the room with him for the next three hours. Did you love him then? I remember when we got home you propped your feet on the brazier and said, 'Rub these tootsies while I rest my eyes,' and I acted like it was the worst punishment." I ran my palm over her soft, cold heel. "Nan, I should have—" My voice cracked. I couldn't go on.

My tears rained down on her oil-slicked skin and beaded off onto the table's top, clustering around her legs.

I stood looking over her, feeling a loss so profound it was as if my chest had cracked open, exposing my fractured heart.

"You should have a pyre, Nan, or be set adrift on the sea. Your family, all of us, should be here surrounding you, saying our intercessions to Merrias."

Who would tell the Arbiter goddess of her good deeds? Who would share the tales that made up the story of her life?

She'd get none of it.

Here in Monwyn, they would bury her and let her rot in a hole filled with dirt and worms.

I shuddered at the thought of her being treated like Imella. Instead of her mortal shell scattering in the wind, or traveling to the ends of the earth upon the waves, she would be entombed, stuck in this Goddess-forsaken land of rock and—

My skin warmed, and the æther vibrated as it gathered in my chest.

"*He* took that rite from us, Nan. The poisonous Gaean King—my sire, my mother's rapist."

The fire in my chest flared. My hands burned as the æther squeezed its way into the very fibers of my muscles. The pressure intensified until it threatened to boil over.

"No." I slid my arms under Nan's neck and knees, and then heaved with all my might. "No. He will never, *ever*, take from me again."

Nan's head fell back as I lifted her, and a foamy, pink liquid discharged from her mouth and nose. The fluid dripped over my arms, but I didn't flinch or recoil. It was a part of her. Nothing that was a part of her could disgust me.

"He will suffer, Nan. He. Will. Suffer."

My arms slid from around her, her torso too slick to maintain my hold. Shifting and grabbing her beneath the arms, I eased her to the floor.

"Rest here awhile." I squeezed her hand in mine before setting off to retrieve a set of large linen bandages. Slipped between us, they were enough to create the friction I needed to continue our journey.

"I will remove his limbs and then his crown." Nan's heels caught on the shards of glass and plant matter on the floor. I hesitated, but it didn't matter. Not anymore. "My mother may have been born of the light, Nan—born of love— but I will not deny the side of me that walks in the darkness."

Sweat rolled down my temples and between my breasts. My muscles shook as I strained to hold on to her and swipe at the door's handle at the same time. I hooked my fingers and shoved.

"What the fuck? You, get the Protector, run!" I heard the guard yell from outside.

A bitter wind rushed past me, dispelling the shed's humid air. I inhaled a cleansing breath and knew my actions to be righteous.

"Don't touch the consort! He gave orders. Don't fucking touch her, she—"

I snapped my head around and glared at a man who was frantically running back and forth between the barrel and the door.

"Soldier!" I commanded. "Open this godsdamned door."

The man stopped and stared.

I hit the heavy door with my hip but couldn't smack it hard enough to get myself and Nan over the threshold.

"THE DOOR!" I ordered again.

The whites of his eyes shone brightly as he stood, frozen in shock, but an instant later his brain caught up with his body.

"Consort," he mouthed while holding the door wide. "Consort, you are naked. And it is against the law to, to remove or tamper with a corpse once it's in custody of the healer."

I didn't bother to look up.

"Your healer is dead. And the punishment for desecration is what?" I bit out, continuing to inch my Nan through the mud. My foot splashed in a puddle, momentarily throwing me off balance.

"It's—well, it's," he squeaked, "lashes, uh, lashes until rendered unconscious."

The corners of my mouth tugged down.

"Well, soldier, after you tip that barrel over, unfurl your finest whip and take your best strike." I struggled under the weight in my arms, my words coming out between heavy pants. "Though I'd advise you to render me real damn senseless on your first go-round."

"Tip the—tip... You want me to tip..."

"The barrel. That flaming fucking barrel. Knock it over."

The guard dropped the door, swung his head around, and began walking in circles, searching for his brothers-in-arms who were nowhere to be seen.

"Soldier, get a grip!" I ordered, mimicking the way Cato addressed the men under his command. "Shoulders back, stand tall."

The guard stopped his desperate pacing, but his lips bobbed, trying to form the words that he clearly couldn't voice.

For fuck's sake.

"I'll do it my godsdamned self."

I laid Nan flat and finger-combed her hair again—the soft and silky strands slipped easily through my fingers. Then I straightened her limbs, which had splayed awkwardly on the ice-speckled ground, tucking them close to her sides.

"What the nether is this?" an unfamiliar voice said. "Grab her and I'll get the body. The Protector has yet to finish the autopsy and—"

"He *will not* touch her," I gritted out between clenched teeth. My hands turned blisteringly hot. Smokey white steam curled around my palms and drifted into the night. The guard who was moving toward me raised his arms, stopped in his tracks. "Run along now. Go tell *that* to your Protector."

I stood, stepped over Nan's body, and grabbed the rolled-metal edge of the flaming barrel. No heat, no sear, not the slightest burn reached me as I wrestled and then toppled the makeshift pyre.

"Nether witch. Sister of sin." The guard who held the door finally found his initiative and ran. His comrade stood there pissing himself, the wet spot traveling quickly down his inner thighs.

"Goddess, spare me of her malicious intent."

Sparks flew as logs and embers tumbled out and onto the body of my beloved companion.

Around my feet, the fire engulfed her, no doubt aided by the flammable oil of pine—her hair fizzled quickly, a million tiny red sparks haloing her exquisite face.

Such beauty in the gruesomeness.

I fell to my knees.

"Nanetta of Nortia..." I choked out, gripping her hand in mine, "a little girl's guide. Childless mother." I didn't look away from the morbid sight of her skin as it blistered and bubbled. I held her hand still as the flesh peeled away. "You taught me to experience life on my own terms—supported me. You saw me at my best and worst and loved me unconditionally. You bandaged my scraped knees when I fell on the ice. You walked to your end in my name. Your girl."

I tilted my head to the moon, and the fire swelled.

"Your girl," I sobbed. "My N-nan."

The flames licked my thighs and rose to my shoulders.

"Merrias, hear me. See your faithful servant to the Mother, greet her with your open arms and see her seated in the bosom of the Goddess's love. Th-this is my intercession."

Tears sizzled as they slid down my cheeks, never falling from my chin as they dissipated in the intense heat.

The hand held in mine ceased to exist. I searched my palms, looking for something, anything, that remained of her.

There was nothing. As was right and proper, but soul-crushing, nonetheless.

"Goddess, what use is a Chosen One who cannot save? What's the point of a deity's blood if it cannot drive out the scourge walking amongst us?"

The wind blew, kicking up ash, sending it into a wild spiral that danced within the flames that soared higher with each new gust.

I wept. I allowed myself to wail, screaming my misery at the waxing moon that loomed above. I gave myself permission to feel, truly feel, my loss for the first time.

"You belong to the wind, my Nan, you belong to the—"

A gargling sound pulled me from my lamentation.

I glanced through the flames that distorted my vision.

Dark eyes bore into mine, a dangerous glint in their thin ring of gold. He pulled his blade from the crook of the soldier's neck.

Never dropping my gaze, Cato let the body fall.

"Highness, leave now; she's a sorcer—" As the second guard came running back, Cato snatched the man by his neck and slammed his face into the pointed metal knee cop he wore, once... twice. The soldier struggled momentarily and then ceased his fight.

"Catommandus, control yourself. There are barely enough guards to cover the grounds as is... thanks to the witch." Septimus stepped out from behind Cato, kicking at the bloodied guard. "Filthy succubus that she is."

"Speak ill of my woman again, uncle, and it will be *your* brain matter dripping down my calf."

"Your woman? Hold your tongue, boy," Septimus reprimanded, awareness dawning in his cold eyes. "Your commitment to destroying your idiot bastard brother is laudable, but we cannot afford the stink of scandal so soon after losing Burchard."

"I do not care, Protector Septimus. I no longer fucking care." Cato unclasped his cloak and spun the heavy, gray wool from his shoulders. "Eira, love, move out of the flames."

Septimus's mouth dropped open, just slightly, before he snapped it closed.

My foot sank into the mud as I rose and stepped backward—it hissed and simmered, bubbling around my heel.

Strong arms and soft wool enveloped me. He smelled of horse, leather, and body, but below that were the achingly familiar hints of cedar and clove. He was my shroud, the covering that shielded my heart.

"Wait, Cato, please." His arms loosened, and I bent low, reaching toward the fire. "Gods!" I snatched my hand back. Whatever power that protected me from the flames had disappeared, leaving me vulnerable. I took a deep breath, steeling myself, and reached in again, scooping up a handful of ashes. I cradled the tiny, still-smoldering mound to my chest and turned back to the man who tethered me to sanity.

He glanced at my hands and back to my eyes, nodding his understanding.

Chapter Six

WHAT'S GOOD FOR THE GODDESSDAMNED GANDER

Eira

"Eira, is this your doing?"

I peeked out from the comforting pillow of Cato's chest and glanced around, taking in the scene. The soldier who'd done nothing more than try to keep me from leaving, to keep me safe, lay very much dead upon the floor, surrounded by a group of servants.

"I... Cato, when I left, he was... Oh my Goddess, I..."

"Tuck your head. Do not speak." Cato tugged the cloak up, obscuring my face from sight.

"High-Highness," the strained voice of a young woman floated through the thick wool around my ears. "A plague's upon us. He messed himself to death, he did. And the gods was angry! You left, and the ground opened up, took our king."

"Calm yourself, Marjorna. The new healer arrives soon. He will assess the man and make us aware of the precautions we should take. Plague is nasty business." Cato held me up as if I were another victim of illness.

"And the nether god, Protector... Highness he done came up and—"

"Was it not our king, the devoted follower of the Goddess, who sent the Depraved One back into the ground?"

"I-it was," the servant stammered.

"Then certainly the Goddess watches over us, above all others."

The release of her held breath was audible.

"And no others have come down with this illness?" Cato asked.

"None, Highness, no."

"Inform Lemder that one of the palace soldiers has expired, and there is a mess that requires his attention. Do not go near the corpse. Return to your quarters until you receive word that all is safe."

"Yes, Highness, right away."

Cato took the steps to my apartments two at a time.

"Where is Ambrose?"

"In his room," I whispered into his neck, humiliated by the extent of trouble I had caused in the span of a few hours.

"Jance! On your feet! I will have you stripped of your rank for—"

"I-it was me, Cato. Me again. I sent him to sleep." He hugged me close, but the unmistakably vexed sound of his rough exhalation belied his action.

A groggy Jance opened his eyes and when recognition finally settled in, he shot to his feet, snapping to attention.

"Highness Catommandus! Consort! Are you hurt? I passed out. Hit the floor. Hit my noggin. Lost my spear..." Jance whipped his head back and forth, scanning the ground for his lost weapon. "Are we under attack? Show me the knaves. I shall protect you both with my body, shield you from the enemies." Jance drew his sword. "Take her to safety, Highness," he yelled, "go now!"

"Steady soldier. The adversary was apprehended quickly. It was nothing more than a hungry consort stealing an apple from the kitchens," Cato lied smoothly and reached into the leather bag at his side. He flicked open a buckle and pulled out a bright-green apple. "I'm returning the thief to her husband. He can sort out her punishment."

Jance gave a curt nod and held the door wide before shutting it behind us.

The nauseating sensation of self-consciousness overwhelmed me as the door sealed shut. I tugged one side of the cloak attempting to conceal myself, failing to do so as I cradled Nan's ashes close to my chest.

"Here." Cato sat me in a chair, dug into his satchel, and retrieved a small black pouch. "Store her remains in this, so that you may keep them close." He bent to inspect the soles of my feet, running his fingers lightly over the scraped skin.

"I want them taken to Nortia. I want them scattered in the Penumbrean sea. Her husband lies at its bottom as well."

"I swear it to you." He kissed one of my kneecaps and then the other, his mouth lingering on a new bruise. "Come to me, love." I slid my arms around his neck and he lifted me once more. "Should I prepare myself to find Ambrose lifeless atop a mound of shit?"

His chuckle, meant to lighten the mood, had the opposite effect.

"No... he." I shook my head and squeezed my eyes shut at the same time, praying it was the truth.

Cato strode through the common area and into Ambrose's chamber. My husband sat on the edge of the bed, physically holding each of his eyelids open with two splayed fingers.

"Brother? Are you—"

"Cato..." Ambrose stood quickly, wobbling unsteadily on his feet. "Cato, I—" he choked on his words, never finishing his sentence.

Mossy-green eyes filled with tears and a heart-wrenching sob tore from the man who stood nearly seven feet tall—who'd mutilated a troll and who'd outwitted his adversaries with cunning *and* aplomb. His arms dropped to his sides.

Cato lowered my feet to the floor, and then quickly covered the distance to the bed.

Ambrose circled his arms around Cato's neck and finally let go of his grief.

"Mama's gone. She's gone, Cat—she loved me above all others, never saw me as a chore." Tears of anguish tracked down his flawless face, spilling onto the gray linen of Cato's shirt. "I put her in the ground, our mother," he cried and shook, losing his ability to hold himself upright. "She lies covered in dirt, brother. Her eyes never to open again. She is... she was my first love, Cat."

Cato led Ambrose to the rug-strewn floor, holding him, one arm around his chest and the other supporting his neck. He rocked the big man who lay across his lap, not an ounce of judgment in his expression.

"I know, Ambrose, I know." He tightened his embrace. "Our retribution will be swift."

"Your vengeance is meaningless, Cat. It cannot resurrect her."

Ambrose looked at me with red-rimmed eyes and reached in my direction, "Eira, we need you."

I rushed to them, dropping to the floor, hugging them both to my chest, ensuring our connection.

"Ambrose, nothing can replace what you've lost." I smoothed his beard and then used the hem of the cloak I wore to wipe the moisture from his cheekbones. "But I love you." Ambrose placed his palm over mine and held it against his heart, his tears falling steady. "And Cato loves you too. We will—"

"Eira." Cato's voice turned cold—skin-sticking-to-frosted-metal cold.

I sat back, searching his eyes, removing my hands from Ambrose.

The coward in me wasn't ready to have this conversation with him yet, but the Nortian in me knew I couldn't back down. I loved him more than I could ever imagine loving another... and I just happened to love his brother, too.

I met his gaze, and puffed out my chest, ready to face his anger.

"Cato, when you were gone, I—"

Cato flung back the left side of my cloak, baring my body.

"Your Obligate's brand—where is it? And—" He tenderly cupped my breast in his palm. "And you've removed your piercing. How... Why?"

Ambrose wiped his eyes and then laid a hand on Cato's arm.

"Catommandus, fetch Eira a shirt. I will have food brought. There is much to discuss."

Disbelief was a foreign expression on Cato's normally controlled countenance. His brows furrowed so deeply that two vertical lines ran from his nose to the middle of his forehead and the corners of his mouth tugged down in confusion.

"Go on. She will catch her death in these temperatures, nude as she is."

Cato cleared out, heading to the consort's room, and Ambrose got to his feet. He took my hands in his, pulling me up so fast I had to hop on my toes. He gathered me into his arms and planted a kiss on the top of my head.

"If he becomes enraged, foist the cunt fairies upon him."

I cringed.

"Change your vocabulary or *you* will never be on the receiving end of them again."

"Vagina vipers. Is that better? Pussy pixies...? Twat trolls?" He swatted at my bare rear, but I jumped out of his way, evading his hand with a twist. My maneuver landed me smack dab into the path of a fiercely angry Cato.

Oh fuck.

"Eira, where is the shirt I gave you?" He stalked forward, chin down, eyes up, like a bull ready to charge. "Do you no longer wear it? It has been a week's time. Have you eschewed our commitment so readily? Embraced your fake-husband and tossed me aside?"

Ambrose stepped in front of me, cutting him off.

"Cat, *you* left for a week with little to no information on your whereabouts." He widened his stance. "And Creator's kneecaps... she sleeps with the goddessdamned thing balled up under her pillow. Perhaps you could oversee the washing of the odiferous keepsake."

Cato sailed past his brother and flipped the pillow off my side of the bed, snatching up the wrinkly ball of fabric that I'd stowed there. He snapped the garment straight.

"My apologies to both of you. Eira?" He crooked his finger in my direction and held the garment high. My head emerged from its neckline. "I am sorry, love. The very moment we parted, I turned into the worst of tyrants." He smoothed the garment with his hands, starting first at my shoulders and ending at the curve of my hips. Cato threaded his fingers through mine and led me to the low couch. He turned and sat, pulling me into his lap.

He was home. The colors became richer, the atmosphere lighter.

Ambrose crashed down beside us and draped his long legs heavily across our laps. I ran my fingernail down the sole of his foot, and he kicked out with a yelp.

"Cease your flirtations." Cato caught my hand and pressed the soft skin of my inner wrist to his warm lips. "Ambrose, debrief."

Ambrose waved his hand dismissively but launched in. "Fairly uneventful. Eira turns into an angry little cloud when she is in a particularly shitty mood. It's quite spectacular, really. She gets all shimmery, like choppy water and then puffs out and shoots away—"

"I get choppy?" I asked, curious as to what my shade form looked like. I honestly didn't know.

"Fewer disruptions, wife, impatient little haglet."

I narrowed my eyes in Ambrose's direction but held my tongue.

"Anyhow. Eira was incredibly disoriented before she..." Ambrose wagged his fingers in the air, outlining a sphere that didn't exist, "... puffed. And it seems the Primus-King was the Elderman all along. He threatened to continue taking lives unless Eira, or her mother, *his queen*, returns to his kingdom."

"He will gain neither," Cato growled. Below me, his muscles bunched tightly.

"No, he will not," I agreed, while rubbing the tension from his rock-like forearm.

"That was the primary cause of the understandably foul mood and subsequent shadow poof—Oh! Lemder blackmailed her, if you can even imagine such a thing. He discovered your affair by means of your shared poison plant rash—"

"He will die," Cato said with an air of nonchalance. He smoothed my hair back over my shoulder and slid the tip of his nose along my collarbone.

I shook my head.

"Don't. It's not worth the risk." I gave Cato a pleading look. "The palace's defenses are weak. Cato, I took the lives of over twenty, all told, in minutes, seconds really. Sixteen of those were the men *you* trained."

Gold-ringed eyes studied me.

"It is apparent then that their tutelage was inadequate. My fault alone." Ambrose tapped my breast with his long toes.

"Hello?" Ambrose pursed his lips in a pout. "Back to me, if you will." He leaned forward and snatched the pillow from behind Cato's back, then tucked it under his own neck. "Right. In summary, Eira destroyed the Den after a *magnificent* performance that brought Lemder low... and it just so happens that she tongued a whore, almost fucked Septimus, and then burned our father to a literal crisp." Ambrose clapped his hands loudly and then cupped them around his mouth. "And then, lastly... THE FUCKING NETHER GOD CAME OUT OF THE GROUND WITH NOT ONE BUT TWO DEMON BABIES GIFT-WRAPPED IN ICE!"

Well, that is one way to deliver sensitive information.

Cato stared ahead, working his jaw, grinding his molars together. I reached up to caress his beard, but he snapped his head back as if my touch would scald him.

"Cato, please. Please let me explain," I begged. Underneath me, his leg shook rhythmically. "Cato, I... I ask for your forgiveness. After thwarting Lemder, I backed into Septimus. The Bond with my already heightened sense of emotion was just too much. When you left, *his* Bond seemed to strengthen, and I—"

"How often should I expect your infidelity?" Cato bit out in a flat and emotionless tone. "Eira, I cannot abide—"

"*You* can't abide?" I snapped my head up and looked him in the eyes. "Damn you to the nether, Cato. Do you think I would *choose* to be unfaithful to you? Do you honestly think I *wish* to be assaulted by Septimus... over *loved* by you?"

His eyelids fell. He couldn't bear to look at me.

"Already you lie with Ambrose, Eira, and I have just barely come to terms with that—"

Ambrose pressed his hairy, but expertly manicured toe against Cato's cheek. Cato's nose flared. I could practically see the violence growing within him. I swatted the giant's foot and chastised my husband with a stern look.

"Catommandus, before *you* go placing blame. Was it you or some other thickly endowed gentleman who explained that were it not for the Bond and her magical blood, you would *never* have participated in *our* recent bed sport?" A very serious Ambrose pointed his finger directly at Cato's nose. "Do not blame her for something you will not take the blame for yourself."

My gods.

"Ambrose!"

Cato shot up and tossed me on to the sofa. He marched to the door, his fists balled tightly at his sides. His back expanded and shrank as he seethed in anger.

"Ambrose, did you pay off the whore or kill him? Who is it? I will take care of the—"

"Offilia," I squeaked out. "It was a she... it was Offilia. A mask concealed her face, and I was—"

Cato stopped dead and then twisted slowly on his heels, mouth agape.

"Close your maw, brother. She will crave Eira's tongue for the rest of her miserable life. Suitable retribution for the idiocy of your love-addled boy's brain."

Cato tensed and then stomped away.

I made to follow, but Ambrose held me back and shook his head, warning me off.

"Come back, Cat. Communication is key!" Ambrose shouted. "Where are you going?"

The common room door slammed against the wall.

"Eira lived out her inappropriate penetration fantasy—now it is my turn. In *my* dreams I slowly skewer Septimus's pretty blue eye with a dinner fork," Cato yelled.

"Oh, dear." Ambrose scrambled to his feet, snatched his discarded clothes, and started out the door. "Get to sleep, wife. Even your eye bags bear luggage."

Chapter Seven

LIKE TOUCHING A TIT

Eira

Why I was not *solely* attracted to women was beyond me. Goddess knows life would be simpler without the man-centric requirement to big-chest-brute-walk over every other male in the vicinity. I thought the anglers of Nortia were overstuffed on masculinity, but their big fish stories paled in comparison to the mountain men's need to prove themselves—hair-covered, instinct-driven swine.

After washing and brushing my half-head of hair until it crackled with static, I took a set of shears to a pink flannel nightgown and cut the hem above my knees. The ruffled bottom, along with the dozens of celery-green rosettes, got damned to the waste bin, along with its puffed sleeves.

I inspected my reflection in the mirror.

It still looked like me. Maybe the fine line across my forehead had deepened some, but other than that, it was still the same sloped nose and almond-shaped eyes. No bulbous growths or wart-dotted face that a child Eira imagined when reading of the conjurers in Ærta's corruption-tainted past.

The door to the common room opened loudly.

Great.

I scurried toward my bed, hopping in and snuggling under the ruby-red cover.

Breathe slow. No twitching. Eyes be still. I wasn't above faking sleep if the outcome was much needed alone time.

"Eira?" I heard my name being called from the other room but didn't respond. Instead, I silently counted four seconds between my respirations, mimicking deep slumber. Ambrose would see right through me if I didn't entirely commit to the ruse.

The door I had purposefully shut creaked wide open—the darkness of my closed lids made bright.

"Wiflet, is your tum acting up? I noticed you did not move your bowels at your regular time today and…" Ambrose's voice lowered to a whisper. "She's in here, Cat."

On light feet, both men entered the chamber and moved to either side of the bed.

The sound of shoes hitting the floor and belts loosening was unmistakable, and so was the warmth that spread through my core, flaring out in pleasurable, pulsating waves.

Vagina. You will spoil this. She was a single-minded fiend.

"You did no permanent damage from what I can tell, but Cato, how do you plan on explaining your actions to Aberus?" The telltale thud of Ambrose falling to the plush carpet for his nightly round of pushups made his voice cut in and out. "Brother Aberus… Ambrose's salaciously thick wife attempted to take Uncle Septimus on a boat ride to tuna town," he mimicked Cato's clipped diction, "so I took a stab at his face. By the by, are you aware that your upstanding Protector has pierced his purple-helmed soldier?"

Cato slipped into bed behind me, wrapping his arm around my waist and caging me against his chest. Were I not so focused on my sleeping act, I would have wept for the comfort I found wrapped in his embrace. A part of me, I realized, had been terrified that I'd never experience it again.

Cato snorted.

"One benefit of Father reinstating my title is that I owe not a single soul an explanation of my actions. Not even Aberus, until the crown is officially placed upon his head. Speaking of, has word come from the Mantle yet? They, no doubt, will wish to do the honors Themself."

Ambrose paused between squats. He'd now hold that horse stance until his thighs quivered and gave out.

Cato's hands casually explored my stomach and hips.

Sleep Eira. Sleep, damn you. I begged my hips to stay put instead of pushing back into the length that nestled its innocent self against my rear.

"Yes, Primus Thierry received a missive this morning. Are you paying attention?" A quick exhale burst forth from Ambrose's lungs.

Cato's fingers whispered over my pubic bone.

Down, girl!

"Scoot over, Cat. This bed is much smaller than my own." The cool air rushed along my chest and thighs as Ambrose peeled the covers back.

"Gracious Goddess, look at the scandalous little outfit she's worn for us, all boobs and juicy bits."

Cato craned his neck over my shoulder, his scratchy beard rubbing against my neck as he looked down at my chest.

"The finest set of tits to have ever graced a torso," Cato said, his voice husky and full of appreciation.

Ambrose crawled in, his cold feet seeking the warmth of my own as his hand sought my breast. "Honestly, every part of her is like touching a tit."

I pictured my body, as he described, hundreds of fatty lumps covering my thighs and stomach. *Is that a compliment? Sleep. Eira, you are asleep!* I stiffened ever so slightly but caught myself before I struck Ambrose on his perfect nose. He squeezed my breast gently and stroked my nipple to a hard peak.

"Mmhmm," Cato hummed his agreement. "She feels like the most expensive of silks and molds perfectly to my hands and... other parts."

Better. That's better.

They shared a naughty chuckle like two pubescent boys catching sight of a maid in her bath.

Ambrose rolled over and pressed his rear into my hips.

Little ladle tonight, then. I didn't resist the urge to place my arm through his while stifling a faked yawn. He cupped my hand to his chest.

Cato turned to steel behind me, his entire body reacting to the innocent touch I shared with Ambrose.

"Brother?"

"What, Cato? I am fading."

"Do you love her?" Cato spoke softly.

Oh.

Silence. Stretching, stagnant, silence.

The urge to pop up and run, like a herd of hungry sprites nipped at my heels, nearly made me blow my cover.

"I..." Ambrose paused, "do not know how I feel, in all honesty, and I have nothing to compare it to. She says she loves me because I keep her heart safe, but she most assuredly does not yearn for me the way she does you. She desires my dick, of course, but who doesn't?" Ambrose wiggled his backside against me, nestling closer. "I find myself quite upset if she is not waiting for me when I come to bed. And if she is not on my arm as I walk through the halls, I feel like I left something important back in the room. Is that love, brother?" Ambrose asked, genuinely.

"No, it is absolutely not," Cato said bluntly.

The faintest smile stretched the corners of my mouth. He may have come to terms with the physical aspects of my contract marriage, but the emotional side was an altogether different beast. I made a mental note to have a long discussion with him and ensure he knew my feelings for him hadn't lessened in the slightest.

"You are probably right. You knew within, what, three days? Ah, well. Let us discuss what took place before your departure."

Cato stiffened... and not in the fun way.

"Go on," Cato said, his voice firm.

My heart beat out of rhythm.

"The sex. How do you feel after the..." Ambrose allowed his words to die out.

Cato breathed in deeply and then exhaled slowly, his breath skimming over my cheek.

"To be honest, I have not given it a great deal of thought, but I found the experience pleasant enough."

Ambrose recoiled so forcefully that his thick curtain of hair swung back, covering my face.

"Pleasant? Are you serious, Cat? Pleasant is a picnic on a nice spring day, a-a stroll through the gardens. That night was..."

"Incredible," Cato murmured. "It was incredible. She was amazing taking us both as she did."

"Correct. I was magnificent."

Cato's chest rumbled with a soft chuckle. His lips brushed the skin below my ear.

"And is it something you wish to experience again? Or is it something we should never speak of and chalk up to a rousing bit of pussy sorcery?"

More silence.

"Ambrose. If you are asking if I would want a-a more *husband*-like relationship with you, the answer is no. In my life, there is only room for the woman who lies between us. And though I felt no shame in the act, I have no desire to love another as my spouse. She is my beginning and end. But I find it difficult to deny her anything."

"So, would you join us again? If she wished it?" Ambrose asked. "Though complicated... for me, it felt... complete."

If my heart were an iceberg, it would have melted and formed a new sea.

"I want her to experience the most pleasure in life," Cato said. "If you continue to please her, I am open to the prospect." My heart skipped a beat again, temporarily making me lightheaded. "But if you do not, I will assert my claim—she will belong solely to me." Cato's hand slid up to lie possessively against my chest. "When Father revoked the Protectorate and its restrictions upon me... I considered, briefly, dragging my blade across your neck."

Ambrose rolled over to face Cato, his chest touching my chin. He smoothed his palm down the length of my hip and pressed his knee between my legs.

"Would you care to expound upon that statement?"

"I would not," Cato replied.

Ambrose said nothing, but I felt his head nod against the pillows.

"Should we rouse her and make her aware of tomorrow's little family gather—"

"Gods!" Sharp teeth bit down on my shoulder, jolting me from my ploy. Cato roughly yanked my hips back and ground his arousal into the small of my back.

"There is no need," Cato murmured. "She has been awake the entire time."

His tongue traced the spot, still smarting from his nip.

"Deceitful little harpy," Ambrose crooned in my ear. "And to think we could have been having a *much* more enjoyable evening." He dropped his hand low and squeezed my rear until it stung.

"Nope, too tired." I popped a kiss on Ambrose's jaw. "Goodnight, husband."

A low growl issued from behind me.

"Goodnight, um, shorter husband?" I twisted my head around and placed a kiss on Cato's chin while Ambrose giggled at the dig.

Cato caught my jaw, his eyes blazing as he stared down at me.

"Goodnight, woman." His lips hovered above mine. Heat pooled low in my stomach. The æther blossomed within me, unfurling its petals to the sun that nourished its bloom. "And if a superlative is required, you may refer to me as *thick* husband."

I groaned, stretching up to capture his mouth, my hand seeking his length.

"Ah, ah," he said, tilting away. "Only good girls get rewards." He closed his eyes, a perfectly coy smile stretching across his lips.

He was asleep within minutes... and I was at last content, listening to the sounds of their combined breaths, steady and strong.

The orangey glow of the lamps dimmed as their oil reserves ran low.

But for me, the night was just the beginning.

The dark wisp emerged from the room's corner, settling itself above my eyes.

CHAPTER EIGHT

POSITIVELY PROGRESSIVE

EIRA

"Allaine, add pink to her eye bags and set them with a fine mineral powder. It should brighten that dullness right up." Ambrose affixed a blue baldric across his chest, pinning it with his golden bear's head brooch. From its mouth hung a crown encrusted with diamonds, the points of which were set with teardrop-shaped opals. "Goddess above, Aberus will think I wed a raccoon or a—what did they call the corpses that re-lifed during the war?"

"Awakened," I supplied, not giving a single shit about the purple splotches that were now permanent fixtures on my face. They brought out the green undertones in my eyes.

"Yes, one of those." He pointed down at me, shaking his finger. "I bet they too allowed themselves to become all droopy and dreary. Clawing one's way to the surface is bound to be tough on the fingernails." Ambrose flexed his hand, inspecting each of his filed and buffed digits.

"Not a reader, are you, husband?"

"I beg your pardon. Just the other day, I was enjoying a dissertation on the erotic applications of rock formations and their uses to enhance the human body."

"You were looking at nudes painted on scenic backgrounds?"

Ambrose chuckled; Allaine gasped.

"According to the books I've read, most of the Awakened were Hainan or Talcery soldiers who'd fallen in battle and weren't buried at all. There was no time between skirmishes." I brightened a little and sat up straighter on my stool. "*And* if I recall, desert burial customs revolve around drying the deceased on top of the wide plateaus. Then they grind the remains into powder and fire those into glass beads, which they then wear. I imagine many of Mother Imella's beaded necklaces contain the remains of her ancestors."

The look on Ambrose's face was one of utter horror. It matched the expression of my lady's maid, who was reflexively dabbing a thick layer of powder on my nose, wide-eyed and lips parted in an *O*.

"What?" I shrugged, finding their shock incongruous—they put people in a fucking mud hole. "I think it's a lovely custom. Ouch!" I cried out, covering my eye. It watered profusely, keeping me from staring spitefully at Allaine.

"If you were holding still, instead of spinning tales meant to haunt us in our dreams, I would not have powdered your pupil."

She bopped the tip of my nose with her brush, diffusing a cloud of earthy-smelling mica dust.

"You are such an—*achoo*—asshole, Allaine. If I could make myself look this good on my own, I'd send you packing."

"I *would* send you packing," she chastised my use of contractions. Her gruff puppy giggles filled the room as she moved around me, searching for the best angle to apply her rainbow pile of cosmetics. I was so glad to hear the gritty and growly sound. Laughter had understandably been in short supply in Cordillaria, but I have always found that, especially in the worst of times, it had curative properties.

"Never did I imagine a wife would take up so much counter space." Ambrose shoved his way in front of the mirror, straightening the bejeweled white belt that hung low on his hips. Enameled stiffeners shaped like roses adorned the leather, and malachite-tipped rivets held them in place.

Though he despised the color, I thought he looked striking in his all-white ensemble, a thigh-length woolen tunic, woven in a fine twill pattern. Linen pants that clung to his muscular thighs. Soft leather boots gartered below his knees. I wish he saw what I did, the stark contrast between it and his inky hair, how the color brought out the pink undertones of his pale skin. But I could see in his scowl the utter disappointment of having to don the color of mourning yet again, or maybe it was the constant reminder of his loss.

I slid my hands down the small of his back and gave his rear an appreciative pat. Allaine went whiter than my dress, uncomfortable with such an openly sexual display. Ambrose's lips quirked.

I'd made the right choice.

My eyes settled on our reflections as he moved aside. The power of face paints and skillfully styled hair was not lost on me. From the fragile woman of last night to the beacon of hope and strength I saw now—the transformation was astonishing. My cascade of dark curls fell onto the iridescent silk of my gown—lightest blues and greens reflected as I shifted in the cream-colored taffeta. Another marvel created by the Millanderers. Square neckline, showing a hint of cleavage, silver moon charms glittering in quads across the bust and hips, the voluminous skirts flared out in what must have been a ransom's worth of fabric. The sleeves, a sheer silk, allowed the dozens of bracelets that Ambrose insisted I wear to show. The diamonds and opals glittered like I imagined a sprite's wing would, from my wrist to the middle of my forearm.

Allaine whopped me on the forehead, startling me from my self-assessment. She then palmed the back of my head in her incredibly firm grip.

"Stay straight," she scolded, her eyes narrowing to slits.

One... two... her brother just died... three...four... she's menstruating. I held my tongue instead of calling her a hate-filled sack of fish guts.

"Allaine, how do you find Scion Greggen? You have accepted an offer to dine with him this evening, I understand. Unchaperoned... and in his apartments, no less."

Two precisely pointed arches shot to her hairline, and she turned the same maroon as the coils she'd recently added into her auburn hair.

My mischievous chuckle reverberated off the tiles as Ambrose's reflection winked at me, a conspirator's knowing gesture.

"Oooh! It is not fair that you are in cahoots! What else has he told you? Two against one is... is—"

"—absolutely wonderful." I finished her sentence, glancing up at my husband. "And, if Scion Greggen treats you as well as my Black Bear does me, Allaine, I will cease calling for his head. Most likely."

Allaine balked, but then her face turned soft.

My heart understood. Even if my mind heaved an internal barf.

"A word of caution, lady's maid; Never presume the upper hand when challenging the likes of team Ambeira—Eirbrose?"

"Ambrose! Was that... was that a slight about her arm?" I punched his butt so hard he swayed. "You know very well that I will not cond—"

"The team names...?" I saw it dawn on him. "Oh, snowballs, no! Eira, it's a commonly used phrase and—"

"One you'll endeavor not to use in her presence, please?"

Ambrose turned to face Allaine.

"Allaine, was it hurtful?"

"No, it was fine."

"Tell the truth," I admonished, noticing immediately how she shifted from side to side. She threw me an aggravated look.

"It was not actively hurtful, but, well... it reminded me of my difference." Allaine lowered her deep-blue eyes to the floor, not wanting to meet her sovereign's gaze.

"Then I shall no longer use it." Ambrose nodded curtly.

How positively progressive—and oddly sexy. I trailed my fingernail up the back of his thigh, and he tightened his glutes as I neared his curvy swell.

"Lady Allaine, you are due in the Obligate's quarters to prepare them for temple. Make them aware of the customs, ensure they do not dress in garish colors. Tone down Cinden's hair for Goddess's sake—ugh, like a salmon's innards—and tell Richelle not to giggle, *not once*, for the next two days. Those are direct orders. Now leave. Make haste."

"Yes, Highness." Allaine curtsied and then left in a hurry, most assuredly relieved to be on her way.

Ambrose pulled at the hem of his tunic. His eyes looked bleak once again, even under the beautifully defining swath of eye black he'd brushed on.

I stood, tucked myself under his arm, and wrapped my arms around his middle.

"I find myself in need of a lover's kiss."

In the mirror, his eyes met mine. I rested my palm on the hard plane of his stomach and drew little circles below the notch of his breastbone. Touch soothed him like nothing else, and I knew the next couple of days—the Period of Remembrance—would be difficult for him.

The big man twisted in my embrace and settled his arms around my shoulders. He bent his head, causing his pearl-encrusted braid to fall over his shoulder and land between us. Turning shy eyes to his, I watched as the flames ignited in his thickly lashed gaze. With Cato, I never suffered a moment of insecurity—could spread my legs and bare myself to him with the confidence of the most seasoned courtesan. With Ambrose, I still felt a little out of my depth.

"She would be proud of how you've comported yourself." I chanced another peek at him and blushed at his intensity. "You have acted every bit the prince. Checking in on your citizens, having food baskets sent to those who lost loved ones, financially seeing to the widows, all while both your brothers were away. She sits with your father, looking down, contented in the knowledge she raised her boy well."

Tender fingers settled under my chin, lifting my face.

"Eira, do you think the Goddess gave you to me knowing you would fill the void that her passing has left in my soul?"

I swallowed; my voice held captive to his vulnerable declaration.

"We will never allow their names to be forgotten, husband."

Ambrose nodded and dropped his mouth to my ear as he walked me backward.

"Would you allow me to put a babe in your belly, sooner rather than later, wife? I know our agreement says no, but I—"

I shoved him in the chest.

"You will not impregnate me to soothe an emotional scar. Not happening." I shook my head in emphasis and tried to push away. It was a futile battle against the vice of his arms. "That is *not* a sound reason to bring a babe into the world, I think... maybe?"

Or maybe it is? The thought of a little Nanetta running around my legs eased the deep pressure in my chest that I fervently hoped was just gas.

"Fine," he grumbled. "But I believe I am ready to resume the fine art of baby-making *practice* this evening."

He dipped a fingertip between my breasts and tugged the fabric of my gown, looking down into the gap it made.

"And I think, lady wife, you are just as eager to straddle the saddle." He dragged his finger across my clavicle and gave me a lecherous grin. "Hmmm, would wielding the reins interest you? A crop perhaps?"

"Ambrose..."

"I look mighty fine in full harness. These pectorals outlined in soft leather. Gods, I grow hard at just the mention."

That body covered in leather straps... kneeling beside me... also covered in leather straps... in front of a fully clothed Cato.

Ambrose's lips settled on mine, and I opened my mouth in invitation. The taste of mint and the scent of his freshly washed hair amplified my need for intimacy. Something that I hadn't realized I *needed* at all. I moaned into his mouth and softened my body against his.

"My apologies for the dry patch, wife, especially with Cato unavailable to take up my slack." Ambrose hoisted me up by the rear, and I wrapped my legs around his slim hips, cradling his hardness between my thighs. My back pressed against the cold mirror above the countertop, and his hands came to my breasts, teasing my nipples through the thin silk.

I fisted the fabric of my skirts, pulling the volume above my knees.

"We need to be fast."

Ambrose ran his hands up my silk stockings and then pressed my legs wider.

"I want you coming on my tongue."

I nodded rapidly.

"I can do that," I panted, my passage swelling in preparation. "Quick, though, yes?"

"And then I will turn you over and snack upon your other entrance before I thrust my dick into—"

"Oh, wait!" I smacked his shoulders. "Not now. We can't. We absolutely cannot."

Chest heaving, fingers tugging at the lacing of his pants, he halted his assault on my mouth.

"What? Am I not to your liking? It is this outfit. I am in mourning, Eira."

"Ambro—" His lips sealed themselves to mine again, cutting off my view of his mouthwateringly long length as it jutted free of his pants. He pushed my skirts to my hips, hands frantic.

"I will be quick, Eira, a few thrusts at the most."

"No!" I managed to squeal just before he bit my lip between his teeth. "Thaa swacretons. We ah wawing whaaa!"

He drew back and scowled.

"Come again?"

"The secretions. Ambrose—we are wearing white." I braced my arms against his flat abs. "You know I get messy, and you have a tendency to wave that wand around like you're conducting a full ensemble."

He blinked down at me, a lopsided smile curving the side of his mouth.

"That should not stiffen me further... and yet."

"What's that!" I yelled, pointing over his shoulder.

His head whipped around, following the direction of my finger. His hand fell to the blade at his hip.

I jumped off the counter and ran across the floor, racing into the common room.

"Jance! The door! Jaaaaaance!" I yelled.

The door flew open, smacking against the wall.

"Where is the enemy, consort? Point me to the brigand!"

Jance ran in, spear at the ready.

Ambrose's carefree laugh boomed from behind me, the rich and uninhibited sound filling me with quiet joy.

CHAPTER NINE

TIME FOR TEA. SPILL IT!

EIRA

"We're late because of you!"

"A prince cannot be late," Ambrose replied smugly, his pace that of a leisure-seeking snail.

I rolled my eyes to the cradle and tried to drag my giant fucking husband-by-contract down the royal gallery corridor. He stopped to examine each of his ancestors' paintings, and with each pause I imagined shanking him in the kneecaps... which would slow us more but allow me to remain in control of my dwindling sanity.

"You are undoubtedly the most infuriating man to have ever graced the Great Sphere." Ambrose tsked and stepped closer to a painting that resembled a child's rendering of a dead cat, squinting and scrunching his nose at the piece of "art."

"The Goddess was gracious by not allowing me to spring from the loins of a man who seems to lack cylindrical nostrils. How do you suppose he breathed through those?"

"I do not care. And now, the guests will have no other option but to fasten their eyes on *us* as we sashay into the room as if they owed us their patience," I said, frantically tugging his hand. My anxiety reached yet another tier of discomfort. I was meeting the brother.

The motherfucker I Joined with turned and began taking the tiniest baby steps he could manage.

"Precisely, Eira. Let their gazes rest upon me, wishing they too had a title *and* hereditary perfection." Ambrose stopped, turned, and flexed his two admittedly fine cheeks. "The cut of these leathers... My ass is actually breathtaking."

A lovely blonde servant carrying a stack of papers squeezed by, doing her best not to gawk at Ambrose's double-cheeked dance. I smiled at her apologetically.

"Just like what comes out of it," I muttered under my breath, ushering him toward the door. At least when he was spouting off in vanity, he kept moving.

"You act decent now, wife. But I have a bet going with myself that I can make you soak your underthings *and* your pretty white gown before dessert is served." He snuck up behind me, wrapping his arms around my waist.

"I don't need Aberus to think I'm a—oh high and holy Gammond above—Ambrose... What if he has the Bond?" I whipped around in his arms and snatched his tunic in my fists. "I'm certain that Cato *and* Septimus do and—shit shards! What if it's hereditary? I cannot, *will* not, entertain a third man in the bedroom. The two of you are more than I can handle—one all whiny, one all broody. And how gross would it be? He's Cato's *actual* blood relative. And what if it's not a Fated Bond, and it's the *Mated* kind? You said—"

"Nortia."

"Don't interrupt me. You said he was a big man. How big? You big? Lemder big?"

"He makes Lemder look like a starved waif in a famine. Now, if you will cease your yapping, I can explain to you that Cato has made Aberus aware of the fact that you have the conjuring ability." My eyes welled—not in sadness, but in terror. "He met him early this morning and will be present in the chamber already, along with Bem. Just in case."

Ambrose spun me around and we resumed our walk. It was now *me* taking baby steps.

"Is *that* the real reason we are arriving late?"

Ambrose's full-on beaming smile hit me like a ray of warm sunshine.

"It was *I* who came up with the plan."

I rang my hands together but managed an appreciative nod.

"Well done, husband."

"It was, wasn't it? He knows about Gaea as well, Eira. Aberus is a master strategist. His mind works like no other's... but allow him to mull things over before you go all *Nortia*, if you do not mind."

"I'm sorry? Go all what?" I stopped short and propped my fists on my hips.

"Umm, freezing the fucking ground? Calling forth your frozen babies' daddy? Trying to commit regicide dressed up in your angry little cloud costume?"

The sound of spear butts hitting the marble floor echoed through the hall. The ornately carved doors of the monarchs' apartments opened, and Ambrose practically shoved me the rest of the way down the hall.

As we inched closer, I noticed that the crescent moon representing Lord Gammond decorated the entryway's left panel, surrounded by lilies interspersed between fine knotwork. On the other, a glorious sun whose rays touched the doors' perimeters had been carved in relief. Its background was peppered with triangles and crenellations—I recognized them instantly as the designs of Imella's tattoos.

Ambrose outlined the circle that made up the center of the sun.

"Father had this room renovated after Aberus was born. He was so proud of Mama, and he wanted her to have a special, private sanctuary for her and the family. It was her idea to use geodes from the quarry to make the tiles for the upper walls."

"Oh, my stars."

Three steps past the threshold, a ray of winter light cast a brilliant rainbow onto the middle of the chamber's floor. The window on the back wall was magnificent, artistry in architecture—a wealth of multi-colored fragments formed a glass depiction of a wreath of roses. At its heart, the round window remained clear, allowing viewers to gaze upon the breathtaking scene of two overlapping mountains far in the distance. The light it allowed in glittered across the walls, reflecting off a thousand textured crystals of purple, white, and gold. It was like walking into a lustrous crystal cave.

"Ambrose it's—"

"   a contrast to the morose-looking crew sitting before us   " he flicked his fingers toward a table, where three serious faces watched us like a kettle of hawks on the hunt. My eyes immediately sought Cato's

"Greetings, my brother. And I am so glad to meet you, cons—"

A sob tore from my lips. The make-up Allaine, so painstakingly perfected, was in peril.

I wasn't prepared. I hadn't been told.

Aberus.

It never occurred to me that he wouldn't resemble Cato or Burchard. Nothing but the curls were similar, and even then, Aberus's were black-brown ringlets that reached down his back. Cato's were more like soft flips.

No, Aberus was Imella made over, in structure, in color, and expression. Thoughtful onyx eyes, set deeply on either side of a stately nose, and lips thinner than his brother's, revealed a smile just as tender and inviting as hers had been.

Solemn tears flowed down my cheeks as he rose cautiously from his seat and held his arms wide.

Cato jumped to attention, placing himself in front of his brother just as Ambrose stepped into my path, blocking my view.

"Move your beefy troll's body." I slipped around Ambrose and walked forward, but he trapped my hand, holding me back.

Cato glanced back at Aberus, lines of concern bracketing his mouth. He held his arm out in front of the future king as if that would stop the mountain-ogre-sized man if he wished to break through. Aberus topped out at seven feet or more, and not a bit of him was lanky.

"Eira, are you stable?" Ambrose asked, twisting me around to face him. He dropped his voice and his mouth to my ear. "Your vajeene will become nigh-uncontrollable surrounded by three Bonded men."

"No. Bond," I whispered, yanking my hand from his grasp. "I'm fine."

Ambrose looked up over my head, squinting through one eye and tilting his chin back slowly.

"Aberus, are you compelled to fornicate with my wife?"

I sensed a hulking presence behind me.

"What in the gods' name is that kind of question? She is your wife, brother mine. Have you taken ill? Gracious me. I value morality and a connection to a partner besides."

I twisted on my heels and looked up and then kept looking up.

"Ambrose values a connection *with* his cuddles," I said, taking up for my husband.

"Does he then? I would not have thought it." Aberus opened his arms, and I stepped into the circle of his embrace. "Well met, sister-in-law."

His deep, rumbling laugh vibrated throughout my body.

"If Ambrose is a black bear, surely you must be Thoramika, the four-armed warrior bear of ancient lore."

"I am twice as large as any of the bears I have encountered. Thoramika is my favorite constellation, though. How could she not be after saving the world from the greedy god of... was it agriculture?"

"Not even close. Lou was the trickster god, who fooled Mossius into Joining with a cow. Thoramika, the goddess of metal craft and metallurgy, freed him from a corral made from impenetrable iron." I laughed then, the sound breaking through the sadness that struck me earlier. I suppose that's how grief works, though. Memories and reminders consume you and then life reminds you to breathe.

Cato cleared his throat, but I didn't make to move. I was content to be where I was, tucked in the brotherly hug of Imella's eldest child. It was like hugging my Nan; he was thicker and softer of body. I loved the press of his rounded stomach against mine, and the all-encompassing comfort in his silent acceptance. Unlike hugging Nan or Imella, however, I was fairly certain that, with the expanse of muscle I detected beneath the surface, Aberus would give both Cato and Ambrose solid competition in feats of strength.

"Come now, little sister, I have ordered up a lovely repast of steak and onions—heavily peppered and served with a lump of freshly churned herb butter."

"*I love him,*" I mouthed to Cato.

Our embrace ended as Aberus escorted me to the table, where he pulled out my seat and tucked me in close. *A gentleman.*

Ambrose and Cato took seats to my left and right. They began stabbing slabs of beef, filling their plates with meat on one side and heaping piles of sauteed onions on the other.

Aberus took his time seating himself, and then unfolded and placed a linen in his lap, patting the pristine white cloth with both hands.

"I am afraid my brothers have lost all decorum in my absence," Aberus said while transferring a steak to his plate using the provided serving utensils. "Ambrose, do you mind if I refer to your lady by her first name, or would you prefer 'consort'?"

"Please address her as Consort Fairy Cun—"

"This steak is delicious!" I shouted, glaring at my husband, whose eyes danced in amusement.

"It is indeed," Ambrose agreed. "Especially when you actually ingest its succulence."

Hot prickles of embarrassment raced across my chest. I glanced down at my empty plate but then held my head high as I addressed Aberus, "Eira will do."

The soon-to-be-king cleared his throat, waiting for Ambrose—whose cheeks were stuffed like a greedy chipmunk—to acknowledge him. "Fin bah me. Ah don kur," he said with his mouth full. He waved his knife in the air, motioning for his brother to continue.

"Excellent." Aberus cut a small bit of beef and chewed it meticulously before he spoke again. "Eira, as the remaining woman of this family, it will fall to you to present yourself as the model citizen of the mountain kingdom—grace and morality personified. Like my late mama, and paragon of an aunt, Lilium."

I sat straight, trying to give the impression that I hung on his every word, even as I groaned internally.

"As a Troth trained in both decorum and the art of political savvy, Eira will undoubtedly rise to the occasion." Ambrose didn't attempt to contain the chuckle that slipped out between shoveling food in his face. "Will you force her to sit in the Ladies Loft at the temple?"

"Oh, gods." I hid my muttered impropriety under my linen as I patted it to my lips.

"Absolutely. It is the feminine throne of this kingdom—She will be the exemplar for the next generation of Monwyn women—a shining beacon of propriety and genteel womanhood. She will counsel them on the importance of maintaining their purity—what a gift that she bestowed it upon you brother—At least until I take a wife."

"*I* am to be the inspiration of p-poise and purity?"

Ambrose kicked me under the table.

No. What I *was*, was about to rise up and run the fuck out of here. Give me contracts. Let me negotiate the whale blubber trade or arrange marriages for the lesser nobles but leave me out of this misogynistic morality play.

"Would you please pour and serve the tea, dear?" Aberus asked politely.

"Yes," I chirped a little too loudly. "I would be honored and delighted." This was something I could do without fucking it up. The dining experience and all that came with it was a skill I had honed and then mastered while at Temple Verus.

"Tea!" Aberus boomed in a voice so loud that I jumped in my seat.

A liveried servant, wearing the mountain crest of Monwyn, strode forward, bearing a tray with such reverence that it could have been a reliquary containing the bones of a long-dead Mantle. He placed the tray slightly off to my side and then bowed so deeply that his backswept hair flopped forward, revealing a shiny bald spot.

A throat cleared across the table.

I ignored it.

It sounded again.

"Will you not greet me, *consort*?" Septimus spat out my title while he drummed his fingers deliberately on the tabletop. "I fear Aberus has unrealistic expectations of your capabilities... and integrity."

Do not launch a knife. No knives at breakfast. Butter over butchery.

I made a show of turning up all the downward facing teacups and placing them on their matching saucers. The little clinks of fine pottery filled in the emptiness of an increasingly awkward silence.

"My plan, Protector Septimus, was to ignore you entirely," I said with a brilliant smile and nod in his direction. I didn't allow my eyes to connect with his icy-blue ones. I knew the effect they had on me. This breakfast was uncomfortable enough already.

Cato chuckled like a smug little rat, but Ambrose's glee drowned him out.

With deft fingers, I poured a perfect stream of fragrant tea into each cup, filling them to exactly the same depth.

"Eira, little sister," Aberus said.

"Yes, Majesty?" I dipped my head in his direction.

"Two things." He cut a piece of steak, lifted it to his mouth and glanced meaningfully around at the family. Septimus's plate remained empty. Ambrose's was nearly clean, and Cato was stabbing at his third meat chunk. "Maybe three."

Aberus's brow wrinkled as he prepared his thoughts.

"One: Uncle Septimus is a member of this family and the highest-ranking man in my military; he is to be treated with respect."

Traditional Monwyn male. Why had I assumed he would be otherwise?

"Noted." I successfully kept my nostrils from flaring, focusing instead on mixing a spoonful of cream into each of the delicate cups. *Neutral face, Eira. Keep it contained.* I swallowed hard and then managed a curt nod.

"Second. I am aware that you, like my late father—may his bones be blessed—possess certain *attributes.* Starting today, you will be monitored at all times. I am told your talents are, by our best accounting, in their nascent stages and pose a danger to my citizens."

I pressed my lips tightly, wishing I could argue against his logic.

The æther stirred lightly in my stomach, like a hundred little butterflies waking from their naps. I kept my gaze downcast.

"Third. You broke into the healer's shed. As you know, the area is off-limits to those other than the healer, head gardener, and Protector. It is also my understanding that you removed a body and desecrated it in the back gardens. This is unacceptable and, frankly, disturbing. It smacks of the vulgar behaviors my father displayed, but unlike in his case, I have the authority to curb your excesses. You will be punished."

"Now wait a damn minute," Cato interjected, shoving his plate to the side.

Aberus remained silent as a servant hurried to the table, snatched up the endangered stoneware, and darted away on soundless feet. I tapped my fingernail against the cold metal of a tiny sugar spoon while the chastisement continued.

"Hush, Catommandus. The consort's actions resulted in the deaths of three of my guards, according to Uncle Septimus."

"Aberus, those killings rest upon my shoulders. You will not—"

"Hold your tongue, Cat. The remains of an Emissary—from the holy temple of Verus, no less—were burned like so much kindling, before autopsy or respect could be rendered. The Mantle will be incensed. The sheer level of disrespect committed upon that woman's body was..."

I stopped listening and placed my hands in my pocket, clutching the little bundle of ashes—the only thing keeping me tethered to this moment. *Strength of Nortia, my girl.*

"... furthermore, she allowed the guards to see her unclothed. A woman's body should never..."

The disrespect was not in *my* actions.

The disrespect was in the customs of my people, *Nan's* people.

"... I will not tolerate a woman of my household to carry on in such a way."

My head snapped up.

"Brother Aberus, may I address your concerns?" I asked, using the familial denotation to ease the conversation from its judicial tone.

"You sure as fuck can, consort," Cato blurted out beside me.

"Oh, gods," Ambrose muttered. "Can you not, for once?" He rubbed his fingertips in little circles around his forehead. "Sugar for me, lots of it." The look I aimed his way unmistakably said, "Get your own fucking sugar."

The ice upon which I tread was brittle, but I was no amateur.

"None for me. I prefer the leaves bitter," Aberus said.

Like your soul...

"Give me my cup before it gets cold," Septimus chimed in.

Control, Eira. Play the good wife.

I mixed two little spoons of fine powder into Ambrose's cup, but he pointed his finger in the air, indicating the need for more. I dumped in two more measured heaps and then added two to mine.

"By all means, little sister, you may address the family. You have my permission to speak."

Permission? With hands much steadier than they felt, I passed each man his saucer, managing not to hurl the steaming liquid into any of their smug-ass faces. *See? Control.*

"Thank you, Majesty." I sipped the warm beverage that smelled of jasmine and black tea and let it roll over my tongue. "I believe it is important that you are made more aware of my peculiarities"—I sipped the fragrant drink again, each drink bolstering my resolve—"so that we may continue moving forward."

"Go on," Aberus said with a roll of his wrist.

Ambrose slid me his empty cup and pointed. I was thankful, honestly; it allowed me respite from Aberus's unwavering stare. I poured my husband another cup and reached for the cream and sugar. I squared my shoulders and looked up... directly into Septimus's amused face. His tongue darted out, sweeping along the rim of his teacup.

The pleasant tingling he inspired in my nether regions pissed me right off.

"I would address each of your statements in kind. Number one: Your father engaged in an affair outside of his marriage."

Ambrose's fork clattered to the table.

"Tread lightly, consort," Aberus warned. He leaned forward and tilted his chin down, a gesture Cato commonly used to intimidate others.

"Eira," Cato whispered. "Eira, do not."

"What you may be unaware of is that he and the woman were linked by what the conjuring books describe as a Mated Bond. It's a sexual connection that draws together those who share the likelihood of bearing a child with access to the æther. That initiated his more unpredictable behaviors."

The new king's bushy brows knit tightly.

"Cato, is what she says true?" Aberus snapped his head in his brother's direction, causing his unbound curls to sway around his head.

"It is." Cato scowled, his eyes shooting icy shards toward Septimus. "However, what we must keep in mind is—"

"And this is where I will address your first concern," I butted in. "I share a Mating Bond with your Uncle Septimus, but I do not wish to sully my Joining vows and commitments. Therefore, I choose to keep him at a distance."

Aberus's mouth fell open, revealing a bottom tooth capped in gold.

"Pardon me, sister-in-law, are you saying that you—"

"—want to pound your uncle like a mallet driving a twenty-two-inch tent stake into the ground? Yes."

"You need to eat," Ambrose said with near-bored levels of nonchalance as he dropped a slab of steak on my plate and cut it into bite-sized bits. "You have not touched a morsel."

Aberus turned his head from side to side, his coils bouncing around his face.

"You... you are aware that your wife wishes to bed another?" he stuttered, eyes darting to Ambrose.

Ambrose speared a piece of meat and brought it to my lips. "Eat." I dutifully opened my mouth and chewed the most tender, succulent sliver of bovine I'd ever consumed. "Yes, I am aware and—"

I placed my hand on Ambrose's forearm.

"Husband, my apologies for interrupting again. However, I believe it's important to inform Aberus that I'm also stars-over-the-moon, in love with Cato and share in a Fated Bond with—"

"Holy Goddess above." Aberus smacked both of his giant's hands against his heavily bearded face. "Everyone out!" he bellowed, thunder filling the room.

Two servants scurried out, and Bem followed behind them. Aberus leaned back in his chair, meal forgotten. He crossed his arms and then uncrossed them... and then crossed them again.

"Should I be worried, consort, that you would make a cuck of my brother?"

"Which brother?" I asked, confused by his statement. I mulled over the question in my head and—"Oh! I understand your confusion."

Cato leaned his head toward me, his mouth a fine line. He picked up my hand, placed my palm on the table, and covered it with his own.

"No!" Aberus hollered. The teacup nearest him quaked. "You are—"

"—in love," Cato said, while smoothing the pad of his thumb down the side of my hand. "Yes, brother. Eira is the answer to every prayer my lips have uttered. She is my only experience of color in this dank and dark world. Had I not been bound to the Protectorate, she would be my wife in name. The biggest mistake I have made in life was not resigning the position the instant I understood what has become the central truth of my existence."

Ambrose handed me my tea, and I drank deeply.

"But I took her maidenhead," Ambrose said in an overly merry tone. "That tight little corona gave way, and I showed her the way of pleasure, over and over. Do you remember sweetheart, that first time?"

I choked and sputtered, thankful for the napkin in my lap.

"An admitted whore." Across the table, Septimus stood and began pulling at the fingertips of the leather gloves he wore. "A woman of ill repute cannot be the outward face of this family."

I looked at him askance. *He* was the lord of the Den, not me.

"Septimus, you odiferous green toad, you are simply jealous that she did not allow that pierced dick of yours to slip into her Goddess-blessed cavern. I am honestly sorry for you. Penetrating her is a delicacy, a privilege you will never know." Ambrose brought my hand to his mouth and bit my middle finger between his teeth.

"Please, no more," I begged, pulling my fingers back from his lips.

"Disgusting slut," Septimus hissed. The barbed words sounded seductive coming from his mouth.

Cato rose slowly, facing off with Septimus in clear challenge.

"Cato, sit! This is madness. Uncle Septimus, resume your chair!"

"Nephew, listen to me well," Septimus leaned toward Aberus but kept his piercing blue eyes fixed on mine. "Dissolve this sham of a marriage and give her to me. Taming her will be my service to Monwyn—breeding her will be my reward."

Aberus recoiled, slowly shaking his head in denial.

"For fuck's sake!" I yelled, throwing my napkin at the table. All heads snapped to me. Aberus looked close to stroke. "Listen up Septimus, if it will end this godsdamned Mated Bond bullshit, go ahead, get one of your colorless nether spawns on me and then leave me the fuck alone." I tugged angrily at my skirts, yanking them above my knees. "Come get it while it's free of charge—I'm running a special!"

Septimus mounted the table, launching himself in my direction, eyes dilated and a heavy erection pressing against his pants. Plates went flying; bowls shattered. Hunks of beef landed on my chest, rolling down my bodice, ruining my beautiful gown.

Cato flung himself at Septimus and met him head-on, driving his fist into the side of his silver head. Septimus struck back in a series of quick blows, opening his nephew up to a savage punch to the solar plexus. Cato collapsed in on himself, doubling over, but came up swinging.

"I will have order in my kingdom!" Aberus stood to his full height. "Uncle Septimus! Catommandus! Do you not hear me?"

"Come, wifey." Ambrose calmly rose and pulled my seat back, steering me away from the ensuing danger. He then rounded the table, collecting the knives that hadn't already hit the floor. He tossed the handful to the far wall, where they rattled noisily against the white wainscotting that covered the lower half of the walls. "Better off that way."

"I will shoot my seed into her womb."

"A dead man can do no such thing," Cato growled. "She is my woman. Mine alone."

"Is she then?" Ambrose popped a brow, watching the two combatants closely. "Come again, brother?"

Cato's hands wrapped around his uncle's neck, but Septimus's face split in an evil grin as he took the unguarded opportunity to strike Cato in the throat—two evenly matched lions embroiled in a fight for dominance.

"If Ambrose divorces her, she becomes my wife. *My. Wife.*" Cato's voice was gravelly, and he punctuated his last two words with cracking slaps across Septimus's face. "You have no claim upon her. She is mine."

Ambrose's eyes darkened, every ounce of his former amusement gone. His shoulders rolled forward, and he clenched his fists in anger.

"No, no, no. Black Bear, hold steady. Brother Aberus? Please?" I begged. I hadn't the physical strength to stop him.

Aberus intercepted Ambrose, grasping him by the shoulder, "Brother, do not give in to this madness."

Ambrose shrugged him off.

"She is *my* wife, Aberus. Before both Goddess and crown."

The table toppled, scattering the remains of the meal across an antique rug depicting a peaceful forest scene of nymphs and woodland creatures.

Ambrose used the opportunity to run forward and wade in. He kicked the fallen table aside, and wretched Cato's arm behind his back, allowing Septimus to land two solid blows to Cato's nose. Blood poured from his nostrils.

I placed my hand on Aberus's forearm.

"Could we speak in private?"

Aberus turned thoughtful eyes to mine. He worried the corner of his lip, a nervous habit that seemed counter to his impressive physical stature.

Tucking my hand into the crook of his elbow, he bent so that I could hear him over the cacophony of the skirmish. "Control, little sister, or lack thereof, is what separates us from the deer roaming in Goddess Maressa's forests. For my father's kingdom... *my* kingdom to flourish, control—yours and theirs—is paramount to its success."

I nodded my understanding. "This level of jealousy and impulsive use of force is the antithesis of what we learned at Verus. Even with all that I have become, peace and prosperity are still my ultimate objectives." *That and annihilating the Primus-King.*

The king nodded.

"Please step to the far corner, if you will." Aberus swept an arm to his right, indicating the location.

I hesitated briefly before tucking myself between a marble statue of Lord Gammond in repose and the wall.

Septimus, head pinned to the floor by Cato's boot, never saw it coming.

Aberus snatched his uncle from the floor as easily as a polar bear seizing a fish from an ice-hole. He hefted him fully above his head and sent him flying.

Holy fuck.

Bits of plaster and dust fell over Septimus's prone form as he demolished a modesty panel which had been exquisitely painted with a rendering of the royal family. The top of its wooden frame followed, clunking loudly against his skull. His eyes rolled briefly before snapping open once again.

"There will be no talk of divorce, Cato," Ambrose grunted. I turned my attention back to him, fearing for his safety. In his rage, however, he was holding his own just fine. Cato had him pinned to the ground, but Ambrose scissored his legs around his brother's waist and began squeezing his powerful thighs together, keeping Cato at an awkward angle and minimizing the punches that rained down on the side of his ribcage. "And you"—*squeeze*—"were"—*squeeze*— "the fool who devised the plan that made her *mine.*"

Aberus marched over, snatched Ambrose's braid at the base of his head, and palmed the lower half of Cato's jaw with his other massive hand. With one mighty heave, he pulled both men to their feet and forced them, half stumbling, into a nearby wall. He held their faces against the polished crystalline surface.

"If you cannot maintain order in our home, I will treat you like the rabble you are acting like. Calm yourselves or cool off in a stone cell. I abhor violence, as you well know, and this is not, let me emphasize it once more, *not* how the members of our noble lineage will conduct themselves. You will right this room, take your seats, and this conversation will continue. Now!" Aberus dropped the brothers, righted Septimus, and with an unbelievable show of dignity walked to his seat.

CHAPTER TEN

THE HIDEY-HOLE OF MY HEART

EIRA

With the furniture back in place, all four men sat in silence, three of them patting their napkins to their various cuts and scratches. The chamber reeked of animosity.

"Allow me to pick back up where I left off," I said in a voice more suited to a cheerful afternoon promenade.

"Please," Aberus replied with a gentle inclination of his chin.

"Issue number two: As for the conjuring, I only became aware of the ability recently. You are correct that I need to learn control." I turned to face Cato. "I need access to Father Burchard's books, specifically those written by Magis Raephin. That, or to find a suitable tutor."

"Where would we find one? Solnna?" Ambrose, whose eye was swelling shut, brushed my hair back over my shoulder. "That is within the realm of possibility, but I cannot leave until Aberus is firmly installed—I am now first in line to the throne."

I rested my palm on his in understanding. The risk would be too great.

"And with the threat of Gaea, love, traveling is not a risk we should take," Cato added, his voice muffled by the linen currently staunching the bleeding from his nose. "The books, however—"

"Will remain under lock and key," asserted Aberus. "Consort, my father, bless him, only became more erratic as he studied the tomes. I cannot give you my blessing."

"Then... I can't ensure the safety of those around me. Aberus, please take a chance and get to know me. I came here for this kingdom; I came here to give the people their king back and—"

"—and he died, consort, the fault of which lies at your feet."

Like a bolt to the chest, his words pierced me deeply.

"We are leaving." Cato took my hand, threading his fingers through mine. "Come with me. Nothing binds me to this place now; I will take you to my own lands in Basilia. We can be there before the Gaeans even know we have left."

Ambrose grasped my thigh under the table.

I shook my head at Cato, but clutched his hand between both of mine.

"Aberus," I met the eyes of the eldest brother. "In addressing issue number three: the Emissary whose body I removed and subsequently burned." Tears brimmed, but I held them in check. "She was my dearest, closest companion in this world, and I buried her as she would have wished. And I would take the same actions three times over." I released my hold on Cato and withdrew the tiny pouch from my pocket. "This is all that remains of her."

Cato frowned as he looked at the black drawstring bag.

"Eira, where are the *rest* of her remains?"

"The rest of them?" I repeated, looking around at a table of confused faces.

"When we sealed the bag, it was plump. It is now—"

"I-I mixed them into my tea," I admitted in a soft whisper.

"Cannibalism," Aberus gasped. Septimus grinned like a cat who caught a mouse in its claws.

I turned to Ambrose.

"I was thinking about the Taleery ash beads, and... it seemed like the best way to have her with me, like your mama's people would have done... Ambrose, you had some as well. She always liked you, and I figured you wouldn't... I should have asked."

"Do... do what?" Ambrose pressed the back of his hand to his forehead. "I grow faint." He swayed, and I grasped his shoulder, lending support. "I am going to vomit. Fetch me a pail. Fetch it now."

"Weakling," Cato muttered under his breath. He reached down, procured a chipped teacup, and held it out. He cupped his hand under mine and lifted the pouch of Nan's ashes.

The tears freed themselves then—fat drops of loss, but also love.

"I know you didn't care for her much."

He smiled softly. "I will *always* love her for how deeply she loved you."

I shook a bit of ash past the broken rim.

"A pail, Bem!" Ambrose screeched, lurching toward the door.

With his fingertip, Cato captured a tear that was falling down my cheek, dipped it into the gray-colored soot, and then pressed the finger to his tongue.

"In this life and the next," he said. His eyes softened, and he leaned his blood-streaked face to mine, only to halt when a firm hand clamped down on his shoulder.

"Cat, you are nothing if not committed, but until I can wrap my head around this literal farce of a situation, keep your distance. She is *legally* married to your brother," Aberus said, casting a shadow over us both.

"Then you should prepare my prison cell *now*, brother." Still gazing into my eyes, Cato jerked his shoulder free, captured my waist, and yanked me to his chest. His lips settled on mine and in an instant, the world around us faded away. This man was my everything.

"Catommandus Odelguard!" Cato flew backward. "What the nether has gotten in to you? Where have you stowed the disciplined man that was my brother? I am stunned, absolutely appalled. This is Ambrose's woman, his property, and you will respect their union."

Cato fought against the arms that bound him.

"Aberus, you have never known the man I *wish* to be."

"And who is that? A philanderer? A man lacking in moral direction?"

The door opened.

"Aberus, he loves her. Can you not tell?" A green-faced Ambrose staggered into the room, looking worse for wear. I took his clammy hand in mine and reached up with my other to smooth an errant hair from his forehead.

"I am aware. Only love can turn a man into a fool this witless. But this is not Taleer, or even Gaea. Plurality is *not* a part of our kingdom's customs. It is illegal in this state."

Aberus shifted, releasing Cato, and looked Ambrose squarely in the eye, "Tell me you are perfectly fine with Catommandus pawing at your wife, and that you are perfectly happy to watch them kiss and caress while we entertain the dignitaries from Nortia or-or Solnna."

Ambrose sneered.

"I am not at all fine with *those* things, Aberus, you buffalo's ass." Ambrose's throat worked up and down and he covered a gurgling belch with his palm. "We have discussed perimeters and discretion in public—"

"Discretion? Ambrose, you flung open a door allowing a handful of servants a view into the room where Cato was thigh humping the woman bound to you before Goddess and peers."

Ambrose waved one hand dismissively and held his stomach with the other. "They just need to fuck it out and—"

"My ears." Aberus's hands flew over his curls, blocking the sound of his brother's voice. "My ears cannot handle what you are saying. Am I correct in thinking that you *share* this woman? You are both *actively* fornicating with *this* woman… under the roof of *this* palace?"

Cato glared down his swollen nose. "You think I would give up the Protectorate and *not* be fucking her? You are clearly not fit to wear the crown upon your head."

Holy shit.

Angry Aberus was terrifying.

He swelled up to double his size, and his dark eyes splintered under heavy black brows. He pushed the sleeves of his gray-knit sweater over bulging forearms and then bent closer to Cato's face.

"Guards!"

Fingers of fear gripped me tightly around the throat.

"No!" I wedged myself between them and threw my arms wide. "I will stay away. Please to the gods, please don't lock him in a cell. The thought… I can't breathe." My hand flew to my chest as the sound of armored men running through the hall echoed around us. A dark cell was far too similar to the horrid graves in which they buried their dead.

"See that you do, consort, for I am duty bound to uphold the laws and customs of Monwyn—family or otherwise." Aberus loomed over me, his authority palpable.

Ambrose laced his fingers through mine and positioned himself to support me.

Cato moved toward us, determination in his gold-rimmed irises. I held up my palm, halting him mid-stride, and turned into Ambrose's chest. For a moment, I thought I might faint dead away.

"You will *not* keep me from her," I heard Cato say in a flat and tightly controlled voice.

"No. I will not have to. My sister-in-law is more intelligent than the both of you and has made the proper choice—what is *that*?"

"Fucking nether," Ambrose muttered. "Eira, Troth face. Now."

Serene-faced and prepared for an encounter, I quickly wiped under my eyes and tossed my curls over one shoulder. I pressed my back against Ambrose to cover the eyeball-shaped makeup stains I'd left on his once immaculate tunic.

The "that" was Richelle's plump behind, bouncing around a corner backward. She hopped forward—presumably peeking around the wall—and then shuffle-bounced backward on her toes, concealing herself once more.

How she thought she could hide her mass of orange-red curls was beyond me. They spilled beyond the wall every time she hid.

Aberus waved off the guards that now stood at our perimeter. "You are no longer needed. Thank you for your haste."

I followed the king's line of sight. His obsidian eyes landed on the big bottom encased in the palest of orchid pink. Aberus hooked his hands together around his back and bent slightly at the hip, inspecting her with a down-turned mouth.

Like the graceful dollop she was, Richelle—entirely unaware of her surroundings—shuffle-bounced backward... heading in our direction.

"Richelle," I called out, plastering a false but believable smile on my face. "Do turn around. I'd like to introduce you to—"

"Eira, hush, I am pursued," she whispered-yelled back, waving her petite hand behind her. She was only ten feet away and closing in at an astonishingly high speed.

"She has no awareness," Aberus said, his brows shooting up to his hairline.

"None," Ambrose replied matter-of-factly.

"Eira," Cato used the distraction to move closer, but I sidestepped him, ignoring the tick in his jaw and the lethal way he held his hand on the hilt of his blade.

There is nothing I can't endure for him.

"*Richelle*, ahem, I would like to introduce you to—"

"Someone who can order your mouth sewn shut—oh Goddess!" Richelle twirled around; hands pressed to her pink cheeks. "Eira, please tell me you know I didn't mean to say something so insensitive"—She stopped abruptly. "Gracious, you're built sturdy." She smiled up at Aberus, scrunching her delightful button nose. She then walked directly past him, threw her arms wide, stole me away from Ambrose, and rocked me from side to side.

"You look lovely in white, Eira, but you should take more care, or at least cover those big bosoms with a linen." She grabbed the hem of her gown, spit on a section, and then began scrubbing at my chest. "What were you eating?"

"Steak."

"Steak? I was served chilled cucumber soup. I will waste away here."

"Richelle? My most wonderful friend." I tried to bat away her hands.

"Hmmm?" She patted my left breast, amused by its jiggling, and then reached to scour the right.

Aberus took a very formal, very dignified step in our direction.

"Troth Richelle, you mentioned being pursued. Is a man in this palace making untoward advances? Do you find yourself in need of a savior?"

Richelle dropped her dress and faced Aberus fully on.

"Oh, no, it's not like that. Come with me." She tucked her hand under Aberus's forearm and pulled him along. "Do you know little Mae?" she asked.

"I do not."

"Truly?" Richelle paused and gave her head a disbelieving shake. "Maihon's little girl, as cute as a fairy, hair as blonde as butter?"

"No, I am afraid I have yet to make her acquaintance."

Richelle sang out a high-pitched sound of surprise.

"Well, you won't have to wait long, I'm sure. We are in the midst of a rousing game of hide and seek, and she is an excellent seeker. I'm only half-good at hiding, you see; I tend to forget my role and end up caught while exploring the artwork or ogling one of those fine Monwyn guards." Richelle burst into uproarious laughter and turned to catch my eye.

I smiled back, baring my teeth in a clear "shut the fuck up," expression.

"Anyhow, I didn't catch your name, my big fellow."

"It's Aberus."

"Well, Aberus, I'm not sure if I have a hidey-hole big enough for you to fit in, but if you'd like to play, we'll give it our best shot."

Ambrose snorted behind me, and I kicked him in the shin.

Aberus kept his face as neutral as a Scion on Assignment day, but he couldn't obscure the warm blush that spread across his bronze skin.

"I am honored by the invitation but must resume my duties. Perhaps we will—"

"—see you at temple tonight?" Richelle asked, her smile as friendly as ever.

The king nodded.

"Great! I'm off. If you meet up with a tiny blonde, don't tell her you've seen me. Eira, I can see your nipples through the fabric now. You should probably change. Bye, Catombrose!"

Richelle flounced off in a wave of pink skirts.

"Eira, this is nonsense. You will stop, and you *will* listen to me."

I strolled through the dead, dreary gardens, ignoring Cato as if I were entirely alone.

Allaine was at my back, ordered by Ambrose to stay no less than ten paces away if I was in the presence of nobility, five feet if it were a male commoner, arm linked through mine if it was Septimus. Jance walked behind *her*, spear in one hand, longsword at his hip, short sword on the other, dagger on his thigh, dagger in his boot.

I nodded at a passing servant, who stopped to curtsy. Her arms were full of dried flower stalks and white ribbon.

Cato inserted himself directly in my path. I stared at his chest, knowing that any eye contact would send the æther spinning.

"Tell me honestly. Would he lock you up? Toss you into a dungeon?"

"I do not fucking care if he—"

"Answer me." I waved at another couple of servants, who smiled as they too ran by with laden arms.

"Aberus does not mince his words, but there is also not a cell in this palace that I could not escape from."

Cato reached for me, but I drew back, evading his touch. Bile rose in my throat. Sweat beaded on my forehead.

"Perhaps when you were Protector. But you no longer are and… and the thought of not being able to see you… thinking of you surrounded by dirt and grime and rats and worms and—"

"You have never seen a prison cell, I take it?" He smiled his condescending half-smile.

"No, and this isn't a time for levity."

Cato lunged and gripped my arm tightly, holding firm when I attempted to pull away.

"Where you are concerned, I am nothing but serious. Now listen to me."

Jance cleared his throat as he moved forward.

"I will snap your neck before you can clear your sword, officer. Now, take two steps back and you may *both* face away."

Allaine immediately turned. Jance, just enough that he could still see us in his periphery.

"Whether he understands it or not, you are my wife, just as much as you are Ambrose's. *We* were bound under the Goddess's sky, and if you think that doesn't take precedence over the words of some old fuck in red robes—"

"Cato," I reached out and then dropped my hand to my skirts, shooing away some imaginary bug.

He closed his eyes and breathed deeply, doing his best to stay grounded.

"You are the husband of my soul, and we will figure something out. But until Aberus can come to terms with us, or until... I don't know what," I tossed my hands into the air, "you must keep your distance."

"I will do no such thing."

"You will." I lowered my voice. "Cato, my heart, I won't be able to control the shadows if they lock you away. What I am capable of—the annihilation of all in my path—you have not witnessed firsthand. You may threaten to burn this city to the ground, but I will eviscerate it. I will wipe it from the memories of men if you're taken from me." My chest burned as the words tumbled from my lips, and my hands shook as the æther begged for its mate. I could barely maintain dominion over my body. My passage swelled as if encouraging me to move forward, and I was flooded with a slick heat that demanded the man standing in front of me.

Cato's nostrils flared as if he could scent me. He unbuttoned the top closure of his shirt, the open collar giving me a glimpse of the dark hair at his chest.

He played the game... and he played it well.

"Do. Not," I warned.

His fingers moved to the next button, and I closed my eyes against the sight.

"Or what?" he asked, his voice lust-thickened, deep and drunk on desire.

"A-Allaine!" I shouted over my shoulder.

My ever-dutiful lady's maid hurried to my side.

"Reporting for duty, consort." She saluted like a soldier, balled fist to shoulder and then slid her hand through my elbow.

"We must prepare for temple. Good day, Prince Catommandus." I ripped the words from my lips.

"That is, like, five hours away." Allaine shook her head and scrunched her shoulder to her ear.

"*Allaine.*"

"Fiiiiine. Come on."

CHAPTER ELEVEN

IF ALL I HAD WAS A SPOON

EIRA

"We're up to our twat in a snowbank with no sun in sight."

Ambrose scowled at me while sorting a few tendrils of my hair.

"Your backwoods euphemisms fall on deaf ears, I am afraid. Everything will work out. Aberus will come to terms, but until then... wrap your siren's lips around my dick, yes?" Satisfied with my hairstyle, he kept his head low and ducked his lips to mine. "That will ensure a thaw."

"At a Joining?" I glared at Ambrose while tapping my foot on the wooden floor. "You want me to drop to my knees in the middle of the Ethens family shrine, minutes before the ceremony begins?"

"No." Ambrose leaned around me and peered into the small but lovely building located half an hour's ride from the palace. "But only because you cannot reach my cock while kneeling." He ran his hand down his bearded jaw. "The pew however, I think would put your chin at my pubic bone and—" he closed one eye and held up his thumb like an artist framing a portrait, "—your dark hair would be stunning, haloed by the powder-blue and gold backdrop."

I glanced around at the small but beautifully appointed room. The walls, of course, were the familiar beige stone that was the entire town and palace, but these contained a vein of shimmering gold that flowed in thin, concentric rings. Interesting. I moved closer to examine what seemed entirely unnatural.

"Oh, Ambrose look." I sucked in a quick breath, awed. The bands were not rock features at all, but prayers from the Common Book that were chiseled in a precise yet bold hand, no more than a quarter inch in height. Each letter gleamed, gilded in gold leaf. "Perhaps I should have considered

Ethens's proposal," I muttered under my breath while trailing a finger lightly along the wall. This magnificent tribute to the divine surely cost a fortune.

"I am a literal prince, you second-guessing harpy—an astonishingly handsome, tall *and* muscular prince at that. You got the fairytale, and yet some sparkly walls have your head turning?"

Ugh, petulant Ambrose. I recognized the biting quality of his snark. He would soon morph into hateful ogre Ambrose.

"Pants down. Now," I pressed him back toward a tiny, recessed room, meant for prayer and reflection. "Mean Ambrose needs to stay the fuck away while we are dealing with upset Eira and raging Cato." I palmed the bulge between his legs, coaxing it to life. "The whole godsdamned palace will fall down around our ears."

"Yes. Take command." His hands flew out, one gripping the marble ankle of the god Josa, the other clutching the curved beak of the hawk that perched upon the shoulder of a statue of the goddess Meressa. "I am your big, strapping soldier, and I have just entered your barracks without permission—"

A choir began to sing—the sound was otherworldly. An ethereal collection of youthful voices blended and swirled in intricate polyphony.

"Shit, shit, shit." I jumped back, took Ambrose by the hand, and stood in front of him as we awkwardly shuffled our way down a short aisle.

"I do not enjoy delay play, Eira," he whispered as he nodded to the three men located in the fourth pew. "This is the longest dry spell I have *ever* endured. I haven't even taken a self-guided tour of Mount Ambrose since, well, since the balcony. Since... and down he goes."

"Shut up. Or at least lower your volume." I inclined my chin to an older man who I recognized as an ally in the mass assault on Scion Greggen. He bowed his head in allegiance, and we continued forward.

"He-he didn't even pay me my due respect. Did you see that? Eira, I demand you stop your quest to feminize this kingdom."

"Hush."

"Do not hush me."

As the highest-ranking guests to attend, we slid into the very first pew and sat.

As the music swelled, Cinden appeared in the right alcove and Ethens in the left.

"Oh, Ambrose... usually I hate attending these things, but just look at her."

Joining of convenience or not, Cinden was glowing—which may have been the pregnancy or the hundreds of candles that lit the sanctuary—I chose to think that maybe it was just, perhaps, a hint of happiness.

A priest all but skipped down the middle aisle, an exuberant smile stretched across his young face. His patchy beard resembled scraggly bits of wool fluff, and he had the excited eyes of the sled dog puppies back home. He raised his hands and invited the couple to his sides.

Cinden was a vision. Her pale-gray gown matched the altar cloth, evoking silver stars disappearing in the morning sky. Cinden had told me that, Ethens had procured the exquisite silken fabric for both the bride and the altar to be a "reminder of our most sacred day" each time he attended temple. Not even the Millanderers could boast of a fabric of such unique construction—clever dying techniques and fine threads of silver gave the impression that the cloth progressively became more metallic. The hem gleamed as pure as the silver in Ambrose's crown. Her bodice was strewn with diamond-encircled emeralds that clustered more thickly around her neckline and seemed to merge with a collar of overlapping wrought silver leaves that spread over her shoulders and down her arms.

Allaine had worked her magic and taken Cinden's hair from a sugary pink to cool blonde, highlighted by rose strands. Her brown complexion and velvety brown eyes gleamed through the green and gold powders used to enhance her features. She was perfect.

Ethens wore a gray, nondescript suit. No flash, no bright red shoes or fuchsia pants, just a modest man in the most modest of clothing. I noticed he did allow for a bit of color—the ring in his ear that now marked him as Joined was the exact shade of pink as Cinden's pout. And his eyes... they spoke volumes. He was enchanted by the woman who agreed to be his.

"This will be my fourth Joining to date, and I will tell you they are by far the most superb of the sacraments I perform." The priest dropped his arms and held his hands out, palms open to the couple, who each offered a hand of their own. "When the Goddess granted each of us admittance into this blessed world, she opened up our hearts and bestowed upon us the ability to love... and love is what brings us together this evening."

Ambrose leaned in close. "Do you remember our big day? Hmm?" His breath tickled my ear.

"Of course," I whispered back, "it was like, last week, Ambrose. Now hush." I smiled to myself and kept my eyes trained to the front. The priest placed Cinden's slender hand into Ethens's. My heart broke, noting the little quiver of her bottom lip.

Stay strong, Cinden... for the little love growing in your belly.

She had to be an absolute mess. She had found her lifemate, but now she was pledging to another. Maybe on the other side of Merrias's blade...

A bout of sniffles pulled me from my thoughts.

Stars above. Tears streamed down Ambrose's cheeks and into his beard. I procured a linen from my cloak pocket, my fingers brushing up against the little pouch of ashes stored there as well.

"My sweetest Black Bear, you were the most handsome man that day. When I saw you walk the aisle, time froze."

I dabbed the linen gently below his eyes, wiping away the eye black that started to run.

"You gifted me my Mama that day, Eira. Because of you, I have *that* memory and not just the one where I see her suspended from those ropes." His big, warm hand came to my face, cupping my cheek. "The Goddess must love me, yes?"

"Without doubt, Ambro—" His brow shot up. "Husband," I corrected.

"And you love me?" His mossy eyes searched mine, their color illuminated by the soft glow of candlelight.

"Yes. I do love you."

He nodded his head slowly, as if trying to convince himself.

"You would move mountains for me?"

I thought about his question as he gazed at me, his hope brittle.

"Even if the only shovel I had was a spoon."

Ambrose frowned.

"A spoon? Eira, that is nonsense. Go all angry puff and explode the damn thing." He snatched the linen from my hand and dabbed the corners of his eyes. "Now shush, I do not want to miss their vows."

CHAPTER TWELVE

THE MOUNTAINS THEY DO RISE

EIRA

"**Y**our Highness, consort, thank you for providing us with the royal carriage. Our bond continues to solidify—my hat, take my hat, Cinden."

Bent over and hurling, Cinden's deep, guttural grunts permeated the air, along with a sickening stench. She filled the gray flat cap to its brim.

"Out the window, Eira. Aim! Good Goddess, I have never once heard of the sympathetic vomits."

As I emptied the contents of my stomach, it flew out the window, splattering the side of the shiny black vehicle.

"It's the smell, and... and the speed. If we could simply slow down, I could..."

Another wave of a cheesy-smelling stank hit my nostrils and doubled me over.

"They have carriages in Gaea, yes?" Ethens asked.

"N-not like these," Cinden said, laying her head back against the royal-blue padded seat. "Life is slower there, not so-so fast-paced."

Good girl Cinden, keep up the ruse.

"We do *not* have carriages in Nortia," I moaned, clutching my stomach. If I were looking for a silver lining about hurtling through the town in a cramped, enclosed space, my vomiting would at least help sell Cinden's story.

"We cannot slow. Ethens took ten minutes licking her mouth clean instead of kissing her chastely and sealing the deal. A prince being late to the king's Mourning Service—can you even imagine?" Ambrose grumbled.

"It was a lovely—*gag*—if intimate kiss, Ambrose." I shot a compassionate smile to Ethens, whose cheeks were turning pink. He was adorable. "My nose burns. Give me my hanky back."

Ambrose reached into his vest pocket, huffed loudly, and tossed it on my lap. "This was to be the memento of a poignant moment."

I blew my nose, extracting the stinging remnants of my regurgitated dinner.

"Burn it when you are done, wife."

The carriage came to a jarring halt, and Ambrose hopped up from his seat, flinging the door open, striking the face of the footman who came to aid us.

"Out. Fast. Eira, I will escort you to the Ladies' Loft. Allaine will meet you there. I will take my place with the men in the front. Cinden—"

"Relegated to the back—Allaine filled me in," Cinden said in resignation.

"You may join Eira for the musical interlude but then, out. Do you hear me? She plays an important role tonight."

Cinden cocked her head to the side.

"You've not heard?" I blinked at her innocently. "The new king of Monwyn has graciously bestowed upon me the official title of 'Most Virtuous Vagina in the Land.'"

"You?" Cinden's loud, tinkling laughter filled the carriage as Ambrose dragged me along. "Has the king seen your tits yet?" I heard her yell, even as her voice faded away behind me.

Ambrose froze, statue still. "I forbid your breasts to make an appearance." He leaned down, bringing his nose to mine. "Do you remember what to do?"

"Yes… and I've let *them* know their roles as well," I muttered, nodding in the direction of my wranglers.

Allaine fanned her fingers in greeting. Jance pounded the butt of his spear on the ground. Both stood at the bottom of a grand staircase whose railing was made entirely of gold filigree.

Cinden slipped her arm into my elbow, bowing to my personal escort as we strolled by, and together, we marched up the stairs and onto the balcony.

From the second level, we had an expansive view overlooking the congregation.

Aberus sat on the throne his father had once occupied. The crown of Monwyn sat on a table next to him, atop a white cloth that reached the floor. He'd not be permitted to wear it until after his coronation took place. I thought about trying to explode his big head with the sheer force of my will but calmed, remembering I might actually be able to.

The temple, the same one in which Ambrose said his vows *at* me, was at capacity, yet it was easy to find my men. Ambrose tucked himself next to Cato in the front pew, their heads immediately dipping together in conversation.

Music began all at once, startling me with the magnitude of its volume.

On the dais, arranged in a *U,* was the largest collection of instrumentalists I'd ever witnessed in one place—their combined sound was glorious, if a little overwhelming. Horns, stringed instruments, and drums were all present in multiplicity, and a tiny woman—old as the dirt itself—led them with a flurry of motions that looked a lot like Cato and Ambrose's secret sign language.

Tonight was all about music.

The god, Josa, would be present in this holy house and would send our prayers—laments and joys both—to the cradle as an offering to the pantheon.

Cinden and I leaned over the half-wall of the balcony and studied the crowd. I scooted closer to her side and snuck my arm around her waist.

"Are you okay?"

That lip wobbled again.

"No, but I will be," she replied weakly. "M-my husband is a very good man. He will be a brilliant father." She rubbed her still-flat stomach unconsciously.

"If you don't wish to answer, I understand, but have you… been intimate with him yet? We can explain away a month, but not much more. And with your wedding pushed back because of the Nether Lord's appearance…"

She turned and looked me in the eye, biting her bottom lip while she ginned goofily.

"It… it won't fit yet," she chuckled, "but we've been increasing my ability steadily since the night of the bedding."

"Cinden," I said, the trepidation clear in my voice.

"*Eira,*" she repeated, mocking my concern. "I'm a trained Troth. I've had him ejaculating in, on, and around every orifice I own. I hand-humped him with just his tip in my entrance and made a whole deal about craving his spill. He'll have an entirely new list of proclivities by the time I'm through with him."

I pressed my lips in a tight smile.

"Somehow I don't doubt it."

"I need to sit."

We turned to the three ornately carved chairs that sat behind us, the middle one taller than its flanking counterparts. Each had a prayer book atop its ostentatious purple-blue cushion, and as I stacked them in the leftmost chair, my eyes fell on the initials stamped on the leather volumes. *L. Septimus, Duchess*—*Queen Imella Monwyn*—and *Lady K. Septimus*. I traced my fingertip over the letter *K*.

Of course, Kairus would have attended temple with her mother when she lived here. I smiled, picturing her turning all of Baldorva on its head, issuing orders to the slavers and making demands of the Warlord. She was made for that Assignment.

Cinden flopped gracelessly into a chair and pulled both of her legs up, shoving her feet under her bottom. She laid her head back and sighed.

"The exhaustion and sickness should pass in a couple of weeks, I think."

She nodded faintly while pressing her lips firmly together.

We sat in silence, listening to the strings and horns as they played a somber melody. I rubbed the spot between her thumb and forefinger, having remembered from my momma that it might help settle her.

I studied my friend. She was such a brat, but also much more intelligent than she let on—much more shrewd than many would ever give her credit for.

A sudden, disturbing thought flashed like lightning in my mind, and a prickling heat washed over me. My stomach knotted.

"Cinden, have you met the Primus-King?"

"Of course."

Then she *had* to have known the man presenting himself as the Primus-King at my Joining was an imposter.

"And... and you spoke with him at the Joining? Was he well?"

"Goddess no." She popped a soft-brown eye open. "I avoided him like the boil plague. Why?"

The shadows swam in my periphery. Was she lying? Was she a spy? His spy, the fucking Primus-King's?

"It's just that he looks different from what I imagined, much different from how Ozius described him to me at Verus."

She visibly saddened at the mention of her lover's name.

"Oh, well, the Scion live at the palace. They stay until they are of age. The Troth don't. I was introduced to our ruler right before my hair was colored. He blessed me with his own hands. I'll never forget it."

"When was that?"

"Oh, I must have been five, maybe four."

My vision settled, and the radiating heat across my chest stilled.

"I remember thinking him quite handsome. Gentle eyes, a funny blue color. Quick to smile. I imagine he's gone all white and crusty now, but we couldn't see a thing but the top of Ambrose's fat head at the Joining. You know, in Gaea, the temples are constructed in the round so the entirety of its worshippers may take part. Ethens says he will construct a circular temple in our northern holdings to celebrate our union."

I scrubbed my palms against my face.

"Jealous?" Cinden giggled and plucked at the ribbons that secured a creamy-white, fur-trimmed half-coat around her shoulders. "Simply green with—"

The music came to an abrupt end.

"Shit! Get, go!"

Cinden hopped up, and I brushed down the wrinkled skirts of her dress while she re-secured her coat. She flew to the steps, and I ran to my designated spot on the balcony... it was time.

A line of priests, perhaps a dozen, flanked by rows of priestesses on either side, processed down the long aisle that Ambrose and I traversed so recently. The smell of lavender and woodsy incense traveled from the front of the temple, where the prayer fire was being lit, all the way to the back, bringing with it a nostalgia for simpler times and rituals shared with those now gone. The religious sisters peeled off and stood in front of the dais, forming a wall of red. The priests stepped up and then configured themselves in a circle around the fire-filled urn.

"We pray to the Mother." The presiding priest raised his palms to his forehead and covered his eyes. "According to our faith, King Burchard has met his judgment. He stood on the blade, no doubt found to be righteous by Merrias, and now spends his eternal home in the hands of She Who Which No Greater Can Be Conceived. Take this time to transition from sorrow to rejoicing. No longer will the sounds that surround his memory be somber, for our kingdom's father, Burchard, walks the path of divinity."

The circle of priests dispersed, clearing the dais.

"In accordance with his wishes, written by his hand in his last testament and will, King Burchard requests his favorite song, "What the Mountains Provide," be performed in his honor, by none other than Prince Catommandus of Basilia."

Do what?

The congregation erupted.

"It is a rare honor that we hear the voice that moved us beyond emotion in our younger days."

Squinting in disbelief, I leaned over the railing to get a better view.

Sure as shit, Cato stepped from an alcove to deafening applause. The atmosphere of the temple buzzed with anticipation. Young ladies craned their necks; men shifted in their seats. A gaggle of mothers waved their hankies, vying for his attention. One yanked at the neckline of her daughter's bodice, showing off her round bosom.

I thought I'd seen grumpy Cato—I was mistaken. He glared with open hostility at the assembled masses, eyes narrow, mouth tight. He marched to the dais like he was attending his own court martial.

In the front row, I caught the shake of Ambrose's broad shoulders—I didn't think he was weeping. Aberus held his balled fist over his mouth, and I could see the twinkle in those obsidian eyes from here.

Oh, gods. Josa, Lord of Glory, He Who Gave Us Beauty in Sound, take Cato by the hand. Hold your brother in your arms as he embarrasses himself for the sake of his dead father.

Absolutely horrified for him, I pressed my palms to my stomach.

Cato positioned himself in front of the musicians, back rigid, shoulders squared. He tugged angrily at the wrists of his sleeves and inhaled, expanding his chest widely.

The harpist struck the opening chords of the melody, and Cato opened his mouth while I sent up another vehement prayer...

"Sheltering the land,
The mountains they do rise.
An ever-stalwart presence,
The mountains do provide."

"Holy fuck." *Holy actual fuck.* He held the last note of the stanza in a clear and shockingly pure baritone.

"Amethyst peaks in the evening light,
An opal that gleams when snow covers their height.
We build our homes from the stone they provide.
The glorious mountains of Monwyn do rise."

The shock to my senses was so profound that I couldn't force my mouth to shut.

Even singing a song about rocks, Cato was... I peered down at the women who sat in the back of the temple—it wasn't just me. The old and young alike wore swoony faces, all puckered lips and promise-filled eyes. Their lusty sighs and unabashed moans were audible from the second goddessdamned story.

I patted myself on the back. Yeah; I was fucking with that.

I didn't even hear the words of the last verse, too enamored by the celestial sound pouring from the man that *I* got to nail. The way he breathed, so controlled and confident as he gave the song life. *Gods.* My nipples stiffened to hard points as I added a new category to my own list of *proclivities*… voice kink… song slut… oratory aphrodisiac? Whatever it was, it was hypnotic.

The song ended—I never wanted it to end—and the masses went wild, surging to their feet and clapping their hands above their heads. Men hugged and patted each other on the backs like they were the ones who blessed our ears with their talents.

"Again! Again, Highness!" a woman screamed like a demon had entered her body.

"It has been decades since that voice was heard!"

"He is back. Monwyn's child prodigy returns!"

My eyebrows snapped to my hairline. Child prodigy? Voice of a godsdamned man-siren they mean. What in the actuality of Ærta was Cato's childhood like?

Amid the applause that was growing louder by the second, Cato grimaced at the crowd, gritting his teeth. He curled his top lip and snarled before pivoting on his heels and marching off the same way he entered. The crowd, overcome by the return of their musical genius, tossed large stalks of dried white hydrangeas onto the dais, and, *nether*, a woman below me passed clear out. Three priestesses rushed to her side and began fanning her while removing her heavy overcoat.

Ambrose and Aberus were outright cry-laughing now, wiping at their eyes and hee-hawing like the assholes they were. The thunderous applause squelched their guffaws.

The presiding priest raised and then lowered his hands, calling for order.

"We all remember fondly our angelic Kitten raising his voice during our High Holy Day celebrations. You are now invited and encouraged to lift your own voices as our prayers continue through song. Let our king hear us from his new home above."

The familiar sound of "Creator Goddess, Lordess of Light," floated up to the balcony. My part was soon to come. Thank the Goddess above, it didn't involve singing of any kind. My voice should only be heard by drunks in a tavern, or maybe a babe in desperate need of comfort.

The two lines of priestesses held their arms high as the notes swelled. In their hands, they held the prayers of the faithful. They began their solemn procession to the flaming urn, and I watched, my heart lighter, as they placed each scrap of paper one by one into the fire.

I breathed deeply, touched by the sight of thousands of fond memories and well wishes from the citizens across the kingdom.

The arched ceiling filled with smoke until a priest pulled a tassel that opened a small window at the uppermost point of the sanctuary. Like a storm cloud, the smoggy grayness lowered, but never met the heads of the assembly. The heavy scent of burning parchment reached me, and another, more subtle aroma took me back to searching hands, panted breaths, a star-studded sky.

Cedar and clove.

"Do not look away, Eira. Face forward."

I gasped out loud but did as I was told, keeping my eyes fastened on a group of priests kneeling at the four corners of the covered altar. My heart pounded against my ribcage.

I breathed him in, the man for whom I'd forsake the Goddess herself, letting his scent infiltrate my every pore.

"Did you kill Jance? Allaine?"

His soft chuckle, closer now, was the music that moved my soul.

"I scaled the staircase from its side. Neither of them saw me—and I will order your husband to appoint a new guard upon our return to the palace."

"Cato, if Aberus sees you—"

"He will not," he said in a tone so certain, so matter-of-fact, that I believed him... or convinced myself that I did. "And you will rid yourself of the ridiculous notion that you can keep yourself from me. You cannot."

"I can. I possess a much stronger will than you think, and the thought of you locked away bolsters my resolve." And it did. I would not, could not, allow him to be imprisoned.

"Sweetheart?"

"Yes?"

There were a few beats of silence between us.

"Lift your skirts for me, love."

My eyes rolled back as my lids fluttered shut. The æther that gathered in my chest shot to my stomach and then lower. That delicious pulse that mimicked my heartbeat took up residence in my goddess-given gem.

"No. Cato, if we are caught..."

"I will explain to our captor that my hands forget themselves when I cannot touch you—they act of their own accord. Then I will put a blade to their throat. It is quite simple. Now, lift. I won't ask again."

"But Ca-Cato. Aberus is a man of his word." I tucked my arms behind my back and bent my head as if in reflection, protesting even as I followed his order. Bit by bit, I worked up the fabric that trailed down my legs, scrunching the silk in my hands without disturbing the gown's front. "You said so yourself."

"Higher, love. Show me what I desire more than the air that sustains me."

The crescendo of voices and instruments softened, and I heard the telltale sound of a belt unbuckling.

"The tops of your stockings tease the curves of your ass. So fucking beautiful. I long to feel the silk slide around my hips while my cock is ensconced in your heat."

Gods. Oh, gods. I would not... *could not* deny this man.

My breaths became erratic. I hastily tugged the gown above my hips, tilted my rear and perched the roll of fabric on the small of my back. With each shift of my shoulders, the rub of my gown's bodice sensitized my breasts. I wanted his fingers there, gliding over my naked skin, pinching and flicking my peaks to stiffness.

"Your undergarment, pull the strings. Release them and hold them out behind you."

I exhaled slowly, as I was trained to do, attempting to slow my heart, trying to restrain my arousal. The fear of being caught by Aberus, or worse yet, the entire upper echelon of Monwyn society, almost stopped me... but even that didn't outweigh the thrill of knowing he wanted me enough to risk it all.

I plucked one side of my ties and then the other.

"Soaked already? I have yet to begin, wife." He caressed my palm as he slid the silk garment from between my fingers. "Your scent, Fira. Gods, I am hard as fucking granite, and my hand brings me not an ounce of the pleasure that you do."

I heard him spit, and a soft groan followed. My knees nearly buckled. I gripped the banister in front of me to keep stable. The image of him handling and jerking his cock was my undoing.

"Mmm, your color deepens. Show me more, love."

I leaned forward, resting my elbows on the banister, listening to the clicking of his belt buckle and his soft grunts as he stroked himself faster. I placed my fingertips on my forehead, hoping the guise of prayer would cover the redness I knew seared its way across my cheeks.

"What is that you pray for?"

"You, Cato. Always you." My voice was nothing more than a breath lost in the notes of another song.

"Take one step back—no—don't look around."

"But I want—"

"Face. Forward."

I complied, slowly placing one foot behind the other.

Calloused fingers slid up my thigh until they cupped my rear. Cato squeezed and then lightly shook my cheeks.

"Your body is perfection—soft skin, unfathomable curves." He traced the cleft of my bottom, reaching lower until he met the telltale dampness of my longing. "You do realize that there will come a time that I proclaim you as my own, yes?" He ran a finger through my wetness, one long motion, opening me from clit to entrance. A finger settled, poised to bring me the pleasure. My hips sought him, rocking back as he fed me the tips of two fingers. "It will be done publicly, before Aberus and any others who care to bear witness. This is not negotiable. Now look up and play your part."

The music stilled—my cue.

Goddess above.

I quickly adopted a face of sweet serenity a mere second before the audience stood and turned to face me.

Every eye was on me—their paragon of virtue. I nodded at the demurely dressed women, relegated to the sanctuary's back, and then lowered my head in reverence, paying my respects to Aberus, who stood and proclaimed, "Give us your blessing, Mother Monwyn, and in return, we pray your womb bears us strong sons."

Sons. Of Course.

I placed both hands over my heart and then gestured, spreading my arms to the hundreds of eager faces that now looked upon me.

Two fingers slipped into my passage, spreading me and finding that delicious spot deep within.

"Our daughters will lord over these sheep," Cato muttered from below me.

"Oh, oh, Goddess." My head fell back, and my lips parted. The fingers inside me rocked, hooking upward as they thrust. "M-mother above."

"The Goddess imbues her!" the priest cried out from below.

Cato's lips brushed softly against my lower back. He rubbed his coarse beard along my rear, licking the flesh at intervals as he moved from top to bottom. "Take me, give me purpose. I am your body to command." The words stumbled out of their own accord as Cato slid my clitoris between the love-slick fingers of his other hand. I bucked, my rear pressing into his face.

"The consort's words float on the sacred smoke to the Creator's divine ears," the priest intoned. "Let us give her thanks!"

The crowd bowed in unison and then turned back to the dais—all but one. Septimus's fine brow arched inquisitively. His eyes lingered, roaming over me before finally shifting.

My walls constricted—release nearly upon me.

"Not yet, Nortia."

Cato pulled away, and I clamped my lips together to keep from crying out.

A hand twisted into the roll of fabric at my hips and slowly pulled me backward.

"Widen your stance." I obeyed, and Cato's hands slid between my inner thighs. "Another step back... good... now lower yourself slowly as you sit upon *your* throne."

As I descended, he lifted my legs, hooking my knees over the velvet-covered armrests of the chair—his broad tip snugged against my widespread entrance.

"Can you support yourself? Hold entirely still? If you move, we risk discovery."

"I'll damn well try." I white-knuckle gripped the arms of the seat, clamping my fingers around them tightly. Testing the integrity of my position and the chair itself, I did my best to hover just above him.

"If it collapses, love, I will console myself by fucking you on the floor," Cato whispered. He reached between us and held his hard length, repositioning himself slightly. "Remain motionless. Allow me to honor you." His thighs tensed beneath me. "Gods Eira, I've missed this." His arm slipped around my waist, anchoring me. With an excruciating slowness, he lifted his hips, parting my walls and filling me with the familiar pressure I craved more than any other vice. He thrust up slowly, pulling out when my tight ring met his dryer skin, and beginning again, working himself in with my wetness.

"Cat, Cato, I—"

"Keep silent. Face neutral. Do not allow your lips to part. Do not allow them to see your pleasure. *That* is mine to enjoy."

"I am beyond caring what they might see. Fuck me. Please don't torment me."

"Eira, sweetheart, the ways I could find to torture you... besiege your spectacular body..." Cato tightened his hold on my waist, seating himself fully, his thighs flush to my backside. He ground, moving his hips like a wave that didn't fully crest, slowly churning and flowing beneath me. "And though now I can think of nothing more titillating than hearing the clicks of the rack as it spreads your legs... we are in the Goddess's house. I will pay homage to her greatest creation."

His hand dipped under the back of my gown and around my widely parted thighs. He held my vulva snuggly.

"I want you naked, Eira, yanking my hair, those claws leaving streaks of blood on my back."

My breath caught in my throat, and my arms shook. While so deeply embedded, he rolled his pelvis rhythmically and then pressed the thick part of his hand against my clit, rubbing it in steady, circular motions. My passage flooded, allowing his erection to glide more freely.

"Your breasts in my hands, nipple rolled between my lips. Gods, I would spend myself in—where would you have me come, darling?"

"My mouth," I whispered without hesitation. I recalled the first time we were intimate at Verus. How he had worshipped me with his tongue, how I'd returned the favor, much to his surprise. "And then inside me wi-with my legs draped over your shoulders."

Cato groaned into my back, his breath tickling a path across my neck, his lips warm through the silk.

"Do your miss your monster... the warrior-king?" He vibrated the tips of his fingers against the sensitive flesh of my clit in a fast back-and-forth motion. "I can hardly control him when you are not near me."

"Yes, yes. I need him. Want him. Don't stop, please—I'm so close."

"I will never stop," he gritted out. "Aberus won't stop me." He reared his hips below me, thrusting hard. I clutched the chair arms, securing myself as much as I could. "Ambrose won't." He fucked up into me once and then again, his cock growing harder—it was more glorious than when I rode him and took all the pleasure for myself. "And *you* won't stop me, Eira."

A loud moan bubbled up from my chest, completely out of tune with the melody being played.

Any other man's possessive-ass declaration would have my eyes rolling... and not from desire. Cato's? His proclamation was my undoing. I wanted his domination, desired to feel small and secure in his arms... beg him to control me as he saw fit.

The side of Cato's hand entered my mouth, sealing off my cries.

I bit down and pressed my own hands over his, determined to stifle the whimpers.

I dragged my tongue across his skin, tasting my salty response mingled with the taste that was him.

And he abandoned control.

I fell forward, thighs falling from the armrests, a hand pressed to the middle of my back. On all fours now, he captured my hips and drug me back against his cock, spearing me in a single swift movement.

My orgasm coursed through me, hazing my vision, casting the rest of the world to shadow as I floated amongst the stars. I spasmed and pulsed, swelled around him while he took his pleasure. Incoherent noises tore from my lips.

"My wife." He grasped the back of my neck, pushing me lower until my breast touched the floor. His other hand tugged me against him as he hammered himself into me. "The very beat of my heart."

His fingers clenched, digging into me.

"My world," I breathed—praying his head wasn't visible over the half-wall as he continued to thrust into me.

Though I couldn't see him, I knew how every plane of his face would look—I had memorized the pout of his lower lip, the way his dark eyes would go out of focus and then snap back to sharpness moments before his release.

He yelled and groaned behind me as he came. With each spasming release of himself, his body shuddered until finally, he lay over me, spent and breathing hard.

"I love you, Eira, and I will never forgive myself for placing this kingdom above you."

"We made that decision together, Cato." I caressed the hands that tightened around my middle. "And you can make it up to me by singing me a romantic song before bed." I heard his scoff above the drumming that started up below us. "Now dislodge yourself and give me my underwear. We don't have time to bask in the aftermath of post-coital delight." I giggled while making to stand, remembering to affix an expression of piety and calm resolve before resuming my post at the front of the balcony.

I scanned the crowd—they were transfixed on a thin man with a massive voice, who was now singing a most impressively high-pitched aria.

"Godsdammed, Ambrose is correct. Your cruelty is without bounds. I risked my life for you just now."

"Underwear." I wiggled my fingers behind my back. "Here, please."

"No."

"Catommandus Odel, middle name, middle name," I said in frustration. "Your *emissions* are slipping down my thighs. Hand them over."

"I cannot, love."

I whipped my head around, still caught up in his spell.

"These are mine, now." He raised the white silk to his nose and inhaled. "And my *emissions* are exactly where I want them."

"That's disgusting." I lunged forward to snatch them from his hand, but with a short run and swift hop he bound over the railing, halting his fall with a hand on the gold acanthus leaves of the stair's dazzling architecture. His precise movements were perfectly silent.

Beneath the filigree banister, I spotted his beaming face. He blew a kiss, and then he was gone.

I peeked down the stairs and caught sight of Greggan, tall and handsome, assisting Allaine in stretching out her seized arm. Her affected hand rested against his forearm as he held her elbow—his warm tone a contrast to her pale skin. It was decidedly intimate for being so innocuous. Allaine jumped at being discovered, but I shook my head and mouthed for him to resume. His returned smile was a kind one.

Ugh, don't make me like you, fucker.

I waddled awkwardly back to the balcony, wide-legged and uncomfortable, just in time to see Cato resume his seat below. Ambrose placed his arm around his brother's shoulder and pulled him closer. Cato, Goddess love him, reached up and sweetly blotted his brother's tears, and then nestled the hanky in Ambrose's hand.

"Blessings from above!" Ambrose hollered so loud I heard him clearly from my perch. "Oh, for fuck's..." I buried my head in my hands.

It was not a hanky pinched between his fingers. Handkerchiefs didn't have ties.

CHAPTER THIRTEEN

HOLY MOTHER!

EIRA

I dipped and then dodged, evading the strike!

Tucking my buns, I sprinted away like a dog caught in the larder.

"Oho! Is someone jealous?" I teased, peeking out from behind the column where I sought refuge.

Ambrose leaned to the left, and I ran right, only to fall for his well-timed feint. He caught my arm, spun me around, and smacked my ass so hard the slap carried throughout the bathing chamber.

"You dirty little nether spawn!" He snatched up my skirt hems and tried pulling the dress over my head.

"Flatten the boobs, Ambrose; it's not coming off if you don't," I squealed as he yanked and shook me inside the cocoon of silk. "Stop! Before you tear it."

His laughter was genuine and deeply reassuring.

"And... jealous? Of course, my dick is jealous. Look, he has spoiled you. Absolutely filthy. I have counseled you *both* on the importance of aftercare. Ugh, you're all streaky and crusty."

I shimmed and rocked, finally emerging from the gown as he tugged it over my head.

"Was it fun?" Ambrose arched a brow and held his arms out.

"It was so much fun." I reached for his proffered hands. "Hugs, hugs, hugs."

And then I was flying.

I broke the surface of the water, all flailing limbs and curses. Sputtering and spitting, I flung the mass of my soaked hair over my forehead and glared up into the smiling eyes of my husband.

"Good Gammond, you're such an asshole!"

Ambrose strode forward and into the tub, parting the water like a ship's keel through the sea. He pulled me against his body, holding me tightly, his arousal stirring, lengthening between us. His wet finger found the divot where my neck and clavicle met, and a warm rivulet of water trickled between my breasts.

"Let's commence tah fuckin,'" he drawled—his mountain accent was awful but oddly adorable all the same.

"Nope, I'm done with water sex unless you know how to keep the lubrication lubricate-y." I pushed away from him, grabbed a jar, and lathered myself from hair to heel. "Pick something else for your well-earned release." I glanced over my shoulder and made a show of rubbing the slick soap over my breasts... while keeping them just out of view.

"Mmm. Let us see, let us see..." He looked around the room, stroking his chin as he thought.

"Also, I'm completely spent of energy after the balcony. Consider me your willing vessel... who wants you to come quickly so we can grab a snack before bed."

Ambrose placed his hand over his heart.

"More endearing words were never uttered, perfect spouse."

His brows drew together, and he pursed his lips.

"Such a serious expression, Ambrose."

"I take my sex seriously."

"Come here." I motioned him over and pointed to the recessed bench. He sat dutifully while I scrubbed his head and then dug my thumbs into his shoulders.

"Do you want to watch me masturbate, wife?" He sighed and let his head rest against the tub's edge as his hand dropped below the water's surface.

I bit my bottom lip, holding it between my teeth. My clitoris pulsed happily to life, beating out a tempo all its own. I dipped my hand into the water, running my finger around his velvety tip before caressing the spot between his penis and sac.

"Actually, husband, a while ago you mentioned the possibility of running yourself between my breasts... That sounded... interesting."

"Interesting indeed." Ambrose skimmed his palm over my nipple before rolling it lightly between his fingertips. He watched closely as it peaked under his touch. "Your pillowy tits will make a cozy home for my cock."

"And I was also thinking..."

"What were you thinking?" His green eyes darkened as his tongue darted out to moisten his lips. I caught the hand that was pumping his arousal and slid it up my body to cup the other breast. I lowered myself, straddling his hips, teasing his erection with my labia.

"I believe you possess the required length to, um... slide between the pillows, and then right into my mouth." I rocked, rubbing my clit along his length. "Is that something you think we might try?"

Ambrose lifted me back to standing and rose, letting the water cascade down his chest. He was so fucking beautiful.

"Oh wife, I think we will need to try it *several* times—to ensure the mechanics are efficient."

"Kiss?" I asked as my back came up against the tub's edge. "Cato didn't give me kisses." I fake pouted. "And though I cherished the forbidden liaison... I missed the intimacy of having his mouth on mine. Can you make it all better?" I blinked up innocently from under my lashes.

"How dare he treat my wife so shamefully?" Ambrose bent low. "Kiss." He settled his soft lips on my mouth. When I slid my tongue across his, his skin went to goosebumps under my palms. "Is it possible that you are more than just a willing vessel this evening? Your body does not keep its secrets well."

"Your Highness!" Jance called loudly from the common room. "Highness!"

Ambrose's head jerked up.

"What for gods' sake? I am trying my damnedest to wet my dick."

"You have been summoned by His Majesty Aberus. You are to come to the Joining chamber at once!"

"The snow babies. Do you suppose—" Ambrose's eyes filled with concern.

I may have levitated from the water.

Ambrose followed, and we dressed still sopping wet—in the first items of clothing we could get our hands on.

We raced from our apartments, soaked hair seeping into our shirts, bare feet slapping against the marble floors. The doors of the Joining chamber opened as we sped down the hallway. A burst of frigid air struck my face as I ran across the threshold.

"What's happened?"

The immaculately dressed triad of Aberus, Cato, and Septimus turned to stare.

"Thank you for joining us. For future reference, if the situation is dire enough to forego dressing, rest assured it will be included in the summons," Aberus said, diverting his eyes from our mismatched and bedraggled outfits.

"Jance!" Ambrose shouted without bothering to look back at the guard. "The next time you come running, yelling at me to make haste, the fucking Nether Lord best have reappeared."

"Sorry, Highness, my apologies Highness, I will endeavor to—"

Ambrose kicked the door closed behind him and then looked down at his ensemble.

"Its fine, husband, you look fine."

Chest still heaving from the run, I patted his forearm reassuringly.

He wore a pair of scuffed-up leathers, barely suitable for hunting, and had paired them with a blue silk vest with scrolling pattern encrusted in lines of rubies and pearls.

Cato cleared his throat. His eyes dropped to my chest meaningfully, and he coughed again, louder this time. When he removed his gray coat, I finally caught on.

"Fucking fuck."

Ambrose's dirty, white undershirt clung tightly to my chest. My sopping hair had made it transparent—a prominent pink nipple and its darker areola was clearly visible in the lamplit room.

"It was only a matter of time, Aberus." I wound up my wet hair and knotted it the best I could atop my head. Cato tossed me his coat, and I hastily buttoned it up. "They've all seen them."

Aberus's mouth worked up and down as he searched for a reply, but I sailed past him on a much more important mission.

They were here. My frozen gifts from the hand of the Depraved One.

I searched them over, checking for any changes. They seemed the same as they had before.

"Thank you, Goddess," I breathed.

I sat on the bed where they lay, and ran my fingers along the two frozen forms, who clung to each other like twins in the womb. My shoulders dropped, and my clenched jaw loosened—they were safe.

"Protector Septimus has explained how these two men have come to be in my palace." I sensed Aberus as he positioned himself behind me. "He reported you called out for the 'daughters of Gaea' and yet, these two appeared instead. As your 'children' the brief stated."

I said nothing, as he hadn't asked a question.

"Do you know the whereabouts of the Gaean daughters?"

I shook my head.

"Have you frozen them? The political repercussions would be insurmountable if you have done something so ghastly."

I scoffed loudly, snapping my head around to face him.

"I didn't freeze *these* two. Evandr..." I reached for him, cupping the Scion's face in my hand. "Evandr is here on account of my blood, I believe. I need access to the Magi's books to better understand, but—"

"And the other?" Aberus interrupted.

My hand drifted along the clean-shaven chin of the umber-complected man.

I shook my head.

"I have spent hours combing through my memories, but I have no recollection of him. Nothing at all."

"Ahem," Ambrose cleared his throat like Cato had earlier. I spared a glance at my crotch, praying *that* pink wasn't visible as well.

"Majesty... I can't place his face, but it feels—in my soul—like we are, in fact, connected."

"Ahhh-heeemm," Ambrose loudly made his presence known again.

"Brother Ambrose, are you well?" Aberus asked while closely inspecting the two frozen figures. He made to touch Evandr but stopped short before making contact.

Cato and Septimus moved to stand at the end of the bed. Septimus, disdain dripping from his every pore, confidently placed his fingers to the spot where the king's would have touched. He snapped his arm back like he'd been burned, cradling his fist to his chest.

"It's like receiving a shock... He is so cold," he said, "and yet *your* witch's hands go unscathed." He covered his eyes in prayer.

I paid no attention to him or the increasing tingling in my passage while in the presence of both of my Bonded men.

"Slight her again, Septimus, and the shock you feel will be my fist shattering your teeth." Cato postured toward his uncle, hands balled into fists.

"Catommandus, my insolent namesake, it is only your youth that allows you to think you could best me. Never forget who taught you, boy."

I looked between them, scrubbing my face with both hands like it could somehow cleanse my brain. "Creator above, it doesn't matter. We've all been so focused on fucking and other frivolities that so much has slipped past us."

A heavy hand came to rest on my shoulder. I looked back into the sorrowful eyes of Aberus.

"That is the most astute statement I have heard since arriving home, little sister."

His endearment melted some of the tension that had characterized our relationship thus far.

"AHHHH-HHHHEEMMMM, godsdammit!" Ambrose shoved his way between Cato and Septimus, wedging himself in between their combined bulk.

"Brother Ambrose, if you have something to say, speak."

Ambrose crossed his arms against his gem-studded chest and pressed his lips into a tight line.

"Yes. Thank you. It is just that... I-I happen to know the identity of the unnamed ice man."

Every eye in the room, baring the babies, settled in Ambrose's direction. My palms began to warm.

"What do you mean, you know? Explain yourself! I can't believe you would keep this from me. What the fuck would compel you to sit on such knowledge?" I skittered across the bed and fisted the sides of his collar, jerking his head to eye level. A line of sewn-on pearls snapped off in my hands, and a wealth of rubies followed, raining down onto the mattress.

"Literally this!" Ambrose attempted to brush my hands away from his chest, but I held tight. "Piss you off and *poof*," he waved his arms around his head, "evil puff-Eira freezes my godsdamned nuts off and casts me into a dirt rift!"

I recoiled. Stung by his words.

"Ambrose, I would never." I took his bearded cheeks in my hands, stunned that he would think I could.

"You might... Eira, I think you are miraculous, but..."

"Tell me, Black bear. Tell me who it is." The thought that he might fear me made me ill.

Ambrose puffed up his cheeks and blew a gust of air directly into my face. "Cato, place yourself between us—"

"Ambrose, now!" Aberus barked.

"His name is Larm." Ambrose's arms shot up between us. He covered his face and then peeked around hesitantly when I didn't cloud out.

"Larm... Larm? Who the fuck is Larm?" I tried to keep the anger out of my voice, but could *not* keep my temperature from rising. My entire body heated, radiated.

"What is your acquaintance with Larm, Ambrose?" Cato asked, pinching the bridge of his nose. He attempted to take my arm, but I snatched it away when I saw Aberus's eyes widen.

Ambrose tried to shrink away, but Cato's arm flew out, impeding him.

"D-do you all remember the time I went on campaign and saved the western coast from the vile scourge of pirates who were attempting to overthrow the kingdom? You know, the marauding and plundering ones—raiding our trade routes and causing all manner of mayhem? They probably would have overthrown the continent had I not thrown myself into wickedness's path and led the navy to stop them."

"Ambrose." Cato pushed his brother forward, causing Ambrose's shins to hit the bed's footboard. "Succinctly."

"Well, you see, after they surrendered, we boarded the ship of the pirate lord. It was difficult to maintain balance on account of the recent deck swabbing—that is pirate speak for mopping. It keeps the deck free of mold and... things were quite slippery."

"If you do not speed this tale up, brother, I will *encourage* your wife to do her worst," Aberus said.

Ambrose squared his shoulders and looked down the bridge of his flawlessly straight nose. "Well, because I had not acclimated to my sea legs, I had to concentrate on keeping stable. An errant wave nearly took me from my feet and... I accidentally ran Larm through with my steel."

"But how did he come to—Ambrose... you didn't!" The æther leapt to my throat, squeezing through the column of my neck. "Swear to me, swear to me you didn't!"

Steam rose around me, a cloud of hazy gray.

"Eira, I had no choice. I felt bad. His innards were slipping out of his body, and he kept yelling 'Why? We surrendered!' over and over until—"

"What is happening?" Aberus shouted over his brother. "I demand to know immediately!"

"How could you, Ambrose?" My cloud of humid, white air started filling the room.

"How could he what?" Aberus bellowed.

Cato mounted the bed and pulled me into his arms.

"Calm down, love," he ran his fingers down the edge of my jaw, "sweetheart, settle yourself. Look around you."

My frazzled nerves began to calm under Cato's hands, but I couldn't look at my husband. I gazed into Cato's eyes, fighting back tears.

"Before Ambrose left, I was terrified he'd be grievously injured or killed while taking on the pirates. I gave him three vials of my blood." I pressed my face into Cato's shoulder and scream-growled in frustration.

"My gods. Protector Septimus, prepare yourself to restrain her."

"Shut the fuck up, Aberus," I shouted over my shoulder.

Ambrose, coming to his senses, shooed the king and Septimus backward and then lowered himself onto the mattress next to me.

"Eira is correct... and I administered those vials to the man you see before you. It's all rather heartwarming, would you not agree?"

Aberus and Septimus shook their heads in confusion.

"I'm going to kill him, Cato." I lunged at Ambrose, but Cato restrained me. "I'm going to gouge his brains out from his giant, disgusting nose holes and feed them to the swine! One of those vials was to be given to you, love. To you, Cato! But matching his ostentatious-ass boots to the color of the decking was more important to him than *your* safety. He squandered what would have saved you had *you* been mortally wounded!"

Septimus gasped and fell to his knees. Aberus placed his hands on his brow and muttered a prayer under his breath.

"Y-you have brought the dead back to the living," Septimus, for the first time in our brief history, looked... frightened. His eyes, so quick to flash in ice-colored fury, went round and glassy, and he shifted back on his ankles, shielding his chest with an arm.

"No. Maybe? I don't know. Evandr's heartbeat was so faint, he was upon death's door, and Gotwig—" I stopped myself, before I shared too much. "The books. I need the books to make sense of things. Father Burchard—"

"Help! Please help!" A cry rang from the hallway.

Septimus ran to the door, sword pulled. He slipped through the crack as Cato jumped from the bed, dagger in hand.

"She's missing, and we can't..."

I knew the voice.

"Richelle?" My heart jumped to my throat. I bolted from the bed, followed quickly by Aberus and Ambrose. "Richelle, what's wrong?" I called out.

Cinden's baby? An otherworldly haunt? A murder... My gods, had the Primus-King struck again?

"Make way!" Aberus belted out from behind me. He all but shoved himself through the door Cato was purposefully holding closed. We spilled out into the hallway and into the distraught path of my friend. She ran straight to Aberus and pressed her tear-streaked face into his arms. Her hair was limp, and lines of dirt caked across her back.

"We've been looking for her since before everyone left to temple. We searched everywhere—just everywhere."

Aberus awkwardly patted her back with the tips of his fingers while she trembled, choking between breaths.

"Who is missing, Madam Obligate? Tell me."

"Little Mae. We must alert the king." Richelle turned pleading eyes to Aberus. "It was her turn to hide and... Maihon is beside himself with worry."

"Protector, form a search party. Catommandus, Ambrose, to the back grounds. I will take the front."

"Yes, Majesty." Septimus saluted, fist to shoulder.

"Oh!" Richelle hopped back and proceeded to brush off the dirt she'd left on Aberus's oversized white sweater. "I-I had not realized—I am—oh gracious, my ap-apologies," she stammered. Head bowed in embarrassment at her blunder, she did her best to hold back her tears.

"Not at all. We will locate the child. Come with me." Aberus banded his mass of curls with a leather thong he kept on his wrist, presumably for that purpose.

Orders received, I ran behind Cato and Ambrose, who outstripped me by a solid ten paces.

We hit the exit to the back grounds and, like the soldiers they were, the men split off to the left and right, keeping twenty feet between them as they combed the grounds.

"Goddess above, I beg you, grandmother Merrias, please don't let her be at the bottom of the rift," I prayed to the darkness. The image of Mae's innocent, broken body was enough to make me regret every action I took that fateful night. The æther formed a steel band around my stomach.

I took off and headed toward the gaping hole in the ground, body shaking as I neared the cavern.

"No!" I reared back. "Goddess no!"

From the shadow of the chasm, the demon shade flitted in front of my eyes.

I swatted at the shadowed cloud that surrounded me. It bobbed and bounced and flew around my head at a dizzyingly fast speed.

"Leave me be!"

The cloud darted away and then flew back toward me.

It repeated the action twice more.

Something was different...

"Do you know where she is?"

The shadow stopped its frantic movements and swelled. Tendrils of shade coiled and grew into a massive nimbus.

"Take me to her."

It disappeared into the dark. With only a second's hesitation, to pray its intentions were benign, I gave chase. My bare feet thudded against the ground in the same tempo as my pounding heart.

Let her live. Please let the sweet child live.

With an electric snap and a sharp but fleeting pain, I took shadow form and surged to catch up with the cloud that was moving too fast for my mortal feet.

Together, we soared through the sky. Below me, Cato combed through the fallow fields. A group of soldiers in the distance searched the few out houses that scattered the grounds. We sailed past the healer's shed and headed toward the thickets where Maihon and Mae's home once stood... before I brought it low.

The shade veered and then swirled in a downward spiral, gaining momentum as it headed toward the muddy ground.

I couldn't stop. I didn't know how.

Fuck, fuck, fuck! Brace!

My form shrank in on itself, seconds before smashing into a large boulder.

And then I was me again—battered and stunned, but in one piece.

I scrambled to my feet and took off through a hedge of dense, scratching brambles that caught on my skin and yanked my hair. I pushed away twigs and leafless branches as I made my way into a clearing.

The soft glow of a moonlit beam bounced off her yellow-blond hair.

The child lay on her side, tucked into a dirt-covered ball. Her upward-turned, almond-shaped eyes met mine, and I winced at the cuts and scrapes that covered her chubby arms and legs.

"Mae, there you are. No sweetling, don't be afraid. It's Eira; we met before. Do you remember?"

"Mae-Mae?" She pointed to her chest.

"Yes, little one. I'll take you home to your papa. I am so glad to see you."

"Baby?" She rolled forward and hugged her shivering arms against her body. She was terrified.

"Yes, you're his baby, and he's so worried and can't wait to have you home."

"Ba-baby, baby," she babbled in her gentle voice. "Two. Me and two here."

I bent low, crouching down beside her, and laid my fingers on her arm. She was freezing. I tenderly stroked her shoulder, not wanting to upset her any further, but needing to get her near the warmth of a fire.

She curled in on herself again.

"Mae, what do you have, little lamb?"

I leaned closer.

"Is that your dolly? We need to get her warm as well. Come with me and—holy Mother above."

My heart ceased to beat.

My eyes could not comprehend what they beheld, but nor could they deny the truth of what lay before me.

The satyr infant tucked in Mae's little arms cried out weakly.

"Mae." I reached out. "I need to help the baby."

"Baby." She turned her small eyes up to mine and nodded. "Hungry."

"Yes, Mae." I nodded back. "You've done a good job taking care of the little. Can I?"

She loosened her hold, and I brought the scrawny, naked bundle to my chest.

The satyr's skin was near-death-cold against mine. The tiny girl was so small that there was no hair covering her face or body, like the satyress the guards butchered just near here, beyond the tree line. Her half-closed eyes showed irises of dark purple-blue, and tiny horn nubs formed on either side of the soft spot in the middle of her head.

Her breaths were fast and shallow, her chest caved in as she desperately tried to bring in air. I placed my palm over her heart and felt it fluttering, like the blurringly fast wings of a hummingbird.

She was near her end.

The shade that led me here appeared, circled my head and then slowed and stopped above the baby in my arms.

Now I understood.

"I'm sorry I didn't come sooner. I am so very sorry."

I clutched the child to my breasts and lent her my warmth while quickly assessing our surroundings. My eyes caught on a silver glint—a tiny beacon.

"Mae, I need to borrow your earring, sweetheart."

Her little fingers went to her ear, but she couldn't remove it by herself.

"Ear, ear," she said, tugging at the lobe.

"Yes, dear." I shifted the satyress in my arms, removed the hoop from her ear, and pierced my finger. Did my blood work on nether born?

The little one latched onto my pinky finger the moment it touched her lips, desperate for the milk I couldn't give her.

Can my tears heal her if my blood doesn't? They splashed down on her small and sunken chest.

"Come, Mae. You've been such a wonderful helper, and we need to get the baby inside. On my back, okay?"

I squatted, the tiny satyress tucked close, while Mae climbed up and wrapped her legs around my waist.

"Hot," she said, laying her frigid cheek on my shoulder. She sighed as she hugged her arms tightly around my neck. "Warm for Mae."

I did my best to shield my small charges as we navigated our way through the sticker bushes. As my flesh tore on thorns the length of my pinky, I was thankful that Maihon had bundled Mae as well as he had. Not for the first time, I wished I could take my clothing with me when I became shadow.

We made it through the bramble safe, except for the puncture wounds that leaked egregious amounts of my blood. Poor Mae, poor courageous child, had endured this, and worse, before I found her.

I braced my legs, feeling weak, overburdened by the physical and emotional weight I bore.

"Cato!" I tipped my head to the dark sky. "Cato, I need you!"

The shade that led me here, that haunted my nights, swooped in front of my face, startling me. It hovered near the satyress.

I suppose, when you loved someone with your whole being, even the promise of paradise wouldn't free you from the need to see them safe.

"If she lives... she will know nothing but love." The shade grew, engulfing the three of us in a kiss of mist. "I promise."

Like a deep breath, a sigh of relief, the shadow expanded in a swirling cloud of shade and then shrank in on itself before streaking off into the night, a glimmering star racing to the Goddess's realm.

Chapter Fourteen

SAVIORS AND SINNERS ARE ONE AND THE SAME

Eira

Cato came barreling through the night, dagger drawn and his face naked with unhidden fury. Behind him, Ambrose loomed like a giant, netherbent on destroying all in his path.

My men—my soul, charging to my rescue... followed closely by my heart.

Mae squealed out in fear, clinging tightly to my neck, constricting my airway.

"The-they're here to help," I gasped, speaking as calmly as I could manage, while wrapping one arm around my back and holding her close.

"Eira, what has..."

"... I'm—" My knees gave out. I panicked and pushed the babe toward Cato, but before I collapsed, his arms were around my hips, supporting all three of us and gently lowering us to the ground. The mud cooled my fevered flesh.

Aberus, Maihon, Richelle, and Jance rushed toward us.

"Jance, alert the Protector... the child is safe."

Jance bolted away as the others came near.

"Aberus, Eira requires a healer." Cato lifted Mae, prying open her fingers, which still clung tightly to my neck, and pressed her into the arms of her weeping father.

"My tot, my best girl. I've missed you so." He hugged her closely. "I'll take her to the palace, see to her scrapes."

Aberus nodded. "Troth Richelle can assist you, Maihon."

The lead gardener inclined his chin. Richelle ran to his side, patting first Mae and then Maihon on their backs.

"Oh Mae, that was the longest someone has ever hidden! Next time, tiny love, let's just hide on the first floor, yes?" Richelle spoke soothingly, pulling the stickers from Mae's hair as they left.

"We need to find milk." I looked down at the baby in my arms. "Goat's or perhaps cow's... Cato, I-please help me." I shifted away from his chest, trying to rise.

"No, love, do not move. You are exhausted, and your skin is torn to shreds."

"Catommandus, step away from her. Now." Aberus barked the harsh command.

Cato's head snapped up.

"I will do no such thing. Can you not see with your own eyes that she is depleted?"

Septimus emerged from the darkness.

"Protector Septimus, this woman has called forth an abomination." Aberus took a step back, and I tightened my arms protectively around the babe. "Remove it and see it slaughtered before burning its corpse."

Septimus moved quickly.

Cato was faster.

Dagger in hand, he threw himself in front of me, pointing the blade straight at Septimus's chest.

"Touch her and your blood will nourish next year's harvests." Cato's stance exuded deadly intent—toes twisted into the dirt, heels lifted just off the ground, hips, knees, and shoulder coiled, a loaded spring. He wasn't preparing for an honorable duel. He was a viper, tensing to strike. "The same to the rest of you." He turned his head to the left and right, glaring at Aberus and even Ambrose, reading their postures, sizing up potential threats.

"Brother?" Ambrose said, inching forward with his palms held up. "Cato, it is nether born, like any troll or pixie."

Septimus dipped and lunged under Cato's arm, so smoothly that I couldn't follow the movement. His fingers brushed my forearm, and then his eyes flashed wide as he fell, tripped by his fast-acting nephew.

"I have no intentions of touching the nether witch." Septimus gulped, his chest heaving. He sprawled flat on his back.

"Quit the act." Cato launched himself toward his uncle, but Septimus rose nimbly, smashing his elbow into Cato's face.

"Still astute, boy." Septimus struck again, his fists and dagger flying in a combination of strikes and thrusts. Cato countered each attack fluidly.

"Catommandus, stop at once," Aberus bellowed. "That is a direct order!"

Cato jerked his chin, acknowledging his brother's command, but he didn't stand down.

Septimus lashed out, blade point first. He targeted Cato's underarm and the chest cavity beneath it. Cato leaned back, just enough for the blade to pass harmlessly by, and then exploded into motion. He shoved Septimus's dagger arm at the elbow, turning him and slamming his own hilt into the older man's temple. Septimus staggered, and Cato drove his knee into his uncle's stomach. The Protector collapsed in an unmoving heap on the ground.

Brother faced brother.

"Aberus, there is much you still need to know." Cato shifted back, taking a step in my direction. "But know where she is concerned, I will make no compromises."

"This is not normal, Cat, and you *will* stand down. The will of your king and the safety of Monwyn trumps your tawdry affair."

Ambrose inched toward Cato as Aberus closed in.

"My *what*, Aberus?" Cato tilted his head to the side and stretched his neck.

"Husband, please," I whispered. I didn't know if I was begging Ambrose to stay out of harm's way or to protect Cato.

"Hush, Eira." Ambrose flicked his eyes in my direction, and took another cautious step toward Cato. "Cat, you are not yourself right now. Your blade is pointed at the king, your brother."

"As we both know, even brothers cannot be trusted."

"Cat, Aberus is not our fath—"

Septimus rolled and lurched from the ground. His fingers curled around the babe's bicep, and she whimpered a pain-filled cry as he twisted her fragile arm.

I struck with an open palm, claws bared, my hand connecting solidly with Septimus's chest.

"You will not!"

In a cloud of blackness, he flew back, his face contorting as he struck Aberus, sending them both careening into a spiral of energy-imbued shadow.

They struck the ground some fifteen feet away, sliding through the mud until Aberus's back slammed into the leg of a stone garden bench.

Like a deep bruise, the center of my palm darkened and cracked. My hand pulsed and stung, a flame put to my palm. I could no longer hold on to the child, could no longer keep myself upright.

Aberus waved to a group of soldiers running to his aid.

"Shackle Catommandus and place him in a cell. He is compromised."

My eyes went hazy. My body gave up its fight.

CHAPTER FIFTEEN

I WUV YOU

EIRA

"Eira? I need you to wake."

Ambrose's soft voice penetrated the fog, but the darkness trapped me so thoroughly that I couldn't respond.

"It is time to come back to me, wife." I felt the brush of his fingertips along my calf. He circled my ankle and slipped down to squeeze my heel.

I wanted to. Truly I did—he needed cuddles, and we wouldn't have long until Cato snuck into the bed and pulled me to his side. But my eyelids were so heavy. I needed sleep. I wanted to lie here and think of nothing more than how perfectly this pillow cradled my head. How ideal the temperature was with my feet sticking out from beneath the light cover that was pulled to my chin.

"Our goat-daughter is persistent in suckling my teat, and I have become most uncomfortable."

Do what?

The fog began to lift; the light infiltrated the thin slits of my eyelids.

"Our wh-what?"

My memories became crisper, like the lamplight stinging my eyes.

"She nursed the water from a rag but cries fiercely unless clamped on. And though I believe we are bonding, I have begun to chafe."

"Chafe?"

My eyes fluttered open. I rubbed my fists against them, trying to dislodge what felt like a pound of grit.

"And I think her wittle-bitty hoofers need to be filed down. They are as sharp as my steel."

"Hus-husband..." I groaned, the words catching in my parched throat.

Mossius give me strength.

Ambrose sat on the end of the bed; the baby latched to his nipple. Her tiny fingers clenched around the hilt of his jeweled dagger.

I tried again. "Ambrose, in no realm is a blade an acceptable plaything for an infant. Put your knuckle in her mouth."

He scoffed, but tossed the knife to the side of the bed and plucked the satyress from his big peck.

An earsplitting squall of discontent made both of us flinch. I covered my ears.

"She gets her lungs from her mommy."

"Are your hands clean?" I asked.

He ignored me, opting instead to make silly faces at the baby, who probably couldn't see more than seven inches from her little button nose. It was adorable.

"Cato!" I bolted upright, tossing the blanket aside.

"Is contained," Ambrose said, unconcerned, as he batted his lashes and made kissy noises. He blew raspberries against the satyress's long-fingered palm. She stared at him, wide-eyed and expressionless, as she waved her other balled-up fist in the air. "At the moment, he is safe where he is." Ambrose tried unsuccessfully to squish his large, bent finger into the babe's mouth. He chewed his lip thoughtfully and then tried the tip of his ring finger instead. "There we are."

"Safe?" A short-lived wave of vertigo twisted in my head. I fell to my elbows, holding my temples tight. "Where he is?"

"Eira, you need rest. Lie back. And yes, I think he is safer where he is for the moment. When you passed out, he went mad. He fought off everyone like some aggrieved lion protecting his pride. It took four guards, Septimus, *and* Aberus to contain him, and even then, they struggled."

"Have you seen him? Where have they taken him? Stop avoiding my question."

"I cannot say for certain as—"

A knock sounded at the bedroom door. Two quick raps.

Jance entered with a tray balanced in one hand, his spear in the other.

Ambrose tucked the satyress's hooves into her swaddling, hiding them from view.

"Highness, consort." Jance did his best to bow. "I bring you food and beverages from the kitchens. Your Highness, you are summoned by His Majesty and are to bring the infant that was found on the grounds... Can you believe anyone could leave their kith and kin in the outdoors? And in cold temperatures. I bet that—"

"Jance, don't judge those whose reasoning you don't know." It was rude of me to interrupt, but I meant every word.

The memory of the shadowy soul shooting towards the sky would not soon leave me. Had it been Nan? The stranded spirit of the slain satyress? Mother Imella? She would have watched over the babe at the expense of her own afterlife.

"Leave the tray and go," Ambrose said. Jance obeyed and placed the meal on the end of the bed. "Relay the following to Aberus. I will see my wife fed and comfortable. Only then will I seek him out."

By the roundness of his eyes, it was clear Jance was uncomfortable with the order, but he saluted, shoulder to fist, before exiting the room.

I tore the cover away and crawled to Ambrose's side.

"Ambrose, husband. He will slaughter this child. His heart is not open. But from the nether or not, she is an innocent."

A shrill cry came from the small bundle in his arms. I cupped her downy-soft head as I clung to Ambrose's side.

"Eira, Aberus is no monster and—"

"—and neither is she," I admonished, sinking my hip into the mattress, doing my damnedest not to give in to my fatigue.

"Dis wittle one? Nooooo. She's a pretty bitty goatling, is what she is."

"But you heard what he said." I placed my palm on his bearded cheek and coaxed his face to mine. His green eyes turned serious, and his lips compressed.

"I will keep her safe. You trust me, yes?"

My stomach twisted itself into knots. I could feel the faintest bit of æther flickering in my chest, warning me to say no, but I nodded.

I did trust him. In our entire history together, he had proven himself steadfast.

"Good. Now," he booped the babe's nose, "I will not weave your sexy wittle shadow mama unwess she consumes that entire bowl of soupy soup." He leaned over and nuzzled my neck with his nose. "I am sure my tardiness will upset the king. However, you, as always, are my priority, wife."

"Ambro—"

"Eat." He reached out and then pressed a steaming bowl into my hands. Then, he took a twisted linen napkin that laid across his thigh and dipped it into a glass of foamy white milk.

"Mama fed the youngest of my sisters this way. Odella's tongue didn't allow her to nurse like the others did. I remember it working to keep her fed until the healers determined what to do."

Oh, Ambrose.

His eyes became glassy as he spoke, and his big shoulders deflated as he encouraged the baby to nurse.

"Mother Imella would be so proud of you, Black Bear, for protecting an orphan and seeing to her wellbeing."

He nodded slowly as he watched the babe suckling on the makeshift nipple. She made quiet, cooing sounds of comfort and smacked her hungry lips as she closed her eyes.

"Like she did for me." He shrugged his shoulder to wipe a tear from his eye. "You know, Eira, she didn't have to accept me as her own. And now I cannot imagine a life where she didn't love me."

I listened to my husband while sipping the piping hot soup from the bowl's rim, savoring the richness of beef stock, tomatoes, peas, and carrots.

"Ambrose, what will we do with her?"

He traced the top of her pointed ear and shook his head.

"I didn't mean to cause strife amongst your family. I just... just couldn't think about her being..."

"Worry about resting. Allow me to lift this burden." Ambrose glanced up, concern filtering across his face. "Shadow-you seems to drain your energy, and you have sustained hundreds of nicks. No matter though, I will have a pound of fatty bacon and a concoction of raw eggs and almond flour sent up. It's a staple in my regimen."

Ugh.

"Please don't go to the trouble." The thought of choking back a thick slime of a grainy egg made me ill.

"It is no hardship... though at some point we must consider the excessive cost of your clothing if you continue burning them away." A half-smile pulled at his lips as he gathered the satyress in his arms and stood. He tucked her under his arm like a sack of flour, upside down, with her face resting in his massive palm. I didn't chastise him, as she seemed content enough.

"I know you will not listen to me, but Eira, don't fret overly much. I will check on Cato and deal with Aberus. All his life he has been taught that conjurers are different and that different is to be feared. We are, all of us, to blame for that... Father might still be here if we'd accepted who he was in the first place."

Ambrose came to my side and tucked the blankets up around my chin, patting them lightly. He took the empty bowl from my hands, placing it on the bedside table.

"Sleep. I will return." He bent down and kissed my cheek. "I lov—oho." His eyes widened as he straightened. "Hmm… I will, uh, mull that over and get back to you." The skin above his dark beard flashed crimson.

Heat flared across my own cheeks.

"I love you, husband." I skated my finger down his wrist, and he squeezed my hand in return. "Will you please tell Cato the same from me?"

"Tell him yourself… when he crowds us both out of the bed tonight."

Ambrose lowered the lamplight to a soft glow before striding from the room.

I nestled deeper into the pillows, listening to his voice fade as he told the baby about the time he was a minotaur and had a tail just like hers.

I closed my eyes, succumbing to the draw of slumber.

The shade wouldn't visit me tonight, and though I had new fears pressing down on me… my tumultuous heart knew a small semblance of peace.

CHAPTER SIXTEEN

YOU MUST

"**W**e are leaving."

I screamed, the sound lost in the pillow.

Septimus.

I thrashed and bucked, trying to unseat him.

The smell of leather and spearmint wafted from the gloved hand that clamped over my mouth as he forced my head back.

He dug his elbow deeply into my spine, the pain so intense that struggling was impossible—I could barely draw in a breath through the agony I was experiencing.

"Ambrose is detained—the infant disposed of."

"N-no." I jerked my shoulder and tried to roll, struggling in earnest to free myself.

"Listen to me—Listen," Septimus hissed into my ear. He eased up slightly and I gulped the air.

"Get off of—ahh!"

He ground his elbow again, so viciously that my vision swam in and out of focus. The shadows, understanding the threat, flickered in my periphery but fell away. I called to them, begged them to aid me—tried to follow them—but to no avail. My exhaustion was so profound that even the normal spark of æther-driven sexual tension Septimus's nearness caused was hardly discernible. Nothing more than a tickle in my stomach, easily overshadowed by panic.

"Why the fuck should I listen? Abuser. Cheater. AMBR—"

He clamped his hand over my mouth, and I sank my teeth into the soft flesh between his thumb and pointer finger. Like chewing through thick tendon, the hide began to give. The thick leather might protect his skin from breaking, but I'd crush his godsdamned bones.

Septimus made no sound, no grunt of pain, nor sign of vulnerability. Silently, he dug his fingertips into the sides of my jaw—driving them deep into the muscles—forcing my mouth open.

"God—St-sto..."

"I carry a missive from Catommandus. He demands we run." Septimus dropped his hand under my chin and tipped my head backward until saliva ran from the corner of my mouth. He increased the pressure until a sharp pain traveled down my spine and both arms. "Bite me again, witch, and I will slide my blade between your ribs."

Eira, fight. Fight!

"Liar." I wrenched my hip to the side and kicked out, but he wound his ankle around my knee and kicked out, splaying my leg wide. The compression on my spine increased twofold, a reed near snapping.

"Spare me your theatrics."

My head jerked to the side, and he bent his face into my periphery. "Ending you would solve a great many of my problems."

Septimus shifted, reaching across his chest. He produced a parchment and held the scrap to the dim lamplight.

"Read it." Again, he twisted my head forcefully until I faced the small square.

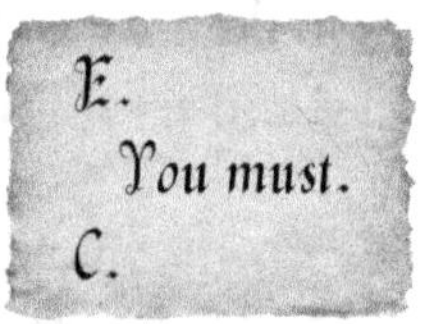

It was Cato's handwriting.

I'd seen it enough—the fine hand, the flourish he made when crossing his *T*'s, the heavy-handed slash instead of a dot that formed his periods.

Please... please. Let this be a nightmare.

That scalding flash of fear—the instinctual response of the body to run or freeze—overcame me. But I fought back against its pull. I would not be the victim. I would not.

Use your brain, Eira.

I beat back the terror and donned the mask of a Troth... I *knew* better than to trust this man.

"You would *never* leave your coveted post, Protector. What game do you play?"

"The Protectorate became worthless the moment you took my brother from me, whore." Spit flew from his mouth as he spat the last word.

A powerful wave of guilt spiraled through my chest. I heard the conviction in his words, but I was no simpleton.

"You'd never do Cato's bidding." I jerked again, only to be immediately subdued. His arm shot past my head, and the blanket found its way around my neck.

"I act on my own behalf." Septimus inhaled deeply, dragging his nose through my hair as he strangled me, twisting and tightening the handful of material. "Cato will be put down, riddled with the corruption as he is—the consequence of your adultery. At least Aberus will have one less obstacle in his path to the crown."

Lips skimmed across my hairline; a telltale thickness pressed into my tailbone.

"Evil." I shifted fast, bucking and slinging my head backward, aiming for his chin. "How dare you betray your kin." He straddled my hips, shoved my face into the bed, and held it there while I fought.

"You and I share a common enemy now, consort. *That* is my reason. The Primus-King took my property. He will know suffering and pay recompense, and you and I will extract it. Now get the fuck up. I have packed our belongings."

"Property? You mean your wife? Lilium's life ended, and even so, you can only think of her as an object in your writ of possessions."

This couldn't be happening.

Septimus rolled away and stood. He threw the covers to the end of the bed and then flung the parchment into my face.

I scrambled to my feet and faced him.

"I'm not leaving. I won't leave Cato or Ambrose while their shit of a brother tries to consolidate Monwyn's power for himself—vengeance is nothing compared to the love between—"

"Aberus has accused you of sorcery. The formal declaration speeds toward Verus as we speak. Cato and Ambrose will be held until the Mantle and the Devotees can determine if they have succumbed to conjuration."

I froze.

"He means to see them hanged, legally," I whispered more to myself than Septimus. "So he can rid himself of his competition and not have to dirty his own hands."

Ambrose had said that Aberus was a master strategist.

"Finally catching on?" Septimus flicked his fingers at me in a discourteous gesture. "And they tout the Troth as intelligent."

My mind spun in circles.

Was Aberus as Burchard had been, paranoid enough to wipe his brothers from the earth? Would he follow in the footsteps of his sire? It was the Monwyn way.

But something still didn't make sense.

I took a step toward Septimus, observing him for tells. There was no flickering pulse. His eyes didn't drift down or to the left. He didn't hide his hands or speak in a pattern different from his norm. I took another step forward, leading with my chest, buying myself some time. I knew the effect I had on him, and I'd use it to my advantage.

I allowed my hips to sway, as I continued forward. His nostrils flared like a dog scenting a bitch in heat. The pupils encased in ice-blue irises grew larger.

"And why, Septimus, am *I* here, instead of locked away, awaiting my *own* death? Aberus could, after all, demand it without religious intervention, based on my infidelity alone. Answer that."

He moved fast, snatching the neck of my gown and yanking me hard against his chest.

"Why do you think I am here, stupid girl?"

His hand surged toward my face.

I flinched hard, ducking behind my arms. When nothing struck me, I opened my eyes again... Shackles dangled from his fingers.

"Make your choice, consort. Your life is meaningless to me either way... but I may spend time with your corpse after I have eliminated you, if death is your decision."

I shuddered at his twisted threat.

Think, Eira. Save yourself. Save your men.

I sought the shadows but fell short again. The attempt made my wrists burn, aggravated my palms, but I couldn't summon the æther.

Bidding my time was my only option. I needed to regain strength, build up my energy... and if it took every drop of æther and destroyed my body, I would finish what I started the night the Nether Lord emerged. Monwyn would no longer know the tradition of sibling murders, because I would level the fucking kingdom and rebuild a life for my men and I—its rubble the foundation for a new path.

A plan began to form. I was thinking clearly now.

The Mantle was due to arrive in a matter of days for Aberus's coronation. My gamble was that Aberus was unaware of the connection that The High Holy One and I shared—that They were a part of my story all along, had knowledge of what and who I was.

Cato was undoubtedly aware that Aberus couldn't legally take the life of a Scion without first consulting the Mantle, and I knew that charges of being conjured *upon* were much different from charges of *being* a conjurer. A conjurer caught in the act was to be executed on sight.

It struck me then. *Nether be damned.*

Cato. My brilliant fucking soulmate.

He knew Aberus *could* eliminate me, legally, while he and Ambrose languished in prison. Aberus had proof of my using the corruption. May even have witnesses who could attest to my conjuring. That was enough to see me hang without consultation. The *infidelity* would serve as the icing on his cake of diplomatic mistruth.

Cato... he was buying *me* time.

By telling me to leave with Septimus, he was ensuring that I stayed alive until the Mantle arrived. And the Mantle would *never* allow my death. They fought too hard to keep my mother and me alive in the first place.

I sprang into action.

"I need something before we go." Lifting my nightgown above my knees, I took off at a run.

"I have procured all necessities. There is nothing you—"

I burst into the common room, Septimus close on my heels.

Two steps in and my foot struck something hard.

"Fuck. What in the—Goddess's mercy." The bodies of a handful of guards lay scattered about the floor. "Mother, see them home," I whispered as I wove my way through, stepping on the stiff fingers of one man and sidestepping the blood pooling around another. There was no time to worry over Septimus's sins.

I ran through my room and into the bathing chamber, collecting a handful of medications and the few coins I stashed away, stuffing them into a drawstring bag.

"Your dagger, give it to me."

Septimus placed a hilt in my hand without question.

I flipped over the chaise lounge that sat near the bathing tub and sunk the blade deep into its fine upholstery. With a quick draw of the knife, the papers I sought fell to the floor.

"What are—"

"It doesn't matter. They are important to me."

I spared a glance at Septimus, who was listening at the door for sounds.

"Return my blade."

"No." I stood up to my not-so-tall height and, in direct challenge, lifted my chin.

His hand captured mine, easily wrenching the blade free. "We run."

CHAPTER SEVENTEEN

MUVVAPHUKA

EIRA

"One horse? One fucking horse. Is this a joke?"

Septimus moved quickly, saddling a steed in the dark barn. A single lamp burned low in the distance, illuminating the stable hand's unconscious body.

"I'm a competent rider, and this stable is full of spectacular fucking horse flesh. Saddle a second."

Septimus spun, his jaw ticking as Cato's would when vexed.

Beautiful fucking tyrant.

"Lower your voice, deceitful bitch."

I balled my fists, forcing restraint.

"If I didn't need your sword arm, I swear to—"

Septimus's hand shot out, shoving me in the chest. I stumbled backward and fell ass-first into a mound of feed.

"Are you kidding me?" I attempted popping up to my feet—like Ambrose could from lying prone—but my fish-out-of-water flops sank my rear further into the grain.

Fucking nether.

During our high-speed escape from the palace, I'd felt confident in my decision, pleased that I had worked out Cato's puzzle. But now? Now, I wanted to sink into the seeds and wallow in depression while my heart broke in two. The thought of spending another day without him had me strangling back a sob. I'd miss Ambrose too... and the frost babies. But the Bond that linked Cato and me, it would shred my chest to ribbons before it lessened its bind.

"Were your brain as competent as your ability to ride, you would realize that two steeds leave more hoof prints than one. Hoof impressions are easily tracked." Septimus tugged a strap, snugging the saddle to the horse's middle. "Even morons can follow them."

I anchored myself back to the glum existence of my current reality.

"I swear to the Goddess, Septimus, I will kill you the moment I can summon these finicky shadows of mine. Your blood will stand out boldly streaked through your old man's hair."

He showed me his back, raised his boot to the stirrup, and tossed a leg over the saddle. I rolled around scattering feed and finally found my feet.

"Ending me would be a favor, consort." He flung his hand in my direction, offering me his palm.

I swatted his gloved fingers aside, opting to step directly on his foot and pull myself up. Behaving like a spoiled princess wasn't normally in my repertoire, but as I twisted the ball of my foot, smashing his toes into the metal stirrup, I felt both smug *and* satisfied.

"Give me some room, for fuck—whoa!"

Before I could adjust the nightgown over my thighs, he kicked our steed into motion, and we charged into the night

"If you cannot stop your sniffing, I will gag you. Do you hear me? Every time you wake, your insufferable snorting and lip-smacking assaults my ears."

I ignored him and shimmied my shoulders around until I found a more comfortable spot on his chest... just like I had the fifth and sixth times I woke to his unfounded slew of insults.

Still dark—we can't have gone far.

The trees still looked the same, and the road was still a road—packed dirt in some places, divots in others. We'd been riding for three hours at most. For the last two of them, I'd given in to my body's need for sleep. The comforting sway of the saddle, the perfect temperature created by the warmth at my back and the cooling winds to my front lulled me into a place between dream and oblivion.

"How far have we gone?" I asked, sitting up straighter in the saddle. I rubbed the heels of my palms into my thighs, the seldom-used muscles already sore.

"It would have been farther if you acted as a woman of the Goddess and contained your whoring ways, *succubus.*" He growled the last word.

"Do fucking what?" I tried to turn my head, but he shoved his finger into my cheek, halting me. *Whatever, asshole.* I arched and pushed the small of my back forward, working out the stiffness that had settled deep in my spine.

"Cease, slut."

"I would appreciate it if *you* acted like a man of the Goddess and spoke to me respectfully, jack-dick piece of shit."

"So you *do* feel my shaft digging into your backside. You and your slut's body revel in inflicting this never-ending torment upon me."

I threw my head back, *just* catching his chin—I'd been aiming for his nose.

"Septimus, you egomaniacal prick. I've not been able to feel my ass since an hour after we departed. My pelvis is smashed into the fucking saddle horn, for Lykksun's sake, and my woolybush will be bald for the chafe of it. If you weren't aware, the practical limit of this fine equine innovation is a single rider."

His palm slapped over my mouth.

I tore at his leather-covered fingers, to no avail.

"It is only your cavern that appeals to me. Your mouth, on the other hand, should be permanently silenced."

"Gwo phuk a twee, muvvaphuka." I thrashed my head from side to side, but he held firm. I gave in and leaned back, hoping his balls got so blue they'd fall off.

We streaked down the road, riding at a breakneck speed, not encountering another soul along the way. I'd hoped to come upon a pack of highwaymen, if only because it would require us to stop. My legs and feet were tingling, soon to be as numb as my butt.

"We will stop and rest soon. Ten minutes."

I nodded, thankful, too battered to continue playing the brat.

To my surprise, just a few seconds after he spoke, we veered from the road and into the forest. The terrain was uneven and littered with rocks and fallen limbs—it was much darker here amid the lush evergreen trees.

Septimus tightened the reins. Our steed slowed.

"Praise Derros. I need to pass water," I said, his snort of disgust in my ear.

"Mind that you leave nothing behind—not a trace. Do not comb your fingers through your hair. Do not allow your skin to contact any surface. Do not—"

My indignant huff echoed around the circular copse of trees.

"I know. I've traveled with Cato. We don't sleep near the horses. We only draw a blade if we intend to use it, blah, blah, blah."

"Insolent cow."

"Cantankerous goat."

Septimus dismounted and held his hand up to aid in my descent. I twisted about and, with as much grace as my numb ass could muster, jumped from the saddle's other side, landing without issue.

"You are without doubt the most mannerless bitch I have had the displeasure of traveling with."

"I'm a gassy bitch as well." I patted my belly crassly. "Stand away." My smirk was hidden in the dark, but I heard him grumbling from the other side of the dappled-gray flank that separated us. The perverse sense of pleasure I received in riling him *might* be enough to see me through the next day.

I inched my way through the darkness, pushing through brambles and brush until I found a suitable place to relieve myself.

Fuck avoiding surfaces. I wasn't riding to wherever we were going with my bare feet and hemline soaked in urine. I leaned against the trunk of a thin birch, assuming the squat, and lifted my ugly nightgown to my navel. The Monwyn dresses I owned were all lovely, but Ambrose, it would seem, preferred me to sleep in godsawful ruffles and florals. It was a mystery to me, but the demure and modest sleepwear got him going. Every time he spotted me in the frumpy fashion he got kittenish, all coy-eyed and flirty. Cato seemed to have no preferences, other than his hands acting as my undergarments.

"Motherfuck." I stepped wider as liquid warmth flowed over my toes.

Eira, dumbass, shoes would have been a more sensible grab than medication or papers.

I swatted and massaged my butt back to life as my never-ending stream continued and, of course... I needed to shit.

Do not be embarrassed. Everybody poops. I grabbed a handful of leaves and began the business.

"Gods, you are foul. It is as if—*gag*—as if—*gag*—you have consumed the rotting flesh of a diseased bovine." The telltale sounds of retching had me chortling. I bore down again, smirking as I did so. "I can hardly draw breath and—"

The smell hit me.

"Septimus!"

I shot up, unwiped urine trickling down my thighs.

It didn't matter. Survival was the only thing that mattered.

"To the horse! Get on the horse!"

I bolted toward our mount, heaved myself up into the saddle, and grabbed the reins.

Septimus came running. He grabbed my wrist and pulled, attempting to unseat me.

"You will not escape—"

"Troll!"

"What?"

"The smell, it's troll."

Snap. Crash.

"Come on! Get on now! There is no time to—"

Crack! The sound of a massive limb breaking from its trunk made the hair on my scalp stand straight.

"Move forward. Now, consort!"

Septimus attempted to pull the reins from my hands, but I held tight.

The grotesque scent of decay and funk permeated the air, coating the woods with its potent stink.

"Gods alive." Septimus's head lurched forward on his neck. He swallowed rhythmically, trying to contain the contents of his stomach.

"We can't take it on. I'm leaving in the next two seconds if you don't—"

He jumped, and my toenail parted from its cuticle, mashed between the stirrup and the thick, twisting sole of his boot.

His bulky body landed in front of mine.

"Silence!" he hissed sharply.

I clenched my teeth together, cutting off my cry. The churning combination of pain and nausea threatened to steal my senses.

I cracked the reins.

The monster emerged just as the horse's hooves dug into the soil.

"Protect us, Creator." Septimus covered his eyes for a snap second, his prayer an earnest plea.

This troll was twice the size of the one we encountered while traveling to Cordillaria. Each of its lumbering steps shattered limbs and yanked boughs from the surrounding trees. The devastation allowed the moonlight to illuminate the creature of lore come to life. Its gray flesh was covered in fuzzy green-and-blue lichen. A pelt of fur hung in tangled twists from its chest to its crotch, and its uncovered feet were easily the size of a copper tub. The troll smashed his way through a cluster of young trees, not bothering to move around them.

"Creator, save us."

"Shut up, Protector!" I whisper-yelled. "Stay silent. Don't draw its attention." I couldn't blame him for his outburst—this was likely the first nether creature, other than the satyrs, that he'd witnessed firsthand—but I needed him to keep quiet.

"Gammond's gonads."

Fuck!

The troll spotted us, his bulging eyes widened in surprise and his mouth gaped open in a snarl that revealed three sharp front teeth and a mouthful of blunted molars.

It snapped off a massive branch from the oak nearest him, severing it with ease from the trunk. The giant being tossed its head back, releasing a sound that was like a bull's gravelly bellow mixed with the thunderous resonance of a lighthouse's fog gong.

"Creator Above, Mother of the Cradle and Earth." Septimus prayed and then gagged.

Vomit splattered hotly on my hands, and I clenched the reins tighter, afraid they might slip my grasp.

"Hold tight, Septimus." I ignored the hot slime coating my wrists, abandoning fear and focusing my full attention on the danger ahead.

The troll started toward us, faster than I'd anticipated, the bulk he hefted around seeming not to slow him. He was gaining on us quickly.

Our mount desperately tried to find his footing but slipped and slid on the bed of fallen pine needles.

Twenty feet out, the troll dropped his club from his shoulder, letting it trail behind him, before swinging it above his head with both hands. It slammed down with enough force to sheer tree tops clear off their trunks. Splinters became projectiles and embedded into wood and ground alike. Bellowing again, the creature tossed the heavy caber up to his shoulder—fifteen feet away and gaining.

We would never make it.

Think like Cato. Like Cato. Like Cato!

Our horse could never outmaneuver the fiend in the dense trees. We wouldn't be fast or nimble enough to escape it. *See something else; what are you missing?*

"Solve your own problems, Eira." My mother's words tumbled from my lips.

"What the fuck are you prattling about? Give me the reins, consort!"

I jerked my hands from his, resolute in what I must do.

We had a path—a reckless one... but the only one.

The monster had cleared our way.

I pulled the reins determinedly, squaring up with the troll... and charged.

"Consoooooort!" Septimus grabbed my thighs and held tight.

Ten feet away. I drove the horse to the left. It responded like it had known my touch its whole life, utterly trusting.

The troll's shadowy profile tracked us. The moonlit outline of his giant arm rose.

I twisted the reins and squeezed my thighs. The horse pivoted, changing directions and charging forth like a winged god of old.

The troll swung.

"Duck!" I screamed.

Septimus flattened himself against the horse's neck and I his back. We sailed beneath the troll's outstretched club—the smell so intense my nasal passages burned raw and saliva rushed into my mouth.

"Yah!" I gave the horse its head, urging its flight. "Yah!"

I chanced a look back. The troll worked to free its makeshift club from the soft ground.

"Holy—ugh." Another waterfall of hot refuse smeared down the fingers of my left hand.

"Get it together, Protec—"

"To the right, there is another to the right!" Septimus yelled, his body going stiff and blocking my view.

A projectile sailed in front of us, smashing into a stump and falling into our path.

"Jump! Septimus, make it jump!"

"WHOA!" Septimus jerked my arms backward. The horse skidded to a halt.

An Ambrose-sized branch sailed through the space between the horse's head and our faces.

"Fuck!" I screamed. "Shit! Fuck!"

Septimus clicked his tongue twice, shook my arms to jostle the reins, and the horse took off again, skirting the blockade. I encouraged the animal to a gallop as we traversed the woods. It seemed our equine companion wanted to be away from the beast-ridden forest as much as we did. Septimus's thick braid flew over his shoulder, and mine. My hair plastered to my scalp.

We rode hard until the trees thinned, until our steed felt safe enough to slow to a trot.

"In the future, you would do well to remember that horses do not *just* jump, *competent horsewoman*. They require guidance and trust—a rider who bonds with them. Only then will nature and instinct allow them to—"

I'll be damned.

Septimus combed his fingers through his mount's mane.

"You like horses? You actually *like* something? I am just—just stunned to silence."

The sound of Septimus's lips popping gave me immense enjoyment, but not as much as the fact that he was still riding in the "ladies' spot" of the saddle.

"I would devote my life to the priesthood if the Goddess gifted me your silence."

I leaned forward, a wry smile on my face, and rested my forehead against Septimus's back, energy crashing.

We rode until we emerged into an open field and passed by a small farmstead. From there, we circumvented a little village of well-kept wooden homes and cantered through a herd of goats who felt no need to move. Next came a grouping of sheep who didn't trust our presence at all—the rams shook their horned heads and stamped out their warnings.

I was spent. Utterly and entirely depleted.

"We will come upon Moonledge soon. It's a good-sized town to the west of Colpass. Before we arrive, we will wash and change."

"Because you vomit like an infant when you encounter something stinky?" I brushed my dried, sick-caked hands along his— "Is that your penis?" I balked. "What the fuck's wrong with you?"

I flung my hands away from his actual godsdamned erection... but experienced a glimmer of arousal in my own traitorous loins.

"The talk of bathing—this nethercursed Bond."

"I understand *that*, but it in no way explains why your penis is out, all unsheathed and not tucked into your clothing. Creator's tits, Septimus, have you been dangling free for the duration?"

He reached back, snatched my elbow and shoulder at the same time, and twisted. I hit the ground with a thud, pain shooting through my leg.

"When we stopped, *consort*, I was fisting myself, attempting to relieve my original predicament. Then you screamed loud enough to wake the entire fucking forest."

My mouth fell open. My legs *wanted* to fall open too, but my anger, thankfully, was winning out, keeping the Bond at bay.

"I didn't call forth the *fucking* troll, if that's your implication."

"I do not imply. I am clearly stating that your whorish conjurer cunt is the reason—"

My fingers curled around a rock. I hurled it, striking Septimus in his beautiful face. A cut bloomed red beneath his eye.

"Oh right," I searched for another missile to let fly. "Blame *me* for your lack of control. For calling forth a nether spawn… accusatory piece of—"

He jumped from the saddle and stalked forward, a disturbing half-smile, half-sneer on his face.

"Back up!" I kicked, striking him in the knee. "Leave me be!"

He caught my foot, crushing my battered toes.

"You will learn your place in the hierarchy." Septimus tore my nightdress first from one arm and then the other, shredding the fabric in his haste. My bared nipples hardened in response to his nearness, even through the haze of fear and foulness we shared. "Fat slut, overflowing your bounds." I tingled, not from the chilly wind whipping across my flesh, but from the thrill of the Bond that tethered us. I hated it—was disgusted by its pull.

He grabbed the waist of my underwear and snapped the ties that fastened them. Fear met fantasy. The thought of him forcing himself between my legs had me swelling and slick.

No. Eira, this is wrong. So fucking wrong.

"Do not touch me!" I lunged up in a final attempt to free myself, but Septimus swatted away my clawed hands and knocked me down. My face hit the ground, but I came up swinging despite the dirt that clung to my lashes and rained into my eyes.

"You tell me—" Septimus bit the tip of his glove and ripped it off his hand, then spit it to the ground. He yanked me up to his face and squeezed my breast roughly before his hand ventured lower. His fingernails scored my stomach and then settled between my legs, holding me like he owned me. Gods… I ached for him with the same ferocity that I detested him. He cupped my vulva. The tips of his fingers pressed against my lips, and I sucked in a breath. "You tell me, consort, which one of us lacks control."

Septimus held his hand up to my face. The dawn's morning light illuminated the shine of my moisture.

"Your disgusting body belies your words, consort."

I panted hard, gasping in my need and my fury. The light flicker of æther became stronger in my chest, as did the feeling of an all-consuming arousal in my womb.

"It is a shame for both of us that guilt cannot be conjured away from one's conscience, is it not?" Septimus flung his arm out and pointed to a small stream in the distance. "Go wash. You smell of shit."

CHAPTER EIGHTEEN

POWERFUL GIRLS BECOME POWERFUL WOMEN

EIRA

"**A**re you supposed to be a scholar or a collector of fine-ish, um, dresses?"

Septimus looked right at home in the color clash of garments he'd donned. Long robes under short ones, an underdress of forest green and gold stripes, a top layer of dark purple, cinched at the waist with a magnificent scarlet and goldenrod inkle-loomed belt.

"Neither. The coastal merchants wear layers of light silk—they can add or remove them as they traverse the various climes." He adjusted the knot of his belt and let the extra length trail to his knee.

"And I am?"

"My shore wife."

I scrunched my nose in question. I'd never heard of such a thing.

Septimus rolled his eyes in exasperation.

"The woman I fuck while on shore leave."

I looked down at the drab green skirt that hit my ankles. It had faded tan stripes and a rust-colored stain shaped like a spoon.

"Begging your pardon... I'll find a more successful salesperson to fuck if this is the state in which you plan to keep me." I pulled the lacings that kept the sides of the too-large beige shirt together and secured them with a doubled knot.

"Your breasts would not accommodate the other costumes I could find, and the noblewoman's dress would not have housed your peasant's paunch."

I narrowed my eyes and imagined exploding his head from the inside out. Could my shadow form shoot through his nostril and hit his brain?

"And yet, you desire *all* of this." I lifted the roll of my soft belly and let it drop, wobbling as gravity took hold.

"Heel," he commanded, snapping his fingers—the same order one would give a dog. In a twist of multi-layered fabric, he turned away, leading his mount to the outskirts of Moonledge.

I trailed behind him, taking my sweet fucking time.

"Does your horse have a name?"

"Yes."

"And that name is?"

Silence.

Fine.

I lifted my sack of a skirt and ran to his side, looping my arm through his elbow.

He stiffened and glared at me through the side of his eyes.

"I *refuse* to be your land wife... shore whore or whatever." I waved at a man carrying two foamy pails of milk and smiled my most winning smile. He tipped his head and grinned back. "Here's our story. We're happily Joined even though my father threatened to deny our coming together on account of your advanced age. We had a small and quick ceremony in Gaea because we thought you would soon perish of an old people's disease, but miraculously the Cult Mossius healers were able to give you a few more years."

Septimus attempted to wrench his arm back, but I held tight as a gaggle of children surrounded us.

"You got coins, sir?"

"Can I pet that horse? Let me pet that horse!"

I laid my head against Septimus's thick bicep and stared up at him with innocent doe eyes.

"Oh, Bem, my soft-hearted, doting husband. Spare a coin for the little whelps?" I batted my lashes and patted his hand but seized it back when a stir of a desire struck low.

Septimus glared down his nose and dug the tip of his boot into the dirt road. He kicked out, and the asshole sent a spray of dust and rocks directly into their little faces.

"Shoo. Begone, filthy vermin."

I staggered back, releasing his arm.

"Septimus, my gods, are you *actually* an awful human? I thought maybe this rescue was the start of your redemption arc."

The boys scurried off, rubbing their eyes, tears streaking down their filthy cheeks.

"You too, get out of here, nasty mite!" Septimus shouted at a little girl who'd held her ground.

She screwed up her face, puckering her lips and dropping her brows. She took a mighty breath as she rolled up her sleeve, and then rammed her small, poorly clenched fist right into his groin.

"Take that!" she yelled, before trying to bring him low with another hit, this one striking his thigh. She grimaced and rubbed her smashed thumb, having tucked it into her palm before letting loose.

Septimus put two fingers on her brown-haired head and pushed, sending her toppling.

"Pitiful girls become pitiful women."

He tsked to the horse and strode away.

"Holy fucking snowballs!" I knelt at the little one's side and helped her stand, knocking the soil from her long-sleeved dress of scratchy gray wool. "Here, let me show you something," I said, squatting down to her level.

"Ya ain't got to show me nuthin'. I'm all grown." She jerked her thumb back and pointed to her chest.

I nodded, agreeing with her assertion.

"You are wise beyond your years, I can tell. Old enough to learn my secret technique."

The fearless child propped her fists on her hips and squinted her eyes into dangerous slits.

"I s'pose so."

"Pull your arm back like this next time, and then make sure you tuck your thumb around your fingers, not inside your fist." I held my hand up in example. "Okay, now show me yours."

She hesitated momentarily, but then raised her balled fist in perfect imitation.

"You learn fast. Now, you want to put the power of your hips into your strike, okay? Like this." I modeled the stance Cato taught me while at Verus, swinging and then following through with a twist to generate power. I punched into the air, snapping hard at the end of the thrust.

"Why you cryin' lady?" the little girl asked, dragging her hand across her runny nose.

"Oh, I... well," I swiped under my own nose, "I miss someone."

Badly. More and more with each step that carried me further away.

"But he would say. 'Never let anyone walk over you, but also remember, you have more intelligence in your brain than you do your hands.' I can tell you're feisty."

"Nope. I'm Imaline." She patted her chest with emphasis.

I smiled and held my hand out.

"So nice to meet you Imaline, I'm... I'm Diantha." I lied and gave her the alias Cato had fashioned for me, what felt like a lifetime ago.

The child didn't shake my hand, but instead, clapped her palm against mine in a fast, loud smack. I passed her one of the coins I'd managed to smuggle out.

"Thanks, lady." Imaline smiled a gaped-tooth smile and then ran off to join her friends.

Septimus was waiting for me, arms crossed, mouth turned down.

Yummy. Gross.

"Where are we headed, Septimus?"

He spun on his heels and stalked away.

I trailed behind his scrumptious self, keeping one eye on his tight buns and the other on the buildings we passed. Moonledge was adorable, the kind of place where you could imagine happy families taking afternoon strolls and little old couples clapping along to the songs that made their toddling grandbabies tap their toes.

All the buildings in the two-road town had their signs painted in a similar theme—bright-yellow lettering on a solid blue background. It was too cold for flowers to be in bloom, but every window around us boasted a box from which herbs and the like could grow. Little white flags stuck out from the dirt currently, an homage to their late king.

"I will repeat myself but once, boy." I tried to dip around Septimus's shoulders to see what type of establishment we'd stopped at, but he shifted continually, purposefully blocking my view.

"See her watered. Brush her down only if you have a clean and stiff-bristled brush. She is to be housed in a fully enclosed shelter. Here are instructions with the precise ratios of grain to grass that her feed comprises. If you cannot produce this product here, send out to Colpass. Is that understood?" Septimus flung a scrap of parchment at the lad, and it sailed to the cobblestone sidewalk.

"Yessir," squeaked the gangly youth, cowering before Septimus's overwhelming presence and ridiculous list of demands. He bent quickly, retrieved the list, and tucked it under his floppy hat.

Finally, certain his nameless horse would survive the next few hours, Septimus handed off his reins and stepped to the side, revealing a charming three-story inn. It looked like a tiny version of a castle in a children's book. Square and made of stone, with a pointed tower on its left and right. It was as adorable as the rest of the town.

The sign above its lone window read, *Stranathan's Stop*. Septimus motioned over his shoulder in a "follow me" gesture and proceeded through the establishment's door.

"Morning, sir, madam." The matron behind the large desk looked up through a pair of bone-rimmed spectacles. She had a halo of soft, gray-streaked brown curls and skin that was fair with pink undertones... just like my Nan's had been.

I closed my eyes and acknowledged my pain until the image of my companion faded. *How long would it be like this?*

Behind the matron, the room was abuzz. The sunbaked men wore several layers of silk robes, just like Septimus had said, and the women a varying array of skirts and last year's dresses. Many were embracing or clasping hands with huge smiles. I bet the lives of merchants and their wives could be lonely, with the time it required apart. But from the looks of it, their reunions were joyous.

"We require a room, madam. First floor, private bathing chamber, room service."

The woman's lips stretched across her face, in a... not quite a smile, not quite a who-the-fuck-do-you-think-you-are grimace. She removed her frames, cleaning the smudges on her sleeve, and then flipped the pages of her ledger.

"Two rooms," I blurted out, as her finger trailed down the occupancies. "Grandfather Bem sometimes forgets I'm a woman now and I no longer get nightmares." I moved next to Septimus and patted him on the hand. "PAPAW, TWO ROOMS, RIGHT? YOU SNORE TOO LOUDLY AND PASS GAS ALL NIGHT LONG."

He clenched his jaw so hard I could see the muscle flex beneath his beard. *I hope you break your fucking molars.*

"He's hard of hearing, madam, um...?"

"Stranathan," she said, still flipping through pages. She turned kind eyes upon me with a knowing nod of her head. "SIR, WE ONLY HAVE A SINGLE VACANCY. WE DO NOT HAVE TWO ROOMS AVAILABLE AT THIS TIME. AND WE DO NOT HAVE PRIVATE BATHING ROOMS. HOWEVER, ALL THE SHARED ROOMS ARE OUTFITTED WITH SUPPORT BARS AND WE CAN PROVIDE ASSISTANCE IF YOU REQUIRE AID GETTING IN AND OUT OF THE TUB."

It took all of me—all of me—not to break into a violent fit of cackling.

Septimus reached into his pocket and then slammed a handful of gold coins onto the desk, causing the matron to jump back. When he removed his hand, it revealed a crack in the desk's once pristine surface.

Madam Stranathan glared in disapproval, brown eyes giving back just as much fire as she was currently receiving.

"Ma'am, do you happen to have a guest in need of a bunkmate?" I asked, thinking on my feet.

She glanced at a group of worn-looking men playing cards.

"Mendell, are you still in need of a roommate? This lady's looking to split costs."

I followed her gaze and let my eyes rake up and down the whole-ass man that was Mendell.

Oh, boy.

With only one eye, a scar that cleaved his bottom lip, and a bright red tattoo of a merman with an ogre-sized phallus... Mendell was... perfect.

"Mendell, I like to sleep on the right side of the room. Is that okay?"

"Yep," the lean but sinewy sailor said in the lowest bass voice that I had ever heard. He snapped his fingers in the air. "You like ham? We could split a ham."

"I do. I love ham. And mermaids." I gestured to his ink.

Mendell's face broke into an endearing, bisected grin. He pulled up the half-sleeve of his mustard-yellow tunic, revealing an entire school of merpeople in various sexual pursuits.

"Do you... you think their vaginas are on the back like that? I just assumed they would be on the front. And I think the labia would—"

"The what?" Mendell inquired.

"The flaps... you know, the lips?" I held my hands together in my best approximation of a vulva.

"Could be. The only one I seen though, they was on the butt end."

"Mendell, you've seen a—"

"Enough!" Septimus thundered, causing the matron to jump again. "A single fucking room. Now!" He slammed his hand down on the desk again, and the pile of coins hopped and clattered, one leaping to its side and rolling off the desk.

The matron curved a hand around the side of her mouth and dropped her voice. "My grandad, may Merrias guide him, was given to fits too, sweetheart. You're a good girl for seeing to him. May he pass sooner rather than later."

"From your lips to the Goddess's ears." I patted my forehead with my fingertips as she scraped the absurd amount of gold from the table to her hand. She picked up her quill and penned *Grandpa Bem and granddaughter* onto a line at the bottom of her book.

Septimus snatched the iron key out of the matron's hand as she offered it and marched toward the long hallway she pointed to. I followed, the lure of an *actual* bed more potent than my need to infuriate my companion.

"Sorry, Mendell, I would have much preferred your company," I said as we passed. He shrugged and looked back to his game.

When we came to room number twelve, Septimus shoved the key into the lock and flung the door wide.

"One bed," I said flatly. "One godsdamned bed." It was a cute bed, with a whitewashed headboard covered in what looked like two or three thick, black blankets, but I could tell from where I stood, that it would only fit one-and-a-fucking-half of me comfortably. *It's like the gods have conspired to make me miserable.*

I scanned the rest of our lodgings. There was a tiny, square mirror on the left wall with a painting of a sailboat nailed into the wood paneling right below it. The only other piece of furniture was a—

"Whoa! Whoa, whoa, whoa. What in the frosty fields are you doing?"

Septimus stared, his eyes wide and his brows high... like *I* was the one casually removing my clothes right now.

He pulled layer after colorful layer over his head, revealing a glimpse of his scarred chest, before he turned and faced a wall. The brown linen pants he wore joined the pile. My mouth went dry at the sight of the tight globes of his perfectly round ass.

Oh, no, no, no. I slapped my hands over my eyes.

"You too, will strip."

"I most certainly will not," I retorted. "You and I both know where that leads."

My breath quickened. My heart palpitated. My passage throbbed. The warmth of my burgeoning arousal pulsed low in my womb. Still, though, the æther didn't boil up and over like it normally did, and for *that* I was thankful.

"Fine, stupid woman, contract mattress fleas. I will rid myself of your company soon enough, so I do not care that you will be eaten alive."

"Mattress fleas?"

I peeked between my fingers and watched as he flipped the mattress and inspected each seam. His flaccid, but still thick penis brushed his muscular thigh as he moved. I dropped one hand to my chest in an effort to calm my racing heart.

"Vermin. They will infiltrate every fiber of the cloth you own and are nigh impossible to kill once they have infested. Do you not know of them?"

I shook my head.

"They're not in the north, no. Too cold, maybe? Are they fuzzy?"

"Absolute idiot," Septimus admonished me. "No, they have armored bodies and sharp teeth. They will bite you and leave poison in your skin. You will pray to the Goddess to be relieved of your burning. You will beg to be flayed rather than suffer the incessant itching."

I was frozen in fear—terrified of the flesh-eating vermin he described. Bugs hadn't been a part of my life until venturing south. And mattress fleas didn't sound as cute as the little eight-legged critters I'd encountered in Monwyn.

Mother, keep me pure.

I dropped my skirt and flung it with my toe, sending it flying toward Septimus's head. He snagged it from the air and grumbled something indiscernible but angry while neatly folding the voluminous garment before stowing it away in his bag.

The æther may not have been as strong as it normally was... but it certainly wasn't silent. It tingled menacingly in my fingertips. *Do it Eira, divest, knock him to the bed, and then strip him of all the essence stored up in his broad-headed wrinkle beast.*

I spun around, took a giant's step and sent myself to the corner to think about what I did. Or what I might do.

"Fuck, fuck, fuck." I knocked my head against the wall, willing my brain to clear and that delicious glimmer *downstairs* to cease.

I heard the mattress shift under his weight.

"Gods," he hummed, "I can smell your desire."

"That's gross." It wasn't gross. I squeezed my eyes closed. But he was still there in my mind's eye... laid back, arms behind his head, his veiny and muscular forearms on display.

Septimus moaned, a long and drawn-out sound.

I went rigid, utterly still, and focused on my breathing.

One... two... three...

The sound of flesh running over flesh made my knees buckle.

My palms slid down the wall, my nails leaving streaks in the soft wooden panels as I dropped to my knees.

"S-Septimus?"

"Pull your blouse up and your panties down, leave your slut ass exposed, and stay silent. The Goddess made women for the male's gaze, though unfortunately gave you a mouth." His voice thickened, and his inhalations deepened.

"Truly? They have no inherent worth? No possible benefit to you but to populate your bullshit sexual fantasies? Not to mention the innumerable contributions to…"

I spun around and met his half-lidded eyes.

My entire being pulsed to the rhythm of his hand, working his rigid length.

His arousal stood proud, curving slightly up toward his stomach. He held himself so tightly while he stroked that his knuckles were white. The three piercings below his head glinted dangerously… drawing me in, convincing me to take a ride… for the sole purpose of breeding, not for pleasure, of course. And if there was no pleasure, there would be no sin.

I shook my head, dispelling the phantasmal dick voice.

Stay strong, Eira. Think of Ambrose, Cato.

"First of all, Septimus, I've fucked two men in my entire life, and I'm in a committed relationship with both of them. Second, the term slut is ridiculous. Only the boorish and unintelligent would even think the word has meaning. The number of lovers a woman has is irrelevant to her worth or who she is. Or is it just that the blood from your antiquated brain has leaked into your mediocre appendage?"

Septimus bit the corner of his bottom lip and smiled. It was disconcerting.

He worked his hand harder.

"Your fat whore's cunt is dripping, consort. Once again, your juices prove the lie in your hateful words."

The wetness between my legs taunted me as it escaped to my upper thighs.

"Both of my men would have come by now." I stifled a fake yawn.

"Insolent, bitch."

"Truant Protector."

His eyes flashed in warning, but again, that smile lifted. His cheek dimpled. His thighs tensed.

He stroked himself faster now.

My own arousal began accelerating, climbing to a painful, pulsing jolt between my legs. I dropped my hand into my waistband, running my fingertips through my curls.

"Failed Troth. Shit conjurer. King murderer."

I dipped two fingertips lower and closed my eyes as they made contact with my swollen clit.

"Absent father," I groaned, rubbing hard circles around my heated gem. "Disappointment of a husband. Lonely, fucking, miserable man."

"Yes," He shouted, hips thrusting, coming hard in waves onto his stomach. His thick streams called to me like a glass of honey-sweetened cream. "I am all of those."

I pleasured myself in fast back-and-forth motions, bouncing on my knees as if he were beneath me.

"Am-Ambrose. Oh, oh gods, Cato." My lashes fluttered involuntarily as I rode my orgasm, catching glimpses of Septimus as he leapt up off the bed and lunged toward me. "Hus-bands." He wound his fist into my hair and yanked my ear to his mouth.

"Shout their names, liar. It's rare for someone to make me come at all. But you..." His hand shot out like a whip, and he shoved his fingers painfully against my sensitive flesh. "A gift for you, consort." I shivered as he smeared an unmistakable stickiness between my legs.

"You are revolting, Septimus. You are absolutely loathso—"

His hand snapped closed around my throat, clenching around the sides of my neck. My vision pulsed to the thrum of my heart, narrowing with each beat. I peered into his eyes, disturbed by the expression of genuine happiness I saw there.

My world shrank... and darkness came.

CHAPTER NINETEEN

VERRA CAKES

CATO

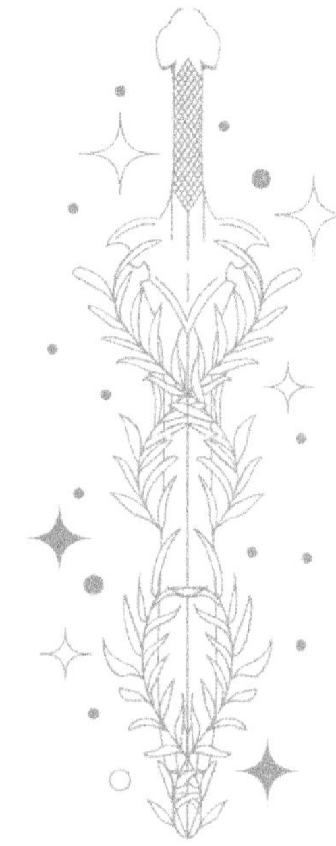

*N*earest weapon... three feet to the left of the furthest bar. Methods of escape, two: cell door, known to the people in the room; blood grate in the floor, leads to cesspool, unknown by others. Greatest threat in the area: me.

"There is nothing vulgar about it, Cato—satyr mommy teats could very well be shaped like mine. You have nothing to go on. Besides, my pectorals rival the amplest-breasted women." Ambrose took a quick step back as I shot an arm through the bars. "Until the wet nurse arrives, she stays put. Remove her and your ears will bleed—they will plead to be ripped from your head."

Adopted brother. Repeat it, Cato. He is not born of the same loins.

I rested my head between two of the steel bars that contained me, frustrated enough to choke the life from him.

"I think, Ambrose, that I am more disturbed by your being here in nothing more than your pants. Did shoes not cross your mind as you padded barefoot through the palace, through the yard, and then through a literal torture chamber? Shall I regale you with the list of viscera and fluids I have personally extracted and watched coat these floors?"

Ambrose peered down at the grime-covered stones and pursed his lips.

"When would I have thought about shoes, Catommandus? Hmm? Before filing her hooves? After she shat a fucking pound of grassy green shit down my shirt? It is a miracle she is diapered at all, what with the tiny tail she has. I tried cutting tail-holes in *your* stockings, Cato, but I am afraid only Aberus's calf was the right size for her sweetest little buns." He wiggled his nose in front of the infant's face. "And everyone knows you keep your punishment paradise immaculate."

"Ambrose! You didn't." Aberus scrubbed at his dense, black beard with both hands. "You know my clothing is specially made, and the Millanderers make such a fuss over the extra material and time it takes. Josa on a jar of jam, just being in a room with those two gives me anxiety."

"Pish, just have Catommandus knit you another pair."

Creator Goddess, mother above, if you have to end their lives to silence them, so be it.

Locking my hands behind my back, I spun on my heels and faced first Ambrose and then Aberus, taking the measure of my quarry.

Aberus sat in the oak chair that I used for interrogation. If he knew the number of fingers I had snapped over its steel-reinforced leather armrests in the last two years alone, he would likely call for the guards to throw it out and burn it. He didn't have the heart for violence, his uncanny resemblance to a mountain troll notwithstanding.

Now, how to get myself out of this mess? If I approach them with anger, they will become more agitated and storm off. If I bark orders, one will fall to the floor in tantrum and the other will "but I am the king" me until I have to bludgeon him, thus increasing the longevity of my sentence.

Persuasion then.

"Brothers, we must come together over more pressing matters."

"More pressing than a conjured nether beast latched on to our brother's man-tit?" Aberus interjected, shaking his massive head of curls in disgust.

"Yes, *Aberus.*" I took a deep breath, pushing down the impulse to lash out at them both.

Taking up the three-legged stool from the cell's corner, I placed it near the bars. I'd show them calm, concerned Cato. I sat and leaned against my prison. The cold metal should have calmed my anger-flushed skin, but all it did was remind me of my Nortian and how I needed to be near her. The only peace in my world was found in her arms.

Gods, she had been fucking fury incarnate, slamming Septimus to the ground with just a wave of her hand. Like it did every time I looked at her, smelled her, *thought* of her, a buzzing surge of energy crackled through my chest and down to my fingertips. She was mine, no matter who tried to lay claim to her.

"Gentlemen, my..." I paused. "Eira sits alone in a room by herself, most likely thinking that you, Aberus—you enormous fucking buffalo of an idiot—are going to have an infant butchered."

Aberus shrugged his shoulders and then slunk down in the chair. If he moved forward even an inch closer, he would be within my reach, and I would snatch a godsdamned bald patch in his head.

"Catommandus, *my* wife is fine. I gave her a snack and tucked her in and—holy nether I cannot even believe I am sharing this with you, but I *almost* told her I loved her."

Pickaxes hammered their way through my skull. The bone-crushing jealousy I had all but thwarted reared its head.

"See. The bars *were* needed," Aberus said. "Were they not between he and us, we would be in a right predicament. And with mother gone, who else remains that can talk him down?" Aberus crossed his legs at the knee and bounced his foot up and down. "I take it you are not as keen on sharing your lady friend as Ambrose is?"

"Again," I gritted my teeth, hating that Aberus was just as astute as our mother had been, "that is *not* the issue at hand. And she is my wife just the same, blessed by the Goddess herself."

"It most certainly is the issue, and unless the Goddess sends me a copy of her contract terms, you are as single as—"

A guard approached the entrance to the chamber.

"Majesty, the woman you called for is here, blindfolded, as required."

"See her in." Aberus waved to the guard and then placed a finger in front of his lips, mouthing "*shush*."

"Lady Trevine, thank you for coming. An abandoned infant was discovered in town, as I am sure you have heard. The little boy suffers from an ailment that has left him mangled and grotesque. The healers say the condition is not contagious, and until the child's mother has been located and punished, we very much hope you will provide us with mother's milk... though we would not ask you to risk your delicate sensibilities by looking upon such a maimed and unfortunate creature."

Daggers shot from Ambrose's eyes as Aberus spoke. The Verus-trained Scion Prince covered the infant's ears as if she could understand what was being said.

"I am honored to aid the Goddess's child, but I am concerned with my modesty, you understand, Majesty. Lord Travine is very particular about where and whom I nurse in front of. It is unseemly to feed in public spaces."

"That's bulls—"

"Of course, good lady." Aberus ran his finger across his neck, threatening me to silence. "I will face the wall and will instruct the guards to do the same." Aberus silently motioned for me to turn my head before motioning to Ambrose, who rose and placed the baby in her hands. He loomed over her with his arms crossed over his chest, and again, Aberus silently commanded him to shield his eyes.

"You may now proceed with your modesty intact, Lady Travine."

Aberus turned his seat around and stared into the spiked wall that made up the room's left side. I had fond memories of that wall. Lord Midguard was the most recent man that I had ended upon the points. His wife had called the guards, and I—the first to charge through the door—witnessed him buttoning his pants as the young woman stared into the ceiling. Instead of being a man, admitting to the heinous act and having his head removed publicly, he refused to talk. No matter though, I enjoyed pressing him slowly upon the spikes, hearing him cry, and would have missed out if the executioner had been involved.

I watched Lady Travine patting the satyress's back. I'd never really questioned the act of breastfeeding, had never seen it done. But as I watched, I couldn't image a more beautiful sight than Eira, raising our child to her chest.

Lady Travine, a woman who, as far as I could tell, was perennially pregnant, pulled her milk-laden breast from the nursing gown, searched for her nipple, and inserted it into the child's mouth. The satyress rooted, shaking her tiny face back and forth, and then latched on quickly.

There was no need to look away—there existed only one set of breasts that tempted me, and I was netherbent on laying my eyes on their naked glory this night. Taking Eira in the Ladies' Loft had only fueled my need to make her mine again. I needed to love her fully, flesh to flesh, lifemate to lifemate. I wanted to push plump red grapes past her lips while we talked about the mundane things that are dear to me—rocks, dogs, the snow stuff she loved to prattle on about. She was the only safe space for the not-so-mundane things—the loss of my parents, the loss of my self-control.

"Oh, he's a hungry little fellow."

Ambrose, the ridiculous man-child that he was, pointed to Lady Travine's chest and gnashed his teeth silently, before squeezing the air with both hands like he was palming the pair.

I shook my head and scoffed silently. He lifted the middle finger that Eira was so fond of flinging up.

"Precious little lamb. Do you have a glass bottle or a cup? I can express a portion for the child to feed on later."

"What kindness. A moment, if you will, Lady Travine. A servant will fetch a vessel." Aberus waved to a non-existent servant.

Ambrose hopped to it, scrambling around a pile of blunted axes, moving flails, and flat shavings of wood that I used to shove under fingernails. The idiot opened the blade storage cabinet and extracted a steel bowl used to catch the testicles of child abusers when castration was required.

I snapped my fingers lightly to get his attention. He glanced in my direction, and I ran my finger along the bottom edge of my lip, indicating that his choice was not a good one.

He signaled back by leaning onto his left foot and dropping his left arm. The sign meant "alternative?"

I stabbed my finger, pointing to a chest across the room.

Ambrose dodged the chains and hooks that hung from the ceiling and flipped open the lid. He immediately found what I had sent him for—a wooden cover that fit snuggly over the tensioning knob of the stretching rack's ratcheting system.

"A cup, fir ya, mum," Ambrose said in his best approximation of a lowborn's voice. He took the baby back into his arms and handed over the makeshift cup.

Lady Travine went to work, pressing her nipple to the cup's edge and squeezing her breast with an expert's hand. It was incredible to behold.

Ambrose slapped his palm over his mouth and clutched the baby to his stomach, doubling over.

Fucking child.

"There we are." Lady Travine held the cup out.

"Thank you, lady. Both the Goddess and Council will hear of your good deed," Aberus said, still facing the wall like the righteous man that he was.

The moment the door shut, he resumed his spot, and Ambrose hopped up on the tall wooden table, where Septimus and I had spent hours honing our bloody craft. He sat cross-legged and sniffed the fresh milk, grimacing dramatically.

"Brothers, draw your attention back to me," I said. "Today was a catastrophe from the moment we—Ambrose, for fuck's sake."

"Eww, brother," Aberus cried, "ewww."

Ambrose dipped his tongue into the vessel a second time, waggling his tongue while staring directly at Aberus.

I pinched the bridge of my nose.

"I was both curious and concerned that the baby may not like it. She seems content, though." Ambrose sniffed the liquid thoughtfully. "It is rather sweet, not what I expected at all. Hmmm, a hint of honey, and very light. Not like heavy cream but..." he sipped again and scrunched his face in confusion, "... Oh, it reminds me of banana." He smacked his lips like a sommelier sampling a fine wine. "I imagine Eira will be flavored like cheese. Would you not agree, Cato? She eats an astonishing amount of—"

Aberus gagged.

"Shut. The Fuck. Up." I grappled with my emotions, clinging tightly to my waning control. On one hand, the thought of tasting what Eira would produce for our child made my chest go tight with an odd and overwhelming sense of love. On the other hand, I knew well that it could be my brother's child she would birth first. I inhaled smoothly, slowing my thoughts as I learned to do long ago. "Gaea. I need you both to focus on Gaea. I have full confidence that Eira will succeed where our father failed. The perverseness of the corruption does not seem to win out in her, like it did him. She needs to understand herself to keep the true enemy at bay. I ask you, Aberus, man-to-man, brother-to-brother, to allow her to study within the confines of the palace or in my lands in Basilia. I will watch over her myself—"

"Catommandus." Ambrose's voice was blade flat. "Where I agree that she should have the chance to hone her abilities, you cannot hold off Gaea on your own, nor can she. And you will *not* be spiriting away with our woman. We come as three, or have you forgotten?"

Like I could forget.

"I have not forgotten, Ambrose. But in light of recent circumstances..."

"You would put your wants first, Cat?" Aberus asked like the judgmental prick he was.

"No. I would put hers first, if given the chance." I reached into the pocket of my leathers and allowed my finger to caress the tiny round of cork I kept there. I twisted the bottle stopper in my fingers, smiling at the memory it conjured—the first night I allowed myself to love her. Originally, I kept the bottle she used to poison me, to identify its contents, but when it turned out to be an abortifacient and not hemlock, I kept a souvenir of her regard for me. "Were I a stronger man, a more intelligent one... I would have put her before you, Aberus—above Father and all of Monwyn."

A shrill squawk came from the bundle in Ambrose's arms.

"Yes, 'ittle bitty Verra cakes, hims is always this dramatic." He fanned his fingers in the little one's face, tweaking her tiny nose.

"Do not name it, Ambrose," said Aberus. "You cannot keep it. It is born of the nether and though you have both suffered brainwashing, it falls to me to make choices that will protect this kingdom."

"Truly?" Ambrose stood, walked to the blade cabinet, and withdrew a thin, sharp knife, the kind that can slide through a man's ribs without leaving egregious damage on the skin's surface. "Here you are, then, my liege." He ducked around a noose, marched up to Aberus, and thrust the baby into his arms. "I do not know the best method of slaughtering a half-goat. I would not suggest the bowels, but perhaps the *V* between her collarbone and neck? That is Cato's preferred way."

Aberus glanced down at the infant, who promptly fell asleep in his big, burly arms.

"For the kingdom, Aberus?" Ambrose whispered, while pressing the razor-like knife into his brother's empty hand. "Whether you wield the blade yourself or call for another to do your bidding, the lives you take are a stain upon your soul."

Aberus stood no chance against *Scion* Ambrose.

"Catommandus, explain to Ambrose why—"

"Not a chance. I love babies, and Eira would actually explode me from the inside out if I let something happen to that kid."

"Oh, that was funny, Cat. Do you think daddy Satyrs call their babies kids? You know, like we do goat babies? Do you get it? Kid?"

I filled my lungs and let the air hiss out slowly, "I think, Ambrose, they are unlikely to speak Ærtan."

Ambrose pressed his fist to his mouth.

"I understood the Nether Lord just fine. Your argument is flawed."

I ran my palms up and down the bars of my prison, growing increasingly exhausted from the cyclical conversation and lack of urgency. I wanted out—needed Eira.

"Can you decide quickly, Aberus? I am due for a wife-cuddling and the clock is ticking."

Aberus glanced between the satyress and the blade, his dark eyes hardening and then going soft once more.

"Majesty! YOUR MAJESTY!"

The blade clattered to the ground, and Ambrose snatched the goatling back, shielding her within the confines of his arms. He kissed her forehead.

Jance came tearing through the door. He dropped to one knee and saluted, fist to shoulder.

"Speak, Jance." Aberus stood. "What is amiss?"

"Majesty. I awoke moments ago, surrounded by the bodies of six slain men. They were littered across His Highness's apartments, and the consort... She's gone."

"Outrageous, she's done it again!" Aberus thundered. "Jance, alert the Protector. Ambrose, Cato, you will—"

"Majesty, tha-that's another issue. The Protector... Majesty, he has vanished."

My soul left my body.

"OPEN THIS FUCKING CELL!"

CHAPTER TWENTY

COLD AS A POLAR BEAR BUTT

EIRA

"All I'm saying is that while masturbation may be the key to not outright fucking, if I'm given a choice, I'd rather it not be in the same room. That smacks of infidelity... which I am disinterested in."

My top half flew forward, and I grabbed the bedpost with both hands to keep from falling. I held tight. It had only taken my knees scraping against the rug-less floor once to learn I had to act fast to maintain my position in the cramped bed.

"You would subject me to self-degradation in a filthy, *shared* restroom? The fact I am spilling my seed anywhere other than where the Goddess intended is vulgar."

"What's vulgar is calling it 'seed,'" I muttered while ramming my hips backward, reclaiming my space. Septimus shoved back, but his buns were no match for mine. His assault ended in a stalemate. "And I refuse to lose any more sleep to your endless dry humping. If I can't sleep, then I can't recharge... no recharge, no Gaean retribution." I jerked my elbow backward, digging it into his ribs. Behind me, Septimus grunted. Unfortunately, it sounded more like a sigh, and less like a sound of pain.

I had no intention of following him to Gaea but needed his protection, and his resources, to put my plan into action, which meant continuing to fuel his notion. Yes, I wanted the Primus-King torn down, but Cato and Ambrose's safety trumped all. Nether, I wasn't sure I *would* face the Gaean again without their support. Yes, I could go all shade puff, but only if I wasn't lying in a puddle of my own anxiety-induced tears.

The bed shook as Septimus flopped over; his imperfectly perfect chest mashed into my back. If I closed my eyes and pinched my nose, I could almost imagine it was Cato.

"How is it that an all-powerful witch is such a weakling?"

"What?" I laughed so hard that the bed creaked below us. "Who said I was all-powerful? Ambrose? He's just awestruck and excited to be railing a real-life conjurer."

"Burchard."

His name hung in the air. A prayer... a memory so real that I had to convince myself that he wasn't in the other room attempting to escape his wranglers. Of course Papa Burchard would have made me out to be some brilliant conjurer. From day one, he believed me to be the most powerful being in the mountains. Never once did his faith wane... he believed in me until the very moment his soul parted from his mortal form.

Septimus shifted, his hips resting against mine. Like the sparkles that danced in the fizzy Solnnan wines, the æther popped around in my chest, more strongly than it had the day before. I worried my lip, chewing the dried skin. Rest would heal my physical body, and that would mean the æther would return in force... but so too would the Bond increase its hold.

"Burchard told me of the power you wield. He said that his daughter could lay waste to our enemies with a wave of her hand."

I blinked back the gathering tears.

"He said that because he cared for me."

"No. He said it because he believed it to be true."

Burchard.

Imella.

Lilium.

My Nan.

When I thought of one, I thought of them all. They all believed in me until their belief got them killed.

"The Primus-King, my father, believes me all-powerful as well." It was the first time I allowed the word to be uttered, even in my head.

Father.

Septimus leaned in, his breath against my ear.

"Father? That explains your mental deficiency. I take it your gluttony comes from your mother's side?"

The forge within my chest bloomed hot, the unnatural warmth spreading to my fingertips and then my hands. I gazed at my palm, where the dark mark appeared the day before. I saw only flesh now, but I knew with certainty that something remarkable lay just beneath my skin.

"Septimus," I whispered, trying to keep the shake of my mounting wrath out of my voice. "One day, I will kill you."

"Mmm, perhaps." He ran a palm down the curve of my waist, and I smacked it away. "My life will end soon, regardless of if you take it or not. And I *do* understand the compulsion to kill. I relished the thought of taking your head when Aberus called for it.”

“Aberus can drown in the Penumbrean sea.”

I wrapped my arms around my chest, attempting to still the æther. Fucking Aberus. I added his name to the ever-growing list of people I would like to see perish.

“Adding treason to your list of crimes, conjurer?”

“And what if I am?” I rolled to face him, my nails biting into his arm, the corded muscles turning to rope as he tried to escape the heat searing his snow-colored skin. I climbed over his body and pressed my forearm into his neck.

“I want you both to fall. Would drop both of your bodies into the same grave as the Gaean king,” I used my weight to bear down on his windpipe.

Septimus sputtered and grabbed my fingers, trying in vain to pry them away while thin rivulets of blood tailed down either side of his bicep. The ruby streaks stained the silver braid that lay under his back. I increased the pressure, admiring the goosebumps that rose on his chest, how his lips slackened, how beneath me his length hardened. I glanced up to his—

“Holy fuck. Your eye!” I let go, and he gasped loudly, smiling like some deviant, panting like he’d just climbed to the summit of Mount Gammond.

“You are incredible, enchantress.”

“And you actually *are* going to die!”

His indignant blue eyes rolled toward the sky—well, one of them did—the other kind of floated in a well of pus. The cut where I hit him with a rock the day before was angry. Violently so. The surrounding skin was inflamed and puffy—a purple blotch with thin, white streaks running through its deep shade.

“Do you feel that?” I grabbed his head and leaned in close to sniff his face. “Oh, gods, you need a healer. That stink is not a good one.”

“No.”

“What do you mean, no?”

“You have seen my body... my disfigurements. An infected cut will never be what lays me low.”

I crawled off him and then stared down, noting the Verus shaped tent of his erection beneath the sheet.

“Let me tell you the story of another dumbass man who wouldn’t see the healer.” I swiped out at his penis with my open palm, but he tucked and rolled away. “My dad, Ulltan. Big fellow, the burliest man’s man in all of Nortia. He’s the same man who is missing the back half of his teeth because 'a little blister ain't never stopped one of Derros's devotees.' It certainly brings him low now, when he has to soak his jerky before gumming it to mush!"

"I do *not* require a caretaker." Septimus sat up, and a stream of milky liquid poured from the corner of his eye, down his cheek and into his beard. "So silence yourself."

I gagged and stepped away. My eyes hazed, and saliva flooded my mouth. Was I not made of sterner stuff? Blood was okay, birth was fine, vomit no big deal, but this...

"On second thought, let it fester. It makes my vagina run as cold as a polar bear's butthole."

I snatched up the satchel on the floor, shrugged into my shirt, and then dug around for my drawstring bag. Maybe one of the vials would—

"Oh, gods, bloody, fucking gods," Septimus said behind me.

"Finally figuring out how bad it is, manly man?" Nothing I brought would help him—conception control, cough suppressant, and a tincture meant for bad breath. Panic had clearly reduced my ability to think the night we fled.

"Mattress fleas... "

I went rigid... motionless.

"Where?" My eyes swept the room. I didn't move for fear of vermin attack.

"They have invaded your tresses."

A stinging stab pierced the knobby protrusion at the top of my spine.

"My gods," I cried, "W-what do I do, Septimus?"

"There is only one thing *to* do."

He produced a dagger from under his pillow.

"No!" I screamed. "Septimus, do not!"

Septimus lunged, and his palm cracked across my face.

"Pull yourself together."

He grabbed a handful of my hair. I cried out in pain.

"What are you doing?"

"What I should have done in the first place."

My chest constricted.

I would die here.

Blade in hand, he struck again.

CHAPTER TWENTY-ONE

TROLLNAIL

AMBROSE

"Like I cannot scent my wife's own brand." I leered down over Cato's aggravating face, cursing under my breath.

His hair looks so fucking stupid—all flips and flops. The grooming set I gifted him for his last name day celebration probably stores his rock collection now... ingrate.

"You have turned over every leaf on the forest floor, Catommandus. I am standing here, telling you, with the full authority of my station, that she has come this way." I raised the dried nugget again, wrinkling my nose at its meaty aroma. "I would bet my life on it. She's quite regular, you know. Sharing the same bathing chamber, I have become overly familiar."

Dark eyes snapped to mine; the weird little ring of gold seeming to deepen in color like some slimy, yellow-eyed toad.

"My concern, Ambrose, lies less in the lump of shit you are *still* inexplicably clutching and more in the godsdamned troll encampment thirty fucking yards from where said turd was found."

Scratching my back on the bark of the tree, I watched Cat knee walk across the moss, pushing aside pebbles with a stick.

"Hmmmmm," I attempted to gain his attention, but he was too engrossed in his inspection of a splintered square. "That is one nasty troll nail." I chuckled to myself, knowing full well it was the remnant of one of Eira's ill-kempt claws. "Blech, even a hangnail makes me cringe."

I studied my own manicured hand. My nails still looked good, despite the damage my mace handle had done to them. The wire grip desperately needed to be rewound and padded now, and the whole thing would need to be scrubbed thoroughly. Troll skulls were remarkably hard on the outside, but just as messy as everyone else's on the inside.

"Do you figure it was the whole Nether Lord thing? You know, the reason that more creaturey things have been cropping up?"

"Perhaps."

"Hmmm. Do you figure Eira left *with* Septimus, or that he took her against her will?"

"I do not know."

"Hmmmm. In your estimation, how long do you think she can reasonably keep from sucking his dick raw? Have you witnessed her obliterating an oyster? One solid slurp and... are you well?"

Those eyes again—so remarkably odd yet lovely, even in a state of rage. Too bad he'll soon wrinkle up like Father—those dry thighs nearly chaffed my taint in our throupling.

Cato bolted up from the ground, turned on his heel, and stalked away.

I followed him, inspecting the ground for myself and rapidly growing bored.

"Cat, we must both bear in mind it is the Dick Bond that perpetuates her desire to rut." He sped up, and I increased my pace, trying to catch up with him. The topic was most important if he was to maintain a cool head. He needed Eira like my flat tum did its girdle, but he was still acting reckless. "My point is, she does not purposefully set out to stir up our combined jealousy."

Cato fled.

I sidestepped a mud puddle, mindful of my freshly polished boots, and took off at a run.

The ass leapt up on his horse and kicked his pony south without once bothering to look back. Simply shameful. What if I were set upon by a libidinous group of criminals? Or-or a naughty group of highwaymen who demanded I slake their lusts?

It was a full ten minutes before my mare caught up to his side. He hid his tells from the world, but I knew he wanted to speak. He kept rubbing the back of his neck and then drawing a breath, only to release it in a loud rush.

"I thought you impervious to jealousy, Ambrose."

Called it.

"'I thought you impervious...'" I mocked in a high-pitched voice and smacked his horse on the flank, causing it to startle sideways.

I fiddled with a loose braid in Lady Azurite Boulder Opal's mane and then flicked a bit of troll brain from her red ribbons.

"Cat? Do you remember when I returned from the mines and Mama gave me this horse? She told me we shared the same peridot-colored eyes."

I smiled at the memory. "Lots of stable hands rode her while I was away at Verus, but she is still *my* horse. If one of them dared claim her, I'd beat them senseless...You would understand the metaphor if you had actually Joined with Eira as I did." Cato soothed horse Ambrose, and I was hit by a pang of longing to see my wife. "As it stands, I will un-join Septimus from his studded dick the moment we find them." I ran my fingers along the blade sheathed at my side. "Try fucking her then, silver-haired serpent."

Cato's nostrils flared. Did he not think I could handle Septimus?

"Did she tell you that? He has piercings, Cato... and his pleasure plonker is thick like yours. My gods, she's probably salivating over it as we speak. Our girl enjoys her ride time."

Never had I seen a man wind himself so tight. His coat pulled across his shoulders as he tensed. He would surely bust a seam.

Cato jumped from his steed and fell to the ground, turned his head to the side, then laid his cheek flush to the road, this time inspecting a hoof print.

"Do you think Verra-cakes is faring well, Cat?"

No answer.

Ethens took it in stride when I dropped my baby goatling at his door before we left. *My* heart, however, burst from betwixt my ribs when I placed her in his arms. She opened those sweetest eyes—with those unusual rectangular pupils—and then let out a squall that reached the Goddess's realm... like I had betrayed her. I clutched my fist to my chest.

I would owe him a considerable debt in the future, but Ethens was *mostly* trustworthy, and Eira found Cinden to be dependable. They would care for our goat girl until we returned, and I'd given them strict instructions detailing her likes and dislikes, ensuring her comfort.

"Cat?"

Silence.

"Catommandus!"

He smacked his hand on the ground as his head snapped around. "What?"

My eyes drew to a speck of vegetation caught between his two front teeth.

"Two things, really. First, there is a thread from Eira's nightgown directly above your head—I changed her into the most adorable floral myself, chartreuse and blush blooms. Here, let me." I slid off my mount and pinched and pulled the long length from the thorny bramble it caught on, winding it into a ball. Cato plucked the fiber from my hands and stuffed it into his pocket. "Second, do you think I am in love if I worry about what *she* will worry over?"

He stared at me as if stricken, mouth agape, eyes sharp. I reached toward him, thumbing his lip, netherbent on scraping the green scourge from his grimace.

"What the fuck are you about?" Like an angry little gnome, Cato flailed, batting at my hands.

Fine. Fuck it. Greet your woman with a cabbage-toothed kiss.

"And no. Absolutely not."

I sighed loudly and then sighed again. The brute was drowning in his own feelings and was completely ignoring mine. He was back to being just as broody and moody as he was before he finally got laid. My most fervent hope was that we could find Eira quickly, stash them in some closet, and she could suck the sulk right out of his cock. Without her, he was only this side of tolerable... and I was lonely.

Back in the saddle, we rode through a herd of loudly bleating sheep. The foolish fluff attempted to stand their ground, but straight was the simplest way to our destination. They learned quickly to part themselves in my presence.

"Catommandus, I require sound advice, brother, and with Mama gone... I have been wracking my mind trying to determine if—"

"Colpass or Moonledge?"

"What?"

"Did they ride to Colpass or Moonledge?"

"Moonledge, naturally." I kicked out at a ram, who was eying my thigh like it was a delicious and thick-assed ewe. "Cat, does it upset you that I might love our woman? The odds are extremely low, however—"

"Why Moonledge?" he asked gruffly, while scowling out over a field.

"I asked first," I huffed.

He did an about-face atop his mount and fixed me with a steely glare.

I looked him up and down like the tiny tot he was. I'd get nothing from him.

"Fine. But clearly, you have never snuck off with a lover. My rationale is as follows: When one's aim is to woo, you take your conquest to a location where anonymity is ensured. Colpass is heavily fortified, and because of your royal decrees, ex-Protector, every soldier has seen or has received a description of both Septimus and Eira. He would, wanting to fuck on the down low, take her to where the chances of being recognized were minimal."

"An astute observation." Cat nodded and then hit me with an expression that concerned me to my core—a slow, smug smile. His eyes grew hazy, and his tongue slipped from between his lips, running along the edge of his full mouth.

Mmmm... Ex-Protector... How might I be of service?

"And I *have* snuck off with a lover, Ambrose: *your* wife, and right under that perfect nose of yours. I have fucked her in a shack, in the middle of a godsdamned field, in the temple's loft with the entire godsdamned court below... and when I find your wife again, I will slip my cock inside of her in front of whatever audience is blessed enough to witness us." Cato winked one of his big brown eyes.

"Ah, yes, the shack fuck. What a lascivious event that must have been... when Mama walked in on you bestowing upon Eira her first anal fissure."

I threw back my head, laughing up at the red-tinted sky, entirely nonplussed by the fury on my brother's face.

Chapter Twenty-Two

Lightning Bolts and Leviathans!

Eira

I was parched—so thirsty that my tongue adhered to the roof of my mouth.

"Cato?" I questioned, smacking my lips slowly, begging for the moisture to return. "Black Bear?" My head was... It wasn't pounding like a headache... but it was sore, so tender I feared injury. Allaine must have adhered the faux fibers too close to my...

"Get up. Fetch me water."

Something was rhythmically tapping my hip over and over, but I couldn't—

"Water, lazy bitch. Bring it to me now."

Septimus.

Right.

"Get your own drink, lofty motherfucker," I grumbled while turning over on my side and hugging Ambrose's thick bicep close to my chest.

"It is I, wife. Trust me to do what is right."

Huh?

My eyes snapped open.

The dirty sole of smelly boot took up my entire field of vision. I shoved off the leather-clad leg I was embracing and sat up, immediately dizzy. The room spun, and I held my forehead in one hand and reached out for support with the other.

I took a deep breath, allowing my equilibrium to right itself... and then took in my surroundings. Sealed wooden walls, sparse furnishings.

The last thing I remembered was... dancing mermaids... ham dinners... mattress fleas and... Septimus's fist flying at my head.

Oh, no.

The æther.

It was back.

I recognized its ebb and flow as I breathed, so much stronger than before. Inhale, and it gathered tightly in my chest. Exhale, and it dispersed down my arms, not quite reaching my fingertips.

I needed air. Needed to gather my thoughts. I glanced through blurry eyes, searching for a place to take refuge. A single glass orb hung from the ceiling, an old-style self-extinguishing light with a wick attached to a float of cork. Two scuffed-up old chairs were tucked tightly under a table in the middle of the room, a painting of two merry little boys with mountains in the background was nailed to the wall. Well-made twine fishing nets hung from the four corners of the chamber's ceiling. One overflowed with bolts of heavy woolens, all-natural colors like grays, creams, and white, another with raw sheep's fleece. I recognized the grassy and sweet smell of lanolin. Nortia traded whalebone combs and bowls for the oil that protected our hands from the constant threat of chap.

"Open the godsdamned door, walk up the stairs, and bring me w-water."

I rubbed at my eyes and ignored the asshole who laid at the opposite end of the tiny bed we shared. My vagina didn't ignore him, though. With the æther roaming through this *finally* rested body of mine, my clit was tingling like a—

He kicked my elbow hard, sending an electric shock of pain through my arm.

"What the fuck, Septimus? Kick me again, and I swear to gods I'll—oh fuck." I scrambled down the length of the bed and gathered his normally pale face in my hands. He was burning hot. Like, Eira-meets-the-Nether-Lord-and-burns-down-half-a-kingdom hot.

Septimus's maimed eye had swollen tightly closed, and the thin, sensitive skin around it was mottled in shades of red and deep purple. Green pus leaked from his tear duct. I palpated his cheek and under his neck. Both were thickened and enlarged, and his veins stood out from under his ear to the top of his clavicle.

"How long has it been like this?"

"Do not touch me, Lil." He shook his head, trying to free himself from my grasp. "I am unclean."

"Septimus, listen to me; I'm going to find—"

"I am not worthy of your touch. But please, Lil... please do not let me find you with him again. He is my brother..." Septimus faded out of consciousness momentarily, thrashing his head from side to side. "I know the child is not mine, Lilium. But Alois and I, we look enough alike—Burchard will not realize she is his. Kairus will be safe here."

Holy shit. Holy fucking cradle-sized shit.

I glanced around frantically, seeking a cup, a pitcher of water.

"Septimus, I'll return. I'm going to find a healer."

Silence.

He said nothing, just stared out through a single, red-rimmed eye.

I got to my feet.

Where the nether are we?

I inspected the new costume I wore. Brown short pants, black tall boots that fit remarkably well, and a flowy linen shirt covered by a baggy blue vest.

"Your heart breaks, but Lilium, it is the way of kingdoms, you know this. Alois cannot stay alive. He threatens Bur-Burchard's succession. Just as the child could..."

Ohhhhhhh. Please stop speaking.

This was bad... and though I was curious to hear what other bits of hidden Monwyn history he would spill, I ran across the floor toward the door but stopped short, stricken again. *Oh, gods.* This pesky fucking vertigo. My head didn't spin this time, but my balance was still not what it should be. I paused until it felt like I was no longer leaning to the left, and then shuffled toward the exit. For stability's sake, I leaned against the threshold, slowly opening the door, and then looked up past a flight of stairs and into the cloud-filled sky.

"Hooo-ly fuck-ing snowballs."

I had assumed the Primus-King would be the first man I offed with a clear intention and a rational mind. I was sorely mistaken.

A gull flew through the sky, its shrill cry mocking.

I charged up the steps but ducked low when I heard the snapping canvas of a gaff sail catching wind above me.

"Boy!" a gravelly voice yelled. "Boy, get back in that thar hull. Storm's a-comin.'" The sailor ran at me, waving his hands above his head and stabbing his finger toward the sky.

Storm.

Storm on the water... The leviathans would shoot lightning bolts from their horned heads and the krakens would surface. That's what Nan always told me about the storms at sea—the thunder woke the creatures, calling them to the surface.

My heart leapt and began pounding so hard I could feel it against my chest wall.

"Listen to me, ya soft-bodied boy child. The sea ain't no place for the breakable. Get back under and hold on tight, ya hur?" He looked over his shoulder, assessing the gray-green clouds rolling in. The peacock feather in his hat flittered wildly in the growing gale. "The Merlann 'as seen her share of Viktos's wrath. We may survive it yet, but there ain't never one storm that's like the last, ya hur?"

Oh, I hur… I hurred him loud and clear.

I planted my body against the wall, hugging the planks like they were my last salvation. The sailor sprinted away, and I dashed back below, making prayers and peace with the divine.

"Septimus!" I screamed, running across the floor. "Septimus, my plan to let you die has changed. I need you!"

I rushed around the cabin, pulling out drawers and rooting through several chests that were nailed in place.

"Please, please, please, please!"

Wait, Eira, idiot.

I swayed across the floor, my feet headed left, and the walls headed right.

"Oh gods, oh gods."

I reached into the ankle of Septimus's boot, withdrew a small blade, and nicked the side of my thumb. There was no sting, the edge so sharp that blood welled immediately. I held his affected lid open and dripped a fat bead of blood directly into his eye. The droplet spread, and a thin film of pink filtered across the entirety of his icy-blue iris. For good measure, I caught his jaw in my hand, pried open his mouth, and drew my finger from the back of his tongue to the front.

And then I sat, wedged my arm around the bedframe, and cried.

The boat rocked in earnest now, and though the furniture didn't move—like a specter playing its nethersome tricks—the nets hanging from the ceiling swayed from side to side.

"Septimus, are you… are you awake?" I couldn't catch my breath. I was so scared. Gods, I'd befriend a cyclops if it meant I didn't have to weather this alone.

One… two… no… no…

My ragged breaths were coming too fast and too shallow—I was drowning in my terror, and I knew that outside the waves were closing in. What would it sound like when the hull cracked open and water gushed through, choking our lives away? Would it hurt for only a few seconds, or would my lungs burn and beg for air until the ocean forced its way down my throat?

Septimus's chest arched high, lifting from the bed. I scrambled up to his side and examined him for signs of life. The scream that tore from his mouth rivaled the clap of thunder that shook the whole godsdamned boat.

"I need you to wake. I can't do this alone." I clutched the collar of the short coat he wore, gripping the heavy wool until my knuckles shone white. I needed to run, flee—be as far from here as possible.

The boat lurched to the right and then abruptly wrenched to the left as wave and wind fought for supremacy. Septimus's heavy body rolled toward the bed's edge, but I shoved against him, securing him by digging my heels into the floor.

A trickling noise and then a telltale slosh confirmed the worst.

Water streamed down the steps and under the door. It didn't puddle. It flowed from one side of the cabin and then shifted, flowing freely to the other.

"Catommandus—son of my heart. Your father's affair is not your fault. I will teach you to har-harden your mind against pain."

Under my hands, Septimus shook uncontrollably. What started as a slight tremor turned to a seizure that had his fingers drawing into his wrists. I scrambled into the bed, carefully rolled over him, and tucked myself under his arm.

"Come back," I cried. "I'm so scared."

I clung to his solid body, desperate to anchor myself in reality.

"The pain is inconsequential, Cato. Push it away. Do not scream. Do not flinch. Your enemies will…"

"Please," I sobbed into his shoulder, giving in to my fear. If I didn't drown in the sea, my tears would pull me under.

"Is-is it so hard to love me, Lil?"

The room tipped. The lamps extinguished

Our bodies met air.

CHAPTER TWENTY-THREE

NO PLOT. JUST AMBROSE.

AMBROSE

"**D**o these come in oxblood? I have something similar in rust, chestnut, and pecan, but what I am looking for is—Cat, come here."

I sandwiched his angry little face between my hands and turned his head until the perfect ray of light beamed into his eyes, illuminating their dark depths. "You see, the reddish-hued reflection, the undertone there. *That* is what I am searching for. Stand still Catommandus."

"No sir, my apologies, Highness, but might I interest you in a fine tan?" The shopkeep drew a hand along the display behind him. The quality of his wares was without question, the details of his footwear and tack just impeccable... but the man lacked a sense of style, an eye for beauty. His shoes may be sturdy, but chunky soles fell out with baggy breeches.

"Tan against this lily-of-the-valley complexion? Ugh, I would prefer to cloak myself in puce. What about your harnesses?" I lifted the sides of leather, rifling through the tall stack, looking for that piece that would just... "You know, Cato," I tapped my fingertip to my chin. "She likes me in black. Her Nortian obsession with the stark color is frivolous, to be sure, but it does send her horse a-hoofing, if you catch my meaning." I wagged my brows at the shopkeep, whose arms lay as slack as his jaws. *Probably years since he's had a rousing hoofing of his own.* "Sir, this deep onyx—oh!—such a lustrous jet. It will be spectacular with my inky tresses."

I tugged out the layer of leather, draped it over my shoulder, and whipped my braid around for comparison.

The man stood corpse-still—not the reaction that I expected.

"Are you suffering from paralysis?"

The mousy little man's mouth worked up and down, "*You* will, uh, b-be wearing the harness y-yourself, then? I-uh—"

Cato shoved me to the side and pushed himself in front of me.

"My apologies. My brother is unaware of when his jokes fall flat. We need a simple repair and—"

"Who the fuck is joking?" Shading my eyes with the edge of my hand, I twisted about, searching for the fool they spoke of. "I see no jester in the vicinity. I know what my wife prefers, and *that* is a palette of deeper hues."

Cato handed over a set of snapped reins.

"If we could just bother you for the replacement, my good man, we will be out of your shop and on the way."

The mercantile began rushing around his shop.

"Absolutely. Anything for you, Prince Catommandus. After what you did to stop that gang of outlaws two years ago, it's on the house. Do you expect your assessment of the fiefs and fields to go on much longer?"

The leatherworker placed a supple new set of reins into Cato's hands, never once making eye contact with me... the literal heir to this blessed kingdom.

Hmmm. I snatched the new equipment from my brother's hands and held them up to the light streaming through the windows.

"Consort Eira, my scrumptious new wife, will wake the whole palace when I slap these against that squishy ass of hers." I bent the length to test it for steadfastness and then struck the reins against my palm, the crack so loud the shopkeep hopped back. "Though we fuck five times daily, she will no doubt demand more." I slid the leather under my nose, inhaling its fine scent. "La, such a difficult life. But, my good man, I fuck for the future of the realm. I fuck for you, for your mother... for Monwyn!"

The merchant gasped, caught up in the spell I wove.

"T-to Mon... To Monwyn." He dipped his head, bowing in respect.

Yes, that's right.

Cato blinked at me stupidly and then clapped the storeman on the shoulder, turning him toward the door.

"No. We will return to Cordillaria within the next day or two. Preparations for the coronation are well underway." Cato nodded to the man respectfully. "Say hello to your lady-wife for me. I have yet to taste an apple pie that rivals hers."

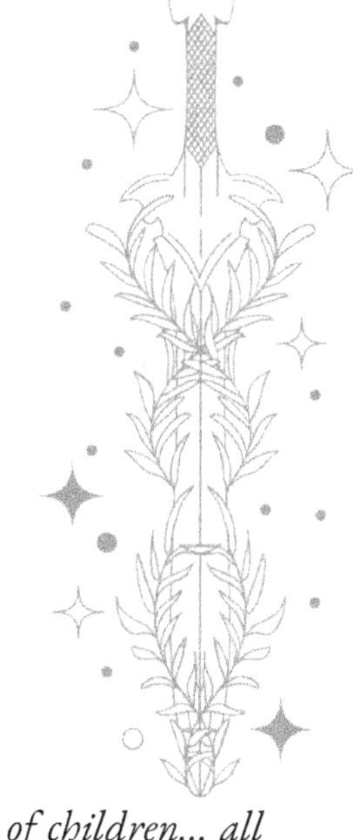

CHAPTER TWENTY-FOUR

SINNONBREAK

CATO

Three armed men. Fourteen soldiers. One thief. Group of children... all thieves. Weapons: one in boot, three at hip and one concealed. Closest location of safety: Colpass. East. Could retreat on foot if required.

"Look at her, just look at her!" Ambrose hefted up and forcefully hugged a wide-eyed waif that asked him for a coin. "She is the spitting image of my Verra."

"Lemme go!" The stringy-haired child wiggled and struggled while a teary-eyed Ambrose rubbed his cheek on her brown mop of hair. "Gods' fucking snowballs!"

I tensed.

"What did you say?" Like a man scalded, Ambrose dropped her to the ground.

She popped up in a rage, a whirlwind of fury dusting the dirt from her little backside. "Girl-child, I have given you an order. Speak by decree of—"

The girl screwed up her grungy face, planted her foot and then struck.

Fist met dick.

"Yahhhhhhh!"

"Gods, alive, I am felled!" Ambrose doubled over, cradling his crotch in both hands.

The girl turned to flee, but I caught her by the scruff of her scratchy gown.

"Child, I offer gold for information." The sharp little miss stilled instantly.

Ambrose leaned his head against a tree trunk while a group of boys yelled from a distance, calling for me to release their friend.

"Do not trust the tiny harpy. Gods fucking dammit, my testicles, Cato—my testes are irrevocably damaged."

I ignored the child wallowing beside me and turned my attention to the shrewd one in my grasp.

"Whatchu wanna know? Huh?" She wiped her nose on her sleeve and crossed her skinny arms over her chest.

"Who taught you to throw a punch like that? Well done, by the way, but next time, continue to follow through, understand? Had you, he would be writhing in a puddle of vomit."

She gazed upon Ambrose with narrowed eyes and nodded her head.

"Ya don't go huggin' those what don't wanna hug."

I smiled to myself. Her clothes were dusty but not filthy, her shoes well made, if a bit scuffed. If I thought her truly destitute, I would take her to Eira and demand to start our gang of girl children sooner than expected. My chest swelled at the thought, tightened until I could no longer draw breath.

"How do ya follow through?" she asked. I released her and slowly shifted my shoulders, modeling the movement for her once and then again.

"Like this?" She thrust her small fist into the air, a perfect scowl on her face. I thought my godsdamned heart would melt.

"Mmhmm, exactly. Now, was it a lady who taught you? Shaped like a goddess, dark hair and ocean-colored eyes?"

"Diantha?" She cocked her head to the side, looking thoughtful. "Yeah, but I think her eyes was just normal eyes."

Diantha. My fucking brilliant woman. Keep leaving me clues, love.

The child pointed us to an inn, and the proprietor there informed us that a very rude and nearly delirious "Grandfather Bem" was kicked out of the establishment this very day. A man named Mendell offered us information on their destination, but only if I split a ham dinner with him. In the end, it took two coins and a sly peek at Ambrose's ass, and he finally pointed us in the direction of Sinnonbreak, a coastal town not a half day's ride from here.

We rode hard, entering the bustling town a few hours after leaving the inn. Unlike the modest and sleepy village of Moonledge, the citizens of Sinnonbreak welcomed us with fanfare, fawning over and parading beside us as we made our way down the main road.

"Cato, we *will* be discussing your attitude," Ambrose said, after hustling to my side. "Or... lack of personality."

"What did they want?" I jerked my head back toward the group of men who had excitedly waylaid him a moment before.

I set a quick pace, doing my damndest not to be sidetracked again. When I was Protector, not a soul dared to stop me. As Prince Catommandus, I made it barely twenty feet past the center of town before being intercepted by the local miners's guild.

Ambrose crowded me to the right. He waved at a group of working women pouring out of the town's brothel.

"And he's single," he sang out behind me, forcing me in their direction. "No... no... no and... you. Yes, you with the birthmark shaped like a lamb shank."

The stretch-marked breasted blonde popped a tit out and then reached for the front of my trousers.

"Do. Not." I bit out. She dropped her hand and folded the tit back into her gown, pouting as she rejoined her sisters.

"You are lovely, dear." Ambrose tossed the woman a coin, which she nestled into her cleavage. "Were I un-Joined I would share in your delights, but alas," he pointed to the glittering diamond hoop in his ear, "my wifey is the jealous type."

We continued toward the coast, nodding to the soldiers who stopped to bow and salute, and placed our fingertips to our foreheads in response to shouted prayers for our safety. Mothers held up their infants, pledging them in service to the mines or military, and fathers brushed off the shoulders of their teenage boys, cueing them to stand straighter. We pressed coins into their hands and kept talking—all the while seeking clues.

For most of the day, it felt like one dead end after another. But I knew if I kept searching, I would find what I sought. Humans and creatures alike left traces of their passage. Sometimes they were as easy to spot as orange calcite in a gray cave or as difficult as finding a stem of salvia in a lavender field. Septimus was an expert huntsman and master of intelligence. I knew I was unlikely to find evidence of his presence... but Eira. She was so amazingly unaware, hopping back and forth between one activity and another, she couldn't help but overshare with everyone she encountered.

I was not surprised when I spotted her hair, of all things, dangling from a rope line at the fiber seller's booth. They must have sold it off for provisions... *and I will be damned...* Septimus's distinctive, dappled gray horse trotted right out in front of us. Either my uncle was losing his touch or something was amiss.

I will choke the life from him.

Instead of immediately pointing out the obvious, I waited to see if Ambrose spotted either of the clues and shifted so that the steed would be in his line of sight. I was aware that my current level of jealousy was inappropriate—and I was *hideously* cognizant of my gruff behavior—but instead of dealing with it rationally and speaking to him about my feelings,

I placated myself by moving pieces of evidence where he could find them, giving him the chance to feel helpful. I would eventually go back to being able to stand him, just not right at this moment.

For fuck's sake. When he did not attend to the obvious, I angled my shoulders, shepherding him toward the marina without him being the wiser.

My ears perked. The dockman, standing within earshot, was blathering on about the three bars of gold in his pocket, "an' all that fair gent wanted t'was a room aboard the Merlann and some pants for his nephew."

Bars of gold were never the currency in a trade-based town.

Slipping indeed, old man.

"Cato, quit diverting the conversation and listen to me."

I rubbed my aching temples, warding off the headache settling between my brows. Ambrose could, in his current position, reach out and flick the forked beard of the exuberant dockman.

"You were fully aware when you pressured us both into the Joining that—yes, madam, your baby is lovely, a true Monwyn prize." Ambrose kissed the head of a squalling toddler once and then again.

I grabbed his shoulders and spun him, swapping our positions, placing him directly next to the bragging dockman. Their fucking arms literally touched.

"Thank you. The sun was in my eyes." Ambrose smiled, waving at the pride-filled mother as she scurried away. "Gammond's wrinkly gonads... Verra makes that infant look like a peeled potato." He tugged at his sleeve while glaring at the man beside him. "Now, Catommandus. First and foremost, the contract was primarily drawn up to ensure Eira's safety. And I know you and she are madly in lust or whatever, but I cannot help that it turns out that I like fucking *and* talking to my wife. We shared her perfectly well in the beginning and—"

"Ambrose."

"No." He stopped abruptly and transformed from the self-centered man of three minutes ago to the dangerously serious one now before me. His mouth tightened, and his brow dropped low. "We are having this conversation. We can either agree to terms, or I, as her legally Joined husband, will enforce a new set of—by gods, is that Septimus's prized steed? Look just there."

Ambrose gripped my biceps and flipped me about, altering our positions once again. Over my shoulder, he pointed to the gray.

Thank fuck.

"Sir, I say, that is a handsome piece of equine flesh you have there. Is she a good ride?" Ambrose hailed the man who was leading the mount away.

I am coming, love.

"Catommandus!" Ambrose hollered after a brief exchange with the handler. "They are bound for Solnna. He has taken my woman hostage and absconded to another realm."

Ambrose took off at full speed, heading toward the pier.

About godsdamned time.

CHAPTER TWENTY-FIVE

WILL I FORGIVE MYSELF?

EIRA

My traitorous hag of a vagina twinkled with effervescent joy while I hurled the sharpest of mental daggers toward Septimus's delight-filled face. He ogled me through his nearly healed eye, like I was a decadent dessert—a thick, creamy custard topped with a heap of brown sugar.

My stomach growled.

"Hur y'ar." The thin slip of a cook plonked two bowls in front of us. "It'll eat." He turned and took his leave.

The moment the door closed, I was on high alert. Septimus was in rare form and had been since he'd ingested my blood.

"How long until we reach Gaea?" I snatched up my bowl and shoveled the oats and… oat-like *things* into my mouth, nudging aside what might be the hard cup of a squid's tentacle or someone's missing molar.

"Gaea?"

"Yes, fucking Gaea."

Septimus sniffed a spoonful of gray lumps, his tongue slithering out to sample the offering.

"This fare is tasteless at best. I require salt."

I curled my lip in a sneer.

"Are you not some super soldier? Did you complain about the cuisine while on campaign as well?" I weighed the crudely carved spoon in my hand, wondering if it was substantial enough to dig out his other eye. "Did you stop and ask the outlaws to borrow their saltshakers? How embarrassing for you."

Septimus dug into his gruel with such violence the bowl sustained a crack.

"What is embarrassing is your hair." He pointed his spoon at my head and grinned.

Did he...? Did he just...?

"You want salt? I'll guide your gorgeous silver head to the fucking salt. I'll hold you below the surface of the sea and you can drink your fill." Little wisps of smoke wafted up from my hands, filling the small space between us.

"You would not survive an entanglement with me." He ladled the mush into his mouth, one spoonful after the other, sat the empty bowl down, and then smoothed his hair back into its lush braid.

My scalp *still* hurt from where he ripped out the faux fibers. I ran my fingers over the tender spot and watched the corner of his mouth hitch up in amusement.

"And you'll not survive if you ever touch me again, Lord 'Why is it so hard to love me? I know she's not my daughter' Septimus."

"Seal your mouth, consort." Though neither his face nor body betrayed him, the light behind his wicked eyes seemed to dim. He stared at my fingertips where I clenched the table's edge. Tendrils of steam licked up and over my nail beds. "You know nothing of which you speak."

"Do I not?" I cocked my head to the side. "Did Burchard know Lilium loved another? Hmm?" The smoke swirled in earnest now, forming a cloud above us. "Look me in the eye when I address you, Septimus."

His light brows shot to his forehead, and ever so slowly, he let his gaze rise to mine.

"Did the Primus-King love your mother when he forced her on her back?"

I slammed my hands on the table and shot to my feet. Flames licked at my fingers—gold and black sparks bouncing from fingertip to fingertip.

"You know *nothing* of my mother, and I will snuff you from existence if you dare mention her again."

He smirked. He just sat back, crossed his arms over his chest and smiled like the deviant he was.

"Hmmm, so touchy when on the receiving end, aren't we?" His fingers flirted with his collar, unbuttoning one and then two of the buttons at his throat. "You think you know things, but remember who you are up against." He spread the two halves of his shirt, bearing his clavicles.

Fuck me. Man chest.

My temperature spiked... my mouth went dry.

The initiative was suddenly his.

Like a netherhound scenting its prey, his nose flared at the corners. Warm, rosy splotches crawled up his neck, and the knowledge of his burgeoning arousal was not lost on me—never lost on me. The Bond chained us tightly.

My nipples stiffened through the thin linen I wore. They tingled and pressed against the fabric that whispered over my unsupported chest. He leered, watching my body respond against my will, his lust palpable.

"You still have yet to figure me out… what makes me… me." A predatory smile stretched across his lips—so beautiful, so very dangerous. "Would you like to know?"

"I think I'm putting together the pieces just fine. Seventh son, too far away from the throne to be important. A political marriage to a woman who preferred fucking your big brother instead of you. Not man enough to let her go, too much of a man to—"

Septimus flew from his seat, clutching my jaw before I could react.

"Wrong again, loud-mouthed bitch."

He drove me backward, slamming my back into a corner, pressing my cheek into the rough-hewn boards. Splinters bit into my temple. I seized his hand and clawed at his fingers, to no avail, as he ground my face into the planks. His lips found the column of my strained neck.

"I *saved* Lilium," he slurred like a drunkard deep in his cups. "Her betrothed, my shameful prick of a brother, watched from afar while a gang of slavers took turns fucking her aboard their ship—she was the example, you see, to keep the other women they had stolen in check. It took me days to catch up with them, and when I returned her and hung the degenerates from the gallows… Alois said that she was no longer worthy to bear his line."

My chest heaved up and down as my brain fought to process what I was hearing. But my focus dissipated to nothingness the moment he sucked on the delicate spot beneath my ear.

"She worshipped him, and I knew she housed his child well before the incident took place. I took her as my wife when he would not."

"Then you chose misery."

"I *chose* to do what was right."

I snapped back to reality and fought to dislodge him—tried desperately to keep his body from pressing further against mine. He was warm, hard, and fit me perfectly.

"When was it *right* to Join with a traumatized woman and impregnate her time and time again? You did her no favors. Keeping Kairus and her locked in your home—yes, of course I know about that—it's disgusting, just like you for forcing yourself upon her, wife or not."

"Forced her?" His barked laughter sent chills through my body. "She snuck into *my* bed, groaning *his* name into my ear. And yes, I prayed each and every time that she would bear me a child—one that would not be taken from me."

"Is that supposed to forgive your actions? The shit you heaped upon your family? The hatred you hurl?"

My vision swam as his fingers dug into the sides of my throat and squeezed, forcing me to my knees. He crowded my space, blocking any chance of retreat.

"Until you, consort, it was that hatred that kept them away from me... that allowed me to find peace in my misery." He forced my gaze to his. The ice in his eyes melted away, replaced by flickering blue flames. "A solitary glimpse of you, and my heart unleashed itself from decades of confinement... and I will not forgive you for it."

"Septimus," I breathed, lost in the poignancy of his tragedy.

"Let me have you," he whispered, voice low, vulnerability in his expression. "Just once, let me taste you, experience you beneath me. Allow me to know what it is to be with someone that I have not paid to pretend... and make it hurt, Eira... make me feel again."

I froze, enslaved by the man who would be my master.

He wrapped me in his arms, pulling me to my feet.

I threaded my fingers through his and pressed his hands above his head. Our lips met.

Chapter Twenty-Six

EMOTIONAL COMPLEXITY

Cato

Sixteen more hours. Two more meals. Lightning strike... two... three... four... thunder. Five seconds... one mile from the ship. Good. The weather would match my mood, and I would welcome the diversion of a storm-tossed sea.

"You have snored atop your enemy's still-warm viscera. You sleep fine when Eira shoves her feet between your thighs and latches to your body like a paralysis demon." Ambrose yawned so loudly it was more a shout. "I can have the captain send in his first mate if you require a cuddle. He is fleshy in a not-as-delicious-as-she-is way but may be an adequate enough substitute until we find her." He scrubbed his beard, finger-combed it to perfection and then did the same to his brows, running a thumb over each to ensure not a hair was in disarray.

I rolled over in the bed that was too soft for my soldier's spine and stared into a pair of solemn eyes. Sometimes I forgot how earnestly idiotic he could be.

"All these years I chalked your senselessness up to your mother being some pock-marked streetwalker and your father an unknown merchant's cock, but it obviously runs deeper than your parentage."

Ambrose huffed and shook his head indignantly.

"And you emerged from the loins of an overweight desert maiden and a broken-tooth conjurer... and yet." Ambrose crooked a finger. "Come here."

"Freeze in the nether," I scoffed, elbowing him in the ribs.

He grabbed my waistband and shirt, tugging me close, but I fought him off.

"Ambrose, for fuck's sake, I'm fine. Leave me be."

"Nonsense." He stopped pulling and opted to instead scoot himself toward me, forcing his arm under my head. "Ho-hold still, dammit. Let me snuggle you. Cease y-your struggles." He closed his arms around me and squeezed me into a vice-like hug. Were we not already sagging in the godsdamned rope-strung mattress, I would have tossed him on his giant fucking head.

"No, Cat, you are not fine." He compressed his arms harder, making it difficult for me to inhale, and then locked me in place with a heavy thigh across the stomach. "We have slept in each other's arms to stave off the cold, shared bath water *and* underclothes. Your dick may have taken a foray into the depths of my gloriousness, and, yes, we fuck the same woman. But we are friends, confidants above all else."

"I would counter these are proof that we are entirely *too* close and that I have earned a measure of personal space." His arm dropped from my chest and settled around my waist; he brought his mouth to my ear.

"Space to be a standoffish little bitch?" His high-pitched giggle filled the cabin, and I would be a liar if I said it didn't alleviate some of the tension between my eyes. "Talk to me, Cato. Man-to-man. Sort-of-lover to sort-of-lover."

Godsfuckingdammit.

I sucked in the air and let it rush out in a single burst. Being able to fully engage when my reason for existing was halfway around the continent was challenging, to say the least.

I gave in... a rarity.

"Ah, Ambrose, I cannot quiet my mind." I sat with my thoughts for a moment, shuffling and stacking them in a way that allowed me to articulate my feelings. "I am running a hundred scenarios through my mind, and at each of their ends, they merge into the same vexing conclusion—we find her, and still, she is not mine." I wrinkled my nose at the tickle of Ambrose's pelt-like chest hair as he forced my head between his pectorals. He stroked the back of my head like I was some fucking pet and whispered indecipherable sounds. How Eira found this pleasant was beyond my reckoning. "Also, what if she *did* choose Septimus?" The question slipped out, and I wished immediately I could take it back and lock it away.

I glanced up at Ambrose. Or tried, but had my head forced back into his fluff.

"Cato?

"What?"

"If she were happy with Septimus and I chose to let her go... would that be a sign that I loved her?"

I swallowed hard, tempering the fear that churned in my gut.

"No." *Now set her aside and go fuck the entirety of the Monwyn army instead.*

A rush of hot air hit my forehead.

"Ah well, kiss my cheek and say goodnight."

"Fuck off," I said, shoving him back and turning to my side.

Wet lips smacked against the apple of my cheek, the wiry hairs of his beard sticking to mine. *Gods, is this what Eira experiences when I kiss her?* I would revisit the beard oil Ambrose gifted me on my last name day. Though frivolous, she might enjoy it.

Finding a more comfortable position, I willed my mind to rest, while the sway of the ship lulled me into a state of blissful semi-consciousness.

Sleep, at least, would hasten our reunion.

"Cato?"

My eyes cracked open.

"What, Ambrose?"

"I like sharing her with you." He shifted again, nestling closer. "I enjoy watching her please you and feel so fucking proud of her when she elicits a response from your surly self. My wife is so confident, so exuberant in giving and taking her pleasure." He drummed his fingers against my hip. "And when she looks at us, like we are her reward, while at the same time knowing she is absolutely worthy of our attentions... It is an entirely new level of emotional complexity compared to my past pursuits, and it makes me—"

"—wish you still prayed to the Goddess, so you could thank her for bestowing upon you her greatest creation?"

Ambrose clicked his tongue.

"I was going to say makes me want to tongue-fuck her tight, ruby entrance while you watch. But your sentiment is sweet all the same."

I opened my mouth to make another acerbic comment but thought differently.

"And why do you think that is, Ambrose?" I inched my hips away from him. The talk of sex and Eira had turned my cock to granite.

"I think, dear Cato, because as much as we think we own her... it is quite possibly the other way around." His hand dropped low, and his fingers wrapped around my arousal, tightening briefly. I closed my eyes and clamped my jaw shut. "I think *this* is all hers." He pressed his hips to my ass, his erection insistent at the crotch of his pants. "And so is this." He released me, my need to spill nearly crushing. "Now, go to sleep." Ambrose shoved me aside and then wormed around. "You will find your relief soon enough. And then I shall have mine."

Chapter Twenty-Seven

TRUTHS BE TOLD, YA HUR?

Eira

"You didn't expect that, now did you?" I panted loudly into the room as I pressed my back to the wall. "Has it ever happened to you before, Septimus?"

"N-no," he stammered.

"Well, so you know, for your future attempts. I... I much prefer fucking people I can stand to converse with for a period of ten minutes o-or longer." My mind grew fuzzy as I peered into Septimus's desire-laden eyes... delighting in the part of his lips... the way his hips jerked in my direction. "And as much as my womb *thinks* it wants to grow your pale little goblin spawn, my head knows better." *I think.*

I swirled my thumb around my clitoris, nearing my climax. My middle and index fingers swept in and out of my body in short, measured strokes. That remarkable sense of tightening pressure strengthened in intensity, and I knew that in seconds all nether would break loose.

"Y-your penis got you in trouble, didn't—oh gods—di-didn't it?" I spread my legs wider and rubbed myself faster as I stared at him from the chair I sat in, hoping the bed concealed my lower half. "Never forget, Septimus, I'm a Troth, first and foremost. Cho-chosen—fuck, fuuuck—by the Goddess." I massaged my breasts and pinched my nipples, reaching into my baggy, half-buttoned shirt, wishing they were someone else's fingers... doing my best not to dive onto Septimus's dick like an orca seeking a seal dinner. "Now, when I—oh, ohhhh, yes—when I finish, I'm going to free your arm, just one, as a courtesy."

"Trickster whore," Septimus groaned loudly, a deep and guttural sound of need. He yanked against the ropes that bound him. His wrists were raw against his bindings, and his erection strained heavily against the crotch of his pants as he struggled to free himself. "Cock-teasing daughter of the Depraved One. I will separate your arms from their sockets."

The sight of him trapped and enraged was fucking decadent.

"Release me. Now." With each inhalation he took, his broad chest strained against the knots of the rope net. "Cut me from this web and replace your fingers with my steel."

"So you can further assault me? I think... no."

My eyelids fluttered shut. I tossed my head to the side and arched my chest as my orgasm—my third orgasm—pirouetted through my stomach and down my legs. My passage pulsed around the two fingers still nestled deeply inside my entrance, and just the barest flick of my thumb on my clit was too much sensation for my body to handle.

"I'm usually a one-and-done kind of woman... Well, that's not entirely true since your nephews came into my life." I slid my fingers slowly from my vagina. "Saying that out loud sounds gross." I laughed. Clearly, orgasms did wonders for stress relief. I stretched my arms up over my head, ready for a nap.

"Consort, my bindings."

"Bindings... right. Yes."

I stood, wiped my fingers on the tails of my linen shirt and, while buttoning my knee-length pants, marveled again at the sight of such a powerful man subdued. In my faked yet sexy-as-fuck tussle, he'd been clueless to my nimble fingers, hard at work, stretching open the rope knots in the empty net above us.

His fault, though. If he couldn't tell the difference between subterfuge and fondling, that was on him. Lashing him to the ceiling had been much easier than I had ever expected—like myself, he was not in control when the Bond crested.

"I assume you are unaware that all—and I do mean all—Nortian children are expert netters?" I yawned deeply, the day's exertion catching up with me. "Netting is a generational craft. The littles practice making pup-sized nets throughout the year and then present them as tribute to the king at the annual Whale Festival." I stretched my fingers and studied my hands. "I suspect I could knot up your chin hairs and catch a fish faster than you could travel to the market and buy one."

"Spare me the tales of peasantry," Septimus sneered, his face pinched in frustration.

"You were ripe for the plucking, Protector."

"Consort! For the gods' sake."

"Fine, fine. Right or left?"

"Left."

"Wait. Answer me first. Where are you taking me if not Gaea?"

I picked at the tight knot, pulling just the precise tangle of—

He struck with one hand, grabbing my neck and pulling me so close the tips of our noses touched.

"Pants." He sucked the air between his teeth as he stared into my eyes. "Unbutton them."

Oh, of course.

His hips bucked into my hands as I reached for his closures.

"The smell of your nectar taunts me," he whispered, lowering his lips to my ear. His silver braid swung and fell over his shoulder, the soft tail whispering against my neck.

"My nectar?" I laughed, still too pleased with his capture to resist egging him on. "I wish my vagina smelled of roses. Or, if I get to choose, maybe lemon cake."

One button undone and he was thrusting into my hands. Another and his head dropped back between his wide shoulders. I popped the remaining two buttons and reached for the ties to his small clothes.

You are going to see a penis—an appendage made for urinating. This is an act of kindness, not an act of the most carnal fucking delight... one of-of cataclysmic proportion!

I steeled myself and pulled the silky ties—immediately the Bond surged in intensity.

His erection was warm and heavy, and though it curved up, pointing toward his navel, it somehow fell into my hands.

Fell. Yes, fell.

My fingers skimmed the velvety skin of his length—a byproduct of the boat rocking, no doubt. It was the same swaying motion that caused my fingers to slide across the three glinting steel bars that ran along the underside of the smooth flesh.

A bead of moisture gathered at his tip.

Life.

The æther flared, my lusts still not satiated.

"You know where this belongs, just as I do." Septimus gathered the droplet on his fingertips, spit into his palm and dragged his fist along his arousal, squeezing tight and then reaching under to cup his sac. I traced the thick vein that ran down the underside of his length with my eyes.

I was mesmerized.

Enchanted. That had to be it... I was enthralled... under a spell, as if charmed by the creatures who swam the seas enticing sailors to their doom.

"Spread yourself. Show me the repulsive gash between your legs."

"No. Absolutely not."

You have a choice, Eira.

I turned away.

"Bend."

Choose to walk away.

"Show me what the Goddess intends for me, Eira," he demanded.

I caught my waistband and began to slide the too-big pants over my hips, moving as if in a dream—this wasn't real.

Make yourself stop.

The gathering wetness at my apex cooled pleasantly, now exposed. I stood and looked back over my shoulder.

"Release me." Septimus yanked at the rope that secured him, his raw skin tearing and welling with blood. The metal anchors tethering the ropes to the ceiling creaked, and I could see tiny fibers parting from their strained twists as he stretched, reaching for me. He was a man parched, standing inches from a well—a starving man, locked away from a feast.

"Choose me, Eira, and we will give the Goddess what she wants. We will walk in her divine light, as she has called us to do." He wrenched the rope again. Fresh blood bloomed through its fibers and seeped, spreading along its length.

"Th-the Goddess. She *has* called us... I want... Septimus."

He circled his hand around his base and glided up his cock. His knuckles turned red as he gripped himself roughly and plunged his hand down again.

"Taste me, enchantress... but score me with your teeth as you do. Leave your mark amongst my scars."

Mark him, Eira. Own him.

I wanted to crawl to him like a fucking peasant, begging her king for a morsel to eat. His scent taunted me: spearmint, clean and sweet... the antithesis of the man himself.

I took a step toward him.

My palms skimmed down his stomach. I trailed my fingernails over his hipbones and down a white scar that cut through the dark-gold curls that were the same color as his brows.

"The gods will it."

I nodded, caught in the tangled spell he wove around me, binding my self-sovereignty.

Dropping my head to his chest, my tongue sought his flesh, licking and lapping, sucking his nipple into my mouth.

"Their will," I whispered, wrapping my fingers around him, working him between our bodies. "Not ours."

"This is our path."

"Our path," I agreed, floating on a current of æther. *Mine.*

I sank my teeth into his chest until I tasted iron.

"Fuck!" Septimus roared. "Enchantress."

Ropes of semen splattered across my pubic bone and hit the hem of my shirt. I scooped the stickiness into my palm. His hand cupped mine, and together we lowered them to my apex.

"*Granddaughter.*"

I stilled.

"Septimus, did you..."

My fingertips tingled with an intense energy that rapidly spread up my arms.

"*Granddaughter,*" a voice whispered.

I jerked my head over my shoulder, seeking her... the goddess Merrias.

"Grandmother? I hear you." I cocked my head, trying to locate the direction of the voice that seemed to be all around me.

"*Come to me. Do not fear the path.*"

I nodded.

"Consort? What is happening?" I stepped backward, and Septimus lunged forward, swinging his arm out to capture me, but I was already out of his reach. He groped for the blade in his boot but came up empty; it was the first thing I'd confiscated after his capture. He began frantically plucking at the knots.

I walked away.

"Eira, stop. Where are you going? A woman cannot be found aboard a Monwyn ship. Your vest. Don your vest and cap..."

His voice faded away as I placed my foot on the step that would take me above.

"*Yes, child, continue forward,*" Grandmother Merrias's voice carried on the winds.

"I'm coming," I answered as I surfaced, shirt opened to my navel, fevered breasts cooling in the night's crisp air.

Shouts broke out across the lamp-lit deck, and shadowy figures ran across the boards.

"Cap'n!" a distant voice hollered. "A siren walks amongst us! Cover yur ears, men!"

"Goddess preserve us..."

I stepped around a sailor who had fallen to his knees, ignoring both his lewd demands and the fingers that fumbled against my thighs.

I continued on, one foot in front of the other, trusting my grandmother to guide me.

A hand caught my wrist and yanked, heaving me against a sweaty chest. Alcohol-laden breath assaulted me when clammy, stiff lips covered mine.

I let the æther flare.

His scream sounded like justice.

"Foolish men. Come to the rail, granddaughter."

Sailors jumped out of my path, some falling to their knees in prayer, others covering their eyes with their caps.

"Climb up, child. Stand tall."

The wind shoved me backward as I scaled the banisters, but I leaned against them, holding steady. There was lightning in the distance... but I knew no fear.

My short hair flew, whipping painfully into my eyes. One foot found the top rail, and I could hear the sea crashing against the ship's prow. The other followed, and I felt the ocean in my veins—unbridled power, infinite authority.

"Derros, keeper of the seas, your servant beckons you." The words tumbled from my mouth of their own accord. "Grant me safe passage."

"Eira!" Septimus yelled in the distance. "Eira, do not!" His voice grew louder, more fearful.

"Now, granddaughter, show these boys what true faith looks like."

I jumped.

Snap!

My shadow raced across the water, twisting and spinning as the black waves reached out, trying to snatch me under. I evaded them, flowing seamlessly between the swells, skating over the white foam when they collided.

There was no direction but forward—my spirit knew the way.

"Offer yourself to Derros, granddaughter. Show him your allegiance—trust him with your life."

I soared into the star-studded sky—praising the Goddess and the glory she built with her divine hands. I was a child of the night, a shadow swimming in infinite darkness.

The crescent above bathed me in its glow as I rose higher and higher.

"Now," Grandmother Merrias said. *"Make your offering."*

I dove, hurtling toward the sea. I had nothing but myself to give.

"Lord Derros, Sinker of Ships, Great Provider, Anchor of Hope. The remains of my ancestors flow within your depths, and I make of myself a sacrifice to join them."

The water opened, parting into a yawning mouth of churning foam. It rose, swirling into a twisting spout supported by the fearsome winds that ripped across the seas.

I drove myself into the center of the massive eddy and plunged into the abyss.

A wreath of bubbles encompassed me, accompanying me downward, pulling me under until I reached the ocean's floor. Like a hastily poured glass of water, the skittering froth quieted, forming a solid, transparent orb around my form.

"Eira, Born of the Light and the Dark, Daughter of Moon and Star." She emerged from the ruins, Mother Merrias, the Goddess's child of judge and jury. She glowed softly in the murk, her celestial body illuminating the darkness. As she moved forward, the shadowed surroundings became visible.

Merrias's light shifted as she rounded a sunken altar whose offering bowl, though still attached, was covered in a green moss that undulated in the water's current. The massive open-jawed head of a fearsome dragon appeared, looming high above us. The ornately carved figurehead, still attached to a sunken ship's stem, seemed to sprout from the sand like a giant wooden orchid, its hull long since disintegrated.

"What is this place, grandmother?"

Colorful fish—bright yellow, blue-striped, and iridescent green—swam in and out of my... ah, I was still in shade form. There was no reaching out to touch them.

Merrias came closer.

"Derros allowed us to breach his underwater realm. Your devout Nortian tribe has long been faithful to him, so he acquiesced to my demand for a space far from mortal ears."

Unlike the fully armored Merrias who once came to me in the dilapidated statue garden of Cordillaria, this time, she appeared in a flowing gown of gray. The diaphanous material of the high-necked garment covered her from throat to foot and rode the currents as she moved. The brown rounds of her areoles showed through the sheer layers, as did the spirals of muted red that began at her collarbone and flowered diagonally across her stomach to her hip—maybe tattoos, perhaps paint? Ropes of pink and cream pearls circled Merrias's wrists and glinted throughout her textured brown hair; rings of gold covered her battle-hardened hands—not a single finger boasted less than three. Her face was devoid of any décor or added color, but despite that, the unique beauty she exuded was more extraordinary than when she showed herself encased in metal and leather.

"We converse in the remains of Lænnan, a coastal city that once existed in the Kingdom of Hain… before the giants doomed it to its underwater grave."

A casualty of the Great War.

Grandmother Merrias stood in front of me. Her eyes roamed over me, taking in my form, inspecting the wisp that I was.

"A battle will soon break out on the gods' plane," she stated plainly, her face not giving any indication of her feelings on the matter. "Though humans will not bear witness to the violence, many, like yourself, will sense its reverberations." She squinted and passed her hand through me. I felt a strong ripple, my form parting and reforming. It was not a pleasant sensation.

"*Why do they fight, grandmother?*"

"You." She spoke without malice, no hint of blame. "They fight over you, my blood."

"*Me?*" A sudden sharp snap and my flailing arms and legs were mine once more. I gasped and struggled, gulping water into the lungs that screamed for the air and found none. I floundered and then kicked, as if by instinct seeking the surface that I knew lay too far above me to reach.

And then, the bubbles that surrounded me pressed into my mouth and ventured down my throat, expelling the water that collected there, providing a barrier. They sealed themselves across my nostrils, and at once I received a refreshing surge of much-needed air as they cycled in and out of me.

Merrias's hazel eyes widened slightly.

"Granddaughter, you had more hair last we met." A tender smile pulled at one side of her mouth. "It is different from the norm, but not unbecoming."

I didn't return the smile, still fighting off the fear of death by drowning. I scrubbed my hands over my face, or at least tried to. The air barrier didn't allow for contact.

"Why me? Why the nether would the gods—fucking Lykksun, Maressa, and Josa—fight over—"

"And Viktos, and even myself… and others your world does not yet know."

I stopped my tirade, pondering her words. *Other gods? War?*

"I need to sit. I grow weary of existing through historic events that I have no control over."

I attempted to kneel but couldn't drop—the buoyancy was all wrong. With both legs crossed, however, I sank slowly and awkwardly from where I'd stood on the ocean floor. When my rear met the stable surface, a tentacled creature morphed as if from the sand itself and scurried away on a multitude of limbs. A cloud of particles, stirred by his flight, fell around me, reminding me I was nothing more than a single speck in a chaotic fucking world. Another feeling that I was tired of.

"Explain yourself, Grandmother. Right now and in puny human terms, not your gilded goddess tongue." I leveled my gaze at Merrias, meeting her eyes full-on.

Her smile deepened.

"Goodness, you are more of me than I thought." She crossed one ankle over the other, and then gracefully sank to a lying position, curling her legs and propping herself up on one elbow.

"I would apologize for my tone, but my lapse in manners is warranted." I rocked back and forth, pushing and pulling against the water's weight, pretending it was Ambrose's arms wrapped around me instead of my own—his murmured, nonsensical sounds of comfort.

Her laugh was deep and husky... the carelessness of her attitude was not at all reassuring.

"Never apologize for your beliefs. Too often, human women feel the need to do so... You all could learn something from the harpies."

I watched the ripples created by my movements, the specks of sand as they floated around me.

"We war over precedence, rank, and power... but it is in *how* we wage battle where you are significant." Merrias dipped her finger into the sand and idly drew a series of lines, dots, and arrows—I'd seen Cato do the same when planning formations. "You will play a significant role." She raked her fingers through the diagram, dashing it away.

"Since last we met, I have discovered that you carry the energy of *two* gods within your body, not one, as assumed. From my line, you house the Mother Goddess. And it would seem the man from whose loins you sprung is himself a carrier."

"The fucking Primus-King? The thought of sharing anything beyond the air we breathe is revolting."

"Yes, him. He is not a conjurer, and it was not through birth that he, like you, received a god's essence."

"That's great. So I contain too many god grains and now you want some back?"

Merrias grinned fully and laughed, a rich and hearty sound.

"No, nothing like that." She waved me off. "It took time, but after *persuading* a lesser deity for the information, I learned that, in exchange for a single mote of divine energy, the Primus-King pledged his kingdom, his children, and all of Ærta to the god who has designs on unseating my mother."

"Who would be so bold as to go against the Goddess?" I inquired.

"Leyometh, Gate Keeper of the Nether, Guardian of Fire."

"Leyometh?" I smacked my palms over my ears. Not that it would stop me from hearing her. "The slavers of Baldorva worship him exclusively, yes?"

"They do." She lowered her chin, nodding once.

"Again, where do I factor into this mess?"

Merrias tilted her head and stared up at the surface, like she could detect something other than darkness.

"Eira, you contain the energy of two gods—the Goddess and Leyometh poured into a single vessel. Your children will house those energies with the potential of a third line running through them... all dependent on whom you are bred to. Can you imagine the strength that your child will possess? Multiply your powers, and if they too are born conjurer... Never has something so powerful been considered, not even in the gods' realm. The child will be unlike any other—they will reverse tides, change the trajectory of the future."

My heart palpitated against my chest wall, and anger rose, a knot in my throat.

"So, it's not about me at all. It's about my worth as a child bearer? Well, I've already got two kids on ice back home. You can have those and leave my womb alone." My mind conjured up an image of Evandr and the pirate Larm.

"The Frostborn? They will eventually rise—through great pleasure and great pain. But it is not them I speak of. It is my next granddaughter."

"Of course," I said, while shoving my fingers through the hair that floated in front of my eyes. Sarcasm dripped from my words.

Merrias sighed.

"Your triple-blessed offspring are what the gods vie for—Eira Verras Chulainn, Obligate born, Conjurer, Twice Blessed."

"Twice cursed," I spat back. "If it's the Bonds you speak of."

"You do not care for the men the gods chose for you?"

My hands fell to cradle my stomach as she arched a brow.

"I care for one of them."

Her smile was knowing, and it made me entirely uncomfortable.

"How much do you know of the Bonds, Eira?" she asked.

I shrugged.

"I've gleaned some knowledge from a few difficult-to-decipher sentences from Magis Raephin's diaries, that and the musings of Father Burchard."

Merrias fiddled with the pearl drops in her hair. Her smile transformed to a sneer, no doubt at the mention of her former lover's name.

"Conjurers, like them, have but an inkling of understanding. The powerful conjurers can achieve Primitive Bonds—create mind-altered lackeys who do their bidding—but only a god can bestow the Mated, Fated, and Infinite Bonds. Well, the gods and *you*. Your doubled deity's blood is how you managed the Infinite Bond with the Monwyn king. So no, it's not *just* your womb that is important."

Her hazel eyes, more brown than green, bore into mine, a reminder that she knew my thoughts whether or not I spoke them out loud.

I felt the momentary pang of emptiness of the missing Bond with Burchard.

Merrias sensed my reaction.

"We feel that loss as well when the Bonds break." She pulled a hairpin from her hair and held it out to me. From thin chains dangled iridescent orbs of cream and pink.

"The gods feel the Bonds?"

"We do. When we grant them, it takes a piece of us, and when they die, that piece isn't restored. It is why we bestow so few."

I studied the strands of pearls that fell from the hairpin as I pondered her words. The pearls were irregular in shape and in color, not the perfect spheres I assumed they were from further away. I slid it into my long bangs, pinning them back.

Merrias rolled and pillowed her head in the cradle of her crossed arms.

"Many a zealot was created by Bond... and many a Mantle as well. The Bonds are how we influence life on this plane in small or large capacities. Naturally, you and I are Bonded through blood. I oversee you, as you are of my line—a gift from my half-human child. Likewise, Leyometh is Bonded to the Primus-King and, because of that, can influence his actions."

"We are puppets then—to be used as you see fit."

Merrias shrugged and continued fiddling with her hair ornaments.

"Lykksun and I struck a deal to place a Fated Bond in your Catommandus. We noticed the immediate attraction between you and realized that together you would produce excellent offspring. Lykksun's charisma paired with my cunning and Leyometh's insight—your daughter could be an æther-wielding warlord or empress, influential enough to reshape humankind."

My child... Cato's child.

Now wait.

"And Septimus! You fucking allowed—"

Merrias's head snapped to the side. Her eyes shards. The icy glare stunned me to stillness.

"Viktos Bonded to him, on my orders. And never question my rationale for the choice. Viktos's determination is unrivaled, and Septimus clever and devout. He is your Safeguard."

My mind moved at the speed of a penguin sliding on ice. *Viktos, Safeguard... fucking storm god.* The pieces fell into place.

"The weather, the godsdamned storms that break out when we are entangled?"

"Are Viktos's way of pushing you together." A full, beaming smile waved over her face, brightening her eyes. "Is a strong chest not the perfect place to snuggle for one so fearful of thunderstorms?" She chuckled. "He and Lykksun fight tooth and nail vying for their candidate to breed you."

Meddling-ass bunch of...

My fingers wrapped around a conch shell, and I launched it toward the lounging goddess.

It caught in a current and fell less than a foot away, rolling backward and resting against my toe. Little brown legs sprouted from its hollow, and it slowly ambled away.

I wished it would have struck her smug face.

"You know what, *Grandma*? You can go right on back to godstown and inform the whole fucking pantheon that they can cut out the breeding bullshit and leave me be." I dug my heels through the sand, leaving deep trenches. "Bunch of manipulating despots, just like the nobles here on the Great Sphere. I'm going to recommend—as the Chosen, Blessed enigma that I am—that Lykksun and Viktos start fucking and raise a bunch of little hot-headed babies of their own."

Merrias smirked, just a quick and bittersweet quirk of her lips.

"Even with your abilities and birthright, you cannot fight the will of the gods, Eira."

I hung my head. What more could I do? My entire life was "the will of the gods" and had been from before I was even born.

"Merrias?" I scooped up a handful of sand and let the granules fall through my fingers, watching until nothing remained.

"Yes?"

"The Nether Lord. He called me Firewalker, nether daughter, and Leyometh, he's—"

"*Now* you are thinking like the spawn of the Goddess of Judgment." Merrias rolled over on her stomach and let her chin rest on her folded hands. Her wise eyes glittered with intent. "Leyometh is the god of flame and son of the nether god himself—which makes *him* your grandfather, just as I am your matriarch." Merrias glanced to her side and then up to the water's surface. "I ask you, Eira, do you suspect it is Leyometh or his father, the Goddess's own netherbound brother, attempting to topple her?"

Holy fuck.

"I—I... " My mind spun in circles, rivaling the most tumultuous current. *Fathers, mothers, rivalries, gods, children...war.*

There was a distinct change in the water's temperature, and I caught sight of the shadowed bodies of large fish—or were they men?—circling above us. The distinct shape of a trident flashed in the aura of Merrias's light.

"Our time ends, Eira. I will find you again—continue on the path you choose."

One minute I was sitting on the ocean floor, the next, I tumbled from a fisherman's net onto the deck of the Merlann. Slimy strips of seaweed stuck to my body, and a bevy of fish flopped beside me.

"A woman! Cap'n, the siren returns!" A man bellowed, shocking the snowballs out of me. His eyes rolled as he swung his cutlass above his head. "Her bits and bobs are hangin' out for tha world tah—"

His words ended in a harsh choke, and he slumped to the deck. A body's worth of blood gushed from his neck, where his head used to be, seeping between the waterproofed planks, spreading in precise lines.

"There is *no* woman aboard this vessel." Septimus bent and gathered me in his arms. I wrapped myself around him, dazed in the face of the violence. "I do hope, sailors of Monwyn, that I have made myself clear."

The murmurs of "of course, sir,' and 'we understand, lord," were a chorus.

"W-we dock in Lykk with'n the hour, sir."

Septimus strode toward the lower level.

"We are not to be disturbed until then, captain, or this ship will mysteriously find itself dashed upon the rocks with its crew never to be found."

He kicked open the door to our chamber, sending it crashing against the wall.

"Lykk? We are bound to Solnna?"

"Yes. You are a pathetic conjurer, a blunt and useless tool."

With me cradled in his arms, Septimus sat on the edge of the rope bed and stared at the open entrance—ready to strike at any who would dare enter.

I pushed against his chest, but he didn't relinquish his hold.

He plucked the pearled pin from my hair and held it to the light.

"Septimus... it-it's so much bigger than we knew."

Chapter Twenty-Eight

LYKK

Eira

"Lykk, capital city of Solnna. City blessed by the sun goddess Lykksun, Lordess of the Harvest, Mother to Derros, and Giver of Light," the ship's captain extolled the lengthy list of her virtues as we docked.

"It is hot."

So miserably hot.

"You need more descriptors to qualify this level of heat, Septimus." I brushed my sweat-soaked bangs off my forehead.

Septimus looked at me askance and batted at the spikes with the back of his hand.

"Leave it be. There's no helping it." I squinted at him while shading my eyes. "Is there help for you being an absolute mule-headed jerk? Septimus, remove your coat. Silk-lined woolens are not conducive to this clime."

Sneer. Scoff. Face of disbelief. Mmhmm, right in that order.

"The Protector of Monwyn will *not* deliver the Assigned Troth of Solnna to the literal queen of said country looking like some bedraggled pauper."

I wiped the perspiration from my temples and pulled up the last pair of pants Septimus had brought in his bag of costumes. Massive, baggy, and striped green and black. My sweat coupled with their low-hanging crotch was already chaffing my thighs. I drew the line when he had insisted that I wear the wool vest for modesty's sake—or more accurately, I tossed the stifling garment into the sea. We'd fought, loudly, and then "compromised" when he held me to the floor and tied the laces of my skintight linen shirt in "knots so taut a Nortian brat couldn't pick them apart."

I studied him. He was on high alert. His eyes shifted back and forth and up and down, landing on and assessing every person who surrounded us—and there were hundreds. Sweat dripped from the top of his silver braid, down the shaved sides of his head, and onto the front of his pristine linen shirt... which was quickly becoming transparent.

"Fine by me. If heatstroke takes you, several of my problems will be solved."

"Does your mouth ever close?" Septimus took me by the arm and steered me down the ship's ramp and into a world teeming with life.

If I closed my eyes and listened, it sounded just like home.

I allowed myself a moment to forget all that weighed on me, clinging to the scrap of nostalgia. The glug of water hitting the docks as the moored ships rode the waves... the bells tolling, striking out the half hour. Men shouting happily in the distance as they made land for the first time in weeks, and the smell of fresh fish. So very far from Nortia and yet, my soul felt more at home than it had in months.

Something tickled my nose.

"Flutterby!" I squealed, frightening away the most beautiful bug that I had only seen drawn in a book. It floated above us, purple and yet blue at the same time, like a stunning, shifting silk. "Glorious gods." Its cobalt and bright orange mate joined in its spiraling circles, tumbling in and around our heads.

"Butterfly, you imbecile." Septimus swatted at the charming pair, so I swatted his face, striking him soundly in the jaw. His nose flared indignantly, but his eyes... they smoldered with a different sort of flame.

Right.

"You are an asshole." My eyes remained fastened on the somersaulting winged worms. "A really attractive... scumbutt."

"Your insults wound me deeply." He rolled his eyes and then turned in a stiff about-face. "I fear you have born me a mortal injury."

We continued through an open-air market, winding in and out of tent stalls, dodging tensioning ropes and steel stakes. The butterflies trailed us as we made our way.

I nodded to a merchant who held up a fine onyx linen with thick white stripes. Nan would look—

"Lazy woman. Keep up." Septimus caught me by the arm again, but I dug my heels in, refusing to budge.

I couldn't breathe. Couldn't swallow down the sadness.

The orange-patterned butterfly landed on my shoulder, as if sensing my grief. Its wings opened slowly, revealing its rainbow of hues, and then folded again, cloaking itself in its solid black underwing. Like life, I suppose, the beauty is always there, even if, temporarily, we couldn't see it. I inhaled, savoring nature's lesson—remembering the pink complexion and soft gray eyes of my companion.

Septimus's beet-red face appeared before mine. The tip of his nose so close my eyes crossed.

"I will tell you what I told Catommandus years ago. Allow no one to see your weakness if you do not wish it exploited."

"How the nether could a merchant exploit—"

Septimus palmed my head and twisted. Sure enough, the merchant had draped five more lengths of black and white fabric over his arm and was brandishing another as he stuck out his bottom lip in feigned concern.

"Whatever," I grumbled.

Septimus batted at the swarming butterflies again. A third—orange and black—had joined in their merry little band.

"I think they're attracted to the color of your old man hair," I teased, jabbing him in the ribs, wishing that for once he would lighten the fuck up.

"If you wish to watch me rip the wings from their bodies, continue wagging your whorish lips."

He would make good on his morbid promise, so I stayed silent, appreciating how the insects dodged around his silver mane, which was even more striking in the brilliant sunshine.

We ventured past a stall whose owner was lifting handfuls of whalebone spoons from a crate and arranging them in a perfect row.

"Septimus, I'm not actually sold on your plan, by the way." I scurried to keep up with him and tucked my arm in his elbow. He glared at our joined limbs. The æther danced, but it would slow down his determined speed-walk and maybe keep him from passing out. His extremely pale skin was already burning. "We snuck away from Monwyn, assumed new clothing and identities, maintained discretion—sort of—but now the strategy is to walk up to the gates, proclaim my title, and, *surprise*, your Obligate came to visit."

"This was *your* plan."

"What?" I shoved him in the sweat-soaked shoulder, but he maintained his vigilant survey of our surroundings.

"You came away from the palace with nothing more than some Solnnan identification papers and a handful of medication. If that wasn't enough, you made it perfectly clear that you require a conjurer if you are to amount to anything more than an out-of-control weakling, so here we are."

He produced my drawstring bag and dangled it above my head.

"I brought the papers as a contingency plan," I swiped, jumping up to reclaim my property, but he jerked it back before I could grab hold, "because you are a creepy motherfucker who I might need to escape from. And frankly, I only needed you to remain alive for a handful of days until the Mantle arrived at Monwyn and I could return. And now, we are on the other side of the godsdamned continent, and you'll soon die of a sun seizure. Take off the fucking coat!" He darted around, attempting to still my grabby hands, but I was too quick wrestling the offending thing from his shoulders. I wrapped the heavy garment into a ball and tossed it to a seller of nicknacks and oddities... nothing odder than a wool coat in Solnna. "Free, good sir—sell it to the next man headed north." The bemused merchant nodded his head and took the costly garment to his rack.

Septimus spun me around and stepped close.

"Does it give you satisfaction to thwart me? To anger me beyond the limits I thought possible?"

I blinked up at him innocently, batting my lashes like the demurest of maidens.

"It sure as fuck does... and if I had this body, I'd never cover it up." *Did I just say that?* I blinked, ogling the saturated linen-molded chest in front of me. The soaked fabric clung to him, showing off the hard planes of his abdomen—his heavy pectorals and the ridges made by his larger scars. If this is how Cato aged, I was in for a lifetime of living out my fantasies.

Septimus's jaw fell to the ground.

"Are you... Is that a blush? Your cheeks are as pink as my puss—"

"Shut. Up," he clipped out angrily. His sun-scalded cheeks bordered on fuchsia now.

A butterfly landed on the top of his head, unbeknownst to him.

I pressed my lips together and held back the chuckle threatening to bubble over. In my current state—anxious, bewildered, afraid for at least six differing reasons—I'd take my joy where I could, and right now, pestering this asshole was my everything.

He stormed away in a huff, remembered himself, and then turned to glare until I rejoined his side.

We came to a tall, stone gate that was flanked on either side by heavy gold fencing. The barrier's patrol consisted of a contingent of guards wearing white tabards stamped with golden suns. Bronze vambraces covered their forearms, and through the hip slits of their heraldic garments, I could see they wore cuisses and greaves of the same metal. All held spears at their sides, but those, surprisingly, looked like replicas of the Monwyn weapons—heavy and forged from steel.

"Septimus, what does Monwyn receive in return for the weapons you trade?"

"Fruit."

"Are the metals you pull from the ground stronger than what they have here?"

"Yes."

"And fruit is valuable enough to trade for weaponry?"

"Yes."

"What's the name of your horse?"

"Daisy." The vein in his forehead pulsed. His eyes nearly bulged from his head.

"Daisy? For the equine monster that charged a troll without one misstep? Are daisies those the little white flowers with the yellow puffball in the middle?"

Septimus's lip curled as he shook his head in disgust.

"Daisies are hearty growers, resilient, and rise year after year."

I patted his shoulder, but he shrugged my hand off. He was violent levels of upset. "We'll buy Daisy back when we return," I promised.

"I will not be returning." He rummaged around in his bag.

"Of course you—"

He snapped around, jaw clenched.

"A Protector who deserts his post may only return when his head is to be mounted in front of the city gates. Wait here, do not move."

He charged off, my stolen identification papers clutched in his hand.

I stood under the shade of a massive purple-and-white striped tent. Flowy curtains formed walls around the pole structure, casting slow-moving shadows across the ground. Vendors gathered under it, preparing skewers of lemons, oranges, and a purple something or another. Others were crushing mint into the bottom of glasses, releasing a sharp yet refreshing aroma.

"Lovely lady, can I tempt you?" I looked up into the acne-spotted face of a young woman carrying dozens of skewers in each hand. Each shined with a glistening coat of melted sugar. She approached me at the same time Septimus returned to my side.

"Four, please."

She nodded, sending her blonde-streaked curls bouncing, and held up both hands, allowing me to select the sticks I wanted.

"The cost is one coin," she spoke softly in Solnnan, while looking up through her lashes at the brute who was doing his best to push himself between us.

"Septimus, buy these please. Four coins each," I lied. He shoved my drawstring bag into my chest and dug into his own satchel.

"Four? That is preposterous." He slapped the coins into her hand, sneering down at her like he sneered at everyone. "Monwyn should be charging three times the market price for the meat we supply them."

I thanked the woman and handed Septimus a skewer. He stared at it like I'd handed him a meal coated in poison.

"Keep whatever rude thing you're going to say in your mouth and instead fill it with this delight." I bit through a citrus slice and had to close my eyes. I thought the fruits we ate in Monwyn were succulent, but these... these were otherworldly. Fragrant, acidic, and perfectly sweet. There were no fruit trees in Nortia, and the food at Verus was tithed from across the continent—maybe some of the flavor was lost in transit. "Surely, this red thing is served at the Goddess's table."

Septimus's eyes went flat.

"What?" I asked, stuffing not one, but three sugar-coated fruits in my mouth. "They're good."

"Not only will you greet Her Majesty stained and frumpy, but with teeth that appear to be infected by a bleeding disease."

I let my eyes roll back and pressed my breasts into his chest, groaning. He tensed.

"What ails you, consort?" He shook me by the arms.

"Septimus, I-I need you to take me. Right now. Feed my weak woman's womb your-your man seed. *Heheheh*. This fruit, it has melted my inhibitions and..."

His mouth gaped, and I stuffed the largest of the juicy, red chunks past his lips, barely avoiding the teeth that clamped shut.

"Now, *Timmy*, she will assume a red grin to be a cultural trait. Perhaps they are stained thusly when a Monwyn leaves their kingdom? Or when one is in mourning?"

"Do not refer to me as *Timmy*."

"I'll refer to you however I please."

Septimus swiped a hand across his brow and pointed to a massive urn that stood at least a story tall. Its fire blazed, and a man stood at the end of a ladder, carefully pouring oil into the basin.

"Why the fuck do they have a godsdamned bonfire burning?"

I ignored him and strolled away, waving at the group of guards who were clearly waiting for us.

"Well met, all! I'm Eira, Troth Solnna. I look like shit, probably smell like it too, but I am incredibly excited to be here."

The guards smiled back... They fucking emoted.

We were absolutely *not* in Monwyn anymore.

The contingent parted, revealing a person dressed in a lapis-colored linen skirt that hung low from their thin hips. The fine, pleated cloth boasted lines of stylized magenta suns and was held in place by a belt of gold plaques studded with purple amethysts. They wore no shirt at all. Instead, their hairless and soft-breasted chest was oiled to a gleam, and covered by a swag of amethyst and crystal necklaces in various lengths and colors—some deep purple, others nearly red.

My chest constricted tightly. Cato, my man, would have regaled me with all the boring details of why each stone was unique... and I would have hung on every dull word.

"And to answer your man's question, the Deathless Flame burns at all times to guide the ship's home and reminds the citizens of our motto... Solnna eternal."

"Solnna eternal!" The guards chanted in unison, striking their spears on their shields.

"What did they say?" Septimus asked, his fingers biting into my shoulder.

I ignored him yet again. He may be high on the societal food chain in Monwyn, but here I outranked him.

"Troth Solnna," the unnamed person held their hand to their heart, "Her Majesty sends greetings and will see you this evening. You and your..."

they bent at the hip, peered around me, and leveled their ocean-blue gaze on Septimus—"escort are to be treated as members of our family." They stood back up and flung their arms wide. "I am Trivio."

I walked calmly into Trivio's embrace, opting not to jump into their arms as I had the other Solnnans in my life. Not because I didn't want to, but because Septimus, who couldn't understand the language, was grumbling so loudly that he was drawing the attention of guards and citizens alike.

I melted into their arms. It made little sense, but just like Richelle, Kan, and Mariad, this Solnnan stranger radiated acceptance.

"You smell like sunshine and vanilla," I said into Trivio's fleshy chest. They were deeper complected, like Cinden, but instead of her rosy undertones, their skin reflected a warm ochre.

"And *you* smell like you've been on a boat for many days."

"Ha!" I laughed freely. "I must look more than a little washed up."

"What did they say? What are you going on about?" Septimus interjected, stepping toward Trivio. I intercepted him with a palm to his chest, keeping him at bay.

I released Trivio, who then motioned our group forward with a bow and flourished hand.

"Septimus, they said you are as handsome as you are hairy."

Icy-eyes glowered.

"Consort... Troth Solnna. You will translate with fidelity or—"

"Or what? You'll turn that ship back around and go home?"

Septimus stewed—literally and figuratively—as five guards and our guide led us to a steep wooden staircase built onto the side of a sandy hill.

Trivio turned to address me.

"The dune barrier surrounds the entire capital. The mounds are maintained and monitored throughout the year, which has ensured our security. Much to her credit, no full-scale invasions have occurred during the queen's reign."

I surveyed the terrain, looking left and then right. The straight line of a manmade blockade stretched as far as the eye could see.

"What an ingenious precaution. Does the sand shift in the wind?"

"It does, yes. Guards and engineers walk the dunes regularly for repair, so that storm or foe alike are met with early resistance."

My breath came quickly from the exertion of the climb, but my efforts were rewarded.

"Holy Goddess above."

Any comparison of Solnna to Nortia ended at the coast.

The city was awash with ivory, green, and gold. Domed buildings rose high from every direction, their beaten-copper roofs shining like the sun itself. The largest structures were built from textured gray stones, while the more abundant wood-framed dwellings were painted white and stood one to four stories tall. Pink and purple curtains hung from paneless windows, some parted wide, blowing in the breeze, others pulled tightly, blocking out the sun's rays.

Tall, limbless trees that didn't look like anything I'd ever seen grew in clusters around the city, and their long, many-fingered leaves fanned back and forth.

As we descended the staircase, the townspeople walked about, embracing and waving to their neighbors. Both men and women wore sleeveless shirts that hit anywhere between their knees and ankles, and the children, no matter their gender, ran around in linen skirts in a variety of bright colors and patterns.

"Solvale Palace is the heart of our world." Trivio pointed to a multi-level wonder, as if I could have missed *it* or the colossal, gleaming sun that sat atop its tallest spire. "Each ray is forged from a different metal found on the Ærtan continent, one for each of the Kingdoms, remembered or remaining. We are, all of us, forged from a single soul."

Septimus pushed forward.

"And look, your escort has made a friend." Trivio eyed the butterfly that still clung happily to Septimus's head.

"What are they saying? Leave nothing out. Your safety is—"

"They said the sun atop the palace is made of various metals, and the silver one reminds him of your handsome glowing beard."

If looks were swords, Septimus's blades would be the sharpest.

He growled low in his throat, and Trivio's tight smile told me that they likely understood the common tongue. *Our secret.*

I waved to an older gentleman sitting on his front porch as we walked through a dusty street. He raised his hand, greeting me in return. We passed through a neighborhood of single-story homes. Greenery covered their roofs and vines snaked down, nearly to the ground. Red and blue berries hung from them in tight clusters.

"Trivio, the plants?" I gestured to the homes.

"The families grow the fruit on their houses and harvest it for the dye makers. In return, once weekly, the palace passes out bread and rice to the families who provide."

"Well, that seems just brilliant, but Trivio, I see little children and elders, but where are the others?"

"Ah, yes. Children, from their seventh year to their fourteenth year, attend tutoring while their parents carry out their daily jobs or service requirements. Citizens from their sixtieth year onward choose between watching over the littlest Solnnans or spending time keeping the grounds tidy or assisting our healers. That is the reason for all the tiny ones toddling around."

"I'll be damned. In Nortia, our elders tend to stay indoors and nap." I faced Septimus. "What do older Monwyns do when they can no longer toil or serve?"

He stared at me blankly.

"They die."

CHAPTER TWENTY-NINE

HARD SHELL. TINY CRACK.

EIRA

After walking the foliage-flanked streets of Lykk, we made our way to the palace through a series of hedge-lined tunnels and archways, all covered in the same greenery as the rooftops. The arches sported fat bunches of orange and yellow berries, and the side walls supported clusters of violet that hung down in cone-shaped bunches. Trivio pointed out which fruits you could eat right off the vine and which would result in a day's worth of tummy troubles—understandably, the troublesome bites were relegated to the higher points of the archways, for the safety of children.

"This is the entrance closest to your accommodations, which are located on the palace's westernmost side. Follow me." With a clap, Trivio signaled an armored duo of women to open the door. "We will assign a servant to each of you. I will report to the queen shortly, and House Steward Salsia will see to your needs until evening."

We came to a whitewashed hallway with four doors. A sweet, creamy fragrance that inspired a warm sense of calm carried on the light breeze that somehow blew through the hallway, ruffling my hair. I placed the smell immediately—it was the same faint aroma that clung to Mariad Keagan, Kan Keagan, and Richelle—my beautiful Solnnan friends. Trivio stopped at the second door in the line. "Troth Solnna, your quarters." They placed one of several iron keys dangling from a set of gold chains on their hip, into the lock and pushed, revealing my home away from home.

"Just beautiful." I did a turn just inside the door, taking in my surroundings. "Trivio, when I imagine the place where the pixies live, it's this." I did another twirl.

"Truly? Pixies?" They made a sour face and then shrugged.

The high walls were pale lavender, the ceiling painted the same but with a massive white sun in its center, outlined in sparkling gold leaf. The wall lamps were just like the ones used in Monwyn, but convex shades made from iridescent abalone shells and tiny mirrors affixed to their chimneys, allowing for a soft glow to bounce off the walls, instead of harsh light. The floors I recognized—huge rectangles of gleaming white marble with tan veins covered the entire surface. I'd bet my buns they were harvested from Monwyn quarries. And I couldn't wait to run my bare feet over the rugs that topped it. They weren't wool but were incredibly colorful, woven tight, and looked substantial.

"Are you familiar with the Solnnan style of furnishing?" Trivio asked.

"Beyond pillows used in the place of couches, not so much."

"Come with me." Trivio walked to the center of the main room and nodded at a short-legged table, surrounded by plump cushions of white striped with celery green. "For entertaining guests or taking your ease, we prefer the intimacy this arrangement creates."

"It's lovely, thank you."

"You are most welcome. Now, the bed and bathing facilities are located through here."

At the back of the chamber, two burnished copper panels formed walls on either side of an arched opening. We walked through them and into a second room that I'd assumed was a balcony, given the abundance of light streaming through.

"Bed to the right, behind the curtain. To the left, a selection of clothing and jewels befitting our Solnnan Troth." Trivio smiled confidently and nodded in my direction. "You will find our sense of dress accommodates many body shapes and sizes. You should have no trouble finding several garments that please you. You will look stunning in that cranberry-and-aqua silk." They lifted a hand to a row of opulent fabrics and gestured toward tall shelves containing glittering headpieces, necklaces, and bracelets. "Salsia can pierce your ears if you wish."

I would be a liar if I said I wasn't tempted by the collection of earbobs on display, but considering my nipple piercing closed up when I became the shade, it would be a fruitless endeavor.

"You are too kind. But I think, Trivio, what will please me most is to wash the sweat from my eyes," I said, wiping away the stinging drips as they fell from my forehead.

They nodded knowingly.

"You will acclimate over time, but until then, the rainbath will soothe you." They motioned us forward and pushed open a set of heavy eggplant-colored drapes. Gold tassels the size of my palm and sun-bleached shells strung in swags from their hems, weighing them down.

We stepped through to a living wonder.

"All the fruits here are edible, and many citizens will bathe and break their fasts simultaneously."

"This... this is a marvel," I said in a stunned whisper.

A half-circle balcony, floored in hand-painted tiles depicting both the sun and phases of the moon, stretched out at least twenty feet past the curtains. The walls—I swung around, wanting to gauge Septimus's reaction to the paradise we walked into—were covered in lush, fruit-bearing vines and flowering trees. Jasmine and something akin to vanilla perfumed the air.

"Septimus..." He was gasping, bent over, palms on his knees. His face was a dangerous color. Even the whites of his eyes were pink on their corners. My fingers went straight to his shirt, but he grabbed my hands and held tight. "No, sir. I need you alive for just a little longer."

And I actually did.

I'd been thinking. If a woman couldn't gain passage on a ship bound to Monwyn, I'd need him to gain my admittance, or at least be there if I were found out again. Only Monwyn merchants would brave the north, to race home before winter truly set in. My other option to get home was traveling alone through the desert... where I would succumb to heat death or the creepy critters I heard prowled the sands.

"Begone." Septimus endured two ties of his shirt being unfastened before he shoved me away.

"Fine. You are such a fucking man." I reached up over his shoulder, plucked a red and brown berry, and popped it into my mouth, all the while shooting him my most unsympathetic look. *Shit.* "Ack!"

The fruit's texture was hairy and dry, and it clung grossly to my tongue. I clamped my teeth together, not wishing to spit its horrid flesh upon the ground and upset my gracious host.

Trivio chuckled and came to my side. They pointed to a waste vessel where I rid myself of the rough little ball. They plucked another from the same tree.

"You peel the lychee. Its outer layer is not the draw. The fruit itself, however, is refreshing." They handed me another from the same tree.

I revealed the almost translucent flesh and held it to Septimus's mouth, but he looked away, refusing it. Shrugging my shoulders, I hesitated just briefly before giving it another go. *Oh... ohhhh.* A floral-yet-sweet burst of flavor tantalized my tongue. I picked another and peeled its outer covering away.

"For a *cooling* rainbath, turn this knob in the morning or evening." Trivio indicated a copper handle that stuck out from the balcony's exterior wall. "If you prefer a sun-warmed experience, turn it from when the sunshine peaks until dusk."

I turned to the knob they indicated and, with a twist of the wrist, the ceiling began to cry.

"Sorcery," Septimus muttered behind me.

"A-fucking-mazing."

Trivio's tinkling laughter filled the space.

I looked up and under the perforated square of copper that extended out from under an overhang, expecting to see a cloud. There was nothing above it.

"You will find cleansers here and lotions there. The wastewater will flow down the sloped flooring and—"

"Provide water to the plant life." I turned my stunned face to theirs and shook my head in awe. "Trivio, this is wondrous." I held my hand under the water, absolutely astonished by the thoughtfulness of the design. "I would like to bathe now, before it gets any warmer."

"As you wish."

Trivio stepped toward Septimus and waved his hand back toward the bedroom.

"Sir, I will show you to your..."

Just as I thought, an Ærtan speaker.

Septimus crossed his arms and stood as stone, narrowing his eyes in distrust.

"These are the rooms in which I stay. Argue and I will remove your hands from your wrists."

I intervened, stepping between them. To their credit, Trivio didn't wilt.

"Septimus, don't be ridiculous. There are guards."

"I trust none of them with your safety. You saw what they wore—I could eviscerate them in a matter of seconds."

"Ooooo!" I stomped my foot on the ground and made note of the surprise on Trivio's face. "Cato is overbearing enough. Pick another personality trait."

"Do you, consort, honestly think that your tiny fists perched upon your child-bearer's hips will dissuade me?"

We locked eyes, but it was I who broke the contest of wills. Septimus, alone in a foreign land, was likely to cause more harm than he would in my bedroom—Goddess preserve.

"It's fine, Trivio. He can sleep in the front room on the pillows."

Trivio didn't hide their disapproval. Their eyes widened and bounced between me and Septimus.

A knock sounded in the main room.

"That will be the servants."

Trivio ushered in a team of six.

The female servants wore two strips of linen cloth, one tied around their breasts and the other around their hips, the tails of which hung to their knees. The single male in the group wore a gray loin covering that tied at the hips, much like my own underwear.

"Our guests require washing. Scour them and then oil their bodies. Offer them the normal services afterward and then see to their hair and cosmetics."

"What did he say?" Septimus asked, as Trivio switched back to Solnnan.

I stifled a yawn and began removing my clothing, excited for the pampering to come.

"They are going to scrub us down and oil us up. The scrub may hurt, but the—"

"No."

"No?"

For perhaps the second time in his life, Septimus made an expression other than his angry scowl or horny scowl. This face was... disgusted scowl. His lips turned down, and his eyes looked... haunted. Hurt?

"Look, I'm crusted over like the barnacles on a boat's bottom." Something about the way Septimus held himself gave me pause. *Is he nervous?* No... but I couldn't place the look. Something certainly had him more out of sorts than normal. "Trivio, we will wash while they set up. Thank you." I didn't turn to look at the servants, too worried I'd see judgment pass over their eyes; they were sure to know I was a woman Joined.

"A-as you wish." Trivio shooed the servants along and all of them disappeared into the main chamber.

I wasted no time tossing my salt-stiffened pants in a heap on the floor. My shirt quickly followed. I turned my body to the breeze, the warm air cooling the sheen of perspiration that coated me. A little hesitant to stand fully under its flow, I reached out and let the sky waterfall cascade over my hands. Once I convinced myself I wouldn't drown, I'd fully commit.

"Consort, I..."

"Have a massive erection?" I joked, dipping the top of my head—just the crown—into the water's flow. "Look, it's become easier for us, I think, with the hands-only protocol we've unofficially established. If we focus on, like, wrinkly grandmas in unattractive underwear or Monwyn men lording over their wives, we can endure the Bond. Yes? Take your time, of course, but you stink."

Septimus growled, still standing in the same spot and still not disrobing. He rocked back and forth on the balls of his feet.

What in the world? I'd fully expected the need to æther blast him when my shirt left my shoulders.

He shifted, crossing his arms over his chest.

A thought struck me.

"Septimus? Does... does my body offend you? I don't know how the Mated Bond affects attraction. You resemble Cato, whom *I* find mind-blowingly handsome, but if it just compels us to mate... I never considered it may be an involuntary reaction of your body and not—"

"Your body pleases me enough to use it."

Damn. Shouldn't have asked. Even his kind of degrading admission sent my twat into a slick spiral. I braved a step forward and immersed myself fully into the water, letting it run over my face and down my shoulders—drowning would be a blessed distraction.

"Then why, with an open invitation to peruse my naked form, are you still standing there clothed?" The question tumbled from my mouth.

"Because," he bit out harshly.

Because.

Naw. Something wasn't right.

Our previous encounters... was he always clothed? On the balcony, when it stormed that night, he was shirtless. I saw the scars that—oh, no. That night I had walked through the doors, interrupting his solitude like our Bond was all the permission required to do so. Even at the inn, he was careful never to face me straight on.

"Is it... are you..." I tried to find the right words, mulling over how they might affect him. I blinked the water from my eyes and turned to face him. "Septimus? Do you not like your body?"

He said nothing, just remained the unmoving monolith. I closed the distance between us, dripping wet from head to toe. He didn't budge as I neared him, but I was truly fearful for his wellbeing.

"I've seen you, and I think you're beautiful... and Septimus, for your health and that alone, you cannot remain in your Monwyn wools. I'm so sorry; it didn't cross my mind that what I find appealing you may see as... as... Can I help you undress?"

He looked down his nose at me, eyes sharp but not overly hostile.

"Look, stay alive long enough for me to kill the Primus-King, save the world from divine turmoil, and get back to my men. Okay?"

I gently laid my hand on his elbow. He didn't pull away.

"Come with me. I won't judge you. I won't breathe a word."

He filled his chest with air, and I threaded my fingers through his, pulling him toward the rainbath.

"Why don't you keep your shirt on? We can wash around it."

He stepped closer, closed his eyes, and nodded.

I kneeled and made quick work of his boots and socks—they smelled horrific.

I stood but didn't look him in the eyes, fearing it may cause him further stress.

And why the fuck do I care if I cause him stress?

Because maybe he hated his body... and I couldn't stand that for anyone. There are so many ways to perceive beauty. His body was a masculine work of art. How could anyone loathe such a testament to survival, the body that I ached for on a primal, instinctual level? But then again, it wasn't me who had to live with whatever had caused his scars.

I didn't allow the hunger on my face to show when I worked his pants and underclothes over his hips. His arousal swelled and colored deeply, and when his erection bobbed as he shifted to allow me to slide his clothes over his feet, the fluttering in my womb began to multiply into a twisting current of desire. In a matter of seconds, a maroon-colored flush crept across my chest. My breasts would soon swell as my nipples tightened; my pupils would dilate.

"Shirt?" I asked. "Off or on?"

He didn't answer, just shook his head and stepped fearlessly into the fall of water.

I joined him, washed my hair fast and then rinsed.

"Turn around."

Septimus complied and turned his back to me.

I seized the thong that held his thick braid and tugged. He flinched hard but stood his ground.

"I just mean to wash it." I slowed my forceful ministrations. He was on edge, and as much as I wanted to end this intimacy quickly, they'd just cause him additional strife.

"And debase yourself like a common serv—"

I smacked his wide back, and he shut his mouth with a snap.

"I wash Ambrose's hair daily. He enjoys it, and so do I, judgmental prick."

"Fine." Septimus stood up more stiffly, straightening his spine and neck.

"Can you, uh, bend down slightly? This is normally not a standing activity for me."

He dropped quickly, squatting on his heels with his elbows draped over his knees.

Monwyn butts. My gods, but they are pert globes of perfection. I willed my eyes away and turned to the task at hand. Raking my fingers through his thick braid, I arranged the strands into a curtain, the tips of which nearly touched the top of his backside. Even his hair was physically warm to the touch—that could explain why so many Solnnan men kept theirs shorn. I lathered the earthy and sweet soap in my hands, admiring the breadth of his shoulders, his strength in his stocky build. I massaged my fingers into his scalp, rubbing hard like Ambrose enjoyed.

"Mmmm." The hummed moan slipped from my lips.

Septimus spun and stood in a single swift motion, catching my wrists in his hands.

The rainbath poured over his head, rinsing the soap from his silvery crown. His shirt was translucent. My eyes riveted themselves to the deep scars that covered his torso and arms—a fresh red cut along his shoulder, the half-missing peach crescent of his nipple.

"How... how did they happen?" He looked over my head, scanning our surroundings once and then again. "Wait, no, I'm sorry. I shouldn't have asked."

The lines between his eyes deepened when he flicked his gaze to mine.

"Violence is how."

I swallowed, feeling guilty for finding his trauma so frustratingly arousing. I forced my face to be neutral, let my shoulders fall, but my nipples betrayed my feigned detachment and peaked against his chest.

Septimus set my fingertips on his collarbone and then traced them to the point of his shoulder.

I didn't speak, and I didn't pull away.

"For each life I have taken, I have removed a piece of my own flesh."

Holy Creator.

I kept my face impassive despite my surprise.

"I pay penance to the Goddess for slaying her children."

That was not what I expected to hear.

His body was a monument to guilt… to shame. And my heart broke for him.

"I… may I?"

He closed his eyes and then shrugged out of his shirt, bearing himself to my gaze.

The æther swarmed, but I hid my base desires where I could—Breathed in slowly; settled my heart. I paid recognition to the self-inflicted cruelty but did not pass judgment. We all grieved differently. Maybe I could convince him to seek a priestess who was trained to help those who stood close to the edge?

I gently rubbed the soap into the fresh wound on his shoulder.

"The sailor I beheaded," he said, tilting his nose toward the laceration. "The bit of blood you forced upon me has caused me to heal faster than normal."

I nodded, understanding.

"It may for some time," I explained as Septimus skimmed his fingers over the back of my hand. "Can I ask you something personal? You don't have to answer me if it's too much."

He shrugged indifferently.

"Pain?"

"Allows me to feel."

"Receiving it or inflicting it?" He slid my hand across his chest to graze his bare collarbone again. My soapy hand glided over his dusting of curls until he flattened my palm underneath his. I felt the steady drum of his heart.

"Both," he admitted. "But your hands are a source of confusion."

I stared straight ahead, not able to peel my eyes from where we touched. "How so?"

His erection nudged my stomach as he leaned in and let his lids drift shut.

"Because under *these* hands," he lifted my other wrist and placed it on his mutilated pectoral, "I would swear that I feel… creation."

Creation.

An avalanche raced down my spine, causing my skin to break into bumps.

"Troth Eira, the tables are ready," yelled Trivio in a surprisingly insistent tone.

I stood rooted, not willing to break from the moment.

"Septimus, he said—"

"I can, through context, surmise the intent of his message, consort."

We pulled apart and completed washing.

"You don't have to participate in the next part, Septimus. Stay out here and dry off. I'll ask a servant to lay clean clothing inside the door where you can dress in private." I encouraged the separation more for my benefit than his.

"Do that."

I rolled my eyes at his brusquely delivered retort and made my way into our apartment with nothing but a towel secured around my chest.

CHAPTER THIRTY

I HAVE SEEN THE LIGHT!

AMBROSE

"Of course I am buying it. When you miss your wife, you search near and far for a gift to show her how desperately you pined for her. Oh wait, you have no wife. My apologies." I lifted another jewel, inspecting its sparkle... or lack thereof, in this case. "It is a wonder she tolerates you at all, Cat." I tossed the azure diamond back onto the tray of gems. "You know, I am beginning to think that your *personality* is the reason you remained a virgin for so long."

I didn't bother to look at my grumpy sidekick; I knew the little imp would burst into angry flames if I continued chiding him.

"Fuck off, Ambrose, and for the Goddess's sake, take those off your face."

"I will not." I held the fourth pair of spectacles up to my eyes again and lowered them, repeating the action several more times. "I am absolutely miffed that both Mama and Father neglected to have my eyes seen too. Was it because I am the adopted child?"

Cato's furious little face shifted in and out of focus as I flipped the frames up and down. "It is like I am truly *seeing* for the first time. The colors are brighter, your pores *much* larger, and I believe... yes, you are, in fact, showing signs of early graying."

Gods, could a spine be stiffer?

"Ambrose, speed up your transaction or I will—"

"Don't be petty because you are aging poorly." I handed my purchases to the merchant and gave him my sauciest wink, hoping for a discount. "WRAP THEM BOTH PLEASE!"

The man's head snapped back, and he hopped away, cowering in a corner.

"Gods, Ambrose, fucking shit Scion." Cato stepped in front of me and held his hands up in a gesture of supplication. The merchant slowly made his way back over. "He speaks another language. He is not hard of hearing."

The merchant began wrapping my acquisitions, but he kept one eye constantly on my delectable form—of course he did. I pursed my lips in a seductive pout. I wanted that discount.

Cat elbowed me in the ribs, driving me back.

"Oh, I'm sorry, Catommandus, *world traveler*." I bent low to ensure he heard me. "If I lack cultural poise, it is because of your meddling in my life. You and our father allowed me to leave the kingdom but once, and even then, *you* tagged along. Ugh, just pay the man."

"Thank you, sir." Cato tossed a few gold coins into the man's hands, nodded, and then rudely shoved the package into my stomach. "Now put your ugly spectacles away and seal your lips when we approach the gate."

Cato marched away while I perched my new gold frames on my noble nose.

I chased him through the bazaar.

"Can you imagine how Eira is faring in this heat?" I asked when I caught up to Cato. "If she gets upset and goes all toasty tits, she is liable to burn the entire city to the ground."

Cato said nothing, just stomped his way to the massive garrison gates that lay between us and the palace.

"Prince Catommandus of Monwyn, born of His Majesty Burchard, traveling in the presence of Prince Ambrose, second in line to the Monwyn throne." He thrust his identification papers into the faces of a group of guards. "We demand admittance."

The most handsome of the guards looked Cato up and down like the thirsty, horny lecher he probably was. I leaned over Cat's shoulder and glared hostilely at the man who dared allow his beady little eyes to roam over my wife's plaything. How dare he? Eira would never share Catommandus with anyone but—holy mound of troll turds. The writing... I could see "citizen of Monwyn" clearly written across the parchment's top. I angled the glasses from my face and then set them back again. A miracle. A veritable miracle of humanity.

"State your business, *Prince* of Monwyn," the guard yelled from behind the gate.

He didn't believe us—the knave. Sarcastic piece of peasantry. I would handle this riffraff.

"We seek a bride for my brother." I shoved my way in front of Cato and struck a confident pose, one palm draped over the hilt at my hip, the other in an open gesture of enthusiasm. "The representatives who attended my recent Joining spoke endlessly of the fertile beauties who call the Solnnan lands their home."

A figure approached, ambiguous in stature and dress. They bowed low, finally showing us the respect we were due.

"Yes. We recently received a missive from King Burchard that he sought a wife for the reclaimed *Prince* Catommandus. And with his passing—Goddess keep him—King Aberus must quickly take a bride, hmm?"

A quick mind, but no match for this cunning diplomat.

I drove my heel into Cato's toes and ground down hard, shutting his mouth before he could tell the man otherwise.

"Indeed. My brothers find themselves lonely as they are forced to witness the state of bliss my wife brings to me. Did she arrive on time?"

They nodded, playing right into my hands.

"I can only imagine the energy she brings to your kingdom, Highness. Your lovely wife, our Assigned Troth, is as effervescent as our wines." They clapped their hands merrily and grinned, showing two rows of gleaming white teeth. "I left her and her companion in the rainbath just a few hours ago."

"Oh, that's just lov—"

Do fucking what?

I smiled so serenely, nodding my head, that the Goddess no doubt wept in her gilded throne up above.

"Come again?" Cato barked from behind me. "She was left in a fucking what? And I most certainly am not here for a wi—"

"Hush brother." I blocked Cato with my bulk as he tried to sidestep me "Such a rude little gnome—needs a woman with claws." I bowed my head in a gesture of thanks. "I am delighted to hear my consort arrived safely I demanded she take a different ship as a measure of precaution. Could you imagine the devastation if the *entire* royal family were to meet Derros in an ill-fated maritime misfortune?"

"Goddess forbid," our host said. "That was clever thinking on your part." They tapped a finger to their temple and from the side of their mouth asked the guard, "Are the papers authentic?"

"They are well in order," came the response.

I tightened my pectorals and stood taller, pleased with myself.

"Well then. Welcome to Solnna, most noble mountain sons. I am Triv-io!"

Chapter Thirty-One

"P"

Eira

"What's the scent? I've smelled it on people, in the cleansers, in the air."

"Coconut," said a face sweeter than Cinden's. "You can eat it, moisturize your skin with it, cook with it. It's our most versatile commodity, and that is its natural scent."

Salsia, as she introduced herself, greeted me with a hug that rivaled one of Nan's polar bear embraces. I burst into tears, of course, and the rosy-cheeked, fae-blessed woman patted my back and let me cry for a solid five minutes before coaxing me onto the sheet-covered table. For that reason alone, I was obligated to love her.

"This might be the only aspect of Verus that I miss." I laid back, naked as a newborn, while she rubbed the buttery soft moisturizer into my sore hip. I didn't even realize until now how much being god-hoisted back on the ship's deck had battered me. "After poisoning us or making us battle the Scions, the Devotees usually treated us to something similar... before more suffering." I chuckled under my breath while Salsia pressed her thumbs deeply into my calves.

"Do you wish to proceed with the hair removal? You are *very* furry. Are the northern folks hairier on account of the cold?"

"Noooo," I drawled out. "But also, maybe?" I kicked out in reflex as her hands found my ticklish foot. "I had the hair removed once, but it's too painful to maintain."

She tsked, and I looked over my shoulder. Salsia, a young woman with her hair combed into a tail atop her head, gave me a look that clearly read "wimp."

"I worry the Assigned Troth of Solnna may look out of place when she arrives to dinner with opossum pelts strapped to her legs."

I took the hint as she tapped her fingers on the backs of my knees.

"Ugh, I'll do the calves. *Just* the calves."

Salsia did a terrible job of stifling her laughter, which only became louder as her gaze drifted up and over my head. I followed her widening eyes.

Oh, gods.

"Septimus, discomfort or not, you can't wear the coat with that. I know you have—"

Wack! He brought the back of his hand across the cheek of the young servant, who had rushed forward and tugged at his heavy garment, most likely misunderstanding my comment.

"Do you speak *this* language, dog?" Septimus glowered over the cowering boy.

I scrambled to my feet, shoved myself in front of my *Safeguard*, and threw protective arms up, blocking him from youth huddled at my back.

Heat twisted from the center of my chest down my arms.

"Never lay your hands on a servant," I hissed. "Never!" I bent low and pressed my palm to the young man's face, hoping to ease the sting. His hazel eyes were wide with fear.

"The idiot attempted to pry the coat from my body. Is theft not a crime here?"

I urged the poor thing to his feet, my face sympathetic, and then wheeled on my fucking Bonded Mate.

"He tried to keep you from dying and looking absurd, you high-strung piece of shit." I balled up my fists and puffed out my chest. "Septimus, number one: You can't wear the wool. It's too fucking hot. Two: I refuse to present you to the queen of *this* country while you mock her culture by wearing a filthy-ass coat and body odor-soaked shirt atop one of the finest fabrics I've *ever* laid my eyes on."

He glanced down at the royal blue-and-vermillion pleated skirt he wore while gritting his teeth. The knee-length garment was magnificent, the dyes rich, and the silver disks sewn onto the tips of the crescent moon's pattern were spectacular, unlike anything I'd encountered back home.

"Frippery. I am clothed like the most indecent of whores."

"Oh, indeed. Goddess, protect me from the allure of your sculpted shins."

I wanted nothing more than to punch the uptight ogre in his pierced dick, but even more, I didn't want the palace servants to think that I was complicit or condoning of vicious attacks. I turned to the male servant who was now on his feet, albeit standing at a distance.

"My husband, Prince Ambrose, received a gift of thick arm cuffs from this kingdom. Can something similar be procured? As well as several necklaces, like Trivio wears."

The servant nodded and scurried away.

"I will *not* be wearing *any* of the foolery he brings forth."

"Or you'll remove his fingers?" I cocked my hip to the side. "Chop off his arms?" My arms pushed my breasts up as I crossed them, and Septimus's eyes flicked straight to my cockeyed nipples. "You *will* wear something presentable. And you *will* apologize when he returns."

He bent and brought his face inches from mine.

"*Will* I?"

"Surely, as the nether is frozen." I stretched my neck until my nose touched his.

"And *you* will be making me." His cruel laugh was as damnably seductive as his stupid face.

"Do it and I'll give you a kiss."

That probably shouldn't have been my first offer... fucking Bond.

He fake gagged.

"A pittance. I do not crave your kisses. Why would I even consider such an offer?"

"You don't?" I asked in a tone more surprised than I intended. *Am I offended? Should I be offended?* "What do you want in order to not look like the patchwork motherfucking pirate of the high seas? And sex is off the table," I whispered, the last part for his ears alone.

"I'd prefer it on the table anyhow." He tilted his head to the side and smirked.

"Septimus," I warned.

"Your screams then." Like the lowest point of a flame, his eyes smoldered blue. "That is my price."

"You get those on account of your existence."

I hated the smile that curved his sinful lips.

"The hair removal... I perform it."

"You? Debasing yourself like some 'common servant'?"

He arched a brow, awaiting my answer.

"I will do it *if* you lose the coat, *and*—"

"Deal."

"I'm not done with negotiations." I inched closer, invading his personal space. "You will, sincerely, apologize to the servant. You will also provide him compensation for a week's worth of pay in reparation for the poor treatment he received." I challenged him head-on.

His jaw ticking as he considered my proposition.

"Is it the apology that has you pondering this long? That says a lot about you." I twisted on my toes and sauntered toward the table, purposefully swaying my hips. "But I'm telling you... this hurts... a lot."

I bent a knee on the table and leaned forward, shifting my leg, so that Septimus would see a quick flash of my prettiest pink, and then laid flat on my stomach.

Was it wrong to exploit him? Most likely, but his outfit was as criminal as his actions.

I wound my hair around my finger awaiting his answer.

He snatched a chair and dragged it in our direction, then propped his feet next to mine—the dirt from his scuffed, leather tall boots flaked off, soiling the sheet.

Derros's dick. Could I get him into sandals if I let him slap me around?

Salsia brought a waist-height table to our sides, doing all in her power to suppress her bemused expression at Septimus's silly ensemble.

"Solnna's wax is more refined than any other used on the continent—our apiaries supply wax for silk batiking and skincare. It starts with a deep respect for the bees, including giving them access to the blooms they love the most. Your skin will be soft and smooth, and glow from within."

"Excellent. Now, Salsia, you will teach my companion how to properly apply and remove it."

"I will what?" She balked, her eyes darting between mine and Septimus's.

"You heard correctly." I nodded animatedly. "Because of the outright, disgusting levels of misogyny practiced in Monwyn, my marriage contract states that only a man of my family can touch me. So he," I flicked my fingers toward Septimus, "will be doing the removal."

"B-but the lotion was okay?" Salsia questioned, while drumming her fingers on the top of a small yellow jar.

"Mmhmm, I can see why there is confusion. Lotion is fine. Putting something *on* my body, like helping me to cover myself, is acceptable, but taking something off... that's a punishable offense unless it is done by a male family member. Strange custom, isn't it?" The lies rolled so easily off my tongue.

"You mean entirely fucked up?"

"Quite." I nodded in agreement.

"And you chose to be there? To live in a place so regressive?"

"I did," I said with a resigned sigh. "If you ever meet Prince Ambrose or his delightful brother, you'll understand why."

"What is she saying, and why did you mention Monwyn?" Septimus asked, moistening his lower lip with his tongue, unintentionally causing delightful little pulses of blood to rush to my core.

"She is saying she will show you the proper technique and then you will take over." Septimus looked up at Salsia dismissively but motioned for her to proceed.

"Salsia, please go slow and overemphasize the—GAMMOND'S GLORIOUS GLACIERS!"

Well, that was one way to douse the flames between my legs.

In quick and blinding succession, she ripped the wax once, twice, and a third time from the back of my thighs. The fine hairs of my rear were subjected to the same brutal treatment. After every pull, she pressed her cool hand against my flesh, which did little to ease the sting—perhaps her touch was a gesture of solidarity.

I gripped the sides of the table with both hands and squeezed.

"My turn," Septimus muttered, rubbing his palms together.

"Starfish next," Salsia sang out while her confident hand slid between my cheeks.

My eyes widened, but before I could do more than protest, my hams parted, and a hot glob of goo coated my puckered flesh.

"Translate the following: pull swiftly with the grain of the hair so the initial swipes aren't as painful."

"Septimus, she says 'pull swiftly with th'—GODSFUCKINGDAMMIT!" It wasn't so much a scream that followed, but an earsplitting squeal that sent Salsia running around the table to my front. She squished my cheeks—my face cheeks—in her hands.

"The front is much less sensitive, Troth Solnna." She pointed downward and put her hand over her heart.

Behind me, Septimus dragged in a ragged breath.

"It sure as fuck will be, because I'm not doing it."

I bolted off the table, plucking at a remnant of wax still clinging to my asscrack.

I made it three steps.

Septimus snatched me around the waist. He lifted me over his shoulder and then hauled me back to the table. My back hit the leather, forcing my breath from my lungs... and then his eyes loomed above mine.

"We continue," he whispered.

"I think not."

"Do it for the emotional wellbeing of your poor little serving boy," Septimus simpered, his voice mockingly sweet.

Oooooh!

"Do it then."

"This is normal, Troth Solnna?" Salsia asked, her concern clear. "If you are in danger, tell me. I will alert Trivio, and we will have him arrested."

I gripped the edge of the table, digging my nails into the soft top.

"He wants my screams... I'll give him my silence," I said in Solnnan.

Septimus smeared pearlescent blue wax over my shin and calf and then used both hands to rip the whole godsdamned section off.

I stifled a yawn.

"Hmm." Septimus tsked and went for the wax again. He smoothed it over my upper thigh, this time going against the direction in which my hair grew—exactly the opposite of how Salsia had shown him.

This motherfucker.

Blue eyes, like the sky, drilled into mine. He tucked his bottom lip into his mouth and yanked.

My thigh streaked red as a wildfire swept across my skin.

"This is all making me rather sleepy, Septimus. I'll pass the time with a short nap."

I crossed my arms behind my head and closed my eyes.

I needed to vomit. To cry. A hug. It wasn't the worst pain I'd experienced—not by far—but it brought up echoes of other injuries I'd suffered. Pushing those away, I thought of Cato, my disgruntled songbird, enduring the isolation of prison, of Ambrose having no cuddles or nighttime kisses, of the little motherless goatling whose life Aberus so callously took.

"You're doing well, Troth Solnna, and your companion is... thorough." Salsia leaned over and inspected his work, nodding appreciatively. "If being a brooding ass doesn't work out for him, he could find work on my staff."

I laughed at the thought of Septimus in a loincloth, which helped relax my entire body. I opened my eyes, staring up as if bored.

Septimus jerked his hand back.

Holy hounds of the nether.

My labia departed its vaginal home like a soul speeding to the cradle.

Tears leaked from my eyes, but I played it off as a symptom of another yawn, dabbing their corners as I opened my mouth wide.

"You can take it, consort." Septimus's throat worked up and down as he spoke. His voice was low and thick. "I have seen you laugh in the face of agony... Firewalker, Flesh Eater." He peered down at the hands still working their way around my body, spreading, ripping. "Your strength is what makes me weak for you... not your submission. Gods above, when at last I take you... I want your battle. Bite me, scream *just* for me... *your* Protector."

His hands hovered just above my vulva.

Pain tore through my most sensitive area as he yanked one last blob of wax from the middle of my curls.

I gritted my teeth but made no sound.

"Septimus, you will never have access to that part of me. *Never.*"

"Sure, sure." He nodded. "Continue thinking that while you writhe in anticipation. But until then..."

He glanced down between my legs and chuckled.

I followed the path of his eyes.

"Salsia... fetch more wax. Go now." The woman shot off, and I came up swinging. "I'll fucking kill you!"

Septimus darted right and evaded my fist.

"It is clear you learned the subtle art of faking it from priest-esses—whores remain observant, even when they feign calm."

He walked toward the closet, shrugging off his coat as he fled. I gave chase.

"You fucking branded me... you marked me with a godsdamned letter?" I hefted my lower stomach, looking down at the travesty. A perfectly *P*-shaped patch of dark hair mocked me. The letter was flawlessly rendered and, like the black-and-white skin of an orca, contrasted wildly with the pale flesh beneath.

"The *P* is for Protector," he said in the over-animated voice you would use when teaching a child their letters.

My face fell.

"*P* is for punching your godsdamned face!" I balled my hand and struck, smashing my fist into his jaw a moment before launching another

A long-winded and satisfied sigh filled the alcove.

"More." He ducked and grabbed my rear, hoisting me into the air, pressing my back into the copper partition. "Do your worst, enchantress. You are made for this... for me."

My legs wrapped around his lean waist, and his hips hammered up and into my apex. His rigid, silk-covered cock settled against my clitoris, rubbing the sensitized flesh. He angled his head to the side, exposing his neck. My tongue shot out, tasting his skin before I grazed a prominent tendon and bit down.

He relaxed in my arms but forced his neck harder into my teeth.

"Gods above, harder."

My eyes drifted shut. The smell of him was intoxicating. Spearmint and sun and...

"You're beautiful, Septimus," I whispered into his ear. "So flawed, so beautiful, but I don't want this..."

"The storm that rages between us is—"

A knock sounded sharply against the chamber door.

Septimus dropped my legs to the floor and took off at a run, pulling a dagger from the back of his skirt.

Voices rose in the front room, and the telltale sound of a scuffle ensued.

"You, boy, will not survive this fight—hotheaded lout, just like the rest of them," a muffled voice declared.

Salsia must have altered the guards.

"Pull your weapon, diminutive gnat," Septimus answered.

I jerked a random dress from its hanger, tossed it over my head, and ran toward the ruckus.

"Septimus, stop—"

I froze in place.

"*This* is the Monwyn you settled on? It's no wonder the Primus-King slipped past your defenses." The red-rimmed eyes of my small-framed instructor met mine.

"Gotwig?"

"We are to proceed to the queen's chambers at once." Gotwig eased the knife from the nick on Septimus's throat. He produced a handkerchief from his pocket and offered it to my furious, and handily subdued, Safeguard. "Eira, I'm pleased to see you alive."

Chapter Thirty-Two

AMBROSE, FOR FUCK'S SAKE!

Ambrose

"**I** am spouseless, Ambrose? Is that how you see my relationship with her?"

I spun in a circle, admiring the shrubbery. He would eventually calm and see the genius of my design. I was entirely unworried and stopped to cup a fragrant white bloom to my nose. *Delightful.*

"Cat, your plan was what? Force your way through the gates, toss her over your shoulder like some demented piglet, and stake claim on that which you do not legally own? This is not Monwyn, and she is not *your* property."

Cato scrubbed his hands through his greasy mop of hair and ratty beard while I made my way to a seat where I could more readily enjoy the view.

"The true crime here is that your ass remains so perky despite following no regimen." I tensed my outer thigh and kicked out to inspect my diminishing musculature. "My glutes headed south with the ship." I settled into the cushy chair and steepled my fingers while Cato bathed.

Suds ran down his face and formed a ring around his gross little feet. He growled, an angry sound that wavered in and out with the tempo of his over-vigorous scrubs.

"Are we to believe that she and, and fucking *Septimus* bathed in this contraption... together?" Cato slapped the rainbath's knob, halting the water's flow. He shook himself like a sopping dog, spraying water on everything in a five foot radius, including myself. "I swear to the Goddess, I will kill him, Ambrose. I will bludgeon his reckless skull and then blister her ass with my bare hand."

My eyes narrowed.

"Unless it is meant to bring her pleasure, you will not lay a hand upon my wife." I dropped my foot to the floor and rested my elbows on my knees, his comment striking an odd chord within me.

Cato whipped around. He closed the distance between us, dick swinging, body dripping, and stood in front of me, tensing and releasing his hands.

Delicious. How I never saw it until Eira pointed out his grizzly charm is beyond me.

"You should recall, and recall quickly, who plays the lead in this tangle of a relationship."

I groaned inwardly.

"Yes, Papa." The moment the words left my mouth, my cock began to stiffen. What fun Eira and I could have—on our knees, or her below me, and he above. I wanted to gnash my teeth at the sexy little anger-sprite scowling over me, but he was in no mood for loving. My aim was to *not* suffocate him out our newly formed triad. Not for my sake of course—my wifling's precious puss satisfied my urges, surprisingly enough—but so that she would stay. If given the chance to run, whether she admitted it or not, she would go with Cato. And where would that leave me? No head scratches, no one to braid my hair or cuddle me the way I had come to require before settling into sleep. The others had never stayed the night.

"Call me that again, Ambrose, and see if you make it home."

I sighed, drowning in my feelings, and glanced between my legs. I missed the warmth of her lips as she kissed her way up my dick, the way she'd circle my anus with her unafraid little finger while trying to take all of me down her throat. An impossible task, but gods how she tried. I held back the sob that demanded I set it free. Eira was my lusty counterpart, happy to try all the salacious fantasies I could concoct. And unlike the others, it wasn't because she'd "claimed the prince" or expected a reward of some sort—she was just down to fuck. And I think perhaps, finally I'd found my...

"Oh, good gracious. Catommandus, take note. Their fine fabrics do not conceal an erection, not even a little." A solid eight inches of cock tented proudly from the skirt I chose—a regal Nortian black with thin cream stripes. "It does, however, cling to all the right places."

Cato snatched up the damp towel I had cast off after bathing earlier.

"Ambrose, for fuck's sake." He rubbed his head until his hair stuck up like the quills of a porcupine, then hurled the damp cloth at my offensively long member.

"What?" I tucked my stiffened desire into the belt at my waist, trying to conceal its fervor. "You soaped your broad beast while discussing my wife's lush and fuckable form... and you expect me not to react? Ludicrous."

Cato fought a tunic over his head, his fury making him sloppy. His arm found the neck hole, and a seam groaned its agony as he tried to force his way through.

Yeesh.

"I'll see that Eira fucks the ever-loving anger from you before I satisfy myself in her woman's-well... but I will be dammed if she's forced to mount you while you look like something a troll regurgitated. Fetch my combs."

Chapter Thirty-Three

The Gods Are Not Without Humor

Eira

"Evandr?" Gotwig asked.

"Is in Monwyn, with another of your kind," I whispered, still unsure if my hunch about what they were was correct. "He sleeps encased in ice."

Gotwig slowed his decisive steps and clasped his hands behind his back.

"And the two Monwyns that swore to protect you?" he asked snidely, switching the conversation to Solnnan while glancing at Septimus who trailed a few steps behind.

A servant pressed herself to the wall as we passed. Gotwig bowed to her as if she were the highest of court nobility.

"Incarcerated by the new king." I tossed my chin in Septimus's direction. "He's their uncle."

Gotwig's thin mouth pressed firmly. "Yes, the resemblance between him and the restored prince is remarkable."

"Then you are aware of—"

"Everything."

Of course he was. I wouldn't put it past him to have moles in all the kingdoms. But I knew something he wouldn't.

"Gotwig... Merrias, she—"

He placed his finger to his lips and shook his head. "Like Verus, these walls have ears."

I nodded, and together we strode through the palace's narrow but breezy corridors. There was no time to take in the ornate shell ornaments that hung from the ceilings, or the tall, white statues placed in the center of every hallway's juncture. We came to a staircase that wound its way upward in a tight coil. Gotwig took the steps two by two, his haste triggering my anxiety.

My palms sweat; I held them up to catch the cross breeze that flowed through the arrowslits that powdered the walls. My heart beat harder than it should, whether I was climbing to the top of a sky-high tower or not.

At the stairways end, there was a single door—bronze, with heavy bands of steel fortifying each corner, attached with rivets the size of my palm.

"Your mongrel stays put," Gotwig sneered.

I turned around to translate and came face to face with "my mongrel's" bare torso. My eyes rolled back in my head at the sight of the scarred-up and ravaged expanse. Septimus tensed his pecs, knowing well the reaction he elicited.

A brilliant-orange butterfly flitted through the nearest window and landed on his silver head. He didn't feel it and narrowed his eyes in confusion at the grin I wore.

"You are to stay put. Guard the door."

"No." He glared over my head at Gotwig. "We do not know these people."

Septimus inched forward. I held my palms up to stop him, but he pressed all of his luscious self against me.

Gotwig flipped open his timepiece and then snapped it shut, nonplused.

"Honestly, Gotwig, he'll cause us *more* issues if left to his own devices, I'm afraid." I bolstered my arms against his glorious chest, but Septimus didn't slow. My feet slid backward on the tile floor.

"Keep your dog on a tight leash if he must be present."

An arm shot past my head, lashing out toward Gotwig. I popped Septimus on the nose and the butterfly took flight. "Cut it out."

"An animal in need of training." Gotwig blinked slowly, settling his unguarded stare of disapproval on the Monwyn.

The grind of metal on metal halted the standoff. The door opened, inch by slow inch, as two pairs of hands pushed on its edge, straining under the weight of the barrier.

"Servants, out. Guards, to your post," Gotwig called out.

Five, maybe six men filed out the door and down the steps, followed by four women armored in steel from head to toe. Each of them, tall, statuesque figures of toned perfection, dwarfed me with their magnificent, muscled bodies. Ambrose would applaud their clear commitment to a regimen. Their solid chest pieces were sculpted to imitate bare breasts, the nipples replaced by small brass suns. Skirts of articulating metal tassets fastened to their hips. The women's arms were bare, each branded with a stylized half sun, four rays surrounding a semi-circle.

I gawked.

I'd never seen a woman warrior... and neither had Septimus, apparently. He stood so rigidly I thought he might snap in half, and there was no mistaking the disapproving huff of his displeasure. The tallest of the women regarded him as she marched by, letting out a laugh. She was unimpressed. Four of her front teeth had been replaced with what looked like carved wood and a jagged scar crawled down the length of her neck.

"No!" I caught Septimus's hands before he could react to her slight. "This is not Monwyn." His teeth grit together, and a pulse flickered at the bottom of his neck. "Septimus. Eyes on me."

"Good steel, twisted to pornography and given to scullery maids." He frowned, openly hostile, but did as he was told. I clasped his hands, our eyes connected, and the Bond between us surged. "You yourself are dressed more promiscuously than even those debauched bitches. Were we home, I would revoke your travel privileges if you dared show yourself in public as you are."

His gaze dropped to my cleavage. The aubergine gown was essentially two triangular straps, dotted with light-pink pearls, that attached to a flowing skirt right below my breasts. Its hem reached my knees in the front and heels in the back. It provided minimal support for my chest, but my internal temperature hadn't been more comfortable since arriving.

"I'll be wearing nothing but Solnnan fashions when I return. And I'll request to have a hundred dresses sent for the ladies of the court. Aberus can stroke out and you can continue your wet dream."

"Troth Solnna?" Thunder rumbled in the distance. Gotwig approached me from behind. "Troth Solnna, come through."

I tore myself away from Septimus and strode into a chamber that took my breath—and not in a good way.

"What is the use of a solid metal door if there are no walls, or rather—holy shit." I stumbled back, hands seeking the solidness of Septimus. Sweat surfaced on my forehead and palms. The æther strangled in my neck.

"You are quite safe." Gotwig rounded me and blocked the view. "Control your actions... Master your impulses," he whispered.

I choked down the rising panic, sought the calm of his rheumy eyes.

I control myself.

Thunder rolled, a low and long rumble. The room vibrated in its wake.

Me. I can...

A calloused fingertip ran the length of my spine, and a firm hand settled on my hip.

I slowed my respirations, and Gotwig stepped to the side.

Solnna—all of Solnna—circled me. If it weren't for the glare of the lightning glinting off the curved glass panes, I would swear we stood in the sky. I could see it all. The neighborhoods, the scattering of ant-sized people as they ran from the rain.

The room's domed ceiling was white, cream, and gray, painted to resemble the clouds above. Winged creatures of ancient lore peeked from behind the nimbi—a flying horse, a hippogriff, and a harpy watched over us.

Lightning struck in the distance, out over a navy ocean, but the storm clouds seemed to stall against a brightly glowing sun.

"You have Lykksun's blessing, I see."

I dropped my gaze to the woman sitting at a low table in the center of the room. Dark amber eyes shown from a face of glowing brown. Full lips spread into a dazzling smile, a sizable gap between her two front teeth.

"I am Queen Ahn-Lyse, Daughter of Jessum, Granddaughter of the Sol Queen Lykk, from whom this capital derives its name. I welcome you as I would my own daughters, Troth Solnna."

I curtsied low, showing my reverence.

She snorted a most un-queenly sound of derision.

"You are a princess of Monwyn. Do not bow again, woman of rank, Goddess-touched."

Septimus pinched my hip sharply, causing me to yelp.

The queen tilted her head in question, confusion and amusement vying on her face. As she shifted, the gold powder that coated her eyelids and wide cheekbones shimmered.

"It's bullshit, but in Monwyn, women hold zero precedence in the royal lineage, Majesty."

The queen's face pinched.

"I refuse to believe that. Imella was nothing short of brilliant." The queen brushed aside a stack of parchments and then settled her chin on her fist while she studied me.

Tears, hot, and stinging, pricked at the backs of my eyes.

"She was," I agreed. "Memory immortal." I briefly pressed my fingertips to my forehead.

"We received news of her passing just days ago and have lit the fires in her honor. Ærta owes a debt to the matriarchs of Taleer for their sacrifices in the Great War, ones we will never be able to adequately repay."

I nodded my agreement. Imella had more strength, more cunning, than any of the men of Monwyn—Cato and Ambrose included. She endured decades of abandonment and ridicule, yet still held sway over the kingdom and family.

"Please sit."

I glanced at the round table, not sure where to place myself—and then saw the snacks. Food on the high seas be damned. I kneeled on an over-stuffed pink pillow and tucked my legs under my rear, hiding my patchy red welts and missing toenail. Salsia shouldn't catch the blame for Septimus's handiwork.

"I would introduce you to Primus Zuddaz." The queen lifted her hand, indicating the man to her immediate right.

"Primus Zuddaz, it is my pleasure to—wait—are you...? Do we know each other?" I stared hard at Solnna's second-in-command. I couldn't help it. "You look incredibly familiar to me." I abandoned the snacks before me and crawled across the pillows to get a closer look at the man.

Eyes the color of grass, the brightest I'd ever seen, peeked out from under sagging lids. High cheekbones, still prominent through aging skin, reminded me so much of...

"I am often told that the Mantle favors Their sire." The Primus smiled, revealing a perfect set of teeth, pearly and straight.

"Oh, my gods, that's it exactly!" I beamed.

I pictured the Mantle as I had first seen Them—the closest neighbor at Lord Gotwig's luncheon of doom, the day he poisoned the Troth collective with toxic wine. I remembered the Mantle's grin, the wave of Their fingers and the dancing of Their tiered, multi-colored earrings glittering in the candlelight.

"Don't fear life's experiences, instead seek to understand how they will harm or help you in becoming the self of your choosing," I recited the Mantle's words between us, honestly surprised that I recalled them so readily.

"Sound advice. Proof to me that Verus raised Them well," Zuddaz whispered back. His eyes were soft and misted over.

Where the Mantle was lithe of body, Their father was quite broad but looked equally blessed with height from where he sat. And though the Mantle's hair was a dark chestnut, you could see darker black stripes in the Primus's salt-and-pepper hair, a few streaks of the same in his thinning brows.

"You are, Scion, of course, and the Mantle was conceived during the Rite, correct? Did they parade you around in transparent clothes like they did me?"

"Indeed." He nodded enthusiastically. "And though I was proud of my physique then... now, after so many years, the brand upon my hip looks more like a mushroom than a moon." Primus Zuddaz tossed back his head and laughed unabashedly. I couldn't help but join in. His happiness was loud, contagious, and utterly free.

I leaned closer to his smiling face.

"The Rite is so fucked up, isn't it? Brand us like godsdamned heifers and then expect us to feel good enough to fuck for three days."

Zuddaz's eyes flashed wide, and he wheezed between bursts of hilarity.

"Eira Verras Chulainn. You are every bit your mother's child." He wiped the trails of tears from the corners of both crinkling eyes.

I sobered instantly.

"You knew her?"

I scooted closer to the Primus, my shoulder touching his, suddenly needing to be nearer to him—to any link to her.

My mother. There wasn't a day that passed by that I didn't miss her.

"Knew? I *know* her dear; she still walks the soil." He ducked his head, sensing my concern, and lifted a light hand to my chin, moving my face from side to side. Septimus went all growly, which everyone in the room ignored. "She is well, Eira. Looks just as healthy as she did the morning she appeared at the doors of Verus temple. You were tucked tightly into her belly then."

Zuddaz dropped his hand from my cheek, but I caught it and held it between my palms.

My heart palpitated, skipping a few beats before normalizing again. I breathed through the overwhelming yet tremendous sensation of relief.

"Where is she? Does she look well? When can I see her?"

He patted our clasped hands.

"Vonnie swore me to secrecy, Eira, and *that* secret I will keep. She is one of the most formidable women I know, only second to She Who Sits on the Solnnan Throne." Zuddaz glanced at the queen, who smiled back affectionally. "I wouldn't dare put her in danger by revealing her location... or tempt her fury by squealing. Do you know what she'd do to me?"

"She could freeze, thaw, and refreeze a man with a four-second stare." I hiccoughed between my cries. "And my father?"

"Ulltan? He is ever by her side. Utterly devoted."

I lost it then.

I bent over and buried my head into the pillows and unleashed the worry that had consumed me for months on end.

I wailed. Not the single rolling tear like Kairus could manage. Not the sweet sniffles of a sad Richelle. This was a runny-nose, choking-on-my-saliva level of weeping.

"What did he say to you? Why have you upset her?" Septimus yelled in the common language. "Tell me now or I will render you all—"

"You have no authority to make demands here," the queen said, leveling her gaze at my irate companion. I looked between the two of them. *Shit.* The feral gleam in Septimus's blue eyes alarmed me. I scrambled to my feet, knowing he could turn violent in a matter of seconds. "If Eira wishes you to know something, she will address you." The queen's lips turned down, and her heavily charcoaled eyes tapered. "Who even are you?"

Just in time, I stuck my finger in the middle of his chest. "Hush!"

He balked and then balked again, flipping his head back and snapping it down quickly with bared teeth and tightened lips.

"I will tell you exactly who I am. I am Lord—" Septimus's eyes rolled back.

He slumped to the floor, revealing the impassive face of Gotwig, who now hovered over his prone form.

"Much better," the queen said while pouring herself a drink from the glass pitcher that sat nearest her.

I rearranged Septimus's awkwardly angled arms.

"Your Majesty, this is Lord Septimus, brother of the late King Burchard of Monwyn," I rolled his head back on onto the pillow as it slumped, "and, believe it or not, he's the obstinate and, quite frankly, vile man that Merrias and Viktos found worthy enough to Bond me too."

His head flopped back onto the floor, his chin cracking against the stone. I left it there.

"Pardon me, but what?" A shocked Zuddaz signaled to Gotwig, who turned and walked near a fruit-laden sideboard to retrieve a wheeled seat stationed there. He rolled the chair to Zuddaz, who used his hands to position one of his legs and then the other before lifting himself into the seat. Seeing his entire body now, I knew that I'd surmised correctly. His thighs looked to be double the length of my own, and even having no calves or feet, he was extremely long of body.

Zuddaz wheeled himself to my side.

"You know of the Bonds? When you say Merrias and Viktos, please explain."

"Sh-she's come to me... twice."

It didn't even occur to me until after it was out of my mouth that maybe I shouldn't have shared that much.

Zuddaz and the queen held each other's eyes, then both looked at Gotwig.

My hands began to heat uncomfortably, the æther setting sail from my chest to the tips of my fingers.

Zuddaz reached toward me but stopped short. "May I?"

I looked to Gotwig, seeking advice. I didn't know this man.

"Choose your path, Troth Solnna," Gotwig said.

The Primus knew my mother. He sired the Mantle, but were those enough to qualify him as a confidant? Clearly, he thought laying his hands upon me was important.

I nodded, consenting to Zuddaz's touch.

His large palm, warm and firm, settled between my breasts, right over my thumping heart.

"Can you hear me?"

I jerked my hand to my mouth—it was disconcerting hearing a voice that wasn't Father Burchard's.

"Yes. An Infinite Bond? How did you—"

"No dear," Zuddaz spoke out loud. "Just the ability of a very old conjurer. I could only sustain another word or two before it cuts short. This is a method we use to recognize one another. My queen, were you aware she was—"

"—a conjurer. Yes, Zuddaz, I was," Her Majesty replied, closing her eyes as she spoke. "You know I would never out a conjurer for their own safety... not even to you, old friend. Though we provide safe harbor, even in Solnna the hatred of difference burns as bright as the Deathless Flame."

Septimus began to stir.

From my periphery, I saw Gotwig approach, but I placed my hand on Septimus's chest and shook my head, my eyes still trained on Zuddaz.

"I need him alive."

"Because he is your Fated Bond?" the Primus questioned.

"Gods, I hope not. Septimus is my... my Safeguard, whatever that means. I am Mate Bonded to him... and Fate Bonded to his nephew Catommandus, Prince and former Protector of Monwyn."

Zuddaz slapped himself on the forehead. I would have laughed were it not for the expression of pure horror that flowed across his strong features.

"And you are Joined to the prince's brother?" His brows knit together, but his bright eyes remained round. "The gods are not without humor, it would seem."

I sat back heavily on my heels and held my head in my hands.

"That's not even the half of it," I groaned. "Pass those snacks and gird your loins."

Chapter Thirty-Four

TO KNOW A GODS MIND

Eira

"And this new Monwyn King, Aberus, incarcerated them? I will pen a missive on their behalf and have it sent with our representative. Troth Richelle's brother will deliver it there immediately and see if he can pull sway."

"Thank you, Majesty. I welcome anything that will aid in their release." I inclined my head in thanks and decided to omit the part where I had throat-punched Richelle's piece of shit relation—Representative of Solnna or not, he'd deserved it. I sent a silent prayer to the Goddess that he wouldn't *mysteriously* lose the missive along the way. "The Mantle should reach Monwyn soon, if They haven't already. In my heart, I know They will keep Cato and Ambrose safe, if only temporarily, but I must return to them quickly."

The queen and Zuddaz exchanged a look.

"Troth Solnna, Eira... the Great War resulted from the gods squabbling amongst themselves. And though I agree that stopping the Primus-King from getting his hands on your person is a must, I also feel that preparing Ærta's citizens for an impending battle should be foremost in our minds."

I popped another grape into Septimus's mouth. His hands and legs were bound, but he seemed content enough to remain silent if I stayed in constant contact with his body. It was distracting to have my veins running hot and my passage pulsing while sitting amongst a group of others, but I did my best to focus.

"And I realize, Majesty, that humanity takes precedence over my life and the cruelty shown to Monwyn. But until I know they are safe, I'm afraid I can't focus on either." I looked away, ashamed at not being stronger.

From the corner of my eye, I saw Gotwig nod softly.

"My greatest concern, Eira," Zuddaz shifted, dispersing his weight more comfortably. He then rubbed his hands up and down his thighs. "Is that you must inform the Mantle of what will befall Ærta. My reckoning is that the Primus-King plays a much larger role than we expect and that he seeks you even now. It was dangerous for you to come here. But it will be even more dangerous for you to return."

The queen poured herself a drink from a pitcher of fruit-laden water and brought it to her mouth. She caught a slice of kiwi between her teeth, ran her finger around the glass's rim, and chewed thoughtfully.

"Your other option is to remain, Eira, and allow us to provide for your safety," she said.

Zuddaz drummed his fingers on the table and worried the side of his lip. The action reminded me of Ambrose—my Black Bear. I wanted him close to my side and could all but hear the nonsensical words he would whisper in my ear while rocking me in his arms. And Cato, just a thought and my emptiness increases twofold.

"The Nether Lord presents himself to Eira. He gifts her two Frostborn, creatures strong enough to dominate battlefields and obliterate the most elite soldiers. In all the tomes I've studied, there was only a single mention. I would imagine he is shifting his pieces on the game board of earth... and has been doing so for decades, if not longer. The conjurers may be the only ones who could hold him back if he were to surface again with ill intent. And if the Primus-King supports the Nether Lord's coup..."

The atmosphere in the room changed, darkening as storm clouds seemed to close in on the tower.

The atmosphere felt charged.

"But Primus Zuddaz, how can we know—"

"That's just it, Troth Solnna... We can't know a god's mind... not unless..." He paused, his eyes sharpening.

"Unless what?" I asked, trying my best to connect the dots.

"You said Merrias anticipates your thoughts, correct?"

I bowed my head in response. She had at both our meetings shown awareness of my words and actions before I delivered them.

"Is it possible that ability extends to the Nether Lord as well? You contain his essence through that of his only offspring, just as you do Merrias's."

"I don't know." I shook my head and, as if by instinct, moved closer to Septimus.

"If they can both peer into your mind, can they interact there? Could you, or your offspring, be a kind of conduit between them?"

The thought made me sick.

"It's all conjecture, but what would a divine war be like if you, or the child of your body, allowed one of them to anticipate the other's movements?"

"Catastrophe," the Queen supplied.

"Eira, may I ask you a personal question?" Gotwig said, leaning into the conversation.

I nodded while placing a slice of orange into Septimus's mouth and then one into my own.

"Have you mated with this man?"

Gods.

I hesitated, trying to decide how much to share.

Gotwig's eyes, sharp as his blades, settled on the man at my side.

"Has he forced you?"

Septimus spat the orange from his mouth and strained against his bindings.

"I have not raped her," he gritted out. The word for forced intercourse was the same in Solnnan as it was in Ærtan—and Septimus recognized it immediately. He fought against his bindings.

I swallowed and recalled our encounters. The knife he placed in my mouth. The Den, where I would have let him enter me had it not been for the interruption of Father Burchard. The inn... the ship.

"He—*we* came close." I switched over to the common tongue. "I have consented to, or, more accurately, failed to give voice to my rejection of his advances."

Gotwig lowered his eyes and peered into some unknown distance... like he was sinking back into another lifetime.

"This man, your Safeguard. He acts like the Primus-King did toward your mother, though with more restraint." Gotwig folded his hands and placed them on the table.

The queen cleared her throat.

"Perhaps he was chosen as Safeguard because he possesses a stronger sense of self-control than the Primus-King," she said. "You can take someone by force, at the cost of losing control of your prize. If you can get them to commit willingly, then all the levers of power remain."

"Perhaps the Nether Lord is attempting the same opening gambit, but with different pieces to play this time." Gotwig closed his eyes, and I watched as his thin chest rose and fell. "Eira, in place of Vonnie."

"Consort!" Septimus yelped.

I snatched my hands back from where they rested on his bindings. Smoke wafted from the burned silk.

"Is this... Is this normal for a conjurer?" I held my palms out to Zuddaz, who hesitated briefly before inspecting them up close.

The Primus shook his head and reached for the pitcher, pouring a glass of water and placing it in my hands. "The thermal response is not typical, but this may help. Water is an excellent medium for æther. Your power will interact with it easily, and it has the added benefit of not burning." I focused on the glass... focused on the thought that, though I couldn't change the past, I might be able to alter a parallel future. Tiny bubbles formed at the bottom and began to swim upward, bursting when they surfaced.

My hands started to cool.

"You know, King Burchard had a Mated Bond. It ended when the woman's period stopped coming on, before they even knew she was with child. Perhaps that is why the Primus-King stopped hunting for my mother—she'd conceived me. It would not explain why he now wants her back."

"Soolie was a homewrecking cunt," Septimus said, rolling to his side.

Zuddaz choked, sputtering into his drink. The queen leaned over and thumped him on the back once and then again. She fished the remaining round fruits from his drink and then urged him to take a few sips.

"Soolie is who?" the Queen asked.

"She was the Troth sent to Monwyn du-during that particular Obligate phase," Zuddaz supplied.

I nodded, though my eyes stayed glued to the cup in my hand. Steam rose white and foggy above its rim.

"She died just two years or so after her placement there. Father Burchard said she took her own life. She was Gaean and was ashamed that she had lost her purity without having been Joined. Such bullshit that her kingdom made her feel that way."

"A tragedy," Zuddaz whispered, so low that I could just make out his words.

"Good riddance," Septimus said, loud enough to earn the disapproving looks of all those seated.

"Shut up." I pinched a bit of his chest hair and yanked. "You are in no place to judge—Bonded to me just the same as she was." I faced the group, meeting each of their gazes. "My apologies."

"Don't apologize for the actions of your dog." Gotwig pulled a thin blade from his vest and laid it on the table. "The Primus-King doesn't want Eira's mother because of a Bond. He wants her blood to sustain his life's longevity. Eira's would do the same."

"Holy Creator." Her name fell from my lips... a prayer. "The thought of my mother in the Primus-King's hands... or myself... His lips... drinking from me or-or the child of my body." A shiver wracked me so hard that the hair on my nape stood on end. "Zuddaz, is there a way to render me permanently infertile?"

Septimus sprang to his knees. He lifted his hands high and brought them slamming down onto the table. The burned portions of the silk snapped, and he roughly hauled me to his side.

Gotwig was on his feet in an instant.

"Calm down." I placed a hand on Septimus's arm, which encircled my waist. "Calm," I soothed my Safeguard, laying my head against his chest.

Septimus relaxed against me. His chin came to rest on my shoulder, though he didn't release me from his hold.

"No, Eira, there is no way to alter a single part of a body's functioning. The consequences could be dire, possibly fatal." He glanced down at his lap. "And before we get carried away by the what if's... let us not lose sight of what we *can* control."

"Consort," Septimus tightened his arm, "I will control this situation by busting the Primus-King's skull over his ostentatious throne." He dragged the tip of his nose up my neck, and rested his lips near my earlobe. "Would you give yourself to me then?"

I grappled out of his embrace, embarrassed and aroused.

"It would be a step in the right direction." Pixies danced their sharp toes along my spine, and my nipples pebbled, standing out noticeably as they strained against the light fabric I wore.

Zuddaz frowned. His brow cast shadows over his eyes.

"Under most circumstances, I do not condone the taking of a life—"

"But I do," the queen said in a sharp tone. "My fellow monarch should atone for his sins against her mother *and* his daughter. I will never abide a man so selfish, and if his elimination slows the inevitable course of this war, then I command it to be carried out. Until then, Eira will take shelter in the Conservatory where she can study safely by your side, Zuddaz. When she is powerful enough, she can return to Monwyn."

"The Conservatory?"

"Where conjurers can learn away from the eyes of man."

"I will go tonight." I began working the knot free from around Septimus's ankles.

"No," the Queen interrupted. "You will need to collect your strength before entering. Tonight, we are in need of lightheartedness and will make our way to the Overlook. When you have rested and broken your fast, Gotwig will be your guide."

Chapter Thirty-Five

His Something

Cato

"Where is my wife?" Ambrose's voice echoed through the chamber. In rare form, his anger matched my own.

Palace interior. Small chamber. No windows. Closest escape route... through the gardens. Difficulty of escape? Fucking simplistic. Obstacles? None of immediate concern.

The guard's legs shook, vibrating against the wall as Ambrose held him high, pinned by the neck. The man gasped and choked, seeking his breath.

"Do not quake in fear, simple soldier, for I have saved you from the veritable nightmare that is my brother. Up here he cannot reach you, but by the nether, an inch lower, and he will rip your stomach out through your throat. Now, I ask you once more. Where is she?"

I leapt, using Ambrose's shoulder as leverage, and aimed a punch at the terrified face of the man who had relayed the message that we were to "remain cloistered" until he notified us it was safe.

Safe. The word ripped through my ribs like a bolt fired from close range. Eira wasn't safe—not until her head lay against my chest—and nothing and no one in Solnna was safe if they thought to keep me from her.

Ambrose shrugged his shoulder, causing my blow to glance and my fist to strike the wall.

"Brother, move aside. Allow me to persuade him."

Ambrose's elbow caught me in the ribs, but I managed to snag the guard's overtunic and rip it clear from his body, revealing the curboiled leather he wore beneath. If all Solnnans were armored so lightly, I could lay waste to a dozen men in pursuit of my woman. "A soldier delivering an unlawful demand deserves death."

I jumped again and then feinted right. Ambrose checked me with his shoulder, shoving me backward.

"Prince Catommandus can and *will* put his hand through your chest wall. I have witnessed it twice before and can tell you... it is a slow and messy way to die—*quite* messy, *very* slow, at least until he breaches the cavity below your lungs." Ambrose used his empty hand to push his gold frames up the bridge of his nose while leaning close to his captive's face.

"H-her Maj..."

"Speak up," I growled, beyond furious. "And quit your stammering."

The guard tossed up his hands as his face peaked at its most vibrant shade of purple yet. Ambrose worked his knee between the man's legs, keeping him suspended while relieving the pressure on his throat.

"The queen," the guard sucked air into his lungs, "wishes to ensure the Troth's safety. There is a conflict between your stories and hers," the guard said in a rush. "She bears you no ill will."

I cocked my head to the side, examining him. He appeared truthful, no tells, no ticks... but I still had many tools we could use to verify his statement.

The guard hit the floor with a heavy thud.

"Catommandus, less flailing. Your hair will pull from your braid."

"Fuck off, Ambrose." I eyed the guard. It was doubtful he had the clearance to know the exact position of my woman within these walls, but he *would* have other useful information, like the location of barracks and the names of those who were privy to intel.

"How you continue to lure Eira to your bed is beyond my understanding. Unkempt scraggle-hounds are neither appealing nor attractive, and my wife should only mount the finest."

The guard gulped, his Adam's apple bobbing, and he skittered toward the door like a crab on the sand as I pressed in on him.

Ambrose side-stepped and, without looking, stomped on the soldier's pants, pinning him in place. "Are you judging us, peasant? Catommandus, is he judging us? Is this not the kingdom of openness and freedom, with laws allowing one to love as many as he might?" Ambrose flung his head around to glare at the man, his three intricate, waist-length plaits striking me in the jaw.

I paused in my pursuit.

"That is Gaea, Ambrose."

"No, no." He tapped his index finger on the tip of his nose in the same rhythm as he tapped his foot on the floor. "I distinctly remember being taught at Verus that if a Solnnan couple was infertile, it was acceptable for the husband and wife to choose another male with whom she might breed."

"Yes. That is the case. But plurality before or after conception negotiations is not lawful. Did you even read the primers? Fuck, even I read the primers."

Ambrose's mouth fell into a tight O.

"Should we kill him?"

"I think, *adopted brother*," I looked around, emphasizing my point to the shock-faced soldier, "that would set a poor precedent, and given they only sent a single guard to contain us, he is most assuredly telling the truth."

"Oh, well, yes, that does make a speck of sense. Is it possible that we are both feeling our emotions a little too deeply? And do not chastise me with such a derisive expression. The Troth are the mediators who must know the cultural drivel. We Scion are built for strategy."

Ambrose struck his chest with a fist.

I massaged my temples, willing away the ever-present tension. Knowing Eira was here and knowing that I could have walked into this palace undetected, with its lack of defenses, had me entirely on edge—both because she could have already been in my arms *and* because every second she was not safeguarded could be her last.

I paced.

"You were built for coddling."

Ambrose's face crumpled.

"Our apartments have no locking barrier from the outside gardens, Ambrose. Even an untrained person could climb the hedge wall and gain admittance. The hallways are narrow, which would slow an army, but as the fuckwit now cowering in the corner has found, that simply disallows him from evading a man like me."

I dropped to my heels and looked the guard in the eyes.

The soldier's weakness disgusted me. I would slice his quivering fucking lips from his face to keep from witnessing their trembling any further. A single day and I was already done with Solnna.

"Hear me, coward. You will point me in the direction of Troth Solnna, or I will crush your knuckles one by one."

Ambrose sighed.

"Cato, please do not... unless I am standing outside of a five-foot radius." He drew his fingers in a circle around himself. "When you use your hilt to bust bones, the splatter range is honestly quite impressive, but not as impressive as this silk." He gestured to the tiny fucking skirt he insisted on wearing. I'd explained to him it was a head covering meant to keep one's neck shaded from the sun, but he'd wholeheartedly disagreed.

The guard broke.

I knew the very moment he gave up, saw his throat working up and down as he climbed the door at his back. He lifted his arm, pointing south.

"Sh-she's at the beach."

"You should *start* with the truth the next time you encounter us." I balled up his shredded tunic and launched it at his face. "Now, run back to your commander like the pathetic urchin you are, and tell him that Catommandus, Prince of Monwyn, will be speaking to him soon. Go."

I stood, slapped Ambrose on the back, and strode from the room. His footsteps quickly fell in synch with mine.

"Look there." I pointed to a couple walking through an outdoor court-yard. "We follow them. See how the woman is continually adjusting her garment? She wishes to impress, and her partner, he wipes his forehead from nerves, not heat." Sure enough, the man shook his hands out in front of himself, and then rubbed them together worriedly. The woman smiled reassuringly at the shorter fellow and gave him a curt nod. "My guess, Ambrose, is that they are to be in the presence of royalty. If the queen is as intelligent as I am led to believe, she will have Eira by her side. It is easier to keep someone secure when all eyes are watching."

We walked behind the couple, keeping our distance but acting as tourists might—stopping to smell a towering red flower here, inspecting a statue of Derros there. Neither of us would have passed for a Solnnan. The men we had seen thus far preferred shaved heads and chests, and their beards were missing or trimmed close.

"His dick is fatter than yours, Cato," Ambrose chuckled, while point-ing toward the set of stone testicles that hung just above his head.

"You are a child." I fake-peered at the hibiscus flowers that surrounded the alabaster god, keeping my eyes on the couple that would lead us to our target. "We move."

The sun sank low, and the winds picked up, but lamps lit the manicured lawn we traversed, as well as a surprisingly large throng of children gath-ering under an archway. The tiny tots and their siblings had dressed as sea creatures, and their ranks seemed to swell by the second.

A wayward hair tickled my temple, and the temperature seemed to rise. An intimately familiar sensation settled over me. A deep and comforting calm... like the night Eira and I said our vows under the moon and stars.

She was near.

I sped up, passing the couple who had stopped once again to check their appearances and smooth the wrinkles from their skirts. A staircase loomed ahead, climbing steeply up the man-made barrier that protected the city. I surged forward and took the steps two by two.

"Cat," Ambrose whispered, coming up behind me as we crested. He laid a heavy hand on my shoulder. "Before you run into the middle of what is likely a lovely and highly formal state dinner, find the restraint that went missing the second Eira drew your dick into her silken mouth. You have not played the royal for well over a decade, and it shows."

I nodded and took a few deep breaths. He was, even if I hated to admit it, correct.

"And do not eye fuck her in front of an audience. She is my wife." Ambrose dropped his voice as a tiny jellyfish and a chubby-faced shark waddled by. "We are here for you to peruse their eligible women-stock. Right?" Ambrose exaggeratedly nodded his head. "Our mission is to secure matches for the two prize Monwyn bulls. We do not know what the queen has been told, and we stick to our initial story until we find out." Ambrose plucked the glasses from his face and hung them from one of the fifteen gemstone necklaces he wore. "Now, how do I look?"

I gave him a quick once-over.

"Fine."

He chewed on his pink-painted lips.

"The thread of gold woven into my braids is not too much? Is my eye black too intense?"

I sighed.

"You are handsome. Let us proceed."

Ambrose giggled like a fucking woman.

"You are also handsome." He reached out and smoothed an errant hair back into place while I stood motionless. "Gods, I need to taste her vertical smile like I need beef to sustain my bulk."

Stab him, Cat. The sand will accept the blood offering—easy clean up.

"I may actually kill you."

"Mmhmm." One corner of Ambrose's mouth hitched up. "Come on... and remember, you are the *true* Prince of Monwyn."

He looked at me like a mother sending her child to military training for the first time, adjusting my neckline, smoothing my sleeve.

"Ambrose, you are every bit the prince. Do not sell yourself—"

His eyes softened as he clapped me on the shoulders.

"Brother, I know what the people think of me—and could not give two shits—but tonight, it is you who must remember... the blood that runs through your veins is that of King Burchard and the last matriarch of Taleer. Walk tall. Remain at all times above them."

My throat constricted, but I shoved away my grief. I would mourn my parents in my time. I stood straighter, brushed off the front of my tunic, and checked for the dagger that was tucked into the back of my belt.

We turned and made our way down the steps, walking slowly, as if we had no care in the world.

In the distance, a massive boulder jutted out from the sand and waves, glowing in the last remnants of the day's light. That magical, sparkling black rock was not native to this area.

"Ambrose, lay your eyes on that megalith. Do you think it came from the top of Mount Gammond?"

A low, appreciative whistle was his response.

"Perhaps sent here when Verus was built?"

"What could move such a thing, brother?"

Ambrose picked up his pace, jogging in the direction of the stone.

"Royalty does not run. Time belongs to us. Right?"

"Catommandus, you would dare separate a Monwyn boy from such a magnificent rock?"

I chuckled and ran after him.

On the other side of the colossal boulder, the beach was glowing from a hundred torches staked into the sand. A massive canopy of the most ostentatious gold-and-pink damask rippled in the breeze and then sank as the wind calmed. The same wind whisked away the clouds above, revealing a million of the Goddess's stars twinkling in a navy sky.

Fuck me.

The celestial splendor paled in comparison to the woman dancing barefoot under the shell-covered chandelier. Like the poets who rambled on about love, my heart fluttered at the sight of her. When I returned home, I would make it a point to apologize to the court composer for my dismissal of his fanciful words.

"Ambrose, there she is…" Her hair was short now, dark and thicker in the middle than it was on the sides. She kicked up a foot as she swayed, revealing a glimpse of the soft flesh of her thighs. *Gods, she should always wear short dresses.* My woman was a vision. Eira was beauty made flesh—thoughtfulness and warmth.

My blade disappeared from my waistband.

"And she's dancing with Uncle motherfucking Septimus."

Ambrose bolted, knife in hand.

"Do not," I hissed. "Ambrose, halt."

There was no stopping him.

I gave chase at a decidedly not royal speed.

Whether it was the abstinence rage finally catching up with him or the sight of his wife smiling up at the man who respected piles of refuse more than he did his kin... it did not matter.

"Ambrose, look out!"

He collided with a lobster-child—who landed safely on its massive crustacean's tail. Ambrose picked up the stunned sea creature, patted it on its wobbling stalk-eyes, and then continued charging across the sand.

His fumble was my gain.

Elbows pumping and heels digging, I launched myself at his waist, wrapped my arms around him, and twisted hard to my left, throwing us both to the ground. Ambrose fought hard, but grappling was *my* gift. He reared and kicked beneath me, bucking his hips, attempting to throw me off. Extending my knees over his arms, I disarmed him and tossed the knife aside.

"Cato. Off me now." His eyes burned bright; his lip curled back. He contorted his face in a rage I knew well.

"Not until you are in control." He struggled again, trying to free the arm I pinned to his side. "Do not let him goad you. Play your role. He is worthless. He is nothing, Ambrose—"

I watched his eyes go cold over the arm bar I held across his neck.

"Yes. But she is *my* something."

Chapter Thirty-Six

THE RIVER SWALLOWS THE VILLAGE

My River Just Happens to Be Less Discerning Than Most. Stupid Bonds... Eira

"At least pretend to enjoy yourself," I hissed into Septimus's ear as he spun us in a tight circle and then pulled me close. He slid his hand from the nape of my neck to the top of my rear. "You wouldn't allow me to dance with any others, including a man of ninety-and-four years, so make your 'Monwyn customs' bullshit appear authentic."

We parted, and I clapped out the beat of the drum while he circled around me, looking over his left shoulder and then right. Ever so methodically, the corners of his mouth tipped up. His eyes bore into mine as a smile emerged, gleaming white. It was entirely disconcerting.

Like the great Nortian glacier incident of my Gram's youth, when a wide river of snow consumed an entire village, a frustrating flow of moisture gathered between my legs. I cursed him in my mind. Even his insincerity gave me the leaky loins.

I'd let my wide river swallow his village whole.

I dug my nails into my palms as the dance came to an end, hoping the pain would dull my other responses. Septimus bowed, every bit the consummate courtier. He took my hand in his and looped my arm around his elbow, deepening his grin and revealing two adorable dimples that settled deeply within his cheeks.

He inclined his head to a nobleman as we strolled past.

"You are salivating. Is the bitch finally in heat?"

"On second thought... scowl, Septimus. Knit that brow and resume your thin-lipped, angry face."

"Our next dance is a low country reel!" a herald shouted from his place on the royal dais.

I tried to break free, to seek another partner, but Septimus held tight and steered us in the direction of the water lapping at the shore.

"Consort," he said in a low, melodic voice, watching my chest as it rose and fell. "Had I known wearing this fool's expression would get me closer to your cunt..."

"Hush, foul-mouthed tyrant." I shoved against him in earnest, no longer under the scrutiny of a hundred inquisitive Solnnan eyes. "You know nothing."

The waves crashed and then whispered around dozens of rock formations that peppered the beach. Naturally, Septimus led us toward the largest, most shadowed outcropping. I planted my heels in the sand, resisting, before the Bond and our intimate surroundings made it impossible.

Instead of jerking me along, he stopped and trailed his fingertips down the soft skin of my inner arm.

"You shiver for me, not for the night's chill." His smile softened, but his eyes remained shrewd and full of intention. "Have you allowed yourself to imagine the potency of our coupling? You will fight me, and I will fuck you until you are raw and pleading. Then I will fill you with my seed, allow you to orgasm as you beg me to grace you with my child."

I turned from him, seeking the dais, rubbing my arms, fighting the Goddess-given instinct that screamed I was his.

"I have, and that is precisely why I am removing myself from this situation."

He caught my arm and slung me around to face him.

"Why do you cower from what we could become?"

"Cower? Is it cowardice when an addict chooses a healthier path? Or to leave an abusive spouse that you still love? Our coupling would be divine, the aftermath cataclysmic."

Cruel hands dug into my waist, spinning me, shoving me into the dais. The wind-roughened wood caught the fabric of my dress, seeming to hold me in place. Above me, I saw the driftwood throne—sun-bleached branches, twisted into a formidable-looking high seat. Her Majesty sat there now, watching over her court.

Septimus dropped his head, running his straight and prominent nose, Cato's nose, along the bridge of mine. Thunder rumbled far off in the distance—I felt its resonance between our bodies.

"Are you a woman who requires foreplay, then? The slow and seductive mingling of tongues?"

I closed my eyes, breathing him in. The pumping in my chest and the pulsing in my core synched with the waves crashing into the shoreline.

"Is it love you desire? Eira," he whispered. "Like the false expressions I wear, I could pretend to love you—might even convince myself that I do." He held out his hand, like an invitation to the next dance. "Give yourself to me."

He slid one arm around my waist as I placed my palm on his.

"Let me love you, comfort you." He pressed my head to his shoulder—strength and surety engulfed me. The gesture provided what I'd been missing from the moment I stepped foot out of Cordillaria. "I will end the life of any man who threatens my broodmare." He laughed low in his throat, the sound haunted and tinged with cruelty.

I balled my fist and punched, catching him squarely in the jaw. His head snapped to the side but returned just as quickly, his disconcerting smile spreading wide.

"Partner up for our next dance—a western Nortian jig!" the herald called out above us.

I struggled against him, furious that I was still susceptible to his horseshit. He snagged my elbow and dragged me back, the sand seeming to aid his cause. I rounded in fury and raked him across the face with my claws. Four lines flared red against his moonlit flesh, matching the crackling bolt of heat lighting that reflected red in his pale eyes.

Above us, Viktos murmured his encouragement.

"Yes, enchantress, fight me." He gathered the hem of my dress, pulling it over my hip, high enough to expose my silk-covered backside. "Resist if you must... but you *will* let me in." Septimus's fingers rounded my cheek, edged along my crevice, and spread me.

The wind picked up—a low, hollow whistle raised the hair on my arms as it rushed between the beach's rock features and the dais. The scent of coconut and sea spray tangled in the air, twisting my senses into knots. I craved his taste, remembered the ferocity of his mouth on mine.

Lightning struck.

"I don't want this." The wind took my words and spirited them away into the deepening sky.

"Eira." I watched how his mouth moved as he said my name, luring me with his siren's call. "I offer you the Primus-King's head, or, if you prefer, will restrain him while you take it from his shoulders. I will end him for us. Fuck you in a pool of his cursed blood." Septimus's arousal pressed into my pubic bone. His silk skirt and the downy hair on his thighs whispered against my bare legs. "I vow this to you. All I ask—"

"Bring him to me," the words spilled from my mouth, "rid the world of his progeny..." I expanded my lungs, the smell of rain heavy in the air. "I will bear your—"

Through the racing clouds, the last ray of the sinking sun flashed, washing my hands in a soft-orange glow before dying away.

"We welcome to the Overlook, Prince Ambrose, second in the line of Monwyn succession, and His Royal Highness, Prince Catommandus, Warden of Basilia!" the herald's voice rose above a low rumble of thunder.

I didn't trust my ears.

"They can't—it can't..."

A loud applause rent the air. The uneven staccato of clapping hands was just as tempestuous as the conflicting emotions crowding my mind—confusion, joy, the overwhelming need to fall on my knees to give praise.

"We welcome you to Solnna, Sons of Monwyn!" It was the queen's voice now. I looked up and made out a sliver of her raised arm between the thrones.

"From your womb," Septimus shook me, dug his fingers into my shoulders, diverting my attention. His eyes were... soft, serene. "We will create the future."

A bolt of lightning cracked across the sky.

I wrenched away and ran, charging around the dais and trudging up the hill that gave it its height.

"Cato!" I screamed, hoping my voice would carry above the music. "Ambrose!"

I turned the last corner, falling once in the shifting sand and surged toward the pavilion.

I saw Ambrose first.

Tears poured in a deluge down both cheeks.

"Husband!" I yelled. He stood heads above all others on the abalone-studded platform, so handsome, so regal.

He rotated on his heels and waved like he'd seen me as recently as breakfast. He was perfection.

I was a mess—wind-mussed hair, nose running, makeup streaming down my face.

Cato stepped from Ambrose's shadow, and a cry tore from my chest.

I ignored the stares and raised brows tossed my way as I ran through a crowd of revelers; the wind drying my tears.

"I'd always assumed Nortians to be frigid. I'd be if I lived there."

"A love match, then? How sweet. It's no wonder she chose to stay in those dreadful mountains."

My men were free, alive, and whole.

Ambrose slid in front of Cato, blocking my view. He crooked his finger and gave me a wink. I dashed up the dais, weeping and sputtering, and when I hit the last step, I leapt.

"My bear," I cried out. "My Black Bear." He caught me, stumbling backward, as I wrapped my legs around his hips and held tight. I buried my mouth in his neck and breathed in his spicy scent while I sobbed.

"Wifling, my sensitive spouse, it has only been a few days," Ambrose called out with a playful affect to his voice. He laughed and gave my behind a pat, much to the amusement of the crowd.

"Newlyweds," Cato said beside us, groaning in mock irritation.

Ambrose's lips found my temple.

"Play the part, Troth," he murmured.

Play the part. Play the part. I was tired of playing.

"We have come shopping for a bride. My consort lives to make matches... dare I say she made the most scrumptious one for herself?"

I nodded against him, agreeing.

"Highness Ambrose, you are too much," the queen said in a heavily accented lilt beside us.

"Much too much," Cato added.

"How"—*kiss*—"how"—*kiss*—"did"—*kiss*—"you get free?" I couldn't help myself. I pressed my lips to his jaws, his shoulders, his neck.

"Sister-in-law, how lovely to see you again."

I jolted, knocking the top of my head against Ambrose's chin as Cato's words settled between us.

"Sister-in-law? Cato, how dare you sister-in—"

Ambrose crushed his mouth to mine in a bruising kiss. I answered his ferocity with the force of my own.

"Still sappy, I see," Cato said, aloof and disinterested. "Such an abysmal quality in a wife."

My head snapped up. "Oh, no sir, you will not—"

Ambrose pressed his tongue between my open lips. I squealed in aggravation until he moaned low in the back of his throat. Oh. He missed his wifling, too. I gave in... to the familiarity... to the absolute inferno that he breathed into the kiss.

"Ahem. Well then," Trivio's voice cut through my lust-addled mind. "Prince Catommandus, while the lovebirds continue to catch up, allow me to introduce the most elite and eligible women of Solnna. We have a wide selection to offer you: beauty, high station, proven bearers—if your focus is securing an heir."

"Se-uring whaa—" I shoved back as Ambrose maneuvered his teeth around my tongue and trapped it between his bite.

In my peripheral vision I watched as Trivio danced around Cato and clapped his hands. "The queen herself has curated the offerings."

"Tha whaaa?" I open-mouth shouted, tongue still clamped between my husband's teeth.

No Troth mask I could don would assuage the thorny vines of jealousy that began slithering around my chest, wrapping themselves around my neck.

My skin heated.

Ambrose released me and then squished my face between his massive pecs, subduing me in his bear-like embrace.

"Wet me gwoo! Wet me—"

"Yes, darling, let us take refreshment while my brother peruses the potentials."

"Appropriate seating has been arranged. Please follow me, Highness, consort," said Trivio.

"Sweetling, I know you miss me, but darling," Ambrose laughed good-naturedly and his volume rose as he walk-hugged me backward, "what you're demanding would set the sands aflame." He freed me and settled me with a stern look that I knew meant "get a grip." He waved away Trivio, who gestured to an empty seat. "No, no, one will do. My wife sits upon my lap for all state business back home."

Ambrose flopped down into his seat.

A collective gasp rolled around the Pavilion.

"Makes sense now!" A merry voice yelled from the assembly.

"I'd have missed that too!" Another called out.

I looked down and pressed my lips into a hard line.

"H-husband, your um." I pointed.

"Your cock's out, brother." Cato came to my side and glanced down.

"Oh, my word!" A woman's voice rang behind us. "Gracious Goddess above."

Six flaccid inches of him dangled between his legs and over the seat's edge. It shimmered... His penis shimmered, like the fucking gilded sun that perched on the palace's highest spire.

"It was supposed to be a surprise," Ambrose muttered, batting at his barely-there-skirt. "Ah, well. Wife, weigh down this fine fabric." He pulled me onto his lap, right between his spread legs. "Majesty, roll out the finest flesh you have to offer the mountain monarch... and his brother."

The queen stood, the gauzy periwinkle chiffon of her multi-layered gown shifting in the wind.

"The most powerful of our women have put themselves forward for consideration," she said while wrapping a fur-lined indigo silk around her shoulders. With a flick of her fingers, a line formed. The citizens who attended the soiree closed in, pressing their eager selves to the stairs.

"Eira, turn down the heat, sweetheart. Cato's eyes are for none but your succulent self." His long arms encircled my waist, hugging me snugger, when all I could think to do was leap from his arms. "I missed you, by the way. More than I thought possible."

I remembered my commitments. That I loved two and not one.

"Ambrose." I twisted up, tucked my legs in, and curled my arms around his neck. "I missed you too." Stretching, I placed a kiss on the corner of his mouth. "I haven't known peace since you walked from our room." Tears threatened again, but Ambrose laid his mouth gently on one of my lids and then the other, staunching their flow.

"Bellan of Summervale, second daughter of Her Majesty's brother!" The herald called.

A tall woman mounted the steps to the dais, her arms spread as wide as the smile on her face. Her skin gleamed golden, and her hair swung in fat spirals down her back. She strode across the platform confidently in her asymmetric dress. The aqua-blue and purple scarves of her train shimmied and hopped behind her.

"Fuuuuuuck, Ambrose, she's gorgeous."

A servant bowed, offering an assortment of wines. I took a pink-colored potion and tipped it back. "She's carved like a masterwork statue."

The woman walked straight up to Cato, who stood with his hands folded behind his back. She struck a pose so confident I wished all young women could see her shine, emulate her self-love. Cato circled her, studying her from every angle.

"I am skilled in the arts of weaving, baking, and calligraphy."

"Oh, gods, her voice is as smooth as the silk she wears," I whispered, hiding my mouth behind my glass.

Cato paused behind her, assessing her like a mare he wished to purchase. He dropped his head close to the juncture of her shoulder and inhaled, filling his chest with her scent. His eyes flicked up to mine.

"I will allow you to peer upon my body if you wish it, Prince Catommandus."

My breath caught. Jealousy raged through me like a massive, green ogre netherbent on destruction. The intensity in his gaze called to the æther gathering in my chest. *Mine.* Those deliciously dark eyes pierced right through me.

I swallowed hard, ready to commit crimes, if so much as an inkling of interest twinkled in their expressions.

Ambrose's mouth found the sensitive skin below my ear.

"He's talked nonstop about burying himself in your warm pot of honey. So unsheathe your claws from my thighs."

I loosened the hold I was unaware I had on him.

Bellan's graceful hands parted the robe-like dress she wore, revealing the most wonderfully small and pert breasts.

Cato huffed, the most snobbish of sounds, never once looking at the goddess offering herself up for his view. She was magnificent, slender yet soft in the most feminine of ways.

"I am dissatisfied with the thickness of her thighs. Aberus might enjoy her, though," Cato said, dismissing her with a sneer. He fucking sneered.

The woman gasped at his callous comment.

I polished off my wine and clunked the glass down on a servant's tray.

"Catommandus Odelguard Lefwinis Borko, whatever your other names are, her thighs are exceptional!" I popped up out of Ambrose's lap, and he scrambled to right his skirt.

"Bellan, you are stunning, and he is a pig. You can do better than some second son. You would be sublime on the arm of Nortia's heir. He would better match your divine stature. And I could make the introductions. You taking notes, Trivio?"

Cato's eyebrows shot to his forehead.

"Next," I yelled in Solnnan, swirling my fingers in the air. I shooed Cato to the side and waved up the next contestant.

"Lin Drelada, third child of Her Most Royal Majesty, cousin of Scion Lok, who received his Assignment just this year!"

The person who emerged—holy, glorious Goddess above. "Can we keep them?" I mouthed while looking back at Ambrose. His giggle was response enough to let me know he appreciated the sensuous intensity in their sinewy form as much as I did.

Ambrose hailed me back to his side, where I reluctantly perched upon his knee. He drew sweet, small circles on my hip.

"I think Cato would disown the both of us."

"Probably."

The fuchsia paint on their lips complimented Lin's deep complexion. Lithe of body, thin of hip. Two rings of gold studded with amethyst encircled their finely muscled arms—one above their elbow, another above their biceps. Swags of pearls dripped from the delicate creations. A curved sword hung sheathed at their side, which pulled my attention to a set of thighs that would rival Ambrose's.

"Tree trunks. Good gorgeous Gammond above."

"If he complains about those legs…"

Cato looked up to Lin Drelada and sighed like he'd been served his least favorite food. He circled them once and then again. "State your worth."

I tensed. Ambrose clutched my hip.

"He said what?" I hissed. I pushed the non-existent sleeves up my fore-arms. "He needs a wallop, and I'm just the wife to see it through."

"Hush." Ambrose spanked my thigh.

I shimmied back against Ambrose and crossed my arms in a huff.

Lin Drelada peered at Cato from the side of their eye.

"I am proficient in armed combat. I have trained under Her Majesty's personal Gilded guard and have earned fame subduing criminals on the sea and the land," they said in a smoky voice.

"Gods, they are perfect for him," I muttered to Ambrose while watch-ing Lin stiffen as Cato smelled them and scowled.

"They *are* him."

I pursed my lips and turned back to the inspection.

"Do you like rocks?" I called out.

Cato stopped dead. Only his lips twitched.

"No," Lin Drelada replied curtly.

"Reading?" Ambrose asked.

"No."

"Hmmm, not sure you're his type, then. Are you, um… are you not required to disrobe?"

I clapped like a happy seal in sardine season.

"Oh, good question husband, yes please, I think that should be standard for—"

"Too frigid," Cato announced to the shocked crowd, then stepped away from this latest divine creation, dusting the hem of his fluttering half-sleeve.

"Frigid? Did you leave your brain on the boat?" I admonished. "Lin Drelada, were I unwed—"

"Not nearly warm enough for me, consort Eira. I require a fiery woman to satisfy my most basic of needs." Cato flicked his tongue over the corner of his mouth.

Oh, well then.

I shivered at the way he looked at me, and my hands itched where the æther stirred in my palms. Ambrose felt it too and slid his hand along my thigh. Behind me, he purred. "I feel your response, wife. I cannot wait to watch you feel his."

"Next," I squeaked out, squirming in my Ambrose-seat.

Trivio yelled, "Jeall, Lady of the Spire. Mother of Princess Lymmia and Prince Gerrome."

Another beauty with almond-shaped brown eyes took the stairs. Round of rear and waist, she had a chest that easily rivaled my own. She stepped onto the dais, a tiny girl on her hip and a little boy dressed as a glittery-blue lobster holding her hand.

The queen stood, walked forward, and embraced the smiling woman.

"Jeall is a daughter of my body, recently widowed."

The woman, who looked only a smidge like the queen herself, bowed her head. She left the queen's embrace and made her way to stand in front of Cato. The little boy tucked himself behind his mother's flowing skirt and hid his face.

Cato kneeled.

"Why hello, you are certainly a strong-looking young man," Cato spoke softly. "Are you taking good care of your mother?" The small child peered around, and nodded before hiding again. "I lost my papa recently as well."

Two soft brown eyes looked up from under a veil of dark lashes, though he still clung to his mother.

"Where'd he go?" The little prince asked.

"The cradle... with my mama. I have been told it is beautiful there, and the Goddess watches over them... as she watches over us."

I turned to Ambrose, stroked his beard while he leaned into my touch. My heart shattered for Cato, for my husband as well... and for that little innocent face so sad and full of confusion.

"They can see us from up there?"

"Mmhmm." Cato twisted on his feet and pointed up to the twinkling sky. "The stars are windows. When it is night here, the heavens are bright, which is why we cannot see through them ourselves. But they can see us just fine."

"Oh." A sweet but guarded smile lit the boy's eyes.

Cato held his hand out. The child reached for it, hesitantly at first, but then placed his small, perfect palm into Cato's scarred one.

"It was nice to meet you, Gerrome."

I lowered a hand to my stomach, feeling for the first time in my life what I thought was a maternal instinct. I wanted to—needed to—wrap my arms around the mother and her children, soothe their spirits, patch their hole-riddled hearts.

It struck me then. Cato deserved to be a father. He would be a brilliant parent. He was already a brilliant partner. But *our* child—

Thunder sounded in the distance.

No... not thunder.

The ground trembled beneath our feet.

"Off the dais!" the queen shouted. Trivio shielded her head, and they dashed for the steps.

Ambrose shot up. Cato grabbed the little one and helped the mother down the stairs. Warriors appeared from the shadows surrounding the crowd.

A chilly breeze wafted through the tent... cold, not cool.

The crowd looked around, faces drawn in concern.

Lightning branched out over the ocean, crackling white in the dark sky. The bolt fractured, hurling its fury into the sea. The sands vibrated around our feet as the rumbling shook us once more.

"Another storm. Lightning striking the ocean floor. Nothing to worry about." The queen raised her hands, and collectively her people began to relax. I pressed closer to Ambrose's side. Too many storms in too few days for my comfort. I was all too aware of why.

"Sol Mother," Jeall approached the queen, breeching our small circle. "While we are here, I would introduce you to my new maid and her betrothed." Jeall's face split into a massive smile. "They've arrived!"

"Steffani is here? Bring her forth." The queen clasped her hands tightly. She glowed with a joy that wrapped itself around my own heart.

Jeall waved a couple forward, her excitement palpable.

"Steffani dear, we welcome you. How lovely you've become." The queen embraced the gold-clad woman. "I thought your arrival wasn't until after winter?"

Steffani smiled up at Jeall, who beamed back at her. The dark-haired maid was positively overflowing with love.

"Grandfather gave us permission, as Frem was not dealing well with the pollen. And somehow the winter snows had yet to take hold. We rounded the rift without issue."

"The rift! Are you Nortian?" I asked, suddenly excited. I knew the answer to my question when I caught the glint of green and gold ornamentations on her eyeteeth.

Gaean. I went on the defensive but held my face neutral.

"Gaean, but I've been to Nortia twice!" Steffani exclaimed. "It is the most beautiful place. All covered in white and so pure. Oh, and the foxes! They are the cutest animals of all."

I wanted to jump up and down and discuss just how much I loved snow foxes but remained cautious. There seemed to be no malice in her. And not every Gaean posed a threat. Cinden was Gaean, after all. I reined in my anxiety.

The queen released Steffani but draped an arm over her shoulder.

"Steffani and Jeall were childhood friends until Steffani's father fell in love on a diplomatic endeavor." The queen gathered her daughter and hugged both girls closely. "They all lived here as ambassadors until her mother became ill and returned to Gaea seeking a cure. There are no better healers than those of Cult Mossius, but her body was too far gone. May her soul reside in the cradle. Now Steffani returns and is to Join with Fremman, third son of our arch-priestess."

A fleeting pang of sorrow flittered across Steffani's countenance, quickly replaced by warmth when she laid her eyes on her betrothed, a shorter man with a paunch. Frem blushed crimson, his absolute devotion bared for all to see.

"Grandfather still says the prayers for mother at temple."

The queen nodded.

"How that man thinks he can act as king, Primus, and high holy man is beyond me."

The earth ceased its spin.

The queen kept her arm around her daughter, and like the stalwart leader she was, showed no sign that she'd called for the Primus-King's slaughter earlier that day.

Show me the daughters of Gaea.

My vision narrowed, like I was looking down the eyepiece of a telescope.

The earthquake... the Nether Lord.

It was exactly what I'd asked him for... but looking at her, here, now... Did my thirst for revenge truly run that deep?

Ambrose's heavy hands came to rest on my shoulders, rooting me to the sandy floor.

"Catommandus, Eira wishes to retire. Would you see her back to my rooms? I would have a word with Her Majesty."

"If I must." Cato clipped a short bow and turned, sauntering off toward a massive rock that hid the palace from view.

I stared out at nothing. Couldn't move.

Ambrose stabbed his finger into my back, forcing me forward, until we stood beyond the crowd.

"Look at me. Eira, right here. Are you in control?" He pointed at my eyes with two fingers and flipped them around to his. "Cato needs his dick sucked, and you need to occupy your hot hands before you fell a kingdom. Go up there, show him the godsdamned stars, and do not, under any circumstances, leave the room." He dipped his head, searching my face.

I couldn't speak, only nod.

Show me the daughters of Gaea

Chapter Thirty-Seven

WE TOIL

Eira

Cato strode forward, head held high, hands clasped behind his back.

The scent of him, cedar and clove, wafted back to me, mixing with the ever-present whiff of coconut.

I pleaded with myself not to run and bit my lips, commanding myself not to weep. He wasn't a ghost—he was here with me, tangible, real. He nodded to a group of youths huddling in the middle of a dimly lit courtyard and then made a sudden right turn, disappearing into darkness.

"Cato?" I whispered. I caught a glimpse of him at the far end of a covered stone corridor, standing under a lamp, his back against the wall. He flicked a brow at the same time that his half-smile dimpled his cheek. I took off, but before I could reach him, he lifted his hand and twisted the fixture, casting us both into pitch blackness. I dragged my hand along the rough wall and tiptoed forward, letting my fingers be my eyes, until my hand found the lamp, still warm. "Catomman—"

"You are a woman reborn of the shadows, and yet you cannot find me?" he teased from somewhere behind me. His rich laughter rumbled around us, soothing and sweet.

I startled when his hands found my waist, but then melted into him as he turned me into his chest.

"Nothing could see in this blackness, sir." I grinned into the dark—I was so happy, so relieved. Neither the Primus-King nor the fire god Leyometh could steal the joy from my heart.

Cato's fingers caressed the small of my back, rose to my shoulders, and came to rest on either side of my chin.

"I have no need of eyes to see you, love." His rough thumb swept across my lips—traced my nose. "There is no part of you I have yet to memorize."

His wine-sweetened breath tickled my ear. "I could identify you by the circumference of your wrist alone, an outline of the mark on your shoulder, the texture of a single strand of hair."

The normally effervescent bubbles of æther flowed through me, but their tempo changed. Large, slow circles wound themselves around my torso in a gyre that seemed to slow time.

"Cato?"

"Yes, wife?"

Wife.

I lifted my hand and traced my fingertip down the bump in the bridge of his nose, and then allowed it to linger in the notch that formed the bow of his top lip.

"Please kiss me, husband. Please don't make me wait any long—"

His lips touched mine, soft and unhurried.

I threaded my arms around his neck and gave myself over. His freshly trimmed beard pricked my sensitive skin. I welcomed it, just as I welcomed the deep hum that rolled through his chest as the tips of our tongues met. The familiar sound jostled me from the waking dream of the past days, igniting my fingertips, which pulsed and tingled where they touched his sun-kissed flesh.

He pulled away, but his forehead remained pressed to mine.

"I love you, Eira."

"I love you, Cato."

He smiled against my lips as they met again.

"No, but Eira, I love-love you." He laughed and nuzzled the tip of his nose against mine. "There are not words enough to tell you the depth of my devotion."

"You don't need eyes; I don't need words." I ran my fingers over the closely shaved sides of his head, reveling in how soft the shorter stubble felt as I brushed it. "D-did Ambrose force you to groom?"

"He did. Were I left to my own devices, Eira, I would not have waited another second. I would have—"

"Stormed the gates and slaughtered the men, women, and sea-creature children?"

"Correct."

We laughed together then, the sound more meaningful than words.

"Eira?" he breathed.

"Yes, Cato?"

"I know we have much to discuss, but might I implore you to... oh, I don't know... turn around and allow me to fuck you against this wall? Only so I can concentrate on literally anything other than my cock. I find myself incapable of conversation and unable to concentrate on the very pressing matters of killing a sitting monarch, killing my own uncle, and killing my brother for the farce he just put us through."

I feigned a gasp.

"Because of your Dick Bond?" I said jokingly while stroking a finger down his chin. I couldn't stop touching him.

"Hardly." He pushed his chest against mine as he inhaled the scent of my hair. "Every day I imagined walking hand in hand." He threaded his fingers through mine and brought my knuckles to his lips. "I kept hearing your voice, the adorable fucking way you hold out your vowels when you speak. I wanted your advice... your thoughts when I was floundering, but you were not there, and because of that, I was not whole."

I shivered as he pressed our locked hands over my head and walked me backward.

"I believe you have found your words, husband." My voice barely rose above a whisper.

"And every night... Eira, I have had a red-hot nail hammered through my toe and been kept without food for three weeks—neither compared to the state of torment in which I found myself. I dreamed of you, of us, sitting in front of the fire, reading and laughing and sharing snacks. And fucking, of course. Gods what I do to you in my dreams. I fisted myself in a godsdamned privy that stank of sour man and rotting fish while imagining your legs spread for me as you sat the Monwyn throne."

I slapped a hand over my mouth to stifle the laughter that escaped me.

"Oh no, my love... Did Ambrose not offer his services—Ouch!" His palm slapped against my backside with a sting.

Cato dipped low, hauled my legs around his waist and pressed my back into the wall.

"I can tell you from experience that your slit provides me triple—quadruple—the pleasure of that man's ass... and of course he offered... but by Derros, let me have my fill of you before he enters into the equation of our lovemaking again."

I squeezed my thighs, pulling him closer, wanting more of him.

"Mmm—so hard. You must have missed me fiercely." I slid my hand between our bodies, grasping his thickness through the tunic he wore, adjusting him to lay against my sex.

"If I come inside of my pants, you will have no one to blame but yourself."

I ground my silk-clad lips against him.

"You have a tongue and fingers... *I* will be fine."

His hand shot up, grasping my neck. He squeezed gently and guided my head up.

"Did your time with Uncle Septimus turn you into a full-fledged monster, you little shit?"

"Cato," I groaned. He rolled his hips languidly, parting my thighs further. My underwear stuck to my slickness—my perfect organ, preparing for pleasure. "I'm ready for you, now."

"Then let us adjourn to our apartments." He shifted and with a flick and click, the lamp nearest us flamed to life.

"No. I can't wait that long." My greedy hands parted his deep neckline and spread out over his chest. Goddess bless the Solnnan clothiers.

Sounds of hushed laughter came from the end of the hall.

We were discovered.

"Evening, all." Cato twisted away from the wall, still holding me up by the rear. "I am the Prince of Monwyn, and this is my princess." Cato kissed me once more, in full view of the others. He then bowed, dumping my head backward. I gave an inverted smile to the group of elders. "Allow me to introduce you to Troth Eira, my wife."

The amused chuckles continued until Cato allowed me my feet and took my hand.

One woman blushed. Another hid her smile behind her handkerchief.

Cato took my elbow and led me forward, but I hesitated, searching his eyes.

"Ambrose?" I questioned.

"Just give me this moment, yes?" His eyes crinkled, not with desperation, but with a near boyish charm. A crooked grin tugged at the corner of his mouth.

"Lead the way, my prince."

Cato's throat worked up and down, and he glanced away.

"Esteemed nobles, allow me to introduce you to my heart song, Eira of Basilia."

Did I imagine the slight hitch in his words, or the misty glaze that clouded his eyes?

"A love match?" said a rotund lord. He smiled down at his even more rotund wife. Her hair was thinning, and she had a sickly pallor, yellowish, with purple splotches dotted across the translucent skin of her arms. "I can always recognize one on account of my own."

"Very much so," Cato replied, while taking and bowing over the woman's hand.

"Then, like me, you are among the wealthiest of men. I am Lord Soltair, and this is my Elliz."

The notes of a song floated through the air, a softly sung yet complex harmony.

Cato's brows creased as he turned his head, determining the location of the sound.

"There is... singing every night, a love-lovely tradition... and... way to wind down," the lady offered, wheezing and gasping nearly every other word.

A burst of nostalgic warmth lit within me, spreading from my mind's eye to my limbs. Sunshine and happiness, a deeply brown face, a smile that still had my heart—Kan Keagan.

"My childhood mentor told me of the singing. He said... even on the worst of days, when nothing seemed to be as it should, when everything was out of place... the voices reminded him that something beautiful remained."

The group nodded their heads and glanced meaningfully at one another.

"Well met, young lovers." They shuffled away, humming along to the tune that clung to the breeze.

We stepped out of the hallway and into the moonlit night. Cato hugged me from behind, resting his chin on my shoulder as he swayed with the lyrics of the song, "What do they mean, love?"

I leaned into him, dropped my head back to his shoulder, and listened.

"For our children we toil... their futures bright as Lykksun's light. May they know prosperity greater than our own... and peace in their days." I whispered into his ear, kissing his jaw between translations.

"My gaggle of girls will most assuredly know abundance. Their papa will see to that," he chuckled, "but I doubt there will be much peace."

"Still, no boys?"

Cato shook his head. Though I couldn't see his face, I knew well the wistful expression he'd wear. The same he wore whenever he imagined our future.

"No. I have the strangest feeling that 'girl papa' might be the greatest role I play in life. All my little Eiras running around, demanding cake and collecting rocks."

I froze. The perfect image he painted shattered—a rock cast at the surface of a frozen pond.

"Eira, are you well?" He lifted my heating palm and laid it against his cool cheek, turning me in his arms.

"Cato, so much has happened: Merrias, Septimus, a conflict between gods. Choices must be made."

"Is that all?" He shrugged. "That is simple... I choose you."

CHAPTER THIRTY-EIGHT

MY GIRL

CATO

"**P**erfect, goddess. Pure love."

I meant every sweet word that fell from my lips, but at this moment, I would say whatever it took. I needed to fuck—to bury myself in her warmth and thrust into her until she was screaming and clawing her nails down my back. Until she was contracting around me, shuddering as my name fell from her lips.

I wanted her messy. Covered in my scent.

"Gods, fuck," she gasped as her ass hit the door.

I may have been a little too rough, but she knew what she was doing. I gazed into her ocean-colored eyes as she pawed at my tunic-covered cock, twisted her palm over my tip, and then scored her nails down my length.

"Cato, hurry."

"I am trying but—fuck, love, hold on."

She was doing her best to press the door handle but became distracted by the sliver of chest that she'd unearthed when attempting to rip off my clothes.

"I just need your penis free." She caught my nipple in her mouth and bit down over the fabric. My cock swelled to near pain. "I'll do the rest."

"Shit, sweetheart. Hang on." My hips thrust into her hands, seeking the relief she was most willing to provide.

"No."

No? Normally, I would have laughed at her outright refusal, but she was stone-faced serious.

Her talons dug into my biceps.

My back hit the door.

Fuck.

"Is this all I am to you, Eira, a magnificent cock to mount?"

"Yes. Get my tits out. Now." She ran her tongue over my nipple again, thoroughly soaking the fine fabric. My dick jerked; my sac drew up tight. Already a pressure built low in my spine. Her desire was my defeat. "Can't wait. You'll come in my mouth first, because I've missed that and the sighs you make... and the way your hands tighten in my hair. And then I want it from behind, with your fingers working my clit—Fast side-to-side motions. Do you understand?"

Her hand dropped low, flipped up my hem, and dove into my underclothes. Soft but insistent fingers slipped through the slickness at the crown of my erection and were out and pressed to her lips in an instant.

Died. I have died at the hands of a marshmallow.

She moaned, tasting me. My godsdamned eyes rolled to the back of my head when her tongue slipped between her two fingers, seeking more.

Troll guts. Severed bowels. Dying pets. Anal prolapse. Flipping breathe Catommandus, you absolute weakling.

"Too much? Did I—was that icky? I've just missed you so—"

She paused and took a step back. Those dark, arched brows of hers flattened above worried eyes.

"No." I feigned calm, clicked the handle, and opened the door, sweeping a hand to the chamber. "It was the exact opposite of... icky."

"Then hurry, or I'm headed back to mount the big toe of that statue we passed."

I chuckled.

"Your way with words, Eira, are—oof!" She hit me hard, and I staggered backward into the room, bringing her with me. Her hands were everywhere, tugging, demanding, caressing.

My underwear was gone.

"How the fuck did you manage—"

"Kiss. Now."

She climbed me like a rock face, but I caught her hands and locked them behind her back.

"Cato!" she cried out. "Cato, I..."

I knew she was desperate, but her fervor was making me wish for more than a quick coupling. I wanted to take my time with her, to take her to the edge and watch her writhe and thrash above me while she came on my lips. Then I would fuck her for my enjoyment, push those thighs back and let go.

"What is it that you want, love?" I asked, watching the storm clouds gather behind her eyes.

She stomped her foot—that angry little foot of hers—and my cock bucked into her soft belly.

I cherished a loving Eira, but an indignant one undid me.

"Stop being cruel. You know exactly what I want."

"Do I?" I play-acted confusion and let my eyes scan the room, earning me a grimace. Her full, rosy lips pressed together tightly. They would soon do the same around my cock, while I held her face in my hands and thrust into her mouth. And she would take me deep—gods, how she took me.

I retreated backward, and she moved forward, not even realizing she did so. I was pursued, the opposite of my preference.

In an instant, her lovely face morphed from irritated to hurt, to absolutely fucking furious. My blood pumped through my veins so violently I could hear it pulse in my head.

A worthy adversary.

"You know, a woman of Monwyn would never allow such unbecoming expressions to ruin her lovely countenance. Propriety demands—"

Her eyes bugged.

"What will propriety *demand* when I knock you to the floor and straddle your *face*?" She spat the last word.

I splayed my fingers and peered down at my nails before knocking a bit of non-existent lint from my chest. "Hardly a threat. The promise of your thighs pressed to my cheeks while I watch your breasts bounce above me will encourage me to even greater acts of cruelty."

Tears. Actual fucking tears brimmed in her eyes. Her lip quivered.

The room seemed to fill with a golden light as my eyes dilated. The sound that came from my chest was more growl than groan.

"On. Your. Knees." I gritted out the words, no longer in a playful mood. I needed her, and she required me.

Eira dropped on command, and her dark forelock fell over her eyes while she nibbled on the corner of her full lip. Her thick thighs peeked out from under her hem and her breasts swayed gently.

"The gods favor me, their son of destruction."

Her head snapped up, eyes wide. Something changed in her carriage.

"They do Cato, both of us. Truly. Merrias revealed that we were attracted *before* the Bond was created." She pressed her forearms together and wrang her hands. "We are real—this is real. Not just the scheming hands of a manipulative god."

"I could have told you that."

"What?"

I crooked my finger at her, and she crawled toward me, just as I prayed she would. Her breasts hung heavily, allowing me a view down her plunging neckline.

I dropped my hand and cupped my length, outlining its size, showing her the effect she had on my body. I reached below my tunic and ran my fingers over my erection, letting her glimpse the power she held over me. She gazed upon my member like it was some important relic—or a fucking slice of cake.

"At Verus, I was very much in control until the third night of the rite. Everything changed then. Even though I had made the decision to keep you... my feelings compounded. Do you remember I tried to claim you in front of Evandr? Before he pummeled me into submission?"

She nodded while I combed my fingers through her hair, tucking back the renegade sweep of brown and clutching a handful. I guided her forward.

"You went all warrior-king." Her eyes deepened. My woman liked to be chased, to be dominated and reminded that even in a world where she was powerful, so was I.

"Yes." I stroked the pad of my thumb across her full bottom lip. Her tongue darted out, flicking over its pad, and she ran her fingers, all ten of them, up my cock, base to tip. I sucked in a breath and let it out slowly while she worshipped me. "I was aware, then, that something had changed." She bowed her head, eyes still on mine, and traced her tongue over my divot.

Her warm mouth closed over my head. At the same time, she reached between my legs to weigh my sac and skim her nails lightly over the flesh beneath. I held her gaze, intoxicated—she was the only drug I would risk indulging in.

Eira inched her lips down my cock, pulling back when she hit dry skin and then beginning again, gliding down in the wetness she'd left behind. She was groaning... sucking me off.

Did I deserve her? I didn't give a damn. She was mine.

She rocked back, but I halted her retreat and pressed my arousal further into her mouth. She hummed happily and then relaxed the muscles of her throat to take me further. That tongue of hers somehow still managing to work me, cupping and rubbing. The impatient brat curled her palm around my dick and began pumping me.

"Eira, love," I breathed, feeling my cock leak a precursory bit of come. "As far as talents are concerned, I believe this to be your area of—"

"Catommandus!"

Eira reared forward, gagged hard on my dick, and then shot backward, throwing her hands up in surprise.

"For fuck's sake!" I shouted, snapping my skirt down.

"Rinse your sweat-soaked testes before you park that wagon in my wife's shed... nasty piglet."

Fucking Ambrose. I'll kill him. It would take less than three minutes.

His conceited ass strolled across the floor in nothing but the horrific, tall, tight underwear that he insisted on wearing to bed. Like a king presiding over his kingdom, he pointed his finger at us both.

"Goddess, Ambrose, you scared me to death." Eira stood and marched over to my idiot of an adopted brother and slapped him on the chest. "Why are you here? You gave me instructions, and I'm doing my best to follow them."

I looked down and beheld the saddest dick known to mankind—raging and abandoned.

"I grew bored and decided to do some reading."

Eira snapped her head back at me, concern and shock on her face.

I shrugged.

"Ambrose?" She took him by the elbow and hand, like an infirmary patient, and led him toward the bedchamber. "Black Bear, sweet man, are you well?"

"Of course I am, have you yourself not gazed upon all this sun-pinked—" He paused and tilted his head to the side, taking in the mauve-tipped nipple that peaked from her triangular strap. "On second thought... I *am* feeling rather puny." He stopped short and pressed the back of his hand to his forehead.

"Are you fevered? Ambrose, did you drink the seawater? Don't be embarrassed if you did. I know you require salt after your regimen, but husband, the ocean's water can make you incredibly ill."

She patted his arm and led his deceitful ass away.

Ambrose leaned back just a second before they cleared the copper wall leading to the bedchamber. He batted his long lashes in my direction and had the audacity to smirk.

"Ambrose!" I gave chase.

I whipped around the wall to find Eira in the process of tucking him in like a godsdamned child.

Low bed. Round, no corners. Possible weapons in bedside stand. Glass of water, stack of books. Nearest escape route. Back veranda. Closest visible weapon: dagger hilt sticking out from under the pillow.

"Cato, lower your voice. My head simply cannot take the jarring volume at which you speak. Go wash your dick." He gestured in the direction of the rain bath, and then let his arm fall weakly, like he could no longer support the weight.

"Get up." I snatched the light, silky blue blanket from his body. "I am going to give you a compelling reason to call a healer."

Eira shoved herself in front of me and jabbed a finger into my chest, her glorious tits heaving, distracting me from the true enemy.

"Go wash and fetch him some broth." She whipped the blanket from my hands and flung the thin fabric out with a snap, letting it fall in place over Ambrose's long legs. "I'll ensure he's well, and then we can—what are those?"

"What?" Ambrose looked around while he slid his spectacles up his nose.

Eira pointed to her own face, drawing her finger in a circular motion. She purred like a godsdamned cat.

"Oh, these?"

"Mmm-hmm."

"I found them at the local mercantile when I was shopping for your gift."

"My gift?"

"Indeed, wifey, I will get that later, but..." Ambrose cast his eyes down shyly, "do you still find me fetching in my new eyewear?" He picked up a book from the bedside table and ran his fingertip over the spine, caressing it like a lover's back. "Might I say that these shiny new spectacles reveal that your curves are even more succulent than I had previously assumed?"

He waggled his ridiculous, manicured brows and gnashed his teeth like some absurd fucking shark.

"I... oh, yes, husband. They are, um, quite becoming."

"You'll *becoming*..."

Eira's tinkling giggle filled the space.

I held back my groan of disbelief. They were so fucking ridiculous. *My woman was succumbing to the flirtatious tactics of the idiot actor, who was doing nothing to conceal the rising bump below the sheets. I could clearly see the pink spreading across the bridge of her nose.*

"That's because all bodies are delicious bodies... right?" she said, tracing small circles on her shoulder, unconsciously swaying her hips as she stood over him. She patted his arm.

"Quite so," Ambrose crooned, his voice having gone all low and husky. "And from the show I walked in on, you would know just as well as I." Ambrose opened the book and lifted it to his face. "Feel free to continue as you were. It won't bother me." He faked a cough—a pitiful hacking sound.

"No. Ambrose, we can wai—"

I grabbed two handfuls of her luscious ass and dumped her face-first onto the bed. "Fine by me, brother."

Chapter Thirty-Nine

IT CALLS TO ME

Eira

"**C**ato, he's ill!"

I wrestled with the blanket that blinded me, struggling on account of being ass up.

"Spread yourself."

"Do what?" I pushed up onto my elbows and braced my hands on Ambrose's shins.

"You heard me." Cato grabbed my thighs and parted them wide. He tucked a finger into my underwear and slid his knuckle up and down my labia. "And if this scheming idiot is to be a consistent irritant in our relationship, he better get used to watching or know when to stay gone."

Cato shoved me down, and my breasts mashed into the mattress.

"Ambrose, do not move from where you sit. You will watch me fuck your wife until you understand *exactly* where you fall in the hierarchy of this tangled triad. Am I clear?"

"Cato, you don't get to make that choice for him."

Ambrose cleared his throat... and then he slid those gold-rimmed glasses up on his nose again. He raked those glorious green eyes over my body, tucked his bottom lip under his top, and slowly nodded up at Cato.

"Use your words... prince of Monwyn," Cato growled while smoothing his hands over my rear.

"Yes, sir," Ambrose said, inhaling so deep his chest enlarged. He leaned back into the pearlescent lavender cushions to take in the display, but not before sneaking an arm below the covers.

"Hands where I can see them. This is a reminder, not a reward."

Ambrose nodded and rested both palms on his thighs.

Cato tugged my arms behind my back and laced his forearm through my elbows, holding them captive. He lifted and my shoulders came flush with his chest. My back bowed and my chest jut proudly as he used his other hand to drag my straps down, revealing one breast and then the other, presenting each to Ambrose.

"What part of her do you desire the most?" Cato asked.

He pinched my nipple, rolling the sensitive peak in his fingers.

Ambrose's eyes grew hazy, clouded over by lust.

"Cato, husband, I—"

"Hush, love." He pinched harder, silencing me. "Answer me, Ambrose."

"I... her mouth. Never has another been so enthusiastic about swallowing my dick." A small spot of the blanket covering Ambrose's lap darkened, moisture escaping his erection ensconced below. "Not even the hired professionals, be they he, she or they."

Lust tore through me.

Cato towed up the hem of my dress, the material catching on my breasts, hoisting them until they fell free. Ambrose nodded appreciatively while I halfheartedly struggled in Cato's grasp.

"Her mouth is otherworldly, I agree, but it is what lies between her legs that I long for."

"Gods, yes." I pressed my backside firmly against Cato's arousal. His thick head pulsed where it rested against the small of my back. He released me and placed his hands on my hips, twisting the ties of my underwear around his fingers.

"Ambrose, how should I fuck your wife?"

"Immediately is how," I said, my breath coming in heaves while I squirmed, seeking any amount of friction with the body behind me.

Cato dipped his head low and pressed his cheek to my temple. "I did not ask *you*, consort."

Holy fucking Creator above.

"Slow, Cat. Make her beg for you."

Cato pulled both sides of my laces at once and let my remaining covering fall to the bed, baring me to their eyes.

"Oh my. Nips granite hard, thighs quivering, Cato, we are in for a night of—what the fuck is that?" Ambrose tossed the cover aside and threw himself forward. "I said, what the fu—"

"You are not free," Cato hissed. Ambrose balked and then stilled. His eyes flicked back and forth between us. "Good man. You have always taken orders well."

I whimpered as my slick trickled down my inner thigh. Commander Cato was even more alluring than his sweet, loving counterpart.

"Catommandus... sir, if I may?"

"What?" Cato snapped at Ambrose, irritated by the distraction as he smoothed his lips down my neck.

I sighed, tilting my head, giving him better access.

"I am afraid, brother-in-arms, that Eira has contracted... the gonorrhea."

Like finding ice chips in your undies, his words ejected me from my sensual head space.

"What? Do fucking what?"

"With whom have you lain?" Ambrose knee-walked across the bed. His eyes were angry shards of the darkest jade. He dropped on all fours to inspect me, peering straight at my vulva.

"Was it Septimus and his disease-laden prick? You deserve the fire of his ill-gotten lesions, harlot!"

"WHAT!?" I screamed so loud both men covered their ears. "I haven't *lain* with him or any other, you accusatory bastard."

Ambrose's eyes sharpened. Cato gripped my arms painfully.

"Bastard? Eira, how dare you fling my parentage in my face? And the proof, my unclean spouse, is in your mottled and patchy pubes." He flung his arm out, his finger pointed at my crotch. "Infection courses through you!" He wrenched me away from Cato and tossed me on my back.

"Look, brother." I couldn't tell if Ambrose's eyes were glassy from fury or lament, but my over-dramatic husband's concern was obvious.

And so was my rage.

My foot collided with my husband's stomach. He doubled over, but only briefly. Cato's hand circled my ankle.

"I grow tired of being tossed around and it not ending in orgasm. Cato, I don't have a disease, godsdammit, not unless I contracted it from you or the overgrown ass." I kicked out, my heel making purchase with Cato's shoulder. He ignored it, and Ambrose caught the fist I leveled toward his head. "Unhand me."

Together, they pinned me to the bed.

Cato scrunched his nose up and peered closely at my vulva like he was deciphering some impossible-to-crack code. He flicked questioning eyes up to mine, the apple at his throat bobbing.

"Eira?" he questioned.

For the love of the Goddess and all that is holy.

"It is not the pestilence, nor a sex-plague. It's a letter *P*!" I hollered. "Okay? And it's a bit inflamed because of the wax. My specialist was... new. If you notice, my legs and other areas are also lacking their downy softness."

"Ahh," Cato said, his voice gone smooth, a smile curving his lips. "You recreated our first time. Do you remember, love, at Verrona's pub? You were worried I'd find your hairlessness less attractive." He allowed his fingers to trail from my hip to knee. "I do not mind if you prefer it. But why the shape? It is a bit distracting."

Ambrose chuckled and poked his finger into the bald and angry red center of the letter.

"It stands for pussy," I snapped, outright lying, but not feeling nearly as bad as I should for doing so.

"Oh, I approve, lady wife," said Ambrose thickly. He caressed my knee as he guided it to the side. "There never was a more enchanting pussy. Do you suppose you can fairy cunt me this evening? Hmm?"

I rapidly nodded my head.

"She lies."

I shook my head, glancing wide-eyed and falsely innocent between my husbands.

I do lie. I do.

Cato's eyes narrowed.

"How often has the word 'pussy' fallen from those lips, Ambrose? And do you not feel she said it with a little too much conviction?"

Ambrose gasped and tossed a hand over his heart. "You are right, brother. Our plague-ridden strumpet makes to deceive us."

"And *my* woman would *never* lie to me," Cato growled.

She just did. I couldn't lower the brows that rose to my forehead.

"Fine. You are right. It's a *P* for pubis," I tried again, this time imbued with so much sincerity I almost believed myself. "It's a Solnnan custom for Joined women, just like the ring in your ear. It was a gift... for Ambrose... like his painted penis. I loved that by the way Black Bear, I—"

"Brother mine, how many Solnnan women would you venture to have fucked?" Cato shifted his unbelieving eyes to Ambrose.

Ambrose chewed the side of his mouth thoughtfully and glanced up to the ceiling.

"Oh, let me see, I would estimate a number," he ticked off the count on his fingers, "somewhere in the low twenties, give or take a few I may be overlooking."

"And?"

"Annnd?" Ambrose furrowed his brow.

Cato's eyes widened in emphasis.

"Annnnd? Oh!" Ambrose placed his pointer finger under my chin and turned my head to face him. "And none of them were marked with a *P* or any other alphabetic representation of a spoken language." He shook his head slowly and clucked his tongue. "Eira... how *dare* you violate the sanctity of our Joining vows?"

"You just admitted to violating a great many Joining vows."

"I would never, and you know it."

"I maintain my innocence."

Cato wrapped his fingers around my chin and turned my face to his. "You will confess."

"Th-there is nothing to confess." I looked down my nose, entirely unprepared to discuss how close I came to coitus with their evil uncle.

"Very well then," Cato shifted and brought one of his knees between mine, followed by the other. He pulled his tunic over his head in that teasing way that all men seem to do, grabbing the fabric at the back of his neck and hauling it off in one swift motion. "Ambrose, remove those hideous shorts and kneel behind me. Our woman would never betray us."

My mouth went dry... desert in a godsdamned heatwave dry.

Ambrose rolled to his back, disrobed, and flung his shorts away with his toes. He saddled right up to Cato's back, looking directly over his head... and then carefully removed and folded his spectacles, to lay them aside.

Cato's broad shoulders, tanned and powerful, bulged as he crossed his arms over his broad chest. Gods alive, I wanted to run my hands through the curls there and trace his scars with my tongue. My body began to pulse anew—palms tingling and growing warm. My men were my favorite snack.

I allowed my eyes to drift from Cato's chest downward until they fastened on his thick and heavy length. His broad-headed erection jutted out from his hips, taunting me. My mouth actually watered.

"Knees back," Cato commanded.

I pulled them back and let them fall.

Magnificent Troth. I chucked to myself.

"See how she yearns for us? Look at how her slickness escapes her." Cato swept his finger along my inner thigh and then held his hand over his shoulder. "Taste."

Ambrose locked his eyes to mine, bent over, and drew Cato's finger into his mouth, his cheeks hollowing as he sucked. He moaned softly, and I swallowed hard in response. My respirations were becoming more erratic by the second.

"I've changed my mind, Cat; I will take her *P*-marked pussy. You continue having fun with her mouth."

I nodded, pouring all of my enthusiasm into the gesture. "That configuration will suit my needs just fine."

"No, Ambrose. She will receive no pleasure until she speaks to us truthfully."

"Wait, Cato, I thought..."

Cato inclined his head, the challenge clear in the set of his jaw.

A game of wills then.

"Will I not?" I reached between my legs and spread my lips, circled my clitoris, and then dipped low. Though his lids didn't move, Cato's eyes sharpened, the ring of gold becoming more prominent in his dark eyes. *Yes, my love, let us play.*

"You believe your fingers can compete with what *I* provide?" Cato glanced down at his cock, a smug look on his face. "Think you can win, *Troth*? I survived twenty and nine years before you deflowered me—you will not last nine minutes."

Cato dropped his arms back and grabbed Ambrose's wrists. He wrapped the larger man's arms around him and brought his palms to his chest.

"Feel me, Ambrose."

Green eyes rounded.

I stopped breathing.

Ambrose moved a tentative hand and then paused.

"Cato, are you sure?"

He nodded, just once.

"What I want most in this life is to please my mate," Cato said with an edge of steel in his voice. "I am well aware that your hands on my body sends her into a state of frenzy. And her pleasure heightens my own."

Oh fuck.

Ambrose grinned, his eyes pinned to mine. His palms coasted down Cato's chest, stopping at his nipples and then inching lower to spread across his stomach. My toes curled into the blanket, and I fisted my hands into tight balls. What was it about them touching? Plenty of Monwyn men held hands and kissed their male partners. My reaction to their love didn't come close to stirring this eagerness within me. I allowed myself to imagine another pair of masculine hands gliding over Cato's chest and a bolt of jealousy hit me so profoundly that little tendrils of smoke wafted up from where my nails dug into my palms—Oh... I loved it because they were mine.

They both saw the smoke, of course; wicked smiles were their answers to my obvious distress. Ambrose licked two fingers and then swirled them around Cato's nipple. It hardened to a delicious peak.

"Not as responsive as yours, wife, but I would bet my life that he'd prefer my tongue there instead... like yourself." Ambrose pinched Cato's sensitive skin, and Cato's jaw clenched tightly. "Please to the gods tell me you have sucked her plump, pink tits as you burst inside of her? She tightens her walls when you do and shoves all that flesh into your face like the greedy girl she is."

Oh, he has, Ambrose.

"Oh, I have." Cato gathered Ambrose's hands and slid both downward, coasting over the hard planes of his stomach, following the path of his dark hair.

"Gracious, my nasty little harpy is going to mess the sheets if we continue," Ambrose said. He glanced lazily between my legs and then lifted his eyes back to mine.

"If she wants my cock... she knows how to earn it."

Earn it?

I got to my knees, letting my sternum and then the curve of my stomach drag along the tip of Cato's erection. A little trail of moisture gleamed between my breasts. I shifted to catch its shine in the lamplight.

"Oh love, unclench your jaw, before you break a tooth," I said in a voice dripping with sugar. I looked around the room, and my eyes landed on the glass of fruit-infused water Ambrose brought back from the beach. I leaned over, snatched it up, and drank down the contents, the liquid helping to cool the fire raging through my veins.

"Getting too warm, love?"

I cocked a brow and stared him down.

"You tell me, *love.*" I fished a slice of peach from the glass and slid it along my tongue. "Mmmm." I moaned at the acidic yet sweet flavor. I drew the morsel down my throat, enjoying the cool, silken sensation. "Ambrose?"

"Yes, Eira?" he replied immediately.

I circled one of my nipples with the plump fruit and then the other. They hardened to two spectacularly beautiful points.

"Hungry?"

"Yes." Ambrose sprang from behind Cato, but a hand shot out, caught him around the hips, and held fast. "Catommandus, let me go. My wife has a desperate need, and as her husband, I am duty-bound to assuage it."

Ambrose struggled to no avail.

"I too have a need," Cato crooned. He blew me a kiss, and I swore to the goddess his dark eyes reflected pure evil. *Nefariousness abounds.*

"Hold!" Cato barked the command and Ambrose stilled. He lifted Ambrose's hand, holding it in his own.

"Spit."

Ambrose didn't hesitate.

Cato licked his full lips... and then spat on top of Ambrose's saliva.

"Sir, you have spittle still clinging to your—"

"Lick it off."

Ambrose's chest heaved, as he dipped his head, the most obedient of soldiers. He flicked his tongue along the bottom edge of Cato's lip.

"Holy fucking glorious Goddess," I groaned, watching my fantasies play out in front of me.

Cato raised a questioning brow.

"What was that? I do not think I heard you. A little loud—shit."

Ambrose fisted Cato's cock and stroked down his length, effectively silencing him.

"Dreams come true," I whispered, watching Cato's eyes grow hazy as he held his spine rigid. Ambrose drug his hand back up and then set his pace, holding my gaze.

"Do you prefer it like me, sir? A tighter squeeze on the base, lighter pull on the head, followed by a quick jerk?" Ambrose asked, modeling the technique.

The æther frenzied, shooting and zigzagging between my limbs and core. I was frantic in my need, desperate to become a part of their act. The discarded glass rolled down an indention in the mattress and settled against my knee.

The game is not lost.

"What... what are you doing?" Cato panted.

I gripped the vessel, held it between my legs, and lowered myself in bobbing increments. The narrow glass was cool as I experimented, letting its smooth rounded bottom fill my entrance. It slipped easily into my passage with no catches or maneuvering—not all unpleasant as I bottomed out and rose again... not at all.

"I'm participating. Husband, fast or slow, sweetheart? You decide."

Ambrose's chest heaved as he watched me bounce as he hand-fucked Cato. Cato's face remained impassive, but he couldn't hide the pupils that dilated nearly as wide as his irises.

I rode the glass harder.

"Eira, love, all eight inches of Ambrose are—"

"Nine and a half." Ambrose squeezed Cato's cock, causing his hips to jerk forward.

"Godsdamn. Nine and a half inches of him could be yours, instead of gliding through the pre-cum he is dribbling so carelessly on my back."

I was going to pass out. The possibilities, the imagery... I dropped to my back, no longer able to support myself on my knees. I pressed the glass between my legs and tapped my clit with three fingers, so close to coming.

"Goddess, it is beautiful... I can see *inside* her. I am blessed from above. Let me go, Catommandus. It calls to me!"

"Come to me, Black Bear, yes... I need you. Gods, how I need you."

Ambrose lunged, but Cato twisted his arm, capturing him. I shoved the glass deeper, begging it to relieve the mounting pressure inside me, but it wasn't enough. I needed my men to satiate me. I wanted them thrusting, pushing into me, taking from my body.

I was through. I couldn't win. I didn't *want* to win.

"It's a... *P* for... for... Protector. Your asshole relation tore the hair out. He marked me like a farmer would their prize heifer in a county contest." My face pinked as the stinging fingers of embarrassment scraped their nails along my chest.

Cato's gaze darkened.

"You are wrong," he gritted out. "You continue to lie, Eira."

"I don't. I swear to the gods I don't."

Cato shook off Ambrose, doubled over, and pressed his palms flat on the bed. He stalked toward me, moving one limb at a time. I pushed off my heels and skittered backward as he snatched the glass from my hand and sent it crashing into the wall.

"Please Cato, I am not lying to you."

"Oh, you are... but let *me* now inform you of the truth. This *P*..." His hand caught my ankle and yanked, pulling me down the mattress, my legs on the outside of his. He cupped my vulva, the heel of his palm snug against my over-sensitive gem, while his fingers settled against my wet heat. "It stands for *prince*."

He spread my moisture over his cock and lined himself up with my entrance.

The little explosions began the moment his crown parted me.

"Cato." I bucked my hips to meet his, my release near. "Please."

"*Prince* Catommandus," he growled thickly keeping his hips still. "Fuck her impertinent mouth, Ambrose. Until she learns to address me properly."

Tears of euphoria stung my eyes, clouding my vision. I didn't see Ambrose move, but when his hand clasped the back of my head, turning me to his blunt tip I welcomed him in. He sank himself deep, tasting of salt and sweet coconut.

"Such an inviting mouth," Ambrose said, his words blending into a long and drawn-out moan. "Would you like to try again, wife, to tell us to whom you belong?" He cupped my cheeks and took his pleasure, his tip hitting the back of my throat with each slow plunge.

I tried to speak, but it came out as a gargle of confused sounds.

"Cato, take her hard. She clearly needs the reminder."

My mate pressed my thighs back and let his weight bear down on me. He paused, bent low, and placed a kiss in the middle of my chest.

Ambrose caressed the edge of my jaw and then cupped the juncture where his erection slid through my lips.

"Gods! Oh, gods!" Hips slammed into mine so hard I swore I could see Merrias wielding her sword.

The world shattered around me as I came. My entire body tensed around the men I'd chosen, overflowing with physical and emotional release.

Cato hammered into me.

"Prince," the explosive sound of my cry thundered through my chest. "My prince," I wailed between Ambrose's deep plunges.

A second orgasm ravaged me. The æther traversed my veins, not merrily like a bubbling sweet wine, but with a dark, intense churn that stole my breath.

I came down slowly, beyond satiated, tears of relief spilling from the corners of my eyes and into my hair.

"You did beautifully, love, but now Ambrose would like his chance to move in you."

"Cato, I don't think I can—"

"Hush, love, you can…"

Cato pulled from me, and Ambrose took up his position. His big hands slipped beneath my rear and tilted my hips.

Slowly, he entered me and didn't stop until his head snugged up to my cervix.

"Mmmm, the cunt fairies are out. And how kind of Catommandus to have bathed you in his essence first. When we Joined, I worried I would never again know the pleasure of fucking a lover's semen from the blessed passage of another. There is nothing remotely like it." Ambrose looked at Cato. "I adore the sloppiest of seconds."

I closed my eyes and gave in—listened to the æther swimming through my ears, felt the perspiration, every single bead of it, where it sat upon my skin.

"Now, Cato, watch. Look beyond jealously, and see the beauty of what can transpire between us."

Cato nodded, pressed his body to my side, smoothed the hair back from my forehead and rocked me to the rhythm of Ambrose's slow thrusts. "I love you." He skimmed his finger over my swollen bottom lip. "I know peace again."

His eyes smiled. The gold ring surrounding his pupils reflected the lamplight, giving his deep-brown eyes a warm, red cast.

"I love you, Cato."

Our lips met.

Ambrose encouraged me to wrap my legs around his slender waist. I hooked my ankles together and squeezed, demanding he go deeper if he pleased.

"Ah, ah. You will take too much and blame me for your discomfort in the morn—"

I tore my mouth from Cato's.

"All of it."

Ambrose moaned, dropped low, and captured my nipple between his teeth. He ran his tongue roughly over my flesh.

"Peach... Cato..."

Without having to ask, Cato latched onto my right breast, swirling his tongue around my areola. He groaned, his chest rumbling against my side. His hand found my vulva, and he used the pads of three fingers to stimulate my clit. He rubbed it hard and fast in a side-to-side motion while Ambrose plunged into me like a man gone wild.

"Thank you, Goddess," I prayed. "Thank you."

Ambrose picked up his speed but was still holding back. I ran my fingers up their necks, clasping them tightly to my breasts as they worshipped me. The æther spiraled downward, coating my womb and slipping through my walls.

"All of you, Ambrose, do not deny me." I let my legs fall, draping one over Cato's hips.

Ambrose grunted harshly as he received the æther and drove forward.

I screamed, the delight and pain mingling, shooting me toward another completion. I sucked in the air, and my eyes flew open.

Blue eyes—icy blue—stared into mine.

"Oh, Goddess."

Septimus leaned against the balcony wall, the curtain fluttering behind him.

He acknowledged me with a nod and placed his fist to his shoulder in a soldier's salute.

The æther jolted, like it was trying to leap from my body to its Bonded mate.

He felt it too. His lips parted in surprise.

"So good, such a good wife." Ambrose jerked his head up, blocking my bleary-eyed view. His mouth slackened, and his eyes turned soft. "You have ruined me for any others."

I came again, wailing out the cries of a trance-like ecstasy.

Ambrose pulsed between my legs, the ropes of his release wetting my thighs as he slowed his hips.

The three of us lay, limbs tangled, bodies calm.

After the blissful glow of lovemaking faded, Cato carried me to the rain bath and together, the three of us stood bathing in the night-cooled water and moonlight.

Even though they both protested, on account of "you have to be exhausted after that," I took my time scrubbing them both while dotting kisses over their chests and arms.

When it was my turn, Cato soaped his palms and, ever so gently, parted my labia and cleansed the evidence of our reunion from my thighs. I leaned back against Ambrose's chest and yawned, stretching up to scratch his beard. The silly man shook his leg like the happiest of puppies.

"You are almost as cute as Verra when you are sleepy." He kissed the top of my head. "She doesn't get nearly as warm as you do, however."

I stiffened.

"Pardon me? Who?"

"Oh, yes. Well, you left, and she and I—"

I spun around, nearly knocking Cato backward.

"*She* and you *what*?" I demanded, hands balling and finding my hips. "Who the fuck is Verra?"

"Eira," Cato whispered from behind me.

"Don't 'Eira' me," I twisted around and faced Cato, who pressed forward and smashed me between him and Ambrose.

"Calm down, jealous love. Would you truly be so upset if he left, and it were just you and I?" He tipped my chin up and looked at me with laughter in his eyes.

I stomped, splashing water around our ankles. "Who *the fuck* is Verra?"

My hands began their annoying heat. Steam rose where droplets hit them.

"Your daughter," Cato stated matter-of-factly. "My, um, goat niece."

"W-what?" My mouth worked up and down, my head not understanding what my ears heard. "She's... The satyress is alive?" My voice hitched, stuck in my throat.

"Of course she is. I told you I would take care of everything. And... and I named her after you, because you are strong, just like she shall be—Eira Verras and baby Verra."

"But... Aberus?"

"Aberus is a massive softy despite looking like the—"

"I'll still not forgive him for imprisoning you. Don't ask it of me."

Ambrose wrapped his arms around me and Cato. Squished between the two of them, I could hardly draw air.

"Imprisoned? I was never detained." Ambrose dropped one hand to my rear and squeezed my cheek. "And imagine my shock when I discovered that my wife had abandoned her husband and only child."

"Wait what?"

"Quit rocking me, Ambrose, stay still for gods' sake," Cato said. Ambrose increased his sways.

Not imprisoned? The goatling alive?

"Cato, allow me to comfort you. It is step two in our slow incline to intimacy."

"Ambrose. As I have told you, I do not wish for us to be—"

I birthed myself from between their combined embraces.

"Eira, love, where are you go—"

"To murder your uncle."

CHAPTER FORTY

WHISPER TO YOUR WORLD

EIRA

My brain woke long before my body was ready.

Ambrose snored softly. His behind pressed tightly into the curve of my spine, and one of his feet was trapped between my crossed ankles.

My breasts snugged against Cato's side, and my arm lay in the middle of his chest. The puffs of his uneven breath fluttered my hair, and the thump of his heart below my arms beat too quickly for him to have been at rest.

"Can't sleep?"

I traced the scar that ended at his sternum and smoothed my palm over the hair there. He let out a long-held breath.

"When I close my eyes, you disappear again."

I made to move, but he tightened the arm that held me to his side.

"Cato, I would apologize if I felt that my actions weren't warranted, but I need to explain why I felt they were."

He nodded, encouraging me to continue, always willing to listen.

"Septimus had a missive in what I knew to be your hand. I questioned all aspects of his story, and yet I still fell for his deception."

The admission of my failure left a bitter taste. I forced myself to meet his gaze, but he stared up at the ceiling, mulling over my words. There was no judgment in his eyes, though, and not a hint of doubt.

"He is a master of manipulation, and I place no blame at your feet. Very few stand a chance against his cunning. Eira, if you assessed the situation and concluded it would ensure your safety, you chose wisely. You are resourceful and thoughtful, and though I feared for your safety, I knew I would find you in one piece. Possibly surrounded by the burning pieces of a broken kingdom but..."

His attempt at levity should have dispelled my worry, but it only seemed to heighten my unease.

"And would you blame me if... if we couldn't have a future, Cato?"

He turned to stone under my fingers, sat up, and urged me to do the same. Ambrose groaned until I tucked the blankets more snuggly around his shoulders.

"What has happened?" Cato gave me his full attention. "Are you... have you found... is it Septimus? Have you found that you have feel—"

"Merrias came to me again." I thought about how to put the experience into words. "She called Septimus my 'Safeguard.' My feelings for him remain the same, Cato."

Cato weighed the information, tipping his head from one side to the other.

"A personal guard? In all honesty, the gods could not have chosen better. He has no moral code and fights nearly as well as me. Too bad I plan to kill him before you do."

"You can try." There was no teasing in my voice.

I took his hand into mine and brushed my lips along an old scar.

"But, Eira, why do you question our future? What did Merrias divulge?"

So much, and not nearly enough.

"Cato, you are a prince, and the expectation is that you will reproduce... but I can't be the one to bear your children."

How I managed the words without choking was beyond me.

Cato shook his head, eyes imploring.

"Were I to bring forth a child from a Bonded mate, their life would not be their own. They would become a puppet in the war between the gods. They would be elevated beyond mortal limitations, but, my love, I have learned that the most powerful have the farthest to fall in the end. That is not a life I would thrust on anyone, especially our child. You want a family. It's not fair of me to stand in the way of your dreams. Could you love another? Have the little's you've longed for?"

He hurt. I saw it in the way his lips tensed and in the way the lines formed at the corners of his eyes. And, I knew a similar pain. Giving voice to the idea of him creating life with another made me want to scream, but I could endure it for his happiness—to see the wonder in his eyes as he cradled his babe.

"Come back, Eira." Cato took my hands and folded them between the callused skin of his own. "And answer this. Do I get to keep *you*?"

"You would. Separation from you I could not endure."

"And you wish me to put my child into another?"

Oh gods. My heart lurched, and my skin prickled hot. I wanted to screech out that I would throw him and his fictitious hussy from the highest window of the palace if he dared...but I held my tongue. I was strong. I would endure, just like he did.

"Anxious wife, let me finish." Cato playfully bit the tips of my fingers. "No. I will not breed with another for the sake of fatherhood. Children are a minor part of the equation in a family. It is you that I want more than anything in this world, Eira. My dreams *do* center around family—the two of us together is just as fulfilling to me as the seven of us."

I laughed through the wetness clouding my vision, remembering the night we shared in the cabin outside of Cordillaria—me the mama to his papa with our five imagined girls.

Cato took my face in his hands and popped a loud kiss on my lips.

I studied him... my person. Would our children have his warm-copper skin, my almond-shaped eyes? A deep and intense yearning to see *our* children stirred within me—the physical embodiment of our love.

"There are three of us, *Catommandus*," Ambrose grumbled from behind me. He flipped and flopped, shaking the entire bed as he lifted the covers high and then spooned his long body around my hips. "Reminding you of that fact is quickly becoming tiresome. And, as *we* don't have a Bond, she can still push my progeny from her *P*-marked puss."

"Go back to sleep."

I caught Cato's raised fist and brought it to my heart.

Ambrose grunted unhappily and grabbed me with both hands, pulling me back down to the bed and caging me in his arms.

"Wife?" Ambrose muttered sleepily into my ear.

"Husband?"

"Your gift is on the table." He yawned, releasing a gust of morning breath. "You'll beg to have my babies when you see it."

Cato rolled his eyes so hard I thought I could hear them as they rotated.

"Ambrose, be more considerate of Cato's feelings," I chided, already sensing the storm clouds brewing.

Ambrose walked his fingers up my stomach and patted it twice.

"You know when Cat's going to really sulk?"

I didn't answer him.

"Hmm? Do you know?" He flicked my nipple.

"No, Ambrose, when will Cato sulk?" I smacked his hand away, and he tucked it between my thighs.

"When your sweet slit is off limits to his groin gouging while we are making a perfectly normal, not all-powerful baby." The asshole chuckled.

"You might have to shave *his* initials in your pubes so he can feel relevant." Ambrose flicked his tongue along the shell of my ear... which caused my nipples to go stiff... which Cato noticed immediately, of course.

Oh gods.

"Okay, well." I slapped a palm in the middle of Cato's chest and pushed him back while working my way out of Ambrose's arms. "You two work out your issues. I'm going to conjurer school—may the Goddess guide me and the kingdom survive. Cato, don't kill Septimus today. I'll do it tomorrow."

I kissed my brooding boy on the tip of his nose and leaned back to Ambrose, but before my lips could meet his chin, Cato caught my shoulder.

"He requires your goodnight kiss. Now I demand your morning." His mouth crushed to mine, and I melted into him. He caught my lip, bit down gently, and then swiped his tongue across mine.

"Now you may go."

"Now?" My hands were already making their way south.

He pushed me back and gave a curt nod.

"Not yet—I need my turn," Ambrose interjected, smacking my thigh smartly.

Before he got grabby-hands, I rolled away.

"No. My weak woman's vagina cannot resist the power of your combined magnetism!" I bent and pecked Ambrose on the fuzzy knee, pleased to hear Cato's soft laughter. "Ambrose, wear a longer skirt today, for the good of the people."

There was a knock at the door. Two soft raps.

Gotwig was here, and I was naked.

I crawl-climbed over a tangle of limbs and scurried toward the closet, combing my hands through my hair as I went. Even over the release of my screaming bladder, I could hear the voices of my men.

"You can babysit the older children when we're off making another, Cat."

I thumbed the cap from my conception control and took a swig, and then another for good measure. Ambrose *still* owed me two years before I fulfilled the baby part of our contract. And with the state of the future and the thought of causing Cato pain... perhaps I could convince him to allow Aberus to do the procreating, and we could just... fuck for fun for the rest of our lives? I was not at all bothered by *that* plan.

I dressed quickly, gargled a glass of minty water, and stopped to check in on my naughty spouses before heading to the common room.

Ambrose snored, his cheek resting atop Cato's bicep pillow. Their chests rose and fell in unison.

"I love you," I whispered to my world.

CHAPTER FORTY-ONE

I'LL BE GODSDAMNED

EIRA

"How much further? I grow faint," I gasped, breathing in the humid air. "It's like traversing in a tub."

I knew I was being dramatic, but I was dripping. Beads of stinging wetness poured into my eyes, and despite having chosen what amounted to a barely there underdress, I was boiling. The pale-lavender linen no longer held its shape and bagged off my body. If it continued to sag, I'd have to slice through the straps and then tie them around my neck to remain decent. I hauled the moist fabric up for the sixteenth time, then glanced down at my tan sandals, whose cords crisscrossed and wrapped to right below my knees. At least those were staying put as we walked down a darling cobblestone road in the quaintest area of town. Captivating bursts of colorful plant life flowered over trough-shaped planters that lined the avenue—purples, pinks, and yellows, with variegated greens and blooms the size of my palms.

"Not much further," Gotwig said beside me.

"Thank the gods." I inhaled and found myself enveloped by a nectarous scent, reminiscent of jasmine, but with a hint of vanilla. "How are you not dying?"

His response was sharp side-eye.

Unlike myself, he was fully covered from neck to toe. Long-flowing eggplant-colored pants dragged the ground, and he wore a long, bell-sleeved tunic of white, clasped together at the neck with an opal brooch set in gold.

"What's that place?" I asked for the umpteenth time, this time pointing at a charming storefront with small tables set on the street.

"Another restaurant."

"That's like the fourth restaurant on this street. What's that one?"

"A library."

"For anyone?" I waddle-jogged to the shop's door, holding my chafing thighs apart, and peered through the glass that read "Literary Gems and Parchment Craft" in Solnnan. Floor-to-ceiling bookshelves contained a rainbow of tomes. I saw a section for cookbooks, one for religion, and another for children. There was even a chair in the back of the store and little personal pillows spread around it. I could just imagine an elder reading to a gaggle of the little ones.

"Troth Solnna."

"Huh?" I eyed a section called "Love Tomes," and began devising a strategy to convince Gotwig to make a detour before returning to the palace. It would be the ultimate test of my Troth skills.

"The destruction of Ærta will not delay while you play tourist."

Right. Focus.

I turned and nodded, but my attention immediately caught on the storefront across the street. A chain of golden wire hearts ran across both the bottom and top of the whitewashed building. I pointed.

"Family planning. The Solnnans require couples to attend counseling sessions in their third year of being Joined. They find it cuts down on infidelity and divorce."

"I think that's brilliant, honestly. A few weeks with Ambrose and already I could use an intervention. What's that place?" I pointed to a small blue building, wooden, with two enormous windows, one of which was painted with big block letters, "Smell the Flours."

"That—finally—is where you will learn to command that which flows through you, gods-willing."

"That's the school?" I crossed back over the street. The warm and wonderful smell of yeast grew stronger as I approached the unassuming shop. "Does magic smell like bread?"

"Bread smells like bread," Gotwig mumbled, reaching my side. He opened the door, and together, we stepped into one of my dreams. Solnnan cakes, pink, pale yellow, and blue, lined the bakery's back counter. Some were multi-tiered, some boasted crowns of fluffy spun sugar in various hues. I was immediately drawn to a frosted cake of white, with rounds of kiwi laid around the border of its cream-covered sides. Woven grass baskets around the room's perimeter overflowed with bread—seed-covered and plain, long loaves and rounds.

"All I need is butter, Gotwig... That's all, and my life is complete."

"Follow me. Eat nothing as you pass."

"Are you serious? You bring me here, and the expectation is that I—Oh," I dropped my voice low. "The loaves have been conjured upon. What happens if you eat one?"

Red-rimmed blue eyes rolled so hard they disappeared, leaving nothing but the whites.

"Empty bowels are best for the path we take."

My stomach ceased its growling and instead flipped and then flopped. I grumbled as we walked between two counters and headed to a back door. If the five or six bakers saw us, they gave no indication. One heaved a large bag of almonds to his shoulder and walked straight at Gotwig, who stepped out of his way. The workers just kept on kneading, mixing, and stretching blobs of dough which they then held to the light.

"Mind your step, Troth Solnna."

Gotwig waved me through a door positioned between two stoves. It slammed closed, hitting me on the heels. I scurried forward and ducked behind my teacher.

"Magic?"

"Springs."

I tip-toed around to investigate the mechanism and poked it over and over with my finger. The door opened and shut as if it were itself living—Solnna was amazing.

"The rest of the continent has yet to catch on. They fear modernity. Come along."

The back room was bursting with stacks of flour and sugar. A giant canister of salt, with a scoop the size of my hand, sat against the back wall, and mixing bowls that Ambrose could bathe in were stacked to the left. Pine cabinets lined the left wall, each with dozens of cubbies and drawers.

I headed to the right, inspecting a string hanging from the ceiling. Sweet-smelling, shriveled up brown pods hung by the hundreds. It was vanilla. I knew its scent straight away.

"Ahem," Gotwig cleared his throat.

"I'm taking this seriously, I promise. It's just all so interesting... so different." I strolled across the stone floor, noting that bright-white flour filled the grout lines that separated the stone tiles, and the room was somewhat hazy from the constant movement of finely ground ingredients.

"Remember, Troth Solnna. Do not give in."

"What?"

He twisted the knob of the drawer labeled "pepper" and the entire cabinet—taller than I was—came away from the wall. Gotwig passed through the opening.

"Step through." His voice echoed. I placed a tentative foot over the threshold, seeing nothing but darkness ahead.

"Shit!" The cabinet slammed closed, and the familiar sputter of a lamp coming to life hit my ears as light filled the space. "Will there ever be a time you aren't portentous in your delivery?"

Gotwig pursed his lips and walked to the end of what was just a hallway.

"Your tutelage begins." He crooked his fingers.

My stomach churned. Nothing was ever as it seemed with my instructor, but there was nothing to do but follow.

"Strength of Nortia and all that." I smiled flatly, nodded, and—dropped to the ground.

My face struck the floor, pain shooting through my cheekbone and temple.

This was my death.

The æther, each individual speck within me, died. Once effervescent and light, they dropped, one by one, weighing me down as if coated in steel.

Goddess... Creator Mother. Watch over Cato. Send Ambrose love.

I couldn't move. Couldn't speak.

My mind still worked, and my vision was intact, although poorly focused and fastened on the handle of a butter churn against the wall.

Nan? Momma? Be with me, please—

"The Awakened, I think, lack souls."

I could still hear him.

As he stepped in front of me, Gotwig's purple-clad legs took up the entirety of my narrow view.

"I believe that is the reason we are able to guide conjurers through this ordeal without experiencing the effects." He crossed one foot over the other and then sat.

I stared at his slowly rising chest, and the small silver dagger brooch he wore.

"Evandr is a highly requested guide already."

Evandr. An Awakened... my Frostborn.

"He is charismatic in his tactics. You will find I am not."

Gotwig wrapped his thin arms around his knees. His hands were more scarred than Cato's and lacked the tips of several fingers, the mark of a hard life, of a child enslaved... of a man who escaped only to find his death in Gaea and rebirth at the hands of my mother.

"If you want what is beyond the door, you must endure, Eira. You must reach the other side on your own."

How the fuck am I supposed to do that? How? I'm dying. My life is—

"I recommend thinking about your *why*. What will you gain by reaching the other side? A means to end the Primus-King from afar? An incantation that will loosen the ties of the Mated Bond that pulls you from your heart's desire?"

What? Was that even possible? Could I rid myself of Septimus without taking his life? And the Primus-King... remove him from this world without risking my own life and the lives of those I loved? Was it... could it...

Stabbing, searing pain spiked through my temples. My vision flashed; my lungs shuddered.

Eira, pass out! I screamed inside my mind. *Please, Goddess! Dim the light of life within me, I implore you.*

"Ah, a flutter of your lash. That is admirable progress for such a short length of time." Gotwig rustled around, and a handkerchief appeared before me, cutting off my view of his sunken chest. He blinked in and out of focus. "Hmm." He dabbed the starched white linen on the corner of my eye and below my nose. It came away stained with bright blood. "We don't want this to fall into the hands of just anyone." He folded the square and pocketed it.

Make this stop, Gotwig, please. I beg you...

The pain was an icepick to the skull. I was a frozen fish and a Nortian mother chiseled away at me, chipping off portions for her stew.

Hours passed.

Between intervals of wiping my face and laying his cool hand on my forehead, I spiraled in and out of agony.

"Let me see." I heard the telltale sound of Gotwig's timepiece snapping shut. "I believe it is time for a story."

A story? I sobbed. Though no sound issued from my body, the laments and wails of suffering resounded inside my mind.

Gotwig rested his hands against my temples, applying pressure to the sides of my throbbing head.

"I met a Scion when I was a much younger man, recently Awakened. The Scion was not at all like your husband, Scion Ambrose. This man was quiet, reserved, never boastful." Gotwig paused. "Many assumed his introversion was due to being born missing the lower half of his extremities."

Zuddaz? Just come out and say it, Gotwig.

He shifted his hand to my forehead and then closed and opened my eyelids, once and then again. The moisture revived my drying eyes, relieving some of my discomfort.

Thank you. Even the smallest consolation felt monumental.

"He was often overlooked and questioned his status as Chosen One, thinking it a mistake, a fluke of the officials when recording his birth in the annals at Verus. Why would the Goddess choose someone with such an affliction to lead, after all?"

Allaine. She felt similar. Goddess, I missed her smiling face, her blunt candor. I prayed she was well, and that she was not the Primus-King's next target on account of her proximity to me.

"During his training, this particular Scion could not fulfill many of the requirements of the physical Maneuverings and opted instead to engage his mind. He cloistered himself in the Study for days, pouring over maps and tomes, learning all that he could. And it was there that he met the love of his life. His Lifemate, as she would call him."

Zuddaz had a Lifemate? She was a Gaean then. No others used the moniker.

"Anyhow, the Troth started to skip her classes in order to spend time with the Scion, much to the aggravation of the previous Mantle... but love will find a way and all that drivel." Gotwig waved his hand dismissively. "They loved in secret, or so they thought, and made plans to flee."

I should have fled with Cato. Should have run toward a new life.

"To make this incredibly long story short, the Mantle saw an opportunity, and placed the two Obligates together during the Rite. It was during their consummation that his ability revealed itself. The Scion nearly burned the temple to the ground when they... well, you know. I understand things became quite toasty during your own Bedding ceremony."

Oh, my gods. How the little mite knew everything never ceased to impress me. Fuck, it wouldn't surprise me at all if Ethens or Lemder or even Richelle were in his pocket. I made a mental note to find the leak.

"Here is where the story gets interesting." Gotwig reached for my arm and lifted it above my head. He then pushed my shoulder and rolled me onto my back. Relief poured through my limbs as the æther fell from my front and settled along my spine, their weight still pinning me firmly to the floor. He tilted my head until I registered his face.

"The Troth's courses stopped. She stayed at Verus per tradition, and the Scion was sent off to his Assignment. Naturally, as a conjurer, he was placed in Solnna for his own safety."

The door opened, spilling the sounds of the bakery into the hall. Gotwig met the eyes of a blonde woman and nodded. She sidestepped me and continued forward without issue, returning moments later with a bundle of papers. She left without paying us attention.

"Their babies were born nine months, exactly, from the date of the Rite, squabbling and squawking, all pink and wrinkled. Their birth had been incredibly difficult on the Troth. Your mother's blood was what allowed her to live."

Twin births are so difficult. Such strength to bring two babes into the world. I'd only ever attended one with my Momma. The mother was beyond exhausted well before the second babe was delivered.

"Interestingly enough, the first child was born in the earlier part of the evening, and then as midnight passed, the second was born, just as the Goddess's sign appeared in the sky." Gotwig sighed and blinked. Then he sat staring as if I were supposed to jump up and run across the hall.

"Think, Eira. Use your brain."

I can't hear my thoughts over the pain, asshole. Truthfully, it was letting up some, his story distracting me from my suffering.

"Having been separated from her Lifemate and knowing her Rite-born children would be taken from her and raised at Verus, the Troth became inconsolable, especially when it was determined that the eldest child would step into the position of the next Mantle, while the younger would return to the Goddess."

Return to the... There is so much wrong with our religion.

"You see, there is no precedence for multiple births in the Holy Books, and two Riteborn fighting over the highest throne on the continent was simply too risky."

Too risky? Utter bullshit. Nonsense rules for imagined dangers.

"Because of the intensity of her depression and, if I inferred correctly, worry over the divine consequences of infanticide of a Chosen One, the previous Mantle struck a mutually beneficial deal with the king and queen of Monwyn. That is where the mother was Assigned. The monarch agreed to adopt the second child, raising him where the Troth could watch him grow until he was called to Verus. In return, Monwyn was given the allowance to name a Devotee of their choosing and could claim the Scion as their own Obligate. Have you connected the pieces, Eira?"

Monwyn's adopted Scion...

I lurched up, reaching for the sky.

"There she is," Gotwig said.

I jerked once more, and the specks of æther began to crackle.

"What was his name, Eira?"

A strangled, wordless cry hissed from my dry throat.

"Pardon me, I didn't understand you," Gotwig said blandly. He pulled a knife from someplace and dug the dirt from beneath his nails.

"Amb—"

"Go on."

"Ambro-se." His name came out, barely a whisper.

Ambrose was Zuddaz's child and...

Like the last piece of a puzzle snapping into place, the full picture revealed itself.

"Soolie," I croaked. *Soolie. Father Burchard's Mate Bond.*

"Yes, I do believe that was the Troth's name."

The image of the Mantle burned through my mind: bright-green eyes, the color of thick fall grass, sharp nose, and dark hair. They were tall and thin, lovely of face. Their eyes, a replica of Zuddaz's in shape and gentleness. *Ambrose, my Black Bear.* His lips were fuller and nose more prominent, but the shape was similar. And his body type, broad and long, just as Zuddaz was built.

Pain be dammed... Ambrose had a family. He had a father and sibling still walking this earth. His story would have a beginning, after all.

Merrias, hear me! My chest constricted, pressure building, increasing as I fought the invisible force holding me hostage.

Blackness seeped into my vision... but I was used to the dark.

Come to me, my shadows. Come!

Gotwig's fingers rested on my cheek.

I felt my body rock. I *made* my body rock.

The tiny specks of steel—my æther—began to vibrate.

Let me up. Let me the fuck up!

"Are you struggling still? Not yet strong enough to control what binds you? I will regale you, then, with another story. Its theme is also bondage. Tell me, Eira, are you familiar with the method Boldorvans use to put their criminals to death?"

I followed my shadows as they led me toward the periphery of my eyes.

"They list the accused's crimes on a scrap of fabric and bury that deep into their windpipes."

I stilled.

Listening to his words, I chose not to cross into the other realm.

"Then they sew the offender's mouth shut so that their crimes remain with them in the beyond. Finally, they are hanged unto death. Not an easy punishment to endure," Gotwig whispered. "Not an easy punishment to carry out by oneself." He rubbed his neck, looking off into some unknown distance.

Nan. Baldorva. The Primus-King. The link between Gaea and Leyometh, the sole god of the slaver Baldorvans, solidified further. The

Primus-King had used the Boldorvan manner of punishment to... Images flashed in my mind, flying in and out in quick succession. Nan slumping to the ground. The Primus-King's face. The message I retrieved from her mouth.

What was their link? What was I missing?

How had the fucking Primus-King carried out the hanging of three women and made it back to the Den? Who was his accomplice?

No.

"No!"

My scream pierced my own ears.

Blackness seeped from my body, engulfing the small room in darkness.

"Greggen... Greggen is the Primus-King's man..."

My heart thumped heavily against my chest. Once, twice, and then a third time. My hands pulsed; my palms grew hot and heavy.

"Control, Eira," Gotwig yelled from inside the swirling shade. "Control it. Channel it!"

Channel it? Oh, I'll fucking channel it.

Shards of black fire shot from my palms. The crackle of electricity as it arced to the ceiling made my hair stand on end.

The door opened, and a heavy hand struck the middle of my chest. Gotwig's icy hands gripped my biceps.

"Well, that didn't take nearly as long as it could have," Zuddaz said. "The color is impressive, Troth Solnna. Painful to the touch, though."

The shade twisted into fat ropes that spun wildly in the air and then disappeared, dissipating as the æther broke free from the steel that had confined it. It swarmed within me, renewed.

I gulped the air, kicking out, feet thudding against flesh.

"Let me go. I have to get back!" I raged and fought against the men who held me in place.

Zuddaz struck my chest again with the flat of his palm, and I slumped, the wind knocked from my lungs.

"Your vendetta must wait, Troth Solnna. Now the work begins."

I gazed into Zuddaz's green eyes... Ambrose's eyes.

CHAPTER FORTY-TWO

IT'S ME, HI, I'M THE FLEDGLING... IT'S ME

EIRA

"Lady Monwyn? Troth Solnna? Hello there..."

Giant fingers snapped loudly in front of my eyes, startling me. My unfocused gaze sharpened.

"I-I'm sorry, Primus Zuddaz." I ran my hands through my hair and chewed the inside of my cheek while processing the thoughts tumbling and twisting through my mind. I flashed him a smile that I knew didn't reach my eyes, and his warm hand came to rest over mine. Still a shit Troth... He saw right through me.

Zuddaz squeezed my fingers in a knowing gesture.

"Though your mind is no doubt plagued by thoughts of tyrant kings and the gods' musings, what you can learn here will make your path less burdensome."

I nodded to placate him, but my mind was only on one thing—running a knife across Greggen's deceitful throat. Though when Cato and Ambrose discovered his betrayal, I would have to fight them for the honor.

"Eira, you will slaughter more than you will save if you don't obtain dominion over your abilities. Gotwig tells me that already you have taken lives."

My stomach sank and then soured.

"More than sixteen," I agreed. "Ones that I'm still not sure I regret taking." My voice was strained, but I spoke the truth.

Zuddaz nodded solemnly.

"The longer your powers go unchecked, the more the æther will override your good senses. You can reconcile your actions by telling yourself the soldiers you killed were wrongdoers... but what happens when you slice through a schoolroom? Sear the thinning flesh of the elders who oversee the young ones?"

The memory of Papa Burchard's burned body surfaced.

I swallowed back my grief.

Though I didn't want to second-guess my past decisions, he was right, and I knew it. The lives of innocents should never be an accepted cost in the game of vengeance.

"Lilium. Imella. Nan." The litany fell from my lips, a prayer. "Burchard, little satyr."

Zuddaz scrunched his eyes, worry lines webbing from their corners. On instinct, I reached up and smoothed his concern-wrinkled forehead with my thumbs.

His mouth dropped into a little *O.*

"I'm... Gracious, I'm so sorry. I—"

"Not to worry." He looked away shyly. "Do you enjoy cooking?"

Not the question I expected.

"Cooking? No. Maybe? I enjoy eating, but cooking in Nortia is literally plucking pickled vegetables from a jar, reanimating dried meats, or slicing off raw whale flesh."

"Hmmm, yes, well, my normal analogies will fall flat then. Do you play any type of physical sport? Rock ball, javelin toss, um, wrestling?"

I gestured to my thick thighs and soft tummy, hoping my expression didn't come across as completely incredulous.

"I have run for my life on an occasion or two but prefer wrestling in the sheets to the arena."

Zuddaz threw back his head and let out an uproarious belly laugh.

My Black Bear's grizzly old twin. Oh shit, he has a twin! The Mantle. I longed to watch them toss their heads and laugh together and hug and learn to love one another, making up for lost time.

Tears stung the backs of my eyes, and I could feel my cheeks turning rosy.

"I rather think your husband would take offense to incorporating that methodology." Zuddaz giggled between mopping tears of laughter from under his eyes. The sound warmed my pained heart. "Do you... Well, what *do* you do?"

"Fish."

"Fish?"

"Fish." I nodded. "Ice fishing, pier fishing. Big fish, little fish. I love fish. I'm Nortian."

Zuddaz tapped his finger against his chin and wheeled himself backward.

"I can't say that I share the same zeal for your aquatic hobby, but I think we can make do."

I followed him with my eyes and surveyed the small room.

In my mind, I'd pictured the conjuring Conservatory of Solnna to be something at least as grand as the Study at Vcrus. Where were the brilliant rainbows formed from the spines of a thousand books? There were no cauldrons or jars of preserved fairy wings. There were not even fancy marble tiles or gold-leafed decorations.

This little space was decidedly boring.

It was a simple square room with simple wooden walls, painted a creamy yellow ivory. Several three-tiered bookshelves lined the back wall, but there were at maximum forty, maybe fifty books on each. They were all bound in basic tanned leather and boasted no gilding or stamps.

Zuddaz went to the left side of the room to rummage through a worn, antique apothecary cabinet. It was full of bandages of all sizes and jars of salve.

"Bites, bruises, burns, convulsions..." I absentmindedly fingered a divot in the aged table I sat at as I read the labels out loud. "Pixies, poison, punctures, wraiths... pixies and wraiths?"

"Oh yes, those are the most common creatures to spring up when a conjurer with little training splinters the realms in these parts. Pixies are maniacal little shits. If you see one, just wop it like you would a spider before they bite you, or you'll be begging me to fetch the ointment." Zuddaz waved his hand in front of his face like he was shooing away a nuisance fly. "Their nips pack a brutal punch and itch for days."

"In Monwyn, it's satyrs, trolls, and centaurs. I think I'll stick to those over wraiths." I shivered involuntarily. Satyrs and centaurs were one thing. They still had an element that seemed human.

Zuddaz stilled, his hand poised above the drawer he'd pulled open only seconds ago.

"Oh... oh well then. I was going to start you off with a wand like I do the fledglings, but if those are what you are bringing forth, there is no need." He shut the drawer with a snap. "The littles generally require a conduit to channel the aether until their fine motor skills advance. What skills did your Monwyn mentor teach you?"

I slapped my palms on my thighs.

"So far, I can unlock a lock... some of the time, explode occasionally, and turn into a death cloud of doom and destruction. Oh! I can run through walls."

Zuddaz blinked and smiled a tight smile.

"The Evanesce—passing through barriers—is a rare ability. Exploding is incredibly common, though. It is often how we locate initiate conjurers, if we can get to them before they are hanged, of course. The, uh, doom cloud is not anything I've ever encountered. Not typical at all in my recollection."

"Is anything typical in conjuring?"

He stared at me blankly. "Well... yes, actually." He wheeled himself back to the table and removed two wooden blocks from the satchel that hung from his armrest. He twisted and used them as chocks for his chair. "Conjuring works the same from person to person. It's just another part of you and is very much like... um... tossing out your fishing line—"

"Casting," I said, moving my joined hands back and forth, making the motion of sending bait out over the water.

"Yes, casting, then. So, think about how that feels, as if the pole... Is that the proper terminology?" he asked cheekily, giving me a wink.

I laughed. "Yes, yes, it is."

"Good." He mimicked my movements. "Think of your arm as your pole, the fishing line your æther. The ball of string at the bottom of your pole is your energy store. Do you feel your æther? Wound tight in the center of your chest?"

"All the time. I feel it at every moment unless... Sometimes when I am near Prince Catommandus, it settles." I held his eyes, but it took effort.

Zuddaz leaned forward, his posture open, his eye contact strong.

"I do not pass judgment on the working of one's heart—mine or any others." He glanced down at the hands I was wringing in my lap. "May I?"

He reached out, palm up, and I placed my hand into his.

"Do you see this deep groove, the line that runs from the vein on your wrist to midway up your palm?"

"I do."

"Not all, but many conjurers possess this same line. Close your fingers slightly, see how it lengthens even further. You want your æther to run in a straight line from your chest, through your veins, to this line in your hand. The explosions are the side effects of you not sending it through the... fishing line, if you will. May I pull from you?"

I nodded my consent and then sensed the tiniest tingle near my navel.

"Good gods. You're ripe to bursting." Zuddaz tremored, like Richelle, after taking a swig of strong drink. His wide smile was infectious, and I couldn't help but grin back.

"Pulling from you feels like ingesting far too much of the coffee bean drink."

Zuddaz cast his hand forward and cupped his fingers, pointing them toward a storage bin of quills. The bin slid across the battered surface of the table as he guided it to the left.

"Now watch closely. Like hooking a fish, I think... you feel the bite and then can choose to push or pull against its weight to aid in reeling in the catch. Move naturally, and remember, most importantly, ask the object to move. There is life in everything and even the most insignificant bloom should be treated with respect."

The bin shifted right, sliding in a perfect line to stop in its original location.

"Primus Zuddaz? Hypothetically speaking... if my plans were to use an object to rid the continent of a couple of assholes *and* to help stave off a divinely instigated war, would I still need to ask nicely, or can æther read the room?"

Zuddaz clapped his hands together and tucked them under his chin. His arched brows furrowed.

"You would, uh, yes, need to encourage the implements you *might* use to carry out said plans."

I inclined my chin. The Primus-King and Greggen. I wanted them gone. All lives have inherent worth and all that, but they threatened me and mine—snuffing them out and sending them to the other side was the best use of my powers. Grandmother Merrias could decide their fate then.

"Eira... Eira?"

"Hmm?"

"You are heating the room to uncomfortably hot levels... and I grew up in the desert." Zuddaz pulled a linen from his satchel and blotted his forehead.

"Apologies." I sat up straight and focused. "Fishing line, cast and reel, move stuff."

"Indeed, follow the light to make the æther flow, and then feel for the weight of the quill bin."

I cast out my arm.

"The light doesn't lead me anywhere; only the shadows respond."

Wood splintered and cracked as the bin struck the wall. Feathers scattered in the air and then floated gracefully around us until landing on the floor.

"Lykksun's elbows," Zuddaz whispered. "Troth Solnna, you will need to practice patience and restraint."

I dropped my forehead to the table and let my arms hang past my knees. "I have heard that often."

"Well, like everything, it can be learned. Try again."

"Fuuuuuck."

"How many hours have passed?" I asked, helping Zuddaz regain his seat yet again. "And I am so, so sorry."

Ope! Zuddaz is clearly the parent who blessed Ambrose.

I gathered the charred sides of his once-glorious, shimmering, red-and-gold silk tunic together and held them closed over his thighs, preserving what modesty he had left. He pushed up on his armrests and pulled the material out from under his rear, using the extra volume in the skirts to cover himself.

"I accepted your first and ninth apology, Eira." He exhaled in exhaustion.

"Can you convey my request for forgiveness to the rest of the... what do you call a group of conjurers? Is it like animals—a band, bloat, or colony?"

"We are collectively called a wisdom, but the mundane will often use the term coven. And yes, I will inform them that a fledgling with the strength of a tempest tore the room to shreds." He chuckled despite the absolute carnage surrounding him. "Eira, you have come far today. Already you are able to channel the æther into a more focused line than when we began."

I walked around the room and peeled the two remaining strips of paint from the now bare wooden wall, cupping the remnants in my hands. I focused. The edges ignited, turning bright orange and then black, and I cradled the burning mass until nothing but ashes remained.

"In all honestly, new scorch marks on the floor... a few pen nibs stuck in cabinets—the damage is inconsequential," Zuddaz said, tilting his head toward me. I plucked the metal pen tips from the cabinet face, inspecting each to see if any might be salvageable.

"Prince Ambrose will, I'm sure, foot the bill for a new table... and set of chairs." I gestured to a pile of wooden legs and debris. "And the scribal supplies. Speaking of, how are these books still intact?"

I sliced my hand through the air, toward the tomes on the back wall.

"Protective wards are in place; do you see the letters?"

I moved closer, squatted down, and ran my fingers over the words carved in the wood facings of each shelf. They looked nearly identical to the ones on the tattoo that wrapped around Cato's thigh.

"They are incredibly difficult to put into place, and only a mighty conjurer has the power to undue them."

"Papa Burchard attacked Prince Catommandus and broke one of these... his ward. Cato's mother Imella knew a wise woman who lived near the fire mountain—she inked it into his skin."

"Ah yes, Mildra. She's a nasty old goat, but she knows the craft well. Her journal is on the shelf."

I did a double take, glancing quickly from Zuddaz to the shelf and then back again.

"Journals?"

"Mmhmm. We have very few *actual* texts on conjuring. So we are constantly gathering information from those experiencing it firsthand."

I searched for the conjurer in question.

"Mildra, here it is, and... Cyra Fabia? The instructor from the Grooming? The one who told me I smelled of fish and talked me into a tit piercing? Tall woman, statuesque, nose like a glorious hawk? Takes pride in styling and dressing royals and nobles alike?" I asked.

"Indeed. She is a delight, is she not?"

"Is she?" I remembered her differently: prideful and judgmental, despite her humble beginnings.

"Skilled conjurer, the best Evanescer I've ever witnessed. I imagine she could pass through a wall of steel if she put her mind to it. Former Primus Meridett, who teaches Matters of State, is also one of us."

I knew I had to look ridiculous staring at him with my mouth hanging open. But nothing, *nothing* at all, had indicated that my instructors had been æther wielders.

"I'll be damned, Zuddaz, damned straight to the nether." I lowered to my knees, once again surprised at the true reach of the conjurers. They were amongst us and had been for some time, despite the legalities and the fear surrounding them. "What about Mariad Keagan?"

"Goodness, no. He's as unmagical as they come."

I traced my finger down the line of journals.

Belle Bæsic, Brid Hale, Demeter, Devon, Faye Nightfae, Jes Campos, Krista Flower, Meagbest, Persepha, Ris, Træcy...

"Holy fuck!" My eyes landed on a volume, about the width of my thumb. "Ulltan? Ulltan." I snatched the thin journal and rifled through the pages. There was no fucking way. "'The orcas got beached. I pulled the water to them. They swam right on out again. Movin' big water is getting' easier.'" I could hear my father's voice as I read the words out loud—simple speech, gruff tone. "This is my father, my *dad*... This is *my* Ulltan. I just assumed he fished and ate jerky in large quantities and—"

The tears poured freely down my cheeks, splattering and dotting the pages. I quickly mopped them up with the hem of my dress.

"And can shift the earth and move water faster than even your 'Papa' Burchard. You will find *his* journal just there." Zuddaz pointed to the top shelf.

Just like the other tomes, "Burchard" was written on the spine in simple, black, blocky letters. I slid the volume from between Ankerly and Byrne and opened its pages.

"'Finally, able to shape the water at my command, I can send spheres from one side of the room to the other. This could benefit the old men who break their backs toiling in the gardens and back fields.'" On another page: "'I must find my way to Solnna again, and soon. I cannot squelch the need to pull the æther, even from my own child, and have started drawing others to me, by means that are quite embarrassing to speak of. When whores are sent to me, I do not lie with them; I pull from them until they can no longer walk, no longer take the air into their lungs.'"

But these accountings were...

"Zuddaz... these are recent happenings. How in the nether—"

"Another magi's trick... this one mine." He beamed, pride etched on his features. "All the conjurers who live outside of Solnnas protection have a tome. When they follow the light, or, in your case the dark, they enter the other realm. In that space, objects can be linked across great distances.

I nodded while blotting my tears. Not fully understanding how, but grasping the concept.

"And Eira... I have studied texts from across Ærta and beyond, and what I have learned is that darkness does not imply evil. It is entirely neutral. There are shadows only *because* there is light. Adversity and growth are correlated—I believe there is no cosmic 'good' or 'evil.'"

Zuddaz motioned for me to shelve the journal that I squeezed to my chest.

"Before you return to your mountain home, I will add yours to the shelf. We check them daily for news and updates. It is how we move so quickly when a conjurer is found or when one needs assistance."

"Will a day pass where my soul isn't shocked to its shoes?"

Zuddaz thought for a moment, still gathering his shredded tunic in his lap. "All of the diaries, both the miracles and tragedies told, read to me like

the stories parents tell: a faltering first step, a bloodied knee, a first word…
an empty nest."

"Can I read them?"

"Of course, but realize you may learn things you'd rather not know."

I reflected on his words and then turned back to the shelves. "And Eira,
leave it for tomorrow. You have come far today, despite the wreckage." He
arced an arm around the room. "It's nearly dinner time, and I'm starving.
It takes a great quantity of food to keep me in this fine round shape." He
patted his stomach. "Her Majesty and I are meeting with your husband to
discuss a possible Joining arrangement for—"

"Say Aberus and Aberus only, or I'll burn away the rest of that garment."

Zuddaz's eyes twinkled with an inner light.

"Aberus, yes. Only Aberus. No one told you that His Highness Catommandus marched directly into Her Majesty's private quarters in the middle
of the night? He made it abundantly clear he was not here to be matched.
And then sought permission to hunt his uncle like a stag on royal lands.
That is an interesting family you have aligned yourself with."

Though I didn't allow my face to show it, I was entirely unaware that
he'd left our bed.

"Your Fated Bond is gray in his morality but highly committed to protocol… an unusual combination."

I pictured Cato, back straight, head held high, formally asking the
Queen for clearance to murder his own relation while she clutched her
nightgown around her neck.

"He is… exactly as you describe."

CHAPTER FORTY-THREE

EEWW. THAT'S NASTY... BUT ALSO...

EIRA

"Zuddaz is unaware of the existence of his second child." Gotwig strolled next to me, hands clasped behind his back. For all the world, you would assume he was simply taking a leisurely stroll through the humid gardens of the palace, not conversing about the existence of a child born a Chosen... of two Chosen... conceived during the Rite itself.

My husband.

I understood what Gotwig *wasn't* saying. *Consider what you do with the information, Eira.* And I understood why. Not only were feelings involved, but the highest throne of Ærta risked being contested if the information fell into the wrong hands.

"And Greggen?" My palms burned just saying the name—though instead of that unrestrained feeling I associated with the whirl of uninhibited power, the energy flowed from my chest through my arms to my hands... and then cycled back to my center. This felt more measured, with just a single day of training. What could a month do?

We nodded to a set of guards on patrol and then slowed as we approached my chamber door.

"I don't have the physical proof of Greggen's duplicity, Troth Solnna, but..." He tipped his head to the side and tapped his lips. The *but* said volumes. "When all the clues point in a singular direction..."

I had no reason to doubt him. Gotwig had proven to me time and time again that he *was* the proverbial fly on the wall. He kept his eyes wide open, his ear to the ground, and his lips sealed tightly—unless he was certain.

Gotwig's sparse brows drew together as he studied me.

"What?" I asked, feeling overly scrutinized.

"The Eira I knew at Verus would be halfway to Monwyn by now. She was brash, impulsive and headstrong."

"I must be maturing," I said, accepting the compliment.

"Doubtful."

I chuckled instead of feigning offended surprise. He'd know the difference.

"You're not wrong. If you must know, I've been plotting his demise since the moment I rose from the floor."

He gasped the most sarcastic inhale I'd ever heard.

"Plotting is the first step in learning restraint—a toddler's step—but growth, nonetheless."

I huffed, ready to inform him that *he* was the size of a toddler, but held my tongue.

"Good evening, Troth." He leaned around me and opened my chamber door. A warm breeze behind my back ruffled the wisps of hair that were plastered to my head by Solnna's wet heat. Gotwig made to leave but hesitated, turning his head in my direction.

"Eira. When you fully flesh out your plans, I offer you my services. Kings topple hard when kicked from their thrones. Do not forget the ones they land on."

"The nobles?" I whispered. "They too shall face their fates."

"No. Humanity, Troth Solnna. Do not forget those that rely on him for their well-being."

Gotwig strolled away, the unobtrusive man he was, no shuffling steps, no swinging arms. I watched him disappear down the hallway, all the while wishing it were he and not the Primus-King that was my natural sire.

Papa Burchard's parting words rang like a gong in my head, and I uttered them softly into the distance between us. "'Yes, child, and we will seek our retribution, but not at the expense of your humanity.'"

Wearier now, I padded across the dimly lit room and stopped when my eyes caught on the patterned-yellow package on the communal table. The fragrant and heavy perfume of jasmine filled my lungs.

Ambrose's gift. My sweet husband. *And he has a father. A living, real, conjurer father.*

I smiled to myself, untying and unraveling at least three feet of butter-colored wool before the contents rolled into my palm. My breath caught, and the æther bounded in my chest, lightened, skittering around joyfully.

"Oh, Ambrose."

Six glass flowers rested in my hands, all long-stemmed, crafted to be as lifelike as their real-life counterparts. I knew one was a rose, another a daisy. I didn't know the names of the other four, but one had the shape of a fluted glass, and another splayed petals like the spire above. The last two were soft pink and sky blue.

"A wise woman once told me that a surefrost way to tempt a Nortian to your bed was to give her flowers... I wish I had thought of this."

Cato. His rich voice flowed over my shoulders, caressed my skin, and settled deeply into my heart. I'd not expected him to be here. As a prince of a neighboring kingdom, duty mandated he play the part and attend state functions.

"I am a poor example of a husband, it would seem. Maybe that is why my brother bears that coveted title."

I glanced up from the precious bouquet in my hands.

The Goddess's love enveloped me, and I experienced a profound sense of blessing—the knowledge that it was togetherness that made this world worth living in. He stood, leaning on the jutting wall that separated the two rooms, ankles and arms crossed.

His warm-copper skin caught my eye first. I loved the contrast between my snowy complexion and his sun-burnished hue. Creator above, his body drew my attention next. My mate was hewn from rock, literally built from working in the Monwyn mines, the physique of a workman and soldier.

I dropped my gaze, appreciating him fully. He wore only his Monwyn undergarments, white linen, stopping at the top of his thighs. Muscular thighs, hair-covered calves, one with a serpentine scar twisting around it, the other—I giggled as Cato wiggled his partially amputated toes.

"I think you're doing admirably on the husband front." I grinned in the face of his insecurities. "And your incredibly delicious body makes up for much of what you lack."

His brow slanted

"To me. Now." He flicked his fingers in a come-hither gesture and walked to meet me halfway.

And there goes the æther. It flew around me, sparkling and popping, shooting stars in a night sky. It knew to whom I belonged.

"Free your hands." Cato took the delicate green stems and placed them into an empty cup on the table. Light danced off the arrangement, increasing the glass's luster. "And also, I am in my underwear because it is so fucking hot here, otherwise I would have greeted you properly clothed in—"

"You can always—and listen to me closely, sir—always greet me dressed as you are, or in less if you'd prefer."

His mouth curved appreciatively as he picked up a pitcher and poured a stream of lemon water into an empty glass. He pressed the rim to my bottom lip, watching me intently as I drank deeply.

"I would ask that you do the same. The hardly-a-garment, Solnnan short dress is by far my favorite on you. It makes walking around in public more problematic for myself, but my discomfort is entirely worth it for the view." He twisted the cup around and placed his lips on the same spot I drank from, tipping the glass back and draining its contents. His tongue darted out, catching a droplet. "Tell me what is churning in that beautiful head of yours."

Churning? Mind? What? That Goddess-blessed gem that resided between my legs took on a deep, pulsing rhythm. Never had I wished harder that I was a drinking vessel.

"Goodness me, wife." Cato set the glass down and then covered his nipples with his hands. "Avert your leering eyes," he teased.

We broke into easy laughter, the combined sounds a calming salve smoothed over the parts of me that hurt. But that's how it was with him, my never-ending source of peace.

He reached for me, but I held up my palms. If he wanted to know what was on my mind, we'd need to avoid touching.

"The minute you walked in, love, I could read that expressive face of yours. Brows drawn and teeth nibbling that lush bottom lip, you were clearly distressed." His calloused thumb swept the edge of my jaw. "And then those ocean-colored eyes grew soft. Did *I* cause that reaction? Kiss me if I am correct."

He stared down his nose, with false pretension, and I clenched my teeth, trying hard to keep serious... I failed and squealed with excitement as I launched myself into his arms. He caught me under the rear, hefting me up. I wrapped my legs around his waist while he spun us in a tight circle.

"Yes! Yes, yes, yes! You are absolutely, one thousand times correct."

Cato chuckled low in his throat while I peppered his face with kisses and finger-combed his beard. He deposited me on the table's edge and then lowered himself onto the overstuffed pillow at my front.

"Wait! Before I tell you about my day, have you killed Septimus yet?" I asked half-jokingly, remembering that murder was his entire agenda for the day.

He circled his finger around my knees and then ran them up my thighs, ducking his head under my dress—ignoring my question. He stroked my hipbones and then fingered the ties of my whisper-thin silk underwear—another Solnnan luxury, true silk, not the shiny fakes merchants sometimes tried to pass off.

"Cato." I tapped him on his shoulder. "Your uncle?"

He grumbled, irritated to have his exploration interrupted.

"No. Though he wants it to seem like he has vanished, there are signs of him all around us... He is getting sloppy in his dotage."

"I could have told you that." My head lolled to my shoulder as I savored the light scratch of his nails on my inner thighs.

"Elaborate if you will."

"Hmm?" I fidgeted, trying to feel more of his skin on mine. "Oh. Yes. Septimus." The thought of that asshole, coupled with the feelings my true mate was inspiring, made it hard to focus. "Last night, when we were... um..." *He's going to hit the ceiling. Rip the wax off.* "Welp, he was watching us fuck."

Fingers sank into my hips as my words sank into his head.

"And you did not think before now to mention that my blood relation spied on our lovemaking."

"While you were railing me alongside your *actual* brother? Nope. My mouth was full at the time."

"Adopted brother... whom I was *not* raised with. Furthermore, Ambrose is—wait." Cato's eyes narrowed, but it didn't hide the spark I saw flicking in their depths. "You devious little Troth. You nearly diverted me, well-played." Cato plucked my ties and folded my underthings neatly before setting them off to the side. "Concerning Septimus, I find that I am thrilled that he bore witness to me claiming his cock's desire." Nicked-up hands, battle-hardened palms, slid between my thighs and parted them wide. "Do continue recounting your day."

My pulse fluttered. I could feel the beat of my heart in the sensitive skin of my wrists and the tips of my fingers, coming to life at his touch.

"How in all of Ærta am I supposed to rehash the day with your fingers—Cato, no! I've sweat buckets all day. You can't possibly mean to—"

"I absolutely, *possibly* mean to." His head dropped.

I pushed him away from my crotch, stretching back the sides of his face until he looked like a smooth skinned snow seal. He pushed against me just as hard, determined to get his face under my dress. *Nope.* I could smell my mustiness from here.

Divert, Eira. Divert!

"Wait!" I cautioned. He glanced up, and I quickly slipped my arms from the straps of my baggy dress, shimmying my shoulders just enough to draw his attention. Cato sat back like a trained hound and took my breasts into his hands, fixated.

Men were so simple, even the highly intelligent ones.

"You look at them like you haven't seen them before." I arched my back, thrusting them more completely into his palms.

"And? I lived in the mountains all my life. I am still just as awestruck by their majesty."

Butterflies fluttered in my stomach.

"Put. A. Baby. In. Me. Let them become a decorated war general—a Goddess-blessed mega-queen of some sort. I'm a Chosen One, and I'm mostly fine. They will be fine. We'll be fine."

Oh. It seems women are just as simplistic.

Cato's thumb and index fingers closed around my nipples, pinching and rubbing them until they hardened to points. His pupils expanded into his dark-brown irises, the band of gold glittering wildly in the contrasting hue.

"A compromise then, Madam Troth. After all, I passed up an invitation to an eleven-course dinner to get you alone. And I *am* hungry, Eira... famished."

He lifted his lashes.

Welp. My body responded to the intensity of his unwavering gaze.

He'd won. And he knew it, too.

"Fine. You want to tongue-lap my ratty-haired, less-than-fresh lady bits? Well, you're a grown-ass man." I spread my legs and leaned back, bracing my hands on the table.

An animalistic growl rumbled through his chest.

"Smells like..." Cato's intent fingers slipped beneath the hem of my dress, going straight for his prize. He languidly drew the tip of his finger down the cleft of my vulva. "Mine."

"That's disgusting." *And yet.* "S-so the compromise is your hand instead of mouth?" I tried to sound flippant, to keep the mood light. "That's good. G-great even. Yes, please."

"Oh, no, not at all. The compromise is..." he twisted his hand and poised his finger at my entrance, "if you look away, I stop."

If I look away? Oh gods.

"Now, debrief. Tell me about your day. You do not seem as overly taxed as you normally do after tapping the æther."

He angled his hand up, slipping his finger into my passage. He held it there, delicately searching for the spot that drove me wild. My head dropped back and I—

He removed his hand.

"Wh-what—"

"Less than three seconds. Repeat the exercise."

"This is torture." I took a steadying breath, filling my lungs to capacity.

"A favored pastime. Again." He slowly inched his finger into me while I struggled to keep my eyes from fluttering shut.

"There was a bakery... I... died on the floor, kind of... no, it was the, oh Derros, oh gods. It was the æther. But like, chunks of heavy—"

"You are making no sense at all. From what I gather, you stopped for cake, and it was so entirely scrumptious that you perished in ecstasy?" Cato—confident and so attuned to every movement I made—stared into my godsdamned soul while smoothing the pad of his thumb over my clitoris, working it in the slowest of circles. "Am I close?"

"No... but I am." I breathed unsteadily.

"Then try again." He smoothed his lips over my lower thigh.

"The bakery is not a bakery."

"Go on." He married his index finger to his middle one, reaching into my depths, caressing the spot he knew would bring me close to collapse. The benefits of aligning myself to a calculating man were not lost on me...

My eyes flew open.

"Cato!" I slid my hips forward, but he withdrew his hand, taking with it my delight. I could have smacked the smirk off his Goddess-blessed, so perfectly kissable face.

"Again," he demanded.

Asshole. Desirable, delicious asshole.

I glanced down. His heavy erection strained against his linen small clothes.

I wanted it. I wanted him in me, spreading me, filling me until I was screaming my satisfaction to the top of the fucking Solnnan sun spire.

Focus, Eira, fucking focus or... or play smarter.

"Cato?"

"Yes, love?"

I inhaled sharply.

"GotwigttoldmeastoryaboutaTrothwhowasactuallySoolieandshewaskn ockedupbyZuddazandtheyhadtwins!OnewastheMantleandonewassenta waysoshecouldwatchhimgrow.DoyougetwhatimsayingAMBROSEHAS AFATHERANDABROTHERANDHESLIKETHEMOSTCHOSEN ONEEVERCHOSEN!" I grabbed his hand and thrust his fingers forward, moaning deeply. "Oh," I rocked my hips, riding his digits, "and the woman your father was Mate Bonded to is Ambrose's mother."

My head fell back, triumphant.

Cato shot to his feet.

"Motherfucker!" I screeched, angry at being edged against my will.

His eyes were the size of a snow owl's.

The door flew open.

"Catommandus, you are no peasant. Have the decency to fuck my wife in a bed and not at the table at which we take our meals. Common trash."

Ambrose sashayed into the room, entirely unaffected by the scene before him, dressed like how I imagine a king of Solnna would, in a pearl-dotted silk skirt worn low on his hips. A wealth of necklaces, diamond and rose quartz, separated by golden, barrel-shaped beads hung from his neck. On his wrists, he wore bracelets of carnelians and pearls that twisted in spirals at least three times up his arms. Black leather sandals ran the length of his shins, and he'd clearly coated his fine chest in a sheen of coconut oil. Were a master painter in residence, I would have begged for a rendering to keep for all time.

He glared at me. A face full of judgment.

"Eira, I must insist that you restore your hair before we return home. You are enchanting, of course, but you are in absolute disarray." He slapped Cato on the shoulder as he flounced by me. "Creator's tits, Cato, loosen up. You cannot possibly please her tensed up as you are. And tell me that isn't the sex face you employ *every* time." He popped his brother under the chin, and Cato snapped his mouth closed. "You resemble a deceased cod."

Ambrose poured himself a glass of water, drank it down, and plucked one of the glass flowers from its holder.

He ran the yellow petal over his lip and winked in my direction.

My heart gave a little thump.

"I love them, Black Bear. More than you know."

"Oh, I know." He pooched his lips and sent an air kiss in my direction. "Ah, yes! Catommandus, you will never guess the reason for my premature return from the canceled dinner... though I bet our plump-butted murderess can." He looked at me expectantly, twisting the glass flower in his palm. "Would you care to share the details of your whereabouts last night?"

What?

"Me? Ambrose, I—"

"Show me the daughters of Gaea," he said in a high-pitched approximation of my voice. "Isn't that what you begged the Nether Lord to do? And then,"—he snapped his fingers—"one of his own pops up a full season earlier than expected... and now she is clinging to life, found early this morning. Her betrothed is doornail dead."

"I didn't... I never left the bed. Cato, you visited the Queen's chamber last night..."

"I went to prove a point about her lack of security, but not to take the life of a—"

"Septimus," we said simultaneously.

"He... Oh gods. I fucked up. I really fucked up." I clutched my short tufts of hair in my hands. "I made a deal with him... I think... fucking Dick Bond."

Ambrose came to my side and dropped low. His touch was soft as he removed my clenched hands.

"Do not destroy yourself, wife."

Tears threatened.

"But Ambrose, I am the cause of so much loss and—"

"No, wife. Not the dead man. I have no concern for he nor she." He combed my hair and attempted to arrange the strands.

For fuck's sake.

"A man is dead. A woman injured. Ambrose, don't you see? *I* brought this upon them. My words, spat out in anger, came back to haunt me. The full erasure of the Primus-King's lineage. How many Gaeans will die with Septimus turned loose? On a contract I'm not sure I made."

Ambrose raised the yellow flower to his lips and bit its sun-shaped head clear off, crunching it between his teeth.

"What the fuck Ambrose?" I screeched, clutching his jaws in my hands.

"What? Do not cast judgment."

"Ambrose! Your mouth—why in the nether would—"

He reared back and swatted at my hands.

"I am hungry. What part about 'dinner was canceled' did you fail to comprehend? I am famished. Are you so selfish as to not share your gift?"

I pulled his lips up, inspecting them for the dozens of cuts I knew would be there.

He held the stem to my lips, and I flicked out my tongue. The sweet and sour flavors of orange, mixed with a hint of vanilla and mint, flooded my tastebuds.

I pressed my palms to Ambrose's cheeks.

"You may be the most thoughtful man in existence." I kissed his sticky lips and then sat back, lost in his eyes—pupils blown, half-lidded. "And the most exasperating."

"You know how the most *obedient* wife in existence would show her thanks?" His voice dropped low.

"By cringing at the use of the word 'obedient'?" He spun the tart stem along my bottom lip and then pressed it against my tongue.

"She would fix the bird's nest atop her head, take her husband to acquire sustenance, and then spit shine his dick—twice—upon returning home."

My eyes drifted to Cato, who remained rooted in place, wearing an expression of abject shock.

CHAPTER FORTY-FOUR

BIG BOYS

EIRA

The scent of saffron and a hint of rose wafted through the air outside of the quaint restaurant that Ambrose had decided smelled the most scrumptious... after denying six others. The ambiance was wrong at two of the locations, the chairs not stable enough at another, and the last three... apparently their patrons could not "keep their fucking eyes off my wife's ample curves."

I was quickly approaching the level of hunger that negatively affected my ordinarily sweet-as-sugar personality, but I managed to nod at a little girl and then wave at a smiling couple who held hands as they strolled down the walkway.

Life truly didn't begin in the city of Lykk until the sun went down. It was much too hot for many of their industrial activities to take place during the day. In the distance, I could see the giant outdoor vats where Solnna's most sought-after export, magnificently dyed silks and linens, were being processed. Steam floated up from dozens of cast iron tubs as workers lifted out yards of colorful fabrics with their oar-like paddles. I'd love to strike a deal to have some of the lively materials sent to Nortia. Convincing the fishers to line the insides of their heavy fur clothing with fuchsia, diamond-patterned silk would take some doing, but I think they would love the softness against their often chapped skin.

And I bet I could negotiate a discount. The scent of whale-based oil was heavy in the air as city workers climbed ladders to light the pink blown glass globes that lined both sides of the road.

"Eira. E-i-r-a, Eira!" Ambrose said, punctuating each letter with a clap. "Get back here at once. My stomach sings the song of starvation."

"And yet it is *your* persnickety palate that kept us from food." I jogged back toward Ambrose, who was tapping his toe impatiently, and Cato, who was... watching my breasts bounce. He made no attempt to hide the lusty look on his face—and as I read the promise in his eyes, my expression mirrored his.

Cato cut a fine figure in a gray-purple tunic. The color brought out the deep copper tones of his skin and highlighted the gold streaks that ran through his hair. Though it covered his torso, and the short sleeves fell past his biceps, there was no hiding the breadth of his shoulders or the glimpse of chest the deep *V* of his neckline revealed. Three ruby closures matched the red bits of gemstone sewn to the muted-gold trim along its hems.

He hadn't understood why I fell into his arms, cackling, when he walked out wearing his heavy Monwyn boots with the airy ensemble... and was livid when I told him that Septimus had done the same thing upon arrival. Cato claimed it was necessary for "storing his cache of weapons." He'd sulked until I apologized for making such a ghastly comparison.

A single gold necklace lay against his throat, and from it hung a pendant that looked like an old, dried-up piece of cork. The thing was ugly and looked as out of place as his boots, but I'd take him in whatever garment he wore, without doubt.

"This establishment smells promising. The furnishings look substantial, and—watch your step—the clientele is hideous and too old to attempt seducing you." Ambrose ducked under a set of dangling turquoise chimes that tinkled as he held the door wide.

"Welcome, big boys! You have found your way to Nicolai and Maw's! Come here, come here."

A man I assumed to be Nicolai himself tucked us into a corner, directly under a low-hanging chandelier that boasted dozens of beaded strands that alternated between colorful pieces of brushed glass and small, conical shells. The candlelight gave the gray room, stenciled with golden dragon-flies, a romantic feel, as did the open window that ran the width of the front wall. The breeze loosened tendrils of Cato's shorter hair, pulling it free, allowing it to flutter around his temples.

"My mother is on the pans this eve. Her fry skills put the other maw-maws to shame. Ask anyone!" the restauranteur regaled as he placed settings in front of us. "The old ones run from her spatula-wielding prowess... her whisk wisdom... Ask anyone; they will tell you." The tall and lean man flourished an arm and stabbed out as if he held a sword in his hands. "Fowl or fish?" He air-parried and then thrust again.

I looked from a pair of dark eyes to light. My men were salivating. Ambrose sniffed the air, and Cato's stomach complained.

"Both please, and two orders for each. No, three." My stomach matched my mates', a rumble for each of his grumbles.

Nicolai nodded. "Big boys, big foods, yes?"

I smiled and—

"MAMA! Three birds, three fins!" I jumped in my seat, slapping my palm across my chest as Nicolai headed toward the kitchen.

"On edge, love?" Cato asked.

"Murderer's guilt setting in?"

"Ambrose! Keep your voice down. I did no such thing."

Although inadvertently I may have.

"Which brings me to this gem, brother," Cato said, leaning in closer to Ambrose's side. "In addition to potentially committing murder, Eira failed to mention, until an hour ago, that Uncle Septimus was in the audience during last night's... *performance*."

Gammond's gonads.

Ambrose squinted in confusion until, like a flame put to a wick, he realized *just* what Cato was implying. He surged from his seat, but Cato was quick to throw his arm out, halting and guiding his brother back down.

Ambrose transformed from furious to crestfallen.

"Wife. Am I no longer enough? Have you forgotten the Minotaur's dance? The sacred moments as we Joined in the sanctuary of She Who Gave Us All."

Oh, my gods.

His eyes turned glossy, filling with tears.

"Ambrose, Black Bear." I scooted from my chair and folded myself onto his lap. It was a more effective method of calming him than any other. "Why in the world would you think that?"

His chest rose and he let out a long-lived sigh as I stroked his impeccably edged beard, smoothing it beneath my fingertips. He turned the saddest baby seal's eyes on me, round and innocent.

"Last night, there was no fire."

Ouch, Ambrose.

"Truly?" I felt a prickling sting in my own eyes. "I rather thought the experience earth shatter—"

He pinched my lips together.

"The first time our triad fucked, you nearly burned the palace to beams. But... but last night..."

I rested my head against Ambrose's necklace-laden chest and glimpsed back at Cato, whose lips twitched in amusement. Narrowing my eyes, I threatened him silently, knowing he was formulating a jab at Ambrose's expense.

"Last night, I came so hard I thought for a moment I'd passed out."

"You did?" Ambrose's voice caught in his throat. "That would explain the absence of flame."

Derros's dangling dong.

"I think, husband, that I'm learning to better control the æther." I sat up and preened, rather proud of the fact that I didn't torch the Solnnan sheets. "And I think the lack of fornication fire is a great thing, you know?" I petted his chest. "I burned you the last time, something I don't want to make a habit of... This flawless skin is much too precious for that."

Ambrose's pouty lip returned to its normal state of perfection.

"I suppose. But it is time for the three of us to hash this out. Clearly, we are miscommunicating or... not communicating at all and—thank you, sir, this smells amazing—relationships require candidness, especially ones that I presume will last until one of us does something stupid or dies." Nicolai's lashes fluttered as he heaped mounds of fragrant rice onto our plates. To his credit, he let no additional surprise show.

"My money is on Cato meeting the Creator first. I will get my bed back then... but my buns would certainly miss you."

Cato sputtered, spraying rice in a wide trajectory.

Nicolai coughed into his shoulder.

Ambrose smirked in Cato's direction, winking a mossy-green eye.

"Use your inside voice, for fuck's sake."

My men began shoveling food into their faces like they'd never see another meal, pausing only to throw each other disgruntled looks between spoonfuls.

I made to move back to my chair, but Ambrose snugged a big arm around my hips, stilling me. He pinched a bit of glazed, pink-fleshed fish and placed it into my mouth with his fingers. Sweet honey and sour lemon hit my tongue, followed by a peppery burn that was just on the verge of being too spicy. The bit of ruffly green herbs I chewed added another note of divinely inspired complexity to the dish.

"Ahem, your sex sounds remain between the three of us, wife. Inside voice, *please.*"

I peeked open a single eye, catching the jerks of several heads going back to their own meals.

"Still working through some jealousy, Ambrose?" Cato quipped, pointing his spoon at his brother.

"Oho, tiny brother." Green eyes rolled dramatically until they came to rest on Cato. "Perhaps I am. But look who has the girl on their lap."

Ambrose glared at Cato, and Cato gave it right back.

Nicolai appeared over Cato's shoulder with a large pepper grinder.

"Is the summit in your skirt a reaction to the fish?" Ambrose said into the increasingly packed room. "Food fetish, Catommandus? Oral fixation? I am sure we can marry the two, perhaps strap a trout to her mouth and a swordfish to her—"

"Ambrose," Cato cautioned while dragging a finger across his throat.

"F-fish is good for the, um, it's good for the complexion," Nicolai stammered while grinding a small mountain of pepper directly onto the table.

Bless him for trying.

"Applied topically or orally?" I assumed it was another joke, but Ambrose was quite serious. He held a little chunk of pink meat in front of his nose and then pushed up his glasses. "Such a striking color. Reminds me of Eira's pu—"

"Mama consumes it daily and barely looks a day over ninety and four." The slim and exceptionally well-dressed restauranteur cleared his throat, choking as he attempted to refill our glasses. Water splashed over his pitcher, sprinkling the rose-colored tablecloth. "How's the chicken? It's marinated in the succulent juices of..."

Ambrose's eyes twinkled with menace. I slapped my hand over his mouth, blocking whatever lewd comment he was about to make.

"...coconut, cumin, pineapple, and onion."

Ambrose nipped my finger and held it between his teeth.

Absolute rage washed over Cato's visage—nostrils flared, irises dark—as Ambrose made a smacking sound and licked my finger through his teeth.

"Just stop it." I couldn't keep the smile off my face or from my voice. "You're causing a scene. Both of you."

Before diving back into my meal, I caught the eyes of more than one patron. Some, I noticed, turned their bodies in our direction, and one older lady, with a head full of magnificent graying braids, held her plate directly under her mouth, unabashedly taking in the show.

Cato cocked a brow.

"Ambrose, you share in the blame for my "

I stuffed a heaping spoonful of rice into Cato's mouth, cutting him off.

Grains blew from between his lips. One struck me in the eye and stuck to my cheek while other bits rained into my neckline.

Ambrose tossed his head back and joined me in a bout of stomach-cramping laughter, and even Cato smirked while trying everything in his power to hold tight to his typical look of aloofness, despite his bulging cheeks. He chewed through what was twice a normal man's bite, the lines at the side of his mouth more prominent as he struggled to stay serious. "Well pwayed, wuv. Well pwayed."

"I'm sorry. I'll make it up to you." The giggles still had me in their grips, but I managed to pinch a piece of succulent white meat from a half of a fowl and held it to Cato's lips. "The chicken is divine."

I placed the morsel into his mouth, and as I pulled back, his tongue ran along the pad of my index finger.

"Delicious," he hummed. "And what do you know? I believe I *do* have a fixation... Some might say an obsession."

Ambrose began stiffening under my rear as I squirmed in his lap. My mouth worked up and down as I tried to find a clever retort.

"Is there something you would like to say, Eira?" Cato plucked a piece of meat and held it up. "Use your words, love."

I swallowed hard. There was so much I wanted to say. So much I needed to say. Love to profess, a netheruva day to deconstruct and—oh, right.

"G-Greggen helped the Primus-King murder our family."

CHAPTER FORTY-FIVE

A BATTLE WAGED BEFORE BIRTH

EIRA

Cato's eyes.

They didn't go flat as they had when Greggen attacked me so long ago. They didn't spark like they had when he'd stared into the eyes of would-be assassins traveling from Colpass to Cordillaria.

These were the eyes of my warrior-king—dangerous, singularly focused.

The gold ring that surrounded his pinprick pupil glinted like the sharp edge of a knife.

He stood and walked toward the door.

"Cato, wait. You can't just... Cato, stop," I begged, attempting to grab his sleeve as he passed by.

He flung the door wide, busting the top set of hinges from their frame. He was beyond rage—beyond the point where anyone could stop him unless they understood where he had gone.

"Ambrose, he..."

My husband stared at the table, looking at nothing and everything all at once, no doubt recalling the horror of that night he found his mother swinging.

I leapt from his lap, dug around in the pouch he wore at his side, and tossed a handful of coins on the table. The palmful of gold would afford Nicolai a new door, or brand-new building if he wished it.

"Ambrose, please." He blinked back into awareness. "We have to stop Cato."

"I trusted him, Eira—invited him into my home, defended Greggen to you, and encouraged Allaine... *I* put her hand directly into his."

Ambrose stood so abruptly that I stumbled back. His arm came around my waist instinctually, settling me. Then, like a deity netherbent on destroying the Great Sphere, he squared his shoulders and stalked to the door, leaving me behind.

"Fuck, fuck, fuck." I wrang my hands and looked around the room, hoping to find a means to stop them both.

Food fell from the mouth of a patron, plopping to her plate. She stared in rapt attention, her eyes flickering between Ambrose and me. Ambrose sailed out the door, his head smacking against the hanging chimes. His arm shot out and yanked the cluster of bells and gemstones from their hook, then dashed them to the ground. Beads and shells scattered across the floor.

From the open-shuttered storefront, I saw him quickly catching up to Cato.

"Nicolai, I'm so very sorry, I will... will... Please tell your mother the food was amazing."

Mouth agog, he nodded and shooed me out with both hands.

I ran, panting, to catch up with the two men barging down the street.

The good citizens of Solnna parted as the Monwyns split the crowd like a pod of orcas slicing through the surf.

"Cato, we are days from Monwyn. We can do nothing at this moment. We must be level-headed and form a plan." *Fuck me... I am maturing.*

I caught Ambrose by the waist of his skirt, but he didn't slow. I rushed forward, twisted around his big body, and braced my arms against his stomach.

"Eira, stand down. Greggen deserves the death coming to him."

"Ambrose, listen to me. Please."

He went still, standing rigid, clutching his fists at his sides.

"Are you not the woman who sank your teeth into that miscreant's hand... who called upon the powers of the godsdamned Nether Lord to satisfy her need for vengeance?" Ambrose said, his voice overflowing with emotion. "I seek a vengeance of my own."

"We can't rush into this, no matter the pain we feel," I whispered, urging him to look at me. "They were cleverer than us last time. We can't fight them unless we first outthink them. Theirs has been a long game, which they put into place before you or I traveled to the temple, maybe before we were babes out of swaddling cloth. Ambrose, hear the reality of my words." I pressed myself against him. "I feel the same pain... We share the same pain, my heart."

He breathed deeply, shuddering, but nodded.

"Come, we must stop him." Ambrose dropped his arms and took off, his tiny skirt giving passersby peeks of his bare bottom.

I sprinted, picking up but ignoring the sand and sediment that collected in my sandals.

Ambrose signaled to the right and then pointed to an area of the street whose lamps were still dark, gaining on Cato as he did so. *Smart Ambrose.*

I veered.

"Oh, shit!"

Ambrose pounced, launching his nearly seven-foot frame toward Cato's chest, shoving him into a wall.

The impact was terrifying—loud and jarring. Cato's jaw cracked audibly as it met the wood, but it didn't seem to faze him in the least. He fought, skillfully kicking a foot back and hooking it around Ambrose's ankle.

Ambrose struggled to maintain his hold.

"Cat, come back, man."

Cato's head snapped back, catching Ambrose on the chin. Ambrose let out a grunt as Cato wrenched from his grasp.

Fear flashed in my husband's eyes, stunned by the violence in his own brother's murderous gaze.

Cato planted his foot and reached for his knife.

"Stop, now!" My palm met his chest.

Both men took flight, tumbling against the wall before crashing through a doorway.

CHAPTER FORTY-SIX

BOOFLE

EIRA

"Which of you is the impotent party?"

I rushed over the threshold, just in time to hear the succinctly spoken query.

"I understand the sensitive nature of sexual health-related issues, but no one will be forced into this establishment. Is that clear?"

The woman behind the desk repeated herself in the common tongue, unfazed by the two brutes sprawled on the floor.

Ambrose got to his feet first.

"Pardon me? Impotent?" he spat, incensed at the implication. He straightened his skirt over his thighs and kicked Cato in the stomach. "It is obviously not I, but this one who lacks in virility." He waved a hand over his chiseled stomach.

"Ah." The woman came forward with a mountain of scrolls in her hands and squatted next to Cato, who still lay in a daze—he'd clearly taken the brunt of my æther. "Well, all manner of emotions rear their heads when partners find the right woman to carry their precious bundle. All of them are valid." She smiled and tucked a rolled piece of parchment under Cato's hand. "These scrolls may help to ease your worries, and I can assure you that we handle the process with professionalism. If all parties consent, you and I both can be present during fertilization, and I can talk you through every step of the beautiful journey."

Cato blinked, shaking his head to clear the fog. And Ambrose, giant ass that he was, let out a high-pitched laugh.

"Oh indeed, he should absolutely be present to watch me fill this vacant womb." He snatched me by the waist and patted my stomach.

All of a sudden, her eyes were on me.

"Miss, have you carried for a couple before?"

"I... Nope—surely have not."

"I have a scroll for you as well, then. What a lovely gift you offer our fathers-to-be."

I helped Cato haul himself to his feet. When he righted, I tugged at his lower eyelid, searching to see that the warrior no longer drove him... but also checking that he hadn't sustained a concussion.

"Our rooms are brimming with a myriad of the newest aids and devices for you to achieve arousal. We find conception takes place faster when the vagina is naturally lubricated. Though the various oils we keep on hand do work, they just seem to slow the process." She glanced up at Ambrose. "You and your partner may also have the privacy of a room, to ensure the soldier stands straight."

Ambrose's expression looked like something between seasickness and astonishment.

"I assure you, *madam*, my soldier has *always* risen to the occasion. Lead on!" He thrust a pointed finger toward a hallway located behind the woman's desk.

"Ambrose," I chided.

"We have trained several times for the begetting of a spawn, and now we are ready to put our practice to the test... and to ensure paternity is documented by a noble state official such as yourself."

Witnessing the moment someone succumbed to his charm never failed to amuse me.

"I see someone has done their research. The documentation and certification process of our conceptive practices are the number two reason foreigners visit Solnna, after silk, of course." The slight woman with a hairstyle that resembled my own—shorter sides, a pile of tight coils on the top—preened and patted the silver brooch on her shoulder. "I've had nine success stories already and only received my badge twelve months ago. I'll be in line for recognition if I continue *producing*." She laughed at her own joke and turned away to scrounge on the shelves behind her desk.

"Delightful," Ambrose crooned. "Such an endeavor must be rewarded. You are doing the Goddess's work."

Oh, gods help her. Hook, line and—

"From your lips to her divine ears! I'm Kennda, by the way, and I am so excited to be a part of your parenthood journey, uhhh..." She cleared her throat while checking her notes. "Lords Dallingston and... Miss Boofle.

Boofle?

"Cato, make this stop!" I hissed as quietly as I could.

Ambrose walked behind the desk and took the woman's hand in his, tucking it securely in the crook of his elbow.

"Are the rooms entirely private?" Cato asked. "We will not be bothered?"

He's lost his mind.

"We pride ourselves on discretion, sir. Each wall is double thickness, and you will find them padded to dampen any noise that may otherwise stray. Even the doors are sealed at their bottoms. If you are all in agreement, we can begin."

"I will require a thorough inspection of the room first, but lead the way," came Cato's unexpected response.

Ambrose was already guiding her down the hallway.

Chapter Forty-Seven

DICK WALL

Cato

No windows. Single exit. Surfaces padded. Floor heavily strewn with carpets. Two weapons on my person, one on Ambrose. Seven non-lethal objects. Four that could be improvised into weapons.

I made another turn about the chamber, looking for holes, searching for any thinness in the smartly devised padding covering every surface of the ceiling and walls.

"AMBROSE, YOU THIN-COCKED EUNUCH, I AM FULLY AWARE YOU LACK THE ABILITY TO MAKE HER COME," I shouted, bracing myself for my brother's rage.

Nothing. Excellent.

I flipped the handle and opened the door.

Eira stood there, arms over chest, rolling her magnificent eyes at Ambrose, who was flexing his pecs to the beat of "Not all Rocks are Round," a children's song mothers sang to their huskier boys, before they shipped them off to the mines to be shaped into men. Ambrose nearly deafened me with his dreadful tenor...

"Some rocks are square, and some they are long,
Some rocks have texture, but all rocks are strong."

"This is the reason your men have complexes." Eira brushed her short hair from her face as I held my hand out and led her into the room. My fucking chest near exploded in a rush of emotion. I was here. She was mine. We would face the atrocities of the world as one.

"Rocks hold up houses and build roads so strong,
That horses and carriage go rambling along."

Eira's brows shot to her hairline, and she tucked both lips into her mouth to keep silent.

"Yes, love. He has not an ounce of shame about the way he sounds. My ears also seek silence."

"Not that, Cato. He's adorable," she said, glancing back as the idiot Scion and Kennda swayed together in a joyful little dance.

I cringed, taken aback that she could find his off-key warbles anything but painful.

"It-it's all the penises." Eira clutched my elbow and looked into my eyes. *Gods. Is she wheezing?* I laid my palm on her forehead to search for fever and—ah—the laughter she poorly attempted to conceal was seconds away from cracking free. Her lips twitched, and her eyes twinkled. "There are nine of them on that shelf. Do you see them? One shares the girth of my forearm... and what is that?" she whispered, while pointing to a... I had no idea what the fuck it was. A muck-filled scroll case?

"Surface imperfections are fixed in the mines
Polishing happens all in due time."

"That is for masturbating a penis," our conception consultant interjected, having abandoned Ambrose to his song. "If the provider is having difficulty maintaining their erection, this tool works wonders. Please note, there are several to accommodate differing lengths and widths. My recommendation is to load the tube with the thickened coconut oil"—she pointed to a chest filled with glass jars that sat next to an oddly shaped chaise in the middle of the room—"then place over the shaft, and gyrate. Otherwise, the sensitive skin may tug." Kennda shook her hand at crotch level in a most serious pantomime of self-pleasure and nodded in my direction, singling me out.

My woman. Would it not end in a public fucking, I'd bend her over my knee and swat her rear until she begged me to stop. She was literally biting her lips now, squinting at me from a single eye while she puffed out airy laughs from her nose.

I shot her a stern look.

How she ever made it past her first lesson at Verus was beyond me, even if I treasured all of her quirks.

"There are nodes imbedded in each sleeve, made from a substance extracted from our trees—but that's a state secret," our advocate winked, "that many a man finds most pleasant on his appendage."

I sneered at the woman, who went about straightening the shelves while explaining the use of each contraption the Solnnans had invented for self and partner pleasure.

"Doubtful, unless it was made to replicate my wom—"

"—bat," Ambrose supplied, finally strolling into the room. "He calls me his little wombat on account of my stout backside. Isn't that right, *daddy?*"

I plotted his death.

"We understand. Thank you. You may exit." I flicked my finger toward the door. Our insemination instructor bobbed her head and scurried away.

Ambrose, of course, strode right to the wall of dicks assessing each as if they were a visiting sculptor's newest installation.

"My collection in Colpass has more variety; marble, glass, polished wood. But these are not bad and—gods alive, this one... it flops! Eira, examine this creation. It bounces and looks so lifelike. Shall we procure three or four of these titillating implements for home, hmm?"

Eira went to his side and prodded the faux cock. Her look was one of genuine surprise as she tapped and slapped the milky-white appendage while "ooing" in delight.

"For fuck's sake, don't put it in her mouth, Ambrose." I rubbed at the tension mounting in my forehead. *Two absolute sluts. My sluts. But still.* "We are here to form a plan. This room provides more security than the palace, and Eira's revelation requires us to return to Monwyn directly."

The mood sobered instantly. Ambrose tucked Eira's arm into his elbow and both met me where I stood.

"Sit." I motioned them toward an oddly shaped couch—the first I had laid eyes on in this pillow-permeated country.

"No, wifling, like this." Ambrose draped himself over the elevated slope of the chaise's left side, draping his torso over the large hill. "It perks up the ass and allows me to lazy-fuck you from behind... or perhaps you would be open to taking mine... behind that is." He raised his eyes to the dick wall and tensed his glutes rhythmically.

Eira let out a gravelly chuckle and squeezed her thighs together.

My slut.

"May I have the attention of the nymphos in the room? Yes? Anyone?" I tossed my leg over the opposite end of the chaise and sat.

Eira eyeballed me like I was a godsdamned hunk of high-grade blubber as Ambrose sat in the seat's more defined dip opposite of me. He waved the wobbling cock back and forth, testing its flex like a rapier. I motioned her to me, grabbed her by the waist, and dropped her into my lap.

Wrong move, Cato. The feeling that always accompanied her nearness inundated me—the fierce need to keep her safe. A swell of appreciation and a jolt of blinding lust. My body knew the melody of her song and craved to hear its lush and resonating notes. How another human could dissolve one's sorrows with just their presence alone still baffled me, and I thanked the Goddess for her gift the moment my eyes opened in the mornings.

Eira sniffled, and instantaneously, her "warrior-king" demanded to be let free. Like my shadow, he always lurked close. But if I allowed myself to reenter that state, I would dismantle this kingdom board by board, until her tears dried.

"Love?" I skimmed my finger along her spine.

She hiccoughed a small sound of sorrow and I primed, ready to draw blood.

"Like the many-headed dog in *Magika and Menagerie,* I can't resolve a single issue without it growing double for my efforts," Eira said, snuggling into my chest, tucking her head under my chin—the place she belonged. She soothed me.

"What have you done, other than your duty and your damnedest? Do not hold yourself accountable for the failings of others," I consoled her.

Eira reached up behind my head. She loosened the leather thong holding my braid in place and raked her nails through the plait. The pain in my temples subsided under her tender, loving hands.

"Should you remember that as well, Cato?"

I attempted to shake my head, but she held it firmly in place.

"She is right, Catommandus. Cordillaria never saw a breach under your stint as Protector. You could not have saved Momma, nor any of the others. Your focus was exactly where it should have been—securing Aberus. And you, unlike myself, saw Greggen for what he is... a murdering criminal whose allegiance lies with a country of debasing slavers."

I ran my knuckles down Eira's jawline, uncomfortable with them praising my failures.

Her pupils dilated, a dark orb swimming in a color that I could never properly name. Ocean eyes—sometimes a stormy gray-blue, at other times tinted lagoon green. She worried her bottom lip, and that was all it took to flood my imagination... her legs spread wide, her soft and slick flesh bared.

No doubt she felt my cock go to stone beneath her—inappropriate timing or not—I fucking throbbed. The urge to sink my fingers into her hips and unload myself into her tight passage warred in precedence with the more pressing matters. But I was learning to restrain my perpetual need for release—had been training and testing my limits since the first time I took her.

"We must make haste back to Monwyn before another woman falls. Were those not the Primus-King's words to you? That the slaughters would continue if you or your mother were not presented to him? I imagine Greggen, being his man, would have the means to carry out his orders at any time."

"They were, yes." Eira's eyes welled, and tears fell to her cheeks. I leaned forward and kissed them away. "Cato, I agree we must return swiftly, but I feel I should return to the Conservatory once more before we leave. Zuddaz and I can continue to communicate if I have a journal set up in the room. Though my arrival here was inadvertent, it would be senseless to throw away continued instruction. If nothing else, it may convince Aberus that I am not a monster with nefarious intent."

I heard the wisdom in her words.

"Though I cannot comprehend how you plan to communicate from such a distance, I agree with your assessment. And as you have said, there is nothing any of us can do at this juncture."

Ambrose sat up at attention. "The Primus-King knew that his Boldorvan lackey—fucking Greggen—would be Assigned to Monwyn to ensure his threat came to fruition, didn't he?"

It was rare to hear the lethal edge in my brother's voice.

"And if it wasn't the Boldorvan, the odds were stacked that one of his other filthy Gaean Scion would have been Assigned there. Godsdamned political bullshit."

He sounded like Eira. She was rubbing off on him, too.

"Allaine may already be dead... or Richelle." Eira choked out the words while reaching for Ambrose's hand, linking us together. "Cinden would be a target as well. I'm so worried."

My failure to shield her from such a profound loss made me furious... the prospect of returning to freshly dug graves enraged me beyond what I once knew was possible. The Bond heightened my emotions threefold.

"And the Mantle is due there any day, if They have not arrived already."

Ambrose's words struck a chord in me. I mulled them over, trying to surmise the Primus King's intentions. I needed to know my opponent so well that I could anticipate his moves before he made them.

"My fear is that the Mantle may be the *actual* target," I said, sitting up, adjusting Eira so that I could curve my arm more securely around her. I could feel her fear, sense her rising panic. She deserved my truth though—she was forged from stronger steel than most armor. "Can you imagine the fallout if Their demise occurred when Monwyn's Protector deserted his post and both heirs left to 'procure a bride'? The entire continent would ostracize us, put us under embargo, cut off the basic supplies to our people. Aberus's sovereignty and legitimacy as a whole would be subject to question. And who, if not the Mantle, would act as judge? The Gaean Devotee perhaps?"

It was the perfect setup to ensure continent-wide chaos—for leaders to topple and land to change hands.

"Greggen, undoubtedly, has a line of communication with the Primus-King. Do we imagine he sends information to Baldorva as well?" Ambrose asked, thinking like the Scion he was trained to be.

"Baldorva and Gaea are in collusion, brother, I am sure of it. But we do not know the nature of their link. Is it true allegiance to the god Leyometh or, Goddess strike them dead, do they all want claim to Eira's bloodline for their own ends?"

"Or is it just her blood they seek?" Ambrose leaned forward, dropping his feet to either side of the couch. His eyes were cold, heartless. He would lay his life down to protect my woman; it was the primary reason I tolerated his feelings toward her. If I fell, I knew he would give all to ensure her welfare.

Eira shivered and wrapped her arms around her waist. "And what of Kairus? Is her Assignment in slaver lands a farce? Do you think Baldorva's pursual of an international trade relationship with Ærta was legitimate or a coverup? My gods, we must get her out of there, Cato. I fear she will become a pawn to manipulate both Monwyn and Verus."

"Septimus must be left alive then, Cato. He possesses the official paperwork and lineage tome that would allow him to retrieve his daughter," Ambrose said. "Perchance under the guise of collecting her for her mother's delayed burial."

I immediately sensed a shift in Eira's presence.

"She's not his daughter." Her eyes went as flat as her voice. "On our voyage, Septimus caught a raging fever. He revealed Kairus to be the child of Alois, who I understand was Burchard's eldest brother. She will be left to rot in Baldorva and my 'Safeguard' won't spare her another thought."

"Is nothing real?" Ambrose slumped back. "Alois was second in line to the throne until Aberus came along. And if a woman were permitted to make a move for the high seat of Monwyn, Kairus's claim would be on par with my own."

"The moment I find Septimus, he can join his vile brothers in their graves." I had more reason than one to snuff him from existence. Fuck, I had a dozen spanning decades.

Ambrose shook his head while scrubbing his fingers through his beard.

"No, Cat. Where I would applaud you for severing the Dick Bond he has with my wife, if we are to believe Merrias herself, he is Eira's Safeguard… and Eira is my priority." Ambrose ran the wobbly dick under Eira's hem and lifted her dress. "Wife, did you fuck him on your journey here?"

"No."

Relief poured through me. I wanted to know—burned with the need to ask—but would have never put her in that position. I understood better than anyone the power behind the Bonds and had imagined them a thousand times. His silver hair falling onto her breasts as he fucked her. Her legs wrapped around his waist, pulling him deeper into her body.

"Did you *want* to fuck him?" Ambrose asked, not leaving well enough alone.

"Yes. And I-I masturbated in front of him and he in front of me, and we… we kissed." My whole body tensed, and Eira turned her face up to mine. "I'm sorry, love, I didn't want to, or rather my body did, even though my brain didn't."

I pressed her head to my chest and said nothing more.

"Do I not deserve an apology? You have twice now—no, three times—cavorted outside of the confines of the Joining bed, and though I allowed and even encouraged you to perform the arousing tongue-tangle of cunnilingus on an ill-deserving trollop, I am beginning to harbor resentment."

Eira crawled across the chaise and attempted to pry Ambrose's arms from across his chest—ridiculous infant that he was.

"I make love to Cato and *you*. And just because I'm attracted to women and have a   a Dick Bond with Septimus, doesn't mean I want to *be* with any of them. My heart is happily at capacity with the two men in my life."

She continued wrestling with his arms, and he continued holding out… but I knew he was no match for her persuasive wiles.

"But, Eira, you mostly want Cato, I know."

The sadness in Ambrose's eyes concerned me, but only briefly. That Eira did not immediately deny what he said gave me a surge of joy that bordered on delirium. She belonged to me, and she knew it.

"No, not more or less, but differently."

"Explain yourself." Ambrose relinquished his arms to her insistent hands and allowed her nearer.

I watched as her Goddess-blessed fingers worked their way into his hair as they had mine, stroking his long strands until he calmed. I was immediately envious—if it were anyone else I would...

"Cato is my wildfire, and you are my soft snow," she spoke to him in a delicate tone.

"And you love snow." Ambrose bopped the head of that fake dick on the tip of her nose.

"I do. And the fire, it's a part of me. It burns intensely in my soul and ignites the beacon that is my existence. And then... then you are there, a cool and calming comfort when I burn too bright."

Ambrose tilted his head to one side and then the other, contemplating the importance of each description.

Eira took the wobble-cock from his hand and tossed it to the floor.

"And the offer still stands, Ambrose. If you ever fall in love, you are free to be free. I'd never keep you from the one who captured your heart. I know the pain that would cause."

I held my breath, wondering if he had finally concluded the true nature of his feelings for her.

"Oh, my gods, speaking of soft snow, Ambrose, we had regular people sex. I meant to ask, but was otherwise occupied: how did you like missionary?"

"What the fuck?" I busted out, disbelieving my ears.

Eira crawled around to face me, making a wide turn on the thin couch. I immediately missed the sight of her ass but the sight that replaced it more than made up for the loss: the face I longed for my children to bear.

"Ambrose had never—you know—man-on-top, regular, old-fashioned sexed before last night." She sort-of-scooted, sort-of-flipped back around and crawled toward him on her hands and knees. "Did you enjoy it? You had reservations a while back."

"Thank you for remembering, and, you know, I did." Ambrose twirled a lock of his hair around his finger. "It was not nearly as mundane as I imagined, the angle worked, the puss was tight... and the eye contact was not awkward."

She laid her head on his chest and pushed her fingers through the hair below his gaudy display of necklaces. She stretched her legs and pointed her toes at me—I kneaded her arch, eliciting a shiver that shook her entire body.

"Brother, are you telling me that you never plowed head-on into her luscious fucking field until last night? I've had sex a total of"—I counted the times Eira and I had been together, remembering every mind-altering instance—"Nine times in my life, and pushing those legs back and mounting her is the purest fucking delight I have ever experi—"

"You counted me, yes?" Ambrose held his spectacles in front of his eyes and squinted at me long and hard. "If you deny our moment, Catommandus, I will disown you... extract you entirely from my life."

Gods above, why had I ever... Right... because Eira was more aroused than I'd ever seen her before, which provoked me into seeking another mind-altering æthergasm.

"He counted you," Eira said. "Because I remember the exact number of times he and I have been together, and he included an extra."

It was a lie. I had not included him, never thought about that night unless someone brought it to my attention. But the way Eira looked at me, her eyes pleading...

"I counted you," I said, looking at him squarely.

Her shy smile of thanks made my chest tighten. I would commit atrocities for that smile... cheat or steal... fuck her husband... A mistruth was nothing.

Ambrose snuggled into the cushioned seat and folded Eira in his embrace, placated once more.

"So, the plan, Cato. What are your thoughts now that you are not raging around the town like an aggrieved bovine?"

"We leave at sunrise. Take a ship north, retrieve our mounts, and make our way to Cordillaria. Eira, we will arrange for an escort to Colpass for your safe—"

"Absolutely not," she fired back at me, "Please continue."

"Eira, do not be—"

"I. Said. Absolutely not." The conviction in her tone matched the seriousness of her face, and I knew I would lose the battle if I pressed. I chose not to. She knew her mind. "I know you are both better at strategy and fighting. But if it comes down to it and Greggen manages to get the upper hand on either of you, I will—"

Ambrose smacked his hand over her mouth.

"She will call up the scariest fucking creature you have ever seen and burn our childhood home to the ground, yes?"

Eira nodded and made some sort of muffled agreement.

"Cat, I think our strategy should be to return as normally as we gave the impression of leaving. Give them no time to flee or sound the alarm. Troth Solnna here, found a suitable bride for our brother, and we have brought her back for his inspection. It would actually fall under Eira's purview if she didn't spend her days fucking and eating—ouch!—you vicious little harpy."

I nodded my approval at Ambrose's plan. Ending Greggen would be easier if he thought us in the dark concerning his allegiance.

Ambrose swatted Eira's ass with one hand and jerked his other from her pearly-white teeth. I watched her flesh jiggle under his palm and stifled a groan. Her body caught me off guard at the most innocuous of times. If the Goddess asked me what my specifications were for a mate, it would be her. I itched to grab her by the round ass and hoist her up around my waist. I would slide her down, feeding myself into her, watching her come apart, begging me to take her. And I would, over and over, until the bed sheets soaked through with our sweat.

"So do we actually bring a bride back? And what if Aberus rejects her?" Eira asked interrupting my salacious thoughts. "Is it safe enough to bring another woman to our home?"

Our home.

"Worst-case scenario Cato Joins with her—problem solved. Another marriage of convenience that could turn out as happy as our own."

I jolted from my dream state, ready to finish what I began outside. My fists tightened on instinct.

"Husband, suggest it again and I will æther blast you in the taint," Eira seethed, her jealous side stroking my ego. "See if I don't. That one," she pointed at me, "fucks a single pussy for the rest of his days."

Ambrose scoffed and stamped a foot on the floor.

"I would die, and you would live happily ever after with your fated dick," he spat with a saucy shake of his shoulders. His eyes narrowed. "That is your plan, isn't it? Do not deny it."

"If the two of you will settle, we can continue."

Two aggravated sets of eyes snapped in my direction.

"We will simply send the woman back if she or Aberus are in disagreement. Pick whichever woman you like, Eira. Send a letter to the queen this eve, informing her of your choice." I waved, entirely indifferent, and watched my woman clasp her hands together and smile so radiantly it caused my heart to beat out of rhythm.

You can take the Troth out of Verus... I laughed inwardly, but then braced myself for the next issue I wished to discuss.

"Ambrose, I have decided to arrive back in Monwyn as Eira's lover... publicly."

Chapter Forty-Eight

PROGRESS OR PERSECUTION?

"**N**o."

"Just no?" Cato arched that perpetually aggrieved brow of his—facial intensification.

He and his bushlike brows could dine upon a rotting twat.

"Correct. Were you confused? It was a complete sentence." I got to my feet and took a guarded stance, foot forward for balance, knees bent for agility. I'd sparred with him enough to be overcautious. "The people of Monwyn will *not* see their prince cuckolded. I am only now, three decades into my life, finding acceptance despite my adoption and lack of parentage, and, furthermore, I will certainly not allow the populace to look unfavorably upon *my* wife. Our children will not bear the insult of having their paternity questioned."

"The father will be one prince or another. I see no conflict," Cato said so callously it made my skin crawl. He knew not but a perfect lineage, had never lived with the endless scrutiny.

"Allow me to point it out in a way that your thoughtless brain can comprehend," I swept my hair up, twisted it into a knot on the top of my head and then closed the arms of my spectacles before hanging them from my opal necklace. "Eira will bear the brunt of slander—the gossip and judgment—not you or I. Our status and cocks will save us. I am ashamed that you would subject her to ridicule so that you could, what, hold her hand in the hallway?"

Eira tapped Cato on the chest.

"You and I aren't having babies, Cato, remember? No godly-manipulated little lives running underfoot." She stood and placed herself between us. "Did we not just have that conversation?"

Cato shrugged, indifferent and seemingly detached. *Bond logic.* More and more he yielded to its power.

"Why conceive with a kitty when you can breed with a bear? Hmm? And if she doesn't wish to bring forth your little scowling bundles of chub, she sure as fuck doesn't have to." I skimmed my nails along the inside of Eira's elbow, intentionally provoking his envy.

Eira offered me a thankful expression. Ocean-colored eyes. That is how Cato described them. I likened them more to the slimy teal algae that grows near the western lakes back home... but no woman wants to hear, "Your eyes resemble the grunge that tempts the fish to its fast-growing plume." No, indeed. *Well, Eira does love fish. Hmm...*

Cato's jaw ticked, wavering as fast as a banner billowing in the breeze.

"Catommandus, it is not fair of you to request this of me."

"I made no *request.*" A superior-than-thou expression slid across his face—eyes peering down his crooked nose, mouth pulled into a severe line.

"Put yourself in my place, Cat. Would you do the same for me if our roles were reversed? Let me answer for you. Fuck no."

My stunted brother-not-by-choice propped one leg over his other and leaned back, folding his elbow behind his head. He plotted.

"Introduce me as *your* lover, then, Ambrose."

Gad!

Silence.

Deafening silence.

I wobbled unsteadily, taken aback. Eira, bless her, recognized the quake in my firm-as-a-tree-trunk thighs and came to my rescue, taking my hand, encouraging me to resume my seat.

"That would accomplish nothing but stirring up conjecture and stories of incest. Fan my face, Eira, swiftly now."

Cato bobbed his foot up and down, totally at ease with the fucking insanity spewing forth from his lips.

"Think about it, Ambrose. The entire kingdom thought my vow of celibacy was because I preferred the company of men or—may they all rot in the nether—animals. What if this whole time it was the man who lorded over the depraved Den of Monwyn who had been my lover all along?"

Were I not so averse to the idea of wrinkling, I would have allowed my face to crumple.

"They would never believe it. Before Eira, I averaged a lover and a half per week. Who would believe that we had been an item for all this time?"

"Ambrose, you preen around the godsdamned palace acting like the fucking king of sensual pursuits. We could say it is a new romance—a fresh proclivity would surprise no one. They'd envy you, if anything."

"Have you thought of your own reputation?"

"I do not give a fuck about my reputation. The only fuck I give is for her." He pointed to Eira, whose hot little paws were generating more heat than air. I stilled her fanning hands.

"Eira, thoughts?" Cato asked.

"It's... not practical. No matter how fervently I long to love you freely."

"See?" I nodded in agreement.

Her admission felled him—stunned him to silence. I hated the look on his face even more than I detested his poorly thought-out suggestion. I never wished to cause him pain, always wanted Eira for him, which is why I agreed to the sham Joining in the first place. *That and a parcel of god-blessed babies fired from a Troth's vajeene.*

"Catommandus, they will see right through it. You are as rigid as an oak tree and stuffy and, honestly, rather boring. They would never believe that—"

"Teach me."

"Teach you what?" I shook my head, confused.

"To tolerate your advances. To enjoy your touch. Eira seems to like them... less than mine, of course. The night of your Joining was pleasant enough. Eira, thoughts?" Cato asked again, looking up through those ridiculously beautiful gold-tipped lashes of his.

"No thoughts, can't breathe."

I chuckled and drew Eira to my side, knowing all too well where her mind had gone.

"Oh, my nasty little wife... thinking with your thirsty... tight... wet... little vagina again."

I lowered my head and brushed my lips across her shoulder.

"Ambrose?"

"What, Cato?" I peered down, ogling Eira's cantaloupe-sized cleavage, and could not resist the need to palm her left side. "I am busy calming the wifey."

"Fuck me while she watches."

THE WORLD WAS BUILT ON TNA

Cato

My eyes crossed from the ear-splitting magnitude of Eira's high-pitched squeal. It deafened me for the next few seconds. But, even with a finger stuck in my ear, I managed to grin, noting with amusement that she reacted to the thought of my being ass-reamed just as she did when presented with a fine slice of cake.

She smacked Ambrose on the chest once and then again.

"Husband, Black Bear, has he gone mad?"

Ambrose was fully engaged in freeing a breast from her neckline, but I knew without question that he'd heard me. I could read him better than any other barring Eira. Her, I knew with an inhuman sense of understanding.

"If I know my woman—and I make it my business to know every inch of her—I would say, Eira, that you would come fully apart watching him thrust into me as I fucked you? Yes?" I asked, aware of how enticing my woman found novel sexual experiences.

"Y-yes," she said shakily. "Yes, I would." Ambrose cupped her perfect breast and immediately my fingers grew jealous. The Creator knew what she was doing when she placed a set of enticing fucking playthings on the front of a woman. Tits alone ensured the population didn't dwindle.

"Cato, are we not the luckiest of men?" Ambrose murmured, running his thumb over her nipple and then around her arcola, in a precise, slow circle. Her nipple peaked and my cock jerked at the sight.

"There is no doubt that we are. So, you will do it?" He could fuck me for the rest of our lives if he complied with my demands, and as long as it delighted Eira.

I stood, unsheathed my weapons and tossed them to the floor, preparing to remove my undergarments.

"No." Ambrose glanced up, cheeks flushed, pupils blown.

"What do you mean no?" I felt oddly offended and entirely disgruntled for being denied yet again. "What happened to 'did you count me, Cato? Blah, blah, blah.'" I pitched forward and clutched a handful of the beads he wore, twisting them around my fist, pulling his face near mine. "I have endured all manner of torture. Unspeakable punishment. When the outlaw Medlow captured me, I was assaulted with the severed limb of a pine tree. Your prick would be nothing comparatively speaking."

Eira's hand came to rest on mine. Instead of pushing me away, she pulled me closer.

"But that's just it, Cato. Ambrose doesn't want to be your punishment."

"What *do* you want? What can I give you that will allow my heart to continue its beat? No torture—nails pried off, glass shards slipped between my tendons—compares to the agony of keeping myself closed off from her." And that was the truth. I was self-aware enough to know that my behavior was increasingly unpredictable since our time at Verus, and that the tensioning of the rope that seemed to bind our souls provoked me to act erratically, even with my training to subdue its temptation. "I have always caused the suffering—perhaps this is my punishment."

I dropped my hand in disgust.

Ambrose stared at me thoughtfully and skimmed his finger across his bottom lip. "No" is what the signal meant. I leaned left and dropped my arm to reply "give me a fucking alternative then."

"Nope," Eira piped up. "Stop the secret speak. Arms to your sides." She shook a furious finger in Ambrose's face and then turned to me. "You too. Now, open those incredibly capable mouths and talk. Ambrose you first."

Ambrose shimmied his indignant shoulders, acting as if he was too important to take part. Eira clawed his braid and yanked.

He groaned, fucking subservient creature that he was. My woman, without uttering a single word, subdued Monwyn's most sought-after bedfellow. Like a quarry caving in, he crumbled to her will.

"Fine," Ambrose said, refusing me eye contact. He dusted off the imaginary dirt on his skirt and stood. "I would be honored to be the first to fish for brown trout in your puckered pond. Eira got the dick virginity, and I think it would be very special to have the other end. But she is correct. Being likened to forcible assault by branch is humiliating, and allowing me to fuck you still won't get me to agree to your scheme. I have a family... or *will* have a family to consider, if the gods don't destroy us all. I want what is best for them."

"Thank you, husband." Eira cupped his jaw, her hand tender, and he leaned into her touch, his strain diminishing. "Now, you, Cato." She snapped her head around, slanting those furious eyes in my direction. She beckoned me to her side.

I held her gaze.

"I want simplicity."

"Oh, well," she laid her head on my shoulder, one arm around Ambrose, one around me. "That's right out of the question, love. God wars, cruel kings... I can't comprehend anything more complex. You can toss that dream right into the sea."

I pressed a kiss to her forehead, and she tilted back to look at me.

"Gods, I fucking love you... even that cruel mouth."

Her eyes went soft.

"Cato, simplicity would mean going back into time somehow. And I would never, ever tempt the fate that brought me you."

CHAPTER FIFTY

ANYWHERE.

EIRA

"We should leave. We must make ready." Cato gestured to the door. "The journey home will take longer as we fight the northern winds." He bent his nose to my head and sniffed me like a puppy dog would: two sharp inhales and then one long, sighing breath. *Adorable.* He was never playful with anyone else, not truly... and it made me feel like I was the fortunate winner of some rare and sought-after prize.

Ambrose moped, his body deflating.

"The Solnnans keep such late hours, and the palace will be alive until nearly sunrise. Could we not... linger a little while?" He hooked his fingers through the straps at my back. "For Eira's sake, that is."

Ambrose tugged and Cato fought to keep me from his brother's embrace but acquiesced to the pouty giant's mewls.

"No. I wish to speak to the kingdom's general, and you will escort Eira to the queen to deliver her choice of bride. The woman will assuredly be caught off guard and must have at least a few hours to prepare before departure."

"How ignoble of you when *this* woman—Eira of the Insatiable Penis Prison—clearly has a need of her own." Ambrose released his topknot, flung his head back, and tossed his unbound hair over his shoulder. "Unlike you, it is my sworn duty as her *actual* husband to see that her basic requirements are met."

Yes, it is.

Cato pinched the bridge of his nose and sidestepped, dodging the arm Ambrose attempted to wrap around his shoulders.

"And you consider fucking akin to shelter and food in its importance? Is that your implication?"

"The choice between shelter and pussy is not a difficult one to make, Cato." The innocence on Ambrose's face would have convinced the Goddess herself of his sincerity. His wink told me the truth though. He'd pick sex. "It is most vexing that my wife must endure the stressors of a divinely acquired Dick Bond. The Goddess clearly placed me in her path to assuage its cloying side effects. Who else but I could *supply* for such an unquenchable *demand*?"

Cato slid his deepest brown gaze to mine as I cozied up closer to Ambrose, suddenly finding myself aware of the *inflation* occurring beneath his skirt.

Cato shook his head. His expression was one of disappointment. "If his economic-terminology-turned-innuendo awakens your passions, I will head back to Monwyn this eve on foot."

Ambrose dipped his head, and his inky tresses surrounded us in a cocoon, cutting Cato from our view. His half-smile smacked of desire, and I was but a simple woman... with a simple woman's needs. When the most handsome man on the continent gave you his undivided, smoldering attention, all parts of you perked up to listen.

"Mmm, wiflet, perhaps some double-entry accounting? Hmm? Allow me to audit your ledger and deposit my liquid assets?"

I bit my lip, a prisoner locked behind the bars of his thick-lashed gaze.

Cato parted the hair curtain with steepled hands.

"Eira. I am physically appalled. My dick has shriveled."

"Hush." I tapped Cato on the tip of his nose. "His word use may be a little off base, but it was you who *invested* in my *assets* earlier, stirring up my fervor... before Ambrose interrupted. Since then, there has been a consistent downward trend in market activity, if you get my meaning."

Ambrose chuckled, shaking in conspiratorial mirth.

"And here I am surrounded by a wealth of penises, a rainbow of colors and shapes, and—"

Cato's face fell, his blank-faced stare penetrating right through me.

"You... you require more cocks than the two you own?" He waved to the wall of penises. "The warm ones... that do all the moving for you?"

I bat my lashes.

"If you must know... I've been contemplating something a little naughty since we walked in... *if* we have the time to spare, perhaps we can—"

"Yeah, sure," Cato tossed his hands, sarcasm lacing his voice. "Strategy formation and procuring passage on such short notice be damned."

"I'm glad you agree. Sit." I pointed to the chaise with one hand, while I tenderly skirted the cleft of Ambrose's backside with the fingers of my other. "You too, big boy." I slapped his taut cheek.

"I am so glad you are my wife." He gnashed his teeth, nipping at the side of my lips.

Sighing, Cato turned on his heels and lowered himself dutifully to the other side of the bean-shaped furniture.

Ambrose pawed at my backside, but I evaded his fingers and took a giant's step forward.

"No. Bad husband." I swatted his forearm. "You sit and watch—keep your hands to yourself." He took off toward the couch.

"This is beginning to sound unappealing."

"Ambrose," I chided. "I want to show you what I learned in conjurer school today. Likely the only day I'll ever get to attend." I tried but failed to keep the disappointment from my voice.

Cato backhanded his brother in the chest, pinning him with an expression that said, "Sit the fuck down and listen." Ambrose held his palms up, a silent apology, and then reclined.

"I am sorry, love, that it turned out this way. Please show us."

"Make it up to me with a song, yes?"

My soul-husband looked as if he'd swallowed a palmful of sour Solnnan sweets, rubbing the back of his neck with a grimace.

Ambrose struck fast, spanking the back of Cato's head.

"Yes, brother, a song."

The two faced off. Tensions mounted.

"Are you aware of how awkward it is to sing *at* someone?" Cato asked, his eyes boring into Ambrose's. "Have you ever, for instance, locked eyes with a man whilst they played the fucking fiddle at you? Were you ever cajoled into a private concert for a visiting princess of Gaea, who said, and I quote, 'The voice of a fae lord… the figure of a fatty slab of beef'?"

"You grew out of your husky phase, Catommandus," Ambrose interjected, patting Cato on the shoulder. "You were roly-poly cute then and have a lovely body today."

The thought of a pudgy son of my own, one with Cato's eyes, made my chest clench. I ushered the thought away.

"Cato, are you willing to have Scion Ambrose commit ear assault with his lilting warbles so soon after his first concert? I just need a little tune for encouragement."

"Fair point." Cato crossed his arms.

"Hateful bitches, both of you," Ambrose grumbled, crossing his legs.

"Upbeat please." I glanced at the backs of my hands and took a deep breath before flipping them over. "Follow the lines, Eira."

Cato nodded curtly and, gods be damned, his hums were just as beautiful as his rich singing voice. I stared at him for a moment, lost in the hypnotic sound, until he flicked his wrist for me to begin. *Right, uncomfortable eye contact.*

"Ahem. I will now present to you"—Cato drummed out a staccato beat on his lap, in perfect time to his jovial tune—"moving things around without burning down the whole house!"

"Boo," Ambrose jeered. "Unimpressed."

I ignored him and rose up on my toes while launching my arms into the air.

"Watch closely, gentlemen."

"Take it off!" A shrill whistle rent the air.

Fucking Ambrose.

I commanded the æther.

That distinct tingle coursed through my arm with no more than a thought. I threaded it, guiding it to my palm, containing the surge that wanted so badly to break free.

A jet-hued cock of carved marble slid a solid three inches to the left.

"Snowballs and sleet fall!" Tears welled in my eyes. It didn't topple; it didn't explode. I squealed, hopping in a circle to face my guys, smiling so hard my face probably read more of insanity than elation.

Cato clapped politely, my devoted courtier through and through. The asshole next to him, the one to whom I was contractually bound, stifled a yawn.

"I demand a divorce. Cato, love, have the papers drawn up immediately."

Ambrose balked.

"Eira, I have witnessed you calling forth the Nether Lord. Comparatively speaking, this is boring. And you know that women cannot initiate divorce in Monwyn, so..."

The phallic projectile missed his mountain-sized head by only half an inch. It embedded in the wall behind him with only the textured testes visible, poking from betwixt the privacy pads.

"You were saying?"

"Eh." He shrugged his big fucking shoulders, and I contemplated launching a full-scale phallus offense.

"Cato. Murder him. Do it now."

"As you command." As swift as a striking snake, Cato shifted his weight, reached back, and grabbed Ambrose by the neck. With a powerful twist of his torso and jerk of his muscle-bound arms, Ambrose took flight, soaring forward over Cato's shoulder.

A strand of pearls and carnelians busted and scattered across the carpeted floor as my husband's back made impact.

"Godsdammit, Cato my—Oof!" Ambrose rolled away from the forearm speeding toward his neck and then lashed out, clutching Cato's throat before another elbow caught him in the stomach. Ambrose came up off the ground like a man crazed, crouching like a bear ready to brawl.

"Come on, little man."

He swiped out.

Cato, anticipating the move, grabbed the waist of Ambrose's skirts and heaved. My Black Bear went down, his knees finding the floor.

They were both grinning and struggling to gain the upper hand. To anyone watching, it would look like a friendly scuffle between soldiers at practice, but for the love of Lykksun, all I could see was Cato thrusting his hips against Ambrose's finely toned bottom, which kept peeking out from his egregiously short ensemble.

I took to my knees and crawled my way over, attempting to insert myself into the sweaty scene, one limb at a time.

"Ahem, excuse me, just um, joining in on the fun."

Cato wrapped his fingers around my ankle while I attempted to back my rear into his lap.

"Ambrose," Cato said. "Look at her... how shameless she is. I wonder. Come closer, sweetheart."

"W-what do you wonder?" I wiggled against him, settling in, the anticipation already churning through me as his erection nudged my rear.

"How your body will react to differing stimuli."

Cato's hand snaked around the back of Ambrose's neck and jerked his head down, leaving only a hairsbreadth between their lips. I was stuck between their heaving chests. "For example, if our lips were to meet, would you saturate your silken underthings? Would your divine little clit swell with need?"

Lady in the cradle. There was hot-handed Eira—scaring my men, making flames burst from the confines of their hearth—but she... she was about to meet fire mountain Eira.

Ambrose's tongue darted out, moistening his lips, his full attention on the man holding him in place. The cool room turned humid, steam rising around us, like the hot rock sheds the fisherman used to warm up back in Nortia.

"I think she quite likes it, sir."

Cato nodded slowly, each movement of his head threatening to bring them closer. Sweat beaded at his temples, just like it did between my breasts. His hand dropped from my waist to my vulva as he ground himself into the small of my back.

"What would her reaction be if our lips were to meet? Hmm?" Ambrose tilted his head down and to the side, their mouths nearly feathering.

Were I not already on my knees, my legs would have buckled.

"There is only one way to know for sure." Ambrose closed his eyes as Cato nudged his knee between my legs.

Cato outlined Ambrose's perfect jawline, trailing his fingers along his dark beard.

"Eira, does the thought arouse you?"

"Y-yes." I arched my back and spread my legs wider. He cupped and hugged my silk-clad center, encouraging me to ride his thigh.

"Mmm, Ambrose, I can confirm that she is both slick *and* scalding. Such an obedient wife receives her reward."

Cato tilted his chin and closed the distance. Their lips met.

Ambrose sighed and Cato chuckled.

Heat surged, æther boiled, but instead of a shock of buzzing energy, I experienced a love-tinged flow of heat circling throughout my body. The beads of sweat on my forehead sizzled and evaporated.

"Breathe, love."

"I don't remember how."

Cato's fingers found my chin. He leaned back, his other hand fisted in Ambrose's tumble of waves.

"Now, kiss." Cato guided our heads forward but held them far enough apart that our mouths didn't meet. The tip of Ambrose's tongue swept along the crease of my lips... but it was Cato's mouth that caught my moan as he forced Ambrose's head away.

Eruption.

His domineering touch drove me to frenzy.

I drove Cato back, shoving him hard against the chaise. He hit the frame with a thud but didn't utter a sound, just stared at me with a hunger that matched my own.

With a will all their own, my hands shoved up his tunic and jerked the string of his linen underclothes, freeing his arousal.

"This is mine and I want it now." I dropped, breasts smashed to the floor, cock in my grasp. Cato only thought he controlled our relations. I dragged the flat of my tongue from his base to his tip, and then nipped the sensitive skin below his crown. "You will let me have my fill." I drew his tip into my mouth, tunneling my cheeks and sucking until he hissed above me.

"Fucking goddess, my perfect fucking goddess." He clasped the back of my head, his fingers interlocking, and directed me down his length, knowing exactly how much of him I could take.

I relaxed my throat and sank lower until the hair that trailed from his navel tickled my nose.

"Wait, love, or I will spend—"

"No. I want to taste—ouch!"

Ambrose struck, smacking my ass so hard I yelped and recoiled. He saddled up against my back and smoothed his hands over my still-stinging rear. "*Don't* talk back."

I sucked in a breath.

Cato arched a brow and nodded appreciatively as a smug grin flowed across his face. In a single fluid motion, not needing his hands for support, he stood and then repositioned himself on the chaise. He crossed his arms behind his head and glanced down at his spit-slicked erection. "Resume."

Holy fuck. What this man did to me.

I crawled forward, ready to devour him, but then hesitated.

Wait. Wait is right.

"Husband?" I looked back at the man who brought comfort to my heart. He may not experience jealousy the same way many did, but Ambrose *was* sensitive to abandonment. "Leave no one out, right? Rule number one."

I held my hand out.

He knee-walked to my side.

I craned my neck as he bent low and placed a kiss on the tip of his nose and then chin.

"Thank you, wife," he whispered, dotting kisses on my cheeks in return.

"Come with me?" I tucked a strand of his sweat-soaked hair behind his ear.

He nodded.

"Anywhere."

Chapter Fifty-One

And Sometimes You Just Laugh

Cato

My woman.

My magnificent woman.

She was entirely unaware that the cock collection hovered, levitating a half-inch off of their shelves. When my lips touched Ambrose's, they had risen behind her like—well, like my cock had—her army to command. I would shove my tongue down that man's sarcastic mouth at the top of every hour to see her come apart like the earthbound goddess she was—breasts heaving in time with her panted breaths, her face flushed as red as the treasure between her legs.

The room sweltered.

Droplets of moisture gathered around the frame of the door and the humidity made breathing difficult, but I'd endured worse.

Watching her kissing another man, for instance, filled me with a bone-crushing dread but also heightened in me a sense of competition.

How far could I push her ability to accept pleasure?

I knew somewhere deep in the recesses of my mind that my self-imposed rule of never bedding a woman was in part due to a fear that none could handle what raged right below the surface. But she met my body's base desires with a ferocity that matched and sometimes outstripped my own. The more she gave, the more I wanted.

Ambrose fanned his reddened face while watching Eira trail her fingernails up and down his erection.

There was a rightness to the heat that engulfed us—the sun goddess Lykksun guided us.

When I returned to Monwyn, I would have a shrine built to honor her. I would venerate her holy name while spilling myself between Eira's legs for the rest of eternity. I would pay homage to the Sol goddess by making Merrias's granddaughter writhe below me, screaming her cries of pleasure into my mouth.

And she *would* bear our child.

I knew deep within my being that we could not outrun our fate. And though Eira feared it, and rightfully so, I could fathom no greater tribute than providing the world with another made in her image.

Eira approached me, leading Ambrose by the dick. *For fuck's sake.* My cock twitched in anticipation. This little game wouldn't end until I sank myself sac-deep into her heat.

"Draw your attention to this ample-bodied sampling of womanhood," Ambrose said, snapping me from my wandering thoughts.

Eira pressed her hips into Ambrose as he drew up against her, a great monolith at her back. I watched with rapt attention as he curled one arm around her waist and wound the other over her shoulder to lie across her chest. He grasped her chin between his fingers and then thumbed her bottom lip. "Fine teeth, serpent-sharp tongue. Possess the ability to suck a lamb shank clean in a single slurp."

"I am demure and soft," she said shyly, casting her eyes to the floor, speaking around the digit. An untrained man might have believed her false contriteness, the innocent bend of her neck, the bashful pout of her lips... but my woman wasn't meek.

I palmed my silk-covered erection and her pupils nearly blotted out her irises.

"Your tits are the only soft thing about you, wife. Have you fucked these plush pillows, Catommandus?" Ambrose weighed first her left breast and then right, shaking them with an effervescent joy.

"I cannot say that I have. You, brother?"

"No." Ambrose's eyes turned serious as he pondered. He tapped her nipple with his finger, like he often did his own chin when deep in thought. "I find I am overly enchanted by her backside, and it waylays me while I work my way to the top."

"I understand."

With a carefully executed takedown, Ambrose bent her over his propped-up knee.

"Gods!" Eira shrieked as she fell.

She dangled, her toes and fingertips barely touching the ground, her ass presented for my inspection. "No! Husband! Eeeeek!"

She fought against him, giggling in between her protests as he pinched and tickled her sides.

"Have you gone shy, wife?"

My cock throbbed painfully as Ambrose parted the succulent cheeks of her rear.

"It's—yes! Yes, I have, Ambrose." She reared and kicked, but he paid her no mind. "Assholes aren't to be put on display. There is a reason they are tucked in so tightly, little shriveled uglies."

"Nonsense."

"Ambrose!" she screeched again. He bent over, dipping his fingers into the now completely melted tub of coconut oil.

"Now, Catommandus, as you have admitted to a lack of... shall we say, exposure to sexual practices—"

"Have I admitted to such?" Entranced by the display before me, I leaned forward, grunting as my cock rubbed against my stomach.

"Watch and I shall demonstrate a technique from my book of conquests. When comparing the reactions of my many lovers, the data clearly shows this is a high-yield maneuver."

My breath caught in my lungs. Ambrose swirled his thumb around her tight flesh, the oil leaving her shiny and slick.

"Oh, Eira, do cease your struggling. Our fella is enraptured."

And I was. There was nothing "uglies" about what I saw.

"This will shut her up. Watch carefully."

Fuck. You could draw hooks through my skin, and I wouldn't look away.

This I liked. For once, the normal scorch of jealousy didn't claw at my back and rip me to shreds. This performance was for *my* benefit.

Ambrose slowly introduced his thumb into her anus, while simultaneously threading his middle and ring finger deep into her passage.

"I... I... give in." She clenched around his fingers, her entrance tightening.

"Remember, Cat. Pause when she hugs—bear down, darling—the digits. As she relaxes, you can either retract or explore further."

Fuck. Me. Ambrose's prattling aside, Eira's reaction was mind-numbingly arousing. Her mouth slacked into a little U as she lost all fight.

"More, Ambrose, please." She tried her damndest to press back, but her toes still didn't touch the floor.

"Faster, who?"

"Fucking bastard."

"No, I am sorry; that's not right either. Cato, as my hands are full, deliver a sound slap to her—"

My hand connected hard enough for my palm to burn. I watched the red handprint rise on her pale skin, fascinated by the wobble of her backside, rippling like the surface of a lake.

"Ouch! Cato, you dog-faced prick." Her arms flapped out in front of her, and she kicked back at me like an aggrieved war horse.

Ambrose grinned, his mirthful eyes locked with mine.

"Eira," He slipped his fingers out and then slid them back home. She moaned a full-throated sound, and the cocks on the wall floated higher. "Cat's hand is gliding up that delicious thickness that hangs between his legs. Shall I describe it for you?"

Eira writhed, grunting, desperate for friction. She fought to twist around, but Ambrose gave no quarter—a power game I could appreciate.

"Let me up now. This is... It's torture," she wailed.

"Catommandus, dip your finger in the oils and join me, would you? It is positively silky."

"The honor would be mine." I dunked my finger into the warm oil. On his next pull-out, I married my digit to his, and we slid seamlessly into her sex.

"Fuck." She breathed in deeply. "Gods, yes."

"She is a greedy woman when it comes to her pleasure," I observed.

My fingers worked in tandem with Ambrose's, caressing her smooth walls, teasing the textured bump that made her thrash about.

"Ambrose, though I may not be a veteran in the ways of sex like yourself, I can share with you the secret to making her come on command."

Genuine surprise sparked across his face.

"Oh, I would find that quite useful."

"Observe." I inclined my head to the side, thoroughly enjoying the game we played. "My woman likes it a little rough from time to time."

"Cato, please, love, please," Eira begged, struggling against our hands.

"Truly? She is always quite gentle with—"

I leaned down and grabbed Eira's ass, squeezing the flesh while I pumped my hand into her with more force. I inhaled the musky scent of her arousal, which combined with the sweet smell of coconut, then sank my teeth into her fleshy cheek, biting until she was screaming. Her passion flooded my hand. Ambrose lowered her just enough so that she could press back at her own pace, rocking on her toes, fucking our combined fingers.

"Hus... bands!" She shouted her orgasm into the padded room.

She was at her most beautiful, surrendering. So full of life, an abundance of lo—

"Get the fuck off me, godsdammit. Enough of this fingering bullshit. Get your dicks out, both of you."

Ambrose threw back his head and laughed. Droplets of sweat shook from his long mane, sizzling when they hit Eira's back.

"You." She pointed at my face. "Lay down."

I threw my hands up in supplication and reclined back into the shallow curve of the chaise.

"Far be it from me to keep you from your appetites," I said, gesturing to my cock. Her mouth fell open, her eyes glittering.

"Yeesh!"

She twisted a clump of Ambrose's hair in her hands.

"Two on one was entirely unfair. Now it is your turn to suffer the same fate, *my love*."

She dropped to her knees, grabbed my cock, and jerked Ambrose's head down offering him her mouth.

I dug my fingers into the plush material of the chaise.

Their kiss was electric. Panting and fevered bodies, tongues and lips clashing.

Jealousy. It seared across my chest like venom through my veins.

Eira tore away from him and jerked my cock, just before I made my move to bust Ambrose in his godsdamned jaw. Pleasure and pain stilled my aggression.

Semen leaked from my tip as I fought to regain control. She bent and gathered it on her tongue.

I groaned, my eyesight going fuzzy when she tapped Ambrose on the chin. His jaw dropped, and she fed him my flavor.

"Mmm, briny, a hint of—"

"Coffee, yes?" she murmured. "Where you are like a citrus soap." Her eyes drifted back to mine, and she pinned me with her angry-ocean stare. "How will you fare in a game of two against one? Or perhaps three? Hmm, my mate?"

She leaned over and picked up the wobbly dick.

"Ambrose, don't move." She dunked it in the oil and then placed it beneath his knees. "It might catch fire. I need to focus."

He nodded rapidly, fawning over her every word. How did he not yet realize he was ensnared? *Idiot.*

Eira took a deep breath, centering herself.

"I need to feel its weight." She moved her fingers methodically in the air, and the cock mimicked her movement, sliding and then stopping.

"I'm going to fuck you both. Okay?"

You could have convinced me that Ambrose stared at the literal Goddess of creation—his eyes shined with such adoration.

I could not see the moment of penetration, but with the wave of her fingers and the sway of his lean hips, I knew.

"That's one. Now for two more. Can you handle us, Cato?" She raised her brow in question, still moving her fingers in time with Ambrose's rise and fall.

I leaned back and closed my eyes. No, I squeezed them shut, attempting to steady my breathing.

Two warm mouths closed around either side of my cock.

"And now we make three," Eira murmured.

"Godsdamn," I hissed. "You could not have prepared me."

My eyes flew open, unable to keep from watching as two tongues glided up and down my length. They met at my crown and shared a kiss, smiling back and forth. Ambrose caressed her arm with the back of his knuckles. She maintained the flip of her fingers, fucking him from behind. His hand dropped to his dick, where he handled himself in the same rhythm with which she took him.

"Eira," Ambrose paused, his mouth going slack. He cradled her cheek. "I need to tell you something."

"What? Right now?" She flicked her tongue over my head and then ran it around its flared edge. "While I'm..." She glanced at her fingers, rolling them up and then down.

"Right now is-is perfect. It has never been more perfect." He nodded. "Please continue, though." He gestured in my direction, and she bent, giving my cock a single languid and tight-lipped suck.

"What is it, husband?" she asked, managing to jack me off while maintaining a conversation. *Wonders never cease.*

"I have had time to think—mmm, a little faster please—and I have finally concluded that, Eira—that's exceptional. My prostate is positively chuffed." He worked his fist faster along his ridiculously long dick. "I want you to know I feel safe to be myself in your presence, and, and you have changed something within me, and the fact is... Eira Verras Chul—"

Nope.

I snatched his throat, yanked, and drove my cock into his mouth.

He gagged and sputtered, while I worked his fool's head up and down until he was moaning and gripping my hips in his hands, words forgotten.

The heat that had somewhat dissipated surged, renewed. Eira groaned and purred as she watched him take me.

Was it a dick move on my part? Most assuredly, but I wanted her to be *only* mine for a little longer—even if my mind recognized she had enough love to go around.

Ambrose gasped for a breath, but I gave him no reprieve.

"You are good, Ambrose, but you are no Eira."

Eira launched a leg over my waist. She bent and bit my nipples and rocked her wet center against my pubic bone, blocking Ambrose from my view.

My gods, I was on the Goddess's plane. There was no other explanation. Her breasts bounced, round and heavy, her head fell back, and she grinned like a chubby, happy feline after consuming its kill.

I inserted a hand between her thighs, middle and ring finger pointed up. She gasped in delight.

Ambrose grabbed her ass, helping her grind above his head.

It was too much. Too much and not enough. I wanted between her thighs. It was where I belonged.

"I am going to come. Ride me, Eira—"

Her little cry, that shy little smile, told me she was near.

She nodded and—

"Helloooo!"

The pressure at the bottom of my spine gave way, and I came hard, spilling myself in thick strands.

The door swung open, and our conception advocate entered the room bright-eyed and scroll in hand.

"No, no, don't stop on my account." She waved her quill in the air. "But if you can, for the records, I will need to see active penetration, taller Lord Dallingston?" She looked at Ambrose, who nodded, closed-lipped.

He hopped up with surprising energy, sat in the opposite dip of the chaise, and pointed to his impressively engorged member.

"Baby carrying Boofle, incoming," Eira moved between us and speared herself on his length. "Docking in progress."

They both chuckled.

They were both so fucking absurd.

Ambrose bucked his hips and Eira cried out. And that's when I made eye contact with the man across the couch. He parted his lips just slightly, the evidence of what transpired between us visible. He looked me dead in the eye, hugged Eira close, and pressed his tongue between her lips.

"Alrighty, I can verify to the state that penetration took place and... and it looks like you, shorter Lord Dallingston, were able to participate to some degree. How wonderful! Next time, try the masturbator cuff. Your flagging member may yet heed the call." She pointed to my shriveled, lifeless cock and then walked out.

The rich vibrations of my laughter mingled with the gasps of the two most important humans in my life as they climaxed together, as if everything about our lives was normal.

"Cat, do you think she saw the cock flock?"

Chapter Fifty-Two

Negotiate or Manipulate?

Eira

"We need to find Septimus. We can't leave him here to prey on the Solnnans. Like a feral animal, we can either release him to Merrias or work to mitigate the damage he can do. He doesn't know the language here and attacks when he feels cornered."

"You mean to let him back into Monwyn?" Ambrose scoffed while taking a sharp left turn. "Cato may allow his head to return, but that is all. You know how seriously he took the Protectorate."

"I do, but seriously, he can't stay here, and Merrias said—"

"I know, I know. He is your sworn protector, Viktos's choice, a Safe-something or other, blah, blah, blah."

After a quick shower, we left to seek an audience with the Queen while Cato searched for Gotwig. He wanted to gather even the most minute details of Greggen's betrayal.

Dropping a volatile piece of information like Greggen taking part in his mother's murder should have involved more finesse and less... ripping off the bandage, as Nan would say. I'd sure fucked that up.

"Are you quite well?" Ambrose, realizing I'd fallen behind, slowed his steps and returned to my side.

I gestured through an enormous, unshuttered window to the picturesque landscape of a moonlit ocean.

"This became more of a warm-weathered retreat when you and Cato arrived and much less of a... fugitive-seeking retribution mission. I know we must return home, and I'm committed to Monwyn just as much as I am you... but the moment we step foot in the mountain lands, our problems return to the forefront."

Ambrose gathered me into his arms, snug and safe. He rocked me gently and made those little nonsensical sounds that soothed me.

"Can you wait until tomorrow to cry, though? Muddoz will think me a poor husband if he sees you consistently in tears in my presence."

Fucking Ambrose. I smiled into his chest. My spirit renewed when I thought of seeing them together—unknown father to unknown son. We would soon remedy that as well, though. Cato and I decided to bring them together in the morning as we broke fast before departure. It would give them time to ask questions and make plans for the future, if they decided they wanted to build a relationship. If not, we would head back home no worse for having made the truth known.

"Zuddaz," I corrected.

"Whatever." Ambrose huffed and then grazed his fingers down my spine. "But, Eira, we will return one day so that you may study. The climate agrees with me, as does the fashion. Perhaps we will travel back to conceive our firstborn?" He batted his lashes. "I will feed you all manner of Solnnan delights while you bake our little bun."

"Is this before or after we assassinate a Primus-King and bury a Scion?"

He rubbed my shoulders, doing his best to free the pent-up stress.

"I feel like 'bun baking' should be, well—to continue the cooking puns—placed on the back burner."

"Nonsense. Did not Merrias herself birth The Child amid tyranny and turmoil?"

I scrunched my nose, thinking back on the lore.

"I'm pretty sure the legend says that the Magis scoured the continent for the finest foods and healers, and even conscripted an army of witches to watch over the palace when his daughter was born."

"Perhaps in some backward Nortian retelling she did. In Monwyn legend, she birthed The Child while on campaign against the Rinarians. You know, the ones that live on the other side of Baldorva. Ah! I hear the loudmouth, Trivio. He rarely strays from the Queen's side."

Ambrose was off again, this time dodging in and out of an increasing number of servants and soldiers. The crowd thickened as we neared the inner sanctum of the palace.

We emerged from a hallway and headed toward an arched door-way where a throng of nobles, dressed in bold hues, dripping with wealth—jade and fluorite necklaces, rings of gold and amethyst, and even diadems—gathered.

While I found myself fading, my energy, mental and otherwise, spent, the people of Lykk were in their element, full of energy, lifting glasses of sweet fruit wine to their lips. The crowd parted for Ambrose, a royal in their midst. They bowed and curtsied as we walked through, and I realized that in this kingdom, they bowed to me too. I raised my head a little higher and stiffened my spine.

Guards flanked the entrance, four on either side of the doorway. Great twists of driftwood decorated the arch, painted white with hammered gold palm leaves at their tops—a beautiful tribute to the flora that surrounded the palace.

In unison, eight spears pounded on the floor, announcing our presence.

We entered a large space, an open-air ballroom capable of holding hundreds of citizens. There were six walls in all—a hexagon-shaped chamber. One wall boasted a star-shaped window, directly opposite a crescent moon. Soft light filtered in through both, shining on a centerpiece that hung from the ceiling. The Solnnans had recreated the sun with what seemed like millions of sparkling gems. The reds, golds, and purple hung on delicate silk threads to form a giant sphere. Swags of diamonds stretched from the side of the globe to each of the six corners of the room, forming rays.

"So many diamonds…"

Ambrose looked up, following my eyes.

"Those are sunstones. Believe it or not, you can use them to locate the sun on the cloudiest of days."

"They're breathtaking."

"*You* are breathtaking."

I gazed shyly at the floor, the marble the color of an orca's slick back. He took my hand in his and with his other hailed Trivio, who appeared ahead of us.

"What is this celebration?" Ambrose asked.

"We celebrate life, Your Highness. One lost too soon, but one surely ascending to the cradle above." They raised their glass high and drained the contents.

That's when I saw it. What I thought were faces of gaiety and ease, were expressions of condolence, those that people wore when they said things like, "She lived to be a ripe old age, your Gran."

"Trivio, we received the news of Frem's sudden death. My heart aches for those who have only memories now."

"His mother, the Arch Priestess of Solnna, will oversee his services." Trivio acknowledged me with a nod and held their arms wide. I stepped into their embrace, inhaling the sunshine that seemed to cling to them.

Ambrose clapped in the chatelaine's face, startling the snowflakes out of them.

"That's nice. Noble servant, I require the presence of your queen and her Primus Mummaz. Make haste."

"I am afraid they are at—"

"I am afraid I do not care at the moment. We leave at sunrise, and before then, we must strike a deal."

Trivio sobered instantly. Their mouth bobbed up and down. "You have chosen a Solnnan bride for your king, then?" A smile broke across their face. "An alliance. Our families tied close."

"Yes, yes. Go negotiate, Troth wife. I will find the Primus."

Trivio proffered their elbow, steering me quickly toward a chamber off to the right of the ballroom. The atmosphere here was very different—not at all a celebration, but somber and sorrowful.

The queen, resplendent in a wrap of the lightest pink silk, shot through with fibers of gold and silver, sat with her daughter, both of them stroking Steffani's back as she did nothing to staunch the flow of tears dripping down her cheeks and onto the queen's raiment.

Around the room's perimeter, red-clad priestesses kneeled in prayer. One however, wearing a collar of iridescent scales, stood holding a torch in her raised arm—the arch priestess, I presumed.

The queen waved us forward but kept Steffani secure, the poor girl's head held in her lap.

"Majesty, there is no way for us to adequately express our sorrow for your loss, or for the assault done upon your person, Steffani." The hollow words fell from my mouth. If this was Septimus's doing... it was also mine.

The queen nodded.

"It was the work of a dissenter, I fear," she said, her face a mask of regal assurance. "The life of a royal is not always one of gold and grandeur, as the commoners assume... but you know that, do you not?"

I inclined my chin.

"Can you expound, dissenters?"

She nodded again as the evening voices floated in the air, their melody mournful.

"Fremmen is—was—the child of our Arch Priestess, whose husband controls the silk industry. We employee many secretive methods to create our most prized fabrics, and there is a faction of Solnnan citizens who were wary of Steffani, a foreigner, Joining to a family with such intimate knowledge of its production." She smoothed Steffani's hair in a comforting caress. "We had arranged for guards for Steffani and Frem, but not until next season, when they were supposed to have arrived. I assumed they were safe within the walls of the palace until that time. It was a gamble I lost."

I accepted her rationale, but I didn't believe her explanation for a moment and would bet my life she didn't either. The Nether Lord brought

Steffani here, the god played his hand... Septimus had attempted to remove her permanently.

"Alas, the kingdom moves on, and I am told you do as well."

"That is correct. We must make haste so as to not miss the king's coronation."

And inform the Mantle Their life may be in danger... and that Their Scion is an imposter... and stop the Primus-King from doing whatever shitty thing he is doing.

"I'd hoped for more time with you, Troth Eira of Solnna. However, I understand the necessity of a rapid departure." Her eyes—shrewd and knowing—drifted from my toes to the top of my head. "You come on a matter of political business?"

"I—Yes, Your Majesty, now seems like an awful time but—"

"Monarchs rarely enjoy downtime." A soft smile carved itself out of her otherwise drawn face. She waved to Ambrose, who had entered behind me, and gestured to the pillows before her. We lowered ourselves while the queen's daughter, Jeall, stared at us nervously, leaning in closer to her mother's side.

"Which of those offered do you wish to present before King Aberus? Jeall, Bellan, or Lin Drelada?"

I bowed my head and lowered my eyes.

"They are all exquisite and are no doubt worthy of pairing themselves with a royal line, but none of them will do."

The Queen's gold-painted brows perched high on her forehead.

"Is this some kind of—"

"No, Majesty, but the woman I would have is none other than Steffani."

Jeall flew out of her mother's hands, launching herself at me, claws bared. Ambrose caught her arms and held her out from his body. I made no move, did not flinch or call her out.

"Who the fuck do you assume yourself to be?" The reddish freckles on the bridge of Jeall's nose nearly disappeared as rage streaked red across her light-brown complexion. "She has this day, this very day, lost her betrothed, and you would suggest—"

"Calm yourself. Now." The queen's hand tightened around her daughter's elbow, pulling her back to her side. "I will hear your reasoning, Troth."

Ambrose squeezed the top of my hip in warning. I placated him, resting my hand on his thigh.

"Of course, Majesty." I prayed the monarch would be able to see through my words. I bowed my head again, contrite, showing deference to the Solnnan queen. "The daughters of Gaea are held in great esteem in the kingdom of Monwyn. Why, the Primus-King himself—who I am sure is a doting grandfather—spoke of establishing a relationship between Monwyn and Gaea at my recent nuptials." Not a lie at all. "Newly established relationships with the lands of green and gold allow for the exchange of items of great importance." Glancing up, I caught the queen's eyes and held them. "Of course, Monwyn would pay a heavy dowry for her hand. Not only in amethyst but in..."

A pregnant silence followed.

"Clear the room." The queen clapped her hands and every she, he, and they exited with haste, skittering out—even Steffani, who had shown no reaction to my words, bereft as she was. Her Majesty walked about the room, listening and looking carefully at every wall. She gazed at a framed painting of Lord Gammond and then passed her palm over her eyes. The painting's eyes flickered momentarily, as spy holes closed. She turned back to Ambrose and I and pressed a finger to her lips.

"You plan to use her as collateral if the Primus-King were to get his hands on your mother?"

"Or any other woman I love. Yes." The moment the words fell from my lips, I knew I would not hesitate to use this woman as a pawn. I would use all means at my disposal. "Relevantly, I do not think it was an angry dissenter who took Frem's life and assaulted her. I believe it to have been Septimus." Anger passed over the queen's visage, a brief but terrifying flash. "Your Majesty, to keep her alive, I need her nearby. Otherwise, I can't ensure he won't strike at her again. As is, I am not sure how she managed to survive."

The queen paced back and forth, her arms crossed over her chest.

"When questioned, Steffani said that the sudden lightning storm scared the assailant away. Viktos saved her."

More like cast his bolts of lightning to drive Septimus to my already occupied bed. I remembered how he'd looked at me, how I'd shattered around Ambrose as he watched my men take me... after he'd taken a life.

"It pains me, but wearing a crown means acting to benefit the greater good, even if your soul screams out for you to do otherwise." The queen raised her head high. "Eira, Troth of Solnna, Steffani's life lies in your hands."

"Goddess guide us."

CHAPTER FIFTY-THREE

FUDGE: A FINE MOTIVATOR.

EIRA

"Eira, Troth Solnna." Zuddaz clapped his enormous hands in my face, startling me from the sleep-deprived dreamscape, where I debated with myself on how to introduce a new father to a new son.

The giddy feeling in my chest outstripped the magnitude of both my tumultuous feelings *and* current set of dilemmas.

They were both here, sitting within inches of each other.

How my repetitious stare-then-giggle combo hadn't given me away was a godsdamned miracle. My eyes darted from child to sire. How could they not see it? How did *I* not see it immediately?

"Pay attention. We have little time with which to complete the conjuration."

I scrubbed my face briskly with both hands. There'd not been time for a wink of sleep after conferring with the queen. We set into action immediately, packing, preparing, and signing contracts. Cato was, at this very moment, escorting a numb and entirely miserable Steffani to the ship that would set sail in a few hours' time. He would join us here when she was settled, and together we would tell Ambrose and Zuddaz. I clenched my jaw.

Like the seagulls that soared, screaming their secrets in the harbor... I was this close to squawking.

"Do you perchance have a leg of fowl? A sliver of fine cheese? Waving cake directly under her nose has the same effect as smelling salts," Ambrose said, with not an ounce of malice in his voice.

"A connoisseur of the edible delights is your lady wife?"

Ambrose tapped his chin thoughtfully and then looked back at his literal fucking twin. Okay, it wasn't nearly as uncanny as the Septimus and Cato level of similarity, but the structure of their cheeks, the graceful, long fingers... I wanted to blurt out the secret, scream it from the spire that watched over the city and announce it to the world. But if Cato, my man of three expressions—hungry, horny and irritated—reacted with such an extreme level of surprise, my *very* sensitive spouse might need healers nearby. For once, I wanted to be delicate, to consider the feelings of both my husband and Zuddaz, whom I didn't know well at all. Like the dark fringe of lashes they shared, I had a feeling that their emotions favored a similar drama.

"Mmm, less of a connoisseur, more of a consumer." Ambrose edged in on me again, continuing to dominate the space between me and the Primus. "But I digress. So," Ambrose pointed to a yellow-brown leather journal. "She will write upon the pages of that book while in Monwyn, and her words will appear, here, in Solnna?"

"Kind of. It took decades to work out the specifics, but essentially, Eira will bind *this* journal to *this* room, by means of her other realm—the place she goes when she conjures—behind the eyes." Zuddaz gestured to the shelves of books behind us. "It's the same premise as Eira being able to see her *actual* body where she left it, when she follows her shadows. It still exists, even if she is away from it."

"Father Burchard has a book here, husband."

Ambrose's eyes went soft, and suddenly my overwhelming need to shout my surprise diminished. He loved his father, flaws and all.

"She's correct. His ideas on conjuring to increase the yield of food production were unparalleled. I would wager not a citizen goes hungry in your kingdom. My sincerest condolences to you and your family after what must be a devastating loss."

Ambrose inclined his head, accepting the words.

"Do you know that Eira and he are the only humans I know who have cemented the Infinite Bond? I've tried it and failed at least two dozen times. Your Father must have been pleased with her progress."

A tender smile graced Ambrose's lips. He rested his palm on my hand.

"He loved her dearly, just as I—Gracious, is that your hungry tum, wifling? Cato promised us a meal after the conclusion of our business."

I shook my head, and then took the journal Zuddaz slid across the table.

"This part is not nearly as daunting as the Infinite Bond, I am sure. As you enter the realm, you will ask the animus of this book to separate itself and join you. You have connected with the spirits of objects before, to ask them to move, for example. This is similar, but you are asking for a shift in spiritual state rather than physical space."

"It's like you expect me to know how to do that," I said, not meaning to sound as sarcastic as I did. "This may take more time than we have. My recent achievements are locking and unlocking a door and bouncing a small object with some regularity."

"She is good at that last one." Ambrose's voice deepened as he popped a brow.

Zuddaz, meet Ambrose, he's your son. I conjure-fucked him last evening with a wobbly cock.

Zuddaz rolled his chair around the table and came to my side.

"Just like the lock, my dear, you ask the life within to do your bidding, which, in this case, is just asking the book to remain on the shelf... while you also take it with you. The æther understands you. It's a part of you, just like at their core, the pages and the bookshelf are of the same material. Go on now, and when you return, we will venture to the bakery and indulge in a lump of fudge before you depart."

Zuddaz motioned for me to begin. I closed my eyes and sought the shadows.

My surroundings were the same as always, though I felt unexpectedly peaceful, like being in this space where only *I* had agency somehow released me from the expectations and obligations of everyone else. I collected the journal from the hands of my physical body and received a rousing round of applause.

"Oho, my shadow harpy, well done!"

I bent and pressed a kiss to Ambrose's cheek, and he raised his fingers to his beard.

With the journal held at arm's distance, I began.

Alright, book. I would very much appreciate it if you joined me.

Nothing.

I think you're a pretty journal, well made, letters stamped with a fine hand. You are a fine testament to bookbinding. Let us... um...share in friendship.

I attempted to call it again... and then again. *Shit.* I hadn't the faintest idea of what I was truly looking for.

Nothing happened. No pages ruffled; no spines introduced themselves.

I inspected the book, turning it about, holding it to the lamplight.

And that's when I saw it.

Why hello, there... I'm glad you came.

The book's animus, its spirit, was hidden in the shadow it cast—was made of its shadow. Under the journal in my hands, moving in sync with my motions was a perfectly replicated tome, gray and not entirely substantial.

I reached out with tentative fingers and picked up the dark form. It was whole, even though it... wasn't. I cradled both volumes close to my chest.

Come with me. I placed the shade-text next to my father's—my real dad's. The man who had given me his name. Eira Verras Chulainn and Ulltan Chulainn. The simple letters on simple bindings meant more to me than any gilded volume could.

I stared at the books, pride wedging its way into my heart.

You'll like it here, and my father's journal will be with you, watching over you.

Before my eyes, the shadow rearranged itself. A swirling mix of particles shuffled and shifted color before taking on a corporeal form. It was then that I noticed there was the slightest difference in color between the physical book in my hand and the one on the shelf. The replica was a few shades lighter. That made sense to me though, like the *me* in this realm, it wasn't quite a perfect mimic.

I scanned the shelf again, trying to commit the names of other conjurers to memory: Ankerly, Campos, Fabia, Garnett, Hale, Kittel, Meridett, Nightfaye, Sanders. I'd never remember them all, but felt a certain level of kinship, nonetheless.

And now, now, it was time to go.

I pressed my fingertips to my eyes and took for myself a moment to pray for guidance.

"She Who Is All-Knowing, Mother Creator, Birther of the Great Sphere, please... please guide your daughter."

The Goddess didn't answer. I didn't expect her to.

I glanced over my shoulder and watched Ambrose merrily tap his fingers on the table as Zuddaz entertained him by making quills take flight, zooming across the room and back.

The melancholy of missed opportunity weighed heavily upon my shoulders.

"We thank you again for the new furniture you so kindly purchased for us, Highness Ambrose."

"You are most welcome, Primus Zuddaz. Consider it repayment for teaching Eira how to um..." Ambrose held up two fingers and rhythmically bounced them up and down.

"Control her explosions?"

"Sure. Sure."

Leaving Solnna after only a few days saddened me, but I would be departing with a full heart. Perhaps, like being queen... there was no downtime for a Chosen One either, especially not one of Merrias's—

Ambrose stood abruptly.

Zuddaz tensed, staring at the table, cocking his head to the side, straining to hear—

My eyes snapped open.

"Eira, wake!" Ambrose screamed, his nose nearly touching mine. He shook me so violently my teeth clacked together. "Eira, now!"

"Bring her—we must flee. And—"

The room quaked as Viktos raged. My chest vibrated, not from the drive of æther through my limbs, but from the thunder crashing overhead.

"Is Septimus near?" I asked groggily, blinking away the fog of snapping between realities. "Tell him to leave and—"

Crack!

Amid the earsplitting sounds of wood splintering and splitting, great swirls of dust flew from the walls, momentarily cutting Ambrose from my view. He scooped me into his arms before my mind could register what was happening.

"Run!" Zuddaz's voice echoed from the direction of the hallway.

Ambrose charged toward the Primus but came to an abrupt stop.

"The door is jammed." He dropped my feet to the floor. "Place your hand on the wall so I do not lose track of you."

I did as commanded and sought the outline of his body through squinted eyes.

"Shield your face, Eira."

I turned my head into the wall just as Ambrose barreled forward, ramming his shoulder into the warped panel.

The pressure changed, my ears popped, and again shards flew, but not due to his heroics.

A high-pitched whistle assaulted my ears, piercing and loud.

This was no storm.

As I scrambled down the hall, feeling my way toward the bakery, my hand encountered spikes of fragmented wood and metal bits deeply embedded into the slats. I nearly hit my head on a large baker's sheet, wrapped around the sconce of a shattered lamp.

"Ambrose? Where are you? Speak to me!"

"I am here, Eira." His hands found my shoulders and immediately they began assessing for injury. "Fall in, closely. Stay behind me. Do you understand?"

The air started to clear, the dust settling. I clutched my journal to my chest.

"Ambrose, you're hurt. Let me—"

He jerked the shrapnel from his forearm and pulled another piece from his thigh. Blood welled from both wounds. He paid neither of them attention, and I nodded, too frightened to do more.

Ambrose stumbled through the wreckage, kicking away broken butter churns and chunks of plaster.

"Zuddaz... he's here, Eira."

My breath caught.

Slumped over the side of his chair, peppered with sharp protrusions, Zuddaz sat motionless.

"Is he?"

Ambrose laid his fingers at the base of the Primus's throat as I plucked the razor-edged splinters from his arms.

"He breathes. Steady heartbeat."

"Thank the gods."

Ambrose gathered the unconscious man, cradling him like a mother would her babe.

I flung the bakery door wide.

Ambrose cleared the threshold, and together, we stepped into carnage.

Chapter Fifty-Four

What's That Saying About Judging a Book?

Eira

Where the bakery once stood, two walls remained. Flour and salt, glass and broken pottery had scattered haphazardly over the stone floor. Bodies lay about, unmoving, battered, and broken.

An unrecognizable smell penetrated my nose. A metallic tang settled on the back of my tongue. The air itself seemed to roll, polluted by a heavy fog of earth and powdered debris.

"Hold on to me, Eira. Do not turn loose."

I tucked my journal into my dress, grabbed the waist of Ambrose's skirt, and we ran. I cradled Zuddaz's head with one hand, trying to mitigate the impact of it hitting Ambrose's back as we fled… or tried to flee. Traversing the wreckage was practically impossible.

We picked our way over the unstable surface of rubble, the remnants of the shops that stood here only hours before. Concrete had crumbled, metal twisted, and wood disintegrated.

"Listen to me. If we are separated, do not go near the merchant's row. Do you hear me? If this is the work of marauders, they will loot first, and"—Ambrose tripped over an upended streetlamp, going briefly to one knee before regaining his balance and righting himself—"and then they will leave quickly."

"Ambrose!" I pointed to the sky.

Two spheres, linked by chain, whizzed past our heads, moving at a speed that rivaled any horse or team-drawn carriage I had seen. The air split in its path, revealing a blue sky, until the dust churned, refilling the void once more.

"Ambrose, what was—"

The weapon's impact was deafening as it struck a building behind us. I covered my ears and froze in place.

"Eira, don't freeze, sweetheart. I have you."

People darted in and out of the fog, crying for the Goddess... wailing the names of their loved ones.

"Get—get her to the palace," Zuddaz, conscious once more, stammered weakly. He raised his hand, and Ambrose shifted his body to a position where they could confer.

"Highness, you will leave me here and go. The queen will shield Eira."

"Absolutely not," I hissed. I'd not leave a man to die, especially the Primus of this land.

"*Scion*. You have been given an order." Zuddaz ignored me and gripped the necklaces around Ambrose's neck, shaking them with emphasis.

Ambrose nodded solemnly.

"One he will ignore. We are not abandoning you in this mess!"

Together we moved toward a clearing some thirty feet away before ducking into an alley that ran between two still-standing shops.

"Zuddaz. We will not—Ambrose, we can't leave him. How can you even think to—"

A shrill, pained scream howled in the distance, drawing nearer by the second.

Ambrose lowered the Primus's body and propped him next to a rain barrel. He shoved me behind his back and sandwiched me into the wall.

"Fuckin' put a knife in 'er throat. Shut the bitch up—loud fuckin' cunt."

"No! No, please, my children need—"

The sobbing wails ended abruptly in a gurgling sputter.

"Creator, Mother Goddess... Father Gammond," I called to the shadows, drawing energy to my body, feeling for the æther and centralizing it in my chest.

My palms tingled. The heat of righteous anger flared across my breastbone.

"Eira, do not. Now is not the time. There are too many civilians about," Ambrose whispered, keeping his eyes focused toward the voices. "Listen for the innocents."

I paused.

He was right. The yelps of children, the shuffling steps of the elders who led them to safety were all around us.

Two men emerged from a dust cloud, both tall and lithe with sinewy muscles and dressed in tabards of yellow ochre and iron gray. A sunburnt, white-blonde man wiped his curved dagger on a towel folded through his black leather belt. The fabric boasted dozens of streaks and stains, rust red and sanguine.

"Shoulda killed 'er before I fucked 'er—what do we have here?"

We'd been spotted.

The other man, auburn-haired and heavily freckled, looked Ambrose up and then down. "A cripple and a fancy man. And the fancy man got a thick bit o' cunt wif em."

The blonde grabbed his crotch in a vulgar gesture.

"Hops, you know I don't fuck 'em fat cunts, but me fist is itchin' to destroy a Solnnan whore's puss—"

Zuddaz struck.

"Fuckin' Mossius! What the—"

Fingers curled and teeth bared, Zuddaz commanded a pinky-thin rope of water from the rain barrel. Like a bolt from a crossbow, the liquid missile shot between the man's eyes and burst through the back of his skull, splattering the contents of his head on the opposite wall.

"What the fuck? Duncan you—"

Zuddaz shifted toward the fair-haired miscreant, balled his hands together and then quickly yanked them apart.

There was no time for me to scream.

Blood and gore coated the ground. It splattered warmly on my cheeks and Ambrose's chest. The man's torso ripped cleanly in half, exposing what lay beneath... gut and organ, tissue and fat. His intestines sagged and fell, piling up on the sandy walkway with a nauseating squelch. His eyeballs rolled, and his mouth worked up and down, shock followed closely by death. The man hit his knees and found his end amid a pool of his own viscera.

"I may be an old cripple," Zuddaz sneered, "but I am not without means. Scion, do your duty. At once!"

One minute I was staring at the fearsome conjurer, the next at Ambrose's back.

He ran, leaping over metal beams and dodging the scalding stream of a busted dye bath.

The air left my lungs as my diaphragm connected with Ambrose's shoulder.

"Ambrose—turn back. He's your fa—"

My dress ripped at its hem.

"Put this over your mouth and nose. We are nearly at the palace—"

Another whirling projectile scudded overhead, impacting a roof just behind us.

The world went gray.

I hit the ground, protecting the back of my head with my arms, but my jaw scraped painfully across rocks and rough stone. My wrist snapped as my body rolled. I heard the crack and felt the sickening twist as the bone bisected.

"Hus-husband?" I shielded my eyes from a momentary burst of sunlight that cut through the dust cloud and shifted atop a pile of rubble—shattered planters, bolts of colorful fabric, now unraveled, a sandaled foot sticking out from under the heavy wooden frame of a fallen wall. "Oh, thank you, gods."

It wasn't him, the sandal too small, the toenails unkempt.

The sound of an altercation drew my gaze further afield.

There he was.

Three shadowed silhouettes lunged at Ambrose, their weapons at the ready.

I rolled to my knees and then stood on shaky legs. My head spun as I stumbled toward them. Like my nightmares, I moved in slow motion.

The slash of a speeding dagger opened Ambrose's bicep from shoulder to mid-arm, and a second, the corner of his mouth. The blade sliced through his flesh so deeply it exposed his lower set of teeth through his cheek.

"No!" I sprang forward, talons at the ready, fingers sinking into the neck of the nearest assailant. I'd not drawn the æther from a living thing since the night I destroyed the back grounds of Cordillaria, but the familiar tickle started around my navel, and the link cemented.

The man screamed an incoherent litany of prayers and curses as his flesh seared red and then charred black. This was no slow pull of energy. I fed from him... devoured his life's essence. His blood boiled, steaming and sizzling until nothing remained of him but a few pieces of glinting gold—melted and no longer a distinguishable trinket.

I turned to the next criminal, catching him by the waist. I pulled from him. I pulled so fucking hard my fingers vibrated and my vision blurred.

"Help me! General!"

"Scream louder. Call your leader to me," I hissed, digging my nails into his fleshy side. "Call all of your brethren. I await them."

The thief jerked and then thrust, stabbing a blade into my shoulder, once, twice, and a third time. My instinct was to run, but I shoved it aside.

"Con-conjurer."

My chest swelled, fueled by his life force.

"Goddess," I corrected.

Before me, his walnut-colored irises bleached from gold, to white, and then to nothing but a clear, congealed mass. His lips sank in, the surrounding skin tingeing purple and then pale ivory.

His heart stopped, and I dropped him to the ground. Discarded like the trash he was.

Locked in combat with the third assailant, Ambrose found himself evenly matched. They wrestled over a long-handled axe, arms locked, bodies intertwined in a violent dance. I made to intervene, but Ambrose dipped low and struck, taking out the man's legs and striking with the heel of his palm. The weapon's haft flew backward, smashing across his foe's face. Ambrose disarmed the man, only to return it, edge first, cleaving through his chest wall.

Ambrose lifted the struggling man by his ratty tabard, preparing to end him. The garment shifted, revealing a brand on the man's neck—a stylized portcullis, a gate with sharp points. "What is this? Who do you represent?"

"It's the sign of... of your... demise." The man spat in Ambrose's face, and the scarlet-tinged saliva landed below his eye.

I crouched, yanked the axe from the marauder's chest, and hacked into his neck.

He never made another sound, not when I cut through his windpipe, or when I peeled and tore the branded flesh from his body. My stomach heaved as the stretch of skin came away in my palm.

Ambrose placed the cast-off axe into my hands, sheathed a curved blade at his waist and removed a small flail from the body of the first man to have gone down.

"Come, Eira. And thank you."

I nodded.

We charged forward, running for what felt like hours through smoke, dust, and rubble. It was likely only minutes before we reached the palace gates.

Trivio stood at the garrison that opened into the city. In front of him were hundreds of warriors, at attention and prepared for battle. The normally jovial chatelaine looked hard, arms over his chest, jaw set. Recognition flashed in his eyes as the dust parted, and he commanded the gates to be opened.

"Thank Lykksun. The soldiers sent to retrieve you reported that the bakery no longer stood."

Trivio waved to a soldier standing off to his side. The woman came forward, bearing a map that she rolled out and presented. Trivio studied the city plan.

"Spears to the wharf. Intercept the next wave before they crest the sand barrier. Send the Captains and Banner Lords orders. They are to goad them from their ships. *My* unit will work to break apart their fleet. Their dragon weapons are like nothing we've seen before—fire propelled from a metal throat." A squad of soldiers saluted and ran between the gates, which were quickly sealed again.

From our place behind the barricade, I saw Solnnan soldiers clashing head-on with the criminals pouring into the city. Their numbers, like Ambrose had predicted, were concentrated nearest the docks.

"Pirates?" I asked my husband, whose eyes were glued to the action.

"It would seem, but they are nothing like those I have encountered," he answered, his voice distorted by the open slit in his cheek. "They hold formation, wear heraldic garments. Pirates do neither."

Reality and pain settled deeply into my bones.

"Cato? Where is he?" The æther swelled, the monster I could become ready to break free. "Trivio, tell me where—"

"After depositing Lady Steffani aboard your ship, Prince Catommandus was the one who alerted us of the oncoming attack. He saw this unnatural fog rolling in from the west." Trivio gestured, his arm cutting through what I'd assumed was the aftereffect of large-scale destruction. "He took command of three of Her Majesty's units and returned to the fray."

"Open the gates!" I shouted, sprinting back to our point of entry. Two guards intercepted me as I attempted to push my way through their crossed spears. "Open them. You have five seconds to make your choice, or I will—Ambrose, let me go."

"I will do no such thing. Remember who *he* is. Cato has lived this life, was raised to command. He would have my head if you charged off and got yourself—"

"Atten-tion!" a herald barked.

Soldiers and citizens, nobles bearing arms, all who stood near, dropped to their knees.

Queen Ahn-Lyse strode toward the garrison, with a battalion at her back—the embodiment of valor.

Were there not an all-out war being fought in front of us, I would have taken more time to appreciate the awe-inspiring figure marching toward me. Bronze armor covered her torso and legs—etched with a scene of Lykksun banishing the scorpion-bodied tyrant called Bezogath. White linen wrappings encased her arms, but her feet were bare and heavily calloused. As she neared, she tied a long strip of cloth around her shorn hair, twisting the length around her head and knotting it at the top of her forehead.

"Zuddaz?" she called out, addressing Ambrose as she approached.

"Alive when we split off," he replied.

She nodded resolutely, no outward emotion on her face.

"Who are they?" I asked. "Do you recognize this?" I held up the raw piece of flesh still clutched in my palm.

She sneered.

"Yes. That is the sigil of Baldorva."

Time froze. Not even my husband's arms gave me comfort.

"The fucking Baldorvans have entered the fray?" Ambrose growled. "Then they choose to forfeit their lives."

The queen flicked her fingers over her shoulder, and a girl, who could be no more than six and ten years, appeared bearing a helmet unlike any I'd ever seen. The queen placed the steel on her head. White and pink feathers fluttered from its bronze crest, and a prominent nasal guard jutted down from her forehead to her top lip.

"Scion." She turned to Ambrose as she tugged a leather strap under her chin, tightening and testing the stability of her armor. "Get Eira to your ship before it's no longer seaworthy."

Ambrose made to move, but I stilled him with a raised hand.

"You think it's me they're after?"

"You think it isn't?" Queen Ahn-Lyse held my gaze, her eyes gentle for a moment before fastening to something over my head and then shifting back. "When you reach Monwyn, secure the Mantle, and raise your Frostborn. I am sending Gotwig to aid you. When you are ready to march against our enemies, Solnna will heed the call."

I could only nod in the face of her courage.

"Open the gate." Her Majesty issued the order and then dropped to a single knee, digging her finger into a clump of wispy beach grass.

"Creator's tits..." Ambrose muttered at my side. "Big, bouncing globes of mystery."

Soil and sand rose, climbing to the queen's elbow and then falling away. She slowly withdrew her arm, revealing a bronze hilt followed by a black blade.

"You're a conjurer, Majesty."

She nodded, raised her empty hand, and then, as if linked through nature itself, pulled a stream of water from the vegetation and fruits that surrounded her. They wilted and shriveled to straw as she twisted the berry-colored liquid around her fist.

"No one here is as they seem."

As if to prove her point, Trivio approached, grim and armored in a full suit of blackened steel, decorated with bronze accents. A team of squires finished securing their spaulders as they pulled on a leather glove.

"The archers are in place, and the volley unit is preparing to fire. Upon their release, your Gilded Guard will intercept any who attempt to flee east. A corridor of safety will open and allow for the Monwyns to escape. Eira, can you clear the fog?" Trivio asked.

Could I clear—

I thought for a moment. Fog is... is water vapor. I could gather it to me like Papa Burchard. Or I could... become the shade and... no, I wasn't sure that would—wait.

"The Deathless Flame. Get me to the beacon and I think I can dispel the moisture from the air."

"I will shield you," Ambrose said, with a confidence that bolstered me. "Majesty, I require a small unit."

"It is done." The queen pointed to three of her Gilded fighters, and they broke ranks and lined up at Ambrose's right side.

He faced them, pointing to the first soldier, a ruddy complected woman with four rows of braids that circled in a halo above her head.

"You will commit yourself to her body. Do not allow but a foot of distance between you. You two, flank me."

My guard came to stand at my side. She took my arm by the elbow and inspected the stab wounds and broken wrist. She fashioned a quick sling from a length of cloth pulled from the pouch at her side, and tucked my arm closely against my body without a single word spoken.

"Eira... my wife." He leaned down, his eyes level with mine. "If I fall, you run. If you are chased, rain your black fire upon them. Leave nothing and no one alive. Aberus will defend you unto his death."

He stood.

"Ambrose?"

"Yes?"

"Take my blood, and don't question me, because I swear to the gods, I can't lose you."

He shifted the silk sling, dipped his head, and swept his tongue across my shoulder.

"Good?" he asked, sparing me a wink.

Within seconds, his pupils enlarged. His head lurched as the strange effects took hold.

"Good enough."

Ambrose retrieved the flail from his waistband, and we shot off, our small, tight unit barreling toward the merchant's row.

Goddess, please let this work.

We dodged smaller skirmishes, leaving those to the city's soldiers, and hid behind a cluster of tall trees.

Children cried, screaming for their fathers. From the corner of my eye, I saw an old man brandishing his cane to defend himself and a little boy. I twisted, changing my trajectory to lend aid, but a Gilded blocked me with her spear, her eyes never straying from our goal.

The grandfather fell, his throat slashed.

"Merrias," I prayed, "Merrias guide him."

The murderer snatched the child up by his tunic. I watched in horror as the little one wailed, tears leaving clean streaks on his dirt-covered face.

Ambrose charged, starting his swing before the æther could fill my chest. He let his momentum carry the weapon to the target, just as I felt for the flail's weight, and commanded the spiked spheres to shoot forward.

I closed my eyes against the grisly sight of metal meeting skull but couldn't deafen my ears from the little one's scream slicing through the stagnant air. The poor child doubled over, vomiting in the street before running back to lay his small body across the old man's chest.

"Ambrose, the boy, let me—"

"No, Eira. Stay the course and more lives will yet be saved." Ambrose pointed to the Deathless Flame. The metal dish, the size of a small temple, burned brightly atop its tall, copper base, oddly normal amid the mayhem of the attack.

I called the shadows and commanded the æther as I watched Ambrose carefully scout ahead.

"He signals. We move," my Gilded guardian whispered.

We dashed toward the beacon, my hands meeting the first rung.

As I climbed, swirling black spirals emerged, buzzing and burning my palms—they crackled in the air, sparking and jumping between my fingers. I inhaled and bore down, clenching my stomach muscles tight, containing the jet-hued shadows that sought to materialize and eviscerate all in their path.

Below me, a woman stepped from behind the fiery beacon, a sword in her hand, and a shield shaped like an inverted teardrop. Two Gildeds ran to intercept the soldier as I reached the Deathless Flame.

The first Gilded fell—a blade run between her ribs.

CHAPTER FIFTY-FIVE

WOMAN ABOARD

EIRA

Heat coiled around me, embracing me—singing its crackling song. Through the flames I watched the armored woman drive her sword into the prone Gilded's back, over and over, teeth bared in a violent frenzy.

More will be saved. Focus, Eira. More lives. More.

I dug my fingers into the embers of the basin and bore my eyes into the attacker, the fury she inspired fueling my resolve. With each stab of her blade, the æther pulsed, wishing to burst forth, to be unleashed in a wild and unhinged barrage. But I held firm, focusing and channeling the energy from my heart to my hands.

A controlled flow of æther met flame, hissing as the two distinct fires mingled between my palms. The orange flames transmuted around my fingers, licking black against my skin. My head throbbed from holding the force in check. My body shook, but I demanded the æther to course evenly and not shatter or explode.

My eyes snapped back to the woman, now locked in combat with the second Gilded. This fog, this unnatural gloom, was aiding the slavers in their cause—it had to be lifted now.

Have faith, Eira.

"Goddess, guide me. Leyometh, Fire Commander, lend me your aid."

My muscles spasmed. Searing pain swept down my arms.

The flames surged upward, the heat intensifying tenfold. I closed my eyes and imagined the stream of æther gathering the yellow flames as they rose, a column that supported and shot them higher.

A single beam of sunlight bathed my face.

The fog dissipated faster than I would have thought possible. When the fire touched it, it instantly burned away.

The flames of black and copper spread through the sky, seeming to feed off the particles.

"More, Eira." My attention was drawn again to the Baldorvan fighter. She rained down blow after blow on the ruddy-faced warrior who used a combination of dagger and æther to parry each of the quick thrusts. "More."

The enemy glanced up, her eyes locking with mine. Recognition filtered across her unusual teal eyes. She spun, crouched, and then drove her weapon up at an unexpected angle, through the neck of the Gilded. The tip of the wicked blade emerged from her nape. The young woman's body slid, its weight impaling her as she fell to her knees.

A shockwave of energy burst from the center of my chest, rolling outward.

Blackfire, as beautiful as the nighttime sky, swelled, curling in on itself, and then erupted, rising so high it outstripped the tallest sun ray on the palace's opulent spire. The vertical column climbed and fanned out, chasing away the fog. Projectiles in its path, arrows and the strange steel rounds disintegrated into ash.

The blazing light of a high sun smiled upon Solnna. Hundreds of arrows loosed, arcing into the sky only to begin their downward flight into the enemy's reserve units, now visible on the shore.

"May Merrias cast you to the nether!" I wailed, my fingers finding purchase on the bottom of the basin. My flames died out, dimming as the wood and oil fuel that supported the fire smoldered. I paused and spoke to my heart—to the æther. *Soothe yourself, calm yourself, Eira. You did it.*

"You will stand down!" I heard the command issue from below the Deathless Flame. I shifted, working my way down the ladder, following the shouts. My clothing had burned away, but my body was unscathed—entirely untouched by what would have decimated another.

Both the Gilded lay dead, lifeless eyes staring out at what remained of their home.

"You will not touch my wife."

Ambrose.

I darted around the beacon's wide base.

He was slick with blood, not an inch of his pale flesh visible through the sheet of ruby-red coating his back.

"She is Leyometh's. Your false ceremonies are meaningless." The Baldorvan warrior struck out quickly, opening small slits of his skin, seeming to toy with him as he countered and blocked. Her swordsmanship easily rivaled Cato's honed skills, and her speed was superhuman.

Ambrose planted his foot, found an opening and let his flail fly on a trajectory toward her face. She blocked him with a reflexive movement of her shield.

"Until I no longer breathe, she is mine. Witnessed by the gods." Ambrose staggered backward under the forceful punch of her shield, followed by the flat of her sword catching him across the ribs.

He fell to his knees, but still fought, hooking his arm around her ankle. She kicked out her other foot, the steel sabaton she wore catching him in the cheek, further ripping the skin that hung loosely from his jaw.

I would kill her with my bare hands.

She struck again.

I ran, feeling the effervescent spark of the shade as it began to—a silvery entity slammed into the Baldorvans back, lifting her into the air and slamming her to the hard ground, her tailbone meeting earth.

Septimus.

A lavender butterfly rode atop his unbound hair, the silver-white mass stained with shades of crimson and rust. It fell around his shoulders in heavy, sweat-saturated shanks. His eyes matched the pale color of the sky above, but the fury within their depths mirrored my own. He rolled atop the struggling figure, his forearm an iron bar across her neck.

His gaze met mine.

The ever-present hunger was there, but so was something else. He dipped his head in question while shoving his arm against her chin, bearing her throat.

An offer to his enchantress.

"He demands her return!" The woman screamed, spittle flying from her mouth.

Septimus reacted swiftly, pulling his dagger, thrusting it between her parted lips. He pried and dug at her tongue and gums as she screamed and bucked, trying to wrestle free of his hold.

Her hand shot out, closing around Septimus's neck. She tore at his skin as he mutilated her face.

I lunged, compelled to share in his madness.

"Your filthy warlord should have come himself!"

The æther responded to me like it never had before—a clear, perfectly controlled path jolted through my arm, springing pitch black from my hand. I drew my arm back and struck. Her head separated from her body; neck sliced clean through by the bladed edge of the shadows.

Septimus stood and kicked the dismembered head. It wobbled more than rolled, coming to a stop at the base of the Deathless Flame. No blood oozed, the lethal wound cauterized by my black fire.

Septimus held his hand out to me, palm up.

"Come with me, enchantress." His eyes burned with a desire that matched the intensity of my own. My soul spoke to his.

"Eira," Ambrose groaned, trying to rise from the ground. He fell to one knee.

I looked between them—my Bonded and my beloved.

Æther-high and adrenaline drunk, my body screamed for its Safeguard. I longed for him to lay me upon the carnage we created together. To build our twisted life.

And I could. I could choose this path.

I offered Septimus my hand.

"W-wife. If you love him... go... slip away and live well."

Septimus's hair floated on the breeze, framing his brilliant eyes. He'd kill for me. He'd take me far from here and protect my life with his own.

But the honesty in Ambrose's voice... the gift of freedom. It was worth more than a lifetime of protection.

I ran to Ambrose's side and helped him stand. He was so battered that he was barely recognizable. A blackening bruise swelled around his eye socket and stretched back to his hairline. He breathed shallowly and painfully, like his ribs were broken. Despite his suffering, he stood tall and inclined his chin in his uncle's direction. I wrapped my arm around his waist, lending him support.

"You have my thanks, Septimus," Ambrose said while tucking his bloodied weapon back to his side.

"You may keep it, false prince," Septimus sneered as he wiped his dagger on his thigh before sheathing it. "I act only to fulfill a promise made. A promise that she will one day keep."

To his credit, Ambrose ignored him.

But my body did not. The divine spell took hold—I wanted to run to him, leaving all else behind. I arched toward him, and he reached out, his hand connecting with mine, something small passing between our palms.

"Enchantress." Septimus leaned forward as he tugged my hand.

Our lips met, and the fine hairs on my nape stood on end. It was as if lightning had struck nearby.

"How dare you," Ambrose cursed, trying his damnedest to swipe out at his uncle.

Septimus pressed his fist to his shoulder, while Ambrose leaned heavily upon me. Whether it was to keep me from fleeing or because his body grew heavy with pain, I didn't know.

"Run, uncle, and keep your life. It is the only grace I will ever bestow upon you again." Ambrose spat on the ground at Septimus's feet. "Place a toe onto Monwyn soil and neither Catommandus nor I will spare you. I will hold the rope from which you hang."

I stared ahead, holding Ambrose tighter while my stomach lurched. He was leaving—I was leaving him, the vile creature that he was—and it destroyed me.

"S-Septimus," his name fell from my lips, a plea.

"Enchantress…" His neck corded, the strain visible across his battered chest and arms.

He turned and sprinted away.

Tears cascaded down my cheeks as Ambrose gathered his energy. Together, we half-ran, half-limped toward the ships in the harbor.

A flag of blue, emblazoned with a golden mountain, waved in the sky.

The presence of enemy soldiers lightened as we climbed over bodies strewn across the docks. Most were dead, but others lingered, waiting for their end. Many more floated in the harbor, bobbing in and out of sight as the current swept them out to sea.

"Ambrose, look!"

Cato appeared at the opposite end of the dock, standing in a beam of sunlight, the lighter streaks that ran through his hair glinting gold.

My relief was profound.

"Thank the Goddess above." Ambrose sighed, his breaths coming more evenly.

Cato ran from the eastern side of the wharf, swords drawn, and from the looks of him, entirely uninjured—even his clothing remained unscathed.

He wiped the sweat pouring into his eyes on the sleeve of his gray linen shirt. He was once more a Monwyn—tan leathers clung to his legs, the tall boots he wore reached his knees, and the hilt of a blade was visible from the left cuff.

"Hello, love." He slowed and sheathed his weapons, long and short swords strapped to his hip. He held his arms wide. "How is it that I take my eyes off you for a single second, and all nether breaks loose?" I glanced up at Ambrose, who nodded and pushed me toward Cato.

Strong arms closed around me.

I inhaled the scent of leather, sweat, and the smell of him—cedar and toasted clove.

"Cato—oh, gods," I cried, clutching my arm. My sling had burned in the Deathless Flame, allowing my limb to swing free.

He gently cupped my maimed wrist, his scowl growing deeper by the second. I yelped again as he prodded the limb, dropping what Septimus had slipped into my hand. When it landed, nestled in the sand, I recognized the pearls from the hairpin Merrias had placed in my hair the night I dove into the sea. I bent to retrieve the sand-coated, blood-tinged object before either of my men could ask what it was. I'd need it to fill the odd gulf of anguish already settling in my bones.

"Eira, up the ramp. The crew is prepared to shove off. Ambrose and I must man the deck as we are several hands short."

Ambrose nodded, saying nothing, holding the two sides of his cheek closed.

Cato's face fell.

"Fucking nether, Ambrose. Finally, a scar to be proud of."

Instead of the anger I expected, Ambrose half-grinned.

"Eira, to the ship, sweetheart. I am ready to be home." My husband glanced at me expectantly, eyebrows raised and eyes wide. He then pointed to the boat and snapped. "And for the Goddess's glory, give her your shirt, brother. The crew will lose all composure if she boards as she is." Cato stripped quickly and covered me, taking care not to disturb my arm.

"Go on, love. We will join you soon."

I didn't wait any longer and climbed the ramp, looking back once to see Cato tuck his body under Ambrose's arm as the larger man slumped nearly to his knees. I'd not run back and risk wounding his pride.

"Ya back again now, are ya, girl? 'Spose I ain't died the last time, so welcome aboard what remains of the Merlann." The ship's captain propped a fist on his hip, revealing a bloodied thigh and a shirt torn to shreds. "Head in an' see to that other girlie. That one's not made fir the sea, ya hur?"

I hurred... but I wasn't sure I trusted myself with the Primus-King's progeny at the moment. I nodded and turned away, but instead of ducking inside the ship's quarters, I rounded the mainmast and hurried to the back of the ship, falling to my knees.

We'd made it safe, even if Solnna might fall.

"Merrias?" I implored, hanging my head. "The gods' war may not spill into Ærta for a lifetime, but you failed to mention that Ærta would descend into madness." I stared at the cheerful sun, perched high in a cloudless sky. How dare its cheerful beams fall upon us when so much blood seeped into the sands of Lykksun's own city?

I hugged my waist, my left arm much weaker than my right. My palms were wet, my heart pounded, and fear lured me into its smothering embrace.

This wasn't over. This was just the start.

"Momma, can you hear me?" I closed my eyes against the harsh light and rocked—imagined myself folded in the security of her arms. "Momma, it's too much now. And I can't—"

Goosebumps raced across my skin, tiny pricks of warning.

The mist, that heavy unnatural fog, seeped over the railing, creeping toward me like the steam rolling off a boiling pot.

I crawled to the ship's side and peered out... right into the eyes of Scion Greggen.

His ship approached us at full sail.

CHAPTER FIFTY-SIX

NO MERCY

EIRA

"Traitor! Greggen, you fucking defector!"

He was here... standing on the bow of the ship not a hundred feet from me. The proud red banner of a Verus Scion waved behind him. Baldorvan filth masquerading as a Chosen One of the continent.

Recognition lit his eyes, and a mask of hatred slid over his handsome face.

Under my feet, the Merlann rocked, her sails unfurling.

"No." I tore out, running the length of the boat, never taking my eyes from my target as he sailed one way and me the other. He spun slowly on his heels as his eyes tracked mine. How dare he come here dressed in Monwyn blue, his hair braided back like the men of the mountains? "Greggen!" Septimus's parting gift bit into my palm as I balled my fists, rage bubbling to the surface.

I sensed bodies beside me; the crew setting the ship in motion, the snap of canvas as the wind took hold, the shift of beams above my head... the voices of two men shouting my name.

None of that would stop me.

I was so close to him, the filthy traitor. Only the railing separated the two ships as I called to the shadows, felt the electric pulses in my—

Cato took flight, and my heart caught in my throat.

He jumped, landed on the Merlann's rails, and pushed off, soaring across the sliver of sea that separated the boats. The malice on his face told me that he too had spotted Greggen—and for a moment, I felt pity for what the Scion would endure when Cato meted out his vengeance... Imella's vengeance.

A bolt sped through the air and pierced Cato's shoulder clean through. He began to plummet.

I snapped—the electric jolt racing through my body, my limbs dissipating to shade. I darted into the sea, begging the droplets to aid me, beckoning them to cocoon my shadowed form. They clung to me like a second skin, and together, we surged upward, cracking the surface—a geyser under Cato's feet—launching him into the air, flipping him haphazardly aboard the enemy ship.

I could have pulled him back into the Merlann, set the ship on course to Monwyn... but I would never forgive myself for stealing his retribution.

He hit the deck, rolling forward, and then leapt to his feet. I reeled forward at an uncontrolled speed until I slammed into a large coil of thick rope.

I was back in my body, dazed by the sudden impact of my poor landing.

"Always you," Greggen said with a curl of his lip. "Slow him if you can." He circled a finger in the air, pointed toward Cato, and then ran.

A dozen brigands—a hodgepodge of Baldorvan riffraff—charged, weapons at the ready.

"Stay with me, Derros," I whispered, as I watched Cato pull a thin stiletto dagger from his boot.

He bent his knees, left foot slightly forward, and stretched his neck from side to side as he waited to intercept the onslaught.

"Be with me, Ocean King, Wave Maker—lend a Nortian daughter your aid."

I closed my eyes, calling to the water that pooled around my feet. I concentrated, struggling to feel the weight of the liquid—it was different from moving an object—lighter and unfocused, nothing to grip, tangible and yet not.

A cold wind... no... a frosty gale breezed through my hair, crystalizing the droplets that clung to my lashes.

The temperature plummeted.

"Nether Lord?" Small, white flecks bloomed around my fingers, the water fogging over and turning to ice. "Whose side are you on, Depraved One, Nether Father? Will you freeze me in place? Let them steal me away and take me to your son's worshippers?" Water froze in a circle around my legs. I tried to break free but couldn't move. "If they bring down my lover, I will slit my own throat. Where will the gods be then? No more pawn... no more Chosen womb."

The freeze tightened painfully around my digits and knees until a ray of sunlight burst through the gathering fog.

"It would seem Lykksun fights for me…"

I yanked and pulled, jerking my hands and feet until the sun-softened ice cracked.

"Eira!" Ambrose stood upon the Merlann's deck. His hands curled around his mouth, one holding his jaw, the other helping to project his voice. "Destroy them! Let yourself loose upon them. No mercy for this lot! Anger-puff!"

No mercy.

"Let fly!" Ambrose ordered, while stabbing his finger through the air.

At his signal, the Merlann's crew sent their boat hooks airborne. At least nine of the barbed tethers found their mark, clawing the railings of the enemy ship. The boats shuddered as they drew together.

I turned, assessing the floating island of slavers and warmongers.

They surrounded Cato, closing in on him.

Three men attacked at once, two closing in from the front, the third charging at his back. One swung a curved saber at Cato's chest, but he stepped away from the blow, snaking his arm out, and redirecting the spear of another man into the sword strike. He gracefully pulled the haft of the spear into his side and spun, wrenching the weapon from the enemy's grasp. In a practiced sweep, he threw his dagger into the man behind him, set the spear in both hands, and thrust into the swordsman's belly. Cato then sent the unarmed sailor to Merrias with ease, the blunt force of a spear butt fracturing his skull.

A blade sliced into Cato's arm—a knife thrown from out of sight. Blood bloomed across his bicep, but it didn't slow him. He spun as another man tried to grapple him from behind, but slammed his forehead into his adversary's nose, busting it wide. As the man reeled, Cato stepped into him, almost like he was trying to move through his opponent, and then the man was spinning over the railing and into the sea.

Two more men took the soldier's place as he fell.

Their mistake.

"Do you not recognize a demon when she stands before you?" I yelled, my arms spread wide, the sun burning hot against my naked flesh. Light illuminated the pools of water that I stepped through, a rainbow of color surrounding each of my feet.

Two heads swiveled my way. Red crescents whispered across their necks, Cato's blade finding flesh.

"Eira, you make my blood run hot." Cato's nostrils flared as I approached. The Solnnan sun glinted off the gold in his eyes. "You are mastery in motion, my heart."

Two marauders fled, turning so fast they distracted the sailor nearest them. He tasted Cato's spear as it sank into the soft spot beneath his chin.

Cato's eyes never left mine—not when I charged and sank my fingers into the necks of two unfortunates and not when I drew their energy so fast that I vibrated as their eyes turned white and their faces sunk in.

"Fucking flawless," he gritted out, driving his knife into one man's eye, disregarding the two who sagged lifelessly to the deck.

"Retreat!" a sailor shouted. "Get below!"

The remaining men scattered.

A bloody arm circled my waist; another cupped my jaw. I ignored the press of the spear shaft against my back, ensnared by the sound of Cato's beating heart, enraptured by the love so plainly evident in his eyes. I brushed my knuckles along his scruffy beard and then traced the scar below his collarbone.

"Cato, I—"

"DO. NOT. FUCK!"

Cato flung his hand out, middle finger raised, aimed toward Ambrose.

"CATOMMANDUS ODELGUARD, DO YOU HEAR ME? THE ENEMY REMAINS!"

The Merlann's crew spilled onto the enemy deck, swords drawn, and gave chase, hacking mercilessly at the Baldorvans—may they rot in the nether.

"Did you hear something, darling?" Cato asked, sliding a palm down to my rear.

My lips parted in answer.

Salt, sweat, and the taste of iron were an unexpected yet heady combination when his lips feathered over mine. The tips of our tongues met, and he hummed, a low, contented sound.

"MY LOVERS ARE FOOLS! THEY ARE FOOLS I SAY!"

Cato smiled against my mouth. "Let them come. My delicious terror of a wife will melt their flesh from their bones."

"IMBECILES! LUSTY ASSED HARLOTS!"

Cato pursed his lips. "Ambrose appears to be upset. Make your way back to the ship?"

"Uh, uh." I shook my head and ran my fingers through the hair on his chest; his erection nudged my belly. "What about Greggen? Cato, you will need my help. There are too many here for one man to—"

"I mean to take him alive, Eira." Cato's eyes went cold. "He will not know the pleasure of a swift death."

I protested, but he silenced me with his kiss.

"Besides which, your contract-husband needs you."

From my periphery, I saw Ambrose heaving a leg over the rails. Cato glanced over, tucked his elbow into his side, and slid his finger from his temple to the tip of his ear.

"What's that one mean?"

"Fall back."

Ambrose stopped, resumed his place on the ship and stood tall, his expression impassive.

"See him mended. He has suffered more injuries than he is letting on. I will be back with you soon."

"But Cato—"

He tilted my head, his thumb painting little circles on my bruised cheek-bone.

"Trust me, yes?"

I rolled my eyes; his crinkled at their corners.

"Fine. I'll go."

"And…" He stepped back, the wind pulling wisps of his hair from his braid. "If I am to die… that you found me worthy in this life will bolster me as I stand upon the blade. It is your name I will utter with my last breath."

He turned and ran, taking with him my heart.

"THANK THE FUCKING GODDESS. EIRA VERRAS, YOU SIL-LY SLUT, AVAST YOUR ASS TO THIS SHIP IMMEDIATELY."

CHAPTER FIFTY-SEVEN

ARE YOU REALLY THINKING ABOUT SEX RIGHT NOW?!

OF COURSE HE IS. BUT OKAY, SO AM I... EIRA

"No, sir. Ambrose, you will sit here and allow me to finish."

"Take this confounded journal, then, and allow me a modicum of comfort."

Ambrose extracted the small book from the back of his waistband; my link to Solnna—if Lykk remained standing. We could still see fighting in the distance, could still hear the crash and clangs of battle. He placed it into my quivering fingers. I'd assumed it lost, burned in the fires of the Deathless Flame, or lying on the streets with so many of the dead.

"Ambrose... thank you. Thank you, my most wonderful husband." I peppered his forehead with kisses. It was the cleanest, least abused part of him.

"Eira, contain your emotions and focus. You are stitching without an ounce of regard for my bone structure. If you continue grappling with your overwrought sensitivity, I will have to try my luck with the healer."

"The *healer* has one eye and three fingers whose nails are caked with grime. Now, head back."

He grumbled but settled, gently squeezing the roll of flesh above my hip.

I passed the needle and thread through Ambrose's torn flesh. He winced as the needle pierced his skin, pulling the gaping sides together, but said nothing about the pain.

"You are so brave, my Black Bear. I would be dead or halfway to Baldorva if it weren't for you." There was no lie, no exaggeration in my words. He had given all of himself to ensure my protection.

"And Cato didn't intervene. It was solely my efforts that saved your precious person, yes?"

I laughed on the inside.

"Yep. Just you. He was off leading some army or something. You were all the Protector I required."

To hear the crew talking about him, Cato had single-handedly doomed an entire ship to Derros, before rallying an army of citizens to barricade the outer gates, slowing the first enemy surge.

"Eira, release your pent-up æther, or I must insist you lay down the sharps."

I pressed my lips in an effort to concentrate.

The extra wealth of energy I'd taken in had me feeling like Cato had forced nine mugs of the coffee bean drink he loved past my lips.

I looked to the enemy ship, which had remained quiet since he'd gone below deck in search of Greggen. It took all of me not to shade-sail back over and end the Scion myself. I'd be quick.

"Wife?" Ambrose lowered his voice. He tried to pull me into his lap, but I pinned him with a gently placed knee between the legs. "You must let him have this. Cato was not there to see his mother fall, to see what they had done to her... and he blames his absence for her death and the death of your Nan. It eats away at him—festers."

"With the æther to aide me, I could subdue Greggen in an instant, could cook him before he recognized his end."

"I could... distract you for a few minutes," Ambrose murmured, his fingers fastening to the buttons of the shirt I'd borrowed from none other than the one-eyed, filthy-handed healer. "You are quite fetching in this too-tight garment, and I am beside myself with the need to bite that tummy flesh peeking from betwixt its buttons."

"You're just beside yourself in general, I think."

I speared another length of thread through the needle's eye, using its point to make the knot as small as possible, saying a prayer that the stitching would hold and allow Ambrose's jagged flesh to knit.

"I want you to take more of my blood."

He shook his head, grimacing—kind of grimacing. One side of his mouth dipped down, the other remained still.

"No. It gives me an everlasting erection, and where I would normally welcome such magnificence, it falls to me to see this ship home—I am *still* the Naval Commander of Monwyn. Which reminds me... you are keeping the booty hidden against my orders." He winked and grabbed a handful of my rear.

I looked pointedly between his legs.

"You can't steer a ship with a fever or... or a gangrenous rot gnawing at your pretty face."

That got his attention. He squinted one of his beautiful green eyes thoughtfully.

"Can I lick your lifeblood from someplace sexy?" He wagged those perfectly arched brows, one encased in a dark bruise.

"You are without doubt—"

"Please! He... oh gods!"

Ambrose bolted to his feet, shoving me behind his back.

"What's happening?" I asked, immediately on alert.

He whipped around, grabbing me by the shoulders.

"Eira, go below." His features darkened, his face a mask of bitterness.

"Ambrose, what's—"

"Listen to me, Eira—Do not defy me." I tried to lunge around him, but he shook me, bringing my attention back.

"Goddess above, please, please!" The voice cried out again, cracking between a despondent sob.

I shoved and twisted, kicked out and thrashed until Ambrose could no longer contain me.

Allaine. It was Allaine.

"Eira, wait."

"Let go!" I took off, could hear Ambrose running behind me.

Two crewmen escorted my lady's maid over the railing. She slumped in their arms, head back, her fae-blessed face contorted in agony, her affected arm appearing stiffer and more seized than normal. She was clothed in only her underdress.

He'd taken her.

Fucking Greggen—the slaver born had stolen her from her home.

Cato emerged from a hatch, dragging the Scion by a rope that secured his hands. His head was covered, encased in what looked to be an old grain sack cinched tightly around his throat.

"He fucking took her, Ambrose. He took her."

Cato's face was one of calm. Not a single emotion could be discerned... but I knew the depths of his fury.

A gash split the top of Cato's forehead, opening his brow and ending at his temple.

"He planned to use her, Ambrose... the whole fucking time." I reached out for the steadying arm of my husband, suddenly off-kilter. "She was next. The... the Primus-King's next sacrifice... the one to bring me to his gates."

My vision swam.

"Eira!" Allaine wailed. "Eira, oh g-gods," she choked on her words.

And then my eyes came to rest on the rusty-red stains at her thighs.

Chapter Fifty-Eight

ÆTHER-RICH

Eira

You can't enslave someone aboard a ship that doesn't exist.

What was one less vessel of evil? Just a bit of flotsam upon the waves.

I soared.

I fucking *ascended* into the skies, screeching madly, a sound that reverberated, carrying beyond my shade form, piercing the ears of those below me.

They fell, clutching their heads, their stunned silence a sound of beauty. *Ah, the first to die.*

Æther-rich, I swelled, making myself so large that the wharf and shore darkened as I blotted out the sun.

I breathed in the rays at my back, basked in the fire that empowered both the sun and myself. There could be no darkness without light.

I peaked in my trajectory, hitting a zenith that satisfied me and then turned, contracting in on myself, tightening, as I barreled toward the hull of the enemy ship.

The little ants... how they tried to scurry away from their fate.

The shrill shriek of my form slicing through the atmosphere announced their deaths. I only wish I knew their names so I could call them out, one by one, before I cut them down.

My impact was as loud as the gongs that called believers to prayer.

Crack! The first deck exploded, a rain of splinters and beams projecting outward. I burned my way through the second deck and then the ship's belly. A boiling surge of saltwater spewed up around me, steam and pressure forcing it back up and into the ship.

I dove through Derros's domain, thanking him, and then headed back to the sky, where I sang the praises of Goddess Lykksun.

Greggen's ship began to take on water. None attempted to swim to shore.

One. Two. Three more ships in the distance.

I hurled myself headlong, a racing mass of destruction.

The sky darkened.

In my periphery, both left and right, shaded forms surrounded me—they came from above and below, from the treetops and sand... taking up my screeching dirge.

Wraiths. Bodies of shadow, tendrils of night blanketing out behind them.

I circled, flew around the army of forgotten souls.

Their faces fractured, flickering between feminine features and twisted nether spawn. Both young and old, they greeted me.

The largest among them bared sharp and jagged teeth, not in threat, but in solidarity. They outstripped me—my shadowed sisters—gathering tightly in a formation of demise.

Below me, orcas leapt from the waters, their black and white bodies smashing into the enemy ships, sending the vessels to their sides in a wash of churning sea foam.

Tridents flew from the hands of a thousand shimmering creatures that surfaced, their scaled tails a myriad of the brightest colors I'd ever seen. They towed the bodies of the living below the surface and did not reemerge.

The Baldorvans panicked... and we feasted on their cries as we plummeted.

CHAPTER FIFTY-NINE

CHILD OF DARKNESS

EIRA

"Eira, come back to me, wife."

"Open your eyes, love. Do it now."

I heard them—my men. Ambrose's call was an aggravated plea, Cato's an order issued with intent.

"Mmmm, kisses would help," I whispered, snuggling my cheek into the soft hair of... I didn't know which one it was and didn't care.

I cracked an eye.

"Oh, it's both of you." I placed a kiss on one hairy pectoral and then one covered in linen, enjoying my spot stuck between them. "Do you think the Queen will allow us to take dinner in our apartments?" I yawned, using Ambrose's body to cover my mouth. "I'm exhausted."

"Ambrose, take her below. The hooks are untethered, and we will soon be on our way."

Cato swatted at a pair of purple butterflies that flew around his head. "Of course, they love you, just as they loved Septimus."

I blinked away the haze of sleepiness and came slowly to my senses. I took in the sails, the mast above my head.

"Did I..."

"Obliterate the Baldorvan contingent in the scariest way imaginable? Yes, yes, you did." Cato chuckled, pressing his lips to my forehead. "It was fucking terrifying. I have never come so close to shitting myself."

"And what about..." I extricated myself from my man sandwich and made my way to the ship's bow on shaking legs, my men trailing me, "Oh thank Goddess, Solnna stands."

The Deathless Flame still burned—perhaps not as brightly as it had before—and the sun-shaped spire stood proudly in the distance, though plumes of smoke rose around it.

A pair of powerful arms circled my waist. Ambrose.

"Are you in need of cuddles, Black Bear?"

"You know me well, wiflet." He spun us, leaning his back against the rail and tucking me into his side. He was back in his Monwyn blues. "You scared me."

"You know what I'll miss most about Solnna?" I asked him.

"The sweets."

"Uh-uh."

"Gotwig?"

"No. Not Gotwig."

I reached around to play with his unbound hair, relishing the opportunity to run my fingers through the inky-black veil.

"What then?"

I drew my finger from his knee up to his thigh.

"You wearing the shortest of skirts."

Ambrose's smile was feline, full of promise and smug satisfaction. He leaned down, resting his chin on my head.

"Eira," he breathed in deeply and exhaled slowly, "I would like to tell you something."

My chest squeezed. I knew he'd been trying to say it for days, and I understood how monumental it was for him.

"Alright, I'm listening."

Ambrose fidgeted, moving this way and that, trying to get comfortable. He soon gave up, though, and set me at arm's length, clearing his throat. The unease in his stance was entirely un-Ambrose and beyond adorable. He shrugged his shoulders and then pulled them back, opened his mouth, and then closed it with a snap.

I peered up, so in love with the man trying desperately to come to terms with his foreign feelings.

He puffed his chest out and clasped his coat's collar with both hands.

"I, Prince Ambrose of Monwyn, next in line to the throne of the mountain kingdom, son of Imella and Burchard—late monarch of Monwyn—would like you, m-my wife, to know, that I am making a formal declaration of..." He paused, his eyes going soft, his hands seeking mine. "Eira, you must know by now that you have changed me... not that you ever intentionally set out to do so. But... I am proud of the man I am with you at my side, and I know that is because... well... Gammond's gonads I am positively sweltering." He sucked in a quick breath. "Eira... what I am trying to say is that... I lov—"

"Ambrose down!" Cato bellowed, charging toward us, dagger drawn.

I threw my arms across my husband's chest, protecting him from a danger I did not see.

Cato hurled his blade in an overhand throw, the knife spinning as it raced past our heads. I scrambled, turning in time to see the dagger sink into the chest of a sailor who had remained on the sinking ship.

"Cato, gods, I thought they were all de—"

"E-Eira." Ambrose's hand found my shoulder and then fell, sliding down my back.

I turned, and then ceased to breathe.

The serrated tip of a harpoon's head protruded through Ambrose's side. His legs buckled.

"Brother. Gods, no!" Cato ran, and fell to his knees, catching Ambrose as he sank to the deck, a trickle of blood gurgling from his parted lips.

"Ambrose!"

His green eyes were wide with fear, his body tense and unmoving.

"C-Cat. Promise me... promise me you will Join with her." Ambrose shivered, his entire body convulsing before going still again. "H-have babies and n-name them a-all after me."

"The healer, get him now!" Cato pointed at the bosun, who took off running. "Ambrose, you will not leave us. That is an order."

A cold wind blew—sharp-toed pixies danced their spiteful rhythm down my spine.

"Cato, your knife. Give it to me now."

He blinked, unable to process my words as he held his brother close, rocking him back and forth.

"Cato. Knife!" I begged, reaching toward him.

He stared at my hand, unmoving... frozen.

I watched in horror as fingers of ice crawled up his neck and over his eyes. Icy white patches sealed over his forehead and spread downward toward his nose. His flesh paled as the water on the deck beaded together and rose around his knees.

I clawed at my biceps, trying to sink my fingers into puncture wounds that no longer existed—healed in my shadow state.

"Gods, no, please don't take them. I pray—"

My head snapped back. The air seeped from my lungs as visions of another plane assaulted me. Merrias, wild-eyed and frantic, was screaming. What was she saying?

She swung her sword, cutting down an armored centaur, and clutched the throat of another with her gauntleted hand, ripping his windpipe from his neck.

She ran toward me as if in slow motion.

Do not save the Scion. He must die. Heed me, granddaughter. The Depraved One is—

"Eira!" Cato screamed.

My eyes opened, the sun blazing down into Cato's face, melting away the ice that covered him.

Blood pooled around Ambrose, freezing as it hit the frigid air. Around the wound, crimson frost formed, staunching the rapid flow.

Granddaughter. Granddaughter, hear me!

A deep cold sank into my bones, and another familiar voice sounded in my mind... a deep rumbling utterance: *Child of Darkness, Child of My body, the Scion yet lives.*

"Eira!" Cato cried out, his voice reaching above those of the opposing deities. "Save him. For me, save my brother." Tears cascaded down his cheeks, freezing in their path despite the sun's heat.

Merrias's voice overtook me again. *Kill the Scion—Take his life. Do as I—*

"Eira, I will give you anything, anything... I beg you," Cato pleaded.

Follow the path of your own choosing, Firewalker, the deep voice said, a roll of thunder in my mind. I could see him then, that monolith of blue-and-white stone... the Nether Lord. There was no fight in him, no violence or aggression, just an overwhelming sense of tranquility.

"Cat," Ambrose rasped, his words barely audible. "I don't want to go... I-I am not ready t-to leave her. Does this mean that I-I—"

"Yes, you colossal idiot, you love her. Stay with me, Ambrose. Tell her yourself, for the Goddess's sake."

Firewalker.

Granddaughter!

I struck, slamming my arm into the harpoon's barbed edge. Blood and blackfire flowed from me, the harpoon's wooden shaft igniting.

Ambrose screamed—a pained and wretched cry that would haunt me until my end. The harpoon's head fell to the deck as my fire danced upon his body, cauterizing his flesh.

I poured myself into him, his skin cold where mine burned hot.

Flashes of a helmed goddess flickered in and out of my head, mingling with those of a Nether Lord sitting upon his throne of rock, his head bowed.

CHAPTER SIXTY

NO WAY

EIRA

W e sailed home.

"Hold me tighter." I traced the prominent vein that stood out along Cato's forearm, and he scooted closer, sheltering me from the storm of my own making.

Together, we held vigil over Ambrose, taking turns to tuck in the scratchy wool blankets that covered him. I'd been able to find a cast-off bit of canvas to place between them and his skin, worried the woolen fibers might work their way into his wounds and cause him more discomfort.

We'd had to secure his legs to the bed with a length of rope. In the first few hours, he'd thrashed wildly and groaned in pain, even in his semi-unconscious state. His wounds, even those I'd sealed, had reopened.

Cato and I sat on the floor near Ambrose's head. My hand lay atop his chest, feeling for any changes in his shallow breaths. Cato's arm enfolded me protectively.

"Thank you," Cato whispered, his lips moving against my neck as he spoke. "Though I do not know—and cannot presume to understand the will of the gods—I was selfish enough to ask you to spare him. Take from me anything you wish."

I shifted, pressing myself against him, seeking his nearness.

"You have already given me what I long for." I tilted my head and pressed a kiss to his chin. "But now I fear the future more than ever. Merrias told me, Cato, commanded me to let him die. To end him. And the Nether Lord... he-he gave me a choice."

"Do you think he will wake half-minotaur, then? Partial nether spawn?" Cato half-heartedly jested while running the tip of his nose along mine. "Will you still find me attractive if he does?"

The smile didn't reach my eyes, but I did my best to muster up some levity.

"Ah, wait. I do have a request of you. Do you think you can be a less jealous second husband when he wakes?"

Cato shook his head.

"I plan to be worse." A mischievous grin appeared on his lips, and he rolled his shoulders, flexing his muscles beneath my head. "I cannot pretend that allowing him to perish did not cross my mind. All it would have taken for you to be mine alone—in my bed—announced to the court as Eira, Consort of Catommandus, was to do nothing." Cato lifted my hand to his lips. "I fight it, Eira, but my want for you is without limit." He dropped our combined hands to his arousal. "Even now."

"No, sir. Don't tell me you thought of ending him and then expect me to, what? Fuck you while he lays there near dead."

"You... Do you think this man would care? That one with the bruised face and cracked ribs? This one?" Cato pointed at Ambrose while peering at me from the side of his eyes. "The one you persuaded me to conjure-fuck because it turned you to flame? The same man who finished me off while you fucked my fingers like the most brazen of courtesans. Forgive me, let us do all in our power to preserve the modesty of the prudish and comatose man."

I did laugh then, covering my mouth so as to not wake Ambrose. Cato nibbled at the wrinkly skin of my knuckles, his hair falling into his face and hiding the lusty gleam in his deep brown eyes.

"Is it so awful sharing me? I find it fairly easy to be shared..."

His teeth skimmed along the shell of my ear, eliciting a tingling sensation that spread across my chest.

"Yes. But my heart and cock will learn, eventually. If only because I know that Ambrose would protect you with his life. Because of that, I'll grudgingly allow his continued presence." He bit down gently on my earlobe, and a rush of air hissed past my lips.

"Mmhmm, yes, that's the reason. My ability to destroy a godsdamned fleet notwithstanding."

Cato sat back, furrowing his brows. He ran the backs of his fingers over my bandaged forearm.

"Sweetheart, please. Seeing you hurt is..."

I shook my head. I knew I could seek my shade form and heal... but I couldn't. I needed to embrace the pain... just as Ambrose was. Just as Cato was. He didn't say it, but the ice that had encased him left his flesh angry and raw, and a fresh scar would no doubt cut a path along his temple.

I lifted my bandage, wincing, and then traced a bloodied digit along his wound. He threaded his fingers through mine.

"There is no future for me unless you are in it. Whether I walk behind you or beside is of little importance." Cato smoothed his lips across my wrist in a featherlight caress. "Now, lament for me quietly. I am off to work the rigging." He stood and headed toward the door. "And Eira... the back room on this level... for your own safety and my sanity, please do not venture there. Allaine is in the captain's quarters, however."

The door shut, and I steeled myself for what was to come.

Allaine.

I rose, smoothed my disheveled hair, and did my best to look more presentable, tugging at the hem of my borrowed homespun shirt. A button popped, and the damn thing shot across the floor, skipping along until it found rest under Ambrose's bed.

"Fuck it all." What was once a tiny gap in the stained beige garment was now a gulf where my stomach stuck out. *Whatever.*

I shuffled on naked feet and leaned over Ambrose, feeling his forehead, and then held my fingers under his nose, assuring myself he still breathed.

"Husband, I'll be gone for no more than an hour. I'll bring back food and tell you stories of my childhood in Nortia to pass the time." He didn't wake, but the corners of his mouth sagged. I lifted his head as gently as I could and freed the few strands of hair caught under his back before fluffing his pillow. "Don't leave me. Okay?"

Guilt gnawed at my insides as I took to the stairs.

Allaine needed... well, I had no Ærtan idea what a person needed after enduring a heinous crime. To talk? To be alone? Normalcy? Was anything normal after—I swallowed hard, choking down the regret of not having seen to her safety before fleeing Monwyn

Sailors nodded but gave me a wide berth as I passed them.

I arrived, but stood as stone, staring at the door of the captain's quarters—fist poised, yet unable to move my arm. I inhaled. In and out... in and then out.

Not about you, Eira. This is not about your anger or discomfort.

I knocked softly and pressed the handle.

Despite the cushy comfort in which the room was appointed, the weight of despair in the darkened chamber felt like a noose slipping around my neck. A single taper burned atop the most ostentatious desk I'd ever laid eyes upon, black-lacquered wood, the legs carved to resemble... fornicating merpeople. *What the fuck is with sailors?*

Above the desk, on a low-hanging ceiling, a blue fish with a tusk-like protrusion stood watch, frozen in time. Rolled-up parchments and what I supposed were navigational tools—bronze implements and calipers—crowded built-in shelves and tables secured to the floor.

The door clicked behind me as I settled my back against it.

"You have destroyed me."

I gasped and threw myself to the side as a shadow bore down upon me.

"I... Steffani, my apologies. I was unaware that you were—"

"Move. I'll not share the same air as my abductor."

She shoved past me, hauling open the door and disappearing into the dark.

Gods. Of course she felt that way, but I—

"E-Eira..."

"Allaine, I'm here."

The shake in her voice. *Mossius, I beseech you, lay your healing hands upon her.* I pressed my fingertips to my forehead. What I wouldn't give to hear her gritty grumble of a laugh instead of the choking voice that accompanied too many shed tears.

"Eira, I... I ..."

"Shhh. You don't have to say anything, Allaine." I moved slowly, deliberately, making her aware of every step I took, not wishing to give her any cause for alarm as I padded over and grabbed the candelabra... that was, of course, adhered to the desk. "Not unless you want to, that is."

I plucked the single lit taper and set it to the nearest lamp before replacing it in its holder. Light filled the room, not in abundance, but enough that I would be able to inspect her for further trauma.

"Allaine, all will be well. We'll see you taken care of, sent to Verus to heal with the priestesses if needed."

Her teary, darkest-blue gaze shimmered, reflecting in the low light.

I studied her.

She leaned heavily against the wall of a receded compartment. Her long legs curled up on the small bed it contained. Dark-russet drapes hung from the sides of the little alcove, drawn back and tucked into decorative metal hooks.

Her arm, wrist, and fingers were bent as tightly as I had ever seen them. She was twisted, her shoulder pulled in toward her chest. Strain etched itself in deep but fine lines across her forehead.

"Allaine," I bleated out, running to her side. "Your arm is..."

"It is a bad day, and I cannot seem to bring it ease."

I pressed my fingers to her shoulder blade, and she flinched, shrinking back.

My heart. It pitched in my chest so intensely that for a moment I couldn't catch my breath.

"Oh, gods, Allaine, I'm so sorry—forgive me. I didn't mean to touch you without your permission."

She shook her head.

"No, Eira, it is alright—just the pain is... Can you rub it here?" she asked, her voice at once fearful and hopeful. She pointed to the joint between her neck and back.

"Of course, anything."

Drawing her shoulder backward like I'd seen her do in the past, I kneaded the heels of my palms into the hard muscles. I prayed to the Goddess to relieve her discomfort.

She sighed, and her tension lessened over the next turn of the clock, but tears still wet her lashes.

"Eira," Allaine whispered. "What are you?"

"Well, I'm a..." There was no use in lying. Half of the continent and what remained of a foreign contingent saw me for exactly what I was. "I'm a conjurer. And I know what you saw must have scared you, but I promise I'm not evil. I'm still me." Allaine laid back and rested her head against my chest. Her eyes drifted shut, and her tears flowed in earnest.

"Do you possess the ability to mend a fractured heart?"

Oh gods, I breathed away the tumultuous churn of æther in my chest.

I shook my head.

"Only time can heal such a wound, but there are steps we can take, people who can guide you through—"

"Can you convince Prince Cato to spare Greggen's life?" She choked out the last word.

I bit back the harsh retort that threatened to erupt—kept my curses to myself.

"Allaine, why would I? He—"

"Because I love him, Eira."

My stomach roiled, and I physically covered my mouth to keep quiet. These things were complex. It wasn't the first time and would probably not be the last time, a woman I knew faced hurt at the hands of a romantic partner. And I knew that the feelings of attachment could still accompany even the worst treatment. Those emotions were still very real—even when they weren't healthy. Septimus had proven this to be true.

"I hear you, Allaine, but h-he was an accomplice to the murder of Monwyn's queen, and my... my Nan. The Princes, King Aberus... they will not permit him to live."

Allaine gripped the hand that I'd placed on her arm. She tilted her head back and held my gaze.

"I *refuse* to believe that he took part in such a crime. Is that the accusation? Not some blustering Monwyn versus Baldorvan vendetta? Eira, Greggen is not capable of—"

"He is absolutely capable! At Verus, he attacked me. He hurt me, Allaine. He was accused of theft early on. He... he... Allaine, he raped you."

She bolted upright and the back of her hand lashed across my face, my head whipping to the side.

I covered my stinging cheek.

"Never speak of my husband as if he were a deviant!"

"But he is a—what did you call him?"

Allaine rocked back and forth, silent tears spilling.

"My husband." She drew in a shuddering breath. "Aberus signed our dispensation. We... we Joined the night before we left."

The æther longed to break free yet again... this time aimed at the head of the senseless fucking king of Monwyn.

"A dispensation? On what grounds did—"

"The Mantle's personal healer encouraged me to travel to Solnna. She said that a warmer climate was ideal for improving conditions like mine. Greggen immediately sought my father and received permission to take me south, but Father and Aberus would only allow it after a proper Joining took place. With the winter freeze starting, we booked passage immediately."

Bullshit.

I refused to believe any of this could be a coincidence. Greggen was a trained manipulator, a master of political intrigue—just as all Scion were.

"The blood then?" I gestured to her legs, something close to hysteria rising in my voice. She tucked them tightly under her rear. "The loss of my corona. We became one last night, Eira. And it was beautiful and what I have always dreamed it would be... until Prince Cato ripped me from my sleep. Eira, Greggen chose me... For once someone chose me, and I them."

Allaine turned her head into the pillow, trying to muffle her cries.

"But the boat... you traveled with Baldorvan marauders. How did that come to pass?"

Her face scrunched in confusion.

"They are merchants, Eira. Just a group of men trading with Solnna, just like all the other countries do. Are you not a Troth? You know well that Greggen was Assigned to Monwyn to secure peace and accord—to exchange goods and goodwill."

No. No fucking way am I believing this.

"Okay. Alright." I got to my feet, palms damp, mind reeling. "I'll make dinner. You need to eat. We all need to eat. You are safe now."

Liar.

Chapter Sixty-One

DAMMIT. GODS DAMMIT ALL.

Eira

"I don't care if you are the god of sea creature cuisine! I'm making food for my family. I will nurture them. I am their healer and will nurse them back to the picture of health—and that starts with soup!"

I stomped.

He stomped back—an open challenge.

You could chop the hostility growing between us with a cleaver.

"Sir, how dare you keep me from my sworn task to care for—"

"This hur is why 'em females is left at port!" The cook—a rail-thin man with an abundance of freckles—brandished a scoopy apparatus between us. With a hop, he sent the wooden weapon in an arc bound for my knuckles.

I snatched my hand back and stood my ground.

"Soup is what the passengers on this floating netherscape need, not another brick biscuit! Emotions run high, master chef, and soup soothes the spirit. Why, my mother would—"

"Yur ma can get hoist with the sail, I reckon!"

The cook towed his arm back as if ready to attack, but I took a page from the journal of Vonnie Chulainn. I crossed my arms, cocked my hip, and tapped my foot in a rhythm that said, "You can damn well try."

"Go on, whop me, motherfucker—I'll put you through the gods-damned wall." I braced for the hit.

"Gahhh! I'm not scurred of no uppity witch." He brought his weapon down on a chopping board with a resounding slap, snapping the head clear off the implement. He turned a shade so violently red that I couldn't distinguish his skin from the receding hairline of his copper curls.

"Perhaps you should be..."

I raised my arm and let the æther roll.

With an aggressive clench of my fist, the board snapped in two.

We stared each other down, his squinty eye ticking, my brows reaching a height I didn't think possible.

"Soup it be, then? Ya wanna make a soup?" His spine-chilling, six-toothed smile nearly undid me, but I held firm, puffing out my chest and letting my aggression show through my face.

"Was I not clear earlier? I. Require. Soup."

The cook threw back his head and let out a scream—or perhaps a laugh—whichever it was... the high-pitched, goat-like bleat disturbed me to my core.

Oh, fuck.

He lunged forward, shaky lips sneering, eyeball squinting, breath foul and in my face.

"Make yurself a mighty fine pot 'en. And serve it on a fine dish ah gold!"

"Goodness, yes. That would raise His Highness's spirits infinitely," I said earnestly, glancing around the tiny galley kitchen, wondering what other small touches might make him feel more at home. "Would you be willing to fetch the dishes?"

The cook's eyes bulged.

Another demonic scream-bleat pierced my ears.

"To the nether with ya, bare-bellied bilge rat!" He ripped at the ties of his grubby apron, wadded it up, and shoved it into my hands as he shoved by. "Scabby sea bass of a flying shadow shrew!"

"Am I to assume there are no gold dish—"

The door slammed in my face, his maniacal scream-laugh following him down the hall.

"Well then." I held the stained fabric between pinched fingers and tossed it into the nearest sink. "This can't be nearly as difficult as a Verus Maneuvering or learning to conjure correctly. Would you not agree, noble carrot?"

I inspected the brilliant-red vegetable, admiring its smooth and shiny skin—how amazing that such bounty could be extracted from the ground.

"My mother said that soup is the simple conglomeration of kitchen scraps. You, too, will be added to the bubbling infusion." I speared my crudité companion with a pronged thingamabob and popped it into a bowl.

"It all starts with boiling water." I located a large, round-bellied pot and placed it atop an already piping-hot stove.

"Now we chop." I rolled up my sleeves and went to work, giving up quickly on making precise cuts. Six of the gorgeous carrots, their abundant seeds removed, potatoes, unpeeled to preserve their nutrients, and grapes, for color, would make a delicious fare. Savory and sweet combinations were delightful on the palate.

Lemons were on hand as well, their rinds yellow and fragrant. I knew the flavor would brighten the broth, so I roughly cut six of them, good ones, the size of my fist, and added them to the thickening stew. I broke a dozen eggs into the mix, remembering that Ambrose liked them as a part of his regimen, and then stirred in a jar full of a flaky spice that smelled light and peppery.

An hour later, I added in three or four fish heads and the bones from a large bin, and finally doled out my labor of love. The kitchen smelled wonderful, and my pained heart was full once more.

Armed with my tray of bowls and cups, I knocked on the door to the captain's quarters, my call having gone unanswered. Was I being a coward by not just walking in? Maybe. Probably. Yes. Yes, I was. But I pushed it behind me on account of my concern for Ambrose. It had been well over the time I promised him. I left Allaine's and Steffani's bowls by the door.

I carefully made my way down the steps and into the ship's hull, balancing my homemade meal, now understanding why my Momma broke down once after dropping a small bin of salt into her bean soup. If I tripped and spilled what took me so long to make, shit, I'd go shadow form, dive into the ocean, and flame fry us a succulent fillet... and also sob. I'd never taken care of my family in this way, and it felt so very important.

The door was ajar, and I popped it wide with my rear.

Cato sat against the wall nearest Ambrose, his head back and eyes shut.

I studied him in the quiet moment—drank in the Goddess's gift. His cheeks were windburned, his shirt rumpled, and yet, butterflies took flight in my stomach. He cracked a single eye, and the sweetest smile tipped the corner of his lips. The fine lines around his eyes turned pale in his reddened flesh.

"Why, Mama, you've made victuals for the little ladies and me?" He stretched his arms and yawned. "I am famished."

I sashayed into the room feeling at once accomplished, but also incredibly shy.

"Here you are, Papa, eat up while I feed the toddler." I handed Cato a wooden bowl. "He's a picky little shit and only eats jerky these days. Also, I only found one spoon..."

"No matter." Cato drank deeply from the bowl's rim.

He sighed contentedly.

Sitting the tray on the bolted-down table, I made my way to my husband's side, tucking in close enough for my hip to touch his thigh.

"Black Bear," I whispered, not wishing to jar him from deep slumber. "Husband?" A hand on his forehead revealed no fever. He was cool to the touch, and his skin was dry. Praise the Goddess.

Cato came to my side and kneeled, placing his empty bowl on the floor. He tenderly squeezed Ambrose's shoulder.

Green eyes gradually opened; their whites tinted red.

"Hello, handsome." I brushed Ambrose's hair back, and he blinked awake. "A few bites if you can? Soup is the Nortian cure-all," I said in a tone as chipper as I could muster. "We'll have you as fluffy as a flurry in no time at all."

How many times would I nurse my men until one of them didn't return to me?

Ambrose turned his head to the wall.

"Where will you be if you skimp on your regimen, *Black Bear*?" Cato teased as he positioned himself at the head of the bed and slid his arms under Ambrose, lifting him into a semi-sitting position. Ambrose reclined against Cato's chest, and Cato gently folded down the blanket that covered his heavily bandaged torso. "Flabby and irregular. That's where."

I blew on the steaming soup before bringing a spoonful to his lips. He remained as stone, staring straight ahead.

"I know you're in pain." It was clear as ice in his glassy-eyed stupor—the quiver of his hands as he attempted to shift on his own. "If I could take it from you... I would bear it upon my own body."

Do not cry, Eira. Do not.

My men had always taken care of me, and seen to my every need. They'd fed me, nursed me through illness, and tried so hard to keep life's cruelty at bay. I longed to do the same for them, and even more importantly, I'd promised Imella that I'd care for them both.

"Please, Amby-bear, for me?"

He slowly parted his mouth but could barely manage a sliver—his jaw was so stiff and swollen. He was frail, and it scared me. I pressed the spoon to his lips, careful not to spill the steaming fare. He slurped it dutifully, and just that small bit of regularity made the tension sink from my shoulders.

"Goddess almighty." Ambrose's head pitched forward, and the orange broth trickled from the side of his mouth. "String the cook up by his toes." He coughed out. "It's—*gag*—positively inedible, and it sears the tongue like liquid flame. I will gut the man myself for serving something so—"

My lips trembled. My heartfelt attempt at domesticity shattered.

"I... I made it."

Ambrose's stitched mouth fell open in a little imperfect *O*.

"C-Cato, was it... bad?" I glanced up, fighting back tears.

Rough knuckles brushed the edge of my jaw.

"Horrendous, love."

My eyes welled.

"B-But Cato, you ate all of it." I wanted to hide my face, conceal the flush of embarrassment that crept across the bridge of my nose, but my hands were full of my failure.

"And soon, I am afraid... it will reappear." He dipped his head low.

I tipped the bowl to my mouth and drank deeply. It couldn't be that—

"Holy fuck." It was tart. Both sour and bitter in the same mouthful and also fishy but not in a good way. The caustic liquid fumed its way into my nose, scorching the sensitive passages, making my eyes and nose weep profusely. "It's a food inferno." I stuck my tongue out, fearful it would actually begin to burn away.

Cato took the bowl, pulled his shirttails from his waistband, and blotted at my dripping eyes.

"Blow, love, it will help."

"I'm not—Cato, I am not a child of two, I will not—"

"Blow," he demanded, pinching the linen over my nose and still managing to hold Ambrose with one arm.

I pushed him away, but he held firm.

"He has tongued your bottom, wife. Boogs are meaningless in the grand scheme." Ambrose patted my hip, sort of. He tapped at my thigh with bent fingertips. The sympathetic look on his face blurred through my tears.

Even through one's pain and the other polishing off a bowl of horrendous slop, their thoughts were to comfort me.

"I give up," I cried. "I g-give up." I blew, firing mucus and what remained of my pride into Cato's hand. "Steffani will think I'm trying to kill her, and Allaine will, too. *Ohmygods*, her heart. Her poor, poor heart." Comforting arms closed around me and rocked me back and forth while Ambrose, gods bless him, made his incoherent sounds of support, tapping my hip. Cato kissed a small path up the column of my neck.

"It is unfortunate that Steffani will never Join with her late man," he said lowly, "but she can make a life in Monwyn and find love ag—"

"Not Steffani," I wailed into his chest. "Allaine, and stupid fucking misogynistic Aberus."

"Allaine and Aberus?" Ambrose gasped and clutched his side. "Their children would bruise the laps of their nannies. Gods, can you even imagine the gorgeous giants?"

"No! Greggen and Allaine. They are man and wife. Aberus mandated a dispensation."

Cato stiffened.

Ambrose leaned back, using the wall to guide himself down until he lay flat on the bed. A new spot of bright red bloomed on his bandages.

"Ambrose, you careless beluga. You've busted a stitch."

Cato's stomach groaned, gurgling so loud that all three of us paused.

"I am alive and mending, Eira—brother, are you well?"

"I require a toilet. Immediately." Cato leapt to his feet, clutching his middle. He tore from the room, leaving the door wide in his retreat.

I cried harder.

"Wife, go to him, please."

I tucked Ambrose's blankets near his chin.

"No, no, you are—"

"Desperately in need of quiet."

Ambrose closed his eyes.

"Oh... yes. Of-of course."

I wept my way to the door and climbed the stairs.

The evening wind tossed my hair into my eyes. I attempted braiding it close to my head as I walked downwind along the ship's side, but realized quickly it was a lost cause. I shuffled around a grouping of wooden bins and ducked under a low-hanging rope.

Unlike some ships, the Merlann's facilities boasted a half-wall to give the user *some* privacy. They even decorated the barrier with little swags of amber beads and chunks of coral.

Ahead, I saw Cato's hairy rear poked out from the privacy wall, giving the seaman something to whistle at before he turned and flopped down, no doubt releasing his bowels in an explosive rush. Lord Gammond, have mercy. There was nothing like a bodily function to test the parameters of a partnership.

I stopped at the wall and cleared my throat.

"Can I get you anything?"

The wind howled in my ears.

"Do... know... Zu... make... gods..."

"Cato, I can't hear you." It was impossible to make out his words, but despite the inconvenience, the privy's placement and the high gale did wonders to waft away the unfortunate smells that might have stuck around otherwise.

"Come around... I care not... me... rope."

"There are some things that should remain a mystery between us, Cato."

"Eira!" he yelled. "I cannot reach the rope."

Oh, boy.

I peeked around the wall. Cato was knees up and struggling to capture the wipe that had rolled a few inches out of his reach. I chased the line, retrieving what was nothing more than the frayed end of an old linen rope and handed it over, holding my breath. Cato, not quite finished, indicated I should sit beside him.

Gross.

I shook my head and sat cross-legged in front of him instead.

"Why did you eat it, Cato?" I couldn't quite make eye contact with him while he tensed. "If it was so bad, why didn't you just say so?"

"L-love," he grunted.

Love.

Of course, love.

Cato frowned, gripped by another stomach cramp.

"Eira, I think we should hold off on revealing Zuddaz's identity. Just until Ambrose's wounds stop reopening." He paused, contorting his face, and then continued. "I am concerned, and assuming the Mantle, his actual kin, is in residence at the palace, I feel it best if the conversation took place with all involved parties. Thoughts?"

"I think it wise, and yes, according to Allaine, They've arrived." I shifted on the rough wood. "Do you think the Mantle is aware They have a sibling? A twin, even."

"Not sure." Cato puffed his cheeks out and pressed his mouth. A muffled toot emitted from below. "Eira, what the fuck was in the soup?"

"This and that." I reached out and fiddled with the buckle on his boot. "Are you nearly done?"

He nodded, cleaned up, and then chucked the wipe back into its hole—the rope it attached to uncoiled and pulled taut as the ocean pulled it under to be cleaned.

In silence, we walked toward the scuttlebutt, my eyes catching on a familiar glint. I scooped up the pearl barrette I must have dropped before turning to shade. Cato lifted a questioning brow, and I raised mine in return—was it silly of me to want a memento from his odious uncle? We washed our hands with the scuttle's fresh water, the scentless lye soap drying my skin.

Above us, the stars glittered brightly in the night sky, and as we walked hand in hand to the back of the ship, the pink haze of heat lightning flashed in the distance.

The ocean was black tonight, but I knew that below, another world existed. Another realm entirely, of a people who came to my aid when called. Cato rested his chest on my back and pressed his cheek to mine. We breathed in synch, gazing out at a rippling blanket highlighted by the moon's glow.

"Did you command the wraiths?"

I pondered my answer, letting myself relive the moment, tightening my hand around Merrias's gift.

"Maybe? But I don't think so. I felt a close tie with them, if that makes sense, but— ouch!" I opened my palm, noting a bit of shimmering green and red peeking from between my fingers.

What the?

I flattened my hand and raised it to catch the moon's light.

"Cato." I spun in his arms, the æther winding tightly in my chest. "Creator, guide us."

"What is it, Eira?"

"Were the ships I sank—were they *all* Baldorvan? We know for sure that those we fought were the slavers, correct?"

"Yes. As far as I could tell." Cato hesitated. "The one the wraiths brought low bore their banners—gray and ochre, a portcullis at its center."

"Septimus." I opened my palm and held up the hair bauble. "He kept the barrette Merrias gave me, but look... look at this, Cato." He inspected the trinket. "There was a fighter he brought low, h-he thrust his dagger into her mouth, to silence her, sever her tongue. Before she died, she'd said 'he demands her return.' I assumed the "he" was in reference to Leyometh or a Baldorvan warlord but..." Cato plucked an ivory-colored cube from amid the pearls. He held it between us.

"Malachite," he hissed, shaking his head in disbelief. The intact roots of the gold-and-green-capped tooth were tangled in the thin chain that linked the pearls. "The fucking Primus-King was ahead of us yet again. They were his people." Cato pocketed the molar, bent at the waist, and laid his forehead on the railing. "Dammit. Gods damn it all. This would explain why they slaughtered the civilians rather than gathering them to be sold."

"Show me the daughters of Gaea," I whispered to the waves. "The fighter... her eyes were the same color as mine."

Chapter Sixty-Two

THE ONLY THING THAT MATTERS

The Kingdom of Monwyn: Eira

Ambrose was pale. His flesh bordering on translucent. The hollows of his eyes were a mottled purple-gray and gaunter than they had been two days ago. He rarely spoke, barely ate, and when the guards carried him to our apartments on a healer's board, he no longer sought the comfort of my chest.

Allaine, Steffani, and three Monwyn soldiers had ridden in a carriage behind ours. Cato had ridden ahead of us, having left two highwaymen dead in his wake. Goddess Maressa blessed us as we traversed her forests. I'd dreamed of her between fitful bouts of slumber. Golden spirals hung to her back, her eyes shrewd as the hawk's that perched upon her leather-covered forearm. She'd assured us safe passage, and for that, I would be eternally in her debt.

I'd nearly come undone when Ambrose lost consciousness right outside of the palace gates.

"Will you stay with him, Eira?" Cato asked as we charged through our apartment doors and into Ambrose's bedchamber. His unmasked worry sent my anxiety soaring beyond what I thought were its previous limits.

"I won't leave his side." Cato nodded, pulled me into his arms and kissed my lips, in full view of the crowd rushing in behind us. "But why isn't he responding to my blood? Why isn't he better already?"

Three women dressed in robes of shifting red-and-gold silk entered on the heels of Bem, who looked... exceptionally well-groomed. His normally stringy and greasy hair was freshly combed, pulled back smooth over his balding pate, and his clothing... it matched. Cato focused on his personal attendant, inspecting him with a curious tilt of his chin.

"The Mantle sent these folks tah y'all." Bem stepped aside.

I froze, using all of my strength to hold my æther in check.

"Do. Not. Touch. Him." I didn't recognize the voice that boomed from my mouth. "No, Gaean, healer or not, will lay their hands on him." I shook with rage, staring at the very same healer who'd pierced my breast at Verus during the Grooming.

"Eira, love, I think we can trust—"

I threw my hand up, silencing Cato.

"I saw the mark upon her at the Grooming. She's Cult Mossius trained, she admitted such herself. You may wear the scarlet vestments of a Verus priestess, but I have seen the double flame scarred onto your back—you have sworn fealty to the Primus-King."

The woman, whose name I never bothered learning while she stuck a needle through my nipple, turned her eyes to the bed, where my husband lay unmoving.

"How astute of you. Solid memory you've got," she said blandly. The healer walked forward, and my chest swelled tight, as if gathering the æther to my core was second nature. "A woman as intelligent as yourself will also recognize then, that your husband is soon to lose his life."

"I will remove your head from your neck if you so much as—" Cato caught my shoulder as I raised my arm, ready to defend Ambrose to the end.

"Troth Eira, Lady Verus… Blessed Child… remember that words uttered, even under immense strain, still hold weight."

As if by divine manipulation, the atmosphere transformed. My anger turned to anguish; my battered soul clung to the words of the serene voice that had guided me toward the path of my own choosing. "Never, Goddess-Born, would I endanger the life of My Scion."

I broke, collapsing to the floor at Their feet.

"That is a lie, Mantle… The Obligate's path is naught but hazard." I folded in on myself and hung my head.

They lowered Themselves and took me into Their peaceful embrace. Layers of tissue-fine, muted-gold silk and an overdress of ruby charmeuse fell in ripples around us. I glanced up and searched Their grass-green eyes—the exact shape as my husband's—and saw in them a reflection of genuine concern.

"May I?" They gestured to the bedside.

"O-of course." We stood and, arm-in-arm, made our way to Ambrose.

Cato kneeled at Ambrose's side, hands to his forehead.

The Mantle lowered Themself, sitting upon the bed's edge, the embodiment of grace and composure. They encouraged me to sit and offered me Their hand when I did, Their cool skin a marked contrast to the unnatural warmth of my own.

"Holiness, if I can't lay my hands on the man, he dies. Already his soul departs." The Gaean paced at the end of the bed, assessing Ambrose. If the daggers that shot from my eyes could kill, she would be nothing but a heap of flesh on the floor. "Troth, use your intelligence. Open your eyes. The tint around his lips, the darkening of his fingertips. I'm not sure which of these men you want to warm your bed," she blinked toward Cato, "but it won't be your husband if you don't let me near."

"Eira," Cato whispered, rising to his feet. "Come with me and allow the healer to—"

"I will not leave him. Not with you, not on the arm of the Goddess herself."

The hurt on Cato's face pinned my heart to the inside of my ribs.

"You should not remain here to see—"

"Don't you dare give up on him." I clasped Cato's forearms. "Don't you—"

"His Royal Majesty, King Aberus of Monwyn does enter!" A herald cried from the common room.

Aberus stormed through the door seconds later, his expression indiscernible under his thick beard and heavily drawn brows.

"Why are the healers not aiding him? Time is of the essence and—you." Aberus glared at me. "If the past tells me anything, you are the reason he lies here. Catommandus, tell me I am wrong?"

A bevy of servants cowered behind the king, too afraid to enter.

Cato attempted to tuck me behind his back, but I waved him away. If his brother needed to bristle and bark to feel useful, so be it. My attention was firmly on Ambrose.

"Aberus," Cato said, his tone lethal, "Did you not learn from our last encounter that she comes first? To me *and* to Ambrose."

"Troth, heed my words. You will contain your witching ways," Aberus pointed a meaty finger at my face, "or I will have you forcibly removed and see your head struck from—"

"Majesty. You will not threaten My Troth in My presence or otherwise," The Mantle said, Their declaration forceful but spoken in a soft manner.

Aberus's mouth closed. Without the bluster to hide them, the gray splotches of fatigue below his eyes were plain to see.

"Pardon me, Your Holiness." The king took a knee before the Mantle and bowed his head. "I am fearful for my brother."

I understood Aberus's anger, even if it was misplaced. The fault lay firmly in the hands of the Primus-King.

The Mantle laid Their palm upon Aberus's shoulder and then waved Their healer forward. "Sister Phaina is My own healer and heads the infirmary at Verus. We will allow her to assess My Scion."

At Their word, the Gaean acted fast, pulling the covers back, exposing Ambrose's ripped and raw flesh. She dug around in her satchel and withdrew several items, laying them in a row.

Many a servant covered their nose and backed out to the common room.

My stomach churned. The putrid scent of necrosis and something even more sinister, something I couldn't identify—sharp and metallic—permeated the chamber.

No scabbing or knitting had occurred. His wound was as jagged as when the harpoon entered his body, and his stitches had pulled through, making the separated edges of his skin appear almost serrated. His stomach was a mutilated cavern of torn muscles and flesh.

Sister Phaina struggled to crawl across the wide bed in her robes but didn't let the tangle stop her. When she reached Ambrose's side, she removed her hood, unclasped the single-point closure around her neck, and shrugged out of the garment, revealing bare and heavily pockmarked arms.

She pressed a palm to Ambrose's stomach and bowed her head while prodding and lifting bits of his flesh with a long pair of tweezers. After capturing the tail of a suture, she pulled the long string free. Sticky pieces of skin clung to what should have held his wound together, but his injury splayed wide, as if the harpoon had just entered his body. The healer brought the fiber close to her face and wafted it under her nose.

"His flesh dies. Call Cyra."

"No, gods, no... please do something. I beg you." I turned to the Mantle, eyes pleading, seeking divine intervention. "Pray to Merrias, implore Lord Mossius to intervene. Mantle, please."

Instead of interceding, They enveloped me in Their arms, my head to Their chest. Incoherent words of comfort whispered in my ear. Their touch was—

Can you hear me, Troth Eira?

My body tensed, but a gentle hand stroked the back of my head.

Yes, I responded, pushing into Their mind.

Give me your trust, child.

"Inform Cyra her presence is required. All but immediate family should exit the chamber," Their Holiness said to the room.

Obeying, guards and servants alike rushed away, some patting damp cheeks, others shaking their knowing heads.

Cyra Fabia—royal dresser, fashion guru, and, according to Zuddaz, adept conjurer—entered the room. Just as haughty as I remembered her to be, she arrived, gliding into the chamber as if she floated on a cloud. She was perfection—Ideal figure, hair immaculate, bronze mica set into the kohl around her eyes.

"The wound was dealt by conjuration," the healer said dryly as she palpated a bluish vein on Ambrose's abdomen.

Cyra nodded, her face serious. As she removed a citron necklace from around her long throat, orange and yellow beads glowed in the lamplight. The expensive jewels dropped from her hands to the rug. Her sleek topaz gown quickly followed.

I gazed upon her naked figure, just as flawless as the rest of her, despite her age. Though I would put her in her sixth decade based upon the mature planes of her face and the sunspots on her hands, her skin was as taut and breasts as firm as a woman in her second decade.

Cyra lifted a foot and mounted the bed, stood over Ambrose, and then descended, laying her body flush against his.

I wanted her dead—how jealously even managed to rear its head at a moment like this was a moral failing, but there it was, spiky and hot.

She's a conjurer, Eira. She studies æther-inflicted injuries at temple Verus. Have faith, daughter.

I hugged the Mantle closer.

Zuddaz. He must have passed the ability to his child.

Mantle, are you aware? Do you know who Ambrose is? His parentage?

Of course, there was no response. Zuddaz himself had explained that popping into each other's heads was a short-lived ability—by the length of our conversation alone, I surmised the Mantle must wield an astronomical amount of power.

"Cyra?" the Gaean healer asked. "What do you see?"

Cyra ran her fingers along Ambrose's sides, smearing blood and gore onto the sheets. She took short, shallow breaths, drawing his scent into her lungs.

She dropped her ear to his heart and stilled.

"He is touched."

"Fatal?" asked Sister Phaina.

The room spun; my vision seesawed. Cato's palm found my back, and another came to lie beside it, bolstering me. Its size told me it was Aberus.

"Perhaps not."

"Praise the Creator," the king said behind me.

"Perhaps so," Cyra murmured, moving her hands once again, this time resting blood-slick fingers on Ambrose's eyelids.

"Enough of the flighty fae speak, Cyra. Can you do that thing or not?"

"I will try, Sister Phaina, but he will suffer. One attempts to take him, the other end him."

"Who attempts to—" Aberus shouted.

"Hush, brother," said Cato, his fingers curving around my waist. "Mantle, with all due respect, I require my wife."

The Mantle's arms fell away, and Cato gathered me close, burying his head into the crook of my neck before easing his hold.

"Ambrose is no stranger to suffering. Do what you must and do it quickly." Cato reached for Ambrose's hand and then threaded my fingers through his brother's long digits... before wrapping his own fingers around both of ours.

Cyra blinked her long-lashed eyes at the Mantle, who inclined Their head.

"Secure him."

Aberus moved fast, taking up position at the foot of the bed and holding Ambrose's ankles. He bowed his head and then, under his breath, began to pray. "Lord Mossius... hear me. Thy divinity knows no b-bounds. Your healing touch is infinite, let brother Ambrose's name be a whisper in your mouth. Son of She Who Bore Us All, your presence alleviates all fear as their time draws near. I ask that their suffering be brief."

A prayer for the dying.

Cyra sat up, straddling Ambrose's legs. She didn't wipe off the dying flesh that clung to her stomach, nor did she wrinkle her nose when a pocket of infection opened and oozed down her leg.

The change in pressure made Ambrose's wound spill over. Thickened blood, the color of dark cherries, dripped down his side and into the bed. "Phaina, sit on his legs. Hold them tight."

With no further instructions, Cyra leaned over Ambrose's face, lifted the inky crescent of his lashes, and peered into the whites of his eyes.

"Start Cyra. He's fading," Phaina said. "Fading fast."

With no warning given, Cyra struck, and my body jerked in response.

She stabbed her finger into the soft notch of Ambrose's throat, pressing her pointed nail forward until blood welled around the tip of her finger.

"Holy Godd—"

Cato yanked me back, holding me in place with one hand.

"Hold steady, love. I have you. I will always have you."

Cyra twisted and cupped her hand as Zuddaz had taught me to do when releasing my æther. She exhaled slowly, and the veins in her face darkened, followed by those of her neck and breasts, the discoloration streaking across her body like lightning crackling across the sky. Her hands tremored.

"But Cato, she's, my gods, she's—"

Ambrose's terror-filled eyes flashed open, rolling about as if he were witnessing some unfathomable horror.

Cyra cried out. Her body shook as if in seizure, but her gaze remained focused.

"Black Bear, I'm here." I squeezed his hand, lent him my strength. Of their own accord, tendrils of shadows coiled themselves around our clasped hands. "Do you remember the first time we touched? You scared me senseless, and I almost careened over Verus's balcony. I never told you... I was so rattled by my attraction to you that I lied to Kairus and told her I was flustered because I... I couldn't find a toilet. And then, when you kissed me, all covered in dirt after the First Maneuvering—gods, Ambrose—I thought my heart would burst from my chest. It still does, every time. Stay with us."

Ambrose screamed—a grating sound that scratched out from his parched throat.

Cyra's face slackened, her mouth falling open and her pupils disappearing behind her lids. The lines of darkness continued down her stomach, appearing on her wrists and hands—her skin paled.

Even with two women planted atop him, Ambrose's back bowed. His heels dug into the mattress, and Aberus patted his soles like he was trying to comfort a colicky babe.

The Gaean healer leaned back and searched for a pulse in Ambrose's ankle. She looked to the Mantle and shook her head.

I pulled away from Cato, crawled to Ambrose, and pressed my forehead to his shoulder.

"Ambrose, listen to me. Listen, please. If you are not here, we can't travel to Solnna and make babies. We cannot wade into the surf while you kiss my fat belly, and you will miss the opportunity to place your littles into their grandfather's arms. We have plans, my heart, and they can't take place unless you are here."

My tears tracked through the film of blood on his shoulder, clearing a path down his arm.

Ambrose trembled. He tried to turn his head, his movements jerky and painful. Convulsions struck him, and gray-tinted saliva wept from the corners of his mouth.

"No more," Aberus hollered. "Do not hurt him with your words as you have with your actions."

Where I touched his fevered skin, my shadows flowed, caressing him as my fingers begged to do once more.

"You have a father, Ambrose, a-and a sibling. We were going to tell you right before the world fell around us. It's Zuddaz, Ambrose. He isn't aware either." A soft gasp came from behind me, the Mantle's intake of air. "And Soolie, the Monwyn Troth. Ambrose, she was your mother. She and Zuddaz loved each other, and Ambrose, your sibling is-is…"

"Ræyel." There were quick movements in the room, a flash of ruby and gold in my periphery. The Mantle appeared on Ambrose's other side, Their face nearing mine. "My name is Ræyel. And I have never known a family."

Ambrose quaked as Cato slipped in beside me.

"Remain, brother. Do not play at being selfless for the first time in your life." A tear escaped those dark-brown eyes, winding down the slight bump at the bridge of his nose. "We have a woman to fight over. A family to have. Ambrose, do not give yourself over. Do. Not."

Cyra shrieked—two tones exiting her throat, not one. She shouted in a deafening crescendo.

Cato threw his body over mine, tucking me into the safety of his side, preparing for what was to come.

And then silence fell.

There were no loud blasts or explosions. Fairies didn't fly from Ambrose's mouth, and no centaurs burst through the balcony.

Cyra lay slumped over Ambrose's arm, looking like she'd aged a decade.

"She'll be out for some time yet," Healer Phaina said, like what had just transpired was a common occurrence. She moved off the bed and retrieved her bag.

We found our bearings as two guards bore Cyra away. Aberus righted himself after having dove to the floor, and the Mantle sat as calmly as They always did, Ambrose's hand held between Their palms.

Ambrose's lashes flickered. Though dull from exhaustion, his eyes no longer appeared distant.

"Husband, Ambrose." I kissed his forehead and then watched as the flesh of a minor wound at the base of his neck knitted, going white and then healthy pink. "When you feel better, I will give you whatever you want—kisses, fairy cunts, head scratches." He turned his head, dislodging me. I skimmed my knuckle along the scar forming on his cheek. "Black Bear, you will heal, and I will—"

"Take someone else from me?"

I reeled back, the sting of his words striking me like a slap to the face.

"Ambrose, we have no reason to believe Zuddaz is dead." I tried to calm the anxiety that gnawed at my insides but failed. "He was—is—capable of handling himself. You saw that."

Ambrose closed his eyes.

"Troth, I need to lance the major wound and see to several other punctures. It will take some time, and I need you to exit." The Gaean healer scratched notes into a green leather journal as she cataloged his lacerations and injuries.

"All of you, get out," Ambrose hissed between clenched teeth.

I placed my hand on his chest, and he shuddered as if my touch sickened him.

"I will remain with the Scion," the Mantle said, taking Ambrose's hand. "My brother."

The Gaean healer crossed her arms over her chest and huffed.

Cato caught my jaw and turned my face to his.

"He lives. That is what matters."

Chapter Sixty-Three

I BETCHA FUCK

Eira

We sat in the solarium, the bright light of a winter sky bending rainbows around the vibrant room—a betrayal of the depression that clawed at my insides. There was no merriment found within the walls of Cordillaria. Not a single smile. No well wishes or utterances of relief.

Like an angry buffalo perched upon a frilly settee, Aberus appeared entirely out of place in the femininely appointed room. After taking a single look at the chair offerings as he arrived, he'd sent a team of servants to fetch a small couch from storage.

The Mantle, poise incarnate, donned a ceremonial veil for the morose gathering—light-gold chiffon embroidered with pink rosettes. It covered Them to Their knees but was so sheer it didn't obscure Their face. Behind Them, Sister Phaina, an exhausted Cyra Fabia, and the Monwyn Devotee—with severely arched brows and a salt and pepper braid—stood watch. The Mantle, as was right and proper, traveled with an entire contingent of guards and advisors from Verus.

Though we sat in separate chairs, Cato's hand rested on my upper thigh, and from the wide-eyed stares and sputters of the servants as they brought in refreshments, I'd figured the scandal would start... yesterday. Like a flash freeze, word of my infidelity would spread around Cordillaria like ice across the surface of the Penumbrean sea.

With a flick of his royal fingers, Aberus cleared the room, and Bem, again looking very dapper, sealed the doors and then scouted around the chamber's perimeter, inspecting every surface and corner. When satisfied with our level of privacy, he dragged a chair to the circle of silence and sat, legs splayed and arms crossed.

"Catommandus, debrief," Aberus commanded.

Cato nodded curtly and launched into a full yet incredibly succinct retelling of our time in Solnna, ending at the moment we rode through the palace gates.

"And Uncle Septimus? What has befallen our relation?"

"Dealt with." Cato's words rang with an unmistakable note of finality, echoing through the room's vaulted ceiling.

Aberus lowered his head and covered his eyes with his fingertips.

Butterflies skittered in my stomach, eliciting a queasy, sick feeling. I'd seen Septimus leave with my own eyes... Between boarding and Greggen's capture, there couldn't have been enough time for Cato to locate and dispatch him.

"Your report is sound, Prince Catommandus, but Greggen is a Scion, and because of his status, he is granted the protection of Verus. My Protection. What proof do you have of his misdeeds, Troth Solnna?"

In unison, all heads swiveled toward the Mantle, but it was my gaze that They held.

I bowed my head respectfully.

"Your Holiness, Lord Gotwig—"

"Has been in Solnna since he escorted Scion Evandr south," said Devotee Monwyn. His glower was so well practiced that he could have been *another* lost relation of the royal family. But I'd not be intimidated by his overpowering presence. I felt the truth to my core.

"That is correct, but you are aware of his capabilities, of who he is, and the intelligence he possesses. He concluded that the height at which the women were suspended necessitated—"

"Greggen's stature is your evidence? Not credible. Many a Monwyn stands nearly to his height. Why, Scion Ambrose is one such—"

Æther flooded my limbs.

"Don't allow his name to pass your lips again, with even a veiled accusation." My expression matched that of the judgmental Devotee. I met him scowl for scowl. "And since we are making accusations, please try your hand at explaining Greggen's appearance in Solnna. I don't believe for a second that the slaver piece-of-shit was ushering Allaine to a more hospitable environment." Cato applied pressure to my leg, just enough to remind me he was there. "You all know as well as I do that Gotwig never speaks unless he's sure."

"I can assure you, Troth Eira, that my advice to Lady Allaine and her husband is sound. The warmer clime does indeed relieve some pains and many with her condition have felt its benefits," Healer Phaina said in her flat affect.

What the nether was wrong with these people? It was like they desired Greggen's innocence. Finished with my tirade but still agitated, I shot from my seat.

Aberus pulled a dagger from his boot faster than I could blink, and Cato hauled me backward.

"For fuck's sake—you odious lot of men." I slapped Cato's hands away, but he twisted me around and dropped me into the chair behind him. "I want a sandwich. I've not eaten in a day… and the servants placed food near the dicks a-and whatever Your Holiness has dangling between your, um… oh, gods. I'm so sorry. Pass me a godsdamned plate."

Aberus sheathed his blade, and Cato procured a platter and set it in my lap. He pointed to a triangle with pink filling and then gave his attention to the assembled group.

"If you require a confession. I will get a confession."

I popped the snack into my mouth and remembered again why Cato was made for me—smoked salmon, creamy, cheesy yumminess and a hint of lemon and pickled caper. It was a combination of home and the Solnnan fare I loved.

"Your methodology for rendering a confession?" the Mantle inquired, Their fine brow arching high.

Pretty sure you don't wanna know.

I tapped Cato on the rear with a celery stalk and, when he acknowledged me, placed a sandwich into his mouth. He pecked his lips against the tip of my nose in thanks.

Aberus turned to the Mantle, nodding. "Prince Catommandus is uniquely charismatic. Why, he once convinced the Monwyn council into making him Protectc—"

"Torture," said Cato nonchalantly, as he took up the space behind the back of my chair.

Sister Phaina looked disgusted—Devotee Monwyn… like he wanted to join in on the "fun."

I was… prepared to overlook my man's flaws. I was aware of Cato's darker history, but until this point, only knew him to employ violence in pursuit of rescuing an aggrieved party. Torture was… calculated cruelty. I watched Cyra Fabia taking notes behind the Mantle's head, her expression one of blatant judgment, lips drawn in a thin line, brows arched.

Aberus cleared his throat.

"And you! Why in the gods's name did you sign off on a special dispensation allowing that frozen fox turd to get his hands on Allaine?" I jabbed the celery in Aberus's direction. "She'd known him for, like, a week."

"How long after introductions were you fucking my brother—pardon me, brothers?"

My mouth flopped open. *Touché.*

"I would have fucked them sooner, but this one"—I speared Cato's thigh with my celery sword— "was all like 'we can't because I'm the Protector, and like, I need a connection, blah, blah, blah' and the other, well, we tried very hard but got interrupted."

Should I have feared the darkening face of the king of Monwyn? Probably, but right now, even his gorgeous head of hair was pissing me off.

Cyra continued her furious scribbling, no doubt detailing every crass word that fell from my lips for the records room at Verus.

"At least for Allaine and Scion Greggen, love and honesty factored into their union," Aberus chided.

Cato's arms snapped around me in a vise as I bolted upright. Vegetables scattered.

The æther swarmed in my chest like an aggrieved hive of bees.

"Yes, that's right," I growled out, stretching my neck toward the mammoth king. "And now, because of the archaic laws you uphold, she has no recourse to dissolve her marriage to a murderer. He violated your mother, Aberus."

Cato forced me back into my seat. He kept his hands on my shoulders.

"Consort, you go too far. Our laws are in place to protect the weaker—"

"Too far? You want too far? How will this factor into your brilliant book of laws... Cato, Ambrose, me, we're *all* fucking now... Dicks in asses, mouths on cocks, vaginas dropping down all over the godsdamned place. You gonna hang me, Aberus? Is that too far for you?"

"For fuck's sake," Cato muttered. "This is perhaps not the time."

Aberus had the grace to look shocked. His grimace caused his fine, white teeth to shine like a crescent moon from his bush-like beard.

The Mantle sat as stone.

Bem chuckled through his thin lips. *Fucking Bem.* I nailed him a look from the side of my eyes.

"My gods." The Mantle raised Their hands, palms up in a gesture of peace. "We have traveled far from the purpose of this gathering. Troth Eira, Mother Merrias—may she ever soundly judge us—advised that you should wake the Frostborn."

"I was, yes—close your mouth, Aberus. They are adopted brothers. Were you and Cat fucking you'd have a reason for"—Cato slapped his hand over my mouth—"wooking wat way!"

The Mantle sighed and began again. "Throughout history, we have knowledge of only two instances of the Nether Lord gifting his Frostborn to humanity. Both during the Great War, given to the queen of Nortia before the northern contingent sailed south, and another to the daughter of a Baldorvan farmer."

"One to great wealth and the other... a laborer?" questioned Cato.

"Yes. And both Firewalkers, those with Leyometh's essence." The Mantle folded Their hands and placed them in Their lap. "The ritual to wake them. Are you prepared to take it on, Troth Eira?"

Am I?

"I—Merrias only said that it would involve great pleasure and then pain. I know nothing more."

The Mantle tipped Their chin.

"The tomes stored in my private library say it involves the selection of a mate—a father. The Frostborn will share attributes from both you and him when they rise."

"Let us hope they do not inherit her mouth," Aberus whispered under his breath.

I ignored him, fully engrossed in what I was hearing.

"I will be her mate—I *am* her mate," Cato interrupted. "Divinely Bonded. No other could take my place." His fingers tensed around my shoulders.

"And then what?" I asked.

"I betcha fuck," Bem interjected.

One... two... three... I closed my eyes and breathed deeply, to avoid shadow-punching Cato's man.

"The history books reveal little more. Like a human birth, I suspect your body will know what to do."

"Fucking bullshit," I whispered, more to myself than the others. "Will I be expected to raise them? Feed them? Do they rise as squiggly, mewling kittens? Will Evandr attempt to suckle my teats? The random pirate on ice... Will he try to run me through when I spoon mushed salt fish in his mouth?"

"Calm down, Eira," Cato said, using a soft voice meant to reassure.

"Calm down? You fucking calm down. It sounds like you get to fuck one out while I... Josa's blessed taint... Do I magically birth those big fuckers? I'm leaving. You all can fig—Cyra, is that Healer Phaina's journal?"

"Pardon me?" Cyra shut the leather volume. I watched the pages intently as they fluttered closed.

"The book in which you are so riveted... it is the same the healer used when assessing Ambrose. Why would you share a diary? Cato. Release me." I rose the instant his grip loosened. "Cyra, let me see it."

The book in question, like mine stored on the shelves in the Conservatory in Solnna, appeared slightly washed out. Not quite whole.

"Consort? What are you on about? Resume your seat at once."

"Aberus. Shut your fucking mouth."

The king sat back, offended by my words. Cyra peered down her indignant nose.

"Your Holiness, command her away from me... her mind is obviously addled. His Majesty is right to fear her."

I stalked Cyra, head down, steps slow.

"Continue, love." I felt more than saw Cato's presence.

I looked at the Gaean healer, pieces locking into place.

"You, healer, encouraged Allaine to sail south. Was it truly for her health, or were you helping to set the Primus-King's stage?"

"You are talking out of your mind, Troth," the healer stated with conviction. She exuded innocence, her stance strong, gaze unwavering.

The Devotee took a step to the Mantle's side as I neared Them.

"Am I, healer? Because, I have a suspicion that the journal which I have seen in both of your hands connects to a companion that lies in Gaea."

The healer took a step back. Cyra clutched the tome to her chest.

"This is preposterous, Holiness. As king of Monwyn, I call for your interven— "

I struck, the æther fully in my command.

With a flash of my arm, Aberus's knife flew from the top of his boot. In a swirl of shadowy æther I slashed my hand through the air and then twisted my hips to thrust forward.

The blade halted, pricking the healer's windpipe and hovering at the base of her neck.

"Confess your crimes," I demanded, still advancing on the healer.

"Holiness, she's in league with the Nether Lord, she will turn against you and—"

Cyra Fabia shot off, running toward the door. The diaphanous scarves wrapped around her neck floated out behind her.

Cato gave chase, Aberus and Bem close on his heels. The men spread out, corralling her into a corner, but she pivoted right and Evanesced, disappearing through the wall. The instruments mounted there scattered across the floor. The jarring clang of a dulcimer sounded on impact.

Beside me, the Mantle stood. They closed Their eyes and bowed Their head.

With a floor-shaking boom, the interior wall burst, wood splintering and flying so far it rained down upon my toes. Cato and Aberus dropped, shielding their eyes. Bem charged through the newly made hole, just as Cyra re-emerged. Her body skated across the floor, dragged by some invisible force. She screamed and kicked, trying to free herself from capture.

She came to rest at the Mantle's feet.

As the dust settled, though her eyes were wide and alert, she lay unnaturally motionless, arms stick-straight at her sides, toes pointed in the direction from which she'd come.

Knives drawn and teeth bared, the men of Monwyn returned, chests heaving. The king sat, and I saw for the first time the rumored beast that the citizens were right to fear. His obsidian eyes glinted like the edge of the sharpest blade, and his brow cast a shadow over his face, making him appear as sinister as the demons of lore.

"The book," Their Holiness said in a tone as calm as if They were leading prayer.

Cato swept down and pried the tome from Cyra's clutched hands. He offered it to the Mantle.

Dancing green eyes swept across the pages and filled with sorrow.

"Cyra Fabia." The Mantle eased Themselves back into a chair. "For two decades, you have stood at my side. We have shared in meals, broken bread, and weathered the storms of gain and loss. Will you choose to repent your transgressions?"

Her face slackened, the ticks and unconscious movements of expression restored. Tears glistened her eyes, spilled down her temples, and sank into the carpet below.

"Holiness," —she paused, collecting her thoughts—"we have betrayed you."

The Mantle nodded and then leafed through a few pages. "She will be made into a Monwyn at the Grooming, the most painful of the transitions and the most difficult placement in terms of freedom. This will dissuade her from that kingdom's Assignment and mitigate the attraction the Scion feels for her. He will seek the fruit of a different tree—not those already found in abundance in his homeland." They shuffled through again. "The blood that Scion Ozius collected was not enough. Sister Phaina was able to obtain more from the Baldorvan Scion, after he assaulted your daughter and needed his hand repaired. The amount is to be split between myself and the priest. I have pulled too much æther from him, ensuring he looks convincingly ill. He will perish without the restorative properties of your daughter's blood, and my skin is again showing the signs of advanced age."

The Mantle stopped reading, Their questioning stare falling on Cyra.

"You exchanged your loyalty for vanity?" Their eyes dimmed.

Her tears came quicker, her mouth contorting into a sneer.

"No one was ever interested in the mind of a cheese monger's daughter... only her fine figure... only her flawless face. The royals do not hire old women to dress them, to fill their courts with finery. Sagging skin and wrinkles are a death sentence in this life."

The Mantle sighed.

"It is a cruel world that does not teach its children that beauty is found within. I am so sorry, Cyra, that you have lived with such pain. How long have you carried out your deceit?"

"Six years."

"And Sister Phaina's?"

"A lifetime," Cyra whispered. She lowered her lashes and fought back a sob.

Their Holiness turned Their attention to the journal again.

"And in the last accounting to the Primus-King, Phaina herself has written, 'Cyra was able to block all divine manipulations, which should have resulted in his death, as his injuries were fatal. Your daughter's blood, however, and perhaps her æther, which seeped black from her hands, countered my efforts. It should also be noted that as I pulled from him, I detected a disruption in his pulse, like your own, indicative of otherworldly alteration.'"

The Mantle closed the book and lowered Their chin in quiet contemplation.

I trembled with a raw, blistering fury as vines of inky black twisted up my wrists.

"She admits to the attempted murder of a son of Monwyn!" Aberus bellowed. He gripped the sides of the settee, his fingers digging into its plush fabric. "I demand justice in His Highness's name!"

"You will have your wish, brother-in-law. For today, I walk in the steps of my grandmother."

The healer quirked her lips at me in an almost devious half-smile.

"Your father will deplete you as he did your mother. Maybe he'll spare you his co—"

I thrust my hand forward, and the floating dagger sheathed itself in the healer's neck. She clawed at the blade as a bead the same hue as her garnet robes bloomed and fell, but I continued walking toward her, propelling the weapon's weight, until it met the resistance of her spine.

"I judge you, Sister Phaina, upon *my* blade."

The woman sputtered on the blood that coursed from her severed artery, but still I pushed.

"May you f-freeze in the n—" Her arm shot out and her fingers closed tightly around my wrist, digging into my skin. I watched, unforgiving, as her fingertips charred, and the room filled with the sickening scent of burning flesh.

The iron-scented evidence of her end pooled warmly at my feet.

"And may she rot." Devotee Monwyn tugged his red robes close to his legs as Sister Phaina, traitor, fell to her knees and then floor.

I rounded, my vision tunneling.

"Cyra, your admission of guilt is meaningless to me. Your actions—"

The Mantle raised a graceful hand, and the room fell silent.

They rose and, in a fluttering of silks, kneeled next to Cyra's panic-stricken face. They took her hand between Theirs and with somberness bowed Their head.

"Goddess of radiant light, grant your daughter strength during her transition. We humbly ask that you embrace her, shelter her, and surround her with your presence." The Mantle placed Their fingertips over Cyra's brow and inhaled a steady breath. "Lord Mossius... hear me. Thy divinity knows no bounds..." Her tears came in earnest as she quietly sobbed. The prayer for the dying reached our ears.

With another deep breath, Their Holiness lifted Their hand, and the light in Cyra's eyes grew dim.

"Prince Catommandus, I give you my permission to question Scion Greggen. This evening, I will oversee the ritual of the Frostborn. Eira, daughter of Verus, make ready."

Chapter Sixty-Four

Eira

I sat in front of my bathing chamber mirror, sickened, staring at myself like it might somehow lift the gloom that blanketed my world.

Did I care about taking the life of the healer? Of course I did. It was no small matter, ending a living, breathing entity. Would I make the same choice again? Every time it was offered.

If her loyalty was to the Primus-King, then she was a threat to those who surrounded me.

I smeared on a second coat of brown shimmer and traced a dark line of kohl above my lashes. Logically, I understood Cyra Fabia's dependence on her outward appearance, and though I'd never learned to value it over my morals... I knew many did—and had to do so—as a matter of survival. In this kingdom, for example, women were taught as children that slim figures, curls to your waist, and heavily plucked brows were indicators of one's youthful vitality—in Solnna it was bold colors of make-up and ostentatious clothing. The Gaeans I knew valued a natural appearance, but dyed their hair and, of course, decorated their teeth in precious stone to show status. And even now, despite Nortia's emphasis on not using them, I employed cosmetics to camouflage my emotional turmoil, polishing it to a pretty shine.

"Eira?"

"In here."

Cato passed over the threshold, washed and dressed, bringing with him more than a modicum of comfort. I smiled at the fine figure he presented. He'd dressed less like a royal, and more like the 'Tommand' I fell in love with at Verus—tailored, gray woolen short coat, crisp, navy linen shirt, tall boots, and his favored white belt. I'd swear that if he were out strolling the streets of Monwyn he'd be mistaken for a kingdom exchequer, a man who counted coins and added up figures.

He neared me and took a knee, his expression grave.

"Is Ambrose okay? Is—"

"When I say you are mine..." He slid a wooden box across the countertop and nudged it under my hand. "What I mean is that we are bound as partners." Cato tapped my fingers and pointed to what lay beneath it. "You have brought a lifesaving perspective to my existence, for you see, my secret to not fearing death was not living a life worth cherishing. You, Eira, changed me—with your joyous chaos and wildly impractical optimism. I value every moment the gods grant us, and because of you, I am learning to value myself as more than a weapon."

He nudged my hand again.

I slid my thumb beneath the hinged clasp, unearthing a bundle of petal green silk that smelled faintly of coconut. Cato untied the white ribbon that held the small bundle closed.

"Cato, they're lovely." I shifted to better capture the light. Two rings, one a slender band of gold, the other a twist of gold and silver, perched upon a bed of crimson velvet.

"Look closely." Cato took the smaller ring and held it up to my eyes. The sun streaming through the window behind us illuminated the shiny rounds.

I steadied his hand with my own and squinted. There was something etched into the band of gold and silver. Two rows of tiny letters.

"I searched for peace in sunshine, on mountain tops, and in dreams," I read out loud, while admiring the blocky text.

Cato nodded and then trailed his fingers over my hand. He slipped the ring over the knuckle of my pinky finger.

"The ring I will wear completes the poem." Cato plucked the larger ring from the silk and held it aloft.

"It found me, instead, in your arms," I breathed, not daring to say more and drown us in yet another puddle of my tears. I didn't think it was possible to hold more love in my heart.

Cato placed the gold band in my palm before splaying his fingers. I settled the ring in its new home, on his right hand.

I looked up and batted my lashes, willing my kohl to stay put.

"No tears, love. Here, I had this made as well. But it never touches the one that I placed on your finger. Do you understand?"

"I-yes. But why?"

He reached into his satchel, held up a much larger band of silver, and then chucked it into a puddle of water on the countertop.

My heart palpitated in an outpouring of emotion, the gesture, defining.

"I must go." Cato kissed my fingertips, lingering over them. He flicked his eyes to mine, tenderness abundant in his expression. "I love you."

"And I you."

He walked away, and I hurriedly rescued the ring intended for Ambrose, drying it on clean linen. Small black letters drew my attention.

Second Husband.

"Cato, you are such an asshole!"

His rich laugh floated back to me as the common room door slammed closed.

I shouldn't be scared.

I shouldn't feel the need to knock.

But I stood there, icicle-stiff, fist poised to strike the door of Ambrose's room. My room—I'd slept in the consort's chamber maybe twice.

"Strength of Nortia. Strength of fucking Nortia, my girl," I muttered, mimicking Nan's always assured tone.

I threw open the door and swallowed hard.

Sitting up, shirtless, book in hand, with those becoming-as-fuck gold frames perched upon his nose, was Ambrose. His hair trailed over his shoulders, the tips hiding beneath the covers pulled above his navel. His color was healthier than it had been: pink undertones where they had been a sallow green. None of his wounds wept.

His eyes flicked up, taking me in, running up and down my body—then went right back to reading.

When he didn't comment on the near nipple-baring gown that I'd worn just for him—in blue, of course, with gold bears stamped on its fabric with rubies for eyes—my resolve wavered. I'd even added faux fibers to my hair, and though they weren't curled, my shining tresses of multi-hued brown hung to my back like a curtain of the finest charmeuse.

Don't cry. Don't cry. Do not, Eira.

Troth face. Activate.

I bit my tongue and flounced into the room, cradling a bowl of soapy water and a pitcher in one arm and a pile of linens and comb in the other.

"Put the book down, husband. It's time to clean you up."

He ignored me—no lift of a teasing brow, not even a sarcastic smirk.

I wanted to turn around, close the door, and bury myself under a pile of blankets, but instead, sat my burden on the side table and propped my fists on my hips.

"Ambrose."

Nothing. No acknowledgment. No flare of his insolent nostrils.

I slipped the book from his hand and quickly glanced over the title: *Most Lovely Minerals and their Meanings When Gifted*. I tossed it on the bed next to *The Male Physique: Desirability in Form*.

"I do not wish to be in your presence, Eira."

Do. Not. Cry.

His use of my name instead of "wife" or "succulent spouse" or even "harpy" hollowed out my insides like the scoop of a spoon into fresh snow cream. I pressed my tongue to the roof of my mouth.

"Unfortunately for you, the hoop in your ear gives me permission to be here. Throw off your covers."

"No. Eira, I am serious." He looked at me then, full on. His green eyes were void of humor or any other emotion that would indicate something other than... disappointment.

Hold the line, Eira.

"No, Ambrose, I am serious. We are committed to each other, yes by contract, but also by something more." I stared at him, praying to the Goddess that he wouldn't deny that he felt something for me... anything.

"No."

"Yes. Ambrose, you fucking toddler." We tussled over the cover, briefly, but in his weaker state, I gained the upper hand and flung it over the books, leaving him naked. "I've come to bathe you. The Mantle and Aberus plan to take a meal with you, and as heir, you will look presentable."

"Presentable is not something I will ever be again. And I can bathe myself." He twisted and dropped his feet to the floor. The corner of his mouth dragged—evidence of his continued pain and the sad state of the stitches I'd tried my best to place. "Remove yourself from my chambers." Ambrose stood to his full height and loomed over me, attempting to use his gigantic body as intimidation.

No. Nope. I was Vonnie's daughter. Fucking Goddess-born for what it was worth.

"Sit. Down." I postured, puffing my chest out, careful not to let my body come into contact with his injuries... and yes, weaponizing my best assets for his perusal. He may have thought himself enamored with my rear, but he was in no way immune to my front charms. "Or I will shadow slap you into some semblance of order."

Like a well-trained puppy, he dropped back to the bed, but stared at my stomach with a flat expression, like I didn't exist.

"Good. Now wipe that pout right off that handsome face of yours."

He grumbled, but the sour smell that poured off him necessitated a thorough scrubbing.

Take my hand, Mossius, turn my stomach into steel.

I tugged at my side lacing, irritated that I'd just got into the tight fucking dress, but I didn't want the lovely taffeta to show water stains and wrinkles at dinner.

Ambrose balked.

"You cannot be serious, using your curvaceous form as a means to sway me. Even teats as fine as yours will not tempt me to forgiveness."

I covered my chest and presented him with my side... so that he couldn't see the quiver of my lip. Silently, I pointed to my laces, seeking assistance.

"Stinky trolls don't get seduced. Untie me."

Ambrose snagged the ribbon and yanked but left me to work out the ladder lacing and shrug out of the dress alone. I tossed it on the back of the couch, several feet away, and bobbed my head, mentally bolstering myself for battle.

I turned.

Hook. Line. And sinker.

I caught the twinkle of eyes on tits before they went dead again, staring straight into nothing. If he thought I wouldn't use my majestic mountains to bring him out of his stupor... he was a shit Scion.

"Let's begin," I said matter-of-factly, reaching for my implements.

His normally sweet and spicy scent was no longer on hand, as Imella made the soap for him, so I'd opted for a cleanser with notes of amber and cinnamon.

"Close your eyes." I dunked the cloth in the fragrant water.

His eyelids drifted closed at my touch, saving me from that dead stare. My shoulders sagged in relief.

Ever so gently, I wiped him clean, taking my time to warm the flecks of blood and patches of dry skin around his stitched jaw, before removing them. With every swipe of my rag, I relived the horror of seeing him maimed.

"Ambrose, where you may now see flaw... I see my protector: a man so selfless he risked everything to save others—to save me."

Silence.

I selected a new linen, clean and unstained, and drew the square over his shoulders and chest. The puncture wounds were healing nicely, but his scars ran deep and would probably remain, despite my blood working through his system.

"These are looking much better."

"Mmhmm," he hummed the unresponsive response.

"Do you want to try another drop of my blood? To see if it will soften the scar tissue and lessen your pain?"

"I do not."

I slapped the dirty rag onto the pile of castoffs.

"Fine." I bent low and smoothed another cloth over his hip and went to work on the crease of the V that pointed to my favorite part of him. That's when I saw it... penis inflation.

Check and mate.

I didn't let on that I'd noticed... instead I leaned into my scrubbing, encouraging my boobs to bounce and wobble like I was a passenger in a high-speed carriage traveling over cobblestones. Arching my spine, I lowered myself to my knees and leaned over the bowl, dunking in a fresh linen.

"Other leg." I passed the cloth over my forehead, feigning fatigue. "Shew, always too hot for me." Lather rained onto my chest, riding the slopes, heading for the valley between my breasts.

Half-mast. Wiles working.

I rubbed vigorously at the dirt on his ankles and worked my way up. The green and purple bruising that ran the length of his calf concerned me, as did the—

"Eira?"

I glanced up.

Full erection.

Eye level.

Clit... tightening.

Control, ma'am. Control. The juncture between my thighs pulsed wickedly.

What was it about that stiffness that turned a crinkly-skinned custard launcher into an object of desire?

Soft nipples. Soft nipples. I chanted in my head. *Dead clitoris. Lifeless clit.*

"Finish your ministrations and disappear."

"Right. Of course. I don't want to upset you."

Asshole, please. You're hooked, and I'm going to reel you in with your own pole.

I adopted a grim expression, let my shoulders sag, played the role of dejected spouse, and then slid the cloth under his heavy testicles, already tight and drawn up. His legs parted, and I pressed back between his cheeks and used two fingertips to draw linen-covered circles around his tight ring of flesh.

He said nothing, but the appearance of a pearl drop at his tip spoke volumes—screamed volumes.

I switched out the linen again, breathing slowly through my nose.

"Do not misconstrue the response of my dick for yearning." His words sliced sharply across my heart. "This is simply a body's natural response."

"I understand." I purposefully hesitated before wrapping the dripping square around his length and drawing it up slowly, from base to tip. "But we have to ensure you are clean to encourage healing. This is not sexual; this is sanitation."

His fingertips curled into the fresh, crisp sheet that covered the bed, and I squeezed my thighs tighter, not ready for him to see my underwear, nor the wetness dampening the thin fabric.

I slid the linen back down, letting it "accidentally" roll away, allowing my skin to come into contact with his hot, smooth flesh.

"Eira, what are you doing?"

"My wifely duties," I said, my voice having gone husky. I glanced up innocently, a question in my eyes.

He flexed his rear and tilted his hips, the heat between us flaring.

His knuckles skimmed the edge of my jaw before he grasped the back of my head.

"This changes nothing," he said, eyes hazing over.

"Of course. Nothing."

He dragged the tip of his cock across my lips, back and forth, watching intently as he did so.

I captured him, and drank him down slowly, licking and running my fingertips along his underside. I knew exactly how he liked to be handled, but I performed at half speed. He was still a man injured.

Lips meeting fist, I languished my attention on his crown and stroked him in a sure and steady rhythm. He gripped the back of my neck and squeezed, urging me to take him harder, deeper.

"Ambrose." I panted out between slow plunges. "Gentle."

"Hush."

He urged me to my feet, and his fingers found the nipples that peeked from between the long hair hanging over my shoulders. He massaged my breasts until his erection glistened with a line of his essence.

"Too much, Ambrose. You can't risk reopening—"

He reached down, pushed his hand into my underwear, tested my wetness, and sank a finger past my entrance.

"Always so ready for me." He carefully worked his finger in and then out, circling a fingertip around my clitoris on each withdrawal. "This is how it should be. Just exquisite."

My head fell back.

"No, I—we can't," I whispered, worried that already we had caused further damage. Shit, I'd wanted his attention, but not at the risk of his health.

Ambrose pulled his hand away, ran his fingers over his erection and held it firm at its base.

"On."

"No, absolutely not." I shook my head.

He fisted my underwear and tugged me forward, his tongue curling around my nipple. He groaned as he sucked the sensitive peak into his mouth and wrapped his arm around my rear.

"You will do as I say, Eira. I am aware of my boundaries." He slipped my underwear to the side of my thigh, not bothering to undo the ties. "On."

I straddled him as he parted his knees, spreading my legs wide. The æther danced. My arousal spiked, and I couldn't speak the words to deny him. I rose carefully, notching his head at my entrance, and then sat slowly—excruciatingly slow—letting him slide deeply until I took him as far as my vagina would allow.

I exhaled a burst of air, struggling to keep myself in control.

"Let me move, husband, allow me to love you."

Ambrose grunted and leaned back, bracing himself with his hands.

His torso was far too bruised to hug close like I normally would, so instead, I reached back and grasped his knees for balance. I rode him gently, rising and falling carefully as I watched for any sign that he may be in pain. It wasn't the best position for gaining my own release, but I didn't care. The look of rapture on his battered face—closed eyes, lips parted, hair falling down his back—was enough to satisfy me.

Staved-off tears flooded my eyes.

"I love you, Ambrose. Whether you're angry, or if you've decided you don't love me in return." Wetness streamed down my cheeks. "All that matters is that you are here."

Ambrose closed his eyes as his hands circled my waist. He stilled my rising motions and forced my hips into a back-and-forth grind. The æther melted down my chest, pooling in my pelvis.

"Husband," I moaned, reacting to the glide of his head over that spot deep within, my clit pressed against his pubic bone.

"Love is not fickle, Eira." He guided me forward until his head lightly prodded my cervix. His understanding of our anatomy allowed for a gloriously over-sensitized stimulation that, with another, could have easily tipped to pain. "I do indeed find myself tethered to you by something more profound than my lusts." He pushed and pulled me faster now, his hips rising to meet mine. Goosebumps flashed across the surface of my skin, my nipples tingled like the tips of my fingers, and the æther dove, winding itself around our bodies.

We came together—the energy surging between and around us, our cries echoing shared affection. I felt him release against my walls, pulsing with every spasm as he poured himself into my body.

"And it is because I love you, Eira—more profoundly than I dared ever to imagine—that I will initiate the process of divorce, so that you may find your life's happiness in Cato's embrace... as it should have been from the start."

CHAPTER SIXTY-FIVE

AH, THE FINE SMELL OF FEAR. HOW INVIGORATING!

CATO

"You smell horrific, Scion." I wrinkled my nose at the rank aroma of stale flesh and body odor. "Bem?"

My personal man hopped off the table and approached Greggen, where he hung from a hook mounted securely to the ceiling, wrists bound in chain. He sniffed the Scion's hip.

"Yup. Bad. Smells o' piss." Bem stuck his tongue out and frowned.

"Scrub him well, then. You know I cannot abide stripping a man of his dignity when he reeks of sewage."

"You are sick, both of you." Greggen fought his bindings, jerking his hands, doing nothing but causing himself additional discomfort where the metal bit into his wrists.

The creaking sound of chain links stirred within me a profound excitement—the part of me that the citizens of Monwyn may have guessed at, but that only Septimus and Bem had witnessed. My brothers knew, of course, and had watched my methods up to a certain point, but neither had the stomach to see through what brought a man's confession. True confessions, not the words they thought I wanted to hear when the pain became too intense.

Other than Fira, little affected me the way this did—gods, I should not have thought of her. My cock stirred. But she and my work were two aspects of my life that required complete isolation from each other. I relished the softness that existed between us and would allow nothing to tarnish that which I held sacred.

Septimus had seen to it that nothing—not the smell of vomit or shit, or the screaming cries of men or women—did so much as make me blink. And even then, it was often to keep the blood spray from my eyes.

I loathed him for his tutelage, let my hate of him fester, and cursed him for making me the monster I knew I could be... until the minute my life intertwined with Eira's. From that moment, I thanked whichever disgusting deity Septimus sold his soul to for having carved me from the hardest granite. Eira would never comprehend the lengths I would go to keep my promise: "There is nothing I would not do for you."

Bem slit the back of Greggen's shirt—Monwyn blue on the back of a Baldorvan—and ripped it from his body. His pants followed, as did the linen underclothes he wore.

"You have lovely skin, Greggen. Nearly the same beautiful, deep hue as my mother's—rest her bones. Yours leans more toward a red tone, and hers yellow-gold, but I imagine what lies beneath will be similar, minus, of course, the rot surrounding your heart."

My captive stared straight ahead, his stubborn gray, bordering on blue, eyes never once drifting.

His first time in a room of torment, then. Were it his second, he would be begging me for his death. But he would soon learn. I was the king who presided over this palace—my scepter a carving knife, my crown made of shattered bone.

I sat back in my chair, *my* throne—heavy ebony, no carving, no frills, just gold hobnails tacking down the apricot leather armrests.

"You are a striking man. As tall as His Highness Ambrose, finely muscled, endowed well enough, I suppose." I glanced between Greggen's legs. What was the use of all that length if you couldn't fill your woman properly? "Did you Join with Eira's maid as a way to ingratiate yourself with my wife? You have harbored an obsession with her since Verus—and of course, I cannot blame you."

Nothing.

They never broke on the first question... but that was typical. Men thought so highly of their own bravery, inflated their perception of their own strength until they convinced themselves they possessed the ability to fight off wildcats and bears. I was never allowed to live in that delusion. Being broken, time and time again, gave me a realistic view of my capabilities, which, in turn, allowed me to pinpoint the weaknesses of others.

"Bem? Have I worked on a Scion?" I thought for a moment, drumming my fingers on the armrest.

"Naw."

"Ah, I do relish a new challenge."

"Wet!" Bem hollered seconds before dumping a bucket of ice-cold water over Greggen's head. He had to stand on a stool to reach, but got the job done with a certain aplomb that other stewards could only hope to mimic. "Wash!"

Bem procured the scrub brush—the same stiff-bristled tool used in our stables—and began scouring. First the head and face, next stomach and ass, finally legs and feet. It ensured all the grime ran down the drain and wasn't reintroduced back to the body. Infection could take a life quickly. Greggen would not be afforded a quick death, so cleanliness was a priority.

"Scion, Bem cleanses you with potash, an amazing mineral mined from our lands and floated after hoisting ore from the ground. It is a powerful astringent. You will notice its bite before long... That is how you know it is working."

Greggen bowed away from Ben's vigorous ministrations, but my man gave chase, running his brush over the Scion's naked flesh. He reddened quickly.

Truth be told, many an admission had poured from the mouths of my prisoners purely from fear of what was to come when the soaps sting set in. Though the caustic cleanser did not produce a *severe* burn, Bem's violent brushing did, and the combination culminated in a heightened sense of terror.

I studied Greggen as he swayed in the air, hung at the perfect height where his toes *just* touched the ground. No change in his breathing, no weakening of his muscles. I draped my knee over an armrest and kicked my leg in boredom.

A different line of questioning, then.

"Why would you select a half-functional woman to bear your children?"

Bem's eyes briefly met mine, a sign that he'd felt a change in Greggen's posture—stiffening or slacking, perhaps.

"Is she such a unique fuck that you would allow her to produce?"

My stomach tightened uncomfortably. Goddess's mercy, discussing sex in terms of a woman other than Eira made me physically ill. I pushed her from my mind and focused.

"Do you force your dick between her seized arm and breast? I imagine fucking such a tight space would be just as, if not more pleasurable, than taking her pretty little cun—"

"Leave her out of this," Greggen growled. It was the first virile sound he'd ever made. Less of a coward than I suspected.

He stared at me, face streaked with soap, his expression one of pure malice. Water cascaded down his face and into his mouth as Bem poured another bucket over his head. He sputtered and spat out the sudsy liquid and then shook his chains, as if this time they would break.

"No. I will not. You see... I still remember the bruises you left on my woman's face. At the time, the law of consequences mandated that I break your legs in retribution, but Eira stopped me. Now I see the wisdom in waiting... snapping Allaine's shriveled, worthless arm as you look on will give me an overwhelming sense of satisfaction."

"You would not dare—"

"Strap his ankles."

"Fucking immoral adulterer." Greggen fought his chains again. Futile.

I would not harm Allaine, of course. I found her company quite amusing, and on my payroll, she'd proven her worth—making me aware of Eira's comings and goings, who approached her, who leered overly long—she was valuable, even if her choice of lovers was... unfortunate.

Bem went to work, installing a set of thick leather cuffs, clicking them into place on a *U*-shaped anchor that stuck out from the floor. I stood and went to the chest on the back wall, procuring a favorite set of instruments. After inventing the new method of torment at the tender age of eleven, Septimus commissioned the wood-burned box, especially for me. He'd been so proud. I recalled his embrace, the joy in his eyes. *You are mine in all but blood, boy.*

"Greggen, are you allied with the Primus-King of Gaea?" I blew dust from the box's lid, frowning. Bem had shirked on cleaning duties, but I'd allow it. Returning to Monwyn and finding the kingdom secure and Aberus alive would earn him a hefty raise, even if he already earned more than the highest-ranking Council member. I gave my steward a once over, taking in his new, stain-free tan coat with fine gold buttons. Perhaps a lady had caught his eye while I was away?

"No," the Baldorvan said gruffly, drawing me from my thoughts.

"Mmhmm. Alright."

I laid the box on the table and smiled at the creature depicted on its front—teeth bared, claws sharp, a portrait of the man-wolf Septimus was helping me grow into. Had I actually possessed the ability to change by the light of the moon, as in the lore, I would have ripped my uncle to shreds.

Sixteen needles of varying lengths were sorted by gauge on one side. Three sets of jeweler's hammers and a pair of pliers were stored in compartments in the other.

"Did you aid the Primus-King in murdering my moth—"

"You are fucking mad. Like this entire goddamned continent. I curse you to the nether, adulterer—sinner!"

He spoke quickly as he thrashed about. Too quickly.

I ran my fingertips along the heaviest of the needles, thought a moment, and then selected the finest, thinnest among them.

"You failed, Lord Scion, to answer my question."

"Because you accuse an ancient of murder. The Primus-King is more invalid than man. He can barely move across the floor without his servant's aid."

Bumps were breaking out over Greggen's skin, the caustic soap and frigid water beginning to work.

With the tools of my trade in hand, I approached the Scion. He stood heads above me, glaring down at me even in the state in which he found himself. I was used to men looming over me—mistaking my shorter stature for weakness. Funny how quickly their perceptions could change.

"Still not an answer." I studied Greggen's ribcage. He was slim but dense, sinewy, and hard-planed. I measured the distance between the bones that spanned his chest. "Let me explain the situation in which you find yourself." I pressed my fingertip into the space between the ribs below his pectoral muscle, near his underarm. "I will insert the first needle here, within the intercostal muscle and cartilage. Be careful of how deeply you breathe after it is set—expand too much, and the needle is lost and cannot be pried out without incising." I pinched the iron point between my fingers and held it to the lamplight, checking for burs... knowing very well it was hammered and buffed to perfection. Every move I made was calculated, every word, every pause and inhale. "If not removed, it eventually pierces the lungs, which do not collapse as quickly as one might expect. It will be an infection or the constant trauma of the metal that will most likely kill you before suffocation can occur."

I located the perfect place to drive in the first pin. Right in the center of a darkening spot where inflammation was setting in around a previous laceration. Less chance of my needle breaking.

Greggen's skin shrank back when I twisted the tip of the sharp pin into his flesh, just enough to stick, nowhere near making it through the dermis entirely.

"Did you meet the Gaean Elderman... Deekon, I believe his name was? Spry fellow."

"Y-yes. What the fuck does he have to do with—*meerka!*"

A single tap of my heavy yet compact hammer and the needle shot forward an inch. The Scion's body jerked, but Bem, having partnered with me in this particular dance before, leaned into Greggen's other side, negating his retreat.

I positioned the second-thinnest needle about a half inch from the last and gave it a twist.

"According to my brother's account, you and the Gaean arrived at the Den together... the same night that three women under my protection were slain."

"Your point being?" Greggen hissed, his eyes boring into mine. "I was there to remove Allaine. Your whore of a brother and his slut wife were using her for some—"

I slammed the heel of my hand into the Scion's jaw with a force so intense his teeth bit through his cheek and into my palm.

"*My* slut wife." Greggen spat out a stream of red and a dislodged molar. "Try again."

"Your wife? A farce. How embarrassing to covet another man's property and pretend—stop!"

I wrenched Greggen's testicles forward and twisted them violently, digging my fingernails into his scrotum.

"Stop!" Vomit spewed from his mouth, nothing but stinging bile as he'd been disallowed food for days. He heaved. "I hu-hung the rope, suspended the ropes from the columns. I knew nothing of the murders. I knew nothing!"

"Lies." Releasing him, I returned to my case of needles. Bem showered the floor with a watering can, coaxing the blood and bile into the drain.

"I am begging you, please... H-he said he was paying Ambrose in kind." I flipped the longest needle into my hand, gripped it, and set it over his heart. "Wait! After the foul treatment I received, beaten by your whole fucking kingdom the day I arrived, I agreed to his jest. Th-the boys with him, a Scion youth and the other... they dragged bags, told me they were the carcasses of swine, a prank about Eira's weight—I assumed he was telling the truth."

"'Assumed?' You assumed that my mother—my beloved, unconditionally loving mother was a godsdamned pig?"

I reared back, repositioned my arm, and then drove the needle through his pupil, yanking the pin free and then slamming it through again, this time pinning his eyelid closed. The needle jerked and ticked as his eyes rolled.

"I swear! I didn't know until—" Greggen wailed and screamed, his eye watering profusely, mucus pouring from his nose, saliva from his deceitful lips. "Leyometh, Leyometh, hear me. Hear your son..."

"Bem, make it stop," I grumbled, returning to my chair.

Faster than a mine collapse, Bem unsheathed his dagger and plunged it into the Scion's eye socket, dislodging the orb like he was digging a splinter from his finger.

"Gracious me, I meant his loud mouth, Bem, you rascal," I spoke to my man as if he were a naughty boy caught in a practical joke.

"Pardon, sir. Yah got tah be specific with ole Bem here." He tapped his dirty blade against his temple, streaking his thin hair with blood.

Greggen's screams stopped. Thank the Goddess. But now his keening wails were the source of the pressure mounting in my forehead. His body slackened, stretching his arms nearly beyond their limit. Soon his shoulders would dislocate.

"Why are you not branded, Scion?"

"I am!" he sobbed. "My hip, I bear Verus's mark. You know this. You see it with your own lunatic's eyes."

"And the Portcullis? Are you too much of a weakling to bear your country's device?"

"Do not compare me to a slave."

Hmm. His comment rankled me.

"You... you think you are somehow better than a human forced to do your work... while you hang here?"

Greggen blacked out, his head slumping forward, chin to chest. I motioned to Bem, who tugged his head back and slapped him awake. A silvery-blue eye refocused.

"I am amused to tell you, Greggen, that I actually believe you. Probably because my own wife has softened my heart." I procured a linen from my satchel and bent to retrieve the pink and white eyeball on the floor. "Bem, here you are." My manservant came to my side, took the little parcel, returned my needle, and then shoved the bundle into his pocket.

"A kindness, sir, thankee." Bem blushed—he always did when he got a prize for his collection. He clipped a bow at the hip.

"I have one remaining question, Scion."

Greggen's lips worked, but no sound came forth.

"Were you sent to Verus already having knowledge of Eira?"

A tear from his good eye streaked down his cheek.

"I... I was."

My hand began to quiver. The same feeling that overtook me moments before turning into what Eira deemed the "warrior-king." I sucked in the air and willed myself back into control.

"To what end?" I asked, clenching my teeth, disgusted by the waver in my voice.

"The warlord. His seer prophesied that Eira—Leyometh's carrier—is to be his queen. I was to report back a listing of her likes and dislikes so he could prepare her stronghold."

I laughed, the sound echoing off the walls.

"Truly? That's good of him." I imagined my shade-sorceress, burning Baldorva to the ground when the man forgot to provide her adequate snacks and hugs. "He is free to attempt swaying her, but she has trouble managing two spouses as is, and I believe she would object wholeheartedly to a third. Bem, take him down. Find the healer and cover up that disgusting hole in his face."

Bem jumped into action, and the Scion dropped to the ground, groaning as he fell.

I steepled my fingers and watched the mite writhe and cry out to his god.

"Welcome to my employ, Greggen. Disregard my orders, and Allaine will soon refer to her seized arm as 'the good one.'"

Chapter Sixty-Six

WHEN THE TRUTH IS TOO PAINFUL

Eira

"**L**ike fuck you will!"

Ambrose's eyes went wide, like he'd spotted a terrifying specter over my shoulder.

"Your penis—your still hard dick—is knocking at my cervix's door and you dare to speak of divorce? In what realm is that okay? Who does such a thing? Y-you think to break off our marriage in the same sentence in which you say you love me? Piece of shit, you lump of mountain-shaped shit. Don't you dare speak of it again!"

"Eira, your happiness is—"

"Not yours to dictate!" I grabbed his cheeks, and the asshole leered at my breasts as they jiggled from the movement.

"Ambrose, eyes up—"

I'd welcome death if I could suffocate in those pleasure pillows.

I thumped him on his perfect nose.

"How are you always so crass? Don't sexualize me while making the solo decision to end our—"

"Pardon? How did I sexualize you? Cease your accusations, quick-lipped harpy."

He shoved his hands under my rear to unseat me, but I clamped my thighs and tucked my feet under his knees, holding steady.

He glowered in response.

"Suffocateinthosepleasurepillows! Is that all I am to you? Cease your mouth, y-you backward Monwyn ballsac. And put this godsdamned ring on." I rolled off Ambrose, unintentionally catching him in the side with my knee. He doubled over, clutching his ribs.

That giant motherfucker belongs to me. Who does he think he is? I'll leash him like a godsdamned bear in a traveling troupe.

Ambrose's eyes rounded, his irises resembling a single pea on a plate of white porcelain. I snatched the silver ring from near the comb and shoved it over his knuckle.

"And don't you ever take that off or so help me I'll—"

The door of the common room opened. Jance smacked the butt of his spear on the marble floor.

"Receiving His Royal Majesty, King Aberus!"

"Fuck!"

Fuck!

"Entering, Lord and Lady Ethens, His Royal Highness Prince Catommandus!"

"Just a minute! Ambrose is being an indisposed asshole!" I scrambled, plucking the underwear from my crack and shimmying into my discarded dress, yanking at the laces the best I could.

"... All stand in the presence of Their Most Holy Savior of Verus, the Goddess's Representative on Earth, They Who Preside over..."

"I never thought I'd welcome Jance's long-winded jabbering." I clambered onto the bed behind Ambrose, combed his hair back, and secured it low on his neck. When finished, I hopped down, dashed to the wardrobe and grabbed a dressing gown from where it hung amid four kings' closets' worth of clothing. "Put this on, one arm at a time." I eased the garment up over his shoulder, careful not to let it scrape along his much-better-looking injuries.

"Do not infantilize me, Eira."

Don't act like a fucking toddler then.

"I am doing no such—" Ambrose's massive paws smacked against my cheeks so hard tears pricked in my eyes.

"Oww muvva fukka, wut tha fuk are you—"

"Eira." His forehead smacked against mine. "I heard you."

"Fine. Fuck. You heard me. Now unhand me so I can blacken your other eye."

"No. You do not comprehend my words." Ambrose shook my head so hard my vision wavered. "Comprehend me, wife. Do it now. Gods above, you must comprehend!"

I jerked away, perplexed by the sudden change in his behavior.

"Has fever set in?" I placed my wrist against his forehead. "We shouldn't have overtaxed your—"

How the fuck do you control this mind speak? Eira, Eira? Do you hear me? Hello?

I ran—the only appropriate response.

"No. No, no, no, no, no."

Cato strolled through the door, tugging at his pearled cuff. At full speed, I flung myself into his arms.

"Eira, if you mean to murder him, love, please take him to the bathing chamber first... the mess..."

"Cato!" I buried my head between his silk lapels. "We're Infinite! The fucking Nether Lord, he... he's bound me to that oaf's brain!"

Such a big mouth she has... but the ass-to-mouth ratio is spot-on perfection.

"Ambrose!" I wailed, "I can hear you!" I hopped up and down, tears streaming down my cheeks and onto Cato's fine wool coat. Who was acting the child now?

"Well, turn it off and assist me. I smell of fresh coitus, and I rather think the Mantle... m-my sibling... will be made uncomfortable by the scent."

Cato's arms stiffened around me, but I didn't have the spoons to soothe his insecurities at the moment.

"You have to turn it off, Ambrose! I can't—"

"Both of you, calm yourselves immediately," Cato commanded. "Obligate masks on until we are able to confer again. Is that understood?"

I nodded into his chest, close to hysterics.

Spoiled little thick-dicked soldier. Always gets what he—

Ambrose! I screamed through the connection.

He jumped back, struck the bed and toppled.

"God's alive." He struggled to right himself, while also pointing in my direction. "I demand, as your master and husband, that you abandon my head at once."

Do what?

"Oh, are we to remain Joined now?" I squirmed, attempting to throw off Cato's arms. "No longer sending out a decree to banish me from your life?" I tried stomping Cato's foot, but he was all too aware of my tactics. "Fuck you and your Monwyn laws."

"Was that—is that an option? I support it wholeheartedly." Cato jerked me against his body, the smell of clove and cedar intensifying. "I shall inform Aberus at once."

"Not on your life, brother." Ambrose winced as he tried to stand. "If you want this testy tyrant to yourself, procure me another of equal or greater value. I no longer have my looks to secure such a match." He gestured to his face as his voice hitched.

The shrill cry of an unhappy infant came from the other room.

"My goatling." Ambrose surged to his feet, grabbing his side. "I am coming, baby Verra. Papa hears you." He took off across the floor, panting from the exertion of only four steps.

I broke Cato's hold and hurried to tuck myself under Ambrose's shoulder, and together we slowly made our way to the common room.

It was the most picturesque of family gatherings.

"Blessed be your Joining, Troth Cinden. May you find happiness in life and never forget the value of your existence," the Mantle's hand hovered above Cinden's forehead.

She nodded, not quite meeting Their eyes.

"Thank you, Holiness." She nuzzled Verra's tiny ear and then checked the amount of milk remaining in a glass bottle. Lord Ethens traced circles on Cinden's elbow and gazed upon his wife, a man entirely besotted.

"Give me the child." Ambrose wasted no time plucking the satyress from the cradle of Cinden's arms. As he brought the little one to his lips for kisses, a bereft expression washed over my friend's beautiful face. Her soft-brown eyes saddened. It disappeared quickly, but I didn't miss the tremble of her lip before she squared her shoulders and handed the bottle to Ambrose.

Cato pulled my chair out and tucked me in close to the table.

"Ahem." Ambrose paused in front of his chair until Cato, rolling his eyes, did the same for him. He sat heavily, wincing, needing a few seconds to adjust before he gazed at the little girl nestled into his arms.

"Look at her round little tummy. Looks like her beautiful mama already. And her downy fur, it's already thicker and more abundant. Has she learned to crawl yet?" Ambrose asked Cinden, all manner of serious.

"You know nothing of children, you ridic..." Cinden fought to keep civil. Normally, she would have called him an offending ogre or laughed in his face. "N-no, it will be some time yet, and with her tiny, precious little hooves, she may not begin with crawling at all."

Ambrose narrowed his eyes, but accepted her answer.

Snuggly little buggly bear. Papa missed you, my lamb... goat.

Aberus clanged a spoon on his teacup, calling for attention.

"Catommandus, with Septimus no longer with us, I have extended an offer, and Lord Ethens has accepted a seat on the Council. To that end, he is now aware of the *issues* we face."

I caught Ethens's eye. *Well played, sir.* Highest-ranking marriage he could hope for and the most prestigious appointment in the kingdom. He winked as Aberus turned away.

"What information have you from Scion Greggen?" Aberus asked, snapping out a napkin and placing it across his lap.

Cuddly cricket wif those wittle horns.

Cato lifted a cup to his lips. The aroma of his coffee drink wafted in my direction.

"The attack on Solnna was fabricated by Gaea. It was convincingly a Baldorvan attack, but they failed to get their details correct when planning their ruse. After conferring with the Scion and matching his information to that of my overseas informants, we confirmed that only the enslaved class of Baldorva bear portcullis brands, not their high-class citizens. The Baldorvans would never allow their slaves to be armed and risk revolt."

Aberus nodded while pondering Cato's words.

"And the murders? Brother, is he innocent?"

"That depends entirely on your definition of innocent."

Cato offered me a sip of his drink, but I declined. The extra boost of energy would do nothing but amplify my growing anxiety.

"Lord Gotwig was correct in his estimation that Scion Greggen took part in the slaughter of our women, though he did not slit their throats himself."

Ambrose's head twitched, but he kept his focus on feeding the babe.

"The Baldorvan warlord, like the entire fucking continent apparently, is aware of Eira's existence and seeks to make her—the earthly bearer of Leyometh's essence—his wife or mate or concubine or whatever the custom is there."

"He can try," I muttered. "Aberus, how would you feel about a third man moving in? No? Not keen on the idea? Ambrose has decided to divorce me, so I'll be spouse-shopping soon."

Aberus's nose flared, just like Cato's, just like Ambrose's. He gripped the dainty teacup in his hand until his knuckles reddened.

"Perhaps, you and I—as a trained Troth—might look at your archaic laws and I can initiate the proceedings myself. How about you grant women the right to divorce, and I'll get right out of your lush head of hair? I hear Baldorva requires glassworks as dowries—do you have some in the treasury?"

Cato threaded his fingers through mine and, in an overt display of possession, brought my hand to his lips.

"I will actually consider it." Aberus fired back, turning a violent shade of red. "If it means ridding my kingdom of your presence."

"You do that." I blew the king a kiss, but Cato snatched at the air, catching the imaginary kiss-missile in his fist.

"Those are mine." He shook his head at me. "Not his."

Ethens raised a brow. Cinden suppressed a smile.

Ambrose snuggled Verra.

The Millanderers will make tiny dresses for you, and little hoof covers. Papa thinks periwinkle will be your color.

"Ahem." The Mantle lifted the veil from Their face and held a glass of wine to Their rose-hued lips. Like a group of chastised children, the conversation ceased.

"Upon my return to Verus, missives will be sent to the continent's four monarchs, summoning them to attend a summit, immediately after the thaw. Their second-born children will travel alongside them and be required to stay at the temple for a duration of two years. If a civil war breaks out, and they or their heirs perish, I will have their spares safe, renewed in fraternity, dedicated to the common cause of the continent." The Mantle paused, sipping again. "If the Primus-King attends the summit, his end will come swiftly. If he declines, the triad of kingdoms will meet him at the gates of Gaea."

You could have heard a veil pin hit the floor.

"When the continent's problems are solved, we will turn our eyes to Baldorva. Prince Catommandus, I would appoint you Ærta's general." The slender fingers on Their graceful hand balled into a fist, the first outward sign of aggression I'd ever seen Them use. "Troth Eira, after waking the Frostborn, you will be under constant surveillance. You must never find yourself in the hands of the Primus-King or that of the Baldorvans. If that fate were to befall you, I ask that you take your own life."

Cato choked and pressed his hand to his mouth.

"Prince Catommandus. Does Scion Greggen live?"

Visibly shaken, Cato collected himself, breathing deeply.

"For now."

Ambrose glanced up, his head swiveling toward Cato.

"Now there's a fucking surprise—show me your teefers, Verra. Nope, still just wittle gummies—I would have thought Greggen floating down the river in bite-sized chunks by now." *I'll slit his throat, my little lady. Uncle Cato is weak. We cannot have that nasty demon walking the fields where we will eat cheese and have races.*

"I am equally surprised, brother Ambrose," Aberus said, while filling his empty cup. The elegant teapot looked like a child's toy in his massive paws.

"Oh? Would you like another? Surprise, that is... we are rife with them these days." Ambrose placed Verra on his shoulder patting her back. "Lord Gotwig has arrived. As we visited, he revealed that my secret father lives—that's right, my undisclosed ancestor. Turns out my old man isn't some whore's customer. He's a Primus. Can you even imagine? Thirty years of lies."

Cinden gasped, slapping her hand to her chest. Ethens looked from side to side, like he'd rather be anywhere other than this chamber.

"Yes, Lady Ethens, that would have been my reaction too, had I been told before the man disappeared in a haze of smoke and netherfire."

"Gotwig? Who is Gotwig and how did he slip past without..." Aberus's words faded away as I whispered through the Bond.

Ambrose?

What? He threw back at me shortly, while tucking Verra into the cradle of his arms.

I laid my palm on his knee, though I kept my face forward, nodding in agreement along with the rest of the chattering group.

I'm so sorry, my heart. Ambrose ran his fingertip down Verra's nose, smiling softly. *Our intent was sound, but we should have informed you immediately, before—*

Ambrose stiffened, his whole body going tense. His eyes squeezed shut.

The pain? Husband, let me help you relieve it. Please.

He rested his hand on mine, his green eyes welling. He glanced down at his untouched plate.

Baby Verra... she isn't safe with us, is she?

"Excellent forethought, Catommandus," Aberus said. "Bem, would you be willing to step up as Protector?"

"He would be an excellent choice. Ambrose, what do you think?" Cato asked, turning to his brother.

Ambrose stood, grunting against the pain as his chair legs scraped across the floor. He turned to me. "Eira, why does everyone leave me?"

All conversation silenced as he limped his way to Cinden.

"Raise her well. If I ever see her sad, I will have Ethens flogged. Aberus, Your Holiness, I feel I must retire. I would like time alone to gather my thoughts about the future." Ambrose kissed the upturned nose that poked out of Verra's swaddle and placed the baby in Cinden's arms. "Good night, all."

He turned toward his bedchamber.

"Ambrose, Black Bear, I—Cato, he needs me." I leapt from my seat to give chase, but Cato caught my hand and stalled my efforts.

"Tonight, we will seek him out together." Cato took my hands in his and thumbed the ring on my finger.

The Mantle rose.

"But now... you must wake the Frostborn."

CHAPTER SIXTY-SEVEN

SACRIFICE DOES NOT REQUIRE BRAVERY

EIRA

"Are you afraid?" Cato asked as we ascended the steps in the wake of the Mantle's flowing robes. I stared at the hands clasped behind Their back—gloved in a supple white leather, encrusted with rondels of seed pearls and sapphires.

"I am... I'm fearful of the ritual itself... the unknown." My toe caught on the edge of a step, but Cato's hands were there to steady me. "Thank you." I resumed the climb. "But I am more fearful for the people of Ærta. For the little ones and babies like Verra—she can't be the only one. And how many nascent conjurers die for their differences?" I stumbled again, and Cato hoisted up my silk train and held it up behind my knees. "Already, I'm imagining the fallout will be astronomical when word spreads across the continent that Solnna was harboring conjurers all along."

Cato paused on the steps, his eyes searching, gleaming in the lamplight as the wheels of his mind turned. He glanced at me.

"The Primus-King will gather the traditionalists—make Gaea a safe harbor for those who stand against the conjurers and what they represent—build an army. With a military that large..."

"He would have the means to take her," the Mantle finished Cato's words, as we walked into the hallway. "Under the guise of condemning her to death, he could keep her locked away, deplete her with none the wiser."

The air cooled, and like the grass must sense the morning dew as it settles on its blades, I could sense them, feel the existence of my Frostborn.

"Well met! Mantle, your Holy Highness, just a moment. I have the door, High One. I'll just grab that for you." Jance jogged forward in a clatter of armor. "Goldmines and mountaintops, it is freezing up here. Is this what it's like in Nortia, consort? Pretty close, would you say?"

I smiled weakly as I walked toward the exuberant guard, nodding. "Very similar, yes."

And it was. The hairs in my nostrils prickled just as if I'd swung open the door and stepped outside back home.

"Here you are. Step right in. Let me get that robe for you, Mantle—wait, can I touch it? Oh, gods, forgive me. I didn't want you to—"

"You are forgiven, child." The Mantle passed through the door.

"Shoot, thanks. Consort, Highness." Jance bobbed up and down as he bowed once, twice, and a third time.

I gasped as we crossed the threshold.

The room sparkled—a glittering-gray cast coating the ceiling, walls, and floor. In our absence, the room had encased itself in a thin layer of ice. Not enough to make things slick, but just enough that when I allowed my fingertips to linger on a wall, I felt an instantaneous melt.

I looked around, taking it in.

There were so many memories attached to this chamber.

Where we now stood is where the audience sat, excited to view my "deflowering" on my Joining night.

My cheeks flushed warmly at the memory.

And there was the bed, where I realized for the first time that perhaps the three of us could be just as happy as the two of us.

They were lying upon it now, my unexpected gifts. Like two babes in the womb, Evandr, and Ambrose's pirate, Larm. They embraced each other, frozen in time.

Behind me, the Mantle's personal servants carried a privacy panel through the door and set it up to the right side of the room, directly in front of the fireplace. I smiled at the ragged line of singed carpet, recalling the first time our triad had loved so fiercely that the flames got out of hand.

Another group, guards, four in total, swept into the chamber. Two stopped at the door, spears by their sides. The others came forward carrying stacks of folded blankets, which they let fly and layered directly in the middle of the floor.

"As you ordered, Protect—Highness."

Cato thanked them as they filed out.

"You thought ahead, my gallant spouse?"

He arched his brow and peered down his nose at me.

"Give me some credit, love. I would not create our first frost child on the hardwood. I am no monster taking his mate in the mud, or dare I say, some shitty shack in the woods." He grinned as he lifted my hand to his lips.

"You are exactly that monster," I said, body easing at his mischievous tone.

Jance pulled the door closed behind him, the click overly loud in my ears. I scanned the frost-covered chamber, allowing myself a few moments to breathe.

"Do you suppose this will be the most awkward thing I ever do?"

"Do not tempt fate, Eira," Cato whispered, shaking his head and scrunching his nose playfully.

After inspecting the privacy panel, Their Holiness waved us forward.

Cato squeezed my hand, and together we moved to stand before Ærta's highest authority. Veil in place and the vapor of Their breath visible in the frigid air, They closed Their eyes.

"The act of intercourse is sacred, bestowed by the divine; however, it is not for my eyes," the Mantle said as They gestured toward the panel-hidden fireplace. Light filled the chamber as the hearth roared to life. They opened Their arms, palms to the cradle above, whispering something under Their breath.

"Eira, Catommandus, you prepared to begin?"

"Yes," Cato answered immediately with a conviction I prayed I could match.

The Mantle turned to me, eyes opening. In their depths, with clear certainty, was the knowledge that I could say no without judgment.

Strength of Nortia, my girl.

"I am ready, Mantle, if you find me worthy."

A soft smile tilted Their lips.

"Prince Catommandus, do you freely give of yourself to this woman?" the Mantle asked. "To take part in what we know so little about? To sustain her through the ritual?"

"For the rest of my life and thereafter." Cato folded me into his chest and placed his chin on the top of my head, his warm breath familiar.

"Troth Eira, Chosen Daughter, Firewalker, do you accept this man and agree to take of his essence?"

"Until I no longer draw breath." I hugged my mate closely, listening to the even beat of his heart.

"From what I understand of the history, the intense heat of a Firewalker will stimulate their rebirth—we know little more than that. Your bodies will understand what nature intends. Eira, are you able to maintain the æther? I do not know its effects if let free in this instance."

"I am. Primus Zuddaz taught me."

Another smile lighted Their face.

"Then let us proceed. I am unaware of the duration required to bring them forth and know nothing of the state in which they will return. Do not stop the ritual for any reason. I will seal the chamber's door."

We nodded in unison.

The Mantle made Their way behind the painted screen, which boasted a springtime landscape of the palace's acclaimed front gardens in full bloom.

Cato and I stood together, wrapped in each other's arms. Neither of us wanting to break apart. The tip of his nose brushed the shell of my ear.

"How funny is it that a week ago I, very boldly, asserted that I would storm a palace and fuck you on the floor of the first room in which I found you... and now we are *asked* to make love—as a means to save the continent, mind you—and I feel as if it is our first time all over again?" Cato whispered.

I chuckled into his chest.

"Are you feeling bashful, Catommandus... Prince of Monwyn... Chosen Frostborn Papa."

I stepped back and took his hand, leading him to the pallet.

"Yes. Yes, I am."

His nervous laughter warmed me.

"Fucking you for fun is, no contest, my favorite pastime. Fucking for the future of the realm while the holiest person in the land sits ten feet away... that is a lot of pressure—I hope my good man rises."

"Me, too," I admitted. "On both accounts."

The pallet was soft. Our feet sank into its many-layered cushion. Cato pressed his forehead to mine and swayed back and forth, like he would soon pull me into the steps of a dance.

"Where would you like to begin, love? You are the brave one this night."

I stretched my neck up, resolved to follow the path to which I'd committed. "Here, I suppose."

"Perfection," he murmured, face descending.

Our lips met, and the æther snaked slowly around the inside of my chest. Little electric tingles sparked a path along my skin and gathered at the points where Cato's body connected with mine—lips, hands, chests, and the side of a foot that only barely touched his.

His mouth was soft and warm, a clear juxtaposition to the rough hands that cupped my jaw and neck.

"Oh gracious, from the stiffening in your pants, sir, I'd say your fears are unfounded."

He kissed me once again, smiling against my mouth.

"Shhh," Cato placed a finger to his lips and flicked his eyes to the panel.

"Sorry," I whispered, poking him in his hard stomach.

"Are you, though?" He looked at me pointedly and angled his head.

I dropped my volume. "Catommandus Odelguard. We've had sex in front of your brother, your mother, her guard, and—"

"And none of those was a nonsexual, high holy human listening from behind a curtain... and you are loud, Eira. *Loud*." He mouthed the last word silently.

I slapped my hand over my mouth to stifle my amusement.

"Consort, wife... should we not carry out this ritual with solemnity?" Cato placed his hand over his heart. "Where are the drums? Where is th-the chanting? Its tomb levels of quiet in here. *They* are sure to hear the—"

"Skin slaps and squelching?"

Cato froze, looked at me sideways, and then tossed his head back and laughed so exuberantly that bits of ice fell from the ceiling, dotting our bodies like snowfall.

"I love you so profoundly, Eira. You have made my life worth living, and fuck me, but I am—"

"Oh... I intend to."

I pushed his lapels wide, and his overcoat hit the floor. Faster than he could respond, I gripped the sides of his linen shirt and ripped, popping two of the dozen buttons.

"Oh, oh well then." Cato raised his brows, surveying the damage.

"Ambrose's naughty books make this seem much simpler," I muttered, yanking on his collar and then giving up and unfastening the next in line

"Here, darling." With a single, sharp jerk, he tore the shirt from his body. The remaining buttons flew, rattling to the floor. "Better, my curvy exhibitionist?"

"Mmhmm, much. Now work on the pants while I play."

I wiggled free from my dress, baring my chest for his inspection, ready to press myself against him. The golden aura around his pupils expanded, and I didn't resist the urge to cup my breasts and offer them up to him instead.

He flicked the leather belt free from its buckle.

"Eira, tell me you find your body as stunning as I do."

"I.." I looked down, assessing my curves, the soft swell of my stomach, the flare of my hips... "I do." I ran my hands down my arms and across my waist, appreciating the body that had seen me through this odd life.

"A blessing, because it would take me a full night to sing you the praises of your form. Though I think I would start with the curve of your should—"

"Pants, Cato. I bet your britches that the Mantle would like to seek Their bed sooner rather than later."

He pursed his lips and scowled.

"Such a demanding bedmate. Where is the romance?" Cato teased. "Ambrose isn't nearly as difficult to please." I leaned in and flicked my tongue over his nipple, watching it peak, and then took it into my mouth, skimming my tongue along its tip before applying more pressure and swirling around his areola. "Pants. Yes?"

They dropped to the floor, just as my legs bent to do the same.

"No." Cato caught my shoulders. "Allow me." He lowered himself to his knees, tracing my cleft with his fingertip as he descended.

He parted me, admiring my sex, and then leaned in.

"Cato—oh, yes." I steadied my hands on his shoulders.

"Mmmm. As you wish, love." His tongue circled the outside of my clitoris as he skimmed his nails down the back of my thigh. He tugged on my hip, and I widened my stance, allowing him greater access. "The taste of you." He sucked my gem between his lips and tilted his head back to watch my response as he rhythmically flicked his tongue. "Is my undoing." He moaned; the deep hum adding to my pleasure. Cato pulled my rear forward with both hands and curled his tongue into my entrance.

"You've a Goddess-blessed mouth." I sank my fingers into his hair, freeing the flips and curls from his tight braid.

"And my hands?" Cato shifted and slid the tips of two fingers an inch into my heat as his tongue found me again. He moved in tandem, digits working, lips drawing, until he nestled snuggly into my passage. I ground myself into his mouth.

"Wicked as the nether."

His brows arched, and he looked at me quizzically.

"Humiliating rites are in my wheelhouse." I winked as he nodded and shrugged. "Lay down, husband."

He did as asked, laying back and stretching out on the cushy pallet—never once allowing his fingers to disconnect from me as he did so.

I kneeled between his legs, eyeing his thick member as it bobbed against his lower stomach. I bent forward and traced the thick vein that ran the bottom of his length, watching him just as he had me.

Cato moaned through pressed lips, fighting to muffle his sounds.

"Don't hold back, husband." He watched intently as his cock vanished into my mouth and reappeared slick and shining.

"It's so hot, love."

"Mmm-hmm. Are you more comfortable now that your penis is—Oh!" I released him, suddenly aware of the steam rising from his hips. He caught me by the back of the head and pressed me back down.

"It's fucking exquisite in this chill."

Heat radiated from my body. My palms itched, sweat beaded on my forehead, and the familiar flush of need spread across my chest as I pleasured the copper-skinned perfection that was my Fated mate. This was meant to be.

"You will make me a papa this night, yes?"

I nodded, mouth gliding along his erection, clamping my thighs for the friction it caused.

"A broad-shouldered, blue-eyed Scion—fuck, love, you are flawless, your method impeccable."

I closed my eyes, basking in the warm glow of his praise, the itchy sensation in my palms giving way to... something unique. The æther collected there, pooling and irritating my skin. I focused on the line of my palm, tempering and holding steady. Swirls, reminiscent of nighttime skies, appeared before my eyes.

It was time to begin.

I wrapped my fingers around Cato's arousal. He shuddered, pulled his knees up, and fisted the blankets tightly.

"You glow, Eira. Your skin is...the whole of you is... black flame."

Cold droplets rained from the ceiling, dotting Cato's skin. Where the pearls of water fell, they sizzled and then steamed. Hot tears slid down my cheeks, joining them, splashing darkness onto his stomach. "Are you ready?"

I crawled up his body, straddling his hips, our bodies hissing where they touched.

"I was ready the day I *sniffed* you, Eira. That first day at Verus."

The chamber turned humid. Moisture permeated the air.

I raised my hips and sought him out.

"Mine forever," he whispered.

"Yours forever," I answered in return.

My passage spread as I sank. He was the perfect stretch with no pain. My moan echoed around the chamber, my breath scalding as it traveled through my lips.

His hands found my hips, encouraging me to lift.

I obeyed, rising and falling, seeking my pleasure until my mind traveled, locking out all but the urge to mate with this man—something ancient, something spiritual, flowed between us.

Cato's mouth fell open, his eyes rolled back, and dark flames licked at the perimeter of his shoulders.

"Gods, oh gods. Cato—love." I impaled myself over and over, riding him, until I felt a tickle at the tips of my breasts. "Give me life."

"Eira," Cato gasped. He sat up, captured my waist in one arm and steadied himself with his other. He thrust hard, bucking beneath me. His teeth latched around my nipple, and he drew upon my breast, sucking me, drinking what felt like boiling liquid.

My head snapped back, my consciousness a wash of color.

"Life," I cried out, digging my nails into Cato's shoulders, feeling the warmth of his blood welling around my fingertips. He yelled around my breast and poured himself between my legs. With each of his pulsating releases, he shook, his muscles constricting and tensing so hard they spasmed under my touch. My body followed his example, my orgasm bolting through me, my passage clamping and tightening until I thought I might lose awareness.

The æther, my gods, it flowed through us in a cyclical rush—him emptying into me as I emptied into him. Connected entirely.

And then the pain came.

I screamed, howling in agony as the muscles in my legs contracted along with those of my back and stomach. Cato clutched me tight, and encircled my waist in his arms. He wheezed hard, riding out a wave of excruciating tremors as the black flames engulfed us.

I did not know how long the pain lasted, only that we wept as it subsided, bound by an inexplicable experience.

My heartbeat slowed. My skin was its normal color.

The room was twice as hot as a Solnnan summer day, and I feared for the Mantle's wellbeing as our bodies released their strain.

Cato, covered in a sheen of sweat and long red streaks, looked toward the Frostborn.

"The pirate. He has thawed, Eira. Look."

I scrambled from Cato's lap.

"Look at him. No longer stiff." I ran my fingertips down the man's arm. "He's warm, Cato. His heart beats."

The Mantle joined us, ignoring our nudity. Their sweat-saturated silks hung from Their body and They struggled to breathe.

"He awakens but does not yet breathe." The Mantle studied the man, curled in a fetal position. They pulled Their glove from Their hand and reached into the man's mouth. "He is filled with fluid."

Water dribbled over the pirate's lips, and he began to splutter and choke.

The Mantle reacted quickly, closing Their fingers and drawing back. A ribbon of water issued from the nostrils and mouth of the Frostborn, whose chest rose and fell with a wracking cough, then evened out to a steady rhythm.

"Mantle? Why has Evandr not changed?" I climbed onto the bed and caressed the still-frozen Scion.

Their Holiness shook Their head, dark hair brushing Their shoulders.

"Both were presented to you. Both will awaken through you and only you. Your mate was found acceptable to wake *this* man." His Holiness pointed to Larm.

Panic welled within me.

"But th-the æther or the Nether Lord didn't find him suitable to wake Evandr? Cato and he are friends, as close as brothers."

"I do not know. At this juncture, everything is speculative. Two Frostborn given is unprecedented, perhaps—"

"Call upon Ambrose and perform the rite again," Cato interjected. "I would see Evandr restored if Eira—love, can you bear the pain again?"

"Without question." There was no hesitation on my part, even if my body felt like it had just endured a seven-hour-long charley horse. "But Cato, he is not out of danger. His wounds seep with little provocation. He could barely make it across the floor. I'm not positive he could make it up the steps."

The Mantle laid gentle fingers on my arm. My muscles seized under Their light touch. I jerked forward in pain.

"It is the Scion's duty to give his life for Ærta," the Mantle said softly, perhaps to temper the blow of the arrow that pierced my heart.

"I-I... Is there no other—"

"Eira." Cato clutched my hand in his.

"Do not ask it of me," I begged. "Not my... *our*, Ambrose."

Cato shook his head, a far-off look in his eyes.

"Do you trust me?"

"Of course, but—"

"Guard, open the door!" Cato leapt from the bed and disappeared, stopping only long enough to pull on his underclothes.

I wept.

"Feel your emotions, daughter. Sacrifice does not require you to be brave."

They opened Their arms, the most human of gestures, and I fell into them, my skin reacting, tensing where we touched.

I couldn't catch my breath.

How would Cato explain the situation to Ambrose? Could the Mantle bolster him through the process somehow?

"Please, call the healers. I'll make the space more comfortable for him."

The Mantle nodded, and we parted.

While They made Their way to the door, I pulled the pillows from the bed and rolled up one side of the pallet, making a sort of nest that would support Ambrose's back.

I would be careful with him. I would rein in the æther—would alter our positioning.

A cramp hit my calf and felled me. Jance was there in a heartbeat, supporting me by the elbow.

"Can I get you a snack, consort? Some water, maybe wine... or the stronger stuff? Not sure what was going on in here, and it is absolutely none of my business, but I think a snack would do you good, and Prince Cato, he ran by looking parched. You know, I think it's sweet they both love you. I hope one day somebody can overlook my flaws. My uncle once told me I lacked the charisma to attract a spouse."

I fell against the guard, and he took me in his non-judgmental arms, patting my naked back awkwardly. His armor scraped my stomach, but I ignored it.

"Love will find you, Jance, and when it does, don't hesitate to tell them, in as many words as you can, how much they mean to you—over and over again."

The sound of struggle came from the hall. Poor Ambrose, huffing in pain.

"Troth Eira, prepare yourself," the Mantle said. They walked across the floor, saturated skirts held tightly in one hand, a glass in the other. They pressed the cup to my palm and encouraged me to break away from Jance. "Drink deeply. The air is stifling."

I shook my head, refusing to quench my thirst.

"If he suffers, I suffer."

Soft and kind eyes, the same shape as Ambrose's, gazed at me tenderly. They glistened with tears of their own.

"Your strength was apparent the moment you took Gotwig's chair at your first lesson at Verus. Ambrose, likewise, is strength personified, in body and in heart."

A muffled cry came from the hall.

I grabbed the Mantle's hand and choked back a sob.

Cato appeared, his brother wrapped in a blanket, cradled like a child.

He threw his burden to the ground.

"Cato!"

He spat on the body that rolled to my feet.

"S-Septimus?"

Chapter Sixty-Eight

WHEN SNOW FALLS

Eira

My body responded in a turbulent inferno of revulsion and desire.

"I washed the filth from his body," Cato gritted out. "Eira, can you?"

"Yes," I hissed, need snaking its way through my body, coiling around my legs like a slithering serpent. "Debasing myself with such vileness does not compare to the thought of losing Ambrose. But Cato, where... how is he here?"

"Ambrose told me he let Septimus go—but my uncle has years of abuse to atone for. Is that not right?"

Septimus's lips quirked as he flung his wet, unbound hair over his shoulder.

Cato lashed out, forcing his uncle's chin back, revealing a face badly bruised.

"Isn't. That. Right?" Cato's voice was steady, but its edge spoke of pure hatred.

Septimus grinned.

Icy-blue eyes peered out from swollen flesh.

The Mantle inserted Themself, raising Their hand, a silent command for Cato to back away.

"Prince Catommandus, you will leave the premises—"

"I will do no such thing." Cato shot to his feet, dropping Septimus, regaining his control.

I rested my palm on his forearm, the heat that accompanied my burgeoning arousal already heating the air.

"Cato, love, don't put yourself in a place of suffering."

He scoffed.

"It is what he raised me to do, Eira, and perhaps this is why. I will not leave your side. Do not ask it of me again. I traverse the path we have chosen." Cato stepped back, crossed his arms over his chest, and stood as stone on the edge of the pallet.

The room rained, weeping droplets from the ceiling and saturating my hair.

The Mantle spread Their arms.

"Lord Septimus, Viktos's Chosen, do you freely give of yourself to this woman?"

Septimus stared up from the floor, confusion on his face.

"What in the gods' name am I being asked to give her?"

"Your dick," I said plainly. "Now hurry up, fist yourself into an erection and let's begin... from behind. I'd prefer not to see you."

Septimus, the nasty fuck, threw his head back, silver hair spreading around his scarred shoulders, and barked a laugh—a sound of triumph. From how quickly his pierced member swelled, he'd need no preparation.

"To that, Holiness, I respond with a hearty, 'oh, yes.'"

I clenched my jaw, attempting to stifle the rush of heat to my passage—already slickness gathered, preparing me. On the outside I might sell the lie, but inside, my body sang, knowing it would finally feel what it had longed for from the moment he walked into the Den.

"Troth Eira, Chosen Daughter, Firewalker, do you accept this man and agree to take of his essence?"

"I do," I said, my voice strong. "Mantle, conceal yourself... quickly, please." I pressed my thighs together and wrung my hands as they began to itch.

Septimus lunged, catching my ankle, just as the last of Their Holiness's silks disappeared. He yanked hard, and I toppled, rear-striking the damp pallet.

"Look, asshole, there's no need for the fight. Just put it in, for fuck's sake."

He swatted my leg aside, opening me to his perusal as he leaned low and drew in a deep breath.

"That's disgusting."

"I have dreamt of this moment, just as I know you have." He stalked up my body, his scarred and muscled chest dragging along my stomach. The head of his cock brushed my calf and then knee, leaving a wet trail in its wake.

My legs parted further, of their own accord, thighs rising to brace his hips.

"Wider." He rose up on his knees and smirked. "I'm a thick man." He grasped his erection and tapped his silver-studded underside against my clit. "As you will soon discover."

I tucked my hands under my hips, interlacing my fingers, wanting to suppress my yearning to explore every inch of his sinfully godlike body.

"Tsk, Tsk. That will never do." Septimus struck, sliding two fingers deep into my passage, flexing his digits as he went.

"Septimus!" I yelled out, the sudden intrusion shocking. I flinched and shoved him as hard as I could, but he held me down while continuing to thrust with no regard.

"I will see you hang," Cato growled from where he stood.

I snapped my fingers in his direction and motioned for silence.

Septimus's hand slid up my sternum and curled around my neck. He bent low and tasted my skin, trailing his tongue between my breasts. He pulled his fingers from my body and made a show of wiping them on the blanket next to my head.

"I will not sully myself in the remnants of my disappointment of a nephew."

My lips quirked into a wry grin.

"*Nephews.*" I reached for him. "Now, kiss me, repulsive viper."

His lips slackened, and for a fleeting moment it appeared as if the lust in his eyes transformed into something softer.

"As you wish, enchantress." Septimus clutched my chin with his sticky fingers.

His head descended.

And I smashed my forehead into his nose, the back of his head clutched tightly in my hands—the snapping sound... one of the most fulfilling my ears had ever heard.

Cato's delighted chuckle was my reward.

"Deceitful woman." Septimus grinned through the blood gushing from his nose and coating the perfect pearls of his teeth. "You are my equal in every way."

"Incorrect. My worth is far above your own."

"Bitch." Septimus clawed at my hips and flipped me to my stomach.

The æther buzzed, arcing between the tips of my fingers.

A hand twined itself into my curls and jerked. I half-crawled, half-fell across the floor until another hand forced my chin up.

I peered into Cato's hard eyes—Septimus flaunting my degradation.

His cruelty knew no bounds.

"There you are, husband." I beamed at Cato, pouring every ounce of love I contained into my expression, despite the pain searing across my scalp. "After he comes—if he is able to finish in the first place—will you remind me of what it's like to be loved by a man? He's whetted my appetites, but only you can satiate my desires."

Septimus twisted his talons until I felt the rip of fine hair from the base of my neck.

Cato shook his head as his anger mellowed. His focus was now on me and not the miscreant at my back.

"You are like no other, Eira, wife of my heart." One side of his mouth tilted in a half-smile.

I winked, and his cheeks dimpled.

Septimus poised himself at my entrance, and heat flared, filling the room. Droplets of perspiration coasted down Cato's temples.

I gritted my teeth, unwilling to give in to the shocking levels of arousal coursing through my core and lower.

I didn't want this, but holy fuck, how I *wanted* this.

My entrance tightened, the rods in his cock burning hot against my flesh.

"Prepare yourself, uncle. For the first and *last* time, you will submerge into the most gratifying depths in existence—like wrapping yourself in warm silk."

"Is it... is it that nice?" I asked, drawing his eyes back to me.

"Oh, my darling, it is without description."

Septimus plunged forward with a shout, his piercings scraping that spot within, his fingers tightening around the front of my neck and squeezing. My vision swam.

"Eira, love, you are doing so well. You are a vision. Beauty in motion."

I bit off a cry, as Cato's sweet words tangled with the physical sensations I was trying desperately not to feel.

"No, sweetheart, take your pleasure. Press yourself against him, just how you like it." Cato dropped his hand to the front of his underclothes, adjusting himself. "Never pain for you, only pleasure."

"Silence, Catommandus," Septimus spat. He reared back and slammed his hips into my backside. My eyes rolled back.

"Try lifting her leg, Uncle... if you can manage the position. Wrap her thigh around your hip and fuck up into her. You will find the cradle and never wish to return."

"Shut up!" Septimus pulled out and twisted me onto my back. He pressed my legs backward and thrust his hips, spearing me in a single solid thrust.

"Performance anxiety?" I whispered. "It happens to the best of us."

A palm cracked across my face.

I smiled through the sting.

"Eira, loving wife, though incredibly amusing, we need him to get off quickly. Insulting one's manhood is not the best means to *that* end," Cato said almost jauntily.

I laughed coldly and snaked my tongue over the blood where my lip had split after hitting my canine.

"And uncle, each mark you leave upon her is a finger I will snip from your hand, unless *she* wishes to carry out the deed."

Septimus snarled; his hair soaked in sweat. He lowered his head and bit my nipple between his teeth, sucking and nipping in time with his thrusts.

I felt the change begin and watched, entranced, as my skin deepened in color.

"Mmmmm. That's—yes." I moaned. "Take me harder."

"Eira, I want you to come. I want him to feel how your walls clench around his cock. That divine wetness that surges when you climax, how you swell, keeping my cock snug within your velvet. Let me see it, wife."

I arched my chest into Septimus's mouth, and he grabbed my breasts, smashing them together until he could pleasure both nipples while hammering his hips.

Cato's words shot straight to my core, along with a healthy surge of æther.

"Glorious fucking Gammond," Septimus ground out. His flawless, marble-white complexion contrasted beautifully against my hands, which were coated in shades of swirling gray and onyx.

"Fairy cunt, even? Gods, Eira, it will haunt him for years to come. Septimus, watch her eyes. They are magnificent, like a kaleidoscope of forest and sea. Darling, wrap your legs around his waist and tilt your hips... there you go, love."

Little sounds of pleasure hummed in the back of my throat. My breasts swelled and began to spill.

"Drink." I tugged a lock of his hair and pulled him down. His fingers bit into my breast, kneading it like a satisfied cat. I struggled against the pain as he dug his nails into my skin. He succumbed to this mysterious abyss of euphoria.

"You will have to end me, nephew." Septimus slowed his hips, no longer thrusting, but rolling into me like a wave upon the water. "Death is the only barrier strong enough to keep me from her."

The cyclical churn of his essence and mine—like an ethereal exchange between souls—bound us.

I came hard, squeezing and screaming, crying out his name until my muscles spasmed and wracked with an agonizing joy.

"He thaws, Eira. Evandr is..."

Septimus followed me over the edge.

"Viktos, Merrias," he prayed as he came, pumping and spilling himself in rushes that throbbed within me. "I have done your bidding, and you have blessed me." His muscles tensed, the tight tendons that ran along his neck standing out sharply. The veins of his biceps roped. I pushed him backward and kicked the middle of the chest, unseating him from my person. He went down, his head smacking the foot of the bed.

"The pain, g-gods, its—Goddess, please, save me!"

Cato was at my side, massaging the muscles of my neck as the spasm continued. I heaved and gagged as a profoundly intense ache claimed my body.

"I have you, love, I am here, Eira. This will subside. The pain will end."

"I-I did... it," I puffed out between breaths. "Do... you... hate me, Cato?"

"No. Never. I am so fucking proud of you." As I was too exhausted to do more than lie there, he folded me into his arms and lifted me from the floor. "So godsdamned proud." He kissed my cheek and nose and then lips.

The pain lessened. My breath returned to normal.

The chamber was a soggy mess and felt akin to sitting in a Nortian warmhouse after a long day of ice-fishing. All that was missing was the smell of whale fat and fire.

The Mantle emerged from Their screen, again, struggling to inhale. Cato bore me to the bed as They went to work, pulling the water from Evandr's lungs. Immediately, his chest rose as naturally as if he were napping.

"It worked, Cato. Evandr is—"

I reached out, caressing one dark head and then another, pale as a snowdrift.

"Evan?" The raw emotion in Cato's strained voice would have been reason enough for me to perform the ritual a hundred times over.

Blonde lashes fluttered against pale cheeks, and sky-blue eyes—exact replicas of Septimus's—opened.

"Cat? Is that... Where in the actual fuck—" Evandr coughed, and a gush of water burst from his mouth, further saturating the mattress.

Cato sat me next to him and then crawled the length of the bed to his friend, raising Evandr's head to rest on his thigh.

"Take it easy, Ev. We will explain everything when you have rested. Your... your new brother is stirring," Cato nodded to the pirate, who seemed to be having a more difficult time waking.

"Do fucking what?" Evandr's head slumped to Cato's lap, bewilderment settling firmly on his features. Cato smoothed back the Scion's hair and patted him on the head like an older brother would his younger.

The pirate's lids fluttered.

"Cato, look." I pointed, and Cato's mouth fell. Larm's eyes. They were deepest-brown, their pupils rimmed in gold. They were Cato's eyes, precise copies.

Below us, Septimus stirred.

It took a moment for his addled mind to register his surroundings, but recognition eventually settled in.

"The gods favor me," Septimus said, grinning, his cheeks dimpling. He rolled to his side and got to his knees, swaying slightly. "I have given them their due."

I leveled him with a cool stare.

"Father Burchard stopped feeling anything for his Mated Bond when she conceived." I jerked my head toward Evandr. "Do you think this counts, or is that too much to hope for?"

Cato's hand found my thigh.

"Ask me in a month's time," Septimus said, rising.

I narrowed my gaze.

"What are you playing at?" Cato asked, suddenly still.

The silver-haired snake chuckled as he rubbed his chaffing wrists.

"I diluted her conception control with some foul concoction the morning we left Monwyn."

My hand flew to my stomach.

"You wouldn't dare," I said, knowing very well that he would.

Septimus walked closer, no shame in the nudity that he once claimed bothered him—his lips curled in malicious glee.

"I am *their* Safeguard—the gods'—not yours, ignorant woman. You have yet to learn... you cannot go against their will."

Bile rose in my throat, and the room tilted and seesawed, throwing me off balance. My hand lurched out, searching for Cato's, my anchor in the ever-brewing storm.

"Eira, do not. We will navigate this together. There is no way to tell if you are—"

I snapped, shade swelling, shadows filling the room.

I would end this now, on my own. I was so sick... so tired of being a pawn in this man-centered world.

And I knew well, though a pawn couldn't become a king... they could sure as fuck end the game.

Shooting up, I took flight. No walls stopped me, no roofs contained me. I Evanesced, until the night greeted me, its shadow-seeking daughter.

I flew in a direction that my soul knew to be right—over mountains, through a storm that spat rain and then snow.

I'm coming, father. Open your gates and receive your ill-gotten child.

I would mow him down, the Primus-King of garbage, and ensure the reason for my life's troubles would never rise again. I needed no man—Mated Bond or other—to lend me aid in this task, I—

Oh, Goddess!

Like a wall of water smashing me into the shore, I fell, tumbling from the skies.

I called to the shadows, but the æther didn't respond.

I broke through treetops, and split branches, my limbs no longer shade.

The earth swallowed me whole as my back met mud and my world went dark.

"H-help... me. Ca-Cato? Black B-bear..."

As I opened my eyes, two hazy, doubled silhouettes came into focus, before disappearing again.

"Goodness Ulltan. I expect flakes to drop from the sky when snow falls, not our daughter. Brilliant shot, by the way."

"M-Momma?"

The End... For Now...

THE OBLIGATES OF ÆRTA

EPIC ROMANCE FANTASY BY AUTHOR E.A. FORTNEAUX

BOOK FOUR
THE FINAL
INSTALLATION
COMING
WINTER
OF 2025

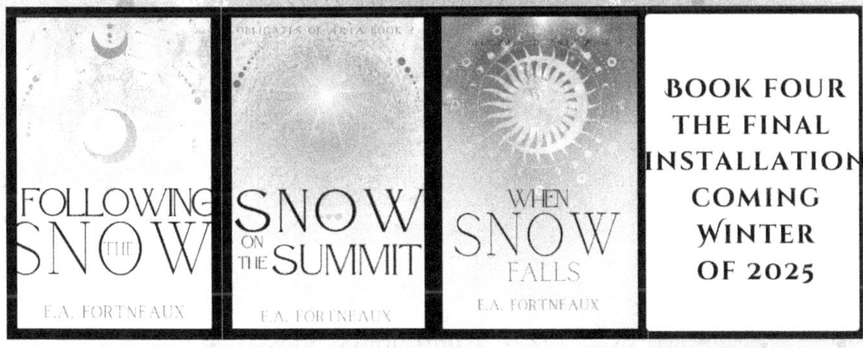

FOLLOW THE QR CODE TO CONTINUE YOUR JOURNEY THROUGH ÆRTA

ARTWORK BY LINA GANEF

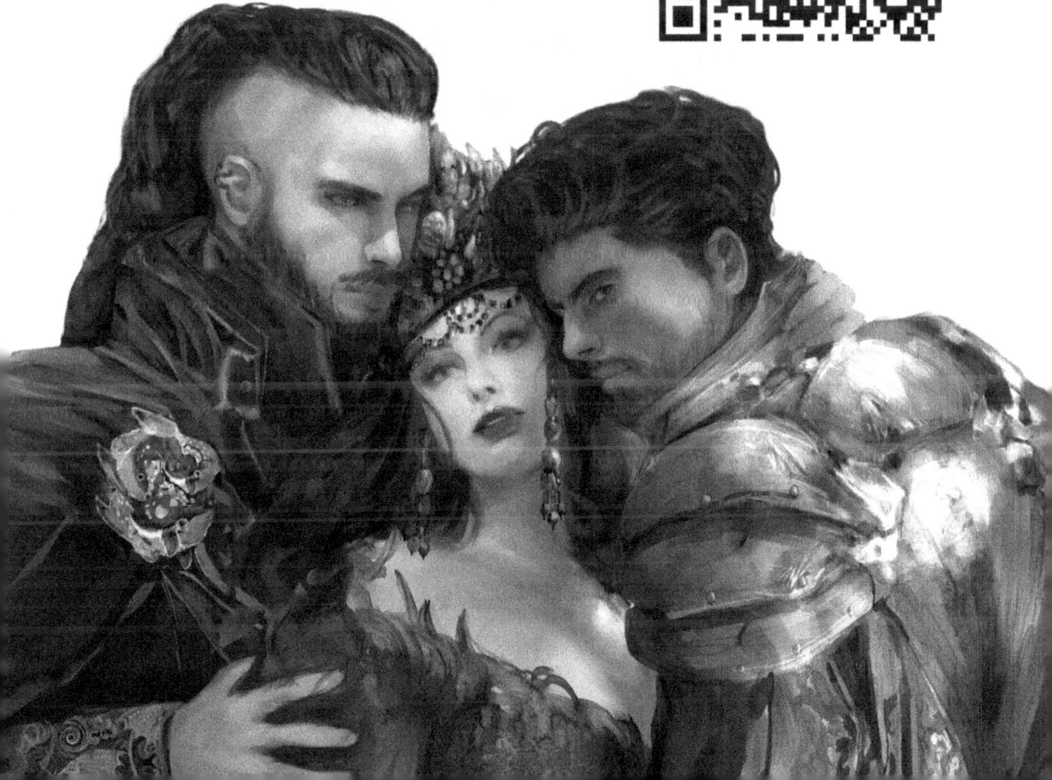

Thank you so much for reading When Snow Falls!

I still can't believe I've published a third book, and I really can't believe people are still reading them! Ha!
The fourth and final book in Eira, Cato and Ambrose's journey, will arrive in 2025, and quite frankly, the thought of it makes me tear up.

Luckily, we still need to find out what the nether is happening to Kairus in Baldorva, and like, was that a little somethin' somethin' going on between Aberus and Richelle?

And like... who does Bem have the hots for?

If you are enjoying the series, please think about leaving a review on social media or the book review sites that you frequent. I really do appreciate it! Also, if you want to chat, feel free to reach out to me on socials. I love hearing your thoughts!

Cheers! E.A.

CONTENT WARNINGS

Abortion (mention of), Abusive relationship, Alcohol, Anxiety, Assault, Attempted murder, Blood, Bones, Bullying, Cannibalism (lovingly so), Cheating (kinda/kinda not), Coercion, Cults, Death, Demons, Depression, Divorce (mention of), Domestic violence (mention of), Dubious consent scenarios, Emesis, Emotional abuse, Fire, Genocide (Mention of a fantastical population), Incest (but not really. Linked through adoption not biology), Kidnapping, Misogyny, Murder, Natural Disaster (Storms, earthquakes), Persecution of a minority (fantastical) population, Profanity, Prostitution, Religion, Scars, Self Harm, Sexual harassment, Sexually explicit scenes (MFM, MM, FF), Slavery (mention of), Sex shaming, Sterilization (mention of), Torture.